THE WAR OF THE RING

THE HISTORY OF THE LORD OF THE RINGS, PART THREE

THE HISTORY OF MIDDLE-EARTH

I
THE BOOK OF LOST TALES, PART ONE

II
THE BOOK OF LOST TALES, PART TWO

III
THE LAYS OF BELERIAND

IV
THE SHAPING OF MIDDLE-EARTH

V
THE LOST ROAD AND OTHER WRITINGS

VI
THE RETURN OF THE SHADOW

VII
THE TREASON OF ISENGARD

VIII
THE WAR OF THE RING

IX
SAURON DEFEATED

X
MORGOTH'S RING

XI
THE WAR OF THE JEWELS

XII
THE PEOPLES OF MIDDLE-EARTH

J.R.R. TOLKIEN

THE WAR OF THE RING

The History of
The Lord of the Rings
Part Three

Christopher Tolkien

HOUGHTON MIFFLIN COMPANY
Boston New York

First Houghton Mifflin paperback edition 2000

Visit our Web site: www.hmco.com/trade.

Library of Congress Cataloging-in-Publication Data

Tolkien, J.R.R. (John Ronald Reuel), 1892–1973.
The war of the ring: the history of the Lord of the rings, part three / J.R.R. Tolkien ; edited by Christopher Tolkien.
p. cm. (The History of Middle-earth ; 8)
Includes index.
ISBN 0-395-56008-X
ISBN 0-618-08359-6 (pbk.)

1. Tolkien, J.R.R. (John Ronald Reuel), 1892–1973. Lord of the rings — Criticism, Textual. 2. Fantastic fiction, English — Authorship. 3. Middle Earth (Imaginary place) I. Tolkien, Christopher. II. Title. III. Series: Tolkien, J.R.R. (John Ronald Reul), 1892–1973. History of Middle-earth : 8.
PR6039.032L6375 1990 90-4732
823'.912—dc20 CIP

Printed in the United States of America

QUM 10 9 8 7 6 5 4 3

CONTENTS

ILLUSTRATIONS

FOREWORD

The title of this book comes from the same source as *The Treason of Isengard*, a set of six titles, one for each 'Book' of *The Lord of the Rings*, suggested by my father in a letter to Rayner Unwin of March 1953 (*The Letters of J. R. R. Tolkien* no. 136). *The War of the Ring* was that proposed for Book V, and I have adopted it for this book since the history of the writing of Book V constitutes nearly half of it, while the first part concerns the victory of Helm's Deep and the destruction of Isengard. The second part describes the writing of Frodo's journey to Kirith Ungol, and this I have called 'The Ring Goes East', which was the title proposed by my father for Book IV.

In the Foreword to *The Return of the Shadow* I explained that a substantial collection of manuscripts was left behind in England when the bulk of the papers went to Marquette University in 1958, these manuscripts consisting for the most part of outlines and the earliest narrative drafts; and I suggested that this was a consequence of the papers being dispersed, some in one place and some in another, at that time. But the manuscript materials for *The Return of the King* were evidently preserved with the main body of the papers, for nothing of Books V and VI was left behind beyond some narrative outlines and the first draft of the chapter 'Minas Tirith'. For my account of Book V therefore I have been almost wholly dependent on the provision from Marquette of great quantities of manuscript in reproduction, without which the latter part of *The War of the Ring* could not have been written at all. For this most generous assistance I express my gratitude to all concerned in it, and most especially to Mr Taum Santoski, who has been primarily responsible for the work involved. In addition he has advised me on many particular points which can be best decided by close examination of the original papers, and he has spent much time in trying to decipher those manuscripts in which my father wrote a text in ink on top of another in pencil. I thank also Miss Tracy J. Muench and Miss Elizabeth A. Budde for their part in the work of reproducing the material, and Mr Charles B. Elston for making it possible for me to include in this book several illustrations from manuscripts at Marquette: the pages carrying sketches of Dunharrow, of the mountains at the head of Harrowdale, and of Kirith Ungol, the plan of Minas Tirith, and the full-page drawing of Orthanc (5).

This book follows the plan and presentation of its predecessors, references to previous volumes in 'The History of Middle-earth' being generally given in Roman numerals (thus 'VII' refers to *The Treason of Isengard*), FR, TT, and RK being used as abbreviations for *The Fellowship of the Ring*, *The Two Towers*, and *The Return of the King*, and page-references being made throughout to the three-volume hardback edition of *The Lord of the Rings* (LR). In several parts of the book the textual history is exceedingly complex. Since the story of the evolution of *The Lord of the Rings* can of course only be discovered by the correct ordering and interpretation of the manuscripts, and must be recounted in those terms, the textual history cannot be much simplified; and I have made much use of identifying letters for the manuscripts in order to clarify my account and to try to avoid ambiguities. In Books IV and V problems of chronological synchronisation became acute: a severe tension is sometimes perceptible between narrative certainties and the demands of an entirely coherent chronological structure (and the attempt to right dislocation in time could very well lead to dislocation in geography). Chronology is so important in this part of *The Lord of the Rings* that I could not neglect it, but I have put almost all of my complicated and often inconclusive discussion into 'Notes on the Chronology' at the end of chapters.

In this book I have used accents throughout in the names of the Rohirrim (*Théoden*, *Éomer*, &c.).

Mr Charles Noad has again read the proofs independently and checked the very large number of citations, including those to other passages within the book, with a strictness and care that I seem altogether unable to attain. In addition I have adopted several of his suggestions for improvement in clarity and consistency in my account. I am much indebted to him for this generous and substantial work.

I am very grateful for communications from Mr Alan Stokes and Mr Neil Gaiman, who have explained my father's reference in his remarks about the origins of the poem *Errantry* (*The Treason of Isengard* p. 85): 'It was begun very many years ago, in an attempt to go on with the model that came unbidden into my mind: the first six lines, in which, I guess, *D'ye ken the rhyme to porringer* had a part.' The reference is to a Jacobite song attacking William of Orange as usurper of the English crown from his father-in-law, James II, and threatening to hang him. The first verse of this song runs thus in the version given by Iona and Peter Opie in *The Oxford Dictionary of Nursery Rhymes* (no. 422):

What is the rhyme for porringer?
What is the rhyme for porringer?
The king he had a daughter fair
And gave the Prince of Orange her.

The verse is known in several forms (in one of which the opening line is *Ken ye the rhyme to porringer?* and the last *And he gave her to an Oranger*). This then is the unlikely origin of the provender of the Merry Messenger:

There was a merry passenger,
a messenger, an errander;
he took a tiny porringer
and oranges for provender.

PART ONE

THE FALL OF SARUMAN

I
THE DESTRUCTION OF ISENGARD

(*Chronology*)

The writing of the story from 'The King of the Golden Hall' to the end of the first book of *The Two Towers* was an extremely complex process. The 'Isengard story' was not conceived and set down as a series of clearly marked 'chapters', each one brought to a developed state before the next was embarked on, but evolved as a whole, and disturbances of the structure that entered as it evolved led to dislocations all through the narrative. With my father's method of composition at this time – passages of very rough and piecemeal drafting being built into a completed manuscript that was in turn heavily overhauled, the whole complex advancing and changing at the same time – the textual confusion in this part of *The Lord of the Rings* is only penetrable with great difficulty, and to set it out as a clear sequence impossible.

The essential cause of this situation was the question of chronology; and I think that the best way to approach the writing of this part of the narrative is to try to set out first the problems that my father was contending with, and to refer back to this discussion when citing the actual texts.

The story had certain fixed narrative 'moments' and relations. Pippin and Merry had encountered Treebeard in the forest of Fangorn and been taken to his 'Ent-house' of Wellinghall for the night. On that same day Aragorn, Gimli and Legolas had encountered Éomer and his company returning from battle with the Orcs, and they themselves passed the night beside the battlefield. For these purposes this may be called 'Day 1', since earlier events have here no relevance; the actual date according to the chronology of this period in the writing of *The Lord of the Rings* was Sunday January 29 (see VII.368, 406).

On Day 2, January 30, the Entmoot took place; and on that day Aragorn and his companions met Gandalf returned, and together they set out on their great ride to Eodoras. As they rode south in the evening Legolas saw far off towards the Gap of Rohan a great smoke rising, and he asked Gandalf what it might be: to which Gandalf replied 'Battle and war!' (at the end of the chapter 'The White Rider').

They rode all night, and reached Eodoras in the early morning of Day 3, January 31. While they spoke with Théoden and Wormtongue in the Golden Hall at Eodoras the Entmoot was still rumbling on far away in Fangorn. In the afternoon of Day 3 Théoden with Gandalf and his companions and a host of the Rohirrim set out west from Eodoras across the plains of Rohan towards the Fords of Isen; and on that same afternoon the Entmoot ended,[1] and the Ents began their march on Isengard, which they reached after nightfall.

It is here that the chronological problems appear. There were – or would be, as the story evolved – the following elements (some of them foreseen in some form in the outline that I called 'The Story Foreseen from Fangorn', VII.435–6) to be brought into a coherent time-pattern. The Ents would attack Isengard, and drown it by diverting the course of the river Isen. A great force would leave Isengard; the Riders at the Fords of Isen would be driven back over the river. The Rohirrim coming from Eodoras would see a great darkness in the direction of the Wizard's Vale, and they would meet a lone horseman returning from the battle at the Fords; Gandalf would fleet away westwards on Shadowfax. Théoden and his host, with Aragorn, Gimli and Legolas, would take refuge in a deep gorge in the southern mountains, and a great battle there would turn to victory after certain defeat with the coming of the 'moving trees', and the return of Gandalf and the lord of the Rohirrim whose stronghold it was. Finally, Gandalf, with Théoden, Aragorn, Gimli, Legolas and a company of the Riders would leave the refuge and ride to Isengard, now drowned and in ruins, and meet Merry and Pippin sitting on a pile of rubble at the gates.

I

In the original opening of 'Helm's Deep', as will be seen at the beginning of the next chapter, the cavalcade from Eodoras saw 'a great fume and vapour' rising over Nan Gurunír, the Wizard's Vale,[2] and met the lone horseman returning from the Fords of Isen, *on the same day* (Day 3, January 31) as they left the Golden Hall. The horseman (Ceorl) told them that the Riders had been driven back over the Isen with great loss on the previous day (Day 2, January 30); and it must have been 'the smoke of battle' that Legolas saw in the evening rising from the Gap of Rohan as they rode south from Fangorn – it cannot of course have been the steam rising from the drowning of Isengard by the Ents (see above). In this original story Théoden and his men, with Aragorn, Gimli and Legolas, took refuge in Helm's Deep (not yet so named) that same night (Day 3).

A chronological dislocation seems to have been already present in this: for the events of Days 1–3 as set out above were fixed in relation to each other, and the Ents must arrive at Isengard after nightfall of Day 3 (January 31); yet according to the original opening of 'Helm's Deep' the host from Eodoras sees the 'great fume and vapour' rising over Nan Gurunír (unquestionably caused by the drowning of Isengard) in the evening of that same day.

II

This time-scheme was duly changed: Théoden and his host camped in the plain on the first night out from Eodoras (Day 3, January 31), and it was in the morning of the second day of the ride (Day 4, February 1) that they saw the great cloud over Nan Gurunír:

> As they rode they saw a great spire of smoke and vapour, rising up out of the deep shadow of Nan Gurunír; as it mounted it caught the light of the sun and spread in glowing banks that drifted on the wind over the plains towards them.
>
> 'What do you think of that, Gandalf?' said Théoden. 'One would say that all the Wizard's Vale was burning.'
>
> 'There is ever a fume above that valley in these days,' said Háma; 'but I never saw anything like that before.'

It is now in the evening of this second day of their ride that they met the horseman Ceorl coming from the Fords, and on the night of this day that the battle of the Hornburg took place. The chronology was now therefore:

(Day 3) January 31 Gandalf, Théoden and the Rohirrim depart from Eodoras and camp for the night in the plains. Ents reach Isengard after nightfall and after the departure of the Orc-host begin the drowning of the Circle of Isengard.

(Day 4) February 1 The host from Eodoras sees in the morning the steams rising from the drowning of Isengard; in the evening they meet Ceorl and learn of the defeat at the Fords of Isen on the previous day; and reach Helm's Deep after nightfall. Battle of the Hornburg.

It seems impossible to avoid the conclusion that the end of the chapter 'The White Rider' (Legolas' sight of the smoke in the Gap of Rohan on Day 2, January 30) escaped revision when the date of the (Second) Battle of the Fords of Isen was changed to January 31.

III

In the original form of what became the opening of 'The Road to Isengard' Gandalf and Théoden, with Aragorn, Gimli and Legolas and a party of Riders, set out from Helm's Deep shortly after the end of the battle of the Hornburg, without any rest; this was on Day 5, February 2, and *they reached Isengard not long after noon on the same day.* As they approached Nan Gurunír

> they saw rising up out of deep shadows a vast spire of smoke and vapour; as it mounted it caught the light of the sun, and spread in glowing billows in the sky, and the wind bore them over the plain.
>
> 'What do you think of that, Gandalf?' said Théoden. 'One would say that all the Wizard's Vale was burning.'

'There is ever a fume above that valley in these days,' said Éomer; 'but I have never seen anything like this before. These are steams, rather than smokes. Some devilry Saruman is brewing to greet us.'

This dialogue was lifted straight from its earlier place at the beginning of the 'Helm's Deep' story (see II above) – with substitution of Éomer for Háma, slain at the Hornburg, and in 'Helm's Deep' a different passage was inserted, as found in TT pp. 131–2, in which what is seen in the North-west is 'a shadow that crept down slowly from the Wizard's Vale', and there is no mention of fume or steam.

The reason for these changes was again chronological: the host on its way from Eodoras is not to see great steams rising from Isengard on Day 4, but the 'veiling shadow' of the Huorns as they came down into the Wizard's Vale. Thus:

(Day 4) February 1 The host from Eodoras sees in the morning the shade of the moving trees far off in the North-west; the drowning of Isengard was not begun till night. At night Battle of the Hornburg.

(Day 5) February 2 In the morning Théoden and Gandalf and their company ride to Isengard, and find it drowned.

IV

The chronology was then changed to that of 'The Road to Isengard' in TT, whereby Théoden and Gandalf and their company do not leave Helm's Deep until much later on Day 5, pass the night camped below Nan Gurunír, and do not reach Isengard until midday on Day 6 (February 3). This chronology is set out in a time-scheme (additions of mine in brackets):

[Day 3] January 31 Ents arrive at Isengard, night. Break in.

[Day 4] February 1 Dawn, they go away north to make dams. All that day Merry and Pippin alone until dusk. Gandalf arrives at Isengard at nightfall, and meets Treebeard. Drowning of Isengard begins late at night. [Battle of the Hornburg.]

[Day 5] February 2 Isengard steams all day and column of smoke arises in evening. [Gandalf, Théoden, &c. see this from their camp below Nan Gurunír.] Huorns return in night to Isengard.

[Day 6] February 3 Morning, Treebeard returns to Gates. Sets Merry and Pippin to watch. Wormtongue comes. [Gandalf, Théoden, &c. arrive shortly after noon.]

This is the chronology of LR, as set out in *The Tale of Years*, though the actual dates are of course different (in LR March 2 = January 31 in this scheme).

*

This, I believe, is how the chronology evolved; but as will be seen in the following chapters, earlier time-schemes appear in the drafts for passages far on in the actual narrative, because as I have said all this part of LR was written as a whole. Thus for example in the first draft of Merry's story of the destruction and drowning of Isengard (in TT in the chapter 'Flotsam and Jetsam') the chronology belongs with the scheme described in II above, and against it my father noted: 'Drowning must not begin until night of Hornburg battle.'

Despite the way in which this part of the story was written, I think that it will in fact be clearest to break my account into chapters corresponding to those in *The Two Towers*; this inevitably entails a certain amount of advance and retreat in terms of the actual sequence of composition, but I hope that this preliminary account will clarify the shifting chronological basis in the different texts.

NOTES

1 The extra day of the Entmoot (TT pp. 87–8) was not added until much later: VII.407, 419.

2 *Nan Gurunír*, the Valley of Saruman, was added in to a blank space left for the name in the manuscript of 'Treebeard' (VII.420 note 9).

II
HELM'S DEEP

A first draft of this story, abandoned after it had proceeded for some distance, differs so essentially from its form in *The Two Towers* that I give it here in full. This text bears the chapter number XXVIII, without title. For the chronology see p. 4, § I.

There was a much-ridden way, northwestward along the foothills of the Black Mountains. Up and down over the rolling green country it ran, crossing small swift streams by many fords. Far ahead and to the right the shadow of the Misty Mountains drew nearer. Beneath the distant peak of Methedras in dark shadow lay the deep vale of Nan Gurunír; a great fume and vapour rose there and drifted towards them over the plain.[1] Halting seldom they rode on into the evening. The sun went down before them. Darkness grew behind.

Their spears were tipped with fiery red as the last shafts of light stained the clouds above Tindtorras;[2] the three peaks stood black against the sunset upon the northmost arm of the Black Mountains. In that last red light men in the van saw a horseman riding back towards them. As he drew near, the host halted, awaiting him.

He came, a weary man with dinted helm, and cloven shield. Slowly he climbed from his horse, and stood there a while, panting. At length he spoke. 'Is Éomer here?' he asked. 'You come at last, but too late and too few. Things have gone evilly, since Théodred fell.[3] We were driven back over the bend of the Isen with great loss yesterday; many perished at the crossing. Then at night fresh forces came over the river against our camp. All Isengard must be emptied; and the Wizard has armed the wild hill-men and the scattered folk of Westfold,[4] and these also he loosed upon us. We were overmastered. The shieldwall was broken. Trumbold [> Herulf > Heorulf][5] the Westmarcher has drawn off those he could gather towards his fastness under Tindtorras. Others are scattered. Where is Éomer? Tell him there is no hope ahead: he should return to Eodoras, before the wolves of Saruman come there!'

Théoden rode up. 'Come, stand before me, Ceorl!' he said. 'I am here. The last host of the Eorlingas has ridden forth. It will not return unfought.'

The man's face lightened with wonder and joy. He drew himself up. Then he knelt offering his notched sword to the King. 'Command me, lord,' he cried, 'and pardon me! I did not know, I thought—'

'You thought I remained in Eodoras, bent like an old tree under winter snow. So it was when you went. But a wind has shaken off somewhat the cold burden,' said Théoden. 'Give this man a fresh horse. Let us ride to the aid of Trumbold [> Heorulf]!'

Forward they rode again, urging on their horses. Suddenly Gandalf spoke to Shadowfax, and like an arrow from the bow the great horse sprang away. Even as they looked, he was gone: a flash of silver in the sunset, a wind in the grass, a shadow that fled and faded from sight. For a while Snowmane and the horses of the King's guard strained in pursuit, but if they had walked they would have had as much chance of overtaking him.

'What does that mean?' said Háma to a comrade. 'Ever he comes and goes unlooked-for.'

'Wormtongue, were he here, would not find it hard to explain,' said the other.

'True,' said Háma, 'but for myself I will wait till we see him again.'

'If ever we do,' said the other.

It was night and the host was still riding swiftly, when cries and hornblasts were heard from the scouts that rode ahead. Arrows whistled overhead. They were crossing a wide vale, a bay in the mountains. On the further side the Tindtorras were hidden in darkness. Some miles ahead still lay the opening of the great cleft in the hills which men of that land called *Heorulf's Clough*:[6] steep and narrow it wound inward under the Tindtorras, and where it issued in the vale, upon an outjutting heel of rock, was built the fastness of Heorulf's Hold.[7]

The scouts rode back and reported that wolfriders were abroad in the vale, and that a host of orcs and wild men, very great indeed, was hastening southward over the plain to gain the gates of the Nerwet.[8]

'We have found some of our men slain as they fled,' said one of the scouts; 'and scattered companies we have met, going this way and that, leaderless; but many are making for Herulf's Hold, and say that Herulf is already there.'

'We had best not give battle in the dark, nor await the day here in the open, not knowing the number of the coming host,' said Éomer, who had ridden up to the King's side. 'What is your counsel, Aragorn?'

'To drive through such enemies as are before us, and encamp before the Nerwet Gate to defend if may be, while the men who have fought rest behind our shield.'

'Let it be so!' said Théoden. 'We will go thither in many [separate comp]anies: let a man who is nightsighted and knows [well the land] go at the head of each.'[9]

At this point my father stopped, and returned to 'It was night and the host was still riding swiftly ...' In the passage just given is the first appearance of Helm's Deep ('Heorulf's Clough') and the Hornburg ('Heorulf's Hold') on its 'outjutting heel of rock'; Heorulf being the precursor of Erkenbrand of Westfold.

Night had fallen, and still the host was riding swiftly on. They had turned northward, and were bearing towards the fords of the Isen, when cries and hornblasts were heard from their scouts that went in front. Arrows whistled over them. At this time they were at the outer end of a wide vale, a bay in the mountains of the south. On its further western side the Tindtorras were hidden in darkness; beneath their feet [> the peaks], some miles away, lay the opening of the great cleft in the hills which men of that land called Heorulf's Clough [> lay the green coomb out of which opened a great cleft in the hills. Men of that land called it Helm's Deep],[10] after some hero of ancient wars who had made his refuge there. Ever steeper and narrower it wound inward under the Tindtorras, till the crowhaunted cliffs on either side towered far above and shut out the light. Where it issued in the vale, upon [*added*: the Stanrock,] an outjutting heel of land, was built the fastness of Heorulf's Hoe[11] (Hold?). Stanrock. [> was built the fastness of Helmsgate. There Heorulf the Marcher had his hold.]

A scout now rode back and reported that wolfriders were abroad in the valley, and that a host of orcs and wild men, very great indeed, was hurrying southward over the plain towards Heorulf's Hold.

'We have found many of our own folk lying slain as they fled thither,' said the scout. 'And we have met scattered companies, going this way and that, leaderless. Some are making for the Clough [> Helmsgate], but it seems that Nothelm [> Heorulf] is not there. His plan was changed, and men do not know whither he has gone. Some say that Wormtongue was seen today [> Some say that Wormtongue was seen in the evening going north, and in the dusk an old man on a great horse rode the same way].'

'Well, if Nothelm be in the Hold or not, [> 'It will go ill with Wormtongue, if Gandalf overtakes him,' said Théoden. 'Nonetheless I miss now both counsellors, old and new. Yet it seems to me that whether Heorulf be in his Hold or no,] in this need we have no better choice than to go thither ourselves,' said Théoden. 'What is your counsel?' he said, turning to Éomer who had now ridden up to the King's side.

'We should be ill advised to give battle in the dark,' said Éomer, 'or to await the day here in the open, not knowing the number of the oncoming host. Let us drive through such foes as are between us and Herulf's Clough [> the fastness], and encamp before the Hold [> its gate]. Then if we cannot break out, we may retreat to the Hold. There are caves in the gorge [> Helm's Deep] behind where hundreds may hide, and secret ways lead up thence, I am told, onto the hills.'

'Trust not to them!' said Aragorn. 'Saruman has long spied out this land, Still, in such a place our defence might last long.'

'Let us go then,' said Théoden. 'We will ride thither in many separate companies. A man who is nightsighted and knows well the land shall go at the head of each.'

I interrupt the text here to discuss some aspects of this story. The names present an apparently impenetrable confusion, but I think that the development was more or less as follows. My father was uncertain whether 'Heorulf' ('Herulf') was the present lord of the 'Hold' or the hero after whom the 'Clough' was named. When he wrote, in the passage just given, 'which men of that land called Heorulf's Clough, after some hero of ancient wars who had made his refuge there' he had decided on the latter, and therefore the name of the present 'West-marcher' (precursor of Erkenbrand) was changed, becoming *Nothelm*. Then, changing again, *Nothelm* reverted to *Heorulf*, while the gorge was named after *Helm*: *Helmshaugh* (note 10), then *Helm's Deep*. The fastness (*Heorulf's Hoe* or *Hold*) standing on the *Stanrock* is now called *Helmsgate*, which in LR refers to the entrance to Helm's Deep across which the Deeping Wall was built.

The image of the great gorge and the fortress built on the jutting heel or 'hoe' arose, I believe, as my father wrote this first draft of the new chapter. In the outline 'The Story Foreseen from Fangorn' (VII.435) Gandalf's sudden galloping off on Shadowfax is present, and 'by his help and Aragorn the Isengarders are driven back'; there is no suggestion of any gorge or hold in the hills to the south. So again in the present narrative he says nothing before he rides off; whereas in TT he tells Théoden not to go the Fords of Isen but to ride to Helm's Deep. Thus in the original story it was not until 'cries and hornblasts were heard from their scouts that went in front' and 'arrows whistled over them' that the leaders of the host decided to make for the Hold; in TT (where the actual wording of the passage is scarcely changed) the host was 'in the low valley before the mouth of the Coomb' when these things happened.

The present text agrees well with the First Map (redrawn section IVE, VII.319). At this time the host was 'at the outer end of a wide vale, a bay in the mountains of the south'; and 'Heorulf's Clough' lay somewhere near the western end of this 'bay'. The First Map is in fact less clear at this point than my redrawing makes it, but the map that I made in 1943, which was closely based on the First Map (see VII.299), shows Helm's Deep very clearly as running in towards the Tindtorras (Thrihyrne) from a point well to the north and west of the 'bay in the mountains' – the Westfold Vale, in the present text not yet named (see note 4).[12]

On the page of the completed manuscript in which the final form of this passage (TT p. 133) was reached the text reads thus: 'Still some miles away, on the far side of the Westfold Vale, a great bay in the mountains, lay a green coomb out of which a gorge opened in the hills.' There is no question that this is correct, and that this was what my father intended: the great bay in the mountains was of course the Westfold Vale. In the typescript based on this, however, the sentence became, for some obscure reason (there is no ambiguity in the manuscript): 'Still some miles away, on the far side of the Westfold Vale, lay a green coomb, a great bay in the mountains, out of which a gorge opened in the hills.' This error is perpetuated in *The Two Towers*.

In this original narrative it was on the night of the day of departure from Eodoras that the host came to the hold in the hills; subsequently[13] it was on the night of the second day (for the chronology see pp. 4–5, §§ I–II). In the later story it is said (TT p. 131) that 'Forty leagues and more it was, as a bird flies, from Edoras to the fords of the Isen', and this agrees very well with the First Map, where the distance is almost 2.5 cm., or 125 miles (= just over 40 leagues). It may have been a closer look at the map that led to the extension of the ride across the plain by a further day. On the other hand, there was also an evident difficulty with the chronology as it now stood: see p. 4, § I.

The original draft continues:

Aragorn and Legolas rode with Éomer's *éored*. That company needed no guide more keen of sight than Legolas, or a man who knew the land, far and wide about, better than Éomer himself. Slowly, and as silently as they might, they went through the night, turning back from the plain, and climbing westward into the dim folds about the mountains' feet. They came upon few of the enemy, except here and there a roving band of orcs who fled ere the riders could slay many; but ever the rumour of war grew behind them. Soon they could hear harsh singing, and if they turned and looked back they could see, winding up from the low country, red torches, countless points of fiery light. A very wood of trees must have been felled to furnish them. Every now and then a brighter blaze leaped up.

'It is a great host,' said Aragorn, 'and follows us close.'

'They bring fire,' said Éomer, 'and are burning as they come all that they can kindle: rick and cot and tree. We shall have a great debt to pay them.'

'The reckoning is not far off,' said Aragorn. 'Shall we soon find ground where we can turn and stand?'

'Yes,' said Éomer. 'Across the wide mouth of the coomb, at some distance from Helmsgate there is a fall in the ground, so sharp and sheer that to those approaching it seems as if they came upon a wall. This we call [Stanshelf Stanscylf >][14] Helm's dike. In places it is twenty feet high, and on the top it has been crowned with a rampart of great stones, piled in ancient days. There we will stand. Thither the other companies will also come. There are three ways that lead up through breaches in the cliff:[15] these we must hold strongly.'

It was dark, starless and moonless, when they came to [the Stanshelf >] Helm's dike. Éomer led them up by a broad sloping path that climbed through a deep notch in the cliff and came out upon the new level some way behind the rampart. They were unchallenged. No one was there before them, friend or foe.[16] At once Éomer set guards upon the [breaches >] Inlets. Ere long other companies arrived, creeping up the valley from various directions. There were wide grass-slopes between the rampart and the Stanrock. There they set their horses under such guards as could be spared from the manning of the wall.

Gimli stood leaning against a great stone at a high point of the [Stanshelf >] dike not far from the inlet by which they had entered. Legolas was on the stone above fingering his bow and peering into the blackness.

'This is more to my liking,' said the dwarf, stamping his feet on the ground. 'Ever my heart lightens as we draw near the mountains. There is good rock here. This country has hard bones. I feel it under my feet. Give me a year and a hundred of my kin and we could make this a place that armies would break against like water.'

'I doubt it not,' said Legolas. 'But you're a dwarf, and dwarves are strange folk. I like it not, and shall like it no more by the light of day. But you comfort me, Gimli, and I am glad to have you stand by me with your stout legs and hard axe.'

Shapes loomed up beside them. It was Éomer and Aragorn walking together along the line of the rampart. 'I am anxious,' said Éomer. 'Most have now arrived; but one company is still lacking, and also the King and his guard.'

'If you will give me some hardy men, I will take Gimli and Legolas here, and go a little down the valley and look for tidings,' said Aragorn.

'And find more than you are looking for,' said Gimli.

'That is likely,' said Éomer. 'We will wait a while.'

A slow time passed, when suddenly at no great distance down the valley a clamour broke out. Horns sounded. 'There are some of our folk come into an ambush, or taken in the rear,' cried Éomer. 'Théoden will be there. Wait here, I will hold the men back to the wall, and choose some to go forth. I will be back swiftly.'

Horns sounded again, and in the still darkness they could hear the clash of weapons. In brief while Éomer returned with twenty men.

'This errand I will take,' said Aragorn. 'You are needed on the wall. Come, Legolas! Your eyes will serve us.' He sped down the slope.

'Where Legolas goes, I go,' said Gimli, and ran after them.

The watchers on the wall saw nothing for a while, then suddenly there were louder cries, and wilder yells. A clear voice rang, echoing in the hills. *Elendil!* It seemed that far below in the shadows a white flame flashed.

'Branding goes to war at last,' said Éomer.

A horseman appeared before the main breach, and was admitted. 'Where is Théoden King?' asked Éomer.

'Among his guard,' said the man. 'But many are unhorsed. We rode into an ambush, and orcs sprang out of the ground among us, hamstringing many of our steeds. Snowmane and the King escaped; for that horse is nightsighted, and sprang over the heads of the orcs. But Théoden dismounted and fought among his guard. Herugrim sang a song that has long been silent. Aragorn is with them, and he sends word that a great host of orcs is on his heels. Man the wall! He will come in by the main breach if he can.'

The noise of battle drew nearer. Those on the rampart could do nothing to aid. They had not many archers among them, and these could not shoot in the darkness while their friends were still in front. One by one men of the missing company came in, till all but five were mustered. Last came the King's guard on foot, with the King in their midst, leading Snowmane.

'Hasten, Lord!' cried Éomer.

At that moment there was a wild cry. Orcs were attacking the [breaches >] inlets on either hand, and before the King had been brought in to safety out of the darkness there sprang a host of dark shapes driving towards the great breach. A white fire shone. There in their path could be seen for a moment Aragorn son of Arathorn: on his one side was Gimli, on the other Legolas.

'Back now, my comrades!' cried Aragorn. 'I will follow.' Even as Gimli and Legolas ran back towards the rampart, he leaped forward. Before the flame of Branding the orcs fled. Then slowly Aragorn retreated walking backward. Even as he did so step by step one great orc came forward, while others stalked behind him. As Aragorn turned at last to run up the inlet, the orc sprang after him: but an arrow whined and he fell sprawling and lay still. For some time no others dared to draw near. 'Sure is the shaft of the elven bow, and keen are the eyes of Legolas!' said Aragorn as he joined the elf and they ran together to the rampart.

Thus at last the King's host was brought within the fastness, and turned to bay before the mouth of Helm's Deep. The night was not yet old, and many hours of darkness and peril yet remained. Théoden was unhurt; but he grieved for the loss of so many of the horses of his guard, and he looked upon Snowmane bleeding at the shoulder: a glancing arrow had struck him. 'Fair is the riding forth, friend,' he said; 'but often the road is bitter.'

'Grieve not for Snowmane, lord,' said Aragorn. 'The hurt is light. I will tend it, with such skill as I have, while the enemy still holds off. They have suffered losses more grievous than ours, and will suffer more if they dare to assail this place.'

Here the original draft ends as formed narrative, but continues as an outline, verging on narrative. This was written over a faint pencilled text that seems to have been much the same.

There is an attack. Endless numbers. Grappling hooks, ladders, piled slain. Riders block breaches with stones from high places, and with bodies. Orcs keep on getting in. Riders lose few men, most at breaches. Orcs once got near the horses. Late in the night the (waning?) moon shone fitfully, and the defenders see a boiling throng beneath the wall. Slowly the dead were piling up.

Wild men in steel mesh forced the north breach, and turning south began to drive men from the rampart. Orcs clamber over. Dawn sees the Men of Rohan giving way all along. The horses are taken away to Helm's Deep, with the King. They make a shieldwall and retreat slowly up towards the Stanrock.

The sun comes out, and then all stare: defenders and attackers. A mile or so below the Dike, from North to South in a great crescent, they beheld a marvel. Men rubbed their eyes thinking that they dreamed or were dizzy with wounds and weariness. Where all had been upland and grass-clad slopes, there stood now a wood of great trees. Like beeches they were, robed in withered leaves, and like ancient oaks with tangled boughs, and gnarled pines stood dark among them. The orcs gave back. The Wild Men wavered crying in terrified voices, for they came from the woods under the west sides of the Misty Mountains.

At that moment from the Stanrock a trumpet sounded. Forth rode Théoden with his guard, and a company (of Heorulf's men?). They charged down crashing into the Wild Men and driving them back in ruin over the cliff.

'Wizardry is abroad!' said [?men]. 'What can this betoken?'

'Wizardry maybe,' said Éomer. 'But it seems not to be any device of our enemies. See how dismayed they are.'

A few lines of very rapid and partly illegible notes follow:

> Their horses were often nightsighted; but the men were not so nightsighted as the orcs. Rohan at a disadvantage in dark. As soon as it grows light they are able to fight. The orcs are no match for the horsemen on the slopes before the Stanrock. Sorties from Helm's Deep and Stanrock. Orcs dive back over wall. It is then that the Wood is seen.

Orcs trapped. Trees grab them. And the wood is full of Herulf's folk. Gandalf has collected the wanderers. [?About] 500. Hardly any of the attackers escape. So hopelessness turns to victory. Meanwhile Herulf told by Gandalf to hold the .... rode .... another force sent .... Eodoras. This is now caught between Herulf and the victorious forces of the King. In a battle on the plain .... terror struck by Aragorn and Gandalf. The host not wishing to rest rides down the fleeing remnant [?back towards] Isengard.

The sentence beginning 'Meanwhile Herulf told by Gandalf to hold the' might possibly, but very doubtfully indeed, be completed: 'eastern rode [*for* road] has resisted another force sent towards Eodoras.'

This then was the original story of Helm's Deep, to become far more complex in its development with the emergence of a much more elaborate system of fortification across the mouth of the Deep (the description and narrative in *The Two Towers* can be followed, incidentally, very precisely in my father's drawing, 'Helm's Deep and the Hornburg', in *Pictures by J. R. R. Tolkien*, no. 26). In this earliest account the 'fastness' consisted only of the sudden natural fall in the land across the mouth of the coomb, fortified with a parapet of great stones; in this there were three 'breaches', a word that my father changed to 'inlets', perhaps to suggest that they had been deliberately made. The nature of the 'hold' of Heorulf on the Stanrock is not indicated; and all the battle of Helm's Deep took place along the line of Helm's Dike.

An isolated scrap of drafting that was not finally used evidently belongs with the original story and may be included here:

Aragorn was away behind the defences tending the wound in Snowmane's shoulder, and speaking gentle words to the horse. As the fragrance of *athelas* rose in the air, his mind went back to the defence on Weathertop, and to the escape from Moria. 'It is a long journey,' he said to himself. 'From one hopeless corner we escape but to find another more desperate. Yet alas, Frodo, I would be happier in heart if you were with us in this grim place. Where now do you wander?'

Written on this same page is an outline in which the radical alteration of the story of the assault first enters.

When Éomer and Aragorn reach Dike they are challenged. Heorulf has left watchers on Dike. They report that the fort of Helm's Gate is manned – mainly older men, and most of the folk of the Westmarch have taken refuge in the Deep. Great store of food and fodder is in the caves.

Then follows story as told above until rescue of King.[17]

Éomer and Aragorn decide that they cannot hold Dike in dark (without archers). The Dike is over a mile – 2 miles? – long. The main host and King go to Stanrock. The horses are led to the Deep. Aragorn and Éomer with a few men (their horses ready in rear) hold the inlets as long as they dare. These they block with stones rolled from the rampart.

The assault on the inlets. Soon drives in as the Orcs clamber up rampart in between. Ladders? Wild men drive in from North Inlet. The defenders flee. Tremendous assault upon the mouth of the Deep where a high stone wall was built. [*Added here but at the same time:* breastwork crowned with stones. Here G[imli] speaks his words. *Reduce description of Helm's Dike* – it is *not* fortified.] Orcs boil round foot of the Stanrock. Then describe the assault as above.[18] Orcs piling up over the wall. Wild men climb on the goblins' dead bodies. Moon ... men fighting on the wall top.[19] Disadvantage of the Riders. The wall taken and Rohan driven back into the gorge. Dawn. Éomer and Aragorn go to the Stanrock to stand by the King in the Tower.

They see in the sunlight the wonder of the Wood.

Charge of Théoden (Éomer left, Aragorn right). [? With day fortunes change.] Men issue on horses. But the host is vast, only it is disconcerted by the Wood. Almost [? the watchers could] believe it had moved up the valley as the battle raged.

Trees should come right up to Dike. In the midst out rides Gandalf from the wood. And rides through the orcs as if they were rats and crows.

My father began a new text of the chapter before important elements in the story and in the physical setting had been clarified, and as a result this (the first completed manuscript) is an extremely complicated document. It was only after he had begun it that he extended the ride from Eodoras by a further day, and described the great storm coming up out of the East (TT pp. 131–2); and when he began it he had not yet realised that Helm's Dike was not the scene of the great assault: 'what really happened' was that the men manning the Dike were driven in, and the defence of the redoubt was at the line of a great wall further up at the mouth of the gorge – the 'Deeping Wall' – and the Hornburg. At this point in the manuscript the story can be seen changing as my father wrote: in Éomer's reply to Aragorn's question 'Shall we soon find ground where we can turn and stand?' (p. 13) he begins as before with an account of the fortification of the Dike ('crowned with a rampart of great stones, piled in ancient days'), but by the end of his reply he is saying that the Dike cannot be held:

'... But we cannot long defend it, for we have not enough strength. It is near two miles from end to end, and is pierced by two wide breaches. We shall not be able to stand at bay till we get to the Stanrock, and come behind the wall that guards the entrance to the Deep. That is high and strong, for Heorulf had it repaired and raised not long ago.'

Immediately after this the Deeping Stream entered, and the two breaches in the Dike were reduced to one: there 'a stream flows down out of the Deep, and beside it the road runs from Helm's Gate to the valley.'[20] At this stage, however, the final story was still not reached, but follows the outline just given (p. 18):

The King and the main part of his host now rode on to man the Stanrock and Heorulf's wall. But the Westmarchers would not yet abandon the dike while any hope remained of Heorulf's return. Éomer and Aragorn and a few picked men stayed with them guarding the breach; for it seemed to Éomer that they might do great harm to the advance-guard of the enemy and then escape swiftly ere the main strength of the orcs and wild men forced the passage.

The story from this point was built up in a textually extremely complex series of short drafts leading to more finished forms, while earlier portions of the chapter were changed to accommodate the evolving conception of the redoubt as the scene of the battle. To follow this evolution in all its detail would require a very great deal of space, and I record only certain rejected narrative ideas and other particular points of interest.

Before the story (TT pp. 138–40) of the sortie of Éomer and Aragorn from the postern gate emerged, the repulse of the attack on the great gates of the Hornburg was differently conceived:

Now with a great cry a company of the wild men moved forward, among them they bore the trunk of a great tree. The orcs crowded about them. The tree was swung by many strong hands, and smote the timbers with a boom. At that moment there was a sudden call. Among the boulders upon the flat and narrow rim beneath the fastness and the brink a few brave men had lain hidden. Aragorn was their leader. 'Up now, up now,' he shouted. 'Out Branding, out!' A blade flashed like white fire. 'Elendil, Elendil!' he shouted, and his voice echoed in the cliffs.

'See, see!' said Éomer. 'Branding has gone to war at last. Why am I not there? We were to have drawn blades together.'

None could withstand the onset of Aragorn, or the terror of his sword. The orcs fled, the hill-men were hewn down, or fled leaving their ram upon the ground. The rock was cleared. Then Aragorn and his men turned to run back within the gates while there was yet time. His men had passed within, when again the lightning flashed. Thunder crashed. From among the fallen at the top of the causeway three huge orcs sprang up – the white hand could be seen on their shields. Men shouted warning from the gates, and Aragorn for an instant turned. At that moment the foremost of the orcs hurled a stone: it struck him on the helm and he stumbled, falling to his knee. The thunder rolled. Before he could get up and back the three orcs were upon him.

Here this story was overtaken by that of the sortie from the postern. In the final manuscript form of this, Aragorn, looking at the gates, added after the words (TT p. 139) 'Their great hinges and iron bars were wrenched and bent; many of their timbers were cracked': 'The doors will not withstand another such battering.' These words were left out of the typescript that followed, but there is nothing in the manuscript to suggest that they should be, and it seems clear that their omission was an error (especially since they give point to Éomer's reply: 'Yet we cannot stay here beyond the walls to defend them').

Gimli's cry as he sprang on the Orcs who had fallen on Éomer: *Baruk Khazâd! Khazâd ai-mênu!* appears in this form from the first writing of the scene. Years later, after the publication of LR, my father began on an analysis of all fragments of other languages (Quenya, Sindarin, Khuzdul, the Black Speech) found in the book, but unhappily before he had reached the end of FR the notes, at the outset full and elaborate, had diminished to largely uninterpretable jottings. *Baruk* he here translated as 'axes', without further comment; *ai-mênu* is analysed as *aya*, *mēnu*, but the meanings are not clearly legible: most probably *aya* 'upon', *mēnu* 'acc. pl. you'.

A curious point arises in Gimli's remark after his rescue of Éomer during the sortie from the postern gate (TT p. 140): 'Till now I have hewn naught but wood since I left Moria.' This is clearly inconsistent with Legolas' words in 'The Departure of Boromir', when he and Gimli came upon Aragorn beside Boromir's body near Parth Galen: 'We have hunted and slain many Orcs in the woods'; compare also the draft of a later passage (VII.386) where, when Aragorn, Legolas and Gimli set out in pursuit of the Orcs, Gimli says: '... those that attacked Boromir were not the only ones. Legolas and I met some away southwards on the west slopes of Amon Hen. *We slew many*, creeping on them among the trees ...' I do not think that any 'explanation' of this will serve: it is simply an inconsistency never observed.[21]

The 'wild hill-men' at the assault on Helm's Deep came from 'Westfold', valleys on the western side of the Misty Mountains (see p. 8 and note 4), and this application of 'Westfold' survived until a late stage of revision of the manuscript: it was still present in drafting for what became 'The Road to Isengard'.[22] Until the change in application was made, the Westfold Vale was called 'the Westmarch Vale'.

In this connection there are two notable passages. The dialogue between Aragorn and Éomer and Gamling the Westmarcher on the Deeping Wall, hearing the cries of the wild men below (TT p. 142), takes this form in a rejected draft:

'I hear them,' said Éomer; 'but they are only as the scream of birds and the bellowing of beasts to my ears.'

'Yet among them are many that cry in the tongue of Westfold [*later* > in the Dunland tongue],' said Aragorn; 'and that is a speech of men, and once was accounted good to hear.'

'True words you speak,' said Gamling, who had climbed now on the wall. 'I know that tongue. It is ancient, and once was spoken in many valleys of the Mark. But now it is used in deadly hate. They shout rejoicing in our doom. "The king, the king!" they cry. "We will take their king! Death to the Forgoil! Death to the Strawheads! Death to the robbers of the North." Such names they have for us. Not in half a thousand years have they forgot their grievance, that the lords of Gondor gave the Mark to Eorl the Young as a reward for his service to Elendil and Isildur, while they held back. It is this old hatred that Saruman has inflamed. ...'

With this compare the passage in drafting of 'The King of the Golden Hall' (VII.444) where Aragorn, seeing on one of the hangings in the Golden Hall the figure of the young man on a white horse, said: 'Behold Eorl the Young! Thus he rode out of the North to the Battle of the Field of Gorgoroth' – the battle in which Sauron was overthrown by Gil-galad and Elendil.[23] On the enormously much briefer time-span that my father conceived at this time see VII.450 note 11.

An extremely rapid initial sketch for the parley between Aragorn, standing above the gates of the Hornburg, and the enemy below shows an entirely different conception from that in TT (p. 145):

Aragorn and the Captain of Westfold.

Westfolder says if the King is yielded all may go alive. Where to? To Isengard. Then the Westmarch is to be given back to us, and all the .... land.

Who says so? Saruman. That is indeed a good warrant.

Aragorn rebukes Westfolder for [??aiding] Orcs. Westfolder is humbled.

Orc captain jeers. Needs must accept the terms when no others will serve. We are the Uruk-hai, we slay!

Orcs shoot an arrow at Aragorn as they retreat. But the Westfold Captain hews down the archer.

On the back of the page in which the new story of the assault entered (p. 17) my father wrote the following names: *Rohirwaith Rochirchoth Rohirhoth Rochann Rohann Rohirrim*; and also *Éomeark Éomearc*. I do not know whether *Rochann*, *Rohann* is to be associated with the use of *Rohan* on pp. 16, 18 apparently as a term for the Riders.[24]

In a draft for the passage describing the charge from the Hornburg the King rode with Aragorn at his right hand and Háma at his left. For Háma's death before the gates of the Hornburg see p. 41 note 8.

Lastly, at the end of the chapter, Legolas, seeing the strange Wood beyond Helm's Dike, said: 'This is wizardry indeed! "Greenleaf, Greenleaf, when thy last shaft is shot, under strange trees shalt thou go." Come! I would look on this forest, ere the spell changes.' The words he cited were from the riddling verse addressed to him by Galadriel and borne by Gandalf ('The White Rider', VII.431):

Greenleaf, Greenleaf, bearer of the elven-bow,
Far beyond Mirkwood many trees on earth grow.
Thy last shaft when thou hast shot, under strange trees
shalt thou go!

His words were not corrected on the manuscript, and survived into the typescript that followed (see p. 420).

NOTES

1 For the subsequent history of this passage see pp. 4–6.

2 *Tindtorras*: earlier name for the *Thrihyrne*; see VII.320.

3 In the first version of 'The King of the Golden Hall' the Second Master of the Mark was Eofored, and when Théodred appears he is not Théoden's son (see VII.446–7 and note 17). The 'First Battle of the Fords of Isen', in which Théodred fell, was now present (VII.444 and note 12), and in a contemporary time-scheme is dated January 25, the day before the death of Boromir and the Breaking of the Fellowship (in LR February 25 and 26).

4 On the First Map (redrawn section IV^{D}, VII.319) *Westfold* was written against a vale on the western side of the Misty Mountains, south of *Dunland* (though afterwards struck out in this position and reinserted along the northern foothills of the Black Mountains west of Eodoras). It cannot be said whether *Dunland*

and *Westfold* originally stood together on the map as names of distinct regions, or whether *Dunland* was only entered when *Westfold* was removed.

5 The change from *Trumbold* to *Herulf*, *Heorulf* (afterwards Erkenbrand) was made while this initial drafting was in progress.

6 My father first wrote *Dimgræf*, but changed it as he wrote to *Heorulf's Clough*; above this he wrote *the Dimhale* (*hale* representing Old English *halh*, *healh*, 'corner, nook of land'), and after it *Herelaf's Clough*, this being struck out. In the margin he wrote *Nerwet* (Old English, 'narrow place'); and at the head of the page *Neolnearu* and *Neolnerwet* (Old English *neowol*, *nēol* 'deep, profound'), also *the Clough*, *the Long Clough*, and *Theostercloh* (Old English *þēostor* 'dark'). *Clough* is from Old English *clōh* 'steep-sided valley or ravine'.

7 Following this my father wrote, but struck out, '*Dimhale's Door*, by some called *Herulf's Hold (Burg)*'; and in the margin he wrote *Dimgraf's gate*, and *Dimmhealh* (see note 6).

8 *Nerwet*: see note 6.

9 The words enclosed in square brackets are lost (but are obtained from the following draft) through a square having been cut out of the page: possibly there was a small sketch-map here of 'Heorulf's Clough' and the 'Hold'.

10 Before *Helm's Deep* my father first wrote *Helmshaugh*, *haugh* being the Northern English and Scottish development of Old English *halh* (note 6).

11 *Heorulf's Hoe*: *Hoe* is from Old English *hōh* 'heel' (used in place-names in various senses, such as 'the end of a ridge where the ground begins to fall steeply').

12 The map redrawn on p. 269 is anomalous in this respect as in many others.

13 The extension of the ride across the plain by a day, and the shift in the date of the (second) battle of the Fords of Isen to January 31, entered in revision to the completed manuscript of 'Helm's Deep': see p. 18.

14 *Stanscylf*, beside *Stanshelf*, has the Old English form *scylf* (*sc* = *sh*).

15 *the cliff*: i.e. the Stanshelf, the great natural fall in the ground, constituting a rampart.

16 Cf. the two versions of the scout's report: 'many are making for Herulf's Hold, and say that Herulf is aleady there' (p. 10); 'some are making for the Clough, but it seems that Nothelm [> Heorulf] is not there' (p. 11).

17 In the first draft the fastness was deserted when the host from Eodoras arrived (p. 13). 'Then follows story as told above until rescue of King' refers to the story in the first draft given on pp. 13–16.

18 This presumably refers to the outline given on p. 16, where the assault was at the line of Helm's Dike, unless some other early account of the assault has been lost.

19 A scrap of drafting has the phrase 'Fitful late moon saw men fighting on the top of the wall'; but the illegible word here is not *saw*, though that may have been intended.

20 It is subsequently said (but rejected) of the Deeping Stream in this manuscript that 'far to the north it joined the Isen River and made the western border of the Mark.'

21 The second of these passages (VII.386) was lost in TT (p. 22). In the fair copy manuscript of 'The Departure of Boromir' as originally written Legolas in the first passage (TT p. 16) said only: 'Alas! We came when we heard the horn, but we are too late. Are you much hurt?'; the fuller form of his opening words on seeing Aragorn, in which he mentions the hunting and slaying of Orcs with Gimli in the woods, was added later (both to the manuscript and the following typescript). It is therefore possible that my father had now rejected the idea that appears in the second passage ('We slew many'), and did not reinstate it again until after the writing of 'Helm's Deep'. But this seems unlikely, and in any case does not alter the fact of the inconsistency in the published work. This inconsistency may have been observed before, but it was pointed out to me by Mr. Ralph L. McKnight, Jr.

22 Another notable instance of the overlapping in this part of the story is found in the name *Erkenbrand*. This appears in late stages of the revision of the completed manuscript of 'Helm's Deep', but it was a replacement of *Erkenwald* (itself replacing *Heorulf*); and *Erkenwald* is still the name of the Lord of Westfold in drafting for what became the chapter 'Flotsam and Jetsam'. See p. 40 note 2.

23 In TT (p. 142) Gamling says: 'Not in half a thousand years have they forgotten their grievance that the lords of Gondor gave the Mark to Eorl the Young *and made alliance with him*.'

24 In addition, the form *Rohir* is found in this chapter; this has occurred in the manuscript of 'The White Rider' (VII.433 note 8). *Rohirrim* is found in the completed manuscript of 'Helm's Deep', but it was not yet established, for *Rohir* appears in the final fair copy manuscript of 'The Road to Isengard' (p. 40), and much later, in 'Faramir' ('The Window on the West'), both *Rohir* and *Rohiroth* are used (pp. 155–6).

III
THE ROAD TO ISENGARD

This chapter was at first continuous with 'Helm's Deep', and when the division was made it received the title 'To Isengard' (Chapter XXIX). The preparatory drafting was here much more voluminous than that of 'Helm's Deep', because the first form of the story had reached a developed form and a clear manuscript before it was rejected. The interpretation of the very confused papers for this chapter is particularly difficult, since it is necessary to distinguish between drafts (often closely similar) for passages in the first version and drafts for passages in the second.

The essential differences in the original version from the form in *The Two Towers* are these: Gandalf and Théoden and their companions left Helm's Deep shortly after the end of the battle (see p. 5, § III); they did not see the Ents as they left the mysterious wood, and they did not go down to the Fords of Isen; but they encountered, and spoke with, Bregalad the Ent, bearing a message from Treebeard, in the course of their ride to Isengard, which they reached on the same day. In this chapter I shall give those parts of the original version that are significantly different from the later form, citing them from the completed manuscript of that version but with certain passages from the initial drafts given in the notes.[1]

First, however, there is an outline that my father evidently set down before he began work on the chapter. This was written in the rapid and often barely legible soft pencil that was usual for these preliminary sketches, but in this case a good deal of the outline was inked over.

Meeting of the chieftains. Éomer and Gimli return from Deep. (Both wounded and are tended by Aragorn?) Gandalf explains that he had ridden ranged about gathering scattered men. The coming of the King had diverted Isengard from Eodoras. But he [Gandalf] had sent some men back to defend it against marauders. Erkenbrand[2] had been [?ambushed] and the few horses remaining after the disaster at Isenford had been lost. He had [?perforce retreated] into hills.

They ask Gandalf about the Trees. The answer lies in Isengard, he said. We go now thither speedily – such as will.

Aragorn, Éomer, Gimli, Legolas, King Théoden and his company and [?a force] .... to Isengard. Erkenbrand. Gamling. Repair of Hornburg.

They pass down a great .... aisle among the trees that [?seems now to have opened]. No orcs to be seen. Strange murmurs and noises and half-voices among the trees. [*Added:* Gandalf discusses his tactics. Gimli describes the caves. *Here the overwriting in ink begins:*]

The sun shines in the plain. They see a tall giant figure striding towards them. The Riders draw swords, and are astonished. The figure greets Gandalf.

I am Bregalad the Quickbeam, he said. I come from Treebeard.

What does he wish? said Gandalf.

He wishes you to hasten. He wants to know what he is to do with Saruman!

Hm! said Gandalf. That is a problem. Tell him I am coming!

What was that, said Théoden. And who is Treebeard?

He was an Ent, said Gandalf. And so is Treebeard.

They hasten and enter Nan Gurunír. There they find a heap of ruins. The great walls of Isengard were burst and flung down in confusion. Only the tower of Orthanc stood alone in the midst of desolation, from which a great smoke went up. The great arch still stands, but a pile of rubble stands before it. On the top of the pile sat — Merry and Pippin, having lunch.[3] They jumped up, and as Pippin had his mouth full, Merry spoke.

'Welcome, lords, to Isengard!' he said. 'We are the door-wardens: Meriadoc son of Caradoc of Buckland is my name; and my companion is Peregrin son of Paladin of Tuckborough.[4] Far in the North is our home. The lord Saruman is within, but [alas, he is indisposed and unable to receive guests. >] at the moment he is closeted with one Wormtongue discussing urgent business.'

'It is possible that we could help in the debate,' laughed Gandalf. 'But where is Treebeard? I have no time to jest with young hobbits.'

'So we find you at last,' said Aragorn. 'You have given us a long journey.'

'How long have you been at Isengard?' said Gimli.

'Less than a day,' said Pippin.[5]

I turn now to the first version of the story, that is the first completed and coherent manuscript. In this, Théoden's words with Gandalf about riding to Isengard (TT p. 149) have a different outcome:

'Nonetheless to Isengard I go,' said Gandalf. 'Let those who are weary rest. For soon there will be other work to do. I shall not stay long. My way lies eastward. Look for me in Eodoras, ere the moon is full!'

'Nay,' said Théoden. 'In the dark hour before dawn I doubted. But we will not part now. I will ride with you, if that is your counsel. And now I will send out messengers with tidings of victory through all the vales of the Mark; and they shall summon all men, old and young, to meet me at Eodoras, ere the moon wanes.'

'Good!' said Gandalf. 'Then in one hour we ride again. ...'[6]

After a brief hour of rest and the breaking of their fast, those who were to ride to Isengard made ready to depart.[7]

The account of the treatment of the men of Dunland and the burials (TT p. 150) reaches the final form,[8] but the description of the departure of the trees in the night and of the valley after they had gone, told in almost the same words as in TT,[9] first entered at this point, whereas in TT it is postponed till much later in the chapter (p. 158). The passage of the wood, and Gimli's description to Legolas of the Caves of Helm's Deep, reach in the completed manuscript of the first version almost exactly the form in TT (pp. 152–3), but with a slight structural difference, in that here the company had already left the trees and come to the road-parting when this conversation took place:

They passed through the wood and found that they had come to the bottom of the coomb, where the road from Helm's Deep branched, going one way to Eodoras and the other to the fords of the Isen. Legolas looked back with regret.

'Those are the strangest trees that ever I saw,' he said ...

Thus at the end of their talk together the old version again differs:

'You have my promise,' said Legolas. 'But now we must leave all that behind. How far is it to Isengard, Gandalf?'

'It is about twelve [*later* > fourteen > eleven] leagues from the bottom of Deeping Coomb to the outer wall of Isengard,'[10] said the wizard, turning round.

'And what shall we see there?' asked Gimli. 'You may know, but I cannot guess.'

'I do not know myself for certain,' answered Gandalf. 'Things may have changed again, since I was there last night. But we shall all know before long. If we are eager for the answer to riddles, let us quicken the pace!'

[*Added:* 'Lead us!' said Théoden. 'But do not let Shadowfax set a pace we cannot keep!'

The company rode forward now with all the speed they could, over the wide grasses of the Westemnet.]

Thus the Caves of Helm's Deep do not receive from Gandalf here the name 'the Glittering Caves of Aglarond', which was only added to the typescript text at a later stage (see p. 77).

The first version of the story now becomes decisively different from that in *The Two Towers* (pp. 154 ff.).

The sun shone upon the vale about them. After the storm the morning was fresh, and a breeze was now flowing from the west between the mountains. The swelling grass-lands rose and fell, with long ridges and shallow dales like a wide green sea. Upon their left long slopes ran swiftly down to the Isen River, a grey ribbon that bent westward, winding away out of sight through the great Gap of Rohan to the distant shores of Belfalas.[11] Below them now lay the fords of Isen, where the river spread in stony shoals between long grassy terraces. They did not go that way. Gandalf led them due north, and they passed by, riding along the high ground on the east of the river; yet as they rode other eyes were turned towards the stony fords and the battlefield where so many good men of the Mark had fallen.[12] They saw crows wheeling and crying in the air, and borne upon the wind they heard the howling of wolves. The carrion-birds were gathered at the fords, and even the bright day had not driven them from their business.

'Alas!' cried Théoden. 'Shall we leave the steeds and riders of the Mark to be picked and torn by fowl and wolf? Let us turn aside!'

'There is no need, lord,' said Gandalf. 'The task would take us long, were it still left to do; but it is not. No horse or rider of your folk lies there unburied. Their graves are deep and their mounds are high; and long may they watch the fords! My friends have laboured there.[13] It is with the orcs, their masters, that the wolves and carrion-birds hold their feast: such is the friendship of their kind.'

'You accomplished much in an evening and a night, Gandalf my friend,' said Théoden.

'With the help of Shadowfax – and others,' answered Gandalf. 'And this I can report for your comfort: the losses in the battles of the ford were less grievous than we thought at first. Many men were scattered but not slain. Some I guided to join Erkenwald, and some I gathered again and sent back to Eodoras. I found that all the strength of Saruman was hurrying to Helm's Deep; for the great force that had been ordered to go straight to Eodoras was turned aside and joined to those that had pursued Erkenwald. When it was known that you, Théoden King, were in the field, and Éomer beside you, a mad eagerness came upon them. To take you and slay Éomer was what Saruman most desired. Nonetheless I feared that wolf-riders and cruel plunderers might be sent swiftly to Eodoras and do great harm there, since it was unmanned. But now I think you need not fear; you will find the Golden Hall to welcome your return.'

They had been riding for about an hour since they left the Coomb, and already the dark mountainous arms of Nan Gurunír were opening wide before them. It seemed filled with smoke. Out of it the river flowed, now near upon their left. Suddenly they were aware of a strange figure striding south along the stream towards them.

This last paragraph was replaced by the following:

They had been riding for almost an hour [> It was close on noon. They had been riding for two hours][14] since they left the Coomb, and now the mountainous arms of Nan Gurunír began to stretch towards them. There seemed to be a mist about the hills, and they saw rising up out of deep shadows a vast spire of smoke and vapour; as it mounted it caught the light of the sun, and spread in glowing billows in the sky, and the wind bore them over the plain.

'What do you think of that, Gandalf?' said Théoden. 'One would say that all the Wizard's Vale was burning.'

'There is ever a fume above that valley in these days,' said Éomer; 'but I have never seen anything like this before. These are steams, rather than smokes. Some devilry Saruman is brewing to greet us.'

'Maybe,' said Gandalf. 'If so, we shall soon learn what it is.'[15]

Out of the steaming vale the river Isen flowed, now close upon their left hand. As they were gazing north, they were suddenly aware of a strange figure striding south along the east bank of the stream. It went at great speed, walking stilted like a wading heron, and yet the long paces were as quick, rather, as the beat of wings; and as it approached they saw that it was very tall, a troll in height, or a young tree.

Many of the horsemen cried aloud in wonder, and some drew their swords. But Gandalf raised his hand.

'Let us wait,' he said. 'Here is a messenger for me.'

'A strange one to my eyes,' said Théoden. 'What kind of creature may it be?'

'It is long since you listened to tales by the fireside,' answered Gandalf; 'and in that rather than in white hairs you show your age, without increase in wisdom.[16] There are children in your land that out of the twisted threads of many stories could have picked the answer to your question at a glance. Here comes an Ent, an Ent out of Fangorn, that your tongue calls the Entwood – did you think the name was given only in idle fancy?[17] Nay, Théoden, it is otherwise: to them you are but the passing tale: all the years from Eorl the Young to Théoden the Old are of little count to them.'

Théoden was silent, and all the company halted, watching the strange figure with wondering eyes as it came quickly on to meet them. Man or troll, he was ten or twelve feet high, strong but slim, clad in glistening close-fitting grey and dappled brown, or else his smooth skin was like the rind of a fair rowan-tree. He had no weapon, and as he came his long shapely arms and many-fingered hands were raised in sign of peace. Now he stood before them, a few paces off, and his clear eyes, deep grey with glints of green, looked solemnly from face to face of the men that were gathered round him.[18] Then he spoke slowly, and his voice was resonant and musical.

'Is this the company of Théoden, master of the green fields of Men?' he said. 'Is Gandalf here? I seek Gandalf, the white rider.'

'I am here,' said Gandalf. 'What do you wish?'

'I am Bregalad Quickbeam,' answered the Ent. 'I come from Treebeard. He is eager for news of the battle, and he is anxious concerning the Huorns.[19] Also he is troubled in his mind about Saruman, and hopes that Gandalf will come soon to deal with him. [*Added:* There is no sign or sound from the tower.]'

Gandalf was silent for a moment, stroking his beard thoughtfully. 'Deal with him,' he said. 'That may have many meanings [> That may have more meanings than one].[20] But how it will go, I cannot tell till I come. Tell Treebeard that I am on the way, and will hasten. And in the meanwhile, Bregalad, tell him not to be troubled about the Huorns. They have done their task, and taken no hurt. They will return.'

'That is good news,' said the Ent. 'May we soon meet again!' He raised his hand, and turned, and strode off back up the river, so swiftly that before the king's company had recovered from their wonder he was already far away.

The riders now went at greater speed. At last they rode up into the long valley of Nan Gurunír. The land rose steeply, and the long arms of the Misty Mountains, reaching towards the plains, rose upon either side: steep, stony ridges, bare of trees. The valley was sheltered, open only to the sunlit South, and watered by the young river winding in its midst. Fed by many springs and lesser streams among the rain-washed hills, it flowed and bubbled in its bed, already a swift strong water before it found the plain; and all about it once had lain a pleasant fertile land.[21]

The description of Nan Gurunír as it was now is almost as in TT (p. 159), but after the words 'many doubted in their hearts, wondering to what dismal end their journey led' there follows:

Soon they came upon a wide stone-bridge that with a single arch spanned the river, and crossing it they found a road that with a wide northward sweep brought them to the great highway to the fords: stone-paved it was, well-made and well-tended, and no blade of grass was seen in any joint or crack. Not far before them now they knew that the gates of Isengard must stand; and their hearts were heavy, but their eyes could not pierce the mists.

Thus the black pillar surmounted by the White Hand is absent. Being on the east side of Isen they cross the river by a bridge, and come to 'the great highway to the fords'. In TT they followed that road on the west side of Isen up from the fords, and it was at this point that the road became 'a wide street, paved with great flat stones'.[22]

Already in preliminary drafting the description of the Circle of Isengard reached almost its form in TT (pp. 159–60),[23] but that of the tower of Orthanc underwent many changes, which can be related to a series of contemporary illustrations. These descriptions, for clarity in my account, I label A, B, C, D.

The description in the preliminary draft is as follows:

(**A**) And in the centre from which all the chained paths ran was a tower, a pinnacle of stone. The base of it, and that two hundred feet in height, was a great cone of rock left by the ancient builders and smoothers of the plain, but now upon it rose a tower of masonry, tier on tier, course on course, each drum smaller than the last. It ended short and flat, so that at the top there was a wide space fifty feet across, reached by a stair that came up the middle.

This description fits the picture captioned 'Orthanc (1)' that was reproduced as frontispiece to Vol. VII, *The Treason of Isengard*,[24] except in one respect: in the text there was 'a wide space fifty feet across' at the top, whereas in the picture the tower is surmounted by three pinnacles or horns (see under 'C' below).

In the completed manuscript of the first version the description begins in the same way,[25] but after 'left by the ancient builders and smoothers of the plain' it continues:

(B) ... a tower of masonry marvellously tall and slender, like a stone horn, that at the tip branched into three tines; and between the tines there was a narrow space where a man could stand a thousand feet above the vale.

This accompanies the drawing labelled 'Orthanc (2)', reproduced on p. 33, where the basal cone is black, and steeper than in 'Orthanc (1)', and the tower much more slender. Against this second description of the tower my father subsequently wrote:

(C) Or – if first picture [i.e. 'Orthanc (1)'] is adopted (but with cone-like rock as in second picture) [i.e. 'Orthanc (2)']:
[a tower of masonry] marvellously tall and strong. Seven round tiers it had, dwindling in girth and height, and at the top were three black horns of stone upon a narrow space where a man could stand a thousand feet above the plain.

This precisely fits 'Orthanc (1)'. It seems likely then that that picture was made after the first description 'A' was written, since it differs from 'A' in that the tower possess three horns at the summit.

The accounts 'B' and 'C' were rejected together and replaced in the manuscript by the following (all this work obviously belonging to the same period):

(D) And in the centre, from which all the chained paths ran, there stood an island in a pool, a great cone of rock, two hundred feet in height, left by the ancient builders and smoothers [> levellers] of the plain, black and smooth and exceeding hard. A yawning chasm clove it from tip to middle into two great fangs and over the chasm was a mighty arch of masonry, and upon the arch a tower was founded, marvellously tall and strong. Seven round

> tiers it had, dwindling in girth and height, and at the top were three black horns of stone upon a narrow space, where a man could stand a thousand feet above the plain.

This conception is illustrated in the drawings 'Orthanc (3)' and '(4)' on the same page as 'Orthanc (2)' and reproduced below (the distinction between the two enters into successive descriptions of the tower in 'The Voice of Saruman', pp. 61–2). On the back of the page bearing 'Orthanc (1)' my father wrote: 'This is wrong. The rock should be steeper and *cloven*, and the tower should be founded over an *arch* (with greater "horns" at top), as is shown in small sketch (3).' He also wrote here: 'Omit the water-course', but struck this out. A stream or 'moat' surrounding the basal cone is seen in 'Orthanc (1)'. In description 'D' the tower stands on 'an island in a pool' ('in the lake', see note 25).

Finally, a rider was inserted into the first manuscript bearing the definitive description as found in TT (p. 160): 'A peak and isle of rock it was, black, and gleaming hard; four mighty piers of many-sided stone were welded into one, but near the summit they opened into

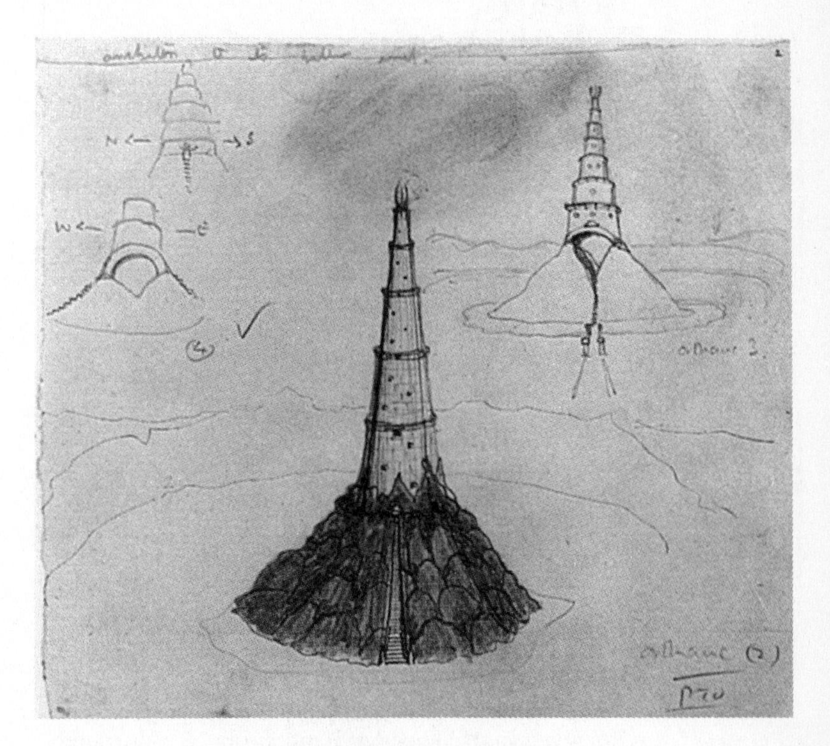

Orthanc '2', '3' and '4'

Orthanc '5'

gaping horns, their pinnacles sharp as the points of spears, keen-edged as knives'. The only difference here from the final text is that my father first wrote that the top of Orthanc was three hundred feet above the plain; but this was changed, perhaps at once, to five hundred as in TT. On this rider he wrote: 'to fit Picture (5)', which is reproduced on p. 34. Here the conception is radically changed, and the 'horns', now four, are no longer a device surmounting the tower of diminishing cylindrical tiers but are integral to the marvellous structure of Orthanc.[26]

The successive versions of the description of the tower differ in the statements made about the name *Orthanc* (the earliest statement on the subject appears in a rejected note to the manuscript of 'Treebeard', VII.419: 'It is not perhaps mere chance that *Orthanc* which in Elvish means "a spike of rock" is in the tongue of Rohan "a machine".'). The preliminary draft, following description 'A', has:

> This was Orthanc, the citadel of Saruman, the name of which had double meaning (by design or chance); for in the tongue of the Mark *Orthanc* signified cunning craft, invention, (machine such as those have who fashion machines), but in the elvish speech it means the stony heart, [?tormented] hill.

The original text of the first completed manuscript, following description 'B', has:

> ... for in the language of the Mark *orthanc* signified 'cunning craft', but in the elvish speech it means 'Stone Fang'.

To this 'Cloven-hill' was added subsequently – when the conception of the great cleft in the basal cone arose. Following the description ('D') of that conception the statement about the meaning of the name is the final form: 'for in the elvish speech *orthanc* signifies Mount Fang, but in the language of the Mark of old the Cunning Mind.' It may be therefore that the translation 'Mount Fang' actually arose in association with the description of the cone as cloven 'into two great fangs'.

From here on the text of TT was reached at almost all points in the manuscript of this version to the end of the chapter,[27] but there are some interesting points in the preliminary drafting.

Gandalf's reply to the opening address of Merry (who declares himself 'Meriadoc, Caradoc's son of Buckland'), ending 'or doubtless he would hasten hither to welcome such honourable guests', originally took this form:

> 'Doubtless he would,' laughed Gandalf. 'But what he would say to find two young hobbits mocking him before his gates I do not know. Doubtless it was he that ordered you to guard his doors and watch for their arrival.'

Pippin's first observation and its effect on the Riders went thus:

> '... Here we are sitting on the field of victory amid the plundered ruins of an arsenal and you wonder where we came by this and that.'
>
> All those of the Riders that were near laughed, and none more loudly than Théoden.

Théoden's loud laughter remained into the completed manuscript, but then his gravity (at least of bearing) was restored and it was removed.

The dialogue concerning hobbits went like this in the draft:

> '... This day is fated to be filled with marvels: for here I see alive yet others of the folk of story: the half-high.'
>
> 'Hobbits, if you please, lord,' said Pippin.
>
> 'Hobbits,' said Théoden. '*Hoppettan*?[28] I will try to remember. No tale that I have heard does them justice.'

In the completed manuscript Théoden said: 'Hobbits? It is a strange name, but I will not forget it.' In the preliminary draft he said subsequently: 'all that is told among us is that away in the North over many hills and rivers (over the sea say some) dwell the half-high folk, [*holbylta(n)*>] *holbytlan* that dwell in holes in sand-dunes...' This is where the word *Holbytla* arose.[29] The manuscript follows this, and Théoden does not say, as he does in TT, 'Your tongue is strangely changed.'

A wholly different and much longer lecture on the subject of tobacco was delivered by Merry in the first of several drafts of this passage:

> 'For one thing,' said Théoden, 'it was not told that they spouted smoke from their lips.'
>
> 'Maybe not. We only learned the pleasure of it a few generations back. It is said that Elias Tobiasson of Mugworth[30] brought the weed back to Manorhall in the South Farthing. He was a much travelled hobbit. He planted it in his garden and dried the leaves after a fashion he had learned in some far country. We never knew where, for he was no good at geography and never could remember names; but from the tale of leagues that he reckoned on his fingers people calculated that it was far South, 1200 miles or more from Manor Hall. [*Here is written* Longbottom.]'
>
> 'In the far South it is said that men drink smoke, and wizards I have heard do so. But always I had thought it was part of their

incantations or a process aiding in the weaving of their deep thoughts.'[31]

'My lord,' said Merry, 'it is rest and pleasure and the crown of the feast. And glad I am that wizards know it. Among the wreckage floating on the water that drowned Isengard we found two kegs, and opening them what should we discover but some of the finest leaf that ever I fingered or set nose to. Good enough is the Manorhall leaf – but this is...[32] It smells like the stuff Gandalf would smoke at times when he returned from journeys. Though often he was glad enough to come down to Manorhall.'

At this time, and still in the same context (conversation at the Gate of Isengard), my father developed Merry's disquisition through three further drafts to a form approaching §2 *Concerning Pipe-weed* in the Prologue to LR. In the next stage, his account to Théoden of the history of tobacco in the Shire[33] proceeds thus:

'It is said that the art was learned of travelling dwarves, and that for some time folk used to smoke various herbs, some fairer and some fouler. But it was Tobias Smygrave[34] of Longbottom in the Southfarthing that first grew the true pipe-weed in his garden in the year 902, and the best Home-grown comes still from that part. How old Tobias came by the plant is not known for certain, for he never told, and the Smygraves own all [> most (of)] the crops to this day.'

'In the far East uncouth men drink smoke, or so I have heard,' said Théoden. 'And it is said that wizards do so also. But I supposed that this was but part of their secret lore, and a device to aid the weaving of their thoughts.'

'Maybe it does, lord,' said Merry, 'but even wizards use it for no better reason than common folk. It is rest and pleasure and the crown of the feast. ...'

The remainder of this draft is as the first, except that Merry here says 'Good enough is Longbottom leaf, but this far surpasses it' (see note 32), and he says that Gandalf 'did not disdain Longbottom if he stayed until his own store was short. Before Saruman took to making worse things with greater labour, he must once have had some wisdom.'

In the next version the context has probably changed to the conversation between the hobbits and Aragorn, Gimli and Legolas after Gandalf and Théoden had gone (see p. 49 and note 8). Here Tobias (not Tobold) Hornblower appears,[35] the date of his first growing of the plant in his gardens becomes 953 ('according to our reckoning'), and Merry says that 'some think that he got it in Bree': to which Aragorn replies:

'True enough, I guess. Bree-folk smoked long before Shire-folk, and the reason is not far to seek. Rangers come there, as you may remember, unless you have already forgotten Trotter the ranger. And it was Rangers, as they call them in Bree, and neither wizard nor dwarf who brought the art to the North, and found plants that would thrive in sheltered places. For the plant does not belong there. It is said that far away in the East and South it grows wild, and is larger and richer in leaf; but some hold that it was brought over the sea. I expect Saruman got his leaf by trade; for he had little knowledge or care for growing things. Though in old days the warm valley of Nan Gurunír could have been made to grow a good crop.'

Finally, and still in the same context, the passage was developed to a form that my father evidently felt had outgrown its place, for he marked it 'Put into Foreword'.[36] Here the date of the first growing of pipe-weed at Longbottom by 'Old Toby' (still standing for Tobias) becomes 'about the year 1050', 'in the time of Isengrim Took the First';[37] and Merry now says of Old Toby:

'... He knew a great deal about herbs, but he was no traveller. It is said he went often to Bree, but he certainly never went further from the Shire than that. Some think he got the plant in Bree; and I have heard it said that Bree-folk claim to have found its uses long before Shire-folk. Certainly it grows well now on the south side of Bree-hill. And it was probably from Bree that the art spread in the last couple of hundred years, among dwarves and such folk as ever come westward nowadays.'

'Meaning Rangers,' said Aragorn smiling. 'They go to Bree as you may remember. And if you really want to know the truth I will tell it you. It was the folk that Bree-folk call Rangers who brought the plant from the South. For it does not belong natively to Bree and the Shire, and only flourishes so far north in warm and sheltered places. Green [Fuilas > Marlas > Romloth >] Galenas we called that kind. But it had long run wild and unheeded. This credit is certainly due to hobbits: they first put it into pipes. Not even the wizards thought of that before them, though one at least that I know took up the notion, and is now as skilful in that art as in all other things he puts his mind to.'

'More than one,' said Merry. 'Saruman likely enough got the idea from Gandalf: his greatest skill seems to have been in picking other people's brains. But I am glad of it, in this case. Among the wreckage floating on the water...'

This version concludes with Merry's saying 'Longbottom Leaf is good enough, but this is better. I wonder where it came from. Do you think Saruman grew it?' And Aragorn replies: 'I expect so. Before he took to making worse things with greater labour, he must have had some wisdom. And this warm valley would grow a good crop, if properly tended.'

The decision to remove most of this to the Foreword had already been taken when the first completed manuscript was written, for here Merry says no more than the few words that Gandalf allows him in TT (p. 163) – with Tobias for Tobold and the date 1050.

Lastly, the conversation near the end of the chapter in the manuscript (there is no initial drafting for this) brings in the meeting with Bregalad on the journey to Isengard, and runs thus:

'It is past noon,' said Gandalf, 'and we at least have not yet eaten. Yet I wish to see Treebeard as soon as may be. If Bregalad took my message, Treebeard has forgotten it in his labours. Unless, as does not seem to be beyond belief, he left us some word with these door-wardens, which their noon-meal has driven from their minds.'

'Bless me! yes, of course,' said Pippin, tapping his forehead. '"One thing drives out another," as Butterbur would say. Of course. He said: Greet the Lord of Rohan, fittingly. Tell him that Saruman is locked in Orthanc, and say that I am busy near the north gate.[38] If he and Gandalf will forgive me, and will ride there to find me, I will welcome them.'

'Then why did you not say so before?' said Gandalf.

'Because Gimli interrupted my fitting words,' answered Merry. 'And after that it appeared that hobbits had become the chief wonder and matter of debate.'

The chapter did not at this time end with Pippin's 'A fine old fellow. Very polite', but went on with 'Gandalf and the King's company rode away, turning east to make the circuit of the ruined Ring of Isengard', which in TT is the opening of 'Flotsam and Jetsam'.

Further abundant drafting, again discontinuous and closely related to the finished text, exists for the second stage in the development of the chapter. Here can be seen the new or altered elements in the narrative as they arose – the postponed departure from Helm's Deep, the Ents at the edge of the Huorn wood[39] that displaced the meeting with Bregalad, the passage of the Fords, the dry river, the burial mound, the Isen suddenly running again in the night. At first, though the time of departure had been changed to the evening, the encounter with Bregalad was still present – but ends differently: for despite Gandalf's message to Treebeard, 'to the surprise of all he [Bregalad] raised his hand and strode off, not back northward but towards the Coomb, where the wood now stood as dark as a great fold of night.' The scene at the Fords likewise evolved in stages: at first there was no mention of the burial mound, then there were two, one on either bank of the Isen, and finally the island or eyot in the middle of the river appeared.[40] The passage describing the departure of the Huorns from the Deeping Coomb and the Death Down (see p. 27) was first moved to stand (apparently) after Gandalf's reply to Legolas' question concerning the Orcs: 'That, I think, no one will ever know' (TT p. 151), for an isolated draft of it begins: 'And that proved true. For in the deep of the night, after the departure of the king, men heard a great noise of wind in the valley ...'[41]

The second main manuscript of the chapter was a fair copy that remained so, being only lightly emended after its first writing. A few details still survived from the first stage: Merry's father Caradoc; Tobias Hornblower and the year 1050; *Eodoras*; and the form *Rohir*, not *Rohirrim* (the two latter being changed later on the manuscript). The assembly at Eodoras is still to be, as in the first version (p. 27), 'before the waning of the moon' (changed later to 'at the last quarter of the moon').

Lastly, in the account of the burials after the Battle of the Hornburg, there were not only the two mounds raised over the fallen Riders: following the words 'and those of Westfold upon the other' (TT p. 150) there stands in the manuscript 'But the men of Dunland were set apart in a mound below the Dike' (a statement that goes back through the first complete manuscript to the original draft of the passage, see note 8). This sentence was inadvertently omitted in the following typescript (not made by my father), and the error was never observed.

NOTES

1 A short section of initial drafting was written on the back of a letter to my father bearing the date 31 July 1942.

2 One would expect *Erkenwald*: see p. 24, note 22. In the first occurrence here my father in fact wrote *Erkenw* before changing it to *Erkenbrand*. It may be that he was for a time undecided between the two names, and that there was not a simple succession *Erkenwald* > *Erkenbrand*.

3 Cf. the outline 'The Story Foreseen from Fangorn', VII.436: 'The

victorious forces under Éomer and Gandalf ride to the gates of Isengard. They find it a pile of rubble, blocked with a huge wall of stone. On the top of the pile sit Merry and Pippin!'

4 *Caradoc Brandybuck*: see VI.251 and note 4. This is the first appearance of Pippin's father Paladin Took: see VI.386.

5 *Less than a day*: this must imply the shortest possible time-scheme (see Chapter I):

Day 3 (January 31) Ents break into Isengard at night and divert the Isen; Théoden to Helm's Deep, Battle of the Hornburg.
Day 4 (February 1) Théoden, Gandalf, &c. to Isengard.

6 This conversation is found in no less than seven separate forms for the first version of the story alone. In one of these Théoden says to Gandalf: 'But would you assault the stronghold of Saruman with a handful of tired men?', and Gandalf replies: 'No. You do not fully understand the victory we have won, Lord of the Mark. The hosts of Isengard are no more. The West is saved. I do not go to an assault. I have business to settle, ere we turn back – to graver matters, and maybe to harder fortune.' — In different versions Gandalf advises Théoden to order an assembly at Eodoras 'on the second day from now' and 'at the full moon four days from now.'

7 In TT the company did not leave for Isengard until the late afternoon, and on the way they camped for the night below Nan Gurunír; see pp. 5–6, §§ III–IV.

8 In preliminary drafting for this passage the bodies of the Orcs were burned; the men of Dunland were still the men of Westfold; it was Gamling who addressed them, not Erkenbrand ('Help now to repair the evil in which you have joined ...'); the dead of this people were buried in a separate mound below the Dike (a statement that was retained in both the finished manuscripts of the chapter, though lost in TT: see p. 40); the slain Riders were buried in a single mound (not two); and Háma, whose death before the Gates of the Hornburg here first appears (see p. 22), was buried among them, yet he gave his name to the mound: 'the [*Hamanlow* >] *Hamelow* it was called in after years' (i.e. Old Engish *Hāman hlāw*, the Mound of Háma). In TT (p. 150) Háma was laid in a grave alone under the shadow of the Hornburg.

9 The Death Down, where the bodies of the Orcs were buried, was first called the Barren Hill ('for no grass would grow there').

10 See note 14.

11 See the First Map (redrawn map III, VII.309), where the Isen flows into the Great Sea in the region then named Belfalas.

12 In the draft for this passage the battlefield 'was but a mile or two away'. — In TT the company crossed the Fords of Isen (by moonlight) in order to follow the 'ancient highway that ran down from Isengard to the crossings'

13 That the slain Riders had been buried by Ents is stated subsequently: see pp. 47, 49, 54. Contrast TT (p. 157): 'More [Riders] were scattered than were slain; I gathered together all that I could find. . . . Some I set to make this burial.'

14 In this version the company was riding fast, but even so my father seems to have been working on the basis of a much shorter distance from Helm's Deep to Isengard: contrast TT (p. 156): 'They had ridden for some four hours from the branching of the roads when they drew near to the Fords.' In a chronology written at this time, when the story was that Gandalf and Théoden and their company left Helm's Deep very soon after the end of the Battle of the Hornburg (see p. 5, § III), he said that they left about 9 a.m. Changing this to the story that they stopped for the night on the way (p. 6, § IV), he said that they left at 3.30 p.m., and noted: 'It is forty miles and they arrive about 12.30 p.m. on *next day*, Feb. 3.' This is followed by notes of distances that are in close agreement with the First Map (see p. 78 note 2), but 'Isengard Gates to mouth of Deeping Coomb' is given as 33 > 41 > 45 miles (cf. p. 27, where Gandalf's estimate was changed from 12 to 14 to 11 leagues).

As well as I have been able to interpret the First Map here I make the distance 1 cm. or 50 miles, and my map made in 1943 agrees. Section IVE of the First Map (VII.319) is stuck onto a portion of IV^{D} that is totally hidden, and it is possible that at this stage the Gap of Rohan was less wide. In any case, considerations of distance as well as of chronology evidently dictated the change whereby Gandalf and Théoden did not reach Isengard till the following day.

15 On the removal of this dialogue from the (revised) opening of 'Helm's Deep' and the chronological considerations that led my father to do so see pp. 5–6, §§ II–III.

16 This extremely squashing (and revealing) remark of Gandalf's to the King of Rohan was subsequently very firmly struck through on the manuscript.

17 Cf. Aragorn's words (at once rejected) in a draft for 'The White Rider', VII.429: 'The Ents! Then there is truth in the ancient legends, *and the names that they use in Rohan have a meaning!*'

18 In the original draft for this passage 'the strange figure came quickly on to meet them until it was about fifty [*written above:* a hundred] yards away. Then it stopped and lifting its grey arms and long hands to its mouth it called in a loud voice like a [?ringing] trumpet. "Is Gandalf with this company?" The words were clear for all to hear.'

19 The page of the manuscript that includes this passage was replaced by another, which introduced little significant change; but in the rejected page Bregalad and Gandalf speak of 'the trees',

and only in the replacement do they call them 'the Huorns'. Several other terms in fact preceded *Huorns*: see pp. 47, 50, 52.

20 In the rejected page referred to in note 19 Bregalad said that Treebeard 'wishes to know what to do with Saruman', at which Gandalf 'laughed softly, and then was silent, stroking his beard thoughtfully. "Hm," he mused, "hm – yes, that will be a problem." ' Cf. the outline for the chapter (p. 26).

21 The original drafting for the description of Nan Gurunír reads thus:

> On either side the last long arms of the Misty Mountains reached out down into the plain, bare and broken ridges half-hidden now in smoke. And now they came upon a strange thing. It seemed to them that ruinous rocks lay ahead, out of which in a new-riven channel came the river, flowing where they stood back into its old course; yet higher up the valley the former bed was dry.
>
> 'Yes, I knew it,' said Gandalf. 'Therefore I drew you this way. We may cross with no difficulty to the Gates of Isengard. As some of you who have journeyed here may know, of old the Isen flowed down, fed by many mountain-springs and streams, until it was already a swift and powerful water ere it left Nan Gurunír – it swept past the walls of Isengard upon the East. That river you claimed as your boundary, but Saruman did not agree. But things have changed. Come and see!'

This was not used at all in the completed text of the first version of the story. It was not the first appearance of the diversion of the Isen: cf. 'The Story Foreseen from Fangorn', VII.436: 'At North end [of Isengard] they let in the River Isen but blocked its outflow. Soon all the floor of the circle was flooded to many feet deep.'

In the passage just cited the meaning must be that the Isen had not been sent back into its former course after the drowning of the Circle of Isengard, but continued to flow in its new channel. Gandalf's words 'I knew it. Therefore I drew you this way. We may cross with no difficulty to the Gates of Isengard' must mean that that is why he had led the company along the east bank of the Isen from the Fords (p. 28), for thus they would only have to cross the dry former bed of the river, to the east of its new course.

22 Later, in 'Flotsam and Jetsam', Merry told (TT p. 171) that when the great host left Isengard 'some went off down the highway to the Fords, and some turned away and went eastward. A bridge has been built down there, about a mile away, where the river runs in a very deep channel.' See p. 56.

23 Differences from the final form were that a part of the Circle of Isengard on the western side was formed of the mountain-wall itself (this was taken up from the draft but rejected from the

completed manuscript in the act of writing); there were two entrances, there being in addition to the great southern arch 'a small gate at the north, near the mountains' feet'; the circle was 'almost two miles from rim to rim' ('a mile', TT); 'through it by many carven channels water flowed, entering as a stream from the mountains beneath the northern gate, and watering all the hidden land'; and the windows in the walls of the circle are described (in the preliminary drafting only) as 'countless dark windows and deep, square-cut, menacing'.

24 This picture was drawn on the back of a page of the examination script of the poet John Heath-Stubbs, who took the final examinations in English at Oxford in 1942.

25 The opening of the description is confused. Apparently my father at first followed the draft 'A' very closely, writing: 'And in the centre ... was a tower, a pinnacle of stone. The base of it, and that two hundred feet in height, was a great cone of rock ...', but altered this at once to 'was an isle of stone, two hundred feet in height, a great cone of rock ...' Subsequently he changed 'was an isle of stone' to 'there stood an island in the lake.' See the description 'D' in the text.

26 On the back of this drawing my father wrote: 'This picture should be combined with old one': i.e. for a final version, which was never made, features of 'Orthanc (1)' should be incorporated. — 'Picture 5' went to Marquette with the second completed manuscript of the chapter, whereas the others remained in England. — The conception of 'Orthanc (5)' is seen also in *Pictures by J. R. R. Tolkien*, no. 27, viewed from the side in which were the stairway and the door.

27 In a draft of the paragraph beginning 'A strong place and wonderful was Isengard' (TT p. 160) these words were followed by 'or *Ang(ren)ost* in elvish speech'. *Angrenost* has appeared before (VII.420); the variant *Angost* occurs subsequently (p. 72).

28 Perhaps *Hoppettan* was Théoden's turning of *Hobbits* into the sounds and grammatical inflexion of the language of the Mark – or else he was merely struck by the resemblance to the (Old English) verb *hoppettan* 'to hop, leap, jump for joy'.

29 *Holbytla* 'Hole-builder' has the consonants *lt* (*Holbylta*) reversed, as in the closely related Old English *botl*, *boðl* beside *bold* 'building' (see my note on Nobottle in the Shire, VII.424).

30 This name can be read either as *Mugworth* or as *Mugwort*, but the latter (a plant-name, and one of the family names in Bree) seems very unlikely as the name of a place. *Mugworth* is not recorded as a village name in England.

31 This passage about tobacco was dashed down in a single spurt without any corrections, and there is no indication that these

sentences were spoken by Théoden; but that they were so is seen from the following draft.

32 The illegible word might possibly be 'grand'.

33 A pencilled note suggests that this should be 'a conversation at [the] feast'. See pp. 72–3.

34 *Smygrave*: with the first element cf. *Smial* (Old English *smygel*). The second element is probably Old English *græf*.

35 With the later change of *Tobias* to *Tobold* Hornblower cf. *Barliman* for earlier *Barnabas* Butterbur.

36 Cf. my father's letter to me of 6 May 1944 (*Letters* no. 66), referring to Faramir, then newly arrived on the scene: 'if he goes on much more a lot of him will have to be removed to the appendices – where already some fascinating material on the hobbit Tobacco industry and the Languages of the West have gone.'

37 *Isengrim Took the First* and the date 1050: in the Prologue to LR *in the days of Isengrim Took the Second* and the date 1070. See the original genealogical table of the Tooks in VI.316–17, according to which Isengrim the First would have been 400 years old at the time of Bilbo's Farewell Party. Since the Shire Reckoning date 1418 (as in LR) has already appeared for the year of Frodo's departure from Bag End (VII.9), Isengrim the First (afterwards Isengrim II) was born in S.R. 1001. According to the genealogical tree of the Tooks in LR Appendix C the dates of this Isengrim were S.R. 1020–1122. — The varieties of pipe-weed from the Southfarthing are here given as *Longbottom-leaf*, *Old Toby*, and *Hornpipe Shag*.

38 On the north gate of Isengard see note 23.

39 In the draft of this scene the three Ents who came out from the trees were not wholly indifferent to the company: 'Silently they stood, some twenty paces off, regarding the riders with solemn eyes.' But this was changed immediately.

In a draft for the passage that follows (TT p. 155), in which Théoden reflects on the Ents and the narrow horizons of the people of Rohan, it is Gandalf who speaks the thought that the war will bring about the disappearance of much that was beautiful in Middle-earth:

> 'You should be glad, Théoden King,' said Gandalf. 'For not only your little life of men is now endangered, but the life of those things also which you have deemed the matter of song and legend. Some we may save by our efforts, but however the fortune of war goes, it may soon come to pass that much that is fair and wonderful shall pass for ever out of Middle Earth. The evil that Sauron works and has worked (and has had much help of men in it) may be stayed or ended, but it cannot be wholly cured, nor made as if it had not been.'

40 The *Fords of Isen* in the plural appears earlier, however (pp. 10, 27–8, 31).

41 For another proposed placing of the description of the passing of the Huorns see p. 70.

IV
FLOTSAM AND JETSAM

The first completed manuscript of 'The Road to Isengard' was originally continuous with Chapter XXVIII 'The Battle of Helm's Deep' (the original title), but I think that the division was introduced at a fairly early stage, with a new chapter numbered XXIX beginning with the meeting of Gandalf and Théoden beside the Deeping Stream after the Battle of the Hornburg. The first completed manuscript of XXIX, of which the original title was 'To Isengard', ran on without break through the later 'Flotsam and Jetsam' and 'The Voice of Saruman', but a division between XXIX and XXX ('Flotsam and Jetsam') was made before it was completed: XXX then included the later 'Voice of Saruman' as well. A very rough and difficult outline for this part of the story in fact begins at the end of 'The Road to Isengard', and the chapter was then expressly to end with the return to Eodoras.

Gandalf asks where Treebeard is?
(Guarding Orthanc, says Merry. Some Ents still demolishing.)
He takes Théoden off.

Aragorn takes the hobbits aside and they sit and eat and chat on the stone heaps. Aragorn smokes. Talk about wizards and tobacco.

Aragorn and Gimli are told about Orc-raid and Treebeard. Merry gives up hope of describing them; says you will see them soon. How shall I describe them to Bilbo? (This was when he first tried to collect his ideas.)

Describes destruction of Isengard. Saruman not strong or brave. Merry tells all he knows about the battles of Ford. How trees dogged orcs.

Treebeard knocks on gates of Isengard. Arrows no good.[1] Saruman flies to Orthanc and sends up fires from floor of plain. Scorched Ents go mad. But Treebeard stops them. They let in Isen River by North Gate[2] and flood the bowl. Terrific fume and steam. Terrible noises, drowned wolves and slaves and smiths. The Ents pull the wall to pieces. They send Galbedirs (Talking Trees) to help Gandalf. They bury dead at Fords.

Gandalf's speech with Saruman. He rides over flooded causeway. Saruman looks out of window above door. Asks how he dares to come without permission. Gandalf says he thought that as far as Saruman was concerned he was still a lodger in Orthanc.[3]

'Guests that leave from the roof have not always a claim to come in by the door.' Saruman refuses to repent or submit.

Gandalf gives Treebeard task of [?caring] for him. 'I do not doubt there are delved ways under Orthanc. But every time water subsides let it in again, till all these underground places are submerged. Then make a low bank and plant trees round it. Guard Orthanc with Ents.'

Théoden thinks a Nazgûl may carry him off. 'Let him!' says Gandalf. 'If Saruman thinks of that last treachery ... cannot pity him for the terrible fate that awaits him. Mordor can have no love [for] him. Indeed what he will do

Say that this must be clear to Saruman himself. Would it not be more dramatic to [?make] Saruman offer help: Gandalf says no – he knows that if Mordor wins he is done for now. Even the evidence that he had made war on us won't help him. Sauron knows that he did so only for [his] own ends. But if we win – with his belated help he hopes to re-establish himself and escape punishment. Gandalf demands his staff of office. He refuses; then Gandalf orders him to be shut up, as above.[4]

They rest the night in the ruins and ride back to Eodoras.

Feast on evening of their return and coming of the messenger – that ominous dark-visaged man[5] should end this chapter.

Another outline (in ink over pencil, but the underlying text though briefer was not greatly different) reads as follows:

Treebeard (and Merry and Pippin) relate events – their arrival at Isengard. They saw Saruman send out all his forces to overwhelm the Riders at Isenford. As soon as Isengard was well-nigh empty, the Ents attacked. Merry and Pippin tell of the terrifying anger and strength of the Ents. Saruman really had little power beyond *cunning*, persuasive words – when he had no slaves at hand to do his will and work his machines or light his fires he could do little himself. All his studies had been given to trying to discover how rings were made. He let his wolves out – but they were useless. A few of the Ents were scorched with fire – then they went mad. They drowned Isengard, by letting in River and blocking the outlet.

All the day they were destroying and making havoc of the outer walls and all within. Only Orthanc resisted them. Then just ere nightfall Gandalf came riding up like the wind.[6] He told them of King Théoden's danger. A considerable force of walking trees had already stalked after the orcs the night before. The Ents now sent a much great[er] force and commanded them all to gather at the mouth of the Coomb and let no *orc* come out alive. A few Ents had gone to Isenford, and buried the dead men of the Mark.

In the margin against the last sentences of this outline is written: 'Shall there be *more* real Ents?' Notably, a sentence in the underlying pencilled text reads: 'The Ents sent a force of walking trees (with split trunks). They crept on in darkness following the victorious orcs.'

There is not a great deal to notice in the scanty initial drafting or in the first completed manuscript as far as the beginning of Merry's story of the attack on Isengard (TT p. 170). The meal provided by the hobbits was not eaten in the guard-house by the gates: Merry and Pippin went off to get the food and returned with it, Pippin explaining that 'There is a door not far inside the old tunnel that leads down into some well-stocked stores' (cf. the outline, p. 47: they sit and eat 'on the stone heaps'). Of Ents, where in TT (p. 167) Pippin says: 'Oh, well, you have seen some at a distance, already', here he says 'Oh well, you have seen Quickbeam' – this being of course a reference to the earlier version of 'The Road to Isengard', where Gandalf and Théoden and their company met Bregalad on their ride from Helm's Deep.[7] And he says also, as in the outline on p. 47: 'But I wish Bilbo could have seen Treebeard: how we shall manage to describe him to the old hobbit, if ever we get back, I can't think.'

In a draft for the discussion of pipes (TT pp. 167–8) Aragorn leapt down from the stone heap and went to the saddle-bags that lay nearby. 'From them he drew out an old cloak, and a worn purse of soft hide. Coming back he wrapped himself in the cloak, and opened the purse, and drew out a blackened pipe of clay.' Before Pippin produced his spare pipe, Merry said: 'There are none to be found. Orcs don't smoke, and Saruman did not give his leaf to his slaves.' And when Pippin said 'Look! Trotter the Ranger has come back!' Aragorn replied: 'He has never been away. I am Trotter and Aragorn, and belong both to Gondor and the North.'[8]

A few other details in the opening of the chapter may be noted. There is no mention of Aragorn's returning of the hobbits' knives,[9] or of Pippin's brooch (TT p. 169). After Merry's story of Grishnákh[10] Aragorn spoke at greater length about Sauron and Saruman:

'All this about the orcs of Lugburz (Mordor, I suppose, from the Red Eye) makes me uneasy,' said Aragorn. 'The Dark Lord already knew too much, and Grishnákh clearly got some message across the River after the quarrel. [But still there are some hopeful points. Saruman is in a cleft stick of his own cutting. Gandalf ought not to have much difficulty in convincing him that a victory for Mordor would not be pleasant for him, now. Indeed' (and here Aragorn lowered his voice) 'I do not see what can save him, except the Ring itself. It is well that he has no idea where it is. And we should do best never to mention it aloud: I do not know what powers Saruman in his tower may have, nor what means of communication with the East there may be.] From your tale it is plain that he thought one of you was possibly the Ringbearer; and Sauron must therefore have the same doubt. If so, it will hasten his attack westward: Isengard has fallen none too soon. But there are some hopeful points. All this doubt may help poor Frodo and Sam. But at any rate Saruman is in a cleft stick of his own cutting.

The part of this text (rather more confused in the manuscript than I have represented it) enclosed in square brackets, was rejected immediately and replaced by what follows ('From your tale it is plain ...'); this was rejected later, leaving only the last sentence. — Lastly, Pippin chants, in addition to *Though Isengard be strong and barred* [*sic*], the Entish *Ta-rūta, dūm-da, dūm-da dūm! ta-rāra dūmda dūmda-būm!* (see VII.420).

In the original draft Merry's story (TT pp. 170 ff.) was at first very different from what it became, and I give this text (written in ink over very faint pencil) in part. Of the opening of his story my father noted on the manuscript that he should know less: 'His account of the war is too detailed.'

'... We came down over the last ridge into Nan Gurunír after night had fallen. It was then that I first got an inkling that the forest was moving behind – or a lot of it was: all the Galbedirs [> Lamorni > Ornómar] were coming, as the Ents call them in their short language (which seems to be an oldfashioned Elvish): Talking Trees, that is, that they have trained and made half-entish.[11] All this must have been happening while you were riding south.[12] As far as I can make out, from Treebeard and Gandalf, the war seems to have gone like this: Saruman opened the game some weeks ago, and sent raiders into the west of Rohan. The Rohan-men sent out strong forces, and they retreated over the fords of Isen, and the Riders rather rashly pursued them right up to the bottom of Nan Gurunír. There they were ambushed by a host of Saruman's folk and one of the chieftains of Rohan seems to have been killed. That must be a good many days ago.[13] Then more Rohan-men arrived coming from Westfold[14] away south, and the Riders still remained on both sides of the River keeping the Isengarders from breaking out of the valley. Up to then Saruman was only fencing; then he struck. Men came up from the land away west, old enemies of Rohan, and the Riders were driven over the Fords. The next stage we were just in time to see.

'As we crept down into Nan-Gurunír – and there was no sign or challenge. [*sic*] Those Ents and their flocks can creep if they wish. You stand still, looking at the weather and listening to the rustling of the leaves, maybe, and then suddenly you find you are in the middle of a wood, with trees all round you. "Creepy" is the word for it! It was very dark, a cloudy night. The moon got up late – and long before it rose there was a deep and sombre forest all round the upper half of Isengard Ring without a sign of challenge. There was a light gleaming from one of the windows in the tower, that was all. Treebeard and some of the elder Ents crept on, right round to within sight of the gates. We were with him. I was sitting on Treebeard's shoulder and could feel a trembling tenseness in him, but even when roused the Ents can be very cautious and patient: they stood still as statues, listening and breathing. Then all at once there was a great stir. Trumpets blared, and all the Ring echoed. We thought that we had been spotted, and battle was going to begin. But nothing of the kind. It seems that news had come in that the Riders had been defeated and driven over the Fords, but were still trying to hold out on the east bank. Saruman sent out his whole forces: he pretty well emptied Isengard. Gandalf says that he was probably in a great taking, thinking that the Ring might have gone to Eodoras, and meant to blot out Théoden and all his folk, before they had time to do anything about it. But there were one or two bits of essential information he lacked: the return of Gandalf, and the rising of the Ents. He thought the one was finished for good, and the others no good, old slow-witted back-numbers. Two very bad mistakes. Anyway that is what he did. I saw them go – endless lines of Orcs, and squadrons / troops of them mounted on great wolves (a Saruman notion?), and whole regiments of men, too. Many of them carried torches, and by the flame I could see their faces. Some were just Men, rather tall, dark-haired, not particularly evil-looking.'

'Those would be Dunlanders,' said Aragorn. 'An upland folk from the west of the Misty Mountains, remnants of the old peoples that once dwelt in Rohan and all about the Black Mountains, south and north.'

The following dialogue, concerning the 'goblin-men' reminiscent of the squint-eyed Southerner at Bree, and Merry's estimate of the forces that left Isengard that night, is much the same as in TT (p. 171), except that Aragorn says that they had had many of the goblin-men to deal with at the Hornburg 'last night' (see note 7), and that there is here no mention of the bridge over the Isen over which a part of the host had passed. Then follows:

'... I thought it looked black for the Riddermark. But it seems in the end the only way in which Saruman could have been overcome. One wonders how much Gandalf knew, guessed, or planned. But Treebeard anyway let them go. He said that his concern was Isengard. "Stone – that we can fight," he said.

'But he sent off a whole wood of the Ornómi[15] down the valley after the army, as soon as the gates of Isengard were shut again. I don't know, of course, much of what happened away south down there; but you will tell us later.'

'I can tell you now briefly,' said Aragorn. 'The Saruman army came down on both sides of the Isen and overwhelmed the men of Rohan, and most of the survivors scattered. A strong force under Erkenwald of Westfold[16] fled south towards the Black Mountains. We met a survivor of the battles of the fords yesterday evening, and were just in time to take refuge in Helm's Deep, a gorge in the hills, before the whole pack came on us.'

'I don't know how you survived,' said Merry. 'But you helped us. As soon as all the army had gone, the fun began here. Treebeard went up and began hammering on the gates. ...'

Merry's account of the Ents' destruction of the gates of Isengard was already in this preliminary draft very close to that in TT (p. 172), but his estimate of Saruman was expressed more largely and with a degree of scornful and rather jaunty assurance that his experience of the master of Orthanc scarcely justified; and Aragorn does not here interrupt him with a more cautious view of Saruman's innate power (indeed the hypnotic potency of the wizard's voice only emerged, or was at any rate only fully realised, when the meeting with him came to be written).

'I don't know what Saruman thought was happening. But all that I have seen since leads me to think that either he was never really a first-class wizard (not up to his reputation, which was partly due to Isengard, and that was not his making to begin with), or he had been deteriorating – relying on wheels and what not, and not on wisdom. And he does not seem to have much heart in any sense: certainly he had been going back in plain courage. The old fool had really become dependent on all his organized slaves. He had a daunting way with him: power of dominating minds and bewildering or persuading them was his chief asset all along, I fancy. But without his armies to do as he commanded, he was just a cunning old man, very slippery, but with no grit. And the old fool had sent all his armies off! ...'

Merry's account (given to Pippin in TT) of Saruman's flight into Orthanc chased by Bregalad, the spouting of fires and gases from vents in the plain of Isengard ('as soon as Saruman got back into his control-room he got some of his machinery working'), the scorching of some of the Ents and the quelling of their fury by Treebeard, is present in the draft in all essentials, though more briefly told (and the horrible fate of the Ent Beechbone does not yet appear). The time-scheme was still at the stage described in § II on p. 5, with the drowning of Isengard beginning later in the same night (31 January) as the Ents came there,[17] and so the story is much condensed in the draft text by comparison with that in TT. Gandalf came to Isengard 'yesterday at nightfall' (i.e. 1 February, the night of the Battle of the Hornburg); and where in TT (p. 175) Pippin says that he was surprised at the meeting of Gandalf and Treebeard 'because neither of them seemed surprised at all', here Merry says:

'... I do not know who was most surprised at their meeting, Gandalf or Treebeard. Gandalf, I think, for once. For from a look he gave us when we first met I have a fancy Treebeard had spotted Gandalf in Fangorn; but would not say anything even to comfort us. He has very much to heart the elvish saw of Gildor's: Do not meddle in the affairs of wizards; for they are subtle and quick to wrath.'[18]

'But Gandalf knew Treebeard was on the move,' said Gimli. 'He knew there was going to be an explosion.'

'But not even Gandalf could guess what that was going to be like,' said [Merry >] Pippin. 'It has never happened before. And even wizards know little about Ents. But talking about surprise – we were the surprised ones: coming on top of the astonishing rage of the Ents, Gandalf's arrival was like a thunderclap. We had very little to do, except try and trot round after Treebeard (when he was too busy to carry us) and see the fun. We had a high time for a moment, when we got left alone, and came in front of a rush of some terrified wolves, and we had a brush with two or three stray orcs. [But when Gandalf arrived, I just stood staring with my mouth open, and then I sat down and laughed. >] But when Gandalf's horse came striding up the road, like a flash of silver in the dusk, well, I just gasped, and then I sat down and laughed, and then I wept. And did he say *pleased to see you again*? No, indeed. He said "Get up, you tom-fool of a Took. Where in the name of wonder in all this mess is Treebeard? Hurry, hurry, hurry, my lad! Don't let your toes grow whiskers." But later he was a bit gentler, after he had seen the old Ent: he seemed very pleased and relieved. He gave us a few minutes of concentrated news, a pat on the head, a sort of hasty blessing, and vanished away south again. We got some more news out of Treebeard after he had gone. But there must be much more to tell. We should have been far more worried and anxious about you, I expect, only it was difficult what with Treebeard and Gandalf to really believe you would come to grief.'

'Yet we nearly did,' said Aragorn. 'Gandalf's plans are risky, and they lead often to a knife-edge. There is great wisdom, forethought and courage in them – but no certainty. You have to do your part as it comes to you; or they would not work.'

'After that, said Merry, 'the Ents just went on and carefully and neatly finished the drowning of Isengard. I don't know what else, do you?'

'Yes,' said Aragorn, 'some went to the Fords to bury the men of Rohan who had fallen there; and to gather all the – what did you say they were called – the Ornómi, the moving woods, to the Deeping Coomb. Aye, that was a wonder and a victory as great as the one here. No orc is left. It was a long night, but the dawn was fair.'

'Well, let us hope that it is the beginning of better things,' said Gimli. 'Gandalf said the tide was turning.'

'Yes,' said Aragorn, 'but he also said that the great storm was coming.'

'Oh,' said Merry, 'I forgot. Not long before Gandalf, about sunset, a tired horse came up the valley with a pack of wolf-riders round it.[19] The Ents soon settled them, though one of Quickbeam's folk, a rowan-ent, got a bad axe-stroke, and that enraged the Ents mightily. On the horse there was a queer twisted sort of man: I disliked him at sight. It says a great deal about Treebeard and Ents generally, if you think about it – in spite of their rage, and the battle, and the wounding of Bregalad's friend Carandrian, that the fellow was not killed out of hand. He was miserable in his fear and amazement. He said he was a man called Frána, and was sent with urgent messages from Théoden and Gandalf to Saruman, and had been captured by orcs on the way (I caught him squinting at Treebeard to see how it went, especially the mention of Gandalf). Treebeard looked at him in his long slow way for many minutes. Then he said: "Hoom, ha, well, you can go to Saruman! I guess somehow that you know pretty well how to find him, though things have changed a little here. But false or true, you will do little harm now."

'We told Gandalf about it. He laughed, and said: "Well, I fancy of all the surprised people he had the worst shock. Poor Wormtongue! He chose badly. Just for a little I feel hardhearted enough to let those two stay and live together. They will be small comfort to each other. And if Wormtongue comes out of Orthanc alive, it will be more than he deserves."'

Against this passage my father wrote: 'No, Wormtongue must come after Gandalf'; and at the foot of the page: 'Shall Wormtongue actually murder Saruman?'

'Well,' he continued. 'Our job was to get rooms ready and prepare stuff for your entertainment. All yesterday and most of last night we worked. Indeed, say what you like, we did not knock off till close on noon this morning. And I don't know if we should even then, only Pippin found two tubs floating on the water'

Here this draft breaks off. The first completed manuscript, from the point where Merry's story begins, was based fairly closely on the draft text (pp. 50–5) in its narrative, but moved far towards the text of TT in expression. The passage about the 'Talking Trees' (p. 50) was developed thus:

'... The Ornómi were coming. That is what the Ents call them in their "short language", which seems to be an old-fashioned Elvish: *trees with voices* it means, and there is a great host of them deep in Fangorn, trees that the Ents have trained so long that they have become half entish, though far wilder, of course, and crueller.'

This was rejected, probably at once, and a passage for the most part very close to that in TT (p. 170) substituted. *Ornómi* was here replaced by *Huorns* in the act of writing and is the point where that name arose. Merry is now uncertain about their nature: 'I cannot make out whether they are trees that have become Entish, or Ents that have become tree-like, or both.'

At first Merry was still going to give a summary and commentary on the course of the war:

'... It seems that news had come in that the [Rohir >] Horsemen had been defeated and driven back across the Isen, but some were still trying to hold out on the eastern bank. We got this out of some of Saruman's men that the Ents captured and questioned. Saruman thought that no more was left of the King's forces, except what he would keep by him to guard his town and hall. He decided to finish off the Rohir with a decisive blow.'

But it must have been at this point that my father noted on the draft (p. 50) that Merry should be much less well-informed on these matters, and the passage just given was rejected and the text of TT (p. 171) substituted: 'I don't know much about this war ...'

Merry now tells (as he does not in the draft, p. 51) that when the great host left Isengard 'some went off down the main road to the fords, but still more turned off towards the bridge and the east side of the river'. This was changed in a hasty pencilled emendation to 'turned off towards where I believe Saruman has recently made a bridge'. See p. 31 and note 22.

Aragorn's brief account of what had happened southwards was still retained from the draft (p. 52), and here he adds the surmise (in the draft Gandalf's, reported by Merry, p. 51) about Saruman's purposes: '... the whole pack came howling after us. They had learned that the King was in the field, so none of them went to Eodoras. Saruman wanted the King and Éomer, his heir, dead or alive. He was afraid that the Ring might get into their hands after the battle from which you escaped.' He also gives the information that the force that fled south from the Fords to the Black Mountains numbered about a thousand men. With this passage cf. Gandalf's remarks to Théoden as they rode to Isengard (p. 29).

Merry's rather overconfident assessment of Saruman was reduced, in stages, virtually to its compass in TT, and Aragorn's intervention now appears, very much as in TT (p. 172), with his emphasis on the peril of private conversation with the master of Orthanc.

In this version a new time-scheme had entered, as is seen from the story of the drowning of Isengard:

'... They calmly settled down to carry out a plan that Treebeard had made in his old head all along: they drowned Isengard. Day was dawning by that time. They set a watch on the tower, and the rest just faded away in the grey light. Merry and I were left alone most of that day, wandering and prying about. The Ents went north up the valley. They dug great trenches under the shadow of the Huorns, and made great pools and dams, and when all was ready, last night, about midnight, they poured in all the Isen, and every other stream they could tap, through a gap by the north-gate, down into the ring. ...'

'Yes, we saw the great vapour from the south this morning as we rode from Helm's Deep,' said Aragorn. ...

'By morning there was a fog about a mile thick,' said Merry. '... Treebeard stopped the inflow some hours ago, and sent the stream back into its old course. Look, the water is sinking again already. There must be some outlets from the caverns underneath. But Gandalf came before the drowning began. He may have guessed or been told by Treebeard what was afoot, but he did not see it happen. When he arrived the digging and damming was not quite finished, but old Treebeard had returned, and was resting. He was only about fifty yards away, soothing his arrow-smarts by pulling down a bit more of the southern wall in a leisurely fashion. ...'

This is still not quite the final time-scheme for the story of the destruction of Isengard (see pp. 5–6, §§ III–IV), because the party from Helm's Deep still reached Isengard in a single day (2 February); so here Pippin tells that it was 'last night' (1 February) that the drowning began, and Aragorn says that they had seen the great cloud of steam as they rode up from Helm's Deep 'this morning'.

All the last part of what would become the chapter 'Flotsam and Jetsam' was discarded from this manuscript and replaced by new pages, in which the text of TT (pp. 174–7, describing the day spent by Merry and Pippin alone while the Ents prepared the diversion of the Isen, Gandalf's coming, and the filling of the Ring of Isengard by moonlight) was reached save for the choice of a different word here and there. But the time-scheme of the rejected pages was still present, with the extra day still not inserted and the time during which the waters of Isen flowed into the Ring correspondingly shorter.[20] On this account the last part of the hobbits' story still differs from that in TT, and Merry ends thus:

'... By morning there was a fog about a mile high, but it was beginning to rise and sail away out of the valley. And the lake was overflowing, too, and pouring out through the ruined gate, bringing masses of wreckage and jamming it near the outlet of the old tunnel. Then the Ents stopped the inflow, and sent the Isen back into its old course. Since then the water has been sinking again. There must be outlets somewhere from the caves underneath, or else they are not all filled up yet. There is not much more to tell. Our part, Pippin's and mine, was chiefly that of onlookers: rather frightened at times. We were all alone while the drowning was going on, and we had one or two bad moments. Some terrified wolves were driven from their dens by the flood, and came howling out. We fled, but they passed by. And every now and then some stray orc would bolt out of the shadows and run shrieking off, slashing and gnashing as he went. The Huorns were waiting. There were many of them still in the valley until the day came. I don't know where they have all gone. It seems very quiet now after such a night. I could sleep.'

But the coming of Wormtongue is now placed according to the direction on the draft text ('Wormtongue must come after Gandalf', p. 55): he came 'early this morning', and the story of his arrival is now much as in TT, though briefer. Aragorn's curiosity about tobacco from the Southfarthing turning up in Isengard appears (see note 8), and Pippin reports the same date on the barrels as in TT: 'the 1417 crop'.

After 'it is not a very cheerful sight', with which the later chapter 'Flotsam and Jetsam' ends, this text goes straight on to 'They passed through the ruined tunnel', with which 'The Voice of Saruman' begins.

NOTES

1 *Arrows no good*: i.e., against Ents.
2 On the North Gate of Isengard see p. 43 note 23.
3 *He was still a lodger in Orthanc*: i.e., Gandalf had never 'officially' left after his enforced residence in the tower.
4 This paragraph was enclosed in square brackets and marked with a query.
5 *That ominous dark-visaged man*: cf. 'The Story Foreseen from Fangorn' (VII.437): 'Return to Eodoras. ... News comes at the feast or next morning of the siege of Minas Tirith by the Haradwaith, brought by a dark Gondorian like Boromir.'
6 The time-scheme here is that described on p. 5, § II.
7 In that version Théoden and Gandalf and their company left Helm's Deep in the morning and reached Isengard on the same day, and so here in answer to Pippin's question (TT p. 168)

'What is today?' Aragorn replies 'The second of February in the Shire-reckoning' (see p. 5, § III). Pippin then calculates on his fingers that it was 'only a week ago' that he 'woke up in the dark and found himself all strung-up in an orc-camp' (i.e. from the night of Thursday 26 January to Thursday 2 February). And again, when Pippin asks when it was that Aragorn, Gimli and Legolas 'caught a glimpse of the old villain, or so Gandalf hints' (as Gimli said) at the edge of Fangorn (TT p. 169), Aragorn replies: 'Four nights ago, the twenty-ninth.'

These dates were changed on the manuscript to 'The third of February', 'only eight days ago', and 'Five nights ago': see p. 6, § IV.

8 In an earlier version of this Aragorn's reply (here assembled from scarcely differing variants) was different:

> 'For a spell,' said Aragorn, with a glint of a smile. 'This is good leaf. I wonder if it grew in this valley. If so, Saruman must have had some wisdom before he took to making worse things with greater labour. He had little knowledge of herbs, and no love for growing things, but he had plenty of skilled servants. Nan Gurunír is warm and sheltered and would grow a good crop, if it were properly tended.'

With this cf. the passages given on pp. 37–9. — The decision, or perception, that the tobacco had not in fact been grown in Nan Gurunír, but that Saruman had obtained it from the Shire, appears in a rider pinned to the first complete manuscript, in which Merry tells Gimli that it is Longbottom-leaf, with the Hornblower brandmarks on the barrels (TT p. 167).

9 The finding of the hobbits' leaf-bladed knives and their sheaths at the site of the battle beneath Amon Hen (TT p. 17) is absent from the draft and the fair copy manuscript of 'The Departure of Boromir' (VII.381).

10 *Grishnákh* was changed on the manuscript at each occurrence to *Grishnák*, a reversion to the original form (VII.409–10). — On the back of this page is a reference that shows it was written during or more probably after June 1942.

11 This is the reverse of what Merry says in TT (p. 170): 'I think they are Ents that have become almost like trees, at least to look at.'

12 Merry was a day out: the march of the Ents on Isengard was in the evening of 31 January, and Aragorn, Gimli and Legolas had reached Eodoras early that morning (see pp. 3–4).

13 The death of Théodred in the First Battle of the Fords of Isen on 25 January (see p. 22 note 3).

14 *Westfold*: see p. 21.

15 *Ornómi*: in the underlying pencilled text the name *Galbedirs* can be read. At the earlier occurrence in this draft (p. 50) *Galbedirs*

was changed first to *Lamorni* and then to *Ornómar* – all these names having the same meaning.

16 *Erkenwald of Westfold*: see p. 24 note 22.

17 Thus Merry says that '*by morning* there was a fog a mile thick', Aragorn says 'we could see the great vapour from the south *as we rode towards the Fords*' (i.e. as the host rode from Eodoras on 1 February), and my father wrote in the margin of the text: 'Drowning must not begin until night of Hornburg battle'.

18 In the first complete manuscript this becomes: ' "Don't be hasty" is his motto, and also that saying Sam says he picked up from the Elves: he was fond of whispering it to me when Gandalf was peppery: "Do not meddle in the affairs of wizards ..." ' For its original appearance see 'Three is Company', FR p. 93. In TT (p. 196) Merry quotes it to Pippin à propos Pippin's interest in the *palantír*.

19 Cf. 'Helm's Deep' in TT (p. 134): 'Some say also that Wormtongue was seen earlier, going northward with a company of Orcs.' But in the present passage in TT (p. 178) Wormtongue arrived alone.

20 In the time-scheme followed here it lasted from midnight on 1 February till the morning of 2 February; in the final story it lasted till the night of 2 February (TT p. 177: 'The Ents stopped the inflow in the night'), = 4 March.

V
THE VOICE OF SARUMAN

Book III Chapter 10 'The Voice of Saruman' in *The Two Towers* is in the first completed manuscript simply the further extension of Chapter XXX (see p. 47). The opening of this part of the narrative is here almost as in the final form (see note 8), but the conversation with Gandalf is much briefer; after Merry's 'Still, we feel less ill-disposed towards Saruman than we did' it continues:

'Indeed!' said Gandalf. 'Well, I am going to pay him a farewell visit. Perhaps you would like to come?'

'I should,' said Gimli. 'I should like to see him, and learn if he really looks like you.'

'You may not see him close enough for that,' laughed Gandalf. '[He has long been a shy bird, and late events may not have >] He may be shy of showing himself. But I have had all the Ents removed from sight, so perhaps we shall persuade him.'

They came now to the foot of Orthanc.

In TT Gandalf's last remarks were developed to: 'And how will you learn that, Master Dwarf? Saruman could look like me in your eyes, if it suited his purpose with you. And are you yet wise enough to detect all his counterfeits? Well, we shall see, perhaps. He may be shy of showing himself before many different eyes together. . . .'

The description of Orthanc in this text at first ran like this:

. . . A few scorings, and small sharp splinters near the base, were all the marks it showed of the fury of the Ents. In the middle from two sides, north and south, long flights of broad stairs, built of some other stone, dark red in hue, climbed up to the great chasm in the crown of the rock. There they met, and there was a narrow platform beneath the centre of the great arch that spanned the cleft; from it stairs branched again, running up west and east to dark doors on either side, opening in the shadow of the arch's feet.

This is the general conception described in version 'D' of the passage in 'The Road to Isengard' (p. 32), and precisely illustrated in the drawing 'Orthanc (3)' reproduced on p. 33. But the text just given was replaced at the time of writing by the following:

... the fury of the Ents. On two sides, west and east, long flights of broad stairs, cut in the black stone by some unknown art, climbed up to the feet of the vast arch that spanned the chasm in the hill. At the head of each stair was a great door, and above it a window opening upon a balcony with parapet of stone.

This is the rather simpler conception illustrated in the drawing 'Orthanc (4)' reproduced on p. 33. At a later stage this was rejected and replaced on a slip inserted into the manuscript by the description in TT, where of course the conception of Orthanc had been totally changed (pp. 33–5, and the drawing reproduced on p. 34).

The description of Orthanc was followed immediately by 'Gandalf led the way up the western stair. With him went Théoden and Éomer, and the five companions.' There is thus no discussion here of who shall go up, or how close they shall stand.

From this point initial drafting (inked over very faint pencil, which is effectively illegible) exists for the interview with Saruman, and this was pretty closely followed in the first completed manuscript. Saruman's voice was at this stage differently described, and this was at first repeated in the manuscript: 'The window closed. They waited. Suddenly another voice spoke, low, melodious, and yet it seemed unpleasant [> unpleasing: its tone was scornful].'[1] This was changed, probably at once, to: 'low, melodious, and persuasive; yet now its tone was of one who, in spite of a gentle nature, is aggrieved.' All else that is said of that voice in TT (p. 183) is here absent; and the description of Saruman is briefer: 'His face was long with a high forehead; he had deep darkling eyes; his hair and beard were white, smudged with darker strands. "Like and unlike", muttered Gimli.'

With the opening of the conversation at this stage (cited here from the completed manuscript rather than from the draft text) cf. the original outline on pp. 47–8.

'Well?' said Saruman. 'You have a voice of brass, Gandalf. You disturb my repose. You have come to my private door without leave. What is your excuse?'

'Without leave?' said Gandalf. 'I had the leave of such gatekeepers as I found. But am I not a lodger in this inn? My host at least has never shown me the door, since he first admitted me!'

'Guests that leave by the roof have no claim to re-enter by the door at their will,' said Saruman.

'Guests that are penned on the house-top against their will have a right to knock and ask for an apology,' answered Gandalf.[2] 'What have you to say, now?'

'Nothing. Certainly not in your present company. In any case I have little to add to my words at our last meeting.'

'Have you nothing to withdraw?'

Saruman paused. 'Withdraw?' he said slowly. 'If in my eagerness and disappointment I said anything unfriendly to yourself, consider it withdrawn. I should probably have put matters right long ago. You were not friendly yourself, and persisted in misunderstanding me and my intentions, or pretending to do so. But I repeat: I bore you no ill-will personally; and even now, when your – your associates have done me so much injury, I should be ready to forgive you, if you would dissociate yourself from such people. I have for the moment less power to help you than I had; but I still think you would find my friendship more profitable in the end than theirs. We are after all both members of an ancient and noble profession: we should understand one another. If you really wish to consult me, I am willing to receive you. Will you come up?'

This passage, whose original germ is seen in the outlines given in VII.212, 436, was developed into that in TT pp. 186–7. The draft text[3] goes on at once to 'Gandalf laughed. "Understand one another? . . ."', and there is nothing said about the effect of Saruman's words on the bystanders; but in the manuscript his speech was changed, apparently at once, to a form somewhat nearer to that in TT (with 'a high and ancient order' for 'an ancient and noble profession'), and this was followed by the passage (TT p. 187) in which the voice of Saruman 'seemed like the gentle remonstrance of a kindly king with an errant but beloved minister'. But here the words 'So great was the power that Saruman exerted *in this last effort* that none that stood within hearing were unmoved' are absent; for of all that precedes this in TT, his long opening trial of Théoden's mind and will, with the interventions of Gimli and Éomer, there is no hint or suggestion in either draft or finished text. The interview is conducted exclusively between the two wizards.

For the remainder of the dialogue between them I give here the original draft:[4]

Gandalf laughed. 'Understand one another? I don't know. But I understand you at any rate, Saruman – well enough. No! I do not think I will come up. You have an excellent adviser with you, adequate for your understanding. Wormtongue has cunning enough for two. But it had occurred to me that since Isengard is rather a ramshackle place, rather old-fashioned and in need of renovation and alteration, you might like to leave – to take a holiday, say. If so, will you not come down?'

A quick cunning look passed over Saruman's face; before he could conceal it, they had a glimpse of mingled fear and relief / hope. cunning. They saw through the mask the face of a trapped man, that feared both to stay and to leave his refuge. He hesitated. 'To be torn by the savage wood-demons?' he said. 'No, no.'

'O do not fear for your skin,' said Gandalf. 'I do not wish to kill you – as you would know, if you really understood me. And no one will hurt you, if I say no. I am giving you a last chance. You can leave Orthanc – free, if you choose.'

'Hm,' said Saruman. 'That sounds well. More like the old Gandalf. But why should I wish to leave Orthanc? And what precisely is "free"?'

'The reasons for leaving lie all around,' said Gandalf. 'And free means not a prisoner. But you will surrender to me the key of Orthanc – and your staff: pledges for your conduct. To be returned, if I think fit, later.'

Saruman's face was for a moment clouded with anger. Then he laughed. 'Later!' he said. 'Yes – when you also have the keys of Baraddur, I suppose; and the crowns of seven kings, and the staffs of the five wizards,[5] and have purchased yourself a pair of boots many sizes larger than those you have now. A modest plan. But I must beg leave to be excused from assisting. Let us end this chatter. If you wish to deal with me, deal with me! Speak sense – and do not come here with a horde of savages, and these boorish men, and foolish children that dangle at your tail.'

He left the balcony. He had hardly turned away, when a heavy thing came hurtling down from above. It glanced off the parapet, narrowly missed Gandalf, and splintered [*struck out:* into fragments] on the rock beside the stair. It seemed to have been a large ball of dark shining crystal.

'The treacherous rogue,' cried Éomer, but Gandalf was unmoved. 'Not Saruman this time,' he said. 'It came from a window above. That was a parting shot from Master Wormtongue, I fancy. I caught the flash of a hand. And ill-aimed. Which do you think it was meant for, me or Saruman?' 'I think maybe the aim was ill because he could not make up his mind which he hated most' (? said Gimli). 'I think so too,' said Gandalf. 'There will be pleasant words in the Tower when we are gone.'

'And we had better go quickly out of stone's throw at least,' said Éomer.

'It is plain to me that Saruman has not yet given up hope [*added:* in his own devices],' said Gandalf. 'Well, he must nurse his hope in Orthanc.'

Here this draft stops, the ending being very ragged. It is notable that in this text there is no mention of Gandalf's summons to Saruman to return to the balcony when he turned away, and so the breaking of his staff does not appear (in the original sketches of the scene in the outlines referred to above, where Saruman was not in his tower, Gandalf took his staff from him and broke it with his hands).[6]

Since there is no evidence at all that the conception of the *palantír* had arisen at any earlier stage or in any earlier writing, this must be presumed to be its first appearance, but the draft does not make it clear whether my father perceived its nature at the moment of its introduction as Wormtongue's missile – Gandalf does not say what he thought of it, nor hint that it might be a device of importance to Saruman. In his letter to W. H. Auden of 7 June 1955 my father said (immediately following the passage from that letter cited at the beginning of *The Return of the Shadow*): 'I knew nothing of the *Palantíri*, though the moment the Orthanc-stone was cast from the window, I recognized it, and knew the meaning of the 'rhyme of lore' that had been running in my mind: *seven stars and seven stones and one white tree*.'[7] On the other hand, in this initial version of the scene he saw the ball of crystal as shattered by the impact, and still in the finished manuscript immediately following this draft he wrote that the ball 'splintered on the rock beside the stair. It seemed *from the fragments*', before breaking off at this point and writing that it smote the stair, and that it was the stair that cracked and splintered while the globe was unharmed. What further significance for the story could it have had if it were immediately destroyed?

The completed text develops the dialogue of Gandalf and Saruman a good way towards the form in TT, though much still remains from the original draft. But there now enters, almost in the final form, Gandalf's summons to Saruman to come back, his final admonition to him, and the breaking of his staff. The crystal ball now rolled down the steps, and it was 'dark but shining with a heart of fire'. In reply to Aragorn's suggestion that Wormtongue could not make up his mind whom he hated most Gandalf says: 'Yes, that may be so. There will be some debate in the Tower, when we are gone! We will take the ball. I fancy that it is not a thing that Saruman would have chosen to cast away.'

Pippin's running down the stair to pick up the globe, and Gandalf's hasty taking of it and wrapping it in the folds of his cloak, were later additions (see p. 79 note 12). Yet that the globe was to be important is now plain. The scene ends thus in this version:

'Yet there may be other things to cast,' said Gimli. 'If that is the end of the debate, let us go out of stone's throw, at least.'

'It is the end,' said Gandalf. 'I must find Treebeard and tell him how things have gone.'

'He will have guessed, surely?' said Merry. 'Were they likely to end any other way?'

'Not likely,' answered Gandalf. 'But I had reasons for trying. I do not wish for mastery. Saruman has been given a last choice, and a fair one. He has chosen to withhold Orthanc at least from us, for that is his last asset. He knows that we have no power to destroy it from without, or to enter it against his will; yet it might have been useful to us. But things have not gone badly. Set a thief to hinder a thief! [*Struck out:* And malice blinds the wits.] I fancy that, if we could have come in, we should have found few treasures in Orthanc more precious than the thing which the fool Wormtongue tossed down to us!'

A shrill shriek, suddenly cut off, came from an open window high above. 'I thought so,' said Gandalf. 'Now let us go!'

The end of the chapter in TT, the meeting of Legolas and Gimli with Treebeard, his parting from Merry and Pippin, and the verse in which the Hobbits are entered into 'the Long Lists', is present in this first completed text all but word for word, save only at the very end, where his last words are brief:

'Leave it to Ents,' said Treebeard. 'Until seven times the years in which he tormented us have passed, we shall not tire of watching over him.'[8]

NOTES

1 The draft has: 'low, rather melodious, and yet unpleasant: it spoke contemptuously.'

2 Though this exchange was subsequently lost, the reference to Gandalf's manner of departure from Orthanc on the previous occasion was brought in at a later point (TT p. 187): 'When last I visited you, you were the jailor of Mordor, and there I was to be

sent. Nay, the guest who has escaped from the roof will think twice before he comes back in by the door.'

3 The draft of Saruman's speech is very close to that cited from the completed manuscript, but after 'We should understand one another' Saruman says 'Building not breaking is *our* work.'

4 Not strictly the original draft, since as already noted it is inked over a faint and illegible pencilled text.

5 The first reference to the Five Wizards.

6 In drafting for the end of the chapter Gandalf's reply to Treebeard's 'So Saruman would not leave? I did not think he would' (TT p. 192) runs thus: 'No, he is still nursing what hope he has. He is of course pretending that he loves me and would help me (if I were reasonable – which means if I would serve him, and help him to power without [?bounds]). But he is determined to wait – sitting among the ruins of his old plans to see what comes. In that mood, and with the Key of Orthanc *and his staff* he must not be allowed to escape.'

7 The need that the *palantír* would come to fulfil had already been felt, as is seen from Aragorn's (rejected) remarks on p. 50: 'And we should do best never to mention it [the Ring] aloud: I do not know what powers Saruman in his tower may have, nor *what means of communication with the East there may be.*'

8 The meeting of Treebeard with Legolas and Gimli and his parting from Merry and Pippin was very largely achieved in preliminary drafting, but was placed at a different point, since it begins: 'The afternoon was half gone and the sun going behind the western arm of the valley when Gandalf and the King returned. With them came Treebeard. Gimli and Legolas gazed at him in wonder. "Here are my companions that I have spoken of to you," said Gandalf. The old Ent looked at them long and searchingly', &c. This was how the part of the narrative afterwards constituting 'The Voice of Saruman' originally began.

VI
THE PALANTÍR

Drafts and outlines for the opening of this chapter show my father very uncertain of the immediate course of events when the company left Isengard. These pages are extremely difficult to interpret and to place in sequence, but I take the one that I give now to be that first written, since it treats as the actual event what would become merely the abandoned plan ('When we came, we meant to go straight from Isengard back to the king's house at Edoras over the plains', TT p. 194).

The sun was sinking behind the long western arm of the mountains when Gandalf and his companions, and the King with his riders, set out from Isengard.

Ents in a solemn row stood like statues at the gate, with their long arms uplifted; but they made no sound. Merry and Pippin looked back as they passed down hill and turned into the road that led to the bridge.[1] Sunlight was shining in the sky, but long shadows reached out over Isengard. Treebeard stood there still, like a dark tree in the shade; the other Ents were gone, back to the sources of the stream.

By Gandalf's advice the company crossed the bridge and then struck away from the river, southward and east, making straight across the rolling plains of Rohan back to Eodoras: a journey of some forty-eight leagues.[2] They were to ride more with secrecy than speed, by dusk and night, hoping to reach the king's house by nightfall of the second day. By that time many of the king's men who had fought at the Fords and at Helm's Deep would be gathering at Eodoras.

'We have gained the first victory,' said Gandalf, 'yet that has some danger. There was a bond between Isengard and Mordor. Of what sort and how they exchanged their news I have not discovered. But the eyes of the Dark Tower will look now in this direction, I think.

'There is no one of this company, I think, whose name (and deeds) is not noted now in the dark mind of Sauron. We should walk in shadow, if we walk abroad at all – until we are ready. Therefore, though it may add to the miles, I counsel you go now by night, and go south so that day does not find us in the open plain. After that we may ride with many men, or ride maybe [??back to the] Deeping Coomb that would be better by ways among the foothills of your own mountains Théoden, and come thus down to Eodoras ... long ravines about Dunharrow.

The last few lines are a ragged scrawl, across which my father wrote (at the same time) 'They meet Huorns returning'. Since against the statement that 'they passed down hill and turned into the road that led to the bridge' he noted in the margin 'No they rode south to the Fords', and against 'the company crossed the bridge and then struck away from the river' he wrote 'No, they go south', it seems clear that it was as he was writing this first draft of the opening that he realised that the company did not in fact make straight for Eodoras but went first to Helm's Deep – and therefore abandoned this text.[3]

In a rejected speech of Aragorn's (p. 67 note 7) there was a suggestion that he had given some thought to the matter, but there is here the first clear expression of the idea that there must have been some means by which news was rapidly exchanged between Orthanc and Barad-dûr. Why Gandalf was so certain of this is not made plain,[4] and one might wonder whether the idea did not arise from the *palantír* rather than the other way about.

On the reverse of this page is an outline that one would naturally suppose to have been written continuously with the text on the other side. That it followed the abandoned narrative draft is obvious from the fact that here the company did not head straight for Eodoras but rode down from Isengard to the Fords. The writing is here exceptionally difficult, not only extremely rapid but with letters idiosyncratically formed.

This was the Orthan[c] Stone [*written above: Orthancstone Orthankstone Orþancstán*] which kept watch on movements in neighbourhood but its range was limited to some 100 leagues?[5] It will help to keep watch on Orthanc from afar.

Night comes swiftly. They come to the Fords and note the river is failing and running dry again.[6] The starry night. They cross and pass the mounds.

They halt under stars and see the great black shadow passing between [?them] and stars. Nazgûl.

Gandalf takes out dark globe and looks at it. Good, he said. It shows little by night. That is a comfort. All they could see [?was] stars and [?far away] small batlike shapes wheeling. At the edge was a river in the moon. The moon is already visible in Osgiliath said Gandalf. That seems the edge of sight.[7]

As they draw near Helm's Deep a shadow comes up like a mist. Suddenly they hear a rustling whisper and on both sides of them so that they are in a lane .... Shadows pass away northward. Huorns. Insert now page 3 of Ch.XXIX.

Next day they ride with many men in the Westfold Vale and .... by [?paths winding] among the mountains. They strike the Dunharrow ravine on the second day. And find folk streaming back to Eodoras. Aragorn rides with Éowyn.[8]

Gandalf looks at the Dark Crystal on the terrace before King's House. They see quite clearly Orthanc – Ents [?moving] ..... water all very [?small] and clear. Horsemen riding over plain from west and north. Strange [?figures of various kind]. And from Minas Tirith. It only shows *lights and men* [?no country].

The reference to 'page 3 of Chapter XXIX' is to the first completed version of 'The Road to Isengard', where the description of the departure of the Huorn wood from the Deeping Coomb was placed before Théoden and Gandalf and their company left for Isengard, and so before they passed through the wood (p. 27). It is clear from the passage of the Huorns at this point in the story that the final time-scheme had not yet been reached (see pp. 5–6, §§ III–IV): Théoden and Gandalf and their company still reached Isengard on the day (2 February) following the Battle of the Hornburg and did not spend the night of 2 February encamped below Nan Gurunír (where in TT, p. 158, they heard the Huorns passing, and after which the passage about the departure of the wood from the Deeping Coomb, and the Death Down, finally found its place).

In this outline there is nothing to suggest that the 'dark globe' was the means of communication between Orthanc and Barad-dûr – indeed, rather the reverse, since when Gandalf looks into it somewhere near the Fords of Isen the range of its sight does not extend beyond Osgiliath (although his words 'It shows little by night. That is a comfort' suggest that he had feared that it might make them visible to a hostile eye). On the other hand, in the preceding narrative draft Gandalf is seen to be much concerned with that question of communication: 'There was a bond between Isengard and Mordor. Of what sort ... I have not discovered.' It seems hard to believe that even though Gandalf had not yet put two and two together my father had failed to do so. A possible explanation is that when he wrote this outline he did indeed already know the significance of the Dark Crystal, but that Gandalf had not yet fathomed the full extent of its range and powers, or did not yet know how to make use of them. Or it may be truer to say simply that in these notes we see the formative moment in which the significance of the Seeing Stone was at the point of emergence: the fateful 'device' – devised long before – which in the final story would prove to have been of vast though hidden importance in the War of the Ring.[9]

A little scribbled note in isolation may be cited here:

The black-red ball shows movements. They see the lines of war advancing. [?Ships are seen] and Théoden's men in Helm's Deep and assembling in Rohan.

The context of this is altogether obscure: for who is seeing these things?

Another text – a brief and tantalising set of notes scrawled down very rapidly in faint soft pencil, vestiges of fugitive thoughts – shows further debate on the meaning of the Orthanc-stone. I cannot see any clear indication of where it would be placed in the narrative, or even of where it stands in the sequence of these preliminary papers;[10] but from various points it seems to have preceded the text that follows it here.

I said that Isengard was overthrown, and the Stone was going on a journey, said Gandalf. And that I would [look >] speak to it again later when I could, but [?at the] moment I was in a hurry.

auctor (No I think the dark globe to be in contact with Mordor is too like the rings)

Gandalf discovers that the Orthanc-stone is a far-seer. But he could not make out [how] to use it. It seemed capricious. It seems still to be looking in the directions in which it was last used, he said.

Hence, vision of the [*added:* 7] Nazgûl above the battlements. He was looking towards Mordor.

Can one see back. Possibly said Gandalf. It is perilous but I have a mind to use it.

He stands back. He has been seen [?bending over it].?

No, he said, this is an ancient stone set in an upper chamber of the tower long long ago before the Dark Tower was strong. It was used by the [?wardens] of Gondor. One also must have been in the Hornburg, and in Minas Tirith, and in Minas Morghul, and in Osgiliath. (Five).

They saw the Hornburg. They saw Minas Tirith. They saw Nazgûl above the battlements of Osgiliath. So Saruman learned some of his news he said.

The bracketing of the words 'No I think the dark globe to be in contact with Mordor is too like the rings' and the marginal *auctor* (meaning that this was my father's thought, not Gandalf's) were added in ink. The implication of these words must be that Gandalf, in the opening sentences of this text, was speaking to a person in Mordor: and if that person was none other than Sauron himself, there is a delightful glimpse of Gandalf telling the Dark Lord that he was busy. — That here only five of the Seeing Stones are named (given a habitation) does not mean of course that at this stage there were only five, but that these were the five Stones of the southern kingdom (Gondor). In subsequent enumerations there were five Stones in Gondor, where in LR there were four.

Lastly, there is a brief outline, ending in a ragged scrawl, that seems to have preceded the first continuous drafting of the chapter in formed narrative.

Conversation with Saruman begins about 3.15 and ends about 4.30 (that is about sunset). Dark comes about 5.30. Gandalf leads them south in the dark – because now they must be more secret than ever. (Wonders what the connexion was between Saruman and Sauron.)

They pass out of Nan Gurunír at about 9 p.m. Camp under shadow of the last western hill. Dolbaran. They will ride fast on morrow. Two men are sent ahead to warn men that king is returning to Helm's Deep and that a strong force should be ready to ride with him. No men more than two or three are to ride openly on the plain. The king will go by mountain paths to Dunharrow.

Then episode of Pippin and Stone.

Gandalf says this is how Saruman fell. He studied such matters. The old far-seers of the Men of Númenor who made Amon Hen and Amon Lhaw One in Hornburg, Osgiliath, Minas Tirith, Minas Morghul, Isengard [Angrenost >] Angost.[11] That is how Saruman got news – though Hornburg and Minas Tirith were 'dark', their balls lost or destroyed. But he tried to peep at Barad-dur and got caught.

Nazgúl.

Feb. 4 They ride to Fords mid-morning (11 a.m.), rest an hour, and reach Deeping Coomb road-fork at 3 p.m. Helm's Deep at about 4. They rest, gather men, and ride by hill-paths lost to sight. Hobbits are given ponies – and Gimli!

Feb. 5, 6 Journey.

Feb. 7 Dunharrow. Joy of people. Éowyn comes forth. The King rides down the mountain valley with Éowyn and Éomund [*read* Éomer] on either side, Gandalf, Legolas, Aragorn beside them. The hobbits and Gimli ...

[?Regency.] Feast. Tobacco. Messenger.

In the previous text (p. 71) it is not actually stated that the Seeing Stones of Gondor 'answered' or corresponded one to another, but the idea was at the moment of emergence, as is seen from my father's passing doubt whether 'the dark globe to be in contact with Mordor is too like the rings', while 'Can one see back' seems clearly to refer to reciprocal vision between one Stone and another rather than to vision of past time. In the present outline this conception is fully present and accepted, and with it the central idea that it was through his knowledge of these matters that Saruman was corrupted, being snared by his use of the Stone of Orthanc to look towards Barad-dûr.

The 'episode of Pippin and the Stone' has arisen (though so far as the evidence goes it had not yet been committed to paper in any form); and the various elements were now coming to interlock in a beautifully articulated conception. The original idea (p. 69) that when Gandalf looked into the dark globe he saw 'small batlike shapes wheeling' will be retained but become Pippin's vision, and the explanation of why it should be that vision and no other (cf. 'It seems still to be looking in the directions in which it was last used', p. 71) will be found in the constant intercourse of Saruman and Sauron by means of the Seeing Stones (itself answering the question of the method of communication between Isengard and the Dark Tower), so that 'the Orthanc-stone [became] so bent towards Barad-dûr that, if any save a will of adamant now looks into it, it will bear his mind and sight swiftly thither' (TT p. 204).

The final time-scheme had now entered (see p. 6, § IV): Théoden and Gandalf and their company came to Isengard on 3 February and left that evening, two nights after the Battle of the Hornburg. It is remarkable that even when the plot had advanced to this stage, with the 'episode of Pippin and the Stone', and the first appearance of a Nazgûl west of Anduin, blacking out the stars (already present in the outline on p. 69), Gandalf was not impelled to ride on ahead in haste to Minas Tirith, but is present at the feast in Eodoras – that feast, often foreseen, which would never in the event take place. For the significance of the reference to tobacco here see p. 37 and note 33. But pencilled notes added to this outline later show the story of Gandalf's sudden departure: 'Feb. 4 Gandalf and Pippin reach Deeping Coomb before dawn', and 'Feb. 4–5 Gandalf rides all night and all day Feb. 5 reaching Minas Tirith at sunset on Feb. 5'.

There are no other writings extant before we come to a first draft of the chapter – which extends however only so far as the conclusion of Gandalf's words with Pippin after his vision in the Seeing Stone (TT p. 199).[12] This was written very fast and apparently set down without any preliminary workings, but the final text of the chapter to this point was achieved at once in all essentials – there are of course countless differences in the expression and a few in very small points of narrative detail, and many of these differences survived into the first completed manuscript of the chapter.[13] The chief difference from the final text comes as Gandalf knelt by Pippin's body (TT p. 198): 'He removed the ball and wrapped it in a cloth again. "Take this and guard it, Aragorn," he said. "And do not uncover it or handle it yourself, I beg." Then he took Pippin's hand and bent over his face ...' Thus Gandalf hands the globe to Aragorn simply as a bearer whom he can trust, in contrast to the story in TT (pp. 199–200), where the charging of Aragorn with the Orthanc-stone takes place at a different point and is given much greater significance through Aragorn's claiming it by right. But Pippin's account of what happened to him when he looked into the globe and '*he* came' was achieved at once in this draft.

From this point there is very little further preliminary drafting, and for almost all the rest of the chapter the earliest available text is that of the first completed manuscript, much of which is written over erased pencil. This manuscript was later given the chapter-number XXXI, and the title 'The Orthanc-stone The Palantir', this being written over an erased title of which only 'The' can be read.

As this manuscript was first written Gandalf in his concluding words to Pippin said a good deal more than he does in TT (p. 199). Some of this was moved to his conversation with Théoden and Aragorn after he had carried Pippin back to his bed: that Pippin had saved him from the dangerous blunder of using the Stone himself, and of Sauron's delusion that the Stone, and the hobbit, were in Orthanc. But here Gandalf goes on:

> 'Very odd, very odd how things work out! But I begin now to wonder a little.' He stroked his beard. 'Was this ball really thrown to slay me after all? Or to slay me if it might, and do something else if it missed? Was it thrown without Saruman's knowledge? Hm! Things may have been meant to go much as they have gone – except that you looked in, not me! Hm! Well. They have gone so, and not otherwise; and it is so that we have to deal with.
>
> 'But come! This must change our plans. We are being careless and leisurely.

Against the paragraph beginning 'Very odd, very odd how things work out!' my father wrote in the margin: 'No! because if Saruman had wished to warn Mordor of the ruin of Isengard and the presence of Gandalf and hobbits he had only to use Glass in normal fashion and inform Sauron direct. ? But he may have wished (a) to kill Gandalf, (b) to get *rid* of the link. Sauron may have been *pressing* him to come to the stone?' He evidently decided that these were unprofitable speculations, and abandoning the direction Gandalf's words had taken returned to an earlier point in his final address to Pippin.

The text in this first manuscript then (with rewriting of some passages, obviously belonging to the same time) all but reaches that of TT (pp. 199–203) as far as Gandalf's opening remarks to Pippin about the Seeing Stones as they rode towards the Deeping Coomb. Only two matters need be noted. When Gandalf gives the Stone to Aragorn (cf. p. 74) he says here: 'It is a dangerous charge, but I can trust you even against yourself', and Aragorn replies only: 'I know the danger. I will not uncover it, or handle it.' Secondly, there is a curious series of shifts in the precise wording of Gandalf's remarks about his failure to understand immediately the nature of the ball thrown down from Orthanc. At first he said: 'I said nothing, because I knew nothing. I guessed only. I know now.' In the first rewriting of this passage he said: 'I ought to have been quicker, but my mind was bent on Saruman. And I did not guess *the full nature of the stone* – not until now. But now I know the link between Isengard and Mordor, which has long puzzled me.' This was again rewritten at this stage to read: 'And I did not guess *the nature of the stone, till I saw it in his* [Pippin's] *hands*. Not until now was I sure.' In further revision of the passage carried out much later it became: 'I did not guess the nature of the stone, *until it was too late*. Only now am I sure of it.' In the final form (TT p. 200) this was changed once more: 'I did not at once guess the nature of the stone. Then I was weary, and *as I lay pondering it, sleep overcame me*. Now I know!' There is, to be sure, among all these formulations no great difference in the actual meaning, but it was evidently a detail that concerned my father: just how much did Gandalf surmise about the *palantír* before Pippin's experience brought certainty, and how soon?

An element of ambiguity does in fact remain in LR. Already in the first manuscript of 'The Voice of Saruman' Gandalf had said: 'I fancy that, if we could have come in, we should have found few treasures in Orthanc more precious than the thing which the fool Wormtongue tossed down to us!' The nature of Wormtongue's missile cannot have been fully apparent to my father himself at that stage: it was in that manuscript, only a few lines above, that he changed, as he wrote, the initial story of the globe's having smashed into fragments on the rock (p. 65). But even when he had fully established the nature of the *palantír* he retained those words of Gandalf (TT p. 190) at the moment when it bursts upon the story – *although*, as Gandalf said at Dol Baran, 'I did not at once guess the nature of the Stone'. But then why was he so emphatic, as he stood beneath the tower, that 'we could have found few treasures in Orthanc more precious' – even before Wormtongue's shriek gave reinforcement to his opinion? Perhaps we should suppose simply that this much at least was immediately clear to him, that a great ball of dark crystal in Orthanc was most unlikely to have been nothing but an elegant adornment of Saruman's study.

At the words 'Hobbits, I suppose, have forgotten them' (the Rhymes of Lore), following Gandalf's recital of the words of the Rhyme *Tall ships and tall kings / Three times three* (TT p. 202), a brief passage of original drafting, written out separately in ink and so not lost in erasure of pencil as elsewhere, takes up: the first framing of Gandalf's declaration of the history of the Seeing Stones, here called *Palantirs*, a word that so far as record goes now first appears.

They [the Rhymes of Lore] are all treasured in Rivendell. Treebeard remembers most / some of them: Long [Rolls >] Lists and that sort of thing. But hobbits I suppose have forgotten nearly all, even those that they ever knew.

And what is that one about: the seven stones and seven stars?

About the Palantirs of the Men of Old, said Gandalf. I was thinking of them.

Why, what are they?

The Orthanc stone was one, said Gandalf.

Then it was not made, Pippin hesitated, by the Enemy, he asked [?at a rush].

No, said Gandalf. Nor by Saruman; it is beyond his art, and beyond Sauron's too maybe. No, there was no evil in it. It has been corrupted, as have so many of the things that remain. Alas poor Saruman, it was his downfall, so I now perceive. Dangerous to us all are devices made by a knowledge and art deeper than we possess ourselves. I did not know that any Palantir had survived the decay of Gondor and the Elendilions until now.

Seven they set up. At Minas Anor that is now Minas Tirith there was one, and one at Minas Ithil, and others at Aglarond the Caves of Splendour which men call Helm's Deep, and at Orthanc. Others were far away, I know not where, maybe at Fornost, and at Mithlond [*struck out:* where Cirdan harboured the ... ships ...] (in) the Gulf of Lune where the grey ships lie. But the chief and master .... [?of (the) stones] was at Osgiliath before it was ruined.

In this passage are the first occurrences of *Aglarond* (see p. 28) and of *Fornost*, which on the First Map was named *Fornobel*, and still so on my map made in 1943, VII.304. Here also is the first appearance of *Cirdan* in the manuscripts of *The Lord of the Rings*.

In the first complete manuscript this was developed towards the form in TT. Gandalf now tells that 'The *palantirs* came from beyond Westernesse, from Eldamar. The Noldor made them: Fëanor himself maybe wrought them, in days so long ago that the time cannot be measured in years.' He speaks of Saruman as he does in the final text; but here he ends: 'No word did he ever speak of it to any of the

Council. It was not known that any of the *palantirs* had escaped the ruin of Gondor. Their very existence was preserved only in a Rhyme of Lore among Aragorn's people.' This was changed to: 'It was not known to us that any of the *palantirs* had escaped the ruin of Gondor. Outside the Council it was not among elves and men even remembered that such things had ever been, save only in a Rhyme of Lore preserved among Aragorn's people.'[14]

The remainder of the chapter in the first manuscript reaches the final form in all but a few respects. There were still five *palantirs* anciently in Gondor, one being still that of Aglarond (translated, as in the draft, 'Caves of Splendour', but changed to 'Glittering Caves').[15] Of the other two, Gandalf still says that they were far away, 'I do not know where, for no rhyme says. Maybe they were at Fornost, and with Kirdan at Mith[l]ond[16] in the Gulf of Lune where the grey ships lie.'

In answer to Pippin's question concerning the coming of the Nazgûl (TT p. 204) Gandalf here says only: 'It could have taken you away to the Dark Tower', and goes on at once: 'But now Saruman is come to the last pinch of the vice that he has put his hand in.' He says that 'It may be that he [Sauron] will learn that I was there and stood upon the stairs of Orthanc – with hobbits at my tail. That is what I fear.'[17] And at the end of the chapter he tells Pippin: 'You may see the first glimmer of dawn upon the golden roof of the house of Eorl. At sunset on the day after you shall see the shadow of Mount Tor-dilluin fall upon the white walls of the tower of Denethor.'[18]

★

In his foreword to the Second Edition of *The Lord of the Rings* my father said that in 1942 he 'wrote the first drafts of the matter that now stands as Book III, and the beginnings of Chapters 1 and 3 of Book V ['Minas Tirith' and 'The Muster of Rohan']; and there as the beacons flared in Anórien and Théoden came to Harrowdale I stopped. Foresight had failed and there was no time for thought.'[19] It seems to have been about the end of 1942 or soon after that he stopped; for in a letter to Stanley Unwin of 7 December 1942 (*Letters* no. 47) he said that the book had reached Chapter XXXI 'and will require at least six more to finish (these are already sketched).' This chapter was undoubtedly 'The Palantír' (not 'Flotsam and Jetsam', *Letters* p. 437, note to letter 47).

In the foreword to the Second Edition he went on: 'It was during 1944 that ... I forced myself to tackle the journey of Frodo to Mordor', and this new beginning can be very precisely dated; for on 3 April 1944 he said in a letter to me (*Letters* no. 58):

> I have begun to nibble at Hobbit again. I have started to do some (painful) work on the chapter which picks up the adventures of

> Frodo and Sam again; and to get myself attuned have been copying and polishing the last written chapter (Orthanc-Stone).

Two days later, on 5 April 1944 (*Letters* no. 59) he wrote to me:

> I have seriously embarked on an effort to finish my book, & have been sitting up rather late: a lot of re-reading and research required. And it is a painful sticky business getting into swing again. I have gone back to Sam and Frodo, and am trying to work out their adventures. A few pages for a lot of sweat: but at the moment they are just meeting Gollum on a precipice.

The 'copying and polishing' of 'The Orthanc-Stone' that my father did at this time is the second, very finely written manuscript of the chapter. Well over a year had passed since the first manuscript of the chapter was written, but not unnaturally no changes of significance were made in the new text: thus Aragorn's reception of the *palantír* remains in the simple form it had (p. 75); Gandalf does not refer to the possibility that Wormtongue might have recognised Aragorn on the stairs of Orthanc (note 17); Aglarond was still one of the ancient sites of the *palantíri* of Gondor, and Gandalf still says that he does not know where the others had been 'for no rhyme says', but maybe in Fornost and with Cirdan at the Grey Havens.[20]

NOTES

1 On 'the road that led to the bridge' see p. 31, where coming in the other direction the company had crossed the bridge and 'found a road that with a wide northward sweep brought them to the great highway to the fords.'

2 In the notes on distances referred to on p. 42 note 14 *Eodoras to Isenford* is given as 125 miles, which agrees well with the First Map (VII.319) and with the statement in TT ('Helm's Deep', p. 131) that it was 'forty leagues and more': see p. 12. *Eodoras to Isengard* is given in these notes as 140 miles (46·6 leagues), which again agrees closely with the First Map (about 2·8 cm.). *Eodoras to Helm's Deep or mouth of Coomb* is 110 miles; in my redrawing this distance is 100 miles (2 cm.), but the map is here very difficult to interpret and I have probably not placed Helm's Deep at precisely the point my father intended: on my map made in 1943 the distance as the crow flies is 110 miles. – The idea that after the visit to Isengard Théoden and his companions returned to Eodoras goes back to the outline 'The Story Foreseen from Fangorn', VII.437.

3 There is a second draft of the opening, which need not be given in full. Here it is noted how they rode: 'Gandalf took Merry behind him, and Aragorn took Pippin; Gimli rode as before with Éomer,

and Legolas was upon Arod at his side'; but this was immediately changed to 'Legolas and Gimli rode together again.' After a further hesitation, whether the company went down to the Fords or passed over the bridge below Isengard and went east, this draft ends:

> Gandalf's plan had at first been to ride straight to Eodoras from Isengard. But he said 'Victory has its dangers', and Théoden had best ride with secrecy now, and with many men. They would return to the Deeping Coomb and send on a messenger, bidding the men who were labouring there to hasten their work and be prepared to ride on the morrow by hill-paths. So now the company rode at a gentle [pace]

4 Cf. *Unfinished Tales* p. 405: 'It needed the demonstration on Dol Baran of the effects of the Orthanc-stone on Peregrin to reveal suddenly that the "link" between Isengard and Barad-dûr (seen to exist after it was discovered that forces of Isengard had been joined with others directed by Sauron in the attack on the Fellowship at Parth Galen) was in fact the Orthanc-stone – and one other *palantír*.'

5 The distance from Orthanc to Barad-dûr on the First Map is 12·3 cm., = 615 miles or 205 leagues. – This is a convenient place to notice that in my redrawing of section IVE of the First Map (VII.319) what I have represented as a small circle on the western side of the Wizard's Vale seems not to be so, but is rather an alteration in the line marking the edge of the vale. At the upper end of the vale is a minute circle that must represent Isengard.

6 The story here was that the Ents (who at the beginning of the draft on p. 68 are said to have gone back to the sources of the stream, leaving Treebeard alone at the gate of Isengard) had at once obeyed Gandalf's parting request to Treebeard (TT p. 192) that the waters of Isen be again poured into the Ring.

7 From Isenford to Osgiliath on the First Map is 8·6 cm., = 430 miles or 143 leagues.

8 Cf. VII.447: 'If I live, I will come, Lady Éowyn, and then maybe we will ride together.'

9 Cf. Gandalf's words in *The Two Towers*, p. 203: 'Alas for Saruman! It was his downfall, as I now perceive'; and in *The Return of the King*, p. 133: 'Thus the will of Sauron entered into Minas Tirith.'

10 It is written in fact on the back of one of the pages of the initial continuous drafting of the chapter (p. 73), but seems entirely unconnected with it.

11 *Angost* was a passing substitution for *Angrenost*: see p. 44 note 27.

12 One of the pages of this draft carries also drafting of the passage in 'The Voice of Saruman' in which Gandalf, seeing Pippin

carrying the *palantír*, cries out 'Here, my lad, I'll take that! I did not ask you to handle it.' See p. 66.

13 I mention the following as examples of such differences in the detail of this part of the story. In Gandalf's talk with Merry as they rode from Isengard (TT p. 194), after saying that he had not yet fathomed what the link was between Saruman and Sauron and that 'Rohan will be ever in his thought', he used again the words found in the soon abandoned draft for the opening of the chapter (p. 68): 'There is no one of this company, be sure, whose name and deeds are not noted now in the mind of Sauron'; but my father bracketed this, with the marginal note: 'No: Gandalf's return hidden.' In the night halt beneath Dolbaran (so written, as also in the outline on p. 72) Merry and Pippin lay not far from Gandalf; when Pippin got up from his bed 'the two guards sitting on their horses had their backs to the camp'; Pippin saw a glitter from Gandalf's eyes as he slept 'Under his long dark lashes' ('long lashes' TT); the *palantír* lay beside the wizard's left hand.

14 This was preserved in the First Edition of *The Two Towers*.

15 As in TT, Gandalf guesses that the *palantír* of Barad-dûr was the Ithil-stone.

16 *Mithond* must be a mere slip, though it was left uncorrected. It is curious that in the next manuscript, made in 1944 (pp. 77–8), the form in this passage was *Mithrond*, corrected to *Mithlond*.

17 In TT 'That is what I fear' refers to additional sentences inserted after 'with hobbits at my tail': 'Or that an heir of Elendil lives and stood beside me. If Wormtongue was not deceived by the armour of Rohan, he would remember Aragorn and the title that he claimed.' But this insertion was made long after (on 'the armour of Rohan' borne by Aragorn see TT p. 127, and in this book p. 304 and p. 317 with note 9).

18 *Tor-dilluin* was emended to *Mindolluin*. The mountain was added roughly to the First Map and not named, but carefully shown on the 1943 map (VII.310). – With Gandalf's forecast that they will come to Minas Tirith at sunset cf. p. 73 (Gandalf reaches Minas Tirith at sunset on February 5).

19 Cf. my father's letter to Caroline Everett, 24 June 1957 (*Letters* no. 199):

> I was in fact longest held up – by exterior circumstances as well as interior – at the point now represented by the last words of Book iii (reached about 1942 or 3). After that Chapter 1 of Book v remained very long as a mere opening (as far as the arrival in Gondor); Chapter 2 [The Passing of the Grey Company] did not exist; and Chapter 3, Muster of Rohan, had got no further than the arrival at Harrowdale. Chapter 1 of Book iv [The Taming of Sméagol] had hardly got beyond Sam's opening words (Vol. II p. 209). Some parts of the

adventures of Frodo and Sam on the confines of Mordor and in it had been written (but were eventually abandoned).

The last sentence evidently refers to the text that I called 'The Story Foreseen from Lórien', in VII.324 ff.

In fact, there is very clear evidence that my father erred in his recollection that the abandoned beginnings of Chapters 1 and 3 of Book V belonged to the time that we have now reached (i.e. the end of Book III); see pp. 231 ff., where the question is discussed in detail.

20 The text has *Mithrond* here, corrected to *Mithlond*: see note 16. – I collect a few further details from this second manuscript. *Palantirs* became *Palantíri* in the course of writing it. – Osgiliath is named *Elostirion* (*Elostirion* being roughly substituted for *Osgiliath* in the first manuscript, but very probably at this time). This change was introduced in a note dated February 9 1942 (VII.423), and appears in the outline 'The Story Foreseen from Fangorn' (VII.435). *Osgiliath* in the drafting and first manuscript of 'The Palantír' was thus a reversion, and *Elostirion* in 1944 another. Finally *Elostirion* was afterwards corrected back to *Osgiliath* on the 1944 manuscript.

Lastly, there was much hesitation about the phase of the moon on the night of the camp below Dol Baran. In the original draft no more was said than that 'The moon was shining' when Pippin got up from his bed. In the first manuscript 'The moon had risen far away but could not yet be seen; a pale sheen was in the sky above the bushes and the eastern rim of the dell'; with this compare perhaps the early notes given on p. 69, where Gandalf looks into the Seeing Stone and says 'The moon is already visible in Osgiliath.' This was changed to 'The moon was shining cold and white into the dell and the shadows of the bushes were black'; but on both the first and second manuscripts my father then shifted back and forth between the two statements, until he finally decided on the latter, which is the reading of TT (p. 196).

On the first manuscript he noted in the margin the following times (which show a much more rapid journey from Isengard than in the outline on p. 72): 'Sunset about 5 p.m. They camped about 6 p.m. This [i.e. Pippin's looking into the *palantír*] happened about 11 p.m. Moon rose 6.34 p.m.' According to the elaborate time-scheme that was made after the introduction of changes in October 1944 (VII.368), the New Moon had been on 21 January, the First Quarter on 29 January, and Full Moon was on 6 February, three nights after the camp beneath Dol Baran.

PART TWO

THE RING GOES EAST

I
THE TAMING OF SMÉAGOL

In his letter of June 1957 cited in note 19 to the last chapter (p. 80) my father said that at the time of this long break in the writing of *The Lord of the Rings* 'Chapter 1 of Book iv had hardly got beyond Sam's opening words (Vol. II p. 209)'. That beginning of a new story of Sam and Frodo in Mordor,[1] for so long set aside, can I think be identified: it consists of a brief narrative opening that soon breaks down into outline form ('**A**'), and a portion of formed narrative ('**B**') that ends at Sam's words (TT p. 210) 'a bit of plain bread, and a mug aye half a mug of beer would go down proper'. The original draft A went thus:

'Well Master this is a nasty place and no mistake,' said Sam to Frodo. They had been wandering for days in the hard barren heights of Sarn Gebir. Now at last on the fifth evening since their flight[2] they stood on the edge of a grey cliff. A chill east wind blew. Far below the land lay green at the feet of the cliff, and away S.W. [*read* S.E.] a pall of grey cloud or shadow hung shutting out the remoter view.

'It seems we have come the wrong way altogether,' went on Sam. 'That's where we want to get, or we don't want to but we mean to. And the quicker the better, if we must do it. But we can't get down, and if we do get down there is all that nasty green marsh. Phew, can you smell it.' He sniffed the wind: cold as it was it seemed heavy with a stench of cold decay and rottenness.

'We are above the Dead Marshes that lie between Anduin and the pass into Mordor,' said Frodo. 'We have come the wrong way – [we >] I should have left the Company long before and come down from the North, east of Sarn Gebir and over the hard of Battle Plain. But it would take us weeks on foot to work back northward over these hills. I don't know what is to be done. What food have we?'

A couple of weeks with care.

Let us sleep.

Suspicion of Gollum that night. They work northward.

Next day footfalls on the rock. Frodo sends Sam ahead and hides behind a rock *using ring*.[3] Gollum appears. Frodo overcome with sudden fear flies, but Gollum pursues. They come to a cliff rather lower and less sheer than that behind. In dread of Gollum they begin to climb down.

Here my father abandoned this draft, and (as I think) followed at once with a new opening (B), in which the text of TT is closely approached at almost all points (but the hills are still named *Sarn Gebir*, and the time is 'the [*struck out:* fourth or] fifth evening since they had fled from the Company'). With Sam's longing for bread and beer this manuscript ends, not at the foot of a page; and it is, I feel sure, the abandoned opening of the chapter to which my father referred.[4] When it was written, in relation to the work on Book III, there seems no way of telling.[5]

'A few pages for a lot of sweat,' my father said in his letter of 5 April 1944 (see p. 78), in which he told me of his turning again to the adventures of Sam and Frodo; and 45 years later one can feel it, reading these pages in which he struggled (in increasingly impossible handwriting) to discover just how Sam and Frodo did in the end get down out of the twisted hills into the horrible lands below.

When he took the chapter up again in 1944, he did not rewrite the original opening (which survives with little change into TT), but taking a new sheet began: 'The sun was caught into clouds and night came suddenly' (cf. TT p. 210). This text, which I will call 'C', soon degenerates into a terrible scrawl and at the end becomes in part altogether illegible.

The sun was caught into clouds and night came suddenly. They slept in turns, as best they could, in a hollow of the rocks, sheltered from the easterly wind.

'Did you see them again, Mr Frodo?' asked Sam, as they sat, stiff and chilled, munching wafers of *lembas* in the cold grey of early morning.

'Yes, once,' said Frodo. 'But I heard the snuffling several times, and it came nearer than it has before.'

'Ah!' said Sam. 'Growing bolder, it seems. I heard him, too, though I saw no eyes. He's after us still: can't shake him off nohow. Curse the slinking varmint. Gollum! I'd give him *gollum* if I could get my hands on his neck. As if we hadn't enough trouble in front, without him hanging on behind.'

'If only I dared use the Ring,' muttered Frodo, 'maybe I could catch him then.'

'Don't you do that, master!' said Sam. 'Not out up here! He'd see you – not meaning Gollum either. I feel all naked on the east side, if you understand me, stuck up here on the skyline with nought but a big flat bog between us and that shadow over yonder.'[6] He looked hurriedly over his shoulder towards the East. 'We've got to get down off it,' he said, 'and today we're going to get down off it somehow.'

But that day too wore towards its end, and found them still scrambling along the ridge. Often they heard the following footsteps, and yet however quick they turned they could not catch sight of the pursuer. Once or twice they lay in wait behind a boulder. But after a moment the *flip-flap* of the footsteps would halt, and all went silent: only the wind sighing over stones seemed to remind them of faint breathing through sharp teeth.

Toward evening Frodo and Sam were brought to a halt. They came to a place where they had at last only two choices: to go back or to climb down. They were on the outer eastward ridge of the Emyn Muil,[7] that fell away sheerly on their right. For many miles it had been falling lower towards the wet lands beyond; here after tending northwards it reared suddenly up again many fathoms in a single leap and went on again on a high level far above their heads. They were at the foot of a cliff facing S.W., cut down as if with a knife-stroke. There was no going further that way. But they were also at the top of another cliff facing east.

Frodo looked over the edge. 'It's easier to get down than up,' he said.

'Yes, you can always jump or fall, even if you can't fly,' said Sam.

'But look, Sam!' said Frodo. 'Either the ridge has sunk or the lands at its feet have swelled up – we are not nearly so high up as we were yesterday: about 30 fathoms,[8] not much more.'

'And that's enough,' said Sam. 'Ugh! How I do hate looking down from a height, and that's not so bad as climbing.'

'But here I almost think we could climb,' said Frodo. 'The rock is different here.' The cliff was indeed no longer sheer, but sloped somewhat backward, and the rock was of such a kind that great flat slabs seemed to have split away and fallen. It looked rather as if they were sitting on the eaves of a great roof of thin stone-shingles or tiles that had tipped over leaving their rough edges upwards.

'Well,' said Sam, standing up and tightening his belt. 'What about trying it? It'll give that flapping footpad something to think about anyway.'

'If we are going to try today we had better try at once,' said Frodo. 'It's getting dark early. I think there's a storm coming.'

The dark smudge of the mountains in the East was lost in a deeper blackness, that was already sending out great arms towards them. There was a distant rumble of thunder. 'There's no shelter at all down there,' said Frodo. 'Still, come on!' He stepped towards the brink.

'Nay, Mr Frodo, me first!' cried Sam.

'Why so eager?' said Frodo. 'Do you want to show me the way?'

'Not me,' said Sam. 'But it's only sense. Have the one most like to slip lowest. I don't want to slip, but I don't want to slip and come down atop of you and knock you off.'

'But [?I'd] do the same to you.'

'Then you'll have something soft to fall on,' said Sam, throwing his legs over the edge, and turning his face to the wall. His toes found a ledge and he grunted. 'Now where do we put our hands next?' he muttered.

'There's a much wider ledge about twice your height below you,' said Frodo from above, 'if you can slide down to it.' 'If!' said Sam. 'And what then?' 'Come, I'll get alongside and try it, and then we need not quarrel about first or second.' Frodo slid quickly down till he stood splayed against the cliff a yard or two to the right of Sam. But he could find no handhold between the cliff-top and the narrow ledge at his toes, and though the slope lean[t] forwards[9] he had not the skill nor the head to make the passage to the wider foothold below.

From about this point the text becomes increasingly rough and increasingly difficult to read: I reproduce a leaf of the manuscript on p. 90 (for the text of this leaf as best as I can interpret it see p. 91).

'Hm!' grunted Sam. 'Here we are side by side, like flies on a fly-paper.'

'But we can at least still get back,' said Frodo. 'At least I can. There's a hold just above my head.'

'Then you'd best get back,' said Sam. 'I can't manage this, and my toes are aching cruel already.'

Frodo hauled himself back with some difficulty, but he found that he could not help Sam. When he leaned down as far as he dared Sam's upstretched hand was just out of reach.

'Lor, this is a pickle I am in,' said poor Sam, and his voice began to quaver. The eastern sky grew black as night. The thunder rolled nearer.

'Hold up, Sam,' said Frodo. 'Just wait till I get my belt off.' He lowered it buckle first. 'Can you grasp it?'

'Aye,' said Sam. 'A bit lower till I get my two hands on it.'

'But now I haven't enough to hold myself, and anyway I can't lean back or get my foot against a stop,' said Frodo. 'You'll just pull me over, or pull the belt out of my hands. O for a rope.'

'Rope,' said Sam. 'I just deserve to hang here all night, I do. You're nobbut a ninnyhammer Sam Gamgee: that's what the Gaffer said to me many a time, that being a word of his. Rope. There is one of those grey ropes in my pack. You know, that one we got with the boats in Lórien. I took a fancy to it and stowed it away.'

'But the pack's on your back,' said Frodo, 'and I can't reach it, and you can't toss it up.'

'It did ought to be but it ain't,' said Sam. 'You've got my pack,' said Sam.

[?'How's that?'] .....

'Now do make haste, Mr Frodo, or my toes'll break,' said Sam. 'The rope's my only chance.' It did not take Frodo long to tip up the pack, and there indeed at the bottom was a long coil of silk[en] grey rope. In a moment Sam [?tied] an end round his waist and ... clutched ... above his head [?with].[10] Frodo ran back from the brink and braced his foot against a crevice. Half hauled, half scrambling Sam came puffing and blowing up the few feet of cliff that had baffled him. He sat down and stroked his toes.

'Numbpate and Ninnyhammer,' he repeated. 'How long's that rope, I wonder.' Frodo wound it [?round his] elbows. '10, 20, 30, 40, 50, 60, 70, 80 hobbit-ells,' he said. 'Who'd have thought it.'

'Ah, who would,' said Sam. 'A bit thin, but it seems mighty tough. Soft to the hand as milk. 80 ells.[11] Well, *one* of us can get down, seemingly, or near enough, if your guess weren't far out.'

'That would not be much good,' said Frodo. 'You down and me up, or the other way. Is there nothing to make an end fast to up here?'

'What,' said Sam, 'and leave all handy for that Gollum!'

'Well,' said Frodo after some thought. 'I am going down with the rope on, and you're going to hold on to the end up here. But I am only going to use the rope for a precaution. I am going to

8

The rope lay [illegible] slack [illegible]
stared at it [illegible] taut, and [illegible]
caught him at unawares. He [illegible]
[illegible]
[illegible]
cy came [illegible] again. [illegible]
[illegible]
[illegible]
[illegible]
The [illegible]
[illegible] below; but [illegible]
[illegible]
[illegible]
[illegible] too difficult [illegible]
[illegible]
[illegible]
[illegible]
¶ In about 10 mins [illegible]
[illegible]
[illegible]
[illegible]
[illegible]
[illegible]
[illegible]
[illegible]
[illegible]
[illegible]. Good luck.

PTO

A page from the first manuscript of 'The Taming of Sméagol'

see if I can find a way down that I can use without a rope. Then I climb up with your help, and then you go down with the rope and I follow. How's that?'

Sam scratched his head. 'I don't like it, Mr Frodo,' he said, 'but it seems the only thing to do. Pity we didn't think out this rock-climbing business before we started. I'll have to stand down there [?staring] and waiting to catch you. Do you be careful.'

Frodo went to the edge again. A few yards from the brink he thought he saw a better point for a descent. 'I am going to try here,' he said. 'Get a purchase somewhere Sam for your foot, but don't let the rope [?saw] over a [?sharp ... edge]. It may be elf-spun, but I shouldn't try it too far.' He stepped over the brink ... There was a ledge for his feet before he had gone his full height down: it sloped gently downward to the right. 'Don't pull on the rope unless I shout,' he said, and he had disappeared.

*The rope lay slack for a long while as Sam stared at it. Suddenly it drew taut, and nearly caught him at unawares. He braced his feet, and wondering [*read* wondered] what had happened and whether his master was now dangling in mid-air at the far rope's end, but not [*read* no] cry came, and the rope went slack again. After a long while as it seemed he thought he heard a faint hail. He listened, it came again, and cautiously he crawled to the brink taking in the slack as he went. The darkness was drawing nearer – and it seemed dim below; but in his grey cloak Frodo if he was there was quite invisible. But something white fluttered and the shout came up clear now. 'It's all right, not too difficult at all except in one place. I'm down. [?I've] 3 ells of rope to spare. Slowly [?to take] my weight ... I'm coming up and shall use the rope.'

In about 10 mins. he reappeared over the edge and threw himself down by Sam. 'That's that,' he said. 'I'll be glad of a short rest. Down you go now' – he described the route as best he could and direct[ed] Sam to hail when he came to the bad place. 'I slipped there,' he said, 'and [?should have gone] but for the rope, a little over halfway down, quite a drop [?start to finish]. But I think I can just ... you.[12] Pay it out slowly and take the weight off on any ledge you come on. Good luck.'

* At this point the text of the manuscript page reproduced on p. 90 begins, and continues to the end of the second paragraph.

With a grim face Sam went to the edge, [?turned], and found the first ledge. 'Good luck,' said Frodo.

... [?time to time] the rope went slack as Sam found some ledge to rest ..., but for the most part his weight was taken by the rope. It was ..... minutes before Frodo heard his call.

First he lowered his pack by the rope, then he cast it loose. He was left alone at the top. At that moment there was a great clap of dry thunder overhead and the sky grew dark. The storm was coming up the Emyn Muil on its way to Rohan and to the Hornburg far away where the riders were at bay.[13] He heard Sam cry from below, but could not make out the words, nor see Sam's pointing hands. But something made him look back. There not far away on a rock behind and overlooking him was a black figure [?whose glimmer(ing)] eyes like distant lamps were fixed on him. Unreasoning fear seized him for a moment – for after all it was Gollum there, it was not a whole ...., and he had Sting at his belt and mithril beneath his jacket: but he did not stop to think of these things. He stepped over the edge, which for the moment frightened him less, and began to climb down. Haste seemed to aid him, and all went well until he came to the bad place.

Perhaps my father was at just about this point when he wrote on 5 April 1944, in the letter cited on p. 78, that 'at the moment they are just meeting Gollum on a precipice'. — From here to the end of the draft there are so many 'bad places' and even sheer drops that I shall not attempt to represent the text as it stands. There follows an account of Frodo's descent: how he slipped again, and slithered down the cliff-face clinging with his fingers till he came up with a jolt, nearly losing his balance, on a wide ledge — 'and after that he was soon down.' There came then the great storm of wind and thunder, with a torrent of rain lashing down; and looking up 'they could see two tiny points of light at the cliff edge before the curtain of rain blotted them out. "Thank goodness you've done it," said Sam. "I near swallowed my heart when you slipped. Did you see him? I thought so, when you started to climb so quick." "I did," said Frodo. "But I think we've set him a bit of a puzzle for those [?soft padding] feet of his. But let's look about here. Is there no shelter from the storm?" '

They looked for shelter, and found some fallen rocks lying against the foot of the cliff, but the ground was wet and soggy; they themselves were not drenched through apparently on account of the elven-cloaks (this passage is very largely illegible). The storm passed on over the Emyn Muil and stars came out; 'far away the sun had set behind Isengard'. The draft ends with Sam's saying: 'It's no good going that way [i.e. towards the marshes] in the dark and at night. Even on this trip we've had better camping-places: but here we'd best stay.'

There was very evidently great need for a better text: my father himself would have had difficulty with this, when the precise thought behind the words had dimmed. He began again therefore at the beginning of the chapter, giving it now its title and number (XXXII) and the completed manuscript ('D') that evolved from this new start was the only one that he made (i.e., subsequent texts are typescripts). The opening of the chapter (text B), which went back to the time before the long break during 1943–4 (p. 86), was written out again, and effectively reached the form in TT (but when the story opens it was still 'the fifth evening' since they had fled from the Company, not as in TT the third: see the Note on Chronology at the end of this chapter).

When my father came to the point where his new draft (C) took up the tale ('The sun was caught into clouds and night came suddenly', p. 86), beyond rounding out the expression and making it less staccato he did not at first change any feature of the story until the beginning of the attempt to climb down – apart from introducing the point that on the last day in the Emyn Muil Sam and Frodo had been making their way along at some distance from the outer precipice, perhaps to explain why it was that they had not observed that the cliff was now less high and no longer sheer; but the long gully or ravine by which in TT they made their way to the precipice when their way forward was blocked was not yet present. The fir-trees in the gully would have a narrative function in the final form of the story, in that 'old broken stumps straggled on almost to the cliff's brink' (TT p. 212): for Sam would brace his foot against one of those stumps, and tie the rope to it (TT pp. 215–16), in contrast to text C, p. 89 ('Is there nothing to make an end fast to up here?' ... 'I am going down with the rope on, and you're going to hold on to the end up here').

My father at first retained the story in C (p. 88) that Frodo followed Sam over the edge and that they both stood splayed against the rock-face together, until Frodo climbed back up again. But as he wrote he changed this: before Frodo had time to say anything to Sam,

The next moment he gave a sharp cry and slithered downwards. He came up with a jolt to his toes on a broader ledge a few feet lower down. Fortunately the rockface leant well forwards, and he did not lose his balance. He could just reach the ledge he had left with his fingers.

'Well, that's another step down,' he said. 'But what next?'

'I don't know,' said Frodo peering over. 'The light's getting so dim. You started off a bit too quick, before we'd had a good look. But the ledge you're on gets much broader to the right. If you could edge along that way, you'd have room enough, I think, to stoop and get your hands down and try for the next ledge below.'

Sam shuffled a little, and then stood still, breathing hard. 'No, I can't do it,' he panted. 'I'm going giddy. Can't I get back? My toes are hurting cruelly already.'

Frodo leaned over as far as he dared, but he could not help. Sam's fingers were well out of his reach.

'What's to be done?' said Sam, and his voice quavered. 'Here am I stuck like a fly on a fly-paper, only flies can't fall off, and I can.' The eastern sky was growing black as night, and the thunder rolled nearer.

'Hold on, Sam!' said Frodo. 'Half a moment, till I get my belt off.'

Having thus got rid of the unnecessary incident of Frodo's going down to the first ledge with Sam and then climbing back again, the new text then follows the former (C) – the failure of the experiment with the belt, Sam's sudden recollection of the rope, and his telling Frodo that they are wearing each other's packs – as far as 'He sat down well away from the edge and rubbed his feet' (p. 89; he felt 'as if he had been rescued from deep waters or a fathomless mine').

'Numbpate and Ninnyhammer!' he muttered.

'Well, now you're back,' said Frodo, laughing with relief, 'you can explain this business about the packs.'

'Easy,' said Sam. 'We got up in the dim light this morning and you just picked mine up. I noticed it and was going to speak up, when I noticed that yours was a tidier sight heavier than mine. I reckoned you'd been carrying more than your share of tackle and what not ever since I set off in such a hurry, so I thought I'd take a turn. And I thought less said less argument.'

'Well meant cheek,' said Frodo; 'but you've been rewarded for the well meaning anyway.' They sat for a while and the gloom grew greater.

'Numbpate,' said Sam suddenly, slapping his forehead. 'How long's that rope, I wonder.'

Here my father abandoned this story, feeling perhaps that it was all becoming too complicated, and rejecting these new pages he returned again, not to the beginning of the chapter, but to the beginning of the draft C, that is to say to the point where Frodo and Sam awoke on their last morning in the Emyn Muil (p. 86), with Frodo now saying, in answer to Sam's question 'Did you see them again, Mr Frodo?', 'No, I have heard nothing for three nights now.' From this point the final story was built up in the completed manuscript D. Some of it was written out first on independent draft pages,[14] but some of the pencilled drafting was overwritten in ink and included in the manuscript. It is plain, however, that the final story now evolved confidently and clearly, and since there is very little of significant difference to the narrative to be observed in those parts of the initial drafting that I have been able to read, I doubt that there is any more in those that I have not.

My father now saw at last how Sam and Frodo did manage the descent from the Emyn Muil, and he resolved their difficulty about leaving the rope hanging from the cliff-top for Gollum to use by simply not introducing the question into their calculations until they had both reached the bottom. In this text the further course of the storm was described thus:

The skirts of the storm were lifting, ragged and wet, and the main battle had passed – hastening with wind and thunder over the Emyn Muil, over Anduin, over the fields of Rohan, on to the Hornburg where the King Théoden stood at bay that night, and the Tindtorras now stood dark against the last lurid glow.

At a later stage (see the Note on Chronology at the end of this chapter) the following was substituted:

The skirts of the storm were lifting, ragged and wet, and the main battle had passed to spread its great wings over the Emyn Muil, upon which the dark thought of Sauron brooded for a while. Thence it turned, smiting the vale of Anduin with hail and lightning, and rolled on slowly through the night, mile by mile over Gondor and the fields of Rohan, until far away the Riders on the plain saw its black shadow moving behind the sun, as they rode with war into the West.

Sam's uncle, the Gaffer's eldest brother, owner of the rope-walk 'over by Tighfield', now appears (cf. VII.235), but he was at first called Obadiah Gamgee, not Andy.

The earlier drafts did not reach the point of Gollum's descent of the cliff-face, and it may be that my father had foreseen it long since. On the manuscript of the outline 'The Story Foreseen from Lórien' he struck out his first ideas for the encounter of Frodo and Sam with Gollum, and wrote: 'Steep place where Frodo has to climb a precipice. Sam goes first so that if Frodo falls he will knock Sam down first. They see Gollum come down by moonlight *like a fly*' (see VII.329 and note 15). But there is no way of knowing when he wrote this, whether when he first began writing 'The Taming of Sméagol', or when he took it up again in April 1944.

In initial drafting the discussion between Sam and Frodo after Gollum's capture, in which Frodo heard 'a voice out of the past', went like this:

> 'No,' said Frodo. 'We must kill him right out, Sam, if we do anything. But we can't do that, not as things are. It's against the rules. He's done us no harm.'
>
> 'But he means to / meant to, I'll take my word,' said Sam.
>
> 'I daresay,' said Frodo. 'But that's another matter.' Then he seemed to hear a voice out of the past saying to him: *Even Gollum I fancy may have his uses before all's over.* 'Yes, yes, may be,' he answered. 'But anyway I can't touch the creature. I wish he could be cured. He's so horribly wretched.'
>
> Sam stared at his master, who seemed to be talking to someone else not there.

At this stage in the evolution of the chapter 'Ancient History', at the point in his conversation with Gandalf at Bag End which Frodo was remembering, the text of the 'second phase' version (given in VI.264–5) had been little changed. The actual reading of the 'current' ('fourth phase') text of 'Ancient History' (cf. VII.28) is:

> '... What a pity Bilbo did not stab that vile creature, before he left him!'
>
> 'What nonsense you do talk sometimes, Frodo!' said Gandalf. 'Pity! Pity would have prevented him, if he had thought of it. But he could not kill him anyway. It was against the Rules. ...'
>
> 'Of course, of course! What a thing to say. Bilbo could not do anything of the kind, then. But I am frightened. And I cannot feel any pity for Gollum. Do you mean to say that you, and the Elves, let him live on after all those horrible deeds? Now at any rate he is worse than a goblin, and just an enemy.'
>
> 'Yes, he deserved to die,' said Gandalf, 'and I don't think he can be cured before he dies. Yet even Gollum might prove useful for good before the end. Anyway we did not kill him: he was very old and very wretched. The Wood-elves have him in prison ...'

It is not often that the precise moment at which my father returned to and changed a passage much earlier in *The Lord of the Rings* can be determined, but it can be done here. When he came to write the passage in the manuscript (D) of 'The Taming of Sméagol', Frodo's recollection of his conversation with Gandalf began at an earlier point than it had in the draft cited above:

> It seemed to Frodo then that he heard quite plainly but far off voices out of the past.

> *What a pity Bilbo did not stab the vile creature, before he left him!*
>
> *Pity! Pity would have prevented him. He could not kill him. It was against the Rules.*
>
> *I do not feel any pity for Gollum. He deserves death.*

It was at this point that my father perceived that Gandalf had said rather more to Frodo, and on another page of drafting for 'The Taming of Sméagol' he wrote:

> Deserved it! I daresay he did / does, said Gandalf. Many that live do deserve death. And some that die deserve life. Can you give it to them? Then be not eager to deal out death even in the name of justice. For even the very wise cannot see all ends. I do not much hope that Gollum can be cured

This was then (as I judge) written into the manuscript of 'The Taming of Sméagol', in a slightly different form:

> *Deserves death! I daresay he does. Many that live deserve death. And some that die deserve life. Can you give that to them? Then be not too eager to deal out death in the name of justice, fearing for your own safety. Even the very wise cannot see all ends. Maybe the Enemy will get him. Maybe not. Even Gollum may do some good, willy nilly, before the end.*

It was certainly at this time that my father changed the passage in 'Ancient History'. Omitting the words 'fearing for your own safety', he joined the new passage into that given on p. 96: '... Even the wise cannot see all ends. I do not much hope that Gollum can be cured before he dies. Yet even Gollum might prove useful for good before the end.' The two passages, that in 'The Shadow of the Past' (FR p. 69) and that in 'The Taming of Sméagol' (TT. p. 221), remain different in detail of wording, perhaps not intentionally at all points.

Lastly, there is an interesting difference between the passage in which Gollum makes his promise to Frodo as it was at this time and as it stands in TT. When Gollum said 'Sméagol will swear on the precious', there followed both in initial drafting and in the manuscript:

> Frodo stepped back. 'On the precious!' he said. 'Oh, yes! And what will he swear?'
>
> 'To be very, very good,' said Gollum. Then crawling to Frodo's feet ...

This was changed at once, again both in draft and manuscript, to:

> Frodo stepped back. 'On the precious?' he asked, puzzled for a moment: he had thought that *precious* was Gollum's self that he

talked to. 'Ah! On the precious!' he said, with the disconcerting frankness that had already startled Sam [*draft text:* that surprised and alarmed Sam, and still more Gollum].

'*One Ring to rule them all and in the Darkness bind them.*
Would you commit your promises to that, Sméagol? ...' (&c. as in TT, pp. 224–5]

The final text of this passage was not substituted till much later.[15]

NOTES

1 For the earliest ideas for this part of the narrative, when Sam crossed the Anduin alone and tracked Frodo together with Gollum, see the outline 'The Story Foreseen from Lórien', VII.328–9.
2 See the Note on Chronology following these Notes.
3 In 'The Story Foreseen from Lórien', VII.328, Frodo put on the Ring to escape from Gollum.
4 An argument against this is that in the 1957 letter my father gave the page-reference II.209, whereas this text extends to II.210. But there are various ways of explaining this, and the evidence of the manuscripts seems to me to count more heavily.
5 Together with these earliest manuscripts of 'The Taming of Sméagol' was found a slip bearing the following pencilled notes, which may very well not have been written all at one time (I have added the numbers)

(1) Account of Rings in Ch. II ['Ancient History'] needs altering a little. It was *Elves* who made the rings, which Sauron *stole*. He only made the One Ring. The *Three* were never in his possession and were unsullied.
(2) Tom could have got rid of the Ring all along [?without further] .... – if asked!
(3) The Company must carry *ropes* – either from Rivendell or from Lórien.
(4) *Emyn Muil* = Sarn Gebir as a knot or range of stony hills. [*Sern Erain* >] *Sarn Aran* the King Stones = the Gates of Sarn Gebir.

With (1) cf. VI.404; VII.254–5 and 259–60. In (2), most frustratingly, I have not been able to form any guess even at the altogether illegible word. (3) seems quite likely to have arisen while my father was pondering the descent from Sarn Gebir (Emyn Muil). On the absence of the mentions in LR of Sam's having no rope, and the absence of the passage concerning ropes at the leaving of Lothlórien, see VII.165, 183, 280. As regards (4), in the long-abandoned opening of the chapter the hills were still called *Sarn Gebir*, but when my father took it up again in 1944 they had become the *Emyn Muil* (note 7). Many ephemeral names to replace *Sarn Gebir* are found in notes given in VII.424. *Sern Aranath* replaced *the Gates of Sarn Gebir* on the manuscripts of 'The Great River' (VII.362 and note 21).

6 This sentence, little changed, is given to Frodo in TT (p. 211).

7 The first occurrence of *Emyn Muil* as written in a text *ab initio*. See note 5.

8 30 fathoms: 180 feet.

9 *leant forwards*: i.e. sloped down outwards from the vertical, what my father earlier in this account called 'backward': 'The cliff was indeed no longer sheer, but sloped somewhat backward.'

10 In the following text the corresponding passage has: 'He cast the end to Sam, who tied it about his waist, and grasped the line above his head with both hands.' In the present text the sentence seems to have been left unfinished and in the air.

11 These figures were much changed. At first, as shown in any case by *hobbit-ells*, my father did not intend the 'English ell' of 45 inches, for by that measure 80 ells is 300 feet or 50 fathoms, getting on for double the height of the cliff as Frodo had reckoned it: whereas Sam thought that the rope of 80 ells would only be 'near enough' to Frodo's guess of 30 fathoms or 180 feet. My father seems first to have changed '80' to '77', and in the margin he wrote '2 feet' and '154'. He then changed '2 feet' to '2½ feet', by which measure 77 ells would give 192½ feet. At some point he struck out *hobbit-* in *hobbit-ells*; and finally he substituted 50 ells for the length of the rope. He had then evidently decided on the measure of 1 ell = 45 inches, according to which 50 ells would be equivalent to 187½ feet, just a little longer than the height of the cliff as Frodo had estimated it. This was the measure in TT, where the cliff was about 18 fathoms, and the rope about 30 ells; taking these figures as exact, there would be 4½ feet of rope to spare ('there was still a good bight in Frodo's hands, when Sam came to the bottom', TT p. 216).

12 The meaning is presumably 'I think I can just hold you', but *hold* is certainly not the word written.

13 See the Note on Chronology below.

14 My father now introduced a further obstacle to the sleuth by using the same piece of paper to write, one on top of the other, drafts for wholly different portions of the narrative.

15 In these texts the word *precious* when referring to the Ring is not capitalised, but capitals were introduced in subsequent typescripts before the passage was changed to the final form.

Note on the Chronology

In this chapter the narrative opens on *the fifth evening* since Frodo and Sam had fled from the Company. That night also they passed in the Emyn Muil, and it was at dusk on the following day (therefore 'the sixth evening') that they made their descent. Since the date of the Breaking of the Fellowship and the flight of Frodo and Sam was 26 January (for the chronology at this period see pp. 3–4, and VII.368, 406), this should mean that the chapter opens on the evening of the 30th, and that they climbed down from the hills on the evening of the 31st. On the other hand, the great storm is described (p. 95) as 'hastening with wind and thunder over the Emyn Muil, over Anduin, over the fields of Rohan, on to the Hornburg where the King Théoden stood at bay that night'. But the Battle of the Hornburg was fought on the night of 1 February (pp. 5–6).

Two brief time-schemes, which I will call Scheme 'A' and Scheme 'B', bear on the question of the chronology of Frodo's wandering in the Emyn Muil relative to events in the lands west of Anduin. Scheme 'B', which begins at this point, is perfectly explicit:

Thursday Jan. 26 to Wednesday Feb. 1 Frodo and Sam in Emyn Muil (Sarn Gebir).

Night Feb. 1–2 Frodo and Sam meet Gollum. (Storm that reached Helm's Deep about midnight on Feb.1–2 passed over Emyn Muil earlier in the night.)

Scheme 'A', also beginning here, has:

Jan. 31 Cold night

Feb. 1 Descend, dusk (5.30). Meet Gollum about 10 p.m. Journey in gully till daybreak.

According to these, it would have been on the *sixth* evening since the flight of Frodo and Sam, not the fifth, that the chapter opens.

Since Vol. VII *The Treason of Isengard* was completed I have found two manuscript pages that are very clearly notes on chronological alterations needed that my father made in October 1944, some four and a half months after he had reached the end of *The Two Towers* (see VII.406–7). On 12 October (*Letters* no. 84) he wrote to me that he had 'struck a most awkward error (one or two days) in the synchronization', which would 'require tiresome small alterations in many chapters'; and on 16 October (*Letters* no. 85) he wrote that he had devised a solution 'by inserting an extra day's Entmoot, and extra days into Trotter's chase and Frodo's journey ...'

These notes refer chapter by chapter to the changes that would have to be made (but not to all). Some of them have been encountered already: the complex alterations to 'The Riders of Rohan' in VII.406; the additional day of the Entmoot in VII.419; and the changes in 'The White Rider' in VII.425. Nothing further need be said of these. But in a note on 'The Taming of Sméagol' the question of the storm is raised;

and here my father directed that the reference to Théoden and the Hornburg should be cut out, because it 'won't fit'. He noted that the thunderstorm over the Emyn Muil was at about five o'clock in the evening of 31 January, while the thunder in the Battle of the Hornburg was about midnight of 1 February, and that 31 hours to travel a distance of some 350 miles was too slow; but no solution was proposed.

I have referred (VII.368) to an elaborate time-scheme that was made after the changes of October 1944 had been introduced. This, being a major working chronology, is in places fearsomely difficult to interpret, on account of later alterations and overwritings in ink over the original pencil. It is arranged in columns, describing 'synoptically', and fairly fully, the movements of all the major actors in the story on each day. It begins on the fifth day of the voyage down Anduin and ends at the beginning of the ascent to the pass of Kirith Ungol; and I would guess that it belongs with the work on chronology in October 1944, rather than later. On this scheme, which I will call 'S', my father afterwards wrote 'Old Timatal stuff' (Icelandic *tímatál* 'chronology').

In this scheme S the death of Boromir and the Breaking of the Fellowship was put back by a day, to Wednesday 25 January.

Jan. 25 Company broken up. Death of Boromir. ... Frodo and Sam cross river eastward and fly into E. of Emyn Muil.

Jan. 26 Frodo and Sam wandering in Emyn Muil (1st evening since flight).

Jan. 27 In Emyn Muil (2nd evening).

Jan. 28 In Emyn Muil (3rd evening).

Jan. 29 In Emyn Muil (4th evening).

Jan. 30 On brink of Emyn Muil. Spend cold night under a rock (5th evening).

Jan. 31 Descent from Emyn Muil at nightfall. Meet Gollum about 10 p.m.
Journey in the gully (Jan.31/Feb.1).

Here therefore the opening of the story in 'The Taming of Sméagol' was on the evening of Jan. 30, and that was explicitly the sixth evening since the flight; but my father was for some reason not counting the first evening in the Emyn Muil (Jan. 25), and so he called that of Jan. 30 the fifth. Perhaps it was the same counting that explains the discrepancy between Scheme B and the text of the chapter (p. 100). And it may well be in any case that the records of these complicated manoeuvres are insufficient, or that there are clues which I have failed to perceive.

In Scheme B, as in the completed manuscript of the chapter (p. 95), it is explicit that the storm over the Emyn Muil reached the Hornburg later that same night; it was moving fast ('hastening with wind and thunder'). In Scheme S, however, this is not so; for (just as in the note of October 1944 referred to above) the descent of Frodo and Sam from the Emyn Muil was at nightfall of Jan. 31, but the Battle of the Hornburg began on the night of Feb. 1. S as written had no mention of the great storm, but my father added in against Jan. 31 'Thunder at nightfall', and then subsequently 'It crawls west', with a line apparently directing to Feb. 1. The storm over Rohan, slowly overtaking the Riders as they rode west across the plains on their second day out of Edoras (at the beginning of the chapter 'Helm's Deep') and bursting over the Hornburg in the middle of the night, was already present when my father came to write 'The Taming of Smeagol'. The storm over the Emyn Muil moving westwards, if not actually conceived for the purpose, obviously had the desirable effect of drawing the now sundered stories, east and west of Anduin, together. The revised passage about the storm in 'The Taming of Sméagol' given on p. 95 was clearly intended to allow for another day in the storm's progress, and implies that Frodo and Sam climbed down out of the hills on the day *before* the Battle of the Hornburg, as in S; and this resolves the problem of time and distance stated in the note of October 1944 by asserting that the great storm did not 'hasten', but 'rolled on slowly through the night.'

But in *The Tale of Years* the relative dating is entirely different:

Scheme S

Frodo enters Emyn Muil	(25 Jan.)	*Day 1*
In Emyn Muil	(26 Jan.)	*Day 2*
In Emyn Muil	(27 Jan.)	*Day 3*
In Emyn Muil	(28 Jan.)	*Day 4*
In Emyn Muil	(29 Jan.)	*Day 5*
In Emyn Muil	(30 Jan.)	*Day 6*
Descent from Emyn Muil	(31 Jan.)	*Day 7*
Battle of the Hornburg	(1 Feb.)	*Day 8*

The Tale of Years

Frodo enters Emyn Muil	(26 Feb.)	*Day 1*
In Emyn Muil	(27 Feb.)	*Day 2*
In Emyn Muil	(28 Feb.)	*Day 3*
Descent from Emyn Muil	(29 Feb.)	*Day 4*
	(30 Feb.)	*Day 5*
	(1 Mar.)	*Day 6*
	(2 Mar.)	*Day 7*
Battle of the Hornburg	(3 Mar.)	*Day 8*

Thus in the final chronology the Battle of the Hornburg took place *four nights after* the descent of Frodo and Sam and the meeting with Gollum. Yet the revised description of the westward course of the storm in 'The Taming of Sméagol' (p. 95) survived into the proof stage of *The Lord of the Rings.* On the proof my father noted against the passage: 'Chronology wrong. The storm of Frodo was 3 days before Théoden's ride' (i.e. 29 February and 2 March, the day on which Théoden rode from Edoras). The passage as it stands in TT, pp. 215–16, was substituted at the eleventh hour: giving the great storm a more widely curving path, and suggesting, perhaps, a reinforcement of its power and magnitude as it passed slowly over Ered Nimrais.

II
THE PASSAGE OF THE MARSHES

The writing of this chapter can again be closely dated from the letters that my father wrote to me in South Africa in 1944. On the 13th of April (*Letters* no. 60) he said that on the previous day he had read his 'recent chapter' ('The Taming of Sméagol') to C. S. Lewis and Charles Williams, and that he had begun another. On the 18th April (*Letters* no. 61) he wrote: 'I hope to see C.S.L. and Charles W. tomorrow morning and read my next chapter – on the passage of the Dead Marshes and the approach to the Gates of Mordor, which I have now practically finished.'[1] And on the 23rd of April (*Letters* no. 62) he wrote: 'I read my second chapter, Passage of the Dead Marshes, to Lewis and Williams on Wed. morning [19 April]. It was approved. I have now nearly done a third: Gates of the Land of Shadow. But this story takes me in charge, and I have already taken three chapters over what was meant to be one!' The completed manuscript of 'The Passage of the Marshes' was indeed first entitled 'Kirith Ungol' (that being still the name of the main pass into Mordor) – for he began writing the manuscript before he had by any means finished the initial drafting of the chapter.

Essential ideas for this part of the narrative had in fact emerged a long time before, in the outline 'The Story Foreseen from Lórien' (VII.329–30) – when he estimated that the chapter would be numbered XXV, eight less than the event had proved. In that outline he wrote:

> Gollum pleads for forgiveness, and promises help, and having nowhere else to turn Frodo accepts. Gollum says he will lead them over the Dead Marshes to Kirith Ungol. (Chuckling to himself to think that that is just the way he would wish them to go.) ...
>
> They sleep in pairs, so that one is always awake with Gollum.
>
> Gollum all the while is scheming to betray Frodo. He leads them cleverly over the Dead Marshes. There are dead green faces in the stagnant pools; and the dry reeds hiss like snakes. Frodo feels the strength of the searching eye as they proceed.
>
> At night Sam keeps watch, only pretending to be asleep. He hears Gollum muttering to himself, words of hatred for Frodo and lust for the Ring.
>
> The three companions now approach Kirith Ungol, the dreadful ravine which leads into Gorgoroth. Kirith Ungol means Spider Glen: there dwelt great spiders ...

A single page of notes shows my father's thoughts as he embarked at last on the writing of this story. These notes were not written as a continuous outline and not all were written at the same time, but I give them in the sequence in which they stand on the page.

Food problem. Gollum chokes at *lembas* (but it does him good?). Goes off and comes back with grimy fingers [?and face]. Once he heard him crunching in dark.

Next chapter

Gollum takes them down into the water gully and then turns away eastward. It leads to a hard point in the midst of the Marshes. Over Dead Marshes. Dead faces. In some of the pools if you looked in you saw your own face all green and dead and corrupted. To Kirith Ungol.

Change in Gollum as they draw near

Gollum sleeps quite unconcerned – quietly at first; but as they draw near to Mordor he seems to get nightmares. Sam hears him beginning to hold colloquies with himself. It is a sort of good Smeagol angry with a bad Gollum. The latter [?grows] – filled with hatred of the Ring-bearer, in longing to be Ring-master himself.

Laid up [?in] rock near gates see great movements in and out. Explanation of why they had escaped the war-movement.

They lie up in day in beds of reeds

Feeling of weight. Ring feels heavier and heavier on Frodo's neck as Mordor approaches. He feels the Eye.

Another page, written at any rate before 'The Passage of the Marches' had proceeded very far, outlines the story thus:

They come to a point where the gully falls into the marshes. Brief description of these (which take about 3 to 4 days to cross). Pools where there are faces some horrible, some fair – but all corrupted. Gollum says it is said that they are memories (?) of those who fell in ages past in the Battle before Ennyn Dûr the Gates of Mordor in the Great Battle. In the moon if you looked in some pools you saw your own face fouled and corrupt and dead. Describe the pools as they get nearer to Mordor as like green pools and rivers fouled by modern chemical works.

They lie up in foothills and see armed men and orcs passing in. Soon all is clear. Sauron is gathering his power and hiding it in Mordor in readiness. (Swart men, and wild men with long braided hair out of East; Orcs of the Eye etc.)

On the far (East) Horn of the Gates is a tall white tower. Minas Ithil now Minas Morghul which guards the pass. It was originally built by the men of Gondor to prevent Sauron breaking out and was manned by the guards of Minas Ithil,[2] but it fell soon into his hands. It now prevented any coming in. It was manned by orcs and evil spirits. It had been called [Neleg Thilim >] Neleglos [the Gleaming >] the White Tooth.[3]

This last passage is accompanied by a little sketch, reproduced on p. 108 (no. I). Until now, the pass and chief entry into Mordor had been named *Kirith Ungol* (cf. the citation from 'The Story Foreseen from Lórien' on p. 104). When contemplating the story ahead as he drafted 'The Passage of the Marshes' my father saw that this was not so: Kirith Ungol was a distinct way through the mountains – and (plainly enough) it is this path that Sam and Frodo are going to take. Concomitantly with this, he was proposing to change the site of Minas Morgul as he had long conceived it, and as it appears on the First Map (see Map III, VII.309).[4] There, the pass of Kirith Ungol was guarded by two towers, one on either side (see VII.349, note 41), and Minas Morgul was away to the west, on the other side of the mountains (i.e. on the western side of the northern extremity of the Dúath, the Mountains of Shadow); whereas now Minas Morgul is to be the tower that guards the pass.[5] A virtually identical sketch to this, in faint pencil, is found on a page of drafting for 'The Black Gate is Closed'. It clearly does not belong with that, however (the later text is written across it), but with the present passage; and accompanying this pencilled version of the sketch is this note:

> It is better for the later story that Minas Ithil (Morghul) should be actually at the Gates of Mordor on its East side.

The scene is thus depicted from the North.

On a page used also for drafting of 'The Passage of the Marshes' there is another sketch of the tower and the pass (also reproduced on p. 108, no. II), very similar except in one important respect: whereas in Sketch I the cleft of Kirith Ungol is placed immediately below Minas Morgul (which thus stands on a high ridge or 'horn' *between* the 'cleft' and the 'pass'), in Sketch II Kirith Ungol lies on the far side of the pass from the tower. The scene is again depicted from the North, for the accompanying text reads: 'Kirith Ungol is *not* the main entrance but a narrow cleft to [S(outh) >] West.' I think it almost certain that Sketch II represents a further stage in the development of the conception, not its first appearance.

Most of 'The Passage of the Marshes' is extant in preliminary drafting (and most of it in excruciatingly difficult handwriting); in this chapter my father made no use of his method of writing a text in pencil and then setting down a more finished version in ink on top of it. The narrative in the draft is not perfectly continuous, and it is clear that (as commonly) he built up the completed manuscript – the only one made of this chapter – in stages. The initial drafting is mostly extremely rough, written at great speed, and in places the completed manuscript (while perfectly legible – it was the text from which my father read the chapter to Lewis and Williams on April the 19th) is itself really the primary composition, constantly corrected and changed in the act of writing. Nonetheless the story of the passage of the Dead Marshes as it appears in *The Two Towers* seems to have been achieved almost to the form of every sentence (apart from certain substantial alterations made very much later) in that week of April 1944.

Only in one respect did the initial drafting differ significantly from the story as it appears in the manuscript. This was primarily a matter of the narrative structure, but I give most of the passage in question, so well as I can make it out, as exemplification. It takes up from Gollum's words 'Snakes, worms in pools. Lots of things in the pools. No birds' (TT p. 234).

So passed the third day of their travelling with Gollum.[6]

All the night they went on with brief halts. Now it was really perilous at least for the hobbits. They went slowly keeping close in line and following every move of Gollum's attentively. The pools grew larger and more ominous and the places where feet could tread without sinking into [?chilly] gurgling mires more and more difficult to find. There were no more reeds and grasses.

Later in the night, after midnight, there came a change. A light breeze got up and grew to a cold wind: it came from the North and though it had a bitter tang it seemed kindly to them, for it bore at last a hint of untainted airs and drove the reeking mists into banks with dark channels in between. The cloudy sky was torn and tattered and the moon nearly full rode among the [?wrack]. Gollum cowered and muttered but the hobbits looked up hopefully. A great dark shadow came out of Mordor like a huge bird crossed the moon and went away west. Just the same feeling came on them as at the ..... they cast themselves down in the mire. But the shadow passed quickly. Gollum lay like one stunned and they had to rouse him. He would say only Wraiths wraiths [?under] the moon. The precious the precious is their master. They see everything everywhere. He sees. After that [?even] Frodo sensed a change in Gollum once more. He was [?even] more fawning [and] friendly but he talked more often in

Kirith Ungol

I

Kirith Ungol is not the main entrance but a narrow cleft to the West.

Minas Morghul

K.U

Morder Gates

II

Two early sketches of Kirith Ungol

[his] old manner. They had great difficulty in making him go on while the moon

The last passage was then rewritten ('After that Sam thought he sensed a change in Gollum again' ...) and the draft continues with a description of Frodo's weariness and slowness and the weight of the Ring that approaches the text in TT (p. 238). Then follows:

He now really felt it as a weight: and he was getting conscious of the Eye: it was that as much as the weight that made him cower and stoop as he walked. He felt like someone hidden in a room (?garden) when his deadly enemy comes in: knowing that he is there though he cannot yet see him the enemy stands at gaze to espy all comers with his deadly eye. Any movement is fraught with peril.[7] Gollum probably felt something of the same sort. After the passing of the shadow of the Nazgûl that flew to Isengard it was difficult to get him to move if there was light. As long as the moon lasted he would only creep forwards on his hands cowering and whimpering. He was not much use as a guide and Sam took to trying to find a path for himself. In doing so he stumbled forward and came down on his hands in sticky mire with his face bending over a dark pool that seemed like some glazed but grimed window in the moonlight. Wrenching his hands out of the bog he sprang back with a cry. There are dead faces ..... dead faces in the pool he cried, dead faces!

Gollum laughed. The Dead Marshes, yes, yess. That is their name. Should not look in when the White Eye is up.[8] What are they, who are they, asked Sam shuddering and turning to Frodo who came up behind him. I don't know said Frodo. No don't master said Sam, they're horrible. Nonetheless Frodo crawled cautiously to the edge and looked. He saw pale faces – deep under water they looked: some grim some hideous, some noble and fair: but all horrible, corrupted, sickly, rotting .... Frodo crawled back and hid his eyes. I don't know who they are but I thought I saw Men and Elves and Orcs, all dead and rotten. Yes yes, said Gollum cackling. All dead and rotten. The Dead Marshes. Men and Elves and Orcs. There was a great Battle here long long ago, precious, yes, when Smeagol was young and happy long ago:[9] before the precious came, yes, yes. They fought on the plain over there. The Dead Marshes have grown greater.

But are they really there? Smeagol doesn't know, said Gollum. You can't reach them. I we tried, yes we tried, precious, once: but you can't touch them. Only shapes to see perhaps, not to touch, no precious! Sam looked darkly at him and shuddered, thinking he guessed why Smeagol had tried to reach them.

The moon was now sinking west into cloud that lay above far Rohan beyond Anduin. They went on and Gollum again took the lead by [*read* but] Sam and Frodo found that he [*read* they] could not keep their [?fascinated] eyes from straying whenever they passed some pool of black water. If they did so they caught glimpses of the pallid dead faces. At last they came to a place where Gollum halted, a wide pool ...... barred their way.

The pools lit by *will o' the wisp* fire reveal dead faces. The moon shows their own.[10]

.... The moon came out of its cloud. They looked in. But they saw no faces out of the vanished past. They saw *their own.* ..... Sam Gollum and Frodo looking up with dead eyes and livid rotting flesh at them.

Let's get out of this foul place!

Long way to go yet said Gollum. Must get to somewhere to lie up before day.

This section of drafting peters out here. In the manuscript the text becomes that of TT at almost all points: the sequence of the story has been reconstructed, so that the change in the weather and the flight of the Nazgûl follows the passage of the pools of the dead faces; and there is no further hint of the idea (going back to the preliminary notes, p. 105) that the beholder's own face was mirrored as dead when the moonlight shone on the pools.

It is notable that in the draft the Nazgûl is said to have been flying to Isengard. In the manuscript as first written this was not said: '... a vast shape winged and ominous: it scudded across the moon, and with a deadly cry went away westward, outrunning the moon in its fell speed. ... But the shadow passed quickly, and behind it the wind roared away, leaving the Dead Marshes bare and bleak.' After the last sentence, however, my father added, probably not long after, 'The Nazgûl had gone, flying to Isengard with the speed of the wrath of Sauron.' The rewriting of the passage, so that the Nazgûl returns and, flying lower above them, sweeps back to Mordor, was done at a later time (see the Note on Chronology at the end of this chapter); but the words in TT (p. 237) 'with a deadly cry *went away westward*' are in fact a vestige of the original conception.

Among various other differences and developments the following seem the most worth remarking.

In the original draft, and at first in the manuscript, Gollum's 'song' (TT pp. 227–8) was wholly different after the first line:

The cold hard lands
To feet and hands
they are unkind.
There wind is shrill,
The stones are chill;
there's nought to find.

Our heart is set
On water wet
in some deep pool.
O how we wish
To taste of fish
so sweet and cool!

There was no reference to 'Baggins' and the fish-riddle.

The story that they slept the whole of the day after they had come down from the Emyn Muil was not present at first. In the preliminary draft of the opening of the chapter Sam, after testing that Gollum was really asleep by saying *fissh* in his ear, did not fall asleep:

> Time seemed to drag; but after an hour or two Gollum sat up suddenly wide awake as if he had been called. He stretched, yawned, got up and began to climb out of the gully. 'Hi, where are you off to?' cried Sam. 'Smeagol's very hungry,' said Gollum. 'Be back soon.'

In the manuscript the final story appears, to the extent that Sam does fall asleep; but when he wakes 'the sky above was full of bright daylight.' This however was changed immediately: Sam and Frodo slept the whole day away, not waking until after sunset, and Gollum's departure to find something to eat is postponed to the evening.[11]

There can be no doubt that the geography of the region in which the Dead Marshes lay had now been substantially changed. It is said in TT (p. 232):

> The hobbits were now wholly in the hands of Gollum. They did not know, and could not guess in that misty light, that they were in fact only just within the northern borders of the marshes, the main expanse of which lay south of them. They could, if they had known the lands, with some delay have retraced their steps a little, and then turning east have come round over hard roads to the bare plain of Dagorlad.

This passage appears in the manuscript, and is found embryonically in the original draft, of which, though partly illegible, enough can be made out to see that the new conception was present: 'They were in fact just within the north-west bounds of the Dead Marshes', and '[they could] have come round the eastern side to the hard of Battle Plain.' The First Map (Maps II and IV^c, VII.305, 317) and the large map based on it that I made in 1943 are entirely at variance with this: for in that conception the No Man's Land lay between Sarn Gebir (Emyn Muil) and the pass into Mordor. There could be no reason for one journeying in those hills to enter the Dead Marshes if he were making for the pass (Kirith Ungol on those maps); nor, if he were at the edge of the marshes, would he by any means come to Dagorlad if instead of going through them he went round to their east. Essentially what has happened is that the Dead Marshes have been moved south-west, so that they lie between the Emyn Muil and the Gates of Mordor – into the region marked 'No Man's Land' on the First Map – and so become continuous with the Wetwang or Nindalf (see VII.320–1 and below); this is the geography seen on the large-scale map of Gondor and Mordor accompanying *The Return of the King.*[12]

In reply to Frodo's question whether they must cross the Dead Marshes, Gollum answered in the original draft (cf. TT p. 233): '"No need. Back a little, and round a little" – his skinny arm waved away north and east – "and you can come dry-foot to the Plain. Dagorlad that is, where the Battle was fought and He lost the precious, yess" – he added this in a sort of whisper to himself.' The manuscript here has the text of TT; but subsequently, in Gollum's explanation of the dead faces in the marshes (TT p. 235), he says: 'There was a great Battle long ago, yes, so they told him when Smeagol was young, long ago, before the Precious came. They took It from the Lord then, Elves and Men took It. It was a great battle. They fought on the plain for days and months and years at the Gates of Mornennyn [> Morannon]' (for the original draft of this see p. 109). Gollum's reference to the story of the taking of the Ring from Sauron was removed much later.

The account of the morning after the night of the dead faces in the pools and the flight of the Nazgûl, and of the lands through which they passed after leaving the marshes, was different in important respects from that in TT, pp. 238–9. The manuscript reads (following an initial draft):

> When day came at last, the hobbits were surprised to see how close the ominous mountains had drawn: the outer buttresses and the broken hills at their feet were now no more than a dozen miles away. Frodo and Sam looked round in horror: dreadful as the Marshes had been in their decay their end was more loathsome still. Even to the mere of the dead faces some haggard phantom of green spring would come ... (&c. as in TT p. 239)

The extended and altered passage that replaces this in TT, introduced at a later stage, was due to considerations of geography and chronology. With this new passage two more nights are added to the journey (see the Note on Chronology at the end of this chapter and the map on p. 117), and during this stage of it they pass through a country seen from the end of the marshes as 'long shallow slopes, barren and pitiless', and described subsequently as 'the arid moors of the Noman-lands'. Here this name reappears from Celeborn's words to the Company in 'Farewell to Lórien' (FR p. 390) and the old maps: see VII.320–1 and above.

An isolated page carries two distinct elements, though very probably both were set down at the same time. The change of the name of the Gates of Mordor in the act of writing from *Ennyn Dûr* (the name on Sketch I, p. 108) first to *Morennyn* and then to *Mornennyn* shows that this page preceded the point in the writing of the manuscript text where Gollum speaks of the dead faces in the pools, for there *Mornennyn* appears (p. 112), but it is convenient to give it here since it concerns the narrative of the end of the chapter (and the beginning of the next).

The famous pass of [Ennyn (Dûr) > Morennyn >] Mornennyn the Gates of Mordor was guarded by two towers: the Teeth of Mordor [Nelig Morn Mel >] Nelig Myrn. Built by Gondorians long ago: now ceaselessly manned. Owing to ceaseless passage of arms they dare not try to enter so they turn W. and South. Gollum tells them of Kirith Ungol beneath shadow [of] M. Morgul. It is a high pass. He does not tell them of the Spiders. They creep in to M[inas] M[orgul].

This text is accompanied by a further sketch of the site of Kirith Ungol, reproduced on p. 114. It is clear from this that the transference of Minas Morgul to become the fortress guarding the Black Gates was a passing idea now abandoned; and it was no doubt at this very point (Minas Morgul being restored to its old position in the Mountains of Shadow a good way south of the Black Gates) that the southward journey along the western side of the mountains entered the narrative. But it is also clear that the Tower of Kirith Ungol had not yet emerged: the cleft of the spiders passes beneath Minas Morgul, on the south side (on the assumption that the scene is depicted from the West); and the original story in the outline 'The Story Foreseen from Lórien' is again present, that Frodo and Sam entered Minas Morgul (but there is here no mention of Frodo's capture).

In the text accompanying Sketch I on p. 108 it is Minas Morghul, above the Black Gates, that was called 'the White Tooth', *Neleglos*; now there emerge (or perhaps re-emerge, from the original two towers guarding the pass, see p. 106) the Teeth of Mordor, *Nelig Myrn*.

It will be seen subsequently (p. 122) that at this stage 'the Gates of Mordor', 'the Black Gates' (*Ennyn Dûr*, *Mornennyn*) were specifically names of the pass, not of any barrier built across it.

The other brief text on this page places Sam's overhearing of Gollum's disputation with himself (foreseen already in the preliminary notes to the chapter, p. 105) at this point in the narrative (though it seems that at this stage my father envisaged them passing a night, not a day, before the Black Gates).

The night watching the [Ennyn D(ûr) >] Mornennyn. It is Frodo's turn to watch. Sam sleeps and suddenly awakes thinking he has

The famous pass of ~~[illegible]~~ Morannon the Gate
of Mordor was guarded by two towers: the Teeth
of Mordor ~~[illegible]~~ Narig Myrn. Built by
Gondorians long ago: now ceaselessly manned.
Owing to ceaseless passage of armies they dare not try to enter.
So they turn to the South. Gollum tells them of
Kirith Ungol beneath shadow of Minas Morgul. This a high

K.U.

pass. He does not tell them of the Spiders. They
creep in to M.M.

The night watching the ~~[illegible]~~ Morannon
it is F's turn to watch. Sam sleeps and suddenly
awakes thinking he has heard his master calling.
But he sees Frodo has fallen asleep. Gollum is
sitting by him gazing at him. ~~[illegible]~~. Sam hears
him arguing with himself: [illegible] versus 'another'.
A pale light and a green light alternate in his eyes.
[illegible] hunger and desire to eat F. But he is
cruelly [illegible]; there's the call of the Ring. His long hand
keeps creeping out and pawing towards Frodo and then
is pulled back. Sam wakes Frodo.

Third sketch of Kirith Ungol

heard his master calling. But he sees Frodo has fallen asleep. Gollum is sitting by him, gazing at him. Sam hears him arguing with himself: Smeagol versus 'another'. Pale light and a green light alternate in his eyes. But it is not *hunger* or desire to *eat* Frodo that he is battling with: it is the call of the Ring. His long hand keeps on going out and paw[ing] towards Frodo and then is pulled back. Sam rouses Frodo.

The actually reported 'colloquy' of Gollum was developed in stages. His references to 'She' ('She might help'), and Sam's passing reflection on who that might be, were added subsequently, doubtless when that part of the story was reached. A change made much later altered what the 'two Gollums' said about Bilbo and the 'birthday present'; roughly in the initial draft, and then in the manuscript and subsequent typescripts, the passage read:

> 'Oh no, not if it doesn't please us. Still he's a Baggins, my precious, yes a Baggins. A Baggins stole it.'
> 'No, not steal: it was a present.'
> 'Yes, steal. We never gave it, no never. He found it and he said nothing, nothing. We hates Baggins.'

Lastly, in the manuscript and following typescripts the chapter ended at the words: 'In the falling dusk they scrambled out of the pit and slowly threaded their way through the dead land' (TT p. 242). All that follows in TT, describing the menace of a Ringwraith passing overhead unseen at dusk and again an hour after midnight, and the prostration of Gollum, was added to the typescripts at a later stage (see the Note on Chronology below).

NOTES

1 My father went on to speak of a letter he had written adjudicating a dispute in an army mess concerning the pronunciation of the name of the poet Cowper (*Letters* no. 61). A draft for this letter is found on a page of drafting for the passage describing the change in the weather over the marshes, TT pp. 236–7.

2 This, I believe, is the first appearance of the conception that the fortresses on the confines of Mordor had been built looking inwards and not outwards.

3 Cf. the *Etymologies* (V.376), stem NÉL-EK 'tooth'.

4 My father had in fact moved Minas Morgul further north from its position as originally shown on the First Map (east of Osgiliath), and placed it not far from the northern tip of the Mountains of Shadow (see VII.310). With this cf. 'The Story Foreseen from Lórien', where Minas Morgul was said to be reached by a path that 'led up into the mountains – the north horn of the Mountains of Shadow that sundered the ashen vale of

Gorgoroth from the valley of the Great River' (VII.333). But Minas Morgul was still on the western side of the mountains (i.e. on the other side of the mountains to the Pass of Kirith Ungol).

5 In notes at the end of 'The Story Foreseen from Lórien' my father had suggested that Frodo should be taken as captive to one of the guard-towers of the pass, and in a time-scheme of that period he changed 'Sam rescues Frodo in Minas Morgul' to 'Sam rescues Frodo in Gorgos' (see VII.344); and again (VII.412): 'The winding stair must be cut in rocks and go up from Gorgoroth to watch-tower. Cut out Minas Morgul.' Now, as it appears, these conceptions were to be fused: Frodo was again to be taken to Minas Morgul, but Minas Morgul was itself the watch-tower above the pass.

6 *the third day:* see the Note on Chronology below.

7 This passage was developed in the manuscript thus, before being changed to the text of TT (p. 238):

> Frodo knew just where the present habitation and heart of that will now was. He could have walked, or flown straight there. He was facing it: and its potency beat upon his brow if he raised it for a moment. He felt like someone who, covered only by a grey garment, has strayed into a garden, when his enemy enters. The enemy knows he is there, even if he cannot yet see him, and he stands at gaze, silent, patient, deadly, sweeping all corners with the hatred of his eye. Any movement is fraught with peril.

8 *when the White Eye is up:* throughout this part of the story Gollum's names for the Sun and Moon were originally the Yellow Eye and the White Eye, not the Yellow Face and the White Face. — TT has here, as does the manuscript, 'when the candles are lit': see note 10.

9 Cf. Gollum's words in TT (p. 235): 'There was a great battle long ago, yes, so they told him when Sméagol was young'. His words in the present draft ('a great battle here long long ago when Sméagol was young') might suggest the far shorter time-span (see p. 21, and VII.450 note 11); but the manuscript had from the first 'so they said when Smeagol was young'.

10 This was no doubt the point at which the idea of the marsh-lights entered (*ignis fatuus, will-o'-the-wisp, jack-o'-lantern*). In TT, as in the manuscript, Gollum calls them 'candles of corpses', and in time-schemes of this period my father referred to the 'episode of the corpse-candles'. *Corpse-candle* is defined in the Oxford Dictionary as 'a lambent flame seen in a churchyard or over a grave, and superstitiously believed to appear as an omen of death, or to indicate the route of a coming funeral.'

11 In the conversation between Frodo and Sam that follows (TT

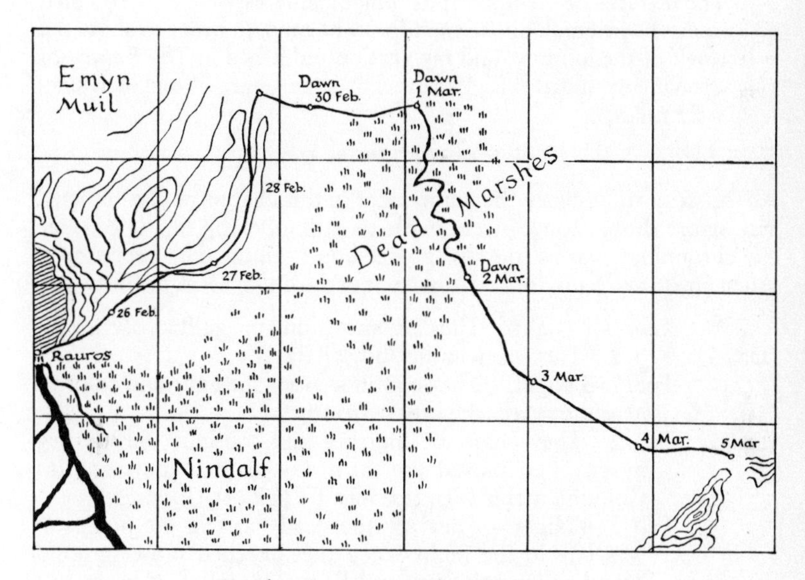

Frodo's journey to the Morannon

p. 231), in Frodo's words 'If we can nurse our limbs to bring us to Mount Doom' the name is spelt thus in the preliminary draft, but the manuscript has 'Mount Dûm': this spelling is found also in the preliminary draft of Frodo's vision on Amon Hen, VII.373.

12 The large-scale map of Gondor and Mordor was closely based on a map of my father's. This included the track of Frodo's journey from Rauros to the Morannon, and I have redrawn this section from the original (p. 117). My father's map is in some respects hard to interpret, for it was made roughly and hastily in point of its actual execution, the 'contour-lines' being very impressionistic, while the Nindalf and the Dead Marshes are shown merely by rough pencil hatching, for which I have substituted conventional reed-tufts; but I have attempted to redraw it as precisely as I can. The features of the uppermost line of squares were only roughed in on the original, above the top of the map, in order to show the track of the journey, and my version published in *The Return of the King* excluded this element. The squares are of one inch side, = 25 miles.

Note on the Chronology

As the story stood when the manuscript of this chapter was completed but before those changes were made to it that belong to a later stage the chronology was as follows (proceeding from the date February 1, when Frodo and Sam climbed down out of the Emyn Muil, p. 100):

Feb. 1–2 Night. They advance along the gully. *(Journey 1)*
(Day 1) Feb. 2 They sleep in the gully all day.
Feb. 2–3 Night. They continue along the gully and come to its end towards daybreak. *(Journey 2)*
(Day 2) Feb. 3 They enter the marshes and continue the journey by day ('So passed the third day of their journey with Gollum', manuscript text and TT p. 234). *(Journey 3)*
Feb. 3–4 Night. They see the dead faces in the pools. 'It was late in the night when they reached firmer ground again', manuscript text and TT p. 236; followed by change in the weather and flight of the Nazgûl. *(Journey 4)*
(Day 3) Feb. 4 When day came 'the outer buttresses and broken hills' at the feet of the mountains were 'no more than a dozen miles away' (p. 112). They were among the slag-mounds and poisonous pits. Day spent hiding in a hole. At dusk they went on (night of Feb. 4–5). *(Journey 5)*
(Day 4) Feb. 5 (Beginning of the next chapter) They reach the Black Gate at dawn.

Both of the brief time-schemes of which the beginnings are given on p. 100 express precisely this chronology. Scheme B was written, apparently, when the story had already reached the departure from

Henneth Annûn, but A accompanied the writing of the present chapter and scarcely extends beyond it. Notably, in A the actual journeys they made are numbered (as I have numbered them in the chronology set out above), and it may well be that '3' against February 3 explains the statement cited above: 'So passed the third day of their journey with Gollum' – for it was the third journey, but not the third day.

Both schemes refer to the flight of the Nazgûl. In B, under February 3, 'Nazgûl passes over marshes and goes to Isengard', with a subsequent addition 'reaching there about midnight'. This is hard to understand, since already in the completed manuscript 'it was *late in the night* when they reached firmer ground again', and that was before the change in the weather and the flight of the Nazgûl. In A it is said that 'Nazgûl goes over at early morning before daybreak' (of February 4), agreeing with the text of the chapter; but Théoden and Gandalf and their company left Isengard on the evening of February 3, and camped below Dol Baran (over which the Nazgûl passed) that night, so that this offers equal difficulty.

In his notes of October 1944 (see p. 100) my father commented, under the heading 'Passage of the Marshes', that 'the Nazgûl over marshes cannot be the same as passed over Dolbaran', and directed that the relevant passage in that chapter, and also that at the end of 'The Palantír', should be changed. It must have been at this time, then, that the description of the Nazgûl's flight over the marshes was altered – it wheeled round and returned to Mordor (p. 110); while at the same time, in 'The Palantír', Gandalf's original words to Pippin 'It could have taken you away to the Dark Tower' (p. 77) were extended by Pippin's further question 'But it was not coming for me, was it?' and Gandalf's reply: 'Of course not. It is 200 leagues or more in straight flight from Baraddur to Orthanc, and even a Nazgûl would take some hours to fly between them, or so I guess – I do not know. But Saruman certainly looked in the Stone since the orc-raid, and more of his secret thought, I do not doubt, has been read than he intended. A messenger has been sent to find out what he is doing. ...'

Scheme S (in which the dates of Frodo's journey are a day earlier than in A and B, see p. 101) has the following chronology:

(Day 2) Feb. 2 Journey in the marshes by day.
Feb. 2–3 Night. 'Episode of corpse-candles' (see note 10).
(Day 3) Feb. 3 Reach slag-mounds at dawn. Day spent hiding in a hole, going on at nightfall. Gandalf, Théoden, etc. leave Isengard at sunset and camp at Dolbaran.
(Day 4) Feb. 4 Reach the Black Gate at daybreak and hide all day. Gandalf and Pippin sight Edoras at dawn.

In the notes accompanying the changes made in October 1944 my father also directed that 'the first Nazgûl' should pass over Frodo and his companions at dusk (5 p.m.) on the evening of February 3 'just about when they start from the slag-mounds', and reach Dol Baran about 11 p.m. 'The second Nazgûl, sent after Pippin used the Stone', despatched from Mordor about one o'clock in the morning of the night of Feb. 3–4, should pass over Frodo at the end of the chapter 'Passage of the Marshes' before they reach the Morannon. This Nazgûl would pass over Edoras on February 4, about six hours later. 'But both may pass high up and only give them faint uneasiness.'

Scheme S is confused on the subject of the flights of the Nazgûl, offering different formulations, but in the result it agrees well with the notes just cited; here however the second Nazgûl leaves Mordor 'at 11 p.m.' or 'about midnight', and it 'scouts around the plain and passes over Edoras at ? 8 a.m.' These movements fit very well with the added conclusion to 'The Passage of the Marshes' (TT pp. 242–3; see p. 115), which I presume was introduced at this time. Thus the unseen Ringwraith that passed overhead soon after they left the hole amid the slag-heaps, 'going maybe on some swift errand from Barad-dûr', was the one that passed over Dol Baran six hours later (on its way to Orthanc to 'find out what Saruman was doing'); and that which passed over an hour after midnight, 'rushing with terrible speed into the West', was the one sent in response to Pippin's looking into the *palantír*.

In the final chronology as set out in *The Tale of Years* two days were added to the journey to the Morannon, during which Frodo and his companions passed through 'the arid moors of the Noman-lands' (see p. 112):

(Day 2) Mar. 1 Frodo begins the passage of the Dead Marshes at dawn.
Mar. 1–2 Night. Frodo comes to the end of the Marshes late at night.
(Day 3) Mar. 2–3 Night. Frodo journeys in the Noman-lands.
(Day 4) Mar. 3–4 Night. Frodo journeys in the Noman-lands. Battle of the Hornburg.
(Day 5) Mar. 4 Dawn, Frodo reaches the slag-mounds (and leaves at dusk). Théoden and Gandalf set out from Helm's Deep for Isengard.
(Day 6) Mar. 5 Daybreak, Frodo in sight of the Morannon. Théoden reaches Isengard at noon. Parley with Saruman in Orthanc. Winged Nazgûl passes over the camp at Dol Baran.

Thus according to the final chronology neither of the unseen Nazgûl that passed over high up at the end of the chapter 'The Passage of the Marshes' (at dusk on March 4, and again an hour after midnight) can have been the one that wheeled over Dol Baran on the night of March 5, nor the one that passed over Edoras on the morning of March 6. A rigorous chronology led to this disappointing conclusion.

III
THE BLACK GATE IS CLOSED

I have already quoted (p. 104) my father's letter of 23 April 1944 in which he said that he had 'nearly done' the chapter which he called 'Gates of the Land of Shadow'. Since in the first fair-copy manuscript of this chapter the text goes on without a break through what was subsequently called 'Of Herbs and Stewed Rabbit', he had probably at that date got well beyond the point where 'The Black Gate is Closed' ends in TT (at Frodo's decision to take the southward road); and this is borne out by what he said on the 26th (continuation of a letter begun on 24 April, *Letters* no. 63): 'At this point I require to know how much later the moon gets up each night when nearing full, and how to stew a rabbit!'

Here I restrict my account to the portion of the new chapter that corresponds to 'The Black Gate is Closed'. This was a part of the narrative that largely 'wrote itself', and there is not a great deal to record of its development; it was achieved, also, in a much more orderly fashion than had been the case for a long time. Here there is a continuous, and for most of its length readily legible, initial draft, which extends in fact to the point where 'The Black Gate is Closed' ends in TT, and then becomes a brief outline that brings Frodo, Sam and Gollum to the Cross-roads and up the Stairs of Kirith Ungol – showing that at that time my father had no notion of what would befall them on the southward road. He headed this draft 'Kirith Ungol' (the original title of 'The Passage of the Marshes', p. 104), sure that he could get them there within the compass of this new chapter (but 'Kirith Ungol' now bore a different significance from what it had when he gave it to the previous chapter, see p. 106).

The draft was followed by a fair copy manuscript (in this chapter called 'the manuscript', as distinguished from 'the draft') which, as already noticed, extends without break through 'Of Herbs and Stewed Rabbit', and here again the first title given to it was 'Kirith Ungol', changed to 'The Gates of the Land of Shadow' (the title my father used in his letter of 23 April), and then to 'Kirith Gorgor: The Black gate is Closed'. At some stage, for some reason, he made a further manuscript of the chapter (ending it at the point where it ends in TT) in his most beautiful script, and this was copied in the first typescript. The chapter number is XXXIV.

In the (first) manuscript the text as it stands in TT was achieved in almost all points without much hesitation in the writing; but there was much further shifting in the names that occur in this region. The opening passage concerning the defences of Mordor and their history differed in some respects from the form in TT (p. 244). The words following 'But the strength of Gondor failed, and men slept': *and for long years the towers stood empty*, are lacking.[1] The paragraph beginning 'Across the mouth of the pass, from cliff to cliff, the Dark Lord had built a rampart of stone. In it there was a single gate of iron, and upon its battlement sentinels paced unceasingly' was first written thus, both in draft and manuscript:

> No rampart, or wall, or bars of stone or iron were laid across the Morannon;[2] for the rock on either side was bored and tunnelled into a hundred caves and maggot-holes. A host of orcs lurked there ... (&c. as in TT)

This was changed in the manuscript as soon as written to the text of TT, introducing the rampart of stone and the single gate of iron; and it is thus seen that up to this point the 'Black Gate(s)' was the name of the pass itself.[3] So also at the beginning of the passage, where TT has 'between these arms there was a deep defile. This was Cirith Gorgor, the Haunted Pass, the entrance to the land of the Enemy', both draft and manuscript have 'between these arms there was a long defile. *This was the Morannon*, the Black Gate, the entrance to the land of the Enemy.' When the rampart and iron gate had been introduced this was changed in the manuscript to 'This was Kirith Gorgor, the Dreadful Pass, the entrance to the land of the Enemy.'[4]

The Mountains of Shadow were still in the draft named the *Dúath*, as on the First Map (Map III, VII.309); in the manuscript the name is *Hebel Dúath*, later changed to *Ephel Dúath* (see VII.310).[5] The 'Teeth of Mordor' are named in the draft *Nelig Morn* (cf. *Nelig Morn* > *Nelig Myrn*, p. 113);[6] in the manuscript they are *Naglath Morn*, which was subsequently struck out and not replaced.

It is convenient to notice here a few other points concerning names in this chapter. The name *Elostirion* for Osgiliath, used in the fine manuscript of 'The Palantír' made earlier in April (p. 78 and note 20), was retained in the draft[7] and in the following manuscript of 'The Black Gate is Closed', with *Osgiliath* later substituted in the latter (TT p. 249). The name of Sauron's stronghold in Mirkwood remains *Dol Dúghol*, the change to *Dol Guldur* being made at a very late stage.[8]

A curious vestige is seen in the name *Goodchild* pencilled above *Gamgee* in Sam's remark 'It's beyond any Gamgee to guess what he'll do next' (TT p. 247). In his letter to me of 31 May 1944 (*Letters* no. 72) my father said:

> Sam by the way is an abbreviation not of *Samuel* but of Samwise (the Old E. for Half-wit), as is his father's name the Gaffer (Ham)

> for O.E. Hamfast or Stayathome. Hobbits of that class have very Saxon names as a rule – and I am not really satisfied with the surname Gamgee and shd. change it to Goodchild if I thought you would let me.

I replied that I would never wish to see *Gamgee* changed to *Goodchild*, and urged (entirely missing the point) that the name *Gamgee* was for me the essential expression of 'the hobbit peasantry' in their 'slightly comical' aspect, deeply important to the whole work. I mention this to explain my father's subsequent remarks on the subject (28 July 1944, *Letters*, no. 76):

> As to Sam Gamgee, I quite agree with what you say, and I wouldn't dream of altering his name without your approval; but the object of the alteration was precisely to bring out the comicness, peasantry, and if you will the Englishry of this jewel among the hobbits. Had I thought it out at the beginning, I should have given all the hobbits very English names to match the shire. ... I doubt if it's English [i.e. the name Gamgee]. ... However, I daresay all your imagination of the character is now bound up with the name.

And so Sam Gamgee remained.

Turning now to the narrative itself, there are only certain details to mention. The distance from the hollow in which Frodo and his companions lay to the nearer of the Towers of the Teeth was in the initial drafting and in both manuscripts estimated at about a mile as the crow flies (a furlong in TT, p. 245). The description of the three roads leading to the Black Gate (TT p.247) was present in all essentials from the outset (they were in fact marked in by dotted lines on the First Map, though not included on my redrawing),[9] as were Frodo's stern words to Gollum (TT p. 248), and the conversation about the southward road; but Gollum's remembered tales of his youth and his account of Minas Morgul (TT pp. 249–50) differed from the final form in these respects. When Frodo said: 'It was Isildur who cut off the finger of the Enemy', Gollum replied: 'The tales did not say that'; then Frodo said: 'No, it had not happened then' (becoming in the second manuscript 'No, it had not happened when your tales were made').[10] Secondly, Gollum's reference to 'the Silent Watchers' in Minas Morgul (TT p. 250) was added to the manuscript, which as written had only: 'Nothing moves on the road that they don't know about. The things inside know.' Thirdly, after Gollum's explanation of why Sauron did not fear attack by way of Minas Morgul (his speech beginning 'No, no, indeed. Hobbits must see, must try to understand'), Sam says:

> 'I daresay, but even so we can't walk up along your climbing road and pass the time of day with the folk at the gates and ask if

we're all right for the Dark Tower. Stands to reason,' said Sam. 'We might as well do it here, and save ourselves a long tramp.'

Thus his jibe at Gollum ('Have you been talking to Him lately? Or just hobnobbing with Orcs?'), and Gollum's reply ('Not nice hobbit, not sensible ...') are lacking. With the expanded text (written into the manuscript later) there enters the second reference to 'the Silent Watchers' (and Sam's sarcasm 'Or are they too silent to answer?').

The brief text given on p. 113 and reproduced with the accompanying sketch on p. 114, in which Kirith Ungol is 'beneath the shadow of Minas Morgul', and in which Frodo and Sam actually enter Minas Morgul, shows that only a short time before the point we have reached the later story and geography had not emerged. But the conception of the entrances into Mordor was changing very rapidly, and the original draft of 'The Black Gate is Closed' shows a major further shift. The conversation following Sam's remarks about the futility of going on a long tramp south only to find themselves faced with the same impossibility of entering unseen (TT p. 251) ran thus in the draft:

'Don't joke about it,' said Gollum. 'Be sensible hobbits. It is not sensible to try to get in to Mordor at all, not sensible. But if master says I will go or I must go then he must try some way. But he must not go to the terrible city. That is where Smeagol helps. He found it, he knows it – if it is still there.'

'What did you find?' said Frodo.

'A stair and path leading up into the mountains south of the pass,' said Gollum, 'and then a tunnel, and then more stairs and then a cleft high above the main pass: and it was that way Smeagol got out of Mordor long ago. But it may [?have vanished] ...'

'Isn't it guarded?' said Sam incredulously, and he thought he caught a sudden gleam in Gollum's eye.

'Yes perhaps,' said he, 'but we must try. No other way,' and he would say no more. The name of this perilous place and high pass he could not or would not tell. Its name was Kirith Ungol, but that the hobbits did not know, nor the meaning of that dreadful name.

As the following manuscript was first written this was not significantly changed (the path and stair are still 'south of the pass'); the passage in which Frodo intervenes and challenges Gollum's story that he had escaped from Mordor, citing Aragorn's view of the matter, was added in a rider to the manuscript later.[11]

Thus Kirith Ungol is now not the pass guarded by Minas Morgul, as in the text given on p. 113, but a climbing stair high above it; it is however very difficult to say how my father saw the further course of the story at this time. In the text on p. 113 Frodo and Sam 'creep into Minas Morgul', which suggests that the story of Frodo's capture in 'The Story Foreseen from Lórien' had been temporarily abandoned – though it is not clear why they should be obliged to enter 'the terrible city'. With the new geography, however, it seems that they are going to avoid Minas Morgul, passing through the mountains high above it. Does it follow that the Tower of Kirith Ungol had already been conceived?

There is nothing in draft or manuscript to show that it had – but that proves little in itself, since in all texts from the original draft Gollum refuses to say clearly whether Kirith Ungol is guarded (cf. 'The Stairs of Cirith Ungol', TT p. 319: 'It was a black tower poised above the outer pass. ... "I don't like the look of that!" said Sam. "So this secret way of yours is guarded after all," he growled, turning to Gollum'). The gleam in Gollum's eye that Sam caught when he asked him if it were guarded certainly means that Gollum knew that it was, but does not at all imply that it was guarded by a tower. I feel sure that Gollum was thinking of the spiders (at this stage in the evolution of the story). The only other evidence is found in the outline which ends the original draft of 'The Black Gate is Closed':

Frodo makes up his mind. He agrees to take the south way.

As soon as dusk falls they start. Needing speed they use the road though fearful of meeting soldiers on it hurrying to the muster of the Dark Lord. Gollum says it is twenty leagues perhaps to the Cross Roads in the wood. They made all the speed they could. The land climbs a little. They see Anduin below them gleaming in the moon. Good [?water]. At last late on the third [day of their daylight journey >] night of journey from Morannon they reach the crossroads and pass out of the wood.

See the moon shining on Minas Ithil Minas Morghul.

Pass up first stair safely. But tunnel is black with webs [of] spiders. ... force way and get up second stair. They [??had] reach[ed] Kirith Ungol. Spiders are aroused and hunt them. They are exhausted.

This does not of course imply that the spiders were the only danger they faced in taking the way of Kirith Ungol, but possibly suggests it.

However this may be, and leaving open the question of whether at this stage my father had already decided that Kirith Ungol was guarded by its own tower, it would be interesting to know whether that decision had been taken when he introduced into the manuscript Gollum's references to 'the Silent Watchers'. The Watchers, called 'the

Sentinels', had already appeared in 'The Story Foreseen from Lórien' (see VII.340–3 and note 33); there of course they were the sentinels of Minas Morgul. Here too Gollum is speaking of Minas Morgul (at this point in the chapter he has not even mentioned the existence of Kirith Ungol). It would seem rather odd that my father should bring in these references to the Silent Watchers of Minas Morgul if he had already decided that the actual encounter with Silent Watchers should be at the Tower of Kirith Ungol; and one might suspect therefore that when he wrote them into the text the idea of that tower had not yet arisen. But this is the merest conjecture.[12]

The passage telling where Gandalf was when Frodo and his companions lay hidden in the hollow before the Black Gate underwent many changes. The original draft reads:

Aragorn perhaps could have told them, Gandalf could have warned them, but Gandalf was ? flying over the green [?plain] of Rohan upon Shadowfax climbing the road to the guarded gates of Minas Tirith and Aragorn was marching at the head of many men to war.

This seems to express two distinct answers to the question, where was Gandalf? — In the manuscript this becomes:

Aragorn could perhaps have told them that name and its significance; Gandalf would have warned them. But they were alone; and Aragorn was far away, a captain of men mustering for a desperate war, and Gandalf stood upon the white walls of Minas Tirith deep in troubled thought. It was of them chiefly that he thought: and over the long leagues his mind sought for them.

In the second manuscript, taking up a revision made to the first, Gandalf is again riding over the plains:

... But they were alone, and Aragorn was far away, a captain of men mustering for a desperate war, and Gandalf was flying upon Shadowfax over the fields of Rohan swifter than the wind to the white walls of Minas Tirith gleaming from afar. Yet as he rode, it was chiefly of them that he thought, of Frodo and Sam, and over the long leagues his mind sought for them.

This was changed afterwards to the text of TT (p. 252):

... and Gandalf stood amid the ruin of Isengard and strove with Saruman, delayed by treason. Yet even as he spoke his last words to Saruman, and the *palantír* crashed in fire upon the steps of Orthanc, his thought was ever upon Frodo and Samwise, over the long leagues his mind sought for them in hope and pity.

On the significance of these variations see the Note on Chronology at the end of this chapter.

The distant flight of the Nazgûl (TT p. 253) and the arrival of the southern men observed and reported on by Gollum differ already in the draft text in no essential points from the final text (except that it is Gollum who calls them *Swertings*); but Sam's verse of the Oliphaunt was not present. It is found in abundant rough workings and a preliminary text before being incorporated in the manuscript; my father also copied it out for me in a letter written on 30 April 1944 (*Letters* no. 64), when the story had reached the end of what became 'Of Herbs and Stewed Rabbit', saying: 'A large elephant of prehistoric size, a war-elephant of the Swertings, is loose, and Sam has gratified a life-long wish to see an Oliphaunt, an animal about which there was a hobbit nursery-rhyme (though it was commonly supposed to be mythical).'[13]

NOTES

1 In a very rough initial sketching of the opening of the chapter, preceding the continuous draft, the reading is: 'They were built by the Men of Gondor long ages after the fall of the first Dark Tower and Sauron's flight, lest he should seek to [?retake] his old realm.' This was repeated in the draft text of the chapter ('after the felling of the first Dark fortress'), but changed immediately to 'after the overthrow of Sauron and his flight'.

2 The earliest sketch of the opening passage, referred to in note 1, has a name that ends in *-y*; it could be interpreted as *Mornennyn* with the final *-n* omitted, but is written thus at both occurrences. For *Mornennyn*, replacing *Ennyn Dûr*, see pp. 112–13.

3 The Old English word *geat* 'gate' is found in a number of English place-names in the sense 'pass, gap in the hills', as *Wingate* (pass through which the wind drives), *Yatesbury*.

4 It seems in fact that my father did not immediately transfer the name *Morannon* to the actual 'Black Gate' built by Sauron, but retained it for a time as the name of the pass: so later in the manuscript text (TT p. 247) Frodo 'stood gazing out towards the dark cliffs of the Morannon' (changed subsequently to *Kirith Gorgor*).

5 Here appear also the plain of *Lithlad* (see VII.208, 213) and 'the bitter inland sea of *Nûrnen*', shown on the First Map (Map III, VII.309).

6 In the text given on p. 113 and reproduced on p. 114 *Nelig Myrn* replaced *Nelig Morn* at the time of writing; yet it seems obvious that that text was written during the original composition of 'The Passage of the Marshes'.

7 The draft text has in fact *Osgiliath* at one occurrence, in the first description of the southward road (TT p. 247): 'It journeyed on into the narrow plain between the Great River and the mountains, and so on to Osgiliath and on again to the coasts, and the far southern lands'. But *Elostirion* is the name in this same text in the passage corresponding to TT p. 249.

8 The name *Amon Hen* was changed at its first occurrence in the manuscript (TT p. 247) to *Amon Henn*, but not at the second (TT p. 252). On the second manuscript the name was written *Amon Henn* at both occurrences.

9 The southward road is shown running a little to the east of Anduin as far as the bottom of square Q 14 on Map III, VII.309. The eastward road runs along the northern edges of Ered Lithui as far as the middle of square O 17 on Map II, VII.305. The northward road divides at the bottom of square O 15 on Map II, the westward arm running to the hills on the left side of O 15, and the northward arm bending north-east along the western edge of the Dead Marshes and then turning west to end on the left side of N 15.

The passage describing the southward road was several times changed in respect of its distance from the hollow where Frodo, Sam and Gollum hid. In the original draft it was 'not more than a furlong or so'; in the first manuscript the distance was changed through 'a couple of furlongs', 'fifty paces', and 'a furlong', the final reading (preserved in the second manuscript) being '[it] passed along the valley at the foot of the hillside where the hobbits lay and not many feet below them.' For one, rather surprising, reason for this hesitation see pp. 172–3.

In the First Edition the description of the topography differed from that in the Second Edition (TT p. 247), and read:

> The hollow in which they had taken refuge was delved in the side of a low hill and lay at some little height above the level of the plain. A long trench-like valley ran between it and the outer buttresses of the mountain-wall. In the morning-light the roads that converged upon the Gate of Mordor could now be clearly seen, pale and dusty; one winding back northwards; another dwindling eastwards into the mists that clung about the feet of Ered Lithui; and another that, bending sharply, ran close under the western watch-tower, and then passed along the valley at the foot of the hillside where the hobbits lay and not many feet

> below them. Soon it turned, skirting the shoulders of the mountains ...

This is the text of the second manuscript.

10 Frodo's meaning must be that these particular tales known to Gollum, concerning the cities of the Númenóreans, originated in the time before the Last Alliance and the overthrow of Sauron.

11 As the rider was first written there was this difference from the text of TT (p. 251):

> For one thing he noted Gollum used *I*, as he had hardly done since he was frightened out of his old bad wits away back under the cliff of Emyn Muil.

This was changed to: '... Gollum used *I*, and that seemed usually to be a sign, on its rare appearances, that Smeagol was (for the moment) on top', and then to the final text.

12 Even if this was so, it cannot be supposed that my father still thought that Frodo and Sam would enter Minas Morgul, and encounter the Silent Watchers there. The outline with which the draft text ends (p. 125) would obviously have said so if that had been in his mind. Moreover, not long after, in his letter of 30 April 1944 (*Letters* no. 64), he said that 'in the chapter next to be done they will get to Kirith Ungol and *Frodo will be caught.*'

13 It is hard to be sure, but it seems from the manuscript evidence that originally Sam's word was *oliphant*, and that *oliphaunt* was used only in the rhyme. — The form is mediaeval French and English *olifa(u)nt*. There are no differences in the texts, except that in the draft version and in the form cited in my father's letter line 11 reads 'I've stumped' for 'I stump', and in line 15 'Biggest of all' is written 'Biggest of All'.

Note on the Chronology

Where was Gandalf when Frodo, in hiding before the Morannon, was thinking of him? Four versions of the passage in question (TT p. 252) have been given on pp. 126–7. The original draft (1) seems to leave it open whether Gandalf was riding across Rohan or was almost at the end of his journey, climbing the road to the gates of Minas Tirith; in the following manuscript (2) he was standing on the walls of Minas Tirith; in the second manuscript (3) he was again riding across Rohan; and finally (4), as in TT, he was standing on the steps of Orthanc.

These versions reflect, of course, the difficulty my father encountered in bringing the different threads of the narrative into chronological harmony. According to the 'received chronology' at this time, the day in question here (spent by Frodo, Sam and Gollum in hiding before the Morannon) was 5 February (see p. 118); while Gandalf, Théoden and their companions left Isengard in the evening of 3 February (pp. 6, 73), camping at Dol Baran that night – the great ride of Gandalf with Pippin therefore began during the night of 3–4 February.

At the end of the fine manuscript of 'The Palantír' that my father had made at the beginning of April 1944 (p. 78) Gandalf had said to Pippin as they passed near the mouth of the Deeping Coomb, following the first manuscript of the chapter: 'You may see the first glimmer of dawn upon the golden roof of the House of Eorl. At sunset on the day after you shall see the purple shadow of Mount Mindolluin fall upon the walls of the tower of Denethor.' This was said, according to the chronology at the time, in the small hours of the night of 3–4 February; and Gandalf was therefore forecasting that they would reach Minas Tirith at sunset on the fifth.

This is the chronology underlying the words of the original draft (version 1). Subsequent shifting in the dates, so that Gandalf and Pippin reached Minas Tirith later and Frodo reached the Morannon earlier, meant that Gandalf was less far advanced in his journey, but his ride across Rohan still coincided with Frodo at the Morannon (version 3). None of the time-schemes, however, allows Gandalf to have actually reached Minas Tirith at that time, and I cannot explain version 2.

The final version 4 of this passage, as found in TT, reflects of course the final chronology, according to which Frodo was in hiding before the Black Gate on the same day (5 March) as Gandalf spoke with Saruman on the steps of Orthanc.

IV

OF HERBS AND STEWED RABBIT

For this chapter, written as a continuation of 'The Black Gate is Closed' and only separated from it and numbered 'XXXV' after its completion, there exists a good deal of (discontinuous) initial drafting, some of it illegible, and a completed manuscript, some of which is itself the primary composition. As in the last chapter I distinguish the texts as 'draft' and 'manuscript' (in this case no other manuscript was made, see p. 121).

On 26 April 1944, in a letter to me already cited (p. 121), my father said that on the previous day he had 'struggled with a recalcitrant passage in "The Ring" ', and then went on to say that 'at this point I require to know how much later the moon gets up each night when nearing full, and how to stew a rabbit!' From drafts and manuscript it is easy to see what this recalcitrant passage was: the southward journey as far as the point where Sam's thoughts turned to the possibility of finding food more appetizing than the waybread of the Elves (TT p. 260).

The original draft begins thus:

They rested for the few hours of daylight that were left, ate a little and drank sparingly, though they had hope of water soon in the streams that flowed down into Anduin from Hebel Dúath. As the dusk deepened they set out. The moon did not rise till late and it grew soon dark. After a few miles over broken slopes and difficult [?country] they took to the southward road, for they needed speed. Ever they listened with straining ears for sounds of foot or hoof upon the road ahead and behind ...

After the description of the road, kept in repair below the Morannon but further south encroached upon by the wild, the opening draft peters out, and at this point, probably, my father began the writing of the manuscript. Here the single red light in the Towers of the Teeth appears, but they passed out of sight of it after only a few miles, 'turning away southward round a great dark shoulder of the lower mountains', whereas in TT this took place 'when night was growing old and they were already weary'.[1] In this text they came to the less barren lands, with thickets of trees on the slopes, during that first night, and the shrubs which in TT the hobbits did not know (being strange to them) were here 'unrecognizable in the dark'. After a short rest about midnight Gollum led them down onto the southward road, the description of which follows.

The precise sequence of composition as between drafts and manuscript is hard to work out, but I think that it was probably at this point that my father wrote a very brief outline for the story to come, together with notes on names. Frustratingly, his writing here has in places resisted all attempts to puzzle it out.

After so much labour and peril the days they spent on it seemed almost a rest. In Gollum's reckoning it was some 20 [*changed from some other figure*] leagues from the Morannon to the outer wards of Minas Morghul, maybe more. Gollum finds food. Night of Full Moon, they see a white ... far away up in the dark shadow of the hills to left, at head of a wide [?re-entrant, *sc. valley*], Minas Morghul.[2] Next night they come to the cross roads. An[d] a great [?stone] figure ... [3] back to Elostirion ... [*Struck out:* Sarnel Ubed.[4] Ennyn. Aran] Taur Toralt [*struck out*: Sarn Torath.] Annon Torath. Aranath. reminding Frodo of the Kings at Sern Aranath. or Sairn Ubed.

But his head was struck off and in mockery some orcs? had set ... a clay ball with ... The red eye was ... [?painted over].[5]

For *Sern Aranath* as the name of the Pillars of the Kings see VII.366 note 21; and cf. TT p. 311 (at the end of 'Journey to the Cross-roads'): 'The brief glow fell upon a huge sitting figure, still and solemn as the great stone kings of Argonath.' It is not clear to me whether *Sairn Ubed* is an alternative to *Sern Aranath*. On this same page, later but not much later, my father made further notes on names (see p. 137), and among these appears the following:

The two King Stones Sern Ubed (denial)
Sern Aranath

The word *denial* makes one think of the description of the Pillars of the Kings in 'The Great River' (FR p. 409), where in the earliest draft of that passage (VII.360) 'the left hand of each was raised beside his head palm outwards in gesture of warning and *refusal*.'[6]

It is plain from this text that at this time the emergence of Faramir and the Window on the West was totally unforeseen, while on the other hand the broken statue at the Cross-roads was already present.

The next step in the development of the 'recalcitrant passage' is seen, I think, in what follows the description of the southward road in the manuscript:

After the labours and perils they had just endured the days that they spent upon the road seemed almost pleasant, though fear was about them and darkness lay before them. The weather now was good, though the wind blowing from the north-west over the Misty Mountains far away had a sharp tooth. They passed on into the northern marches of that land that men once called Ithilien, a fair country of climbing woods and swift falling streams. In Gollum's reckoning it was some thirty leagues from the Morannon to the crossing of the ways above Elostirion, and he hoped to cover that distance in three journeys. But maybe the distance was greater or they went slower than he hoped, for at the end of the third night they had not come there.

This passage was rejected at once, but before this was done 'thirty leagues' was changed to 'twenty', and it was perhaps at this time that a sentence was added earlier, following 'But they were not going quick enough for Gollum' (TT p. 256): 'In his reckoning it was twenty leagues from the Morannon to the crossing of the ways above Osgiliath,[7] and he hoped to cover that distance in three journeys' (where TT has 'nearly thirty leagues' and 'four journeys').

My father now, if my analysis of the sequence is correct, decided that he was treating the journey from the Morannon to the Cross-roads too cursorily; and his next step, on the same page of the manuscript, was to return to the first night (which was that of 5 February):

All that night they plodded on, and all the next. The road drew ever nearer to the course of the Great River and further from the shadow of Hebel Dúath on their left. That second night the moon was full. Not long before the dawn they saw it sinking round and yellow far beyond the great vale below them. Here and there a white gleam showed where Anduin rolled, a mighty stream swollen with the waters of Emyn Muil and of slow-winding Entwash. Far far away, pale ghosts above the mists, the peaks of the Black Mountains were caught by the beaming moon. There glimmered through the night the snows on Mount Mindolluin; but though Frodo's eyes stared out into the west wondering where in the vastness of the land his old companions might now be, he did not know that under

This passage was in its turn struck out. The last words stand at the foot of a page.[8]

It was now, as it seems, that my father decided to introduce the episode of the rabbits caught by Gollum (developing it from the passage where it first appears, given in note 6).

All that night they plodded on. At the first sign of day they halted, and lay beneath a bank in a brake of old brown bracken overshadowed by dark pinetrees. Water flowed down not far away, cold out of the hills, and good to drink.

Sam had been giving some earnest thought to food as they marched. Now that the despair of the impassable Gate was behind him, he did not feel so inclined as his master to take no thought for their livelihood beyond the end of their errand; and anyway it seemed wiser to him to save the elvish bread for worse times ahead. Two days or more had gone since he reckoned that they had a bare supply for three weeks.[9] 'If we reach the Fire in that time we'll be lucky at this rate,' he thought. 'And we may be wanting to come back. We may.' Besides at the end of [?their] long night march he felt more hungry than usual.

With all this in his mind he turned to look for Gollum. Gollum was crawling away through the bracken. 'Hi!' said Sam. 'Where are you going? Hunting? Now look here, my friend, you don't like our food, but if you could find something fit for a hobbit to eat I'd be grateful.'

Yes, yess.

Gollum brings back 2 rabbits. Angry at fire (a) fear (b) rage at nice juicy rabbits being spoiled. Pacified by Frodo (promise of fish?).

Night of full moon and vision of Anduin.

Third night. They do not reach the cross ways. [?Trying] to hasten they journey by day through wood. They come to cross ways and peer at it out of thicket.

The headless king with a mocking head made by orcs and scrawls on it.

That night they turn left. Vision of Minas Morghul in the moon high up in re-entrant.[10]

Here this text ends, and was followed by another draft, beginning precisely as does that just given, in which the story of Sam's cooking was developed almost to the final form. On one of the pages of this text my father pencilled a note: 'Describe baytrees and spicy herbs as they march.' It was thus the cooking of the rabbits that led to the account of the shrubs and herbs of Ithilien (TT p. 258) – 'which is proving a lovely land', as he said in his letter of 30 April 1944 (*Letters* no. 64).

He now returned again to the fair copy manuscript, and without changing, then or later, the opening of the chapter he wrote the story almost as it stands in TT, pp. 258 ff. (from 'So they passed into the northern marches of that land that Men once called Ithilien'). At this stage, therefore, the chronology of the journey was thus:

Feb. 5 Left the Morannon at dusk, and came into a less barren country of heathland. Took to the southward road about midnight (p. 132).

Feb. 6 Halted at dawn. Description of Ithilien and its herbs and flowers. Sam's cooking, and the coming of the men of Gondor.

With the introduction of a long rider to the following typescript text an extra day and night were inserted into the journey between the Morannon and the place of Sam's cooking (see the Note on Chronology at the end of this chapter). At dawn of this added day they found themselves in a less barren country of heathland, and they passed the day hidden in deep heather (TT p. 257); at dusk they set out again, and only now took to the southward road.

At the end of the episode of 'Stewed Rabbit' there is a brief sketch in the manuscript of the story to come, written in pencil so rapid that I cannot make all of it out; but it can be seen that Sam finds that Gollum is not there; he puts out the fire and runs down to wash the pans; he hears voices, and suddenly sees a couple of men chasing Gollum. Gollum eludes their grasp and vanishes into a tangled thicket. They go on up the hill, and Sam hears them laugh. 'Not an orc,' says one. Sam creeps back to Frodo, who has also heard voices and hidden himself, and they see many men creeping up towards the road.

Another page found separately seems quite likely to be the continuation of this outline, and is equally hard to read. There is to be a description of men like Boromir, dressed in lighter and darker green, armed with knives; the hobbits wonder who they are – they are certainly not scouts of Sauron. The fight on the road between the men of Harad and the men of Minas Tirith is mentioned; then follows:

A slain Tirith-man falls over bank and crashes down on them. Frodo goes to him and he cries *orch* and tries to ... but falls dead crying 'Gondor!' The Harad-men drive the Gondorians [?down] hill. The hobbits creep away through thickets. At last they climb tree. See Gondorians fight and win finally. At dusk Gollum climbs up to them. He curses Sam for [?bringing enemies]. They dare not go back to road, but wander on through the wild glades of Ithilien that night. See Full Moon. Meet no more folk.

Strike the road to Osgiliath far down, and have to go back long [?detour] East. Deep Ilex woods. Gollum goes [?on] by day. Evening of third day they reach Cross ways. See broken statue.[11]

The story of the ambush[12] of the Southron men thus seems at this stage to have had no sequel. But from the point where this outline begins (when Sam calls to Gollum that there is some rabbit left if he wants to change his mind, but finds that he has disappeared, TT

p. 264) the final form of the story, partly extant in rough drafting, was achieved without hesitation – with, however, one major difference: the leader of the Gondorians was *not* Faramir, brother of Boromir. At this time he was Falborn son of Anborn (and remained so in the manuscript). Mablung and Damrod, the two men who were left to guard Frodo and Sam,[13] told them that Falborn was a kinsman of Boromir, and that 'he and they were Rangers of Ithilien, for they were descended from folk who lived in Ithilien at one time, before it was overrun' (cf. TT p. 267).

For the rest, Falborn's conversation with Frodo and Sam proceeds almost exactly as does that with Faramir in TT.[14] Mablung and Damrod used 'sometimes the Common Speech, but after the manner of older days, sometimes some other language of their own', but the description of this other tongue (TT p. 267) was added to the typescript that followed the manuscript at some later time. Their account of the Southrons scarcely differs from the final form, but where Mablung in TT (p. 268) speaks of 'These cursed Southrons', in the manuscript he says 'These cursed Barangils, for so we name them' (subsequently changed to the later reading). The name *Barangils* is written on the First Map beside *Swertings* (see Map III, VII.309).

The account of the Oliphaunt was never changed, save only in the name by which the great beasts were known in Gondor (*Mûmak* in TT). In the original draft Mablung[15] cried *Andabund!*, and this was the form first written in the manuscript also. This was changed to *Andrabonn*,[16] then to *Múmund*. These were immediate changes, for a few lines later appears 'the *Múmund* of Harad was indeed a beast of vast bulk', where drafting for the passage has *Múmar*. Soon after, the form *Mâmuk* was introduced in both passages: this was the form my father used in his letter to me of 6 May 1944 (*Letters* no. 66).

Lastly, in the manuscript Damrod cries 'May the gods turn him aside', where in TT he names the Valar; *gods* was preceded by a rejected word that I cannot interpret.

On 30 April 1944 (*Letters* no. 64) my father described to me the course of the story that I had not read:

> ['The Ring'] is growing and sprouting again ... and opening out in unexpected ways. So far in the new chapters Frodo and Sam have traversed Sarn Gebir,[17] climbed down the cliff, encountered and temporarily tamed Gollum. They have with his guidance crossed the Dead Marshes and the slag-heaps of Mordor, lain in hiding outside the main gates and found them impassable, and set out for a more secret entrance near Minas Morghul (formerly M. Ithil). It will turn out to be the deadly Kirith Ungol and Gollum will play false. But at the moment they are in Ithilien (which is proving a lovely land); there has been a lot of bother about stewed rabbit; and they have been captured by Gondorians, and witnessed them ambushing a

> Swerting army (dark men of the South) marching to Mordor's aid. A large elephant of prehistoric size, a war-elephant of the Swertings, is loose, and Sam has gratified a life-long wish to see an Oliphaunt ... In the chapter next to be done they will get to Kirith Ungol and Frodo will be caught. ... On the whole Sam is behaving well, and living up to repute. He treats Gollum rather like Ariel to Caliban.

Since it was not until a week later that he referred to the sudden and totally unexpected appearance of Faramir on the scene, it seems to me that when he wrote this letter he had not progressed much if at all beyond the end of the Oliphaunt episode; for in the manuscript of the chapter that became 'Of Herbs and Stewed Rabbit' the leader of the Gondorians is Falborn, not Faramir, and there is as yet no indication that he will play any further part (cf. the outline on p. 135).[18]

This chapter (including what became 'The Black Gate is Closed') was read to C. S. Lewis on the first of May 1944 (*Letters* no. 65).

This is a convenient place to set down the notes on names added later to the page transcribed on p. 132:

> Change *Black Mountains* to the *White Mountains*. *Hebel* [*Orolos*>] *Uilos Nimr*[*?ais*]
> Alter the *Morannon* to *Kirith Naglath* Cleft of the Teeth
> *Gorgor*
> The two King Stones *Sern Ubed* (denial)
> *Sern Aranath*
> *Rohar?*

To these pencilled notes my father added in ink:

> Not *Hebel* but *Ephel*. *Et-pele* > *Eppele*. *Ephel-duath*. *Ephel* [*Nimras* >] *Nimrais*. *Ered Nimrath*.

With *Kirith Naglath* cf. *Naglath Morn*, p. 122; and on the reference to *Sern Ubed* and *Sern Aranath* see p. 132. On the change of the Black Mountains to the White see VII.433.

NOTES

1 In the manuscript as in the draft, 'The moon was not due until late that night'; in TT 'the moon was now three nights from the full, but it did not climb over the mountains till nearly midnight.'

2 That the illegible word is *re-entrant* seems assured by the recurrence of this word in perfectly clear form and in the same context in the text given on p. 134. In the present text at this point there is drawn a wavy line; this clearly indicates the line of the mountains pierced by a very wide valley running up into a point.

3 The illegible word is certainly not *pointing*. It begins with an *f* or a *g* and probably ends in *ing*, but does not suggest either *facing* or *gazing*.

4 The word *Ubed*, occurring twice here and again in the further notes on names on this page (where it is translated 'denial'), is written at all occurrences in precisely the same way, and I do not feel at all certain of the third letter.

5 Before the words 'The red eye' were written my father drew an Old English S-rune (cf. VII.382), but struck it out.

6 The remainder of this page carries disjointed passages: as elsewhere my father probably had it beside him and used it for jotting down narrative 'moments' as they came into his mind. The first reads:

> that great mountain's side was built Minas Tirith, the Tower of Guard, where Gandalf walked now deep in thought.

On this see note 8. Then follows:

> For a third night they went on. They had good water in plenty, and Gollum was better fed. Already he was less famished to look at. At early morning when they lay hidden for rest, and at evening when they set out again, he would slip away and return licking his lips. Sometimes in the long night he would take out something ..... and would crunch it as he walked.
>
> ..... and lay under a deep bank in tall bracken under the shadow of pine trees. Water flowed not far away, cold, good to drink. Gollum slipped away, and returned shortly, licking his lips; but he brought with him also a present for the hobbits. Two rabbits he had caught.

With Sam's having no objection to rabbit but a distaste for what Gollum brought, and a reference to his prudent wish, in contrast to Frodo's indifference, to save the elvish waybread for worse times ahead, these exceedingly difficult 'extracts' come to an end. It was clearly here that the episode of the stewed rabbit entered; but it seems scarcely possible to define how my father related it to the whole sequence of the journey from the Black Gate.

7 On the continued hesitation between *Elostirion* and *Osgiliath* at this time see p. 122 and note 7.

8 The last sentence is in fact, and rather oddly, completed by the first passage given in note 6, thus:

> There glimmered through the night the snows on Mount Mindolluin; but though Frodo's eyes stared out into the west wondering where in the vastness of the land his old companions might now be, he did not know that under / that great mountain's side was built Minas Tirith, the Tower of Guard, where Gandalf walked now deep in thought.

See the Note on Chronology below.

9 This sentence replaced a form of it in which Sam's reckoning had

been that they had 'a bare ten days' supply of waybread: that left eight.' In the manuscript of 'The Passage of the Marshes', corresponding to that in TT p. 231, Sam said 'I reckon we've got enough to last, say, 10 days now'. This was changed to 'three weeks or so', no doubt at the same time as the sentence in the present text was rewritten.

In TT (p. 260) it is said at this point that 'Six days or more had passed' since Sam made his reckoning of the remaining *lembas*, whereas here it is 'Two days or more'. Three days had in fact passed, the 3rd, 4th and 5th of February (p. 118). In TT the length of the journey had been increased, both by the two extra days during which they crossed the Noman-lands (pp. 112, 120), and by an extra day added to the journey from the Morannon to the place of the stewed rabbit episode (p. 135).

10 *re-entrant*: see note 2.

11 The brief remainder of this outline is illegible because my father wrote across it notes in ink on another subject (see p. 145).

12 It is not clear that it was first conceived as an ambush, which perhaps only arose when the story came to be written – and it was then that my father added to the manuscript at an earlier point 'They had come to the end of a long cutting, deep, and sheer-sided in the middle, by which the road clove its way through a stony ridge' (TT p. 258).

13 In a pencilled draft so faint and rapid as to be largely illegible another name is found instead of Mablung, and several names preceded Damrod, but I cannot certainly interpret any of them.

14 Rivendell is still *Imladrist* and the Halflings are still the *Halfhigh* (see VII.146). Boromir is called 'Highwarden of the White Tower, and our captain general', as in TT (p. 266).

15 Damrod in TT; the speeches of Damrod and Mablung were shifted about between the two.

16 Cf. the *Etymologies*, V.372, stem MBUD 'project': * *andambundā* 'long-snouted', Quenya *andamunda* 'elephant', Noldorin *andabon*, *annabon*.

17 *Sarn Gebir*: an interesting instance of the former name reappearing mistakenly – unless my father used *Sarn Gebir* deliberately, remembering that I had not read any of Book IV, in which the name *Emyn Muil* was first used. Cf. however p. 165 note 7.

18 It is clear that in the manuscript the chapter halted at Sam's words (TT p. 270) 'Well, if that's over, I'll have a bit of sleep.' The following brief dialogue between Sam and Mablung (with the hint that the hobbits will not be allowed to continue their journey unhindered: 'I do not think the Captain will leave you here, Master Samwise') was written in the manuscript as the beginning of the next chapter ('Faramir'), and only subsequently joined to

the preceding one and made its conclusion; and by then Falborn had become Faramir.

Note on the Chronology

The brief time-scheme B has the following chronology (see pp. 118, 135):

(Day 3) Feb. 4 Frodo, Sam and Gollum come to the Barren Lands and Slag-mounds. Stay there during day and sleep. At night they go on 12 miles and come before the Morannon on Feb. 5.

(Day 4) Feb. 5 Frodo, Sam and Gollum remain hidden all day. Pass southward to Ithilien at dusk.

(Day 5) Feb. 6 Full Moon. Stewed rabbit. Frodo and Sam taken by Faramir. Spend night at Henneth Annûn.

There are two other schemes ('C' and 'D'), the one obviously written shortly after the other, both of which begin at February 4. As originally written, both maintain the chronology of B, but both give some information about other events as well, and in this they differ. Scheme C reads thus:

(Day 3) Feb. 4 Gandalf and Pippin pass Fords and reach mouth of Coomb about 2.30 a.m. [*Added:* and rides on till daybreak and then rests in hiding. Rides again at night.]

Théoden sets out from Dolbaran and reaches Helm's Deep soon after dawn.

Frodo comes to the Barren Lands and Slag-mounds and stays there during day.

(Day 4) Feb. 5 Théoden leaves Helm's Deep on return journey. Aragorn rides on ahead with Gimli and Legolas.

Gandalf abandons secrecy and after short rest rides all day to Minas Tirith. He and Pippin reach Minas Tirith at sunset.

At dawn on Feb. 5 Frodo comes before the Morannon. Frodo, Sam and Gollum lie hid all day and go south towards Ithilien at nightfall.

(Day 5) Feb. 6 Frodo and Sam in Ithilien. They are taken by Faramir. Battle with the Southrons. Frodo spends night at Henneth Annûn.

Scheme D, certainly following C, runs as follows (as originally written):

(Day 3) Feb. 4 Gandalf and Pippin begin their ride to Minas Tirith (pass Fords and reach mouth of Deeping Coomb about 2 a.m.). At dawn come to Edoras (7.30). Gandalf fearing

Nazgûl rests all day. Orders assembly to go to Dunharrow. Nazgûl passes over Rohan again.

(Day 4) Feb. 5 Gandalf rides all night of 4–5 and passes into Anórien. Pippin sees the beacons blaze up on the mountains. They see messengers riding West.

Aragorn (with Legolas and Gimli) rides fast by night (4–5) to Dunharrow via Edoras, reaches Edoras at morning and passes up Harrowdale. Théoden with Éomer and many men goes by mountain-roads through south [*sic*] skirts of mountains to Dunharrow, riding slowly.

Frodo at dawn comes before the Morannon. At nightfall Frodo with Sam and Gollum turns south to Ithilien.

(Day 5) Feb. 6 Full Moon (rises about 9.20 p.m. and sets about 6.30 a.m. on Feb. 7). Gandalf rides all night of 5–6 and sights Minas Tirith at dawn on 6th.

Théoden comes out of west into Harrowdale some miles above Dunharrow, and comes to Dunharrow before nightfall. Finds the muster already beginning.

Frodo and Sam in Ithilien; taken by Faramir; battle with Southrons; night at Henneth Annûn.

On the statement in scheme D that Théoden came down into Harrowdale *some miles above Dunharrow* see p. 259. The full moon of February 6 is the full moon of February 1, 1942, as explained in VII.369.

It will be seen that in their dating these time-schemes proceed from the schemes A and B (see p. 118), in which the day passed by Frodo among the slag-mounds was February 4, and in which he came before the Morannon at dawn on February 5. While these schemes obviously belong to 1944, and were made when Book IV was largely or entirely written (pp. 182, 226), it seems clear that they *preceded* the chronological problems that my father referred to in his letters of 12 and 16 October 1944 (see p. 100): for in the second of these he mentioned that he had made a small alteration in Frodo's journey, 'two days from Morannon to Ithilien', and this change is not present in these schemes, C and D.

Scheme D was revised at that time to provide the extra day in the journey from the Morannon to Ithilien, and this was done by revising the dates backwards: thus Frodo now comes before the Morannon on February 4, and on February 5 'lies in heather on the borders of Ithilien' (see p. 135 and TT p. 257); thus the episode of the stewed rabbit still takes place on February 6. Since this scheme only begins on February 4 it is not shown how the earlier arrival before the Morannon was achieved.

It is clear therefore that scheme S was devised following the chronological modifications of 12–16 October 1944; for in S the extra day in the journey from the Morannon was present from its making, and the date of the extra day was February 5 (as in Scheme D revised), because in this scheme the date of the Breaking of the Fellowship was put back from January 26 to January 25 (see pp. 101, 119). The chronology in S I take therefore to represent the structure when my father wrote on 16 October 'I think I have solved it all at last':

(Day 3) Feb. 3 Frodo etc. reach slag-mounds at dawn, and stay in a hole all day, going on at nightfall. Nazgûl passes high up on way to Isengard about 5 p.m. Another one hour after midnight.

Gandalf and company leave Isengard and camp at Dolbaran. Episode of the Orthanc-stone. Nazgûl passes over about 11 p.m.

(Day 4) Feb. 4 Frodo etc. reach dell in sight of Morannon at daybreak, and lie hid there all day. See the Harad-men march in. At dusk they start southward journey.

Gandalf and Pippin ride east. Sight Edoras at dawn. Nazgûl passes over Edoras about 8 a.m.

(Day 5) Feb. 5 Frodo etc. reach borderlands and lie in heather sleeping all day. At night go on into Ithilien.

Gandalf passes into Anórien.

(Day 6) Feb. 6 Frodo etc. camp in Ithilien. Episode of Stewed Rabbit. Frodo captured by Faramir and taken to Henneth Annûn.

[Gandalf and Pippin reach Minas Tirith.]

The original entries concerning Gandalf on February 5 and 6 in this scheme cannot be read after the words 'Gandalf passes into Anórien', because they were afterwards overwritten, but it is clear that as in scheme D he reached Minas Tirith at dawn on February 6.

In this chapter relation to the movements of other members of the original Company arises in the rejected passage given on p. 133, interrupted in the manuscript but concluded as shown in note 8. In this passage, written before the episode of the stewed rabbit and the coming of the men of Gondor had entered the story, Frodo was walking southward through Ithilien, and in the late night of February 6–7 (the second of this journey) he saw the full moon sinking in the West. In its light he glimpsed from far off the snows on Mount Mindolluin; and at that same time Gandalf was walking 'deep in thought' below that mountain in Minas Tirith. When the story was entirely changed by the entry of Faramir it was from Henneth Annûn, before dawn on the 7th, that Frodo saw the setting of the full moon of that night, and in the original draft of 'The Forbidden Pool' appears his sad speculation on the fate of his former companions 'in the vastness of the nightlands' (TT p. 293). When that was written the story was still that Gandalf and Pippin had already reached Minas Tirith.

In the final chronology the relations were altered. Pippin riding with Gandalf on Shadowfax caught as he fell asleep on the night of March 7–8 'a glimpse of high white peaks, glimmering like floating isles above the clouds as they caught the light of the westering moon. He wondered where Frodo was, and if he was already in Mordor, or if he was dead; and he did not know that Frodo from far away looked on that same moon as it set beyond Gondor ere the coming of the day' (*The Return of the King* p. 20). That was still the night that Frodo passed in Henneth Annûn; but now Gandalf did not ride up to the wall of the Pelennor until dawn of the ninth of March.

V
FARAMIR

On the 26th of April 1944 my father said (*Letters* no. 63) that he needed to know how to stew a rabbit; on the 30th (no. 64) he wrote that 'A large elephant of prehistoric size, a war-elephant of the Swertings, is loose' (but made no mention of anything further); on the 4th of May (no. 65), having read a chapter to C. S. Lewis on the 1st, he was 'busy now with the next'; and on the 11th (no. 67) he said that he had read his 'fourth new chapter ("Faramir")' to Lewis and Williams three days before.[1] It seems, then, that what was afterwards called 'The Window on the West' was achieved in not much more than a week. That must have been a time of intense and concentrated work, for the volume of writing that went into this chapter, the redrafting and reshaping, is remarkable. It is also very complex, and it has taken me a lot longer than a week to determine how the chapter evolved and to try to describe it here. In what follows I trace the development fairly closely, since in 'Faramir' there are bearings on other parts of *The Lord of the Rings* and much of special interest in Faramir's discourse on ancient history, most notably in his remarks on the languages of Gondor and the Common Speech (entirely lost in *The Two Towers*).

The various draft-sequences that constitute the history of the chapter are so confusing that I shall try to make my account clearer by using letters to distinguish them when it seems helpful. There was only one manuscript made, titled 'XXXVI. Faramir':[2] this is a good clear text, not extensively emended later, and in it the final form was achieved, with however certain important exceptions. It must have been from this text (referred to in this chapter as 'the completed manuscript', or simply 'the manuscript') that my father read 'Faramir' to Lewis and Williams on 8 May 1944. At this time the chapter began at '"Sleep while you may," said Mablung': see p. 139 note 18.

The original draft for the end of what became 'Of Herbs and Stewed Rabbit', which I will call '**A**', continued on from Sam's 'If that's over I'll have a bit o' sleep' (TT p. 270) thus:

He turned and spoke in Frodo's ear. 'I could almost sleep on my legs, Mr Frodo,' he said. 'And you've not had much yourself. But these men are friends, it seems: they seem to come from Boromir's country all right. Though they don't quite trust us, I can't see any cause to doubt them. And we're done anyway if they turn nasty, so we'd best rest.'

'Sleep if thou wilt,' said Mablung. 'We will guard thee and thy master until Falborn comes. Falborn will return hither, if he has saved his life. But when he cometh we must move swiftly. All this tumult will not go unmarked, and ere night is old we shall have many pursuers. We shall need all speed to gain the river first.'

It seemed to Sam only a few minutes before he woke and found that Falborn had returned and several men with him. They were talking nearby. Frodo was awake and among them. They were debating what to do about the hobbits.

Sam sat up and listened and he understood that Frodo had failed to satisfy the leader of the men of Gondor on some points: which part he had to play in the company sent from Rivendell, why they had left Boromir, and where he was now going. To the meaning of Isildur's Bane he kept on returning, but Frodo would not tell the story of the Ring.

'But the words said *with Isildur's Bane in hand*,' said Falborn.[3] 'If you are the Half-high then you should have that thing in hand, whatever it be. Have you it not? Or is it hidden because you choose to hide it?'

'Were Boromir here he would answer your questions,' said Frodo. 'And since Boromir was many days ago at Rauros on the way to your city, if you return swiftly you will learn the answer. My part in this company was known to him and to all and to the Lord Elrond indeed. The errand given to me brings me into this land, and it is not [?wise] that any enemy of the Dark Lord should hinder it.'

'I see there is more in this than I first perceived,' said Falborn. 'But I too am under command: to slay or take prisoner as [?reason justifies] all found in Ithilien. There is no cause to slay thee.'

Here this barely legible draft ends. At the end of it is written in pencil: *Death of Boromir known*. This is probably to be associated with the following notes written across the outline given on p. 135 (see note 11 to the last chapter):

> Is Boromir known to be dead?
>
> Only by a vision of the boat with a light about it floating down the river and a voice. And by some things of his drifting?
>
> This is Feb. 6. Gandalf only arrives at sunset on Feb. 5 and the Rangers must have left Tirith long before that. Hardly time for messenger from Edoras to Minas Tirith (250 miles).

..... Jan. 31 morning to [Feb. 4 >] night Feb. 3. 3½ days.
Rangers must have left on night of Feb. 3rd.
NO.

On the date 6 February see pp. 140–2. 31 January was the day on which Gandalf came with Aragorn, Legolas and Gimli to Edoras and left with Théoden, riding west across the plains (see pp. 3–5). My father was evidently calculating that a man riding 70 miles a day could have brought the news of Boromir's death by word of mouth to Minas Tirith before Falborn and his men left the city to cross the river into Ithilien, but decided that this was not what had happened.

A new draft text ('**B**'), at the outset clearly written, was now begun, opening with Mablung's words 'Sleep, if thou wilt,'[4] and continuing as in the original draft A (p. 145): there is thus still no suggestion at this point that the hobbits will not be allowed to go on their way (see note 18 to the last chapter), and the leader of the men of Gondor is still Falborn. A was followed closely in this new text (which was a good deal emended subsequently) almost to its end,[5] but at the point where Frodo says 'But those who claim to oppose the Dark Lord would do well not to hinder it' the dialogue moves to the same point in TT (p. 272): 'Frodo spoke proudly, whatever he felt, and Sam very much approved of it; but it did not appease Falborn', and continues almost as in the final form, through the wary conversation about Boromir, as far as Frodo's 'though surely there are many perils in the world.' At Falborn's reply 'Many indeed, and treachery not the least' Sam does not in this text intervene, and Falborn continues: 'But thou askest how do we know that our captain is dead. We do not know it for a certainty, but yet we do not doubt it.' And he asks Frodo whether he remembers anything of special mark that Boromir bore with him among his gear, and Frodo fears a trap and reflects on his danger just as in TT (pp. 273–4). Then follows:

'I remember that he bore a horn,' he said at last.

'Thou rememberest well, as one who hath verily seen him,' said Falborn. 'Then maybe thou canst see it in thy mind's eye: a great horn of the wild ox of the [Eastern wilderness >] East, bound with silver, and written with his name, [*struck out:* worn upon a silver chain]. That horn the waters of Anduin brought unto us maybe [> more than] seven nights now gone. An ill token we thought it, and boding little joy to Denethor father of Boromir; for the horn was cloven in twain as by sword or axe. The halves of it came severally to shore ...'

Falborn's account of how the pieces of the horn were found now follows as in TT (p. 276),[6] ending 'But murder will out, 'tis said'; then he continues:

'Dost thou not know of the cleaving of the horn, or who cast it over Rauros – to drown it for ever in the eddies of the fall, doubtless?'

'No,' said Frodo, 'I do not know. But none of our Company has the will for such a deed, and none the strength unless it were Aragorn. But though it may be a token of ill, a cloven horn does not prove the wearer's death.'

At this stage, therefore, Boromir's death was a supposition in Minas Tirith depending solely on the finding of the pieces of his horn in the river. But now there follows (and at this point my father's handwriting speeded up markedly and becomes very difficult, often a sign that a new conception had entered that would entail the rewriting and rejection of what had preceded, so that what follows slips back, as it were, into a more 'primitive' stage of composition):

'No. But the finding of the horn followed another and stranger thing,' said Falborn. 'And that sad chance befell me, and others beside [*changed to:* 'No,' said Falborn. 'But the finding of the horn followed another and stranger thing that befell me, and others beside]. I sat at night beside the waters of Anduin, just ere the first quarter of the moon, in the grey dark watching the ever moving stream and the sad reeds rustling. ...'

The account of the boat bearing the body of Boromir is for most of its length very close indeed to that in TT (p. 274), and it is here, most curiously, that Falborn becomes Boromir's brother, though he does not change his name: 'It was Boromir my brother, dead.' It is as if he slipped without conscious decision into the rôle that had been preparing for him. What else could he be, this captain of Gondor so concerned with Frodo's story and the fate of Boromir? Foreshortening the actual development, my father wrote in his letter of 6 May 1944 (*Letters* no. 66):

> A new character has come on the scene (I am sure I did not invent him, I did not even want him, though I like him, but there he came walking into the woods of Ithilien): Faramir, the brother of Boromir ...

Falborn's story is different in its ending from the final form:

'... The boat turned into the stream and passed into the night. Others saw it, some near at hand, others from far off. But none dare touch it, nor maybe would even the evil hands of those that hold Osgiliath dare to hinder it.

'[?This] I thought was a vision though one of evil boding, and even when I heard the tale of others we doubted, Denethor my father and I, if it were more, though it boded evil. But none can doubt the horn. It lies now cloven in twain upon the lap of Denethor. And messengers ride far and wide to learn news of Boromir.'

'Alas,' said Frodo. 'For now I do not on my side doubt your tale. The golden belt was given him in Lórien by the Lady Galadriel. It was she who clothed us as you see us. This brooch is of the same workmanship' – he touched the [?enamelled] leaf that caught his cloak about his neck. Falborn looked at it curiously. 'Yes,' he said, 'it is work of the same [?manner].'

'Yet even so,' said Frodo, 'I think it can have been but a vision that you saw. How could a boat have ridden the falls of Rauros and the [?boiling] floods, and naught have been spilled but the horn, and founder not with its burden of water?'

'I know not,' said Falborn, 'but whence came the boat?'

'From Lórien, it was an elven-boat,' said Frodo.

'Well,' said Falborn, 'if thou wilt have dealings with the mistress of magic that . . . .eth [*added:* dwells] in the Golden Wood then they [*sic*] must look for strange things and evil things to follow.'

This was too much for Sam's patience. He stood up and walked into the debate. 'Not evil from Lórien,' he said. 'Begging your pardon, Mr Frodo,' he said, 'but I have been listening to a deal of this talk. Let's come to the point before all the Orcs of Mordor come down on us. Now look here, Falborn of Gondor if that is your name' – the men looked in amazement (not in merriment) at the small . . . hobbit planted firmly on his feet before the seated figure of the captain. 'What are you getting at? If you think we murdered your brother and then ran away, say so. And say what you mean to do about it.'

'I was in mind to say so,' answered Falborn. 'Were I as hasty as thou I would have slain thee long ago. But we have taken but a few minutes in speech to learn what sort ye be. I am about to depart at once. Ye will come with me. And in that count yourselves fortunate!'

Here this second draft B ends,[7] and my father now proceeded to a third version ('C'), beginning at the same point as did draft B (p. 146) with Mablung's words 'Sleep, if you will', and extending no further into the chapter, but C is written on odd bits of paper, much of it very roughly, is not continuous, and contains some sections of the narrative in divergent forms. It seems clear therefore that these pages accompanied the commencement of the completed manuscript.

This third drafting C, in which *Falborn* has become *Faramir*,[8] largely retains the structure of B, while at the same time moving in detail of expression a good way towards the form of the opening dialogue between Faramir and Frodo in TT (pp. 271–6). There were various intricate shiftings and displacements and new conjunctions within the matter of this dialogue before my father was satisfied with its structure, and these I largely pass over. The essential differences from the final form are that Sam's indignation does not explode at Faramir's words 'and treachery not the least', but as in the second draft B at his disparaging remark about Lórien; and that Faramir's tale of how he heard far off, 'as if it were but an echo in the mind', the blowing of Boromir's horn had not entered.

There are a number of particular points to notice. At the beginning of his interrogation of Frodo ('which now looked unpleasantly like the trial of a prisoner') Faramir no longer cites the words of the verse as *with Isildur's Bane in hand* (see p. 145 and note 3), but as *Isildur's Bane upholding*,[9] and continues – in the completed manuscript as well as the draft – 'If you be the Halfling that was named, then doubtless you held it before the eyes of all the Council of which you speak, and Boromir saw it.' In TT (p. 271), when the concluding words of the verse were *For Isildur's Bane shall waken, / And the Halfling forth shall stand,* Faramir says: 'But it was at the coming of the Halfling that Isildur's Bane should waken ... If then you are the Halfling that was named, doubtless you brought this thing, whatever it may be, to the Council of which you speak, and there Boromir saw it.'

When Frodo says that if any could claim Isildur's Bane it would be Aragorn, Faramir replies, both in the draft and in the manuscript: 'Why so, and not Boromir, prince of the city that Elendil and his sons founded?', where in TT (p. 271) he speaks of 'the sons of Elendil' as the founders. The story that Elendil remained in the North and there founded his realm, while his sons Isildur and Anárion founded the cities of the South, appears in the fifth version of the 'Council of Elrond' (VII.144); and this may suggest that that version of 'The Council of Elrond' was written later than I have supposed.

As already mentioned, the sound of Boromir's horn blowing far off was not yet present in this third drafting C; and Faramir still relates the finding of the pieces of the horn before he tells of the funeral boat passing down Anduin. In answer to Frodo's objection that 'a cloven horn does not prove the wearer's death' (p. 147) there now follows: '"No," said Faramir. "But the finding of the shards of the horn followed another and stranger thing that befell me, as if it were sent to confirm it beyond hope."' Thus the words '(that befell me) and others beside' in B are omitted; but in this tale of the boat that bore Boromir's corpse Faramir still declares that he was not the only one to see it:

'Others too saw it, a grey shadow of a vessel from afar.' In yet another revision of this passage before the final form was reached he ends: 'A vision out of the borders of dream I thought it. But I do not doubt that Boromir is dead, whether his body of a truth has passed down the River to the Sea, or lies now somewhere under the heedless skies.'

The remote sound of Boromir's horn blowing only entered in the manuscript, and Faramir there says that he heard it 'eight days ere I set out on this venture, eleven days ago at about this hour of the day', where TT (p. 274) has the same, but with 'five' for 'eight'.[10] As my father wrote this passage in the manuscript he went on, after 'as it might be only an echo in the mind': 'And others heard it, for we have many men that wander far upon our borders, south and west and north, even to the fields of Rohan.' This was apparently struck out immediately.

To Sam's indignant and courageous confrontation of this great man from Minas Tirith Faramir's response in this draft was gentle:

'. . . Say what you think, and say what you mean to do.'

'I was about to do so,' said Faramir smiling, and now less stern. 'Were I as hasty as you I might have slain you long ago. I have spared the short part of [?an hour] in spite of peril to judge you more justly. [?Now] if you wish to learn what I think: I doubted you, naturally, as I should. But if I am a judge of the words and deeds of men I may perhaps make a guess at hobbits. I doubted but you were friends or allies of the orcs, and though the likes of you could not have slain my brother, you might have helped or fled with some picking.'

Here this third phase of drafting (C) ends.[11] — It is curious that in the completed manuscript Sam's intervention has entirely disappeared: the dialogue between Faramir and Frodo in the passage where it originally took place now reaches the form in TT (p. 275) and Faramir no longer expresses so conventional a view of the Lady of the Golden Wood (cf. p. 148).

It is plain, I think, that at this point, at Frodo's words 'Go back Faramir, valiant captain, and defend your city while you may, and let me go alone where my doom takes me', the writing of the manuscript was halted, and that at that time nothing further had been written: in other words, this chapter, in terms of composition, falls into two parts, all up to this point (apart from the absence of Sam's outburst) having been brought virtually to the final form before the story proceeded.

Very rough and here and there altogether illegible outline sketches show my father's preliminary thoughts for its continuation. One of these, impossibly difficult to read, begins at the point where the draft C ends, with Faramir still speaking to Sam: 'But you have not the manners of orcs, nor their speech, and indeed Frodo your master has an air that I cannot ..., an elvish air maybe.' In this text Faramir shows no hesitation about his course and does not postpone his decision, but concludes sternly: 'You shall be well treated. But make no doubt of it. Until my father Denethor releases you, you are prisoners of Gondor. Do not try to escape, if you do not wish to be slain' (cf. the passage given in note 7). Then follows:

In a few minutes they were on their way again down the slopes. Hobbits [?tired]. Mablung carries Sam. They get to the fenced camp in a dense wood of trees, 10 miles away. They had not gone far before Sam suddenly said to Frodo: 'Gollum! Well thank heavens we've lost him!' But Frodo not so sure. 'We have still to get into Mordor,' he said, 'and we do not know the way.' Gollum rescues them

The last three words are very unclear, but I have no doubt that this is what they are – though what story lay behind them will never be known.

Another short text reads as follows:

Faramir says he no longer doubts. If he is any judge of men. But he says that much [more] lies upon it than at first he thought. 'I should' he said 'take you back to Minas Tirith, and if things went ill my life would be forfeit. But I will not decide yet. Yet we must move at once.' He gave some orders and the men broke up into small groups and faded away into the trees. Mablung and Damrod remained. 'Now you will come with me,' he said. 'You cannot go along the road if you meant to. And you cannot go far for you are weary. So are we. We go to a secret camp 10 miles away. Come with us. Before morn we will decide.'

They .... Faramir spoke. 'You do not deal openly. You were not friendly with Boromir. I see S.G. thinks ill of him. Now I loved him, yet I knew him well. Isildur's Bane. I say that this lay between you in some way. Heirlooms do not breed peace among companions. Ancient tales.'

'And ancient tales teach us not to blab,' said Frodo.

'But you must know that much is known in Minas Tirith that is not spoken aloud. Therefore I dismissed my men. Gandalf was here. We the rulers know that I[sildur] carried off the Ruling Ring. Now this is a terrible matter. I can well guess that Boromir, proud, ever anxious for the glory of Minas Tirith (and his own renown) might wish to seize it. I guess that you have the Ring, though how it could ...

The rest of the sentence is illegible. The brief sketch ends with Faramir's words 'I would not touch it if it lay by the highway' and his expression of his love for and desires for Minas Tirith (TT p. 280); the last words are 'I could advise you if you would tell me more.' It is a pity that the passage about the Ring is so brief and elliptical; but the implication must surely be that the rulers of the city knew that Isildur carried off the Ruling Ring because Gandalf had told them. This, of course, was not at all the way in which the story would unfold when it came to be written down.

Another page of even more hasty and staccato sketching takes up from the point reached in the first, and may be its continuation (cf. TT p. 280, where Faramir's words 'it may be that I can advise you ... and even aid you' are followed by 'Frodo made no answer').

Frodo does not say more. Something holds him back. Wisdom? Memory of Boromir? Fear of the power and treachery of what he carried – in spite of liking Faramir. They speak of other things. Reasons of decline of Gondor. Rohan (alter Boromir's words saying he did not go there).[12] Gondor gets like Rohan, loving war as game: so Boromir. Sam says little. Delighted that Gollum seems forgotten. Faramir falls silent. Sam speaks of elvish power, boats, ropes, cloaks. Suddenly aware that Gollum is padding behind. But when they halt he sheers off.

Faramir in accord with law makes them be blindfold as they reach secret stronghold. They talk. Faramir warns him, warns against Gollum. Frodo reveals that he has to go to Mordor. Speaks of Minas Ithil. Moonrise. Faramir bids farewell in morning. Frodo promises to come back to Minas Tirith and surrender to him if he returns.

At this stage, before the chapter proceeded further, Sam's intervention in the initial interrogation of Frodo by Faramir was reintroduced, at an earlier place in the dialogue (at 'and treachery not the least'), and inserted into the manuscript on a rider.[13]

The latter part of the chapter is extant in continuous and for the most part clearly written drafting, with a good deal of my father's characteristic 'over-lapping' – when the narrative takes a wrong direction or is in some respect unsatisfactory, collapses into a scrawl, and is replaced by a new page beginning at an earlier point (thus producing sections of near repetition). This drafting led to the finished manuscript, in which there were still important differences from the text in *Two Two Towers*: it will be seen that at this time there was much development still to come in the past history of Rohan and Gondor.

The new draft ('D') begins (as also does the recommencement of the manuscript, closely based on D) ' "I do not doubt you any more," said Faramir.'[14] The narrative from this point (TT p. 276), as far as Sam's glimpse of Gollum as they walked through the woodland (TT p. 281), already in the draft very largely achieved the final text; but there are some interesting differences.[15]

It is here that the Stewards of Gondor first appear, and the passage concerning them (TT p. 278) was written in the draft text virtually without hesitation or correction, although there is no preliminary material extant. It is notable that from his first appearance in 'The Breaking of the Fellowship' (VII.375–6) Denethor has never been called King: he is the Lord Denethor, Denethor Lord of the Tower of Guard. It seems more than likely, therefore, that this cardinal element in the history and government of Gondor was already of long standing, though never until now emerging into the narrative. The line of Denethor is traced in the draft to *Máraher* the good steward, changed probably at once to *Mardil* (the name in the manuscript); but the last king of the line of Anárion, in whose stead Mardil ruled when he went away to war, was not Eärnur. Both in draft and manuscript he is named *King Elessar*.

Gandalf's recital of his names, as reported by Faramir (who calls him in the draft 'the Grey Wanderer': 'the Grey Pilgrim' in the manuscript), was intricately changed in its initial composition, but apparently developed thus:

> [*Added:* Mithrandir among the Elves. Sharkûn to the Dwarves.] [The name of my youth in the West is forgotten >] [Olórion >] Olórin I was in my youth that is forgotten; [*struck out:* Shorab *or* Shorob in the East,] [Forlong >] Fornold in the South, Gandalf in the North. To the East I go not. [*Struck out:* Not everywhere]

The passage was then written out again in the draft, in the same form as it has in TT, but with the names *Sharkûn* and *Fornold*, this latter being subsequently changed to *Incânus*. In the manuscript *Sharkûn* (for later *Tharkûn*) remains. — Here the name *Olórin* first appears, changed from *Olórion*. On Gandalf's names 'in the South', *Forlong* changed to *Fornold*, I can cast no light; I do not know whether it is relevant that in Appendix F to LR the name of Forlong, Lord of Lossarnach (who died in the Battle of the Pelennor Fields), is said to be among the names in Gondor that 'were of forgotten origin, and descended doubtless from days before the ships of the Númenoreans sailed the Sea.'

Faramir's words about Gandalf's eagerness for stories of Isildur were much changed: 'he was eager for stories of Isildur, though of him we had less to tell, [for Isildur was of the North in Fornost, and the realm of Gondor held from Anárion. > for to Gondor no sure tale had ever come concerning his end, only rumour that he perished in the River being shot by orc-arrows. >] for nought was ever known for certain of his end.' For the first occurrence of the name *Fornost* in the texts, replacing *Fornobel*, see p. 76.

A last point here is that (both in draft and manuscript) Faramir says: 'Isildur took somewhat from the hand of the Unnamed, ere he went away from the battle', where in TT (p. 279) he says 'went away from Gondor'. Cf. 'The Council of Elrond' in FR (p. 265), where Gandalf says: 'For Isildur did not march away straight from the war in Mordor, as some have told the tale', and Boromir interrupts: 'Some in the North, maybe. All know in Gondor that he went first to Minas Anor and dwelt a while with his nephew Meneldil, instructing him, before he committed to him the rule of the South Kingdom.' Cf. also the beginning of 'The Disaster of the Gladden Fields' in *Unfinished Tales*.

At the point where Sam, listening to but not entering the conversation, and observing that Gollum was never mentioned, sees him slipping behind a tree, the draft text (which, since it was soon replaced by another, I will call 'D 1') continues thus:

He opened his mouth to speak, but did not. He could not be sure, and 'why should I mention the old villain anyway, until I'm obliged,' he thought.

After a while Frodo and Faramir began to speak again, for Frodo was eager to learn news of Gondor and its folk and of the lands about them, and what hope they had in their long war.

'It is long since we had any hope,' said Faramir.

These last words appear much later in TT (p. 286). Thus the entire story in TT pp. 281–6 is lacking at this stage: the blindfolding, the coming to Henneth Annûn, the account of the cave, the report of Anborn about the 'black squirrel' in the woods, the evening meal, and Frodo's stories of their journey (although the fact that Frodo and Sam would be blindfolded before they came to the 'secret stronghold' was known to my father: see the outline on p. 152). All this is found in the completed manuscript in virtually the final form.

Faramir's account of the history of Gondor and the coming of the Horsemasters (TT pp. 286–7) was developed in two stages before it was written in the manuscript. Already in the first version (D 1) Faramir speaks very much as in TT of the evils and follies of the Númenóreans in the Great Lands,[16] and of their obsession with death. But after 'Childless lords sat musing in hollow halls, or in high cold towers asked questions of the stars' he continues:

'... But we were more fortunate than other cities, recruiting our strength from the sturdy folk of the sea-coasts, and the hardy people of the White Mountains[17] — where lingered once many remnants of races long forgot. And then there came the men out of the North, the [Horse-marshals >] Rohir. And we ceded them the fields of [Rohan >] Elenarda [*written above:* Kalen(arda)] that are since called Rohan,[18] for we could not resist their rude strength, and they became our allies and have ever proved true, and they learn of our lore and speak our speech. Yet they hold by their old ways and their own speech among themselves. And we love them for they remind us of the youth of men as they were in the old tales of the wars of the Elves in Beleriand. Indeed I think that in [?that] way we are remotely akin, and that they are come of that old stock, the first to come out of the East from which the Fathers of the Fathers of Men were come, Beren and Barahir and Huor and Húrin and Tuor and Túrin, aye and Earendel himself the half-elven, first king of Westernesse. So does some kinship in tongue and heart still tell. But they never crossed the Sea or went into the West and so must ever remain [?alien]. Yet we intermarry, and if they have become somewhat like us and cannot be called wild men, we have become like them and are no longer Númenóreans. For now we love war and valour as things good in themselves, and esteem warriors above all others. Such is the need of our days. ...'

In this notable passage are adumbrated new elements of ancient history that were no doubt long preparing before they appeared in any narrative text, though Eorl the Young had entered in 'The King of the Golden Hall', riding out of the North to 'the Battle of the Field of Gorgoroth' in which Sauron was overthrown (see VII.444 and note 11). That 'between Rohan and Ondor there was great friendship' appeared in the initial draft of 'The Riders of Rohan' (VII.393), and in the outline 'The Story Foreseen from Fangorn' (VII.437), after 'News comes ... of the siege of Minas Tirith by the Haradwaith', was added: 'Théoden answers that he does not owe fealty — only to heirs of Elendil.'

The mention of Earendel as the 'first king of Westernesse' is strange indeed, but I think probably not significant, a passing inadvertence: see further p. 158 and note 26.

This draft D 1 continues on for some way, written fast, and I will return to it; but it is convenient now to turn to the draft that replaced it ('D 2'), and which takes up with Sam's decision to say nothing about Gollum:

'... why should I remind them of the old villain, if they choose to forget him? I wish I could.'

After a while Frodo and Faramir began to talk again, and Frodo asked many questions concerning Gondor and its people and the lands about them, and what hope they had in their long war. He was interested in such matters, but also he wished to discover, if he could, how much Faramir knew of old lore, and how he knew it. He remembered now that at the Council Boromir had shown much knowledge of these things [*struck out:* naming the number of the rings of].

The last part of this was changed to read:

He was interested in such matters, but also he thought of Bilbo. 'He'll want accounts of all these things,' he thought. 'It is long since I made any note in my diary: tonight perhaps, as we rest.' Then he smiled at himself: 'But he lives in the House of Elrond and can have more for the asking than all that is remembered in Gondor! O but well, he'll like it best from a hobbit, personal recollections. He will, if ever I see him again, alas!'

All this was struck from the page subsequently, when the later structure of the narrative was imposed; but the text as written continues (cf. p. 154): '"What hope have we?" said Faramir. "It is long since we had any hope. ...', and then proceeds to develop Faramir's discussion of Gondor and Rohan to a form much closer to that in *The Two Towers*, though still with important differences.

Where in the first version D 1 (p. 154) he said: 'But we were more fortunate than other cities, recruiting our strength from the sturdy folk of the sea-coasts, and the hardy people of the White Mountains', he now says: 'But we were wiser and more fortunate than some; wiser, for we recruited the strength of our people from the sturdy folk of the sea-coasts and the hardy mountaineers of Hebel Nimrath;[19] more fortunate in our foes that became our friends.'[20] Faramir still gives no indication of when the Horsemen came out of the North: 'For on a time there came men out of the North and assailed our borders, men of fierce valour, but not servants of the Dark Lord, not the wild hordes of the East, or the cruel hosts of the South. Out of the North came the Rohiroth,[21] the Eorlingas, and at the last we ceded to them the fields of Kalinarda[22] that are since called Rohan; for long these had been sparsely peopled, and we could not resist the strength of these golden-haired horsemen. And they became our vassals or indeed our allies ...' He continues very much as in TT (p. 287). In the completed manuscript Faramir gives this indication of the date of their coming: 'On a time in the days of Mardil's son there came men out of the North ...' But of course this conveys very little.

Of the origin of the Rohiroth this draft D 2 gives the following version. The passage was heavily emended, and I show the significant alterations:

'... Indeed, it is said by the loremasters among us that they are somewhat our kin in blood and in speech, being descended [from those of the Three Houses of Men who went not over sea into the West >] from those same Three Houses of Men as were the Númenóreans, from Beor and Hador and Haleth, but from such as went not over sea into the West at the calling of the Powers. Thus they have to us a kinship, [such as the Exiled Elves that linger still in the West (of such indeed is the Lady of the Golden Wood) and returned not to Elvenhome have to those who departed. But they have never returned. >] such as the High Elves that do here and there abide still in the West of these lands have to those who lingered and went never to Elvenhome. Such is the kinship of the Lady of the Golden Wood to the folk she rules.[23] And so, as the Elves are divided into three: the High Elves, and the Middle Elves, [the Lingerers the Elves of the Woods >] their kindred that lingered on the shores, and the Wild Elves [the Refusers >] of the woods and mountains, so we divide Men, calling them the High or the Men of [Light >] the West, which are the Númenóreans, and the Middle or the Men of Shadow, such as the Rohiroth and other of their kindred in Dale and Mirkwood, and the Wild Men, or the Men of the Darkness. And of the truth of this their likeness of tongue and heart still speaks. Nonetheless those of Númenor passed over the Sea indeed, even if they after forfeited their kingdom and returned, and so they became a people apart and should remain so. Yet if the Rohir became in some ways more like to us, enhanced in art and gentleness, we too have become more like to them, and do not now rightly claim the title High. We are become Middle Men, of the Shadow, but with memory of other things. ...'

This was very largely retained, as emended, in the manuscript, but with these chief differences: 'they are come from those same Three Houses of Men as were the Númenóreans, from Hador the Golden-haired, the Elf-friend maybe, but from such of their sons as went not over the Sea into the West, refusing the call';[24] there is no mention of the Lady of the Golden Wood; and 'the Middle People or the Men of the Shadows, such as the Rohiroth and others of their kindred in Dale and the upper waters of Anduin'.

The threefold division of the Elves here (lost in *The Two Towers*) is that introduced into the *Quenta Silmarillion* after the return of the manuscript from the publishers at the end of 1937 (see *The Lost Road* pp. 200, 219): the Elves of Valinor; the *Lembi* or Lingerers; and the *Avari*, the Unwilling.

The draft D 1, left on p. 155, continues through Faramir's reply to Sam's remark about the Elves, and this is of great interest. Though a good deal was retained in TT (pp. 287–8) I give it here in full. At the end the writing becomes very fast and the draft ends in scrawled notes. Passages in square brackets are thus bracketed in the original.

'You don't say much in all your tales about the Elves, sir,' said Sam, suddenly plucking up courage: he was rather in awe of Faramir since his encounter on his master's behalf.

'No, Master Samwise,' said Faramir, 'and there you touch upon another point in which we have changed, becoming more as other men. For (as you may know, if Mithrandir was your guest; and you have spoken with Elrond) the Númenóreans were elf-friends, and came of those men who aided the Gnomes in the first wars, and were rewarded by the gift of the kingdom in the midst of the Sea, within sight of Elvenhome whither the High Elves withdrew [*written above:* where the High Elves dwelt]. But in the Great Lands[25] men and elves were estranged, by the arts of the Enemy [who had suborned most men (save only the Fathers of the Númenóreans) to his service] and by the slow changes of time in which each kind walked further down their sundered roads. Men fear and misdoubt the Elves, distinguishing not between the High-elves (that here and there remain) and those that like themselves never went over the Sea. And Elves mistrust men, who so often have served the Enemy. And we grow like other men, like the men even of Rohan who see them not if they pass (or persuade themselves that they do not see), and who speak of the Golden Wood in dread. Yet there are Elf-friends among us in Gondor still, more than among any other people; for though the blood of Númenor is now run thin in Gondor, still it flows there, indeed even Elvish blood maybe: for our kings of old were half-elven, even our first king Elros son of Earendel and brother of Elrond.[26] And 'tis said that Elendil's house was a younger branch of Elros. Some there are of Gondor who have dealings with the Elves, some even still fare to the Golden Wood (though often they return not). One great advantage we have: we speak an elvish speech, or one so near akin that we can in part understand them and they us.'

'But you speak the ordinary language,' exclaimed Sam. 'Like us, or a bit old-fashioned like, if you'll pardon me saying so.'

'Yes,' said Faramir, 'we do, for that is our language. The Common Tongue, as some call it, is derived from the Númenórean, being a changed form of that speech of men which the fathers used, Beren and Túrin and Earendel and those others. [Hence its remote kinship with the tongues of Rohan and of Dale and of Westfold and Dunland and other places.] This language it is that has spread through the western world among all that are of good will, and among others also. But the lords of Númenor spoke the Gnomish tongue of the Noldor to whom they were allied, and that tongue, changed somewhat and mingled, still lives among us, though we do not commonly speak it. So it is that our earliest names were in the High Elvish Quendian, such as Elendil, Isildur, and the rest, but the names we have given to places, and still give to women and men, are of Elvish sort. Often we give them out of the old tales: so is Denethor, and Mablung, and many others.'

Here the draft D 1 peters out, and I return to D 2, left on p. 157, at the same point ('You don't say much in all your tales about the Elves, sir'). In his reply to Sam Faramir here says of the Elf-friends of the ancient wars of Beleriand that they 'were rewarded (such as would take it) by the gift of the Kingdom in the midst of the Sea, within sight of Elvenhome, which they had leave to visit.'[27] And he continues: 'But in the Great Lands Men and Elves were estranged in the days of Darkness ...' He no longer speaks of the men of Rohan being unable to see the Elves, or pretending to themselves that they do not see them if they do, but as in TT says only that they shun them; and he declares, again as in TT, that he would not himself go to Lothlórien, judging it 'perilous now for mortal men, at least to seek the Elder People wilfully.' But his answer to Sam's 'But you speak the ordinary language! Same as us, though a bit old-fashioned like' was substantially changed:

'Of course we do,' said Faramir. 'For that is our own tongue which we perhaps preserve better than you do far in the North. The Common Tongue, as some call it, is derived from the Númenóreans,[28] being but a form changed by time of that speech which the Fathers of the Three Houses [*struck out:* Hador and Haleth and Beor] spoke of old. This language it is that has spread through the western world amongst all folk and creatures that use words, to some only a second tongue for use in intercourse with strangers, to some the only tongue they know. But this is not an Elvish speech in my meaning. All speech of men in this world is Elvish in descent; but only if one go back to the beginnings. What I meant was so: [the lords >] many men of the Three Houses long ago gave up man-speech and spoke the tongue of their friends the Noldor or Gnomes:[29] a high-elvish tongue [*struck out:* akin to but changed from the Ancient Elvish of Elvenhome]. And always the lords of Númenor knew that tongue and used it among themselves. And so still do we among ourselves, those who have the blood of Númenor still in our veins, though mayhap we have changed it somewhat mingling it like our blood with other strains. Thus it is that all our names of town and field, hill and river are in that tongue, and the names of our women and of our men. [*Struck out:* Only in the oldest days did we use the High Ancient Elven for such purposes: of that sort are Elendil and Isildur.] Indeed many of these we still take from tales of the old days: such are Mablung and Damrod, and mine own,[30] and my father's Denethor, and many others.'

'Well sir, I am glad you don't think ill of Elves at any rate,' said Sam. 'Wonderful folk, I think, sir. And the Lady of Lórien, Galadriel, you should see her, indeed you should, sir. I am only a hobbit, if you understand me, and gardening's my job at home ...'

This draft D 2 continues on through Sam's speech (essentially as in TT p. 288), his blurting out that Boromir always sought the Ring, and Faramir's response; but now in its turn it becomes quickly rougher and less formed (for its continuation beyond this point see p. 163) and was replaced by new drafting ('D 3') beginning at 'Indeed many of these we still take from tales of the ancient days ...'

In the text of the completed manuscript the draft D 2 just given was repeated with scarcely any change until towards the end. Faramir now says of the Elvish tongue spoken by the lords of Gondor that 'we can in part understand Elves [*struck out:* and they us] even when they speak to one another secretly', but all that he says in D 2 of the Common Tongue is repeated exactly as far as: 'All speech of men in this world is Elvish in descent; but only if one goes back to the beginnings.' The following sentence in D 2 ('What I meant was so: many men of the Three Houses long ago gave up man-speech and spoke the tongue of their friends the Noldor or Gnomes') was at first taken up in the manuscript, but struck out in the act of writing and replaced by the following (thus eliminating the reference to the abandonment of their own speech by the men of the Three Houses, see note 29):

'... What I meant was so: many men of the Three Houses long ago learned the High-elven tongues, as they were spoken [in Beleriand >] in Gondolin or by the Sons of Fëanor. And always the Lords of Númenor knew these tongues, and used the Gnomish speech among themselves. And so still do we, the rulers of Minas Tirith, in whom the blood of Númenor still flows ...'[31]

And Faramir, giving examples of names taken 'from tales of the Elder Days', adds Díriel to those he gave before.

Among occasional previous references to the Common Speech only once is its nature defined, and there in a wholly different way. This is in an early draft for a passage in the chapter 'Lothlórien' (VII.239 note 26), where it is said that Frodo did not understand the speech of the Elves of Lórien 'for the language was the old tongue of the woods and not that of the western elves which was in those days used as a common speech among many folk.'

With the present passage, in its various forms, concerning the Common Speech and the knowledge of the High-elven tongue of the Noldor among the lords of Gondor may be compared what is said in Appendix F to *The Lord of the Rings*:

> The *Westron* was a Mannish speech, though enriched and softened under Elvish influence. It was in origin the language of those whom the Eldar called the *Atani* or *Edain*, 'Fathers of Men', being especially the people of the Three Houses of the Elf-friends who came west into Beleriand in the First Age, and aided the Eldar in the War of the Great Jewels against the Dark Power of the North. ...
>
> The *Dúnedain* alone of all races of Men knew and spoke an Elvish tongue; for their forefathers had learned the Sindarin tongue, and this they handed on to their children as a matter of lore, changing little with the passing of the years. And their men of wisdom learned also the High-elven Quenya and esteemed it above all other tongues, and in it they made names for many places of fame and reverence, and for many men of royalty and great renown.
>
> But the native speech of the Númenoreans remained for the most part their ancestral Mannish tongue, the Adûnaic, and to this in the latter days of their pride their kings and lords returned, abandoning the Elven-speech, save only those few that held still to their ancient friendship with the Eldar.

There follows an account of the spread of Adûnaic along the coasts before the Fall of Númenor, becoming a Common Speech in those regions, and of the use of it by the Elf-friends who survived the Downfall 'in their dealing with other folk and in the government of their wide realms', enriching it with many Elvish words.

> In the days of the Númenorean kings this ennobled Westron speech spread far and wide, even among their enemies; and it

became used more and more by the Dúnedain themselves, so that at the time of the War of the Ring the Elven-tongue was known to only a small part of the peoples of Gondor, and spoken daily by fewer.

This much more complex conception seems nonetheless not radically different as regards the nature and origin of the Common Speech from that which Faramir presents here: for in both accounts, early and late, the Common Speech was directly descended from the ancestral tongue of the 'Fathers of Men'. It is thus curious to see that by later pencilled correction to the manuscript this was changed, Faramir now saying:

> 'Of course we do ... For that is also our own tongue, which we ourselves made, and here preserve better perhaps than do you far in the North. The Common Tongue, as some call it, is derived from the Númenóreans; for the Númenóreans coming to the shores of these lands took the rude tongue of the men that they here found and whom they ruled, and they enriched it, and it spread hence through the Western world ...'

And at the end of Faramir's discourse on linguistic history, after his examples of Gnomish names in Gondor, he now adds: 'But in intercourse with other folk we use the Common Speech which we made for that purpose.'

Here the idea that the Common Speech was derived from 'that speech which the Fathers of the Three Houses spoke of old' is denied.

In his letter of 6 May 1944 my father continued from the passage cited on p. 147:

> (A new character has come on the scene ... Faramir, the brother of Boromir) – and he is holding up the 'catastrophe' by a lot of stuff about the history of Gondor and Rohan (with some very sound reflections no doubt on martial glory and true glory): but if he goes on much more a lot of him will have to be removed to the appendices – where already some fascinating material on the hobbit Tobacco industry[32] and the Languages of the West have gone.

The passage on linguistic history in the present chapter (with the emendations just given concerning the nature of the Common Speech) survived into subsequent typescripts, and was only removed at a later time; thus the excluded material on 'the Languages of the West' to which my father referred in this letter was not the account given by Faramir.

As already remarked (p. 160), a new 'overlapping' draft D 3 takes up at the end of Faramir's exposition, and in this Sam shows himself as more impressed by what he has been told than in the previous version, and has more to say about Elves before he gets on to the subject of Galadriel. This passage was retained and slightly extended in the manuscript (in which form I cite it here), and it survived in the following typescripts until it was removed from the chapter together with the account of languages that preceded it.

Sam looked at Faramir wide-eyed and almost with awe. To have an elvish name, and even a possible claim to Elvish blood however remote, seemed to him royalty indeed. 'Well Captain, your lordship, I should say, it is good to hear you speak so fair of Elves, sir. I wish I had an elvish name. Wonderful folk they are, aren't they? Think of the things they can make and the things they say! You don't find out their worth or their meaning all at once, as it were: it comes out afterwards, unexpected like. Just a bit of well-made rope in a boat, and there it is: one day it's just what you want, and it unknots itself when you ask it and jumps to your hand. And the boat: I agree with your lordship; I think it rode the falls and took no harm. Of course it would, if that was needed. It was an Elven-boat, sir; though I sat in one for many a day, and never noticed nothing special.'[33]

'I think you are right, Master Samwise,' said Faramir smiling; 'though some would say the White Lady had enchanted you.'

'And she did, sir!' said Sam. 'The Lady of Lórien! Galadriel! you should see her, indeed you should, sir. I am only a hobbit, and gardening's my job at home ...'[34]

I have mentioned (p. 160) that the Draft D 2, now become very ragged, continued on through Sam's description to Faramir of Galadriel, and his blurting out the truth, so long and so carefully concealed by Frodo, that 'Boromir wanted the Ring!'[35] In this draft, where in TT 'Frodo and Sam sprang from their stools and set themselves side by side with their backs to the wall, fumbling for their sword-hilts', and 'all the men in the cave stopped talking', all that is said is: 'Frodo and Sam sprang side by side, fumbling for their swords.' Faramir sat down and began to laugh, and then became suddenly grave. It is clear that he sat on the ground, where they were, in the woods. The last words of this draft before it was abandoned, barely legible, are:

'Do not fear. I do not wish to see or touch it – my only fear is lest I see it and be tempted. But now indeed it becomes my duty to aid you with all that I have. If this is the counsel of Mithrandir, that this [?dreadful] Thing should be sent [?a-wandering] in the borders of Mordor in the keeping of two hobbits, then he is desperate indeed and at his wits' end. Come, let us get to cover as quick as we may.'

It has been seen (pp. 154, 163) that in the drafting (D 1–2) for the latter part of this chapter the entire story of the coming to Henneth Annûn was absent, and the entire conversation that in TT took place there after the evening meal here took place as they walked through the woods. When we come to the third overlapping portion of the draft (D 3), however, at the dénouement, the revelation of the Ring, they are in the cave, and all is as in TT. It is clear therefore that it was only when he had come to the very end of the chapter that my father realised that the long conversation with Faramir had been interrupted by their coming to the refuge; and perhaps it was only now that he perceived what that refuge was: the Window of the Sunset, Henneth Annûn. Drafting for the new passage (TT pp. 281–6, from 'So they passed on, until the woodlands grew thinner ...') is found separately, with very little significant divergence from the finished form. There is no mention of Anborn and the sighting of Gollum in the woods at dusk: this first appears in the completed manuscript;[36] and Faramir says to Frodo and Sam before the meal: 'Do as we do, I pray. So do we always, look towards Númenor that was, and to Elvenhome beyond, and to that which is beyond Elvenhome, Valinor the Blessed Realm.'[37]

On the page of this drafting where appear Faramir's words 'This is the Window of the West' (changed to 'Window of the Sunset') my father wrote many names and forms before achieving *Henneth Annûn*: *Nargalad*, *Anngalad*, *Carangalad*; *Henneth Carandûn*, *Henneth Malthen*; *Henlo Naur*, *Henlo n'Annun*; *Henuil n'Annun*.

NOTES

1 The 'new chapters' were: (1) 'The Taming of Smeagol'; (2) 'The Passage of the Marshes'; (3) 'The Black Gate is Closed' (including 'Of Herbs and Stewed Rabbit'); (4) 'Faramir'. See note 2.

2 Since 'The Taming of Smeagol' was Chapter XXXII, 'The Passage of the Marshes' XXXIII, and 'The Black Gate is Closed' XXXIV, 'Faramir', the 'fourth new chapter', should be XXXV. Its actual number XXXVI implies that 'Of Herbs and Stewed Rabbit' had already been separated off as XXXV – but then of couse 'Faramir' became the fifth new chapter. Perhaps the actual number XXXVI was written in subsequently. See further p. 171.

3 This refers to the form of the 'dream-verse of Minas Tirith' in which the second half ran thus (see VII.146):

This sign shall there be then
that Doom is near at hand:
The Halfhigh shall you see then
with Isildur's bane in hand.

4 Throughout this draft Falborn addresses Frodo as 'thou', but this usage was emended throughout and does not appear in the following text.

5 The men of Gondor were in this draft B 'sitting in a ring, in the middle of which were Falborn and Frodo. It seemed that there was a debate going on.' – Frodo refers to 'Elrond of Imlad-rist': cf. p. 139 note 14.

6 In a rejected version of this 'the other half was found further down the river above Osgiliath by other watchers.'

7 On the same page are written other passages that were presumably potential ingredients in Sam's remonstration to Falborn:

> It's a pity the folks against Mordor fall out so easy. I should have thought it as plain as a pikestaff.
>
> Boromir was on his way to Minas Tirith. We decided not to go that way and went on our own road. Boromir was not dead when we left, but orcs knew of our journey: they attacked us above the rapids beyond Sarn Gebir. What's in it?
>
> I daresay now we made a mistake. I don't know the lie of the lands; but maybe we'd have got there quicker through Minas Tirith. But here we would have come. And if you drag us back there'll be some that do not like it. Boromir would not. Nor Aragorn.

With *Sarn Gebir* here for *Emyn Muil* cf. p. 136 and note 17. – Another passage here, in part totally illegible, is a draft for a more substantial conclusion to the interrogation of Frodo by Falborn: harshly uncomprehending in tone compared to the later Faramir, and suggesting that no further conversation between them had been thought of at this stage.

> 'Thou'rt commanded to go – somewhere. But I too am under command: to slay all that roam in Ithilien unanswerable, or at least to take them prisoner to Minas Tirith. I see no cause to slay you, or at least too great doubt. But to Minas Tirith ye shall go. And if Boromir is there it will ... with you. If Boromir's death be proved it will interest Denethor to speak with those who saw him last before he died. If he [?cometh] doubtless ye will be glad – maybe not. Of your own errand ..... [*the following sentences are effectively illegible*] ..... Maybe if you would say more of the truth and reveal your errand we would help you and not hinder. But if you will not speak I have no choice in my doubt.'
>
> 'Maybe you would, and maybe not,' said Frodo. 'But it is not a matter to speak of to such as you are – not were the walls of [?Mordor] a thousand miles away, whereas they be but a few leagues.'

Also here are inconclusive rewritings of the second part of the 'dream-verse of Minas Tirith'.

8 *Falborn* was emended to *Faramir* (but not consistently) on the

second draft B, where also many other changes leading to the third version C were entered.

9 This line does not appear in the rewritings of the verse referred to at the end of note 7, but *A sign shall be upholden* is found there. It may be that no such form of the verse was ever actually written. The manuscript at first followed the draft, but was then changed to 'But the words said that the Halfling would hold up Isildur's Bane'. *Halfling* for *Half-high* entered by emendation to the second draft B: 'If you be the Half-high' > 'If you be the Halfling'.

10 The date of Boromir's death was 26 January (and in one of the time-schemes the hour of his death is stated to be 'noon'); it was now 6 February, eleven days later. (In the margin of the manuscript my father wrote 'twelve' beside 'eleven', which however was not struck out. This presumably depends on the chronology in time-scheme 'S', in which Boromir died on 25 January: see pp. 101, 142.) In *The Tale of Years* the corresponding dates are 26 February and 7 March, also eleven days later (February having 30 days). In the notes given on p. 146 Faramir and his men left Minas Tirith on 3 February, thus three days before; and both in the draft and in the manuscript he tells Frodo that no members of the Company had reached the city when he left it three days before (where TT has six days, p. 272). In *The Tale of Years* he left on 1 March, thus six days before.

11 A further isolated scrap of drafting may be noticed. It represents presumably unused words of Frodo's when he spoke to Faramir about the boats of Lothlórien: 'These boats are crafty and unlike those of other folk. They will not sink, not though they will be laden more than is their wont when you are all aboard. But they are wayward, and if mishandled' (the sentence ends here).

12 This apparently refers to a passage in 'Farewell to Lórien'. In the fair copy manuscript of that chapter Boromir's original words 'I have not myself been there' (referring to Fangorn) had become 'I have not myself ever crossed Rohan' (VII.282, 293 note 36). This was now changed on that manuscript to 'I have myself been seldom in Rohan, and have never crossed it northwards' (cf. FR p. 390).

13 Rough drafting for this new placing of Sam's intervention is found. In this, rather oddly, Faramir's reply continues on into his astute guessing about Frodo's relationship with Boromir and about Isildur's Bane, and Frodo's quickly smothered desire to 'tell all to this kindly but just man'. In TT this passage, in much more developed form, does not arise until after they have begun their journey to Henneth Annûn. However, this was clearly no more than a sketching of new elements in the dialogue; it was not a

draft for the overhaul of all that had been achieved in the chapter thus far.

14 Cf. the beginning of the sketch given on p. 151. — The passage that precedes this in TT p. 276, from 'For me there is no comfort in our speech together' to 'But whatever befell on the North March, you, Frodo, I doubt no longer' (in which Faramir suggests that some of the Company are still alive, since who else can have arrayed Boromir in the funeral boat), did not enter till later (it was added to the first typescript of the chapter).

15 Various elements are lacking in the draft but are present in the manuscript: such are 'He wished this thing brought to Minas Tirith' (TT p. 278); and the passage concerning Gandalf (p. 279), from 'Are you sure of this' to 'He got leave of Denethor, how I do not know, to look at the secrets of our treasury' — where the draft text reads: '... so much lore be taken from the world. He had leave to look at the secrets of our treasury ...' The draft text has a few features lost in the manuscript: thus after 'There is a something, I know not what, an elvish air maybe, about you' (TT p. 276) it continues: 'And that is not what I should look for, if old tales and rumours from afar told the whole truth concerning the little people.' This was rejected and replaced by: 'Some power greater than the stature of your kind', also rejected. And after 'unlike they were, and yet also much akin' (TT p. 280) the draft goes on: 'Faramir was doubtless of a different temper, but Frodo feared the power and treachery of the thing he bore: the greater and wiser the stronger the lure and the worse the fall.' With this cf. the sketch given on p. 152.

16 *Great Lands*: this survival of old usage remains at this place in *The Two Towers* (p. 286), its only occurrence in *The Lord of the Rings*. At a subsequent occurrence of *Great Lands* in this chapter (p. 158) TT has *Middle-earth* (p. 288), suggesting that its appearance in the first passage was an oversight.

17 *White Mountains: White* was added, but almost certainly as the text was in progress. Cf. the notes given on p. 137: 'Change *Black Mountains* to the *White Mountains*'.

18 The writing of the name *Elenarda* is perfectly clear and unambiguous, and it was not struck out when *Kalen(arda)* was written above it (but see p. 156 and note 22). It is strange to find it applied to Rohan; for this old mythological word derives from the conception of the three 'airs' in the cosmology expounded in the *Ambarkanta*. There it is translated 'Stellar Kingdom', and is another name for the middle region of *Ilmen*, in which move the Sun, the Moon, and the stars (see IV.240–3, 253). — On the name Rohir in the preceding sentence see p. 22 and note 24.

19 *Hebel Nimrath* was the name of the White Mountains written in

the manuscript, subsequently changed to *Ered Nimras*. With these names cf. those given in the notes on p. 137.

20 In the manuscript Faramir says, as in TT (p. 286), 'But the stewards were wiser and more fortunate.' The Stewards of Gondor, ruling in Minas Tirith after the death of the last and childless king of the line of Anárion, have appeared already in the earlier part of the dialogue of Frodo and Faramir (p. 153). In the manuscript Faramir's balance of phrases ('wiser and more fortunate; wiser ..., more fortunate ...') was preserved ('more fortunate, for our most dangerous foes became our friends'); by alteration of the text here at a later time this was lost in TT.

21 *Rohiroth*: see p. 22. In the first of these drafts (D 1) the form is *Rohir* (note 18); in the present draft (D 2) both *Rohir* and *Rohiroth* are found in close proximity. In the manuscript the form is *Rohiroth*.

22 In the manuscript my father wrote *Kalin*, striking it out at once and writing *Calenardan*, then altering this to *Calenardhon*, all these changes being made in the act of writing. See note 18.

23 The difference between these formulations is evidently that in the rejected version the relationship is between the Noldor (such as Galadriel) who remained after the overthrow of Morgoth and those who departed and went to Tol Eressëa; whereas in the second version the relationship is between the Noldor who remained and the Elves who never went to Valinor (such as the Elves of Lothlórien). — Cf. the passage in the chapter 'Galadriel' in VII.248, with note 12.

24 In TT (p. 287) the reading is '*not* from Hador the Goldenhaired, the Elf-friend, maybe ...' This *not* was inserted by my father on a late typescript of the chapter; it was put in very hurriedly, and it seems to me possible that he read the sentence differently from his original meaning — which was certainly 'They may be descended from Hador indeed, *but if so*, then of course from those of Hador's descendants who did not pass over the Sea.' — In the manuscript 'such of their sons' was later emended to 'such of his people', and this seems to have been misinterpreted by the typist as 'such of his sons and people'.

It may be noted here that at the same time as this correction to the manuscript the words 'they became a people apart and should remain so' were changed to 'and should have remained so'.

25 *Great Lands*: here TT has *Middle-earth*; see note 16.

26 This sentence was apparently evolved thus: 'even Earendel our first king and Elros brother [*sc.* of Elrond]' > 'even our first king Elros son of Earendel and brother of Elrond'. See p. 155.

27 It was explicit from the beginning that the Númenóreans were expressly forbidden by the Gods to sail westward beyond the Lonely Isle (see the original outline and the original versions of

The Fall of Númenor in *The Lost Road*, pp. 11, 14, 26). *Elvenhome* here means the Lonely Isle: for that isle lay in the Bay of Elvenhome (cf. *The Lost Road* p. 103: 'the Isle of Eressëa in Elvenhome'); and this is the meaning also in the same passage in TT (p. 288), where the words 'within sight of Elvenhome' are retained — cf. the passage in the *Akallabêth* (*The Silmarillion*, pp. 262–3) where the remote vision from Númenor of Avallónë, haven of Eressëa, is described. This is made certain, apart from any other considerations, by the passage given on p. 164.

28 The word *Númenórean(s)* is variously marked, with an accent on the first syllable or on the third, or no accent. Here the word is written *Númenóreans*, and I have extended this throughout.

29 Cf. the later *Annals of Beleriand* in *The Lost Road*, p. 131: 'the folk of Hádor abandoned their own tongue and spoke with the speech of the Gnomes'; also the *Lhammas* § 10, *ibid.* p. 179.

30 The name *Faramir* does not appear in any earlier writing.

31 By later pencilled correction of the manuscript Faramir's words were changed so that the reference is only to Noldorin: 'many men of the Three Houses long ago learned the High-elven tongue of the Noldor, as it was spoken in Gondolin or by the Sons of Fëanor. And always the Lords of Númenor knew that tongue, and used it among themselves.'

32 On the removal of the history of Pipe-weed from the text see pp. 36–9.

33 With these remarks of Sam's cf. the initial sketch given on p. 152: 'Sam speaks of elvish power, boats, ropes, cloaks.' This was written before the entry of Faramir's account of language (the cause of its loss from the chapter in *The Two Towers*).

34 In neither of the draft versions of Sam's words about Galadriel does Faramir interject: 'Then she must be lovely indeed. Perilously fair', leading (in the manuscript, and in TT) to Sam's consideration of the justice of the word *perilous* as applied to Galadriel; but in both drafts Sam nonetheless says 'I don't know about perilous', and makes the same observations. At this stage he was referring back to Faramir's earlier 'I deem it perilous now for mortal men, at least to seek the Elder People wilfully' (p. 159).

35 In this draft (D 2) Sam's gaffe is preceded by the same words as in TT (p. 289), but he ends: 'and it's my opinion as soon as he first heard of it he wanted the Ring.' Thus he does not refer to Lórien as the place where Boromir (in the words of the final draft, D 3) 'first saw himself clear, and saw what I saw sooner'.

36 The man who saw Gollum was first named *Falborn* in the manuscript, later altered to *Anborn* (this change was actually made in the course of the initial drafting of 'The Forbidden Pool'). In draft and manuscript of 'Of Herbs and Stewed Rabbit'

(p. 136) Anborn was the father of Falborn leader of the men of Gondor in Ithilien, who became Faramir.

37 On *Elvenhome* here (Tol Eressëa) see note 27. The manuscript has the final text (TT p. 285): '... towards Númenor that was, and beyond to Elvenhome that is, and to that which is beyond Elvenhome and will ever be.' Cf. *Letters* no. 211, footnote to p. 281, where the words 'that which is beyond Elvenhome and ever will be' [*sic*] are interpreted as 'is beyond the mortal lands, beyond the memory of unfallen Bliss, beyond the physical world.'

VI
THE FORBIDDEN POOL

The 'fourth new chapter ("Faramir")' had been read to C. S. Lewis and Charles Williams on 8 May 1944 (see p. 144) – 'fourth', because 'The Black Gate is Closed' and 'Of Herbs and Stewed Rabbit' had not yet been separated (see p. 164, notes 1 and 2). On 11 May my father wrote (*Letters* no. 67) that another chapter was in progress, 'leading to disaster at Kirith Ungol where Frodo is captured. Story then switches back to Gondor, & runs fairly swiftly (I hope) to denouement.' On the following day (*Letters* no. 68) he said that 'we are now in sight of Minas Morghul'; and he also quoted Faramir's words to Frodo: 'When you return to the lands of the living,[1] and we re-tell our tales, sitting by a wall in the sun, laughing at old grief, you shall tell me then.' In *The Two Towers* these words stand just before the end of 'The Forbidden Pool'. On the morning of 15 May 1944 (*Letters* no. 69) he read his '6th new chapter "Journey to the Cross Roads"' to C. S. Lewis.

Initial drafting for what became 'The Forbidden Pool' runs on continuously into what became 'Journey to the Cross-Roads', and in the completed fair copy manuscript likewise the two chapters are one, titled 'XXXVII. Journey to the Cross Roads'; the latter title and chapter-break were inserted into the manuscript later, when the first part became 'The Forbidden Pool'.[2] Since my father would not have called his 'new chapter' 'Journey to the Cross Roads' if Frodo, Sam and Gollum did not get there in the course of it, I conclude that this was where they were, beside the broken statue in the ring of trees, when he read his '6th new chapter' to Lewis on the 15th of May (by this time, presumably, he had divided 'Of Herbs and Stewed Rabbit' from 'The Black Gate is Closed', so making 'Faramir' the fifth). In his letter recording this (no. 69) he went on: 'So far it has gone well: but I am now coming to the nub, when the threads must be gathered and the times synchronized and the narrative interwoven; while the whole thing has grown so large in significance that the sketches of concluding chapters (written ages ago) are quite inadequate, being on a more "juvenile" level.'

This part of the story unfolded, once my father began to write it, virtually without any hestitation between rival courses; there is however a little sketch that he wrote for it, exceedingly hard to make out, when all was not yet plain.

They are roused late at night. Moonset over Mindolluin. Sam grumbles at being waked only to see moonlight.

They see Gollum fishing below the pool.

Faramir says he must shoot to kill, or Frodo must help to capture him.

Frodo and some men go out. Frodo calls Gollum and Gollum is caught still clutching a fish.

Faramir warns Frodo against Gollum.

[*Struck out:* Frodo tells him] No it is Gollum.

Frodo begs for his life. It is granted if Frodo will induce Gollum to come and .....[3]

Gollum is caught by guards and brought in.

He [?feigns] great delight at Frodo. Nice fish. Begs him not to delay but start in morning.

They go back to sleep till morning.

They go on through woods by day. No orcs. Farewell. They are out of reckoning, and take long[?er than]

Here these notes end. The sentences 'Frodo and some men go out. Frodo calls Gollum and Gollum is caught still clutching a fish' are marked with a line in the margin, which probably implies that this is the version to be followed, rather than 'Gollum is caught by guards and brought in. He feigns great delight at Frodo.' I cannot explain the rejected words 'Frodo tells him', followed by 'No it is Gollum'.

Drafting for the chapter (much of it in handwriting so difficult that were it not generally already close to the final form parts of it would be virtually uninterpretable) suggests extremely fluent composition, and there is very little to say of it. New elements entered in successive pages of drafting, but the fair copy manuscript, from which the chapter was read to C. S. Lewis on 15 May, reached the text of *The Two Towers* in all but a few minor points.

Minor in itself, but very notable, is what Faramir says of the Moon. In TT (p. 293) he says: 'Fair Ithil, as he goes from Middle-earth, glances upon the white locks of old Mindolluin'; but in the original draft of the passage he said: 'Fair Ithil touches with *her* fingers the white locks of old Mindolluin', and still in the manuscript, where the text is otherwise that of TT, he said: 'as *she* goes from Middle-earth ...'[4]

In the original draft of Frodo's reply to Faramir's question concerning Gollum ('Why does he so?', TT p. 294) he says, in support of his suggestion that Gollum does not realise that men are concealed there, that 'He has night-eyes, but he is nearsighted and I doubt if he could see us up here.' In a second draft of the passage the last phrase became '... and sees to no great distance clearly'; in the manuscript, '... and distant things are dim to him.' Against this, in the second of these drafts, my father wrote (at the same time): 'Make it *not* Gollum who looked out at Morannon – or make it 100 yards' (with '200 yards' written above). But the reference to Gollum's nearsightedness was struck from the typescripts and does not appear in TT, and Gollum remained the one who looked out from the hollow before the Black Gate and saw the 'very cruel wicked Men' coming up the road from the south. My father hesitated much over the distance from the hollow to the road, and this was clearly one of the reasons for it; see p. 128 note 9. — The 'froglike figure' that climbed out of the water as Frodo and Faramir looked down on the pool was a subsequent change from 'spidery figure'.

In very rough and rapid initial drafting for the concluding part of the chapter in TT (pp. 300–2) Frodo says no more of the way past Minas Morghul than that Gollum had said that there was such a way, 'up in a high pass in the mountains'. Then follows Faramir's declaration of the name Kirith Ungol, as in TT. In the fair copy manuscript my father first wrote here:

> 'I do not know clearly,' said Frodo, 'but it climbs, I think, up into the mountains on the southern side of that vale in the mountains on the northern side of which the old city stands. It goes up to a high cleft and so down to – that which is beyond.'

This was subsequently changed to the text of TT. On the earlier idea that Kirith Ungol was on the south side of the valley see p. 113.

At the end of this initial draft my father briefly outlined the further course of the story: the blindfolding of the hobbits and Gollum, the report of the scouts on the strange silence and emptiness in the land, Faramir's advice to go by day through the woods 'skirting the last fall of the land before the river vale', and his farewell. At the foot of this page is a pencilled note only a part of which can I make out:

> K[irith] U[ngol] must not be mentioned before Frodo ... to tell Faramir of Gollum.
> Yes he found the ring many many years ago, said Frodo. He is the means by which all this great matter has been set going.

Two sentences follow in which I can make out nothing at all, except perhaps 'where the ring had been'. But in any case this was evidently a very short-lived idea.

NOTES

1 The original draft of the passage in 'The Forbidden Pool' was almost as in TT: 'If ever you return to the lands of the living ...'

2 A subsequent tentative arrangement was to put 'The Forbidden Pool' with 'Faramir', calling the first part 'Faramir (1): The

Window of the West' (not 'on the West'), and the second 'Faramir (2): The Forbidden Pool'.

3 The illegible end of this sentence looks in fact more like 'visit them' than anything else. If so, the meaning is presumably 'if Frodo can induce Gollum to leave the pool and come up with him to Faramir's presence'; the word is oddly chosen, but these notes were written at great speed.

4 *she* was corrected to *he* on the first typescript. Cf. the *Quenta Silmarillion* in *The Lost Road*, p. 241 §78: 'Varda commanded the Moon to rise only after the Sun had left heaven, but he travels with uncertain pace, and still pursueth her ...'

Another matter concerning the Moon may be mentioned. At the beginning of the chapter, when Faramir waking Frodo says 'the full moon is setting', my father changed this on the manuscript to 'rising'; when they came out from the stairway in the rock the words 'Far off in the West the full moon was sinking' were changed to 'Behind him the round moon, full and majestic, rose out of the shadow of the East'; and Faramir's 'Moonset over Gondor' was changed to 'Moonrise over Gondor'. This would of course make it very much earlier in the night. But all these alterations were returned to the original readings, presumably at once, since subsequently 'It was now dark and the falls were pale and grey, reflecting only the lingering moonlight of the western sky' (TT p. 295) was not changed.

VII
JOURNEY TO THE CROSS-ROADS

I have recounted the original relationship of 'The Forbidden Pool' and 'Journey to the Cross-roads'[1] at the beginning of the last chapter. Preliminary drafting for this second part of the original single chapter runs continuously, in excruciatingly difficult handwriting, as far as the coming of Frodo and his companions to the ridge covered with whortleberry and gorse-bushes so tall that they could walk upright beneath them (TT p. 307).[2] The story to this point differed from that in *The Two Towers*. The journey took a day less: they came to the road from Osgiliath at dusk of the day on which they left Henneth Annûn in the morning; and their taking refuge in the great holm-oak was described at much greater length (cf. TT pp. 306–7, from 'Gollum reluctantly agreed to this'):

Gollum agreed to this, and the travellers turned back from the road, but Gollum would not rest on the ground in the open woodland. After some search he chose a large dark ilex with great branches springing together high up from a great bole like a [?giant] pillar. It grew at the foot of a small bank [?leaning] a little westward. From the bank Gollum leaped with ease upon the trunk, climbing like a cat and scrambling up into the branches. The hobbits climbed only with the help of Sam's rope and in that task Gollum would not help, he would not lay a finger on the elven rope. The great branches springing almost from the same point made a wide bowl and here they [?managed] to find some sort of comfort. It grew deep dark under the great canopy of the tree. They could not see the sky or any star.

'We could sleep snug and safe here, if it wasn't for this dratted Gollum,' thought Sam. Whether he was really as forgiving as he claimed or not, Gollum at least had no fear of his companions, and curled up like some tree-animal and soon went to sleep, or seemed to. But the hobbits did not trust it – neither of them (certainly not Sam) were likely to forget Faramir's warning. They took [it] in turn to watch and had about 3 hours' sleep each. All the while Gollum did not stir. Whether the 'nice fish' had given him strength to last for a bit or whatnot else, he did not go out to hunt.

Shortly before midnight he woke up suddenly and they saw his pale eyes unlidded staring in the darkness.

At the point where this opening draft ended my father wrote *Thunder*. But at this stage there is no suggestion in the text of any change in the weather or in the feeling of the air. Other points worth mentioning are that the staves given to Frodo and Sam by Faramir had 'carven heads like a shepherd's crook'; that the tree of which they were made was first named *melinon* (the last two letters are not perfectly clear), then *lebendron*, and finally *lebethras*, all these changes being made in the act of writing;[3] and that though Faramir warns them against drinking of any water that flows from the valley of Morghul he does not name it *Imlad Morghul* (but the name occurs soon after: p. 223, note 25).

A second draft takes up at the beginning of the passage just given ('Gollum agreed to this'), and the episode of the oak-tree was rewritten. In this text appears the first reference to an approaching change in the weather.

They were steadily climbing. Looking back they could see now the roof of the forests they had left, lying like a huge dense shadow spread under the sky. The air seemed heavy, no longer fresh and clear, and the stars were blurred, and when towards the end of the night the moon climbed slowly above Ephel Dúath[4] it was ringed about with a sickly yellow glare. They went on until the sky above the approaching mountains began to grow pale. Gollum seemed to know well enough where he was. He stood for a moment nose upward sniffing. Then beckoning to them he hurried forward. Following him wearily they began to climb a great hogback of land. ...

After the description of the great gorse-bushes and their hiding in a brake of tangled thorns and briars there follows (cf. TT p. 308):

There they lay glad to be at rest, too tired as yet to eat, and watched the slow growth of day. As the light grew the mountains of Ephel-dúath seemed to frown and lower at them across the tumbled lands between. They looked even nearer than they were, black below where night lingered, with jagged tips and edges lined in threatening shapes against the opening sky.

Away a little northward of where the hobbits lay they seemed to recede eastwards and fall back in a great re-entrant, the nearer shoulder of which thrusting forward hid the view in that direction. Below out of the great shadow they could see the road from the River for a short stretch as it bent away north-east to join the southward road that still lay further off [?buried] in the crumpled land.

'Which way do we go from here?' said Frodo.

'Must we think of it yet?' said Sam. 'Surely we're not going to move for hours and hours?'

'No surely not,' said Gollum. 'But we must move sometime. ..... back to the Cross-roads that we told the hobbits about.'

'When shall we get there?'

'We doesn't know,' said Gollum. 'Before night is over perhaps, perhaps not.'

At this point the second draft breaks down into an outline of the story to come, and the handwriting becomes in places altogether inscrutable.

Gollum away a large part of the day. Reach Cross-roads in fact owing to difficult country not until evening. Start at dusk about 5.30 and do not reach Cross-roads and headless statue until morning [*sic*]. Gollum in a great state of fright. Weather changed. Sky above Ephel Dúath absolute black. Clouds or smoke? drifting on an East wind. Rumbles? Sun hidden. In this darkness they get out of the wood and see Minas Morghul. It shines amid a deep gloom as if by an evil moon – though there is no moon.

Horror of hobbits. Weight of Ring. .... vale of Morghul. Where road went away to the north shoulder and bases of the fortress they turned aside and climbed away southward to other side of V [*i.e.* Vale of Morghul]. Frodo and Sam .... see a track. They are already some way up and the gates of Minas Morghul frown at them when there is a great roll and rumble. Blast of Thunder .... rain. Out of gates comes host led by B[lack] R[ider].

It was in this text that the idea of the great cloud spreading out of Mordor emerged. In a third section of drafting my father returned to the point where the second had become a sketch, following Gollum's words about the Cross-roads: 'The sun that had risen with a red glare behind the Ephel-dúath passed into dark clouds moving slowly from the East. It was a gloomy morning. The hobbits took some food and settled to rest ...'

After Gollum's reappearance from his long absence that day this draft too turns to outline:

When he returns he says they ought to start. Hobbits think something has worried him (or ?). They are suspicious but have to agree. The [early evening >] afternoon is threatening and overcast. At evening they come to the Cross-roads in a wood. Sun goes down bloodred in the west over Osgiliath. Terrible darkness begins.

The completed fair copy manuscript did not in this case reach the form of the story in *The Two Towers*, for Frodo and his companions still only took two days from Henneth Annûn to the Cross-roads, and a major later change was the lengthening of their journey by a further day. This was achieved by the insertion of the following passage into a typescript of the chapter, following the words (TT p. 305) 'The birds seemed all to have flown away or to have fallen dumb':

Darkness came early to the silent woods, and before the fall of night they halted, weary, for they had walked seven leagues or more from Henneth Annûn. Frodo lay and slept away the night on the deep mould beneath an ancient tree. Sam beside him was more uneasy: he woke many times, but there was never a sign of Gollum, who had slipped off as soon as the others had settled to rest. Whether he had slept by himself in some hole nearby, or had wandered restlessly prowling through the night, he did not say; but he returned with the first glimmer of light, and roused his companions.

'Must get up, yes they must!' he said. 'Long ways to go still, south and east. Hobbits must make haste!'

That day passed much the same as the day before had done, except that the silence seemed deeper; the air grew heavy, and it began to be stifling under the trees. It felt as if thunder was brewing. Gollum often paused, sniffing the air, and then he would mutter to himself and urge them to greater speed.

(As the third stage of their day's march drew on ...)

This was retained almost exactly in TT. In the manuscript the text passes at once from 'The birds seemed all to have flown away or to have fallen dumb' to 'As the third stage of their day's march drew on', and thus in this narrative (as in the original draft, p. 175) they came to the Cross-roads at sunset of the second day. They had come to Henneth Annûn at sunset on 6 February (pp. 135, 141); they left on the morning of the 7th, and coming to the Osgiliath road at dusk of that day passed the first part of the night in the great oak-tree; they went on again 'a little before midnight', and passed most of the daylight hours of 8 February hiding in the thorn-brake before going on to the Cross-roads (see further the Note on Chronology at the end of this chapter).

Thus the phrase 'As the third stage of their day's march drew on' referred, when it was written, to the statement then immediately preceding: 'Twice that day they rested and took a little of the food provided by Faramir'; as it stands in TT its reference is less clear.

In this inserted passage occurs the first reference in TT to the heaviness in the air and the feeling of thunder. In the manuscript as in the draft (p. 176) the first reference to the change in the weather does not appear until they set out again and began to climb eastwards, after spending the first part of the night (the second night in TT) in the oak-tree; at this point in TT, by a later change, 'There seemed to be *a great blackness* looming slowly out of the East, eating up the faint blurred stars.' On the following morning, as they lay hidden under the thorns, the manuscript retained the story in the draft: the hobbits 'watched the slow growth of day', and saw the mountain-tops outlined against the sunrise; and here again this was afterwards changed to the reading of TT (p. 308): the hobbits 'watched *for* the slow growth of day. *But no day came*, only a dead brown twilight. In the East there was a dull red glare under the lowering cloud: *it was not the red of dawn.*' Where the manuscript, again following the draft (p. 177), has 'The sun that had risen with a red flare behind Ephel-dúath passed soon into dark clouds moving slowly from the East. It was going to be a gloomy day, if no worse' TT has 'The red glare over Mordor died away. The twilight deepened as great vapours rose in the East and crawled above them.' On the other hand, the further references in this chapter to the darkness (and to the deep rumbling sounds) were already present in the original version, and at the end it is said, almost as in TT (p. 311): 'There, far away, the sun was sinking, finding at last the hem of the great slow-rolling pall of cloud, and falling in an ominous fire towards the yet unsullied sea.'[5]

Comparing the text as it stands in the manuscript with that in TT one might well suppose at first sight that all these careful alterations show my father at a later time (when he had reached Book V) developing the original idea of a great thunderstorm arising in the mountains into that of the 'Dawnless Day', an emanation of the power of Mordor that obliterated the sunrise and turned day into night, that stroke of Sauron's that preceded his great assault. But it is clear that this is not so. That conception was already present. In fact, the essential reason for these changes was chronological, and they are to be associated with the extra day of the journey from Henneth Annûn. The slow approach of the great cloud out of the East had to be advanced at each succeeding stage of the journey to the Cross-roads (see the Note on Chronology at the end of this chapter). It is also true, however, that the rewriting of these passages intensified the Darkness and made it more potent and sinister.

Lastly, another later alteration to the text in the manuscript was the sentence (TT p. 306) 'and the sound of the water seemed cold and cruel: the voice of Morgulduin, the polluted stream that flowed from the Valley of the Wraiths.'

On p. 181 is reproduced a plan of the Cross-roads and Minas Morghul.[6]

NOTES

1 My father wrote the word 'Cross-roads' very variously, but in this chapter I spell it thus throughout, as in TT.

2 Cf. *Unfinished Tales*, p. 99 and note 15.

3 In the fair copy manuscript it was still said that the heads of the staves were in the form of a shepherd's crook, though this was subsequently rejected (see p. 207), but the name of the tree was *lebethron* as first written.

4 In the first draft the form was still *Hebel Dúath*. On this change see p. 137. — This reference to the moon climbing above Ephel Dúath 'towards the end of night' is curious, in view of the opening of 'The Forbidden Pool', where towards the end of the previous night the full moon was setting in the West. The original draft here is even odder:

> The moon rose at last out of [?high] shadows ahead of them. It hardly showed yet any ... of its full light, but already away behind the mountains and the hollow land and the empty wastes day was beginning to grow pale.
>
> 'There comes White Face,' said Gollum. 'We doesn't like it. And Yellow Face is coming soon, sss. Two faces in sky together at once, not a good sign. And we've got some way to go.'

My father was certainly, as he wrote to me on 14 May 1944 (*Letters* no. 69), having 'trouble with the moon'.

In the manuscript the moon is still climbing above Ephel Dúath late in the night; only by a later change does it become 'the sinking moon' that 'escaped from the pursuing cloud' (TT p. 307).

5 The words in TT 'beyond sad Gondor now overwhelmed in shade' were a later addition.

6 At the head of the first stair there is evidently a track and not a tunnel, and therefore the later conception of the ascent to the pass is present (pp. 198–200).

Note on the Chronology

The time-schemes referred to as Scheme C and Scheme D (pp. 140–1) both cover this part of the narrative. Scheme C reads as follows (for comparison with the citations from *The Tale of Years* that follow I have added 'Day 1' etc. in both cases).

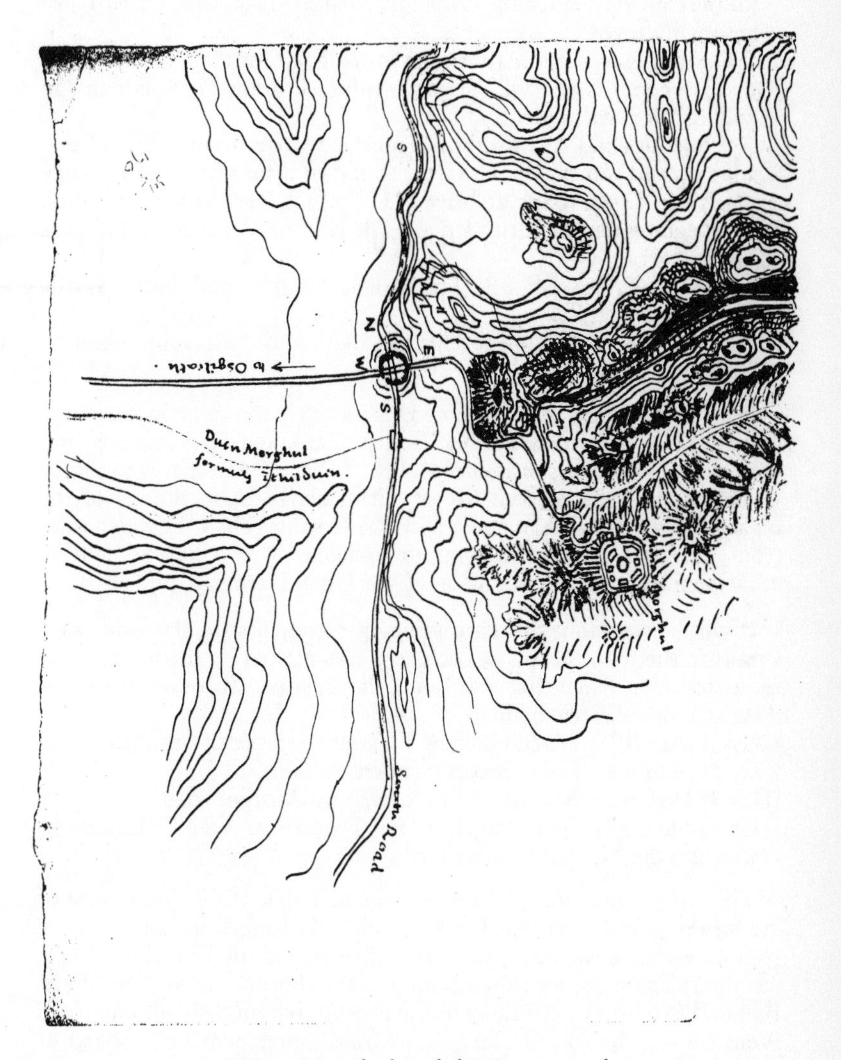

Minas Morghul and the Cross-roads

[Day 1] *Monday Feb. 6* Frodo and Sam in Ithilien. They are taken by Faramir. Battle with the Southrons. Frodo spends night at Henneth Annûn.

[Day 2] *Tuesday Feb. 7* Gollum captured in the Pool of Annûn in the early hours (5.30–6). Frodo Sam & Gollum leave Faramir, and journey all day reaching Osgiliath road at dusk, and go *east* just before midnight.

Faramir leaves Henneth Annûn for Minas Tirith.

[Day 3] *Wednesday Feb. 8* Faramir rides to Minas Tirith late in day and brings news to Gandalf.

Frodo lies hid in thornbrake until late afternoon (Gollum disappears and returns about 4.30). Sound of drums or thunder. They reach the Cross-roads at sunset (5.5 p.m.). Pass Minas Morghul, and begin ascent of Kirith Ungol. The host of Minas Morghul goes out to war.

[Day 4] *Thursday Feb. 9* Frodo etc. all day and night in the Mountains of Shadow.

Host of Minas Morghul reaches Osgiliath and crosses into realm of Gondor.

Here this scheme ends. Scheme D is precisely the same in dates and content, but continues further (see p. 226) and has some entries concerning Théoden's movements: Feb. 7 'Théoden prepares to ride to Gondor. Messengers from Minas Tirith arrive. Also tidings of the invasion of North Rohan and war in the North'; Feb. 8 'Théoden rides from Edoras'. The fully 'synoptic' scheme S also agrees, and in addition mentions the coming on of 'the Great Darkness' on Feb. 8.

It will be seen that this chronology precisely fits the narrative as it stands in the manuscript, i.e. before it was altered by the insertion of the extra day. When that was done, the (relative) chronology of *The Tale of Years* was reached:

[Day 1] *March 7* Frodo taken by Faramir to Henneth Annûn.

[Day 2] *March 8* Frodo leaves Henneth Annûn.

[Day 3] *March 9* At dusk Frodo reaches the Morgul-road.

[Day 4] *March 10* The Dawnless Day. Frodo passes the Cross Roads, and sees the Morgul-host set forth.

The synchronization of Frodo's story with that of the events west of Anduin required both that Frodo should take longer and that 'Day 4' should be the Dawnless Day. Thus in the original story Frodo and Sam see the red sunrise from their hiding in the thornbrake on 'Day 3'; in the final form they are hiding in the thornbrake on 'Day 4', and there is no sunrise, but a red glare over Mordor that 'was not the red of dawn'.

VIII
KIRITH UNGOL

In this chapter I shall describe the writing of the three last chapters of *The Two Towers*: 'The Stairs of Kirith Ungol', 'Shelob's Lair', and 'The Choices of Master Samwise'. As will be seen, this is dictated by the way in which my father developed the narrative.

This is the last part of *The Lord of the Rings* for which precise dating is possible, for when the doors of the Tower of Kirith Ungol slammed in Sam's face my father halted again for a long time, and when I returned to England in 1945 the constant correspondence between us naturally ceased. He wrote on 12 May 1944 (*Letters* no. 68) that 'we are now in sight of Minas Morghul'; and a good part of the work studied in this chapter must have been done during the following ten days, for on 21 May (*Letters* no. 70) he said:

> I have taken advantage of a bitter cold grey week ... to write: but struck a sticky patch. All that I had sketched or written before proved of little use, as times, motives, etc., have all changed. However at last with v. great labour, and some neglect of other duties, I have now written or nearly written all the matter up to the capture of Frodo in the high pass on the very brink of Mordor. Now I must go back to the other folk and try and bring things to the final crash with some speed. Do you think *Shelob* is a good name for a monstrous spider creature? It is of course only 'she + lob' (= spider), but written as one, it seems to be quite noisome.

Adding to this letter on the following day, Monday 22 May, he said:

> It was a wretched cold day yesterday (Sunday). I worked very hard at my chapter – it is most exhausting work; especially as the climax approaches and one has to keep the pitch up: no easy level will do; and there are all sorts of minor problems of plot and mechanism. I wrote and tore up and rewrote most of it a good many times; but I was rewarded this morning, as both C.S.L. and C.W. thought it an admirable performance, and the latest chapters the best so far. Gollum continues to develop into a most intriguing character.

At first sight the references in this letter seem inconsistent: in the past week he had written all or nearly all the story up to the capture of Frodo; he had just spent a day working hard 'at my chapter' (in the singular); and that morning he had read 'it' to Lewis and Williams. There are various ways of explaining this: my guess is that he had at this time got the whole story in draft, which he was still working on, and which he thought of as a 'chapter'; but what he read to Lewis and Williams was 'The Stairs of Kirith Ungol'. That this last is certainly the case is seen from his letter of 31 May 1944 (*Letters* no. 72):

> The rest of my time ... has been occupied by the desperate attempt to bring 'The Ring' to a suitable pause, the capture of Frodo by the Orcs in the passes of Mordor, before I am obliged to break off by examining. By sitting up all hours, I managed it: and read the last 2 chapters (*Shelob's Lair* and *The Choices of Master Samwise*) to C.S.L. on Monday morning.

It had indeed been a great labour. The elements were present: the climb to the high pass, the spider's lair, the webs in the tunnel, the use of the phial of Galadriel, the disappearance of Gollum, his treachery, the attack of the spider, the tower guarding the pass, the coming of the Orcs; but they long defied a satisfactory articulation. Perhaps in no part of *The Lord of the Rings* can the work behind the finished text be more clearly discerned than here.

Already when drafting the chapter 'The Black Gate is Closed' my father had sketched out his idea of the approach to Kirith Ungol (p. 124): there Gollum tells Frodo and Sam of 'A stair and path leading up into the mountains south of the pass, and then a tunnel, and then more stairs and then a cleft high above the main pass'. And in the outline that ends the original draft of that chapter (p. 125) it is foreseen that after leaving the Cross-roads they will see the moon shining on Minas Morghul; they will pass up the first stair, force their way through the tunnel 'black with webs of spiders', and get up the second stair which will bring them to Kirith Ungol; but 'Spiders are aroused and hunt them. They are exhausted.' Whether at that stage Kirith Ungol was guarded by a tower is not clear (see pp. 125–6).

But long before this, my father had written an account of the entry of Frodo and Sam into Mordor, which beginning as outline soon became narrative ('The Story Foreseen from Lórien', in *The Treason of Isengard*, pp. 330 ff.).[1] That story was very largely concerned with Sam's rescue of Frodo from Minas Morghul, which does not concern us here; but the first part of it is very relevant, for my father had it before him in May 1944, and I cite a portion of it again here (taking up the various additions made to the text that were certainly present when he now turned to it).

> The three companions now approach Kirith Ungol, the dreadful ravine which leads into Gorgoroth.[2] Kirith Ungol means Spider Glen: there dwelt great spiders, greater than those of Mirkwood, such as were once of old in the land of Elves and Men in the West that is now under sea, such as Beren fought in the dark cañons of the Mountains of Terror above Doriath. Already Gollum knew these

creatures well. He slips away. The spiders come and weave their nets over Frodo while Sam sleeps: sting Frodo. Sam wakes, and sees Frodo lying pale as death – greenish: reminding him of the faces in the pools of the marshes. He cannot rouse or wake him.

The idea suddenly comes to Sam to carry on the work, and he felt for the Ring. He could not unclasp it, nor cut the chain, but he drew the chain over Frodo's head. As he did so he fancied he felt a tremor (sigh or shudder) pass through the body; but when he paused he could not feel any heart-beat. Sam put the Ring round his own neck.

Then he sat and made a *Lament for Frodo*. After that he put away his tears and thought what he could do. He could not leave his dear master lying in the wild for the fell beasts and carrion birds; and he thought he would try and build a cairn of stones about him. 'The silver mail of mithril rings shall be his winding-sheet,' he said. 'But I will lay the phial of Lady Galadriel upon his breast, and Sting shall be at his side.'

He laid Frodo upon his back and crossed his arms on his breast and set Sting at his side. And as he drew out the phial it blazed with light. It lit Frodo's face and it looked now pale but beautiful, fair with an elvish beauty as of one long past the shadows. 'Farewell, Frodo,' said Sam; and his tears fell on Frodo's hands.

But at that moment there was a sound of strong footfalls climbing towards the rock shelf. Harsh calls and cries echoed in the rocks. Orcs were coming, evidently guided to the spot.

'Curse that Gollum,' said Sam. 'I might have known we had not seen the last of him. These are some of his friends.'

Sam had no time to lose. Certainly no time to hide or cover his master's body. Not knowing what else to do he slipped on the Ring, and then he took also the phial so that the foul Orcs should not get it, and girded Sting about his own waist. And waited. He had not long to wait.

In the gloom first came Gollum sniffing out the scent, and behind him came the black orcs: fifty or more it seemed. With a cry they rushed upon Frodo. Sam tried to put up a fight unseen, but even as he was about to draw Sting he was run down and trampled by the rush of the Orcs. All the breath was knocked out of his body. Courage failed him. In great glee the Orcs seized Frodo and lifted him.

'There was another, yes,' whined Gollum. 'Where is he, then?' said the Orcs. 'Somewheres nigh. Gollum feels him, Gollum sniffs him.'

'Well, you find him, sniveller,' said the Orc-chief. 'He can't go far without getting into trouble. We've got what we want. Ringbearer! Ringbearer!' They shouted in joy. 'Make haste. Make haste. Send one swift to Barradur to the Great One. But we cannot wait here – we must get back to our guard post. Bear the prisoner to Minas

Morgul.' (Gollum runs behind wailing that the Precious is not there.)

Even as they do so, Frodo seems to awake, and gives a loud cry, but they gag him. Sam is torn between joy at learning he is alive and horror at seeing him carried off by Orcs. Sam tries to follow, but they go very speedily. The Ring seems to grow in power in this region: he sees clearly in the dark, and seems to understand the orcs' speech. He fears what may happen if he meets a Ringwraith – the Ring does not confer courage: poor Sam trembles all the time. Sam gathers that they are going to Minas Morgul ...

Sam follows the Orcs as they march off to Minas Morgul, and sees them entering the city; then he follows them in.

My father now wrote a new outline, and it is clear that he wrote it before he had proceeded far with the story that constitutes the chapter 'The Stairs of Kirith Ungol'. The original draft of 'Journey to the Cross-roads' in fact continued straight on into what would become the next chapter, but soon became no more than a sketch. Frodo's sudden crazed dash towards the bridge (TT p. 313) was absent; after scarcely legible words corresponding to the later 'Frodo felt his senses reeling and his mind darkening' follows:

Gollum again drew him away. Not that way ..... he hissed ..... but the sound seemed to tear the air like a whistle. Not that way. He drew them aside and [?shrinking] after him they left the road and began to climb up into the darkness on the northern side of the valley, ... their eyes away from the city on their right, but always looking back again.

It is here that the placing of the high pass (Kirith Ungol) on the north side of the Morghul Vale first appears. Then follows:

They came to a .... and steps and laboured on. As they rose above the exhalations of the valley their track became easier and the [*or* their] steps less heavy and slow. But at last they could go no further. They were in a narrow place where the path or road – if it were one – was no more than a wide ledge winding along the face of the mountain shoulder. Before them it seemed to vanish into the shadow or into the very rock itself.

They halted and at that moment a great red flash lit up the valley. In that place of shadow and pale phosphorescent light it seemed unbearable, suddenly fierce and cruel. Two peaks with notches between sprang suddenly [?black] into view against the [?sudden] fire behind. At the same moment a great [?crack] of thunder ....

There follows an illegible sentence that seems to refer to the great screeching cry, and the text ends with a reference to the coming forth of the host of Morghul.

At this point the new outline for the whole 'Kirith Ungol' story begins. Written at great speed and in pencil, it is often exceedingly difficult to make out, and in one passage very hard to follow.

Description of the endless long black lines. *Rider ahead.* He halts and sweeps glance round valley. Frodo's temptation to put on Ring. At last the host [?passes] away.

The [?storm] is bursting – they are going to Osgiliath and the crossing of the River he said. Will Faramir be across? Will army slay them?

[*Added:* long [?journey] up. Frodo uses phial.]

They pass into the tunnel. Halfway through they find it blocked with webs. Gollum refuses to say what they are. Frodo goes ahead and hews a path with Sting. Sam helps.

At other end after long struggle in dark he finds a *stair*. They can no longer see into valley, as sheer walls of rock are on either side. The stair goes up, up endlessly. [?Occasional] webs across path.

Gollum hangs back. They begin to have suspicion of him. Description of the spiders? There dwelt great creatures in spider form such as lived once of old in the Land of the Elves in the West that is now under the Sea, such as Beren fought in the dark ravines of the Mountains of Terror above Doriath. All light they snared and wove into impenetrable webs. Pale-fleshed, many-eyed, venomous they were, older and more horrible than the black creatures of Mirkwood. Already Gollum had met them: he knew them well. But thought to use them for his purposes.

They come out at last to the head of the stair. The road opens a little. There is still an ominous glare. They see the road [?clearly] .. through a [?narrow] cleft and now the right wall sinks and they look down into a vast darkness, the great cleft which was the head of Morghul Vale. On the left sharp jagged pinnacles full of black crevices. And high upon one tip a small black tower.[3]

What is that tower? said Frodo full of suspicion. Is there a guard? Then they found Gollum had slipped away and vanished.

Frodo is full of fear. But Sam says Well we're up this .... near very top of mountains. Further than we ever hoped to get. Let's go on and get it over.

Frodo goes forward and Sam follows. Sam is suddenly lassooed and falls back. He calls out but Frodo does not come. He struggles up and falls again – something is round his feet. Slashes himself free in a fury of rage. Frodo master he cries, and then sees the great spider that has attacked him. He lunges forward but the creature makes off. Then he sees that there [are] a great number about – issuing out of the crevices, but they are all hurrying forward along the road, taking no further notice of him.

Lines are drawn on the manuscript here, and though the immediately preceding passage was not struck out it was obviously rejected at this point. Its meaning is not immediately plain: does 'him' in 'the great spider that has attacked him' refer to Sam or to Frodo? On general grounds it might seem at first sight more likely to be Frodo: in both the earlier outlines it was Frodo who was the victim, and so also in the version that replaced this. That Frodo would be the victim here also cannot indeed be doubted; but it seems to me certain that 'him' is in fact Sam – precisely because he escaped (and the words 'lassooed' and 'slashes himself free' clearly refer to attack by a spider). Sam had to be delayed in some way so that he was not at hand when the attack on Frodo took place. The first idea was that one of the spiders went for Sam too, but unsuccessfully; my father then saw at once that it was not a spider that came on him from behind, but Gollum. What idea lay behind the statement that the other spiders were all hurrying forward along the path and taking no further notice of Sam is not clear, but presumably they were going after Frodo (instigated by Gollum?).

Returning to the beginning of the last paragraph, the outline continues:

Sam suddenly sees the spiders coming out of crevices. He can't see Frodo and calls out in warning, but at that moment he is seized from behind. He can't draw sword. Gollum trips him and he falls. Gollum tries to get at Sam's sword. Sam has long fight and eventually gets hand on his stave and deals Gollum a blow. Gollum wriggles aside and only gets a whack across his hands. He lets go. Sam is aiming another blow at him when he springs away and going like lightning disappears into a crevice. Sam rushes forward to find Frodo. He is too late. There are great spiders round him. Sam draws sword and fights but they don't seem to [?heed] it. Then he found Sting lying by Frodo's outstretched arm. (2 or 3 dead spiders by him.)

He seizes Sting and drives off the spiders. Frodo lying as if dead. Spiders have stung him. He is pale as death. Sam uses phial. Reminds Sam of his vision in the mirror of Galadriel.[4] All efforts to rouse his master fail. He can hear or feel no heart beat. He is dead. Sam [?falls] first into senseless rage against Gollum [?beating] the stones and shouting at him to come out and fight. Then into a black despair of grief. How long he sat there he never knew. He came out of this black trance to find Frodo still just as he had left him, but now greenish in hue, a horrible dead look with a ....[5]

Sam remembers he himself had said that he had a job to do. Wonders if it has come to him now. He takes the phial and Sting and buckles belt. Sam the two-sworded he says grimly. Prays for strength to fight and avenge Frodo. At that moment he would have marched straight to death, straight to the very Eye of Baraddur.

Two additions were made at the time of writing to the text on this page, the first directed to this point by an arrow: 'Lament see 5c'. This is a reference to the previous outline story, where the words 'Then he sat and made a *Lament for Frodo*' (p. 185) appear on a page numbered '5 continued'. The other addition is conveniently given here, since it is needed to explain the narrative immediately following:

> Orcs have *captured* Gollum – all his little plan of getting Frodo tied up by spiders has gone [?wrong]. They are driving Gollum.

The text continues:

Noise of [?approaching] Orc-laughter. Down out of a cleft Gollum leading comes a band of black orcs. Desperate Sam draws off the ring from Frodo's neck and takes it. He could not unclasp it or cut the chain so he slipped it over Frodo's neck and put it on. As he did so he stumbled forward, it was as if a great stone had been suddenly strung about his neck. At that moment up come orcs. Sam slips on Ring.

Frodo cries – or is Sam's motive simply that [?wishing] to bury Frodo: he won't see Frodo's body carried off. Also wanting to get at Gollum.

To clarify the syntax of the sentence beginning 'Frodo cries' the word *wishing* (?) might be read as *wishes* (sc. 'he wishes'), or *of* might be understood before *wishing*; but even so my father's thought is most elliptically expressed and difficult to follow. However, since immediately beneath these last two sentences he drew lines on the manuscript, implying that the story just sketched was about to be modified, I think that an interpretation on these lines may be correct. 'Frodo cries' is to be understood in relation to the earlier outline

(p. 186): when the Orcs take Frodo he 'seems to awake, and gives a loud cry'. The following words ('or is Sam's motive...') show my father breaking off altogether, and questioning the rightness of what he had just outlined: perhaps this story of Sam's taking the Ring from Frodo because of the approaching Orcs was wrong. Perhaps Sam's only 'motive' (meaning his only purpose, or desire) at this juncture was not to leave Frodo simply lying where he fell (cf. the previous outline, p. 185: 'He could not leave his dear master lying in the wild for the fell beasts and carrion birds; and he thought he would try and build a cairn of stones about him') – and his desire to take revenge on Gollum. I think that some such interpretation is borne out by the revised story that immediately follows.

Make Sam *sit* long by Frodo all through night. Hold phial up and see him elvish-fair. Torn by not knowing what to do. He lays Frodo out, and folds his hands. Mithril coat. Phial in his hand. Sting at side.

Tries to go on and finish job. Can't force himself to. How to die [?soon]. Thinks of jumping over brink. But might as well try to do *something*. Crack of Doom? Reluctantly as it seems a theft in a way he takes Ring. Goes forward on the path in a violent sorrow and despair. [*In margin:* Red dawn.] But cannot drag himself away from Frodo. Turns back – resolved to lie down by Frodo till death comes. Then he sees Gollum come and paw him. He gives a start and runs back. But orcs come out and Gollum bolts. Orcs pick up Frodo and carry him off. Sam plods after them. *Sam puts on ring!* It seems to have grown in might and power. It weighs down his hand. But he can see with terrible clearness – even *through* the rocks. He can see every crevice filled with spiders. He can understand orc speech. But the ring does *not* confer courage on Sam.

It seems they had been warned for *special vigilance*. Some spy of more than usual importance could try to get in somehow. If any were caught messenger to be [?sent]. *Phial taken.* Sam follows up a long stair to the tower. He can see all plain below. The Black Gate and Ithilien and Gorgoroth and Mt. Doom.

Here this outline ends. As revised in the course of its composition, the story now stood thus in its essential structure:

- They enter a tunnel, which halfway through is blocked with webs. Frodo shears the webs with Sting.
- At the end of the tunnel they come to a long stair. (Description of the spiders, which are well known to Gollum.)

- At the top of the stair they see the tower; and find that Gollum has disappeared.
- Frodo goes ahead; Sam behind sees spiders coming and cries out to Frodo, but at that moment is grappled by Gollum from behind. Sam fights him off, and Gollum escapes.
- Sam finds Frodo dead, as he thinks, stung by spiders. He seizes Sting and drives them off; he sits by Frodo all night; puts the phial in his hand and Sting beside him.
- He thinks that he must himself attempt Frodo's task, takes the Ring and sets off.
- But he cannot do this, and turns back; he sees Gollum come out and paw at Frodo, but as he runs back Orcs come and Gollum flees.
- The Orcs pick up Frodo and carry him off.
- Sam puts on the Ring, and follows the Orcs up a stair to the tower.

Comparison of this outline with the old one shows that the new narrative was a development from it, and by no means an entirely fresh start; here and there even the wording was preserved. The single Great Spider had not yet emerged. But (considered simply as a step-by-step structure) it was already transformed, partly through the wholly different conception of the pass of Kirith Ungol, partly through the changed view of Gollum's rôle; and even as the new outline was set on paper his rôle was changed further. At first the Orcs were guided to the spot by Gollum, though he was forced to do so, his own nefarious plan being entirely based on the spiders; but by the time my father had reached the end of it he had decided that Gollum had in fact no traffic whatsoever with the Orcs.

The idea that the tunnel was barred by great webs is present, but since Frodo was able to cut a way through with Sting their presence does not affect the actual evolution of the plot. The words 'Gollum refuses to say what they are' suggest that they entered the story as the explanation of what Gollum's 'little plan' had actually been: and that, I take it, was that Frodo and Sam should be entrapped in the tunnel and so delivered to the spiders. But he had not envisaged that Frodo's elvish blade would be able to cut the strands.

The important element now enters that Frodo went ahead when they issued from the tunnel (and thus Sam had become separated from him when he was attacked by the spiders), although no explanation of this is given.

A very notable feature of this outline is that Sam's clarity of vision when he wears the Ring is not merely retained from the old plot ('The Ring seems to grow in power in this region: he sees clearly in the dark', p. 186), but is greatly increased: he can even see *through* the rocks; in TT (p. 343), on the other hand, 'all things about him now were not dark but vague; while he himself was there in a grey hazy world, alone, like a small black solid rock'. On this question see VII.373–4, 380–1; and for the further development of this element (the effect of the Ring on Sam's senses) see pp. 212, 214.

The fair copy manuscript was built up in stages. From the beginning of the chapter 'The Stairs of Kirith Ungol', as far as 'Frodo felt his senses reeling, his limbs weakening' (cf. TT p. 313), it was developed from the original draft (p. 186) and virtually attained the form in TT; but from this point my father briefly returned to his frustrating practice of erasing his pencilled draft and writing the fair copy on the pages where it had stood. This only extends for a couple of pages, however, and some words and phrases escaped erasure; while on the third page the draft was not erased but overwritten, and here much of the original text can be read. This carries the narrative to the point (TT p. 317) where the host out of Minas Morghul had disappeared down the westward road and Sam urged Frodo to rouse himself; and there is no reason whatever to think that the lost pages of the draft were other than a more roughly expressed version of the final narrative.[6]

But from this point (where the pencilled draft reads: 'Frodo rose, grasping his staff in one hand and the phial in the other. Then he saw that a faint light was welling through his fingers and he thrust it in his bosom') the original narrative diverged, and was followed in the fair copy manuscript (where it was subsequently replaced by the later story). This first form of the fully-written story may be called 'Version 1'. The textual situation at this point is odd and perplexing, but it is sufficient to say here that the opening of this section (of no great length) is lost, both in draft and fair copy, and the story only takes up again with the strange smell that the hobbits could not identify (cf. 'Shelob's Lair' in TT, p. 326).[7]

I feel certain that the lost lines carried an account of the climbing of *the first stair*, leading to an opening in the rock which was *the mouth of the tunnel*, from which the strange smell came (whereas in TT the text at this point tells how after the passage of the ledge the path came to 'a narrow opening in the rock' which was the entry to the high-walled *first stair*). My father still had in mind the series described in the draft text of 'The Black Gate is Closed' (p. 124), where Gollum says 'a *stair* and path, and *then a tunnel*, and *then more stairs* and then a cleft high above the main pass', and again in the following outline (p. 125), where they 'pass up *first stair* safely. But *tunnel* is black with webs of spiders. ... force way and get up *second stair*.' And again, in the original draft for 'The Stairs of Kirith Ungol' (p. 186), when they began to climb up from the valley they came to 'steps'. Further evidence in support of this will appear shortly.

After the obliterated lines the original story continues thus.

... a strange odour came out of it – not the odour of decay in the valley below, an odour that the hobbits did not recognize, a repellent taint on the air.[8]

Resigning themselves to fear they passed inside. It was altogether lightless. After some little time Sam suddenly tumbled into Gollum ahead of him and Frodo against Sam. 'What's up now?' said Sam. 'Brought us to a dead end, have you?' 'Dead end – that's good,' he muttered. 'It about describes it.' 'What's up, you old villain?' Gollum did not answer him.

Sam pushed him aside and thrust forward, only to meet something that yielded but would not give way, soft, unseen and strong as if the darkness could be felt. 'Something's across the path,' he said. 'Some trap or something. What's to be done? If this old villain knows about it, as I bet he does, why won't he speak?'

'Because he doesn't know,' hissed Gollum. 'He's thinking. We didn't expect to find this here, did we precious? No, of course not. We wants to get out, of course we does, yes, yes.'

'Stand back,' said Frodo, and then suddenly drawing his hand from his bosom he held aloft the phial of Galadriel. For a moment it flickered, like a star struggling through the mists of Earth, then as fear left him it began to burn[9] with dazzling silver light, as if Earendel himself had come down from the sunset paths with the Silmaril upon his brow. Gollum cowered away from the light, which for some reason seemed to fill him with fear.

Frodo drew his sword, and Sting leapt out. The bright rays of the star-glass sparkled upon the blade, but on its edges ran an ominous blue fire – to which at that time Frodo nor Sam gave heed.

'Version 1' in the fair copy manuscript stops here, at the foot of a page, the remainder having been taken out of it when rejected and replaced.[10] The next page of 'Version 1' is preserved, however; it was separated from the other 'Kirith Ungol' papers many years ago, and is now in the Bodleian Library at Oxford, among other illustrations to *The Lord of the Rings* – for the verso of the page, in addition to text, bears a picture of the ascent to Kirith Ungol. This was reproduced in *Pictures by J. R. R. Tolkien* (no. 28, 'Shelob's Lair'), and is reproduced again in this book (first frontispiece). That the recto of the page is the continuation of the text from the point reached is assured both by the page-number '[6]', following '[5]' in the fair copy manuscript, and by internal association, notably Sam's words when he sees that they are confronted by spiders' webs: 'Why didn't you speak, Gollum?' (cf. his words on the preceding page: 'Something's across the path... If this old villain knows about it, as I bet he does, why won't he speak?'). The recto reads thus:

Before them was a greyness which the light did not penetrate. Dull and heavy it *absorbed* the light. Across the whole width of the tunnel from floor to floor and side to side were ....[11] webs. Orderly as the webs of spiders, but far greater: each thread as thick as a great cord.

Sam laughed grimly when he saw them. 'Cobwebs,' he said. 'Is that all! Why didn't you speak, Gollum? But I might have guessed for myself! Cobwebs! Mighty big ones, but we'll get at them.' He drew his sword and hewed, but the thread that he struck did not break, it yielded and then sprang back like a bowstring, turning the blade and tossing his sword and arm backward. Three times Sam struck, and at last one thread snapped, twisting and curling, whipping about like a snapped harpstring. As an end lashed Sam's hand and stung like a whip. [*sic*] He cried out and stood back. 'It'd take weeks this way,' he said. 'Let me try Bilbo's sword,' said Frodo. 'I will go ahead now: *hold my star-glass behind me.*' Frodo drew Sting[12] and made a great sweeping stroke and sprang back to avoid the lashing of the threads.

The sharp elven-blade blue-edged sparkling shore through the netted ropes and that web was destroyed. But there were others behind. Slowly Frodo hewed his way through them until at last they came to a clear way again. Sam came behind holding up the light and pushing Gollum – strangely reluctant – before him. Gollum kept on trying to wriggle away and turn back.[13]

At length they came to more webs, and when they had cut through these the tunnel came to an end.

The rock wall opened out and sprang high and the second stair was before them: walls on either side towering up to a great height – how high they could not guess, for the sky was hardly less black than the walls – and could only be discerned by an occasional glow and flicker of red on the underside of the clouds. The stair seemed endless, up, up, up. Their knees cracked. Here and there was a web across the way. They were in the very heart of the mountains. Up, up.

At last they got to the stair-head. The road opened out. Then all their suspicions of Gollum came to a head. He sprang unexpectedly out of Sam's reach forward, and thrusting Frodo aside ran out emitting a shrill sort of whistling cry, such as they had never heard him make before.

'Come here! you wretch,' cried Sam darting after him. Gollum turned once with his eyes glittering, and then vanished quite suddenly into the gloom, and no sign of him could they find.[14]

The verso of the page, numbered '[7]', carrying the picture of the ascent to the pass,[15] has the following text.

'That's that!' said Sam. 'What I expected. But I don't like it. I suppose now we are just exactly where he wanted to bring us. Well, let's get moving away as quick as we can. The treacherous worm! That last whistle of his wasn't pure joy at getting out of the tunnel, it was pure wickedness of some sort. And what sort we'll soon know.'

'Likely enough,' said Frodo. 'But we could not have got even so far without him. So if we ever manage our errand, then Gollum and all his wickedness will be part of the plan.'

'So far, you say,' said Sam. 'How far? Where are we now?'

'About at the crest of the main range of Ephel-dúath, I guess,' said Frodo. 'Look!' The road opened out now: it still went on up, but no longer sheerly. Beyond and ahead there was an ominous glare in the sky, and like a great notch in the mountain wall a cleft was outlined against it — so [*here is a small sketch*]. On their right the wall of rock fell away and the road widened till it had no brink. Looking down Frodo saw nothing but the vast darkness of the great ravine which was the head of Morghul dale. Down in its depths was the faint glimmer of the wraith-road that led over the Morghul pass from the city. On their left sharp jagged pinnacles stood up like towers carved by the biting years, and between them were many dark crevices and clefts. But high up on the left side of the cleft to which their road led (Kirith Ungol) was a small black tower, and in it a window showed a red light.

'I don't like the look of that,' said Sam. 'This upper pass is guarded too. D'you remember he never would say if it was or no. D'you think he's gone to fetch them – orcs or something?'

'No, I don't think so,' said Frodo. 'He is up to no good, of course, but I don't think that he's gone to fetch orcs. Whatever it is, it is no slave of the Dark Lord's.' 'I suppose not,' said Sam. 'No, I suppose the whole time it has been the ring for poor

Smeagol's own. That's been his scheme. But how coming up here will help him, I can't guess.' He was soon to learn.

Frodo went forward now – the last lap – and he exerted all his strength. He felt that if once he could get to the saddle of the pass and look over into the Nameless Land he would have accomplished something. Sam followed. He sensed evil all round him. He knew that they had walked into some trap, but what? He had sheathed his sword, but now he drew it in readiness. He halted for a moment, and stooped to pick up his staff with his left hand

Here the text on the 'Bodleian page' ends, but the further continuation of this extraordinarily dismembered text is found among the papers that failed to go to Marquette.[16] The next page is duly numbered '[8]' and '[9]', and continues as before in ink over pencilled drafting.

– it had a comfortable feel to his hand. As he stood up again, he saw issuing out of a crevice at the left the most monstrous and loathly form that he had ever beheld – beyond his imagination.[17] Spider-like it was in shape, but huge as a wild beast, and more terrible because of the malice and evil purpose in its eyes. These were many, clustered in its small head, and each of them held a baleful light. On great bent legs it walked – the hairs of them stuck out like steel spines, and at each end there was a claw. The round swollen body behind its narrow neck was dark blotched with paler livid marks, but underneath its belly was pale and faintly luminous as its eyes. It stank. It moved with a sudden horrible speed running on its arms, and springing. Sam saw at once that he [*sic*] was hunting his master – now a little ahead in the gloom and apparently unaware of his peril. He whipped out his sword and yelled. 'Look out! Mr Frodo! Look out! I'm —' But he did not finish. A long clammy hand went over his mouth and another caught his neck, while something wrapped itself about his legs. Taken off his guard he fell backwards in the arms of his attacker.

'Got you!' hissed Gollum in his ear. 'At last my precious one, we've got him yes, the nasty hobbit. We takes this one. She'll get the other. O yes. Ungoliant will get him.[18] Not Smeagol. He won't hurt master, not at all. He promised. But he's got you, you nasty dirty little thing!'

The description of the fight is closely similar to that in TT (p. 335), with some difference in the detail of the wrestling.[19] After the second blow, falling across Gollum's back, the text continues:

But it was enough for Gollum! Grabbing from behind was an old game for him – and had never before failed him. But everything had gone wrong with his beautiful plan, since the unexpected web in the path. Here now he was faced by a furious enemy, little less than his own size, with a stout staff. This was not for him. He had no time even to grab at the sword lying on the ground. He squealed as the staff came down once more,[20] and sprang aside onto all fours, and then leaped away like a cat in one big bound. Then with astonishing speed he ran back and vanished into the tunnel. Sweeping up his sword Sam went after him – for the moment forgetful of all else, but the red light of fury in his brain. But Gollum had gone before he could reach him. Then as the dark hole and the stench smote him, like a terrible clap of thunder the thought of Frodo came back to Sam's mind. He span round, and rushed on up the road calling. He was too late. So far Gollum's plot had succeeded.

Frodo was lying on the ground and the monster was bending over him, so intent upon her victim that she seemed not to heed anything else until Sam was close at hand. It was not a brave deed Sam then did, for he gave no thought to it. Frodo was already bound in great cords round and round from ankle to breast, and with her great forelegs she was beginning to half lift, half drag him, but still his arms were free: one hand was on his breast, one lay spread wide, limp upon the stone, and the staff of Faramir broken under him.

At the point where Sam sees that Frodo is bound with cords the underlying pencilled draft stops; the legible fair copy in ink written over it continues, but at the same point declines very rapidly into the handwriting characteristic of initial drafting, decipherable only with labour and in this case often not at all.[21] This continues to the end of the page ('9' in the Version I text, the last page in this numeration), with Sam's attack on 'Ungoliant'. Many words and even whole sentences are totally illegible, but enough can be made out to see that in this earliest form of the story it was Sam's slash with Sting across Ungoliant's belly that caused her to leap back: there is no suggestion of the great wound she suffered when she drove her whole bulk down onto the point of the sword (TT p. 338). When she sprang back 'Sam stood reeling, his legs astride his master, but she a few paces off eyed him: and the green venom that was her blood slowly suffused the pale light of her eyes. Sting held before him, Sam now .... and ere she attacked again he found his master's hand in his bosom. It was cold and limp, and quickly but gently he took from it the glass of Galadriel. And held it up.'

This rough drafting continues on other pages (not numbered on from '9', though that proves little); but I doubt that much more of it, if any, was written at this juncture (see p. 209). The question is not of much importance in the study of the evolution of the story, and in any case it is more convenient to pause here in the original draft.

The fact that my father had overwritten legibly in ink the original draft as far as the stinging of Frodo by Ungoliant suggests confidence in the story, while the sudden change from 'fair copy' to 'preliminary draft' at this point suggests that he now realised that important changes were required. The immediate reason for this may well have been that he observed what he had just written, as it were inadvertently: 'Then with astonishing speed [Gollum] ran back and vanished *into the tunnel.* ... Then as the dark hole and the stench smote him ... the thought of Frodo came back to Sam's mind. He span round, and rushed on up the road calling.' But in this version the far end of the tunnel was immediately succeeded by the agonisingly long second stair, and it was only after they reached the head of it that Gollum ran off (p. 194). The picture of the ascent to the pass contained in this text (see p. 193) shows with perfect clarity the *first stair* climbing up to the tunnel, and the *second* stair climbing away beyond it.[22] It is obviously out of the question that my father imagined that Gollum fled all the way down the second stair with Sam in pursuit, and that Sam then climbed up again! I think that the developing narrative was forcing a new topography to appear even as he wrote (see below).

There seem in fact to have been several interrelated questions. One was this of topography: the relation of the stairs and the tunnel. Another was the time and place of Gollum's disappearance. In the outline (p. 187) he is found to have vanished when they come to the head of the second stair; and in the present version he ran off with a strange whistling cry when they came to that place. And another was the question of Gollum's plan and its miscarriage. My father had written (p. 197): 'But everything had gone wrong with his beautiful plan, *since the unexpected web in the path*.' It certainly seems to be the case in this version that Gollum was very put out when they encountered it in the tunnel: 'We didn't expect to find this here, did we precious? No, of course not' (p. 193); and after the first webs had been cut through Gollum was 'strangely reluctant' to go on, and 'kept on trying to wriggle away and turn back.'

Leaving the 'Version I' text, now reduced to very rough drafting, at some point not determined, my father scribbled on a little bit of paper:

Must be stair — stair — tunnel. Tunnel is Ungoliante's lair. The tunnel has unseen passages off. One goes right up to dungeons of tower. But orcs don't use it much because of Ungoliant. She has a great hole in the midst of path. Plan fails because she has made a *web* across path and is daunted by the phial-light. Stench out of *hole* which phial prevents Frodo and Sam falling into. Gollum disappears and they think he may have fallen in hole. They cut their way out of web at far end. Ungoliant comes out of tunnel.

Thus the series 'first stair — tunnel — second stair' inherent in the Version 1 story is changed. The reason for this was, I think, as follows. The arrangement 'stair — tunnel — stair' arose when there were many spiders in the pass; in the outline the tunnel seems only one part of their territory, and there are webs also across the second stair (p. 187) — the impression is given that all the cliffs and crags bordering the path are alive with them. But with the reduction of the spider-horde to one Great Spider, whose lair is very clearly in the tunnel (where the great webs were), her attack on the hobbits at the head of the second stair, high above the tunnel, becomes unsatisfactory. It was therefore not long after the emergence in Version 1 of Ungoliant as the sole breeder of the terror of Kirith Ungol that this version collapsed, and my father abandoned the writing of it in fair copy manuscript. Associated with this would have been the decision that Gollum deserted Frodo and Sam while they were still in the tunnel.

The plot outlined in the brief text just given is not very clear; but at this same time, perhaps on the same day, my father wrote the fuller note, together with a plan of the tunnels, that is reproduced on p. 201. This also is in the Bodleian Library (see p. 193). The title *Plan of Shelob's Lair* was written onto the page subsequently, since the name of the Spider in the text is Ungoliant(e); cf. note 15.

This text reads:

Must be Stair — Stair — Tunnel. Tunnel is Ungoliante's Lair.

This tunnel is of orc-make (?) and has the usual branching passages. One goes right up into the dungeons of the Tower – but orcs don't use it much because of Ungoliante.[23] Ungoliante has made a hole and a trap in the middle of the floor of the main path.

Gollum's plan was to get Frodo into trap. He hoped to get Ring, and leave the rest to Ungoliant. Plan failed because Ungoliant was suspicious of him — ? he had come nosing up as far as the tunnel the day before? — and she had put a web on near (west) side of hole. When Frodo held up the phial she was daunted for [a] moment and retreated to her lair. But when the hobbits issued from tunnel she came out by side paths and crept round them.

Phial prevents F. and S. falling into the hole; but a horrible stench comes out of it. Gollum disappears and they fear he has fallen in the hole. But they do not go back — (a) they see tower with a light on cliffs at head of pass and (b) while they are wondering about this and suspect betrayal the attack is made: Ungoliant going for Frodo, while Gollum grapples Sam from behind. Ungol[iant] specially wants the star-glass? (Frodo had hidden it again when he came out of tunnel).

Web at end of tunnel?

The plan of the tunnel was mostly drawn in pencil and then overdrawn in black ink. The word pencilled against the minor tunnel to the north of the main passage seems to read 'Bypas[s]'. The pencilled circle in the main passage is marked 'Trap', and the large black circle 'Ungoliant's lair'. Of the two southward tunnels that leave the main one near its eastern end, the westerly one is marked 'Underground way to Tower', and the broad tunnel (drawn with several lines) that leaves this one eastwards will be the way by which Ungoliant emerged to the attack. The last tunnel branching southwards from the main one was added in blue ball-point pen, and is marked 'orc-path'.[24]

Since my father is seen in these notes actually setting down his decision that the second stair preceded the tunnel, it was presumably at this juncture that (leaving aside the question of how far the further story had progressed at this time) he turned back to the point where the faulty conception entered the narrative (see p. 192); and indeed on the back of the first of these notes is found drafting for the new version of the story dependent on the decision (cf. TT p. 317):

> Following him they came to the climbing ledge. Not daring to look down to their right they passed along it. At last it came to a rounded angle where the mountain-side swelled out again before them. There the path suddenly entered into a dark opening in the rock, and there before them was the first stair that Gollum had spoken of.

Then follows the description of the first stair. Thus the 'opening in the rock' was neatly transformed from the mouth of the tunnel into the beginning of the stair (p. 192).

Continuous drafting is found for the revised narrative ('Version 2'), and the story as told in TT was very largely achieved already in the draft as far as the events in the tunnel: the climbs up the Straight Stair and the Winding Stair, the hobbits' rest beside the path, their talk of the need to find water[25] leading to the conversation about tales (written down *ab initio* in a form closely similar to that in TT), their

Plan of Shelob's Lair 16

Winding Stair — stair — Tunnel. Tunnel is Ungoliant's lair.

This tunnel was is of orc-make (?) and has the usual branching passages. One goes right up into the dungeons of the Tower — [but Orcs don't use, [illegible] because of Ungoliant?] Ungoliant has made a hole and a trap in the middle of the floor of the main path.

N E W S

The Tower

Tunnel

Trap

Ungoliant's lair

Gollum's plan was to get Frodo into trap. He hoped to get Ring, and leave the rest to Ungoliant. Plan failed because Ungoliant was suspicious of them — ? he had [illegible] up so far as the tunnel the day before? — and she had posted watch on near (west) side of hole. When Frodo held up the phial she was daunted for moment and retreated to her lair. But when the hobbits issued from tunnel she came out by side paths and crept round them.

Phial prevented Frodo & Sam falling into the hole, but a horrible stench [illegible] of it. Gollum disappears and they fear he has fallen in the hole. But they don't go back — because (a) they [illegible] tower with a light [illegible] at head of pass. or (b) while they are wondering about this and suspect [illegible] the attack is made. Ungoliant going for Frodo, while Gollum grapples Sam from behind. Ungol specially wants the Star-glass? (Frodo had hidden it again when he came out of tunnel).

Hole at end of tunnel?

Plan of Shelob's Lair (1)

realisation that Gollum had disappeared, his return, finding them asleep (with the description of his 'interior debate', looking back up towards the pass and shaking his head, his appearance as of 'an old weary hobbit who had lived beyond his time and lost all his friends and kin: a starved old thing sad and pitiable'), and Sam's unhappy mistaking of his gesture towards Frodo (TT pp. 317–25, where the chapter 'The Stairs of Cirith Ungol' ends). A few passages in TT are lacking in the draft, but they are not of importance to the narrative and in any case they appear in the fair copy manuscript.

A little pencilled sketch appears on the page of the draft where they first see the tower (TT p. 319) – just as there was a picture of the earlier conception of Kirith Ungol at this point in Version 1 (where they had already passed through the tunnel). In the foreground of this sketch is seen the path from the head of the Second Stair, where (in the words of the draft text) the hobbits 'saw jagged pinnacles of stone on either side: columns and spikes torn and carven in the biting years and forgotten winters, and between them great crevices and fissures showed black even in the heavy gloom of that unfriendly place.' The place where they rested ('in a dark crevice between two great piers of rock') is marked by a spot on the right hand side of the track. Beyond is seen the 'great grey wall, a last huge upthrusting mass of mountain-stone' (TT p. 326, at the beginning of 'Shelob's Lair'), in which is the mouth of the tunnel, and beyond it, high above, the 'cleft ... in the topmost ridge, narrow, deep-cloven between two black shoulders; and on either shoulder was a horn of stone' (TT p. 319). A developed form of this sketch is found at the same place in the fair copy manuscript; this is reproduced on p. 204.[26]

The draft continues on into 'Shelob's Lair' without break. Of the narrative constituting the opening of the later chapter there is little to say. In the draft the Elvish name of the tunnel is *Terch Ungol* 'the Spider's Lair'; and the description of the stench from the tunnel is retained from Version 1 (pp. 192–3): 'Out of it came an odour which they could not place: not the sickly odour of decay by the meads of Morghul, but a repellent noisome stuffy smell: a repellent evil taint on the air.' In the fair copy my father first put *Te*, changing it as he wrote to *Torech Ungol* 'the Spider's Hole', and changing this as he wrote to 'Shelob's Lair' (the name *Shelob* having been already devised when he wrote this manuscript). Here he first described the reek from the tunnel in these words: 'Out of it came a stench: not the sickly odour of decay from the meads of Morghul, but a choking rankness, noisome, a reek as of piled and hoarded filth beyond reckoning, tainting even the open air with evil.' But he queried in the margin whether this description was not too strong: if the stench had been so unendurably horrible even from outside 'would they ever have gone in?'; and replaced it immediately with the description in TT (p. 326). He hesitated too about the width of the tunnel.

The new story in the draft version reaches the final form in their realisation that there were side tunnels, and in the things that brushed against them as they walked, until they passed the wide opening on the left from which the stench and the intense feeling of evil came. From this point the draft text reads:

... a sense of evil so strong that for a moment he grew faint. Sam also lurched. 'There's something in there,' he says. 'It smells like a death-house. Pooh.' Putting out their remaining strength and resolution they went on. Presently they came to what almost seemed a fork in the tunnel: at least in the absolute gloom they were in doubt.

'Which way's Gollum gone,' said Sam, 'I wonder.'

'Smeagol!' said Frodo. 'Smeagol!' But his voice fell back dead from his lips. There was no answer, not even an echo. 'He's really gone this time, I fancy.'

'Now we are just exactly where he wanted to bring us, I fancy. But just what he means to do in this black hole I can't guess.' He had not to wait long for the answer.

'What about that star-glass?' said Sam. 'Did not the Lady say it would be a light in dark places? And we need some to be sure now.'

'I have not used it,' said Frodo, 'because of Gollum. I think it would have driven him away, and also because it would be so bright. But here we seem to have come to a desperate pass.' Slowly he drew his hand from his bosom and held aloft the phial of Galadriel. For a moment it flickered like a star struggling through the mists of Earth, then as fear left them it began to burn into a dazzling brilliant silver light, as if Earendel himself had come down from the sunset paths with the last Silmaril upon his brow. The darkness receded from it and it shone in a globe of space enclosed with utter blackness. But before them within the radius of its light were two openings. Now their doubt was resolved, for the one to the left turned quickly away, while the one to the right went straight on only a little narrower than the tunnel behind.

At that moment some prescience of malice or of some evil regard made them both turn. Their hearts stood still. [There was a shrill whistling cry of Gollum?] Not far behind, ... by the noisome opening perhaps, were eyes: two great clusters of eyes. Whether they shone of their own light or whether the radiance of the star-glass was reflected in their thousand facets ..... Monstrous and abominable and fell they were: bestial yet filled

(8

Dimly could be discerned tall piers and jagged pinnacles of stone on either side, and between them great crevices and fissures blacker than the night, where the forgotten winters in the Dark Years had gnawed and carved the sunless stone. And now the red light in the sky seemed stronger, though whether a dreadful morning were indeed coming to this place of shadow they could not tell, or whether only they saw the flame of some great violence of Sauron in the torment of Gorgoroth beyond. Still far ahead, and still high above, Frodo looking up saw, as he guessed, the very crown of this bitter road. Against the sullen redness of the eastern sky a cleft was outlined in the topmost ridge, narrow, deep-cloven between two black shoulders, and on either shoulder was a horn of stone. He paused and looked more attentively. The horn upon the left was tall and slender; and in it burned a red light, or else the red light in the land behind was shining through a hole. He saw now: it was a black tower poised above the outer pass. He touched Sam's arm and pointed.

'I don't like the look of that!' said Sam. 'So, this secret way of yours is guarded after all,' he growled, turning to Gollum. 'And you knew all along, I suppose?'

'All ways are watched, yes,' said Gollum. 'Of course they are. But hobbits must try some way. This may be least watched. Perhaps they've all gone away to big battle — perhaps!'

'Perhaps!' grunted Sam. 'Well, it still seems a long way off and a long way up, before we get there. And there's still the tunnel. I think you ought to rest now, Mr. Frodo. I don't know what time of day or night it is, but we've kept going now for hours and hours.'

'Yes, we must rest,' said Frodo. 'Let us find some corner out of the wind, if we can, and gather our strength — for the last lap.' For so he felt it. The terrors of the land beyond, and the deed to be done there, seemed remote, too far off yet to trouble him. All his mind was bent on getting through or over this impenetrable wall and guard. If once he could do that impossible thing, then somehow the errand would be accomplished, or so it seemed to him in that dark hour of weariness, still labouring in the stony shadows under Kirith Ungol.

In a dark crevice between two great piers of rock they sat down. Frodo and Sam a little way within, and Gollum crouched upon the ground near the opening. There the hobbits took what they expected would be their last meal before they went down into the Nameless Land, maybe the last meal they would ever eat together. Some of the food of Gondor they ate, and wafers of the waybread of the Elves, and they drank a little.

Kirith Ungol

with a malice and purpose and even with a hideous glee and delight such as no beast's eyes can show. An evil mind gloated behind that baleful light.

At this point my father stopped, and noted that the eyes must come first, and then the star-glass (necessarily implying that the eyes of the Spider shone with their own light). An outline follows:

The creature backs away. They retreat up the tunnel. Frodo holds glass aloft and ..... [27] and each time the eyes halt. Then filled with a sudden resolve he drew Sting. It sparkled, and calling to Sam he strode back towards the eyes. They ... [?turned] retreated and disappeared. Sam full of admiration. 'Now let's run for it!' he said. They ran, and suddenly [?crashed] into [?greyness] which rebounded and turned them back. Sam cannot break the threads. Frodo gives him Sting. And Sam hews while Frodo stands guard.

The web gives way. They rush out and find web was over the mouth of the tunnel. They are in the last gully and the horn-pass ... before them.

'That's the top,' said Sam. 'And we've come out of it. Our luck's in still. On we go now, and take the last bit while the luck lasts.'

Frodo ran forward placing his star-glass in his bosom, no thought for anything but escape. Sam follows with Sting drawn – constantly turning to watch the mouth of the tunnel – thinking too little of the craft of Ungoliant. She had many exits from her lair.

Frodo was gaining on him. He tried to run, and then some way ahead he saw issuing out of a shadow in the wall of the ravine the most monstrous and loathsome shape. Beyond the imagination of his worst dreams.

This account agrees well with the plan reproduced on p. 201: they had passed the wide opening on the left which led to the lair of Ungoliant, and the fork in the tunnel, where 'the one to the left turned quickly away, while the one to the right went straight on only a little narrower than the tunnel behind', can be readily identified. But the story has shifted radically from the outline accompanying the plan (pp. 199–200), which apparently never received narrative form, where the story ran thus:

- Ungoliant had stretched a web on the west side of the trap (hole) in the main tunnel. The stench arose from the hole.

- Frodo held up the phial (cutting of the webs is not mentioned) and Ungoliant retreated to her lair.
- By the light of the phial they avoided the hole. Gollum disappeared, and they feared he had fallen into it.
- They left the tunnel, whereupon Ungoliant, having come round ahead of them by a side path, attacked Frodo, and Gollum grappled Sam from behind.

In the very similar short version of this plot (p. 199) it is said in addition that 'They cut their way out of web at far end.'

The story in the present draft has moved much nearer to the final form: they passed the opening to the lair, whence the stench came, and there is no mention of the 'trap' or 'hole' in the floor of the main passage; and they came to the fork in the tunnel.[28] But in this version the phial of Galadriel is used at this juncture, in order to show them which tunnel to take; and turning round on account of a sense of approaching evil the light of the phial is reflected in the eyes of the Spider. My father's direction at this point that the eyes must come before the star-glass clearly means that the eyes, shining with their own light, appeared in the tunnel, and that only then did the thought of the star-glass arise. The remainder of the episode is now essentially as in the final form – except that as they run from the tunnel Sam has Sting and Frodo has the phial of Galadriel.

The fair copy manuscript when it reached this point still did not attain the final story in all respects, and this section of it was subsequently rejected and replaced. In the first stage, the idea in the draft that the phial was used simply to illuminate the tunnel (with Frodo's explanation that he had not used it before for fear it would drive Gollum away) was abandoned, and as in TT it was the sound only of the Spider's approach, the 'gurgling, bubbling noise' and the 'long venomous hiss', that inspired Sam to think of it (thus reversing the decision that the eyes must come first and then the star-glass); the light of the phial illumined the eyes (although 'behind the glitter a pale deadly fire began steadily *to glow within*, a flame kindled in some deep pit of evil thought'). But at this stage the idea that the light did, if only incidentally, show the way to take, was retained: 'And now the way was clear before them, for the light revealed two archways; and the one to the left was not the path, for it narrowed quickly again and turned aside, but that to the right was the true way and went straight onward as before.'[29]

The pursuit of the 'eyes', and the rout of the Spider when Frodo confronted her with the phial in his left hand and the blue-flickering[30] blade of Sting in his right, is in the final form, but my father still followed the draft in making it Sam who cut the web at the far end of the tunnel with Sting. The text here reads thus, from Sam's 'Gollum! May the curse of Faramir bite him' (cf. TT p. 331):[31]

'That will not help us,' said Frodo. 'Come! I will hold up the light while my strength lasts. Take my sword. It is an elven blade. See what it may do. Give me yours.'

Sam obeyed and took Sting in his hand, a thrill running through his hand as he grasped its fair hilt, the sword of his master, of Bilbo, the sword that Elrond had declared to come out of the great wars before the Dark Years when the walls of Gondolin still stood.[32] Turning he made a great sweeping stroke and then sprang back to avoid the lashing [?threads]. Blue-edged, glinting in the radiance of the star, the elven blade shore through the netted ropes. In three swift blows the web was shattered and the trap was broken. The air of the mountains flowed in like a river.

'It's clear,' Sam cried. 'It's clear. I can see the [?night] light in the sky.'

No! Make Sam hold light and so *Frodo goes out first*, and so as he has the light Shelob attacks Frodo.

Sam sweeps up Frodo's sword from ground.

He drops the Phial in struggle with Gollum.

Cut out the staffs.

This is followed by a suggestion, not entirely legible, that the staffs should 'hang on *thongs*', and another that Frodo should tap the walls of the tunnel with the staffs. My father was apparently concerned here with the problem arising from having only two hands. No doubt it was at this time that the reading of the fair copy manuscript of 'Journey to the Cross-roads', where the heads of the staves were still in the form of a shepherd's crook (p. 176 and note 3), was changed to that of TT (p. 303): 'staves ... with carven heads through which ran plaited leathern thongs'. The text continues:

When Sam cannot hew web, Frodo says: 'I do not feel the eyes any longer. For the moment their regard has moved. You take the light. Do not be afraid. Hold it up. I will see what the elven-sword may do.'

Frodo hews the webs asunder. And so the trap as it was planned was frustrated. For though once long ago he [Gollum] had seen it, the nature of that sword he did not know, and of the Phial of Galadriel he had never heard.[33]

They rush out. Sam comes behind and suddenly they are aware (a) of red window (b) of the blue light of Sting. 'Orcs', said Sam, and closing his hand about the phial hid it beneath his cloak again. A sudden madness (?) on Frodo. He sees the red cleft the goal of all his effort before him. No great distance, half a mile. Gain it in a rush. Run! ..... Sam, he said. The door, the path. Now for it, before any can stay us.

Sam tries to keep up. Then the spider attacks, and Gollum.

And so this extraordinarily resistant narrative was at last shaped at almost all points to my father's satisfaction: 'a sticky patch' he described it, achieved with 'very great labour'; and further drafting led to the final text of 'Shelob's Lair' in the fair copy manuscript. Yet even now he seems not to have been entirely confident of the rightness of the story, for the manuscript carries also a second text of the episode in the tunnel (marked 'other version'), and it seems beyond question that this was written *after* the other.[34] It takes up after the words 'a gurgling, bubbling noise, and a long venomous hiss' (TT p. 328).

They wheeled round, but at first they saw nothing. Still as stones they stood waiting, for they did not know what. Then, not far down the tunnel, just at the opening where they had reeled and stumbled, they saw a gleam. Very slowly it advanced. There were eyes in the darkness. Two great clusters of eyes. They were growing larger and brighter as very slowly they advanced. They burned steadily with a fell light of their own, kindled in some deep pit of evil thought. Monstrous and abominable they were, bestial and yet filled with purpose, and with hideous delight: beyond all hope of escape their prey was trapped.

Frodo and Sam backed away, their gaze held by the dreadful stare of those cold eyes, and as they backed so the eyes came on, unhurried, gloating. Suddenly both together, as if released simultaneously from the same spell, the hobbits turned and fled blindly up the tunnel. [*Struck out:* The left-hand opening was blocked with some unseen barrier; wildly they groped and found the right-hand opening, and again they ran.] But as they ran they looked back, and saw with horror the eyes come leaping up behind.

Then there came a breath of air: cold and thin. The opening, the upper gate, the end of the tunnel – at last: it was just ahead. Desperately they threw themselves forward, and then staggered backwards. The passage was blocked by some unseen barrier: soft, strong, impenetrable. Again they flung themselves upon it. It yielded a little and then like taut cords hurled them back once more. The eyes were nearer now, halted, quietly watching them, gloating, glittering with cruel amusement. The stench of death was like a cloud about them.

'Stand!' said Frodo. 'It's no use struggling. We're caught.' He turned to face the eyes, and as he did so, he drew his sword. Sting flashed out, and about the edges of the sharp elven-blade a blue fire flickered.

Sam, sick, desperate, but angry more than all, groped for the hilts of his own short sword, carried so far and to so little purpose all the way from the Barrowdowns. 'I wish old Bombadil was near.' he muttered. 'Trapped in the end! Gollum – may the curse of Faramir bite him.' Darkness was about him and a blackness in his heart. And then suddenly even in those last moments before the evil thing made its final spring he saw a light, a light in the darkness of his mind...

The text continues as in the other version (TT p. 329), but without the sentences 'The bubbling hiss drew nearer, and there was a creaking as of some great jointed thing that moved with slow purpose in the dark. A reek came on before it'; and it ends at *A light when all other lights go out!* There is then a direction to 'proceed' as in the other version.

This also was a good story. There is here a formally simpler disposition of the elements: for Frodo and Sam are caught directly between the monster and the trap – trapped indeed 'beyond all hope of escape',[35] and are saved in the very last nick of time by the Phial of Galadriel.

The Choices of Master Samwise

I left 'Version 1', the original narrative in which there was no encounter with the Spider in the tunnel, and the attack on Frodo took place at the head of the Second Stair (above the tunnel), at the point where my father abandoned that version as a 'fair copy' manuscript and the text precipitously collapsed into fearfully difficult drafting: see pp. 197–8.

It is difficult to be sure of the precise development from this point, because this very rough drafting runs on continuously to the end of the story in *The Two Towers*, being indeed the original setting down of the narrative of 'The Choices of Master Samwise', and yet it cannot have been an uninterrupted continuation of Version 1. The last page that was certainly a part of Version 1 ends with a near-illegible initial account of Sam's attack on Ungoliant and his holding up the phial that he took from Frodo's body (p. 198). The conclusion of the encounter with Ungoliant may belong to Version 1, but not much more, for when Sam, arising from his long trance of despair, composes Frodo's body he says: 'He lent me Sting and that I'll take'. This of course depends on the developed story (Version 2) in which Frodo gave Sting to Sam for an attack on the web at the end of the tunnel while he himself held the phial (see pp. 205–7).

From the point where Sam holds up the phial against Ungoliant the draft continues:

'Galadriel!' he cried. 'Elbereth! Now come, you filthy thing. Now at last we know what holds this path. But we are going on. Come on, let's settle before we go.' As if his wrath and courage set its potency in motion, the glass blazed like a torch – like [a] flash not of lightning but of some searing star cleaving the dark air with intolerable radiance white and terrible. No such light of heaven had ever burned in her face before.[36]

The account of Ungoliant's retreat is largely illegible, but phrases can be read: 'She seemed ... to crumple like a vast bag', 'her legs sagged, and slowly, painfully, she backed from the light away in the opening in the wall', 'gathering her strength she turned and with a last ..... jump and a foul but already pitiable ... [37] she slipped into the hole.'

The declaration that whatever might have been the fate of Ungoliant thereafter 'this tale does not tell' appears in the draft, as does (in very rough form) the passage that follows in TT (pp. 339–40) to the point where Sam composes Frodo's body. Here the draft text reads:

He laid his master upon his back, and folded his cold hands. 'Let the silver mail of mithril be his winding sheet,' he said.[38] 'He lent me Sting and that I'll take, but a sword shall be at his side.' And the phial he put into his right hand and hid it in his bosom. 'It's too good for me,' he said, 'and She gave it to him to be a light in dark places.' There were no stones for a cairn, but he rolled the only two he could find of a wieldy size one to Frodo's head and another to his feet. And then he stood and held up the star-glass. It burned gently now with a quiet radiance as of the evening star in summer, and in its light Frodo's hue ..... [?pale] but fair, and an elvish beauty was in his face, as of one that is long past the shadows.

And then he strove to take farewell. But he could not. Still he held Frodo's hand and could not let it go.

An arrow directs that the placing of the phial in Frodo's hand and Sam's words 'It's too good for me ...' should follow '... as of one long past the shadows'.

The account of Sam's agonized debate was not different from its form in *The Two Towers* (pp. 341–2) in the progression of his thoughts, and his parting words and the taking of the Ring are virtually in the final form; but he does not take the phial, which in this version of the story remains hidden in Frodo's hand. From this point I give the original draft in full.

At last with a great effort he stood up and turned away and seeing nothing but a grey mist stumbled forward towards the pass now straight ahead. But still his master drew him: Sam's mind was not at peace, not really made up. (He was acting as best he could reason but against his whole nature.) He hadn't gone far when he looked back and through his tears saw the little dark patch in the ravine where all his life had fallen in ruin. Again he turned and went on, and now he was come almost to the V [*i.e. the Cleft*]. So the very gate of parting. Now he must look back for the very last time. He did so.

'No I can't do it,' he said. 'I can't. I'd go to the Dark Tower to find him, but I can't go and leave him. I can't finish this tale. It's for other folk. My chapter's ended.' He began to stumble back. And then suddenly to his wrath and horror he thought he saw a slinking thing creep out of the shadow and go up to Frodo and start pawing him.[39] Anger obliterating all other thoughts blazed up again. 'Gollum! After his precious – thinks his plot has worked after all. The dirty –' He began to run silently. There wasn't more than 20 [?yards] to cover. He got his sword out. Gollum! He ground his teeth.

But suddenly Gollum paused [and] looked round, not at Sam, and with all his speed bolted diving back towards the wall and to [the] same opening out of which Ungoliant had come.

Sam realized that Gollum had not fled from him or even noticed him. Almost at once he saw the reason. Orcs! Orcs were coming out of the tunnel. He halted in his tracks. A new choice was on him and a quick one this time. Then from behind also he heard orc-voices. Out of some path leading down from the tower orcs were coming. He was between them. No going back now – Sam would never reach the Pass of Kirith Ungol now. He gripped on Sting. A brief thought passed through his mind. How many would he kill before they got him? Would any song ever mention it? How Samwise fell in the High Pass – made a wall of bodies for his master's body. No, no song, for the Ring would be captured and all songs cease for ever [in] an age of Darkness ... The Ring. With a sudden thought and impulse he *put it on!* [*Added:* His hand hangs weighed down and useless.] At first he noticed nothing – except that he seemed to see much clearer. Things seemed hard and black and heavy, and the voices loud. The orc-bands had sighted one another and were shouting. But he seemed to hear both sides as if they were speaking close to him. And he understood them. Why, they were speaking plain language. Maybe they were, or maybe the Ring which had power over all Sauron's servants and was grown in power as the place of its forging was approached brought the thought of their minds in plain speech direct to Sam.

'Hola! Gazmog,' said the foremost of the orcs coming out of the tunnel.

'Ho you Zaglûn. So you've come at last. Have you heard them? Did you see it?'

'See what? We've just come through the tunnel of She-lob.[40] What should we see or hear?'

'Shouting and crying out here and lights. Some mischief afoot. But we're on guard in the tower and not supposed to leave. We waited but you didn't come. Hurry now for we must get back. There's only Naglur-Danlo and old Nûzu up here and he's in a taking.'

Then suddenly the orcs from the tower saw Frodo and while Sam still hesitated they swept past him with a howl and rushed forward. (Sting must be sheathed.) One thing the Ring did not confer was courage – rather the reverse, at any rate on Sam. He did not now [?rush] in – or make a hill of bodies round his master. There were about three dozen of them in all, and they were talking fast and excitedly. Sam hesitated. If he drew Sting they'd see that. They wouldn't ....: Orcs never did – but 36! They [?*read* They'd] see where he was.

No – above won't do, he must see Orcs from a greater distance and *follow them*. The cleft must be no great distance, 100 yards? from Frodo's body and that 20–30 yards from tunnel. *Cut out Gollum.*

Sam sees orcs coming *down* from tower as he turns back [for the] last time. They seem from afar to spot the little shape of Frodo and give a yell. It is answered by a yell – other orcs are coming out of the tunnel! Then put in the part about his thoughts of *song* as he runs back. Puts on ring and cannot wield sword.[41] Changes it to left hand [*broken staff* (Sam's broke on Gollum)].[42] By that time orcs have picked up Frodo and are off to tunnel. Sam follows. Ring confers language knowledge – not courage.

Sam follows and hears conversation as they go through tunnel. Orcs discuss Frodo. Special vigilance ordered. What is it? Leader [B......] Zaglûn says[43] orders are for messages [*or* messengers] to go to Morgul *and* direct to Lugburz. They [?groan]. Talk of Shelob and the worm (= Gollum).

Big things are on. Only preliminary strokes. News. Osgiliath taken and ford. Army has also left North Gate. [?Other crossing] away up north somewhere and into the north part of the Horseboys' land – no opposition there. We'll be at the Mouths of Anduin in a week and at the Gulf of Lûne before the summer's out – and then nowhere to escape. How we'll make 'em sweat! We haven't begun yet. Big stuff's coming.

Big stick if you don't hurry.

Prisoner is to be stripped naked. Teeth and nails? No. Is he half elf and man – [?there's] a fair blend of folly and mischief. Quick end better. Quick!

They round a corner. Sam sees red light in an arch. Underground door to tower. Horrified to see that tunnel deceived him: they're further ahead than he thought. He runs forward but the iron door closes with a clang. He is outside in the darkness.

Now go back to Gandalf.

[*Added:* Make most of goblin conversation await the rescue chapter?]

In the next stage of development my father returned to the words 'At last with a great effort he stood up and turned away and seeing nothing but a grey mist stumbled forward towards the pass now straight ahead' (p. 211), and now continued thus (cf. TT pp. 342–3):

He had not far to go. The tunnel was some fifty yards behind; the cleft a couple of hundred yards or less. There was a path visible in the dusk running now quickly up, with the cliff on one side, and on the other a low wall of rock rising steadily to another cliff. Soon there were broad shallow steps. Now the orc-tower was right above him, frowning black, and in it the red eye glowed. Now he was passing up the steps and the cleft was before him.

'I have made up my mind,' he kept saying to himself. But he had not. What he did, though he had long to think it out, was altogether against the grain. To stick by his master was his true nature. 'Have I got it wrong,' he muttered. 'Was there something else to do?' As the sheer sides of the cleft closed about him and before he reached the summit, before he looked upon the descending path beyond, he turned, torn intolerably within. He looked back. He could still see like a small blot in the gathering gloom the mouth of the tunnel; and he thought he could see or guess where Frodo lay, almost he fancied there was a light or a glimmer of it down there. Through tears he saw that lonely, stony high place where all his life had fallen into ruin.

What was the 'light, or a glimmer of it' (meaning, I suppose, 'a light, or the glimmer of a light') that Sam saw? It survives in TT (p. 343): 'He fancied there was a glimmer on the ground down there, or perhaps it was some trick of his tears'. Can the original meaning have been that there was a faint shining from the Phial of Galadriel, very probably at this stage (see pp. 210–11) still left clasped in Frodo's hand?

From '"No I can't do it," he said' (p. 211) my father repeated the original text almost exactly, but excising the return of Gollum. When he came to Sam's putting on the Ring he wrote: 'The Ring. With a sudden impulse he drew it out and *put it on*. The weight of it weighed down his hand. For a moment he noticed no change, and then he seemed to see clearer.' But at this point he stopped, marked what he had written with an X, and wrote: 'No! hear[d] clearer, crack of stone, cry of bird, voices, Shelob bubbling wretchedly deep in the rocks. Voices in the dungeons of the tower. But all was not dark but hazy, and himself like a black solid rock and the Ring like hot gold. Difficult to believe in his invisibility.' The account of Sam's understanding of what the Orcs said here takes this form: 'Did the Ring give power of tongues or did it give him comprehension of all that had been under its power [*written above:* Sauron's servants], so that he heard direct? Certainly the voices seemed close in his ears and it was very difficult to judge their distance.' With a reference to the Ring's increasing power in that region and its not conferring courage on its wearer this draft ends, followed by an outline of the salient points in what Sam heard:

> Why such a long delay of Orcs to come? Terrified of Shelob. They know another spy is about. Leader says orders are for messengers to go to Morgul and direct to Baraddur Lugburz. Orcs [?groan]. Talk of Shelob and the Spider's worm [who] has been here before. News of war.

In further drafting the coming of the Orc-bands is described thus:

Then suddenly he heard cries and voices. He stood still. Orc-voices: he had heard them in Moria and Lórien and on the Great River and would never forget them. Wheeling about he saw small red lights, torches perhaps, issuing from the tunnel away below. And only a few yards below him, out of the very cliff as it seemed, through some gap or gate near the tower's foot he had not noticed as he passed debating on the road, there were more lights. Orc-bands. They were come at last to hunt. The red eye had not been wholly blind.

And a noise of feet and shouts came also through the cleft. Orcs were coming up to the pass out of Mordor too.

This conception of three Orc-bands converging survived into the fair copy manuscript, where however it was removed at once, or soon, for there is no further reference to it; here 'orcs were coming up to the pass out of the land beyond', while 'only a few yards off' lights and 'black orc-shapes' were coming through 'some gap or gate at the tower's foot'. In the event (TT p. 343) the Orcs of the tower appeared from the far side of the Cleft.

The draft continues:

Fear overwhelmed him. How could he escape? So now *his* chapter would be ended. It had not had above a page longer than Frodo's. How could he save the Ring? The Ring. He was not aware of any thought or decision: he simply found himself drawing out the chain and taking the Ring in his hand. The orcs coming towards him grew louder. Then he *put it on.*[44]

The achievement of the conversation between the leaders of the two Orc-bands in the tunnel took a good deal of work, extending into the fair copy, and to detail all the rearrangements, shifts of speakers, and so on would require a great deal of space. But there is one draft that deserves quotation in full, for very little of it survived. Here the two Orcs, and especially he of Minas Morghul, are greatly concerned with the precise timing of the various communications that had passed.

In the darkness [*of the tunnel*] he seemed now more at home; but he could not overcome his weariness. He could see the light of torches a little way ahead, but he could not gain on them. Goblins go fast in tunnels, especially those which they have themselves made, and all the many passages in this region of the mountains were their work, even the main tunnel and the great deep pit where Shelob housed. In the Dark Years they had been made, until Shelob came and made her lair there, and to escape her they had bored new passages, too narrow for her [as she slowly grew >] growth, that crossed and recrossed the straight way.[45]

Sam heard the clamour of their many voices flat and hard in the dead air, and somewhere he heard two voices louder than the rest. The leaders of the two parties seemed to be wrangling as they went.

'Can't you stop your rabble's racket?' said one. 'I don't care what happens to them, but I don't want Shelob down on me and my lads.'

'Yours are making more than half the noise,' said the other. 'But let the lads play. No need to worry about Shelob for a bit. She's sat on a pin or something, and none of us will weep. Didn't you see the signs then? A claw cut off, filthy gore all the way to that cursed crack (if we've stopped it once we've stopped it a hundred times). Let the lads play. We've struck a bit of luck at last: we've got something He wants.'

'Yes, *we*, Shagrat.[46] *We*, mark you. But why we're going to your miserable tower I don't know. We found the spy, my lot were there first. He should be ours. He should be taken back to Dushgoi.'[47]

'Now, now, still at it. I've said before all there is to be said, but if you must have more arguments, they're here: I've got ten more swords than you, and thirty more just up yonder at call. See? Anyway orders are orders, and I've mine.'

'And I've mine.'

'Yes, and I know them, for I was told 'em by Lugburz, see? *Yagûl*[48] *from Dushgoi will patrol until he meets your guard, or as far as Ungol top: he will report to you before returning to report to Dushgoi.* Your report was *nothing*. Very useful. You can take it back to Dushgoi as soon as you like.'

'I will, but I don't like [to] just yet. I found the spy, and I must know more before I go. The Lords of Dushgoi have some secret of quick messages and they will get the news to Lugburz quicker than anyone you can send direct.'

'I know all that, and I'm not stopping you taking news to them. I know all the messages. They trust me in Lugburz, He knows a good orc when he sees one. This is what happened: message from Dushgoi to Lugburz: *Watchers uneasy. Fear elvish agent passed up the Stair. Guard pass.* Message from Lugburz to Ungol: *Dushgoi uneasy. Redouble vigilance. Make contact. Send report by Dushgoi and direct.* And there you are.'

'No, I'm not there, not yet. I'm going to take a report back, my own report, Master Shagrat, and I want to know this first. When did you get this message? We set out as soon as possible after the forces left, and we see no sign of you till we're right through the Tunnel – a filthy place and inside *your* area. Then we see you just starting. Now I guess you got that message early today, this morning probably, and you've been drinking since to give you the guts to look at the hole. That's what you think of orders that don't suit you.'

'I've no need to account for myself to you Dushgoi horseboys, Master Yagûl. But if you're so curious to know: the message from Dushgoi was sent out late: things seem a bit slack with the Lord away. Lugburz did not get it till *last night*, mark you, nor me till this afternoon. By which time messages were hardly needed. I'd had my lads out some time. There were very odd things happening. Lights in the tunnel, lights outside, shouting and whatnot. But Shelob was about. My lads saw her, and her worm.'

'What's that?'

The remainder of this text is very rough working for what follows from this point in TT (pp. 348–50). In a following draft Yagool (as he is spelt) says of Frodo: 'What is it, d'you think? Elvish I thought by his nasty smooth peaky face. But undersized.' Here the conversation moves closer to the form in TT, and the long discussion between Yagool and Shagrat about the messages is greatly reduced, though the messages are still given, in very much the same form; but that from Minas Morghul begins *Nazgûl of Dushgoi to Lugburz.* In another brief passage of drafting this dialogue occurs:

'I tell you, nearly two days ago the Night Watcher smelt something, but will you believe me it was nearly another day before they started to send a message to Lugburz.'

'How do they do that?' said Shagrat. 'I've often wondered.'

'I don't know and I don't want to ...'

The manuscript of 'The Choices of Master Samwise'[49] was in almost all respects very close to the chapter in *The Two Towers.* Various points in which it differed as first written have been noticed, but there remain a few others. The following account of Shelob was rejected as soon as written and replaced by that in TT (p. 337):

Shelob was not as dragons are, no softer spot had she save only in her eyes; not as the lesser breeds of Mirkwood was their dam, and her age-old hide, knobbed and pitted with corruption but ever thickened with layer on layer within, could not be pierced by any blade of Middle-earth, not though elf or dwarf should make it and all runes were written upon it, not though the hand of [*struck out:* Fingon wielded it whose] Beren or of Túrin wielded it.

Shagrat's reply to Yagûl's opening sally ('Tired of lurking up there, thinking of coming down to fight?') took this form:

'Tired! You've said it. Waiting for nothing, except to be made into Shelob's meat. But we've got orders, too. Old Shagram's in a fine taking. Your lot's to blame. These Dushgoi bogey-men: sending messages to Lugburz.'

This was rejected as soon as written, replaced by 'Orders to you. I'm in command of this Pass. So speak civil', and with it went the last appearance of the name *Dushgoi* of Minas Morghul. Who 'old Shagram' was is not clear, but he is evidently 'old Nûzu' of the original draft (p. 212), also reported to be 'in a taking', apparently because the garrison of the Tower of Kirith Ungol had been depleted. Possibly he was the actual captain of the Tower, until this point, when Shagrat asserts that he himself is the commander of the pass; but Shagrat's words in the draft cited on p. 216, 'They trust me in Lugburz, He knows a good orc when he sees one' suggest that he was so already.

Lastly, the words of Sam's Elvish invocation (TT p. 339) in his fight with the Spider take in a draft for this passage the same form as they did in the original verse chanted in Rivendell (VI.394), and this form was retained in the manuscript as written, the only difference being *lír* for *dir* in the third line:[50]

O Elbereth Gilthoniel
sir evrin pennar óriel
lír avos-eithen míriel

This was changed on the manuscript to give this text:

O Elbereth Gilthoniel
silevrin pennar óriel
hír avas-eithen míriel
a tíro'men Gilthoniel!

★

It was a long time before my father returned to Frodo and Sam. In October 1944 he briefly took up again the stories 'west of Anduin' from where he had left them nearly two years earlier, but soon abandoned them (see pp. 233–5).

On 29 November 1944 (*Letters* no. 91), when he was sending me the typescripts of 'Shelob's Lair' and 'The Choices of Master Samwise', he said that he had 'got the hero into such a fix that not even an author will be able to extricate him without labour and difficulty.' He had by this time conceived the structure of *The Lord of the Rings* as five 'Books', of which four were written (cf. also his letter to Stanley Unwin of March 1945, *Letters* no. 98); and in this same letter of November 1944 he forecast what was still to come:

> Book Five and Last opens with the ride of Gandalf to Minas Tirith, with which The Palantir, last chapter of Book Three closed. Some of this is written or sketched.[51] Then should follow the raising of the siege of Minas Tirith by the onset of the Riders of Rohan, in which King Theoden falls; the driving back of the enemy, by Gandalf and Aragorn, to the Black Gate; the parley in which Sauron shows various tokens (such as the mithril coat) to prove that he has captured Frodo, but Gandalf refuses to treat (a horrible dilemma, all the same, even for a wizard). Then we shift back to Frodo, and his rescue by Sam. From a high place they see all Sauron's vast reserves loosed through the Black Gate, and then hurry on to Mount Doom through a deserted Mordor. With the destruction of the Ring, the exact manner of which is not certain – all these last bits were written ages ago, but no longer fit in detail, nor in elevation (for the whole thing has become much larger and loftier) – Baraddur crashes, and the forces of Gandalf sweep into Mordor. Frodo and Sam, fighting with the last Nazgul on an island of rock surrounded by the fire of the erupting Mount Doom, are rescued by Gandalf's eagle; and then the clearing up of all loose threads, down even to Bill Ferny's pony,[52] must take place. A lot of this work will be done in a final chapter where Sam is found reading out of an enormous book to his children, and answering all their questions about what happened to everybody (that will link up with his discourse on the nature of stories in the Stairs of Kirith Ungol). But the final scene will be the passage of Bilbo and Elrond and Galadriel through the woods of the Shire on their way to the Grey Havens. Frodo will join them and pass over the Sea (linking with the vision he had of a far green country in the house of Tom Bombadil). So ends the Middle Age and the Dominion of Men begins, and Aragorn far away on the throne of Gondor labours to bring some order and to preserve some memory of old among the welter of men that Sauron has poured into the West. But Elrond has gone, and all the High Elves. What happens to the Ents I don't yet know. It will probably work out very differently from this plan when it really gets written, as the thing seems to write itself once I get going, as if the truth comes out then, only imperfectly glimpsed in the preliminary sketch.

From a letter to Stanley Unwin written on 21 July 1946 (*Letters* no. 105), now more than two years since the doors of the underground entrance to the Tower of Kirith Ungol were slammed in Sam's face, and getting on for two since 'the beacons flared in Anórien and Théoden came to Harrowdale', it is clear that he had done no more. He was then hopeful that he would soon be able to begin writing again; and in another letter to Stanley Unwin of 7 December 1946 (*Letters* no. 107) he was 'on the last chapters'.

NOTES

1 This text went back in turn to an earlier outline, 'The Story Foreseen from Moria', VII.209.
2 At that time *Kirith Ungol* was the name of the main pass into Mordor.
3 The first mention of the Tower of Kirith Ungol.
4 As I have noted in VII.260, Sam's visions in the Mirror of Galadriel were already in the fair copy manuscript of 'Galadriel' almost exactly as in FR (p. 377); the actual words used in the manuscript of this vision were: 'and now he thought he saw Frodo lying fast asleep under a great dark cliff: his face was pale.' When my father wrote this the words of the outline 'The Story Foreseen from Moria' (VII.209) had already been written: 'Gollum gets spiders to put spell of sleep on Frodo. Sam drives them off. But cannot wake him.'
5 The illegible word might possibly be 'grin'.
6 The fair copy manuscript, with some correction and addition from the time of composition, reaches the text of TT, pp. 312–17, in all respects save one: the passage describing Frodo's dash towards the bridge is still absent. The manuscript reads here:

   ... Frodo felt his senses reeling and his limbs weakening.

   Sam took his master's arm. 'Hold up, Mr Frodo!' he whispered, but his breath seemed to tear the air like a whistle. 'Not that way! Gollum says not that way – thank goodness! I agree with him for once.'

   Frodo took a grip on himself and wrenched his eyes away.

   The reading of TT, introduced later, thus in part returns to the outline given on p. 186.
7 In general I do not go into the detail of textual problems, but this is a very unusual case, and the reconstruction of the evolution of the story to some degree depends on the view taken of it; I therefore give here some account of it.

   Page 4 of the manuscript, on which the pencilled draft though overwritten can mostly be read, ends with the words: 'Then he saw that a faint light was welling through his fingers and he thrust it in his bosom.' Page 5 was likewise originally a page of rough, continuous, pencil drafting. The top of this page, some 14 lines or so, was erased, and the *later* narrative was written in this space (ending at 'and there it suddenly entered a narrow opening in the rock. They had come to the first stair that Gollum had spoken of', TT p. 317). Towards the end of this short section, however, the erasure was not complete, and the following can be read: 'not the odour of decay in the valley below ..... that the hobbits could recognize, a'. Thus the original narrative was here entirely different, for within a short space they are already at the mouth of the tunnel.

The strange thing is that from this point the original pencilled draft (continuing with 'repellent evil taint on the air'), not erased any further but overwritten, was *overwritten with the earlier narrative* ('Version 1'). Thus as the text in ink stands on this page it reads:

> ... and there it suddenly entered a narrow opening in the rock. They had come to the first stair that Gollum had spoken of [TT p. 317].
>
> repellent evil taint on the air.

The text following on from 'that Gollum had spoken of' is found on another sheet. The only explanation that I can see is that my father for some reason left the first (approximately) fourteen lines in pencil, and only began to overwrite it in ink at an arbitrary point ('repellent evil taint on the air'). The first part of the page thus fell victim to erasure and re-use when the later story had come into being, but from the point where it had been overwritten in ink the earlier story (Version 1) could not be so used, and was merely struck out.

8 This version of the sentence is found in isolation on a slip, slightly different from and beginning slightly earlier than the form of it that can be read in the pencilled draft (see note 7).

9 With 'then as fear left him it began to burn' cf. the derived passage in 'Shelob's Lair', TT p. 329: 'then as its power waxed, and hope grew in Frodo's mind, it began to burn'; cf. also 'As if his indomitable spirit had set its potency in motion, the glass blazed suddenly' (TT p. 339).

10 This much of 'Version 1' (struck through) was preserved in the manuscript because the page carried a portion of the later story also, as explained in note 7.

11 The Bodleian page '6/7', like page '5', is written in ink over the underlying pencilled draft. At this point there is an adjective, describing the webs and ending in *-ing*, which my father could not read; he therefore merely let the pencilled word stand, without writing anything on top of it.

12 The words *hold my star-glass behind me* are underlined in the original – possibly because my father was emphasising to himself that Frodo had actually given the phial to Sam, though whereas in TT (p. 334) Sam did not give it back to Frodo, later in this version (p. 198) he takes it from Frodo's hand during his fight with Ungoliant.

Frodo drew Sting: on the previous page '5' of the manuscript Frodo had already drawn Sting (p. 193), but this, I feel certain, is no more than an oversight, and does not call into question the succession of the two pages.

13 In the margin is written here: 'Dis. into a side hole?', where 'Dis.' obviously stands for 'Disappears'. This was added later, when my father was pondering the idea that Gollum in fact disappeared while they were still in the tunnel.

14 At the foot of the page is written in pencil: 'Make Gollum come reluctantly back.' This clearly belongs with the underlying pencilled draft; when over-writing the draft in ink my father put a query against these words.

15 The caption of the picture, *Shelob's Lair*, was added afterwards; at this time the name of the Great Spider was Ungoliant (p. 196).

16 At the time of writing, page 4/5 of 'Version 1' is in the United States, page 6/7 in England, and page 8/9 in France.

17 This is the first appearance of the one Great Spider (as opposed to many spiders).

18 On the name *Ungoliant(e)*, derived from *The Silmarillion*, see the *Etymologies*, V.396.

19 When Sam twisted round as Gollum seized him from behind, in TT Gollum's hold on Sam's mouth slipped, whereas in Version 1 it was his hold with his left hand on Sam's neck that slipped (down to his waist). Thus it is not said in Version 1 that 'all the while Gollum's other hand was tightening on Sam's throat'. When Sam hurled himself backwards and landed on Gollum 'a sharp hiss came out of him, and for a breathless second his left arm that was about Sam's waist relaxed' (in TT 'for a second his hand upon Sam's throat loosened'). Sam's second blow, falling across Gollum's back, did not break the staff, and the third blow aimed by Sam was with the staff, not with his sword.

20 Sam's staff was not broken at the second blow, as it was in TT; see notes 19 and 42.

21 The handwriting is so difficult that my father pencilled in glosses here and there where he had evidently been puzzled by what he had written not long before. – It is often the case with a very difficult preliminary draft, which can really only be deciphered by recourse to the following text, that some particularly puzzling word or phrase cannot be solved in this way: another expression appears in its place; and in such cases one may often suspect that my father could not make it out himself. Cf. note 11.

22 On the right is seen the 'Wraith-road' from Minas Morghul rising to the main pass in this region (p. 195).

23 The brackets round this sentence, seen in the reproduction, were put in subsequently, and probably the question mark also. On the tunnel being the work of Orcs see p. 215.

24 I cannot read the word at the bottom of the plan of the tunnels, also in blue ball-point pen, though possibly it also reads 'orc-path'.

25 Here appears the name Imlad Morghul (see p. 176).

26 On lines 3–4 of the page reproduced on p. 204 are the words 'where forgotten winters in the Dark Years had gnawed and carved the sunless stone.' In TT (p. 319) the words *in the Dark Years* are absent. Seven lines from the bottom of the page the text reads: 'or so it seemed to him in feeling not in reason', with pencilled correction to the reading of TT: 'or so it seemed to him in that dark hour of weariness, still labouring in the stony shadows under Kirith Ungol.'

27 The illegible words look most like 'flies back'. If this is what they are, the meaning must be very elliptically expressed: Frodo flees and the eyes pursue, but every time he turns round holding up the phial the eyes halt.

28 A trace of a stage in which the 'trap' or 'hole' in the floor of the tunnel was present as well as the branching ways is found on a slip carrying very disjointed drafting:

> Suddenly a thought came into Frodo's mind. Gollum, he had been ahead: where was he? Had he fallen into that awful lurking hole? 'Gollum! I wonder whether he's all right,' he muttered. 'Smeagol!'
>
> Groping in the dark they found that the opening or arch to the left was blocked a few feet inside, or so it seemed: they could not push their way in, it was
>
> he called or tried to call Smeagol! But his voice cracked and
>
> They tried first the opening to the left, but quickly it grew narrower and turned away mounting by long shallow steps towards the mountain wall. 'It can't be this way,' said Frodo. 'We must try the other.'
>
> 'We'll take the broader way,' said Frodo. 'Any passage that turns sideways .....'

29 Frodo's cry here has the form *Alla Earendel Elenion Ankalima*, and *Alla* remained through the following texts, only being changed to *Aiya* after the book was in type.

30 The word *flicked* in TT p. 330 ('but at its edge a blue fire flicked') is an error for *flickered* which was missed in the proof.

31 Perhaps for no other reason than that this section of the manuscript had become very ragged through emendation, and would have to be replaced, it had well before this point degenerated into rough pencil, at the end becoming an outline very hard to read.

32 The reference is to *The Hobbit*, Chapter III 'A Short Rest', where Elrond, speaking of the swords Glamdring and Orcrist taken from the trolls' hoard, says (in the text of the original edition):

'They are old swords, very old swords of the elves that are now called Gnomes. They were made in Gondolin for the Goblin-wars.'

33 This sentence ('For though once long ago he had seen it ...') was at first retained in the final fair copy manuscript, with the addition: 'neither did he understand his master.'

34 It is clearly written in the 'fair copy' style, but with some repetition and other features pointing to immediate composition, and it was corrected subsequently in pencil; I cite it here as corrected.

35 These words are used also in the story in *The Two Towers* (p. 330), but there only Shelob knows of the web at the end of the tunnel.

36 If this part of the draft did in fact belong with Version 1 there had been no encounter with the Spider in the tunnel, so that when this scene (surviving of course in TT, p. 339) was first written this was the first time that she had been confronted with the light of Earendel's star in the Phial of Galadriel.

37 The words 'foul but already pitiable' are read from a subsequent gloss of my father's. He gave up on the next word and wrote a query about it; it may perhaps be 'scuttle'. The words 'but already pitiable' are notable. In TT there is no trace of the thought that Shelob, entirely hateful and evil, denier of light and life, could ever be 'pitiable' even when defeated and hideously wounded.

38 This goes back to the original outline 'The Story Foreseen from Lórien' (p. 185), as does Sam's thought of building a cairn of stones, and the phrase later in this passage 'an elvish beauty as of one that is long past the shadows', which survives in TT.

39 Cf. the initial outline, p. 190: 'Turns back – resolved to lie down by Frodo till death comes. Then he sees Gollum come and paw him. He gives a start and runs back. But orcs come out and Gollum bolts.'

40 The first occurrence of the name *Shelob* (see p. 183).

41 Cf. the sentence added earlier in this draft at the point where Sam puts on the Ring: 'His hand hangs weighed down and useless.'

42 In the original account of Sam's fight with Gollum his staff was not broken (notes 19 and 20); this was where, and why, that element entered the story. The words 'The staff cracked and broke' were added to the fair copy (TT p. 335).

43 This is obscure. A proper name beginning with B, possibly *Ballung* or something similar, is followed by a sign that might represent 'and' or 'or'; but 'and' would mean that *Leader* and *says* were miswritten for *Leaders* and *say*, and though in this exceedingly rapid script words are frequently defective or miswritten the sentence reappears (p. 214), and there the words are

again *Leader* and *says*. Perhaps my father intended 'or' and was merely hesitating between two possible names for the Orc.

44 On this page of drafting is a hasty pencilled sketch of the final approach to the Cleft, and a little plan of the tunnel. In the first of these the place where Frodo lay is marked by an X on the path, and just to the left of it in the cliff-wall is the opening from which Shelob came. Another entry is seen in the distance at the top of the steps leading to the summit of the pass, at the foot of the cliff on which the Tower stands.

The plan of the tunnel is reproduced here. It will be seen that it differs from the elaborate earlier plan reproduced on p. 201 in that only one passage is shown leading to the left off the main tunnel at the eastern end, curving round and leading to the Tower.

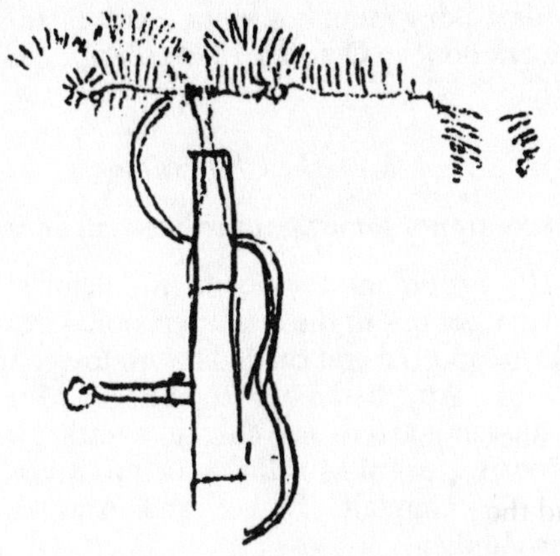

45 With this account of the origin of the tunnels cf. the outline accompanying the plan (p. 199): 'This tunnel is of orc-make (?) and has the usual branching passages.' It survived into the fair copy, where it was subsequently replaced by that in TT (p. 346).

46 The names of the leaders of the Orc-bands were rather bewilderingly changed in the drafts (and some transient forms cannot be read). At first (p. 212) they were *Gazmog* (of the Tower) and *Zaglûn* (of Minas Morghul), and in another brief draft of their genial greetings they become *Yagûl* and *Uftak Zaglûn* – so written: *Zaglûn* may have been intended to replace *Uftak*, but on the other hand the double-barrelled Orc-name *Naglur-Danlo* is found (p. 212). The name *Ufthak* was subsequently given to the Orc found (and left where he was) by Shagrat and his friends in Shelob's larder, 'wide awake and glaring' (TT p. 350). In the present text the names were at first *Yagûl* (of the Tower) and *Shagrat* (of Minas Morghul), but were reversed in the course of

writing (and in a following draft the names became reversed again at one point, though not I think intentionally). At this point, where the Orc from Morghul is speaking, my father first wrote *Shag*[*rat*], changed it to *Yagûl*, and then again changed it to *Shagrat*. See note 48. — *Yagûl* was replaced by *Gorbag* in the course of writing the fair copy.

47 *Dushgoi*: Orc name for Minas Morghul.

48 The text actually has *Shagrat* here, but this should have been changed to *Yagûl* (see note 46).

49 The story of the ascent of the Pass of Kirith Ungol was early divided into three chapters, with the titles which were never changed; the numbers being XXXVIII, XXXIX, and XL. See my father's letters cited on pp. 183–4.

50 After the verse my father wrote: 'such words in the Noldorin tongue as his waking mind knew not', striking this out at once.

51 This was work done in October 1944: see pp. 233–4.

52 Cf. VII.448.

Note on the Chronology

Time-scheme D continues somewhat further than does C (see p. 182):

Friday Feb. 10 Frodo and Sam come to Shelob's lair early in the morning. They get out in the late afternoon – nearly at top of the pass. Frodo is captured and carried to orc-tower at night.

Saturday Feb. 11 Attack at dawn on besieged Minas Tirith. Riders of Rohan suddenly arrive and charge, overthrowing the leaguer. Fall of Théoden. Host of Mordor flung into River.

Sunday Feb. 12 Gandalf (Éomer and Aragorn and Faramir) advance into Ithilien.

Time-scheme S goes no further than February 8.

Pencilled entries were added to February 11 in Scheme D: 'Sam at the Iron Door early hours of Feb. 11. Sam gets into orc-tower. Rescues Frodo. They fly and descend into Mordor'; and 'Ships of Harad burnt'.

PART THREE

MINAS TIRITH

I
ADDENDUM TO 'THE TREASON OF ISENGARD'

After the publication of 'The Treason of Isengard' I came upon the following manuscript page. It had ended up in a bundle of much later writings concerned with the events of Books V and VI, and when going through these papers I had failed to see its significance. It is in fact the concluding page of the first of the two outlines that I gave under the heading 'The Story Foreseen from Fangorn' in VII.434 ff.; and since it represents my father's earliest recorded conception of the events of Book V this seems the best place to give it. I repeat first the conclusion of the part printed in Vol. VII (p. 437):

> News comes at the feast [at Eodoras] or next morning of the siege of Minas Tirith by the Haradwaith. ... The horsemen of Rohan ride East, with Gandalf, Aragorn, Gimli, Legolas, Merry and Pippin. Gandalf as the White Rider. ... Vision of Minas Tirith from afar.

The text begins in the same pale ink as was used for the earlier part of the outline but soon turns to pencil. At the head of the page is written (later, in a different ink): 'Homeric catalogue. Forlong the Fat. The folk of Lebennin' (see p. 287).

Battle before walls. Sorties from city. Aragorn puts the Haradwaith to flight. Aragorn enters into Minas Tirith and becomes their chief. Recollection of the boding words (as spoken by Boromir).

The forces of Minas Tirith and Rohan under Aragorn and Gandalf cross the Anduin and retake Elostirion. The Nazgûl. How Gandalf drove them back. Wherever the shadow of the Nazgûl fell there was a blind darkness. Men fell flat, or fled. But about Gandalf there was always a light – and where he rode the shadow retreated.

The forces of West worst Minas Morghul [*written above:* Morgol] and drive back the enemy to the Field of Nomen's Land before Kirith Ungol. Here comes the embassy of Sauron. He sends to say that [*Here the ink text ends and is followed by pencil, the word* that *crossed out*] to Gandalf and Aragorn that he has got Frodo the Ringbearer captive. (Dismay of Aragorn.)

Sauron's messenger declares that Frodo has begged for deliverance at any price. Sauron's price is the immediate withdrawal of all forces west of Anduin – and eventual surrender of all land up to west of Misty Mountains (as far as Isen). As token Sauron's messenger shows Sting (or some other object taken – the phial?) taken when Frodo was prisoner – this would have to be something Sam overlooked [*written in margin:* mithril coat]. But Gandalf utterly rejects the terms.

'Keep your captive until the battle is over, Sauron! For verily if the day goes to me and we do not then find him unharmed, it shall go very ill with you. Not you alone have power. To me also a power is given of retribution, and to you it will seem very terrible. But if the day is yours then you must do with us all that remain alive as you will. So indeed you would do in any case, whatever oath or treaty you might now make.'

Gandalf explains that Frodo is probably *not* captive – for at any rate Sauron has not got the Ring. Otherwise he would not seek to parley.

The story must return to Sam and Frodo at the moment when Gandalf and Aragorn ride past Minas Morghul. ? And go down to moment when Ring is destroyed.

Then just as Gandalf rejects parley there is a great spout of flame, and the forces of Sauron fly. Aragorn and Gandalf and their host pour into Gorgoroth.

Part of Battle could be seen by Frodo from [?his] tower while a prisoner.

With the last part of this text compare the second part of the outline 'The Story Foreseen from Fangorn', VII.438.

II
BOOK FIVE BEGUN AND ABANDONED

(i) Minas Tirith

My father recorded years later (see p. 77 and note 19) that before the long gap in the writing of *The Lord of the Rings* in 1943–4 he had written the beginnings of Book V Chapters 1 and 3 ('Minas Tirith' and 'The Muster of Rohan'); but 'there as the beacons flared in Anórien and Théoden came to Harrowdale I stopped'. A preliminary question is whether the abandoned opening of 'Minas Tirith' still exists and can be identified.

What is certainly the earliest of several 'beginnings' ('**A**') consists first of a few lines clearly written in ink:

Pippin looked out from Gandalf's arms. Though he was awake now he felt that he was still in a swift-moving dream. Still the world of grey and green rushed by and the sun rose and sank and the wind sang in his ears. He tried to reckon the time, but he could not be sure.

From this point the text is continued in a rapid pencilled scribble:

Two days ago it was that he saw the sun glinting on the roof of the king's great house, and then he had slept, dimly aware of the bustle and a coming and going about him. Coming of Nazgûl. Then more darkness and wind, and then again. Yes, this must be the third riding. The stars seemed to be fleeing overhead.

He stirred. Where are we, he said.

Passing [?through] the land of Anórien, which is [?a realm] of Gondor, said Gandalf. Now we have turned southward. Dawn is at hand. Open your eyes.

Beacons. Messengers riding West.

Description of Minas Tirith and its immense concentric walls.

They come to presence of Denethor and hear news which Gandalf supplements.

Gandalf remains hidden [?communing] with himself. Pippin on the battlements. The allies come in. Faramir returns. War and siege. Gondor defeated. Ships of Harad. New force from North. Episode of the Palantír and Gandalf.

No sign of Riders.

This pencilled continuation was obviously written all at one time, and it was written therefore *after* May 1944, when Faramir, whose return to Minas Tirith is mentioned here, entered the story of *The Lord of the Rings*: it is new work on the story after Book IV had been completed. That the brief initial passage in ink ('Pippin looked out from Gandalf's arms ...') should be separated from its pencilled continuation by a long interval seems to me so unlikely as to be out of the question. Far more probably my father abandoned it because he had changed his mind about Gandalf's riding by day, and (as he often did in such cases) then sketched out the changed conception very rapidly (see the Note on Chronology at the end of this chapter).

This was followed by a further draft of the opening ('**B**'), a single page roughly written in ink that went no further than the errand-riders racing from Gondor to Edoras. I give this brief text in full, ignoring a few subsequent changes in pencil.

Pippin looked out from the shelter of Gandalf's cloak. He was awake now, though he had been sleeping, but he felt that he was still in a swift-moving dream. Still the dark world seemed to be rushing by, and a wind sang loudly in his ears. He could see nothing but the wheeling stars, and away to the right vast shadows against the sky, where the mountains of the south marched by. Sleepily he tried to reckon the time, but he could not be sure of his memory. This was the beginning of the second night of riding since he had seen the pale gleam of gold in the chill dawn and had come to the great empty house upon the hill in Edoras. There he had slept only dimly aware of much coming and going and of the great outcry when the winged flier had passed over. And since then riding, riding in the night.

A pale light came in the sky, a blaze of yellow fire was lit behind dark barriers. For a moment he was afraid, wondering what dreadful thing lay ahead; he rubbed his eyes, and then he saw it was the moon rising full out of the eastern shadows. So they had ... for four hours since dusk![1]

'Where are we, Gandalf?' he asked.

'Anórien the realm of Gondor is still fleeting by,' said Gandalf.

'What is that?' said Pippin, suddenly clutching at Gandalf's cloak. 'Fire! I thought for a moment it might be a dragon. I feel that anything might happen in this land. Look there is another!'

'On, Shadowfax!' cried Gandalf. 'We must not rest this night. Those are the beacons of Gondor calling for aid. War is kindled. See, there is the light on Amon Thorn, and a flame on Elenach;

and look there they go speeding west, Nardol, Penannon, Orodras, and Mindor Uilas on the borders of Rohan. Haste!'

And Shadowfax leaped forward, and as he sprang forward he neighed pricking his ears. Neighing of horses answered and like shadows flying on a wild wind riders went by them thundering west in the gloom.

'Those are post riders,' said Gandalf, 'riding from message post to message post – bearing tidings and summons. The message will reach Edoras by nightfall tonight.'[2]

This text was followed by another single page ('C'). This was typed by my father in the 'midget type' which he used in his letters to me from 7 July 1944 (see the beginning of no. 75 in *Letters*) and frequently until October of that year; and thus this one sheet carries the story as far as the point where Shadowfax passes through the narrow gate in the Pelennor wall (RK p. 21) – the text stopping just before the name *Pelennor* would appear (see p. 277). The final text was now very closely approached. The names of all the beacons (now seven, not six) are here in the final form: Amon Dîn, Eilenach, Nardol, Erelas, Minrimmon, Calenhad, and Halifirien on the borders of Rohan. There are however a few differences. Gandalf here tells Pippin that the message-posts were at distances of 'every fifty miles or so, where errand-riders were always in readiness to carry messages to Rohan or elsewhere' (in RK, p. 20, no distance is mentioned, and Belfalas is named as another destination of such errands). The passage in which Pippin, falling asleep, thinks of Frodo runs thus:

He wondered where Frodo was and if he was already in Mordor, little thinking that Frodo on that same night saw from afar the white snows under the moon; but the red flames of the beacons he did not see, for the mists of the Great River covered all the land between.

On this see the Note on Chronology at the end of this chapter.[3] — The leader of the men at the Pelennor wall is here named Cranthir, not Ingold.

The next stage in the evolution of 'Minas Tirith' was a complete, or nearly complete, draft text; that the page 'C' preceded it and was not an abortive start to a typescript of it is certain (e.g., the leader of the men at the wall is now Ingold).

My father here set a most curious puzzle. The datum is that (as he said) he abandoned 'Minas Tirith' about the end of 1942, as 'the beacons flared in Anórien': the story only went 'as far as the arrival in Gondor'. A single typescript page ('C') does precisely that, and when I first studied these papers I felt certain that it was the 'abandoned opening'; but it is clear and obvious that 'C' was developed from 'B' and that from 'A', and in 'A' there is a reference to Faramir, who only entered the story in 1944. Moreover 'C' was typed with a special type which my father seems only to have begun using in 1944. The emphatically underlined words in A '*Beacons. Messengers* riding West' certainly suggest that this is where those ideas actually arose; but how could they have done so, since 'the beacons flared in Anórien' already in the original opening of 1942? I was therefore forced to the conclusion that that was lost.

But this conclusion is wrong; and there is very clear evidence that my father erred in his recollection. The solution lies in a passage from his letter of Thursday 12 October 1944, which I have cited before (p. 100), but not in full:

> I began trying to write again (I would, on the brink of term!) on Tuesday, but I struck a most awkward error (one or two days) in the synchronization, v. important at this stage, of movements of Frodo and the others, which has cost labour and thought and will require tiresome small alterations in many chapters; *but at any rate I have actually begun Book Five* (and last: about 10 chapters per 'book').

I had taken (in view of what he said years later) the words that I have italicised to mean that my father had begun 'Minas Tirith' anew, and supposed that in this brief reference he simply passed over the fact that the beginning of the chapter (and the beginning of 'The Muster of Rohan') was long since in existence – or else that the earlier beginning had now been rejected and set aside. But the words are much more naturally taken to mean what they say: 'I have actually begun Book Five' – on 10 October 1944, *ab initio*; and if they are so taken the entire problem disappears. The abandoned opening is not lost, and it is indeed the curious isolated page 'C' in 'midget type'; but it was written in 1944, not 1942. The page 'A', preceding 'B' and 'C', is indeed where the ideas of the beacons and the westbound errand-riders first emerged – and since it was written in 1944 the appearance of Faramir represents no difficulty. Thus in his letter of 29 November 1944 cited on p. 219 my father could say that 'Book Five and Last opens with the ride of Gandalf to Minas Tirith ... *Some of this is written or sketched*': it had been 'written or sketched' in the previous month.

The reason for this error, made many years later, is easy to see: for there was indeed a long hiatus in the writing of 'Minas Tirith' (and 'The Muster of Rohan'). But it fell not in the long halt of 1943–4, between Book III and Book IV; it fell in the long halt between October 1944 and the summer of 1946 (see pp. 219–20), after Book IV was completed. That this is so is strongly supported by the time-schemes. I have argued (p. 141) that the schemes C and D preceded the chronological problems that emerged in October 1944, while scheme S represents their resolution. All three, however, deal both with Frodo and Sam on the one hand and the events in Rohan and Gondor on the other; and it seems therefore very probable that they are all to be associated with the new narrative opening at that time. It was precisely because my father was now, in the latter part of 1944, returning 'west of Anduin' for the first time since he finished 'The Palantír' that the need for all this chronological synchronisation arose. See further the Note on Chronology at the end of this chapter.

The first full draft of 'Minas Tirith' belongs of course to the final period in the writing of *The Lord of the Rings*. This text was left behind in England; but apart from this, almost all manuscript material from the final period (Books V and VI), including outlines and initial draftings, went to Marquette University in the original consignment of papers.

(ii) The Muster of Rohan

The original draft for the opening of 'The Muster of Rohan', here called '**A**', is a rapidly pencilled text in my father's most difficult script, some of which has defied repeated attempts to decipher it; I give it here as best I can. The opening paragraph was rejected as soon as written, but it was not struck through. It may be mentioned before giving the text that it had long been known that Théoden would return from Isengard through the mountains to Dunharrow: see the outlines given on pp. 70, 72 (written before Gandalf's sudden departure for Minas Tirith on Shadowfax had entered). In LR the journey of Théoden, Aragorn and their company from Dol Baran is described in 'The Passing of the Grey Company', but that had not yet been written.

Morning was come again, but dim still lay the deep dale about them. Dark and shadowy the great woods of fir climbed upon the steep sides of the ... hills. Long now it seemed to the travellers since they had ridden from Isengard, longer even than [?the] time of their weary journey.[4]

Day again was fading. Dim lay the high dale about them. Night had already come beneath the great woods of murmuring firs that clothed the steep mountain-sides. But now the travellers rode down a steep track and passing out of the scented sighing gloom of the pines they [?followed a] ...... they found themselves at the ... where it passed into a wider vale. The long vale of Harrowdale. Dark on the right loomed the vast tangled mass of Dunharrow, its great peak now lost to sight, for they were crawling at its feet. Lights twinkled before them on the other side of the valley, across the river Snowborn[5] white and fuming on its stones. They were come at last at the end of many days to the old mountain homes of folk forgotten – to the Hold of Dunharrow. Long it seemed since they rode from Isengard. [?It was] ... days since they rode from Isengard, but it seemed ..., with little else but weary riding. So King Théoden came back to his people.

As dusk fell they came to the river and the old stone bridges that [?were there]. There they sounded a horn. Horns answered gladly from above. Now they climbed up a winding path which brought them slowly up to a wide upland field set back into the side of the great [?bones of Dunharrow. Treeclad walls half embraced it].[6] The Snowborn issued and fell down with a waterfall. The rock behind was full of caves that had been bored and cut with great labour in the rock walls. Legend said that here was a dwelling and a [?holy] place of forgotten men in the Dark Years – [?before ever] the ships came to Belfalas or Gondor was built. What had become of them? Vanished, gone away, to mingle with the people of Dunland or the folk of Lebennin by the sea. Here the Eorlingas had made a stronghold, but they were not a mountain folk, and as the days grew better while Sauron was far away they passed down the vale and built Edoras at the north of Harrowdale. But ever they kept the Hold of Dunharrow as a refuge. There still dwelt some folk reckoned as Rohir, and the same in speech, but dark with grey eyes. The blood of the forgotten men ran in their veins.

Now all [?about] the vale on [?flat] sides of the Snowborn they saw ... and ... of men, fires kindled. The [?upland plain] was filled [?too]. Trumpets rang, glad was the cry of men to welcome Théoden.

Éowyn comes forth and greets Théoden and Aragorn.

Gandalf's message tells her to hold assembly at Dunharrow.

This is not the House of Eorl. But [?that is guarded]. Here we will [?hold] the feast of victory so long delayed, and the [ale >] ... ale[7] of Háma and all who fell.

The torchlit stone hall.

Merry sat beside Théoden as was promised.[8]

Éowyn brings in the cup for the drinking.

Even as Théoden drains it the messenger comes.

Aragorn had already arrived and greets King Théoden[9] side by side with Éowyn.

Halbarad sister-son of Denethor.[10] He asks for ten thousand spears at once.

Men are [?gathering] in the East beyond the Inland Sea of Nurnen, and far north. Eventually they may assail the East

Emnet, but that would not come yet. Now Orcs have passed south through Nargil pass in the Southland beyond [?River] Harnen.[11]

I postpone discussion of this earliest conception of Harrowdale and the Hold of Dunharrow to the end of the next version. This, which I will call '**B**', began as a fully articulated narrative in ink and in clear script, but swiftly collapsed. The opening passage was much corrected both at the time of writing and subsequently; I give it here as it seems to have stood when my father abandoned it.

Day was fading. The high valley grew dim about them. Night had already come beneath the murmuring firwood that clothed the steep mountain-sides. Their path turning a sharp shoulder of rock plunged down into the sighing gloom under dark trees. At last they came out again and saw that it was evening, and their journey was nearly at an end. They had come down to the edge of the mountain-stream, which all day they had followed as far below it clove its deep path between the tree-clad walls. And now through a narrow gate between the mountains it passed out, and flowed into a wider vale.

'At last!' said Éomer. 'We are come

Here my father stopped. Perhaps at once, he added in pencil 'to Harrowdale', then struck out Éomer's words and continued the text in pencil, which soon becomes difficult to read, and finally as nearly impossible as text A.

They followed it, and saw the Snowborn white and fuming upon its stones rush down upon its swift journey to Edoras at the mountains' feet. To their right, now dark and swathed in cloud, loomed the vast tumbled mass of great Dunharrow, but his/its tall peak and cap of snow they could not see, for they were crawling under the shadow of his knees. Across the dale before them lights were twinkling.

'Long now it seems since we rode from Isengard about this hour of the day,' said Théoden. 'We have journeyed by dusk and night and by day among the hills, and I have lost count of time. But was not the moon full last night?'

'Yes,' said Aragorn. '[Five >] Four days have we passed on the road, and now six remain before the day that you appointed for the assembly at Edoras.'

'Then here at Dunharrow maybe we can rest a while,' said the King.

They came now [?under] dusk over a stone bridge across the

river; and when the head of [?his] long line had passed it a man sounded a loud call upon [a] horn. It echoed in the valley, and horn[s] answered it from far above. Lights sprang out and men rode forward to meet them. King Théoden was welcomed back with joy, and he rode on with Éomer and Aragorn and his company up the steep winding path that led to the Hold of Dunharrow on the mountain's knee. No foe could climb that way while any defended it from above. [Looking back] Merry was riding now on a pony furnished for him at Helm's Deep. With him [?went] Legolas and Gimli. They looked back and long after they had climbed high they could descry in the grey dusk below the long winding line of the Riders of Rohan still crossing by the bridge. Many men had followed Théoden from Westfold.

So at last they came to the Hold – the mountain homes of long forgotten folk. Dim legends only now remembered them. Here they had dwelt [and had made a dark temple a temple and holy place in the Dark Years] in fear under the shadow of the Dark Years, before ever a ship came to Belfalas or Gondor of the Kings was built. That was in the first [?reign] of Sauron the [?Great] when Baraddur first was founded, but they had ... [?him] and built a refuge ...... [?that no enemy] could take. There was a wide upland [field > ?slope] set back into the mountain – the lap of Dunharrow. Arms of the mountain embraced [it] except only for a space upon the west. Here the [?green bay] fell over a sheer brink down into Harrowdale. A winding path led up. Behind the sheer walls of the vale were ..... caves – made by ancient art. [?Water fell in a fall over the .... and flowed ... the midst ...]

When the men of Gondor came [?there] the men of this place lived for a while [?owning] no lord of Gondor. But what became of them no legend knew. They had vanished and gone far away.

As my father wrote the end of this text he drew two little sketches of the Hold of Dunharrow, and this page is reproduced on p. 239 (see also note 6). These sketches show his earliest imagining of the Hold very clearly: a natural 'amphitheatre' with caves in the further rock-wall, and a stream (in text A stated to be the Snowbourn) falling down from the heights behind and over the central door, thence crossing the open space ('the lap of Dunharrow') and falling again over the lower cliff up which the path climbs. It is less easy to be sure of the situation of the Hold in relation to Harrowdale. When Théoden and his company enter the dale 'the vast tumbled mass of great

Dunharrow

Dunharrow' is on their right; Dunharrow is the name of the mountain (on the First Map, IVE, VII.319, 'Dunharrow' is written against the mountain at the head of the great valley extending south-west from Edoras). They crossed the Snowbourn by a stone bridge; the path, steep and winding, then led them up to the Hold 'on the mountain's knee'; and the 'amphitheatre' was open to the west. The most natural interpretation is that the Hold was on the far (eastern) side of Harrowdale, and near the head of the valley.

The references in A to the Hold having been preserved as a refuge, and to 'the torchlit stone hall' in which the feast was held, are explained and expanded in subsequent texts.

Text B was followed, no doubt immediately, by a third version ('C'), clearly written in ink, which however again stops at the same point. Here the entry of the Riders into Harrowdale is described in very much the same way as it is in B:

They followed it [the mountain-stream] and saw it spring with a last leap into the Snowbourn River that white and fuming on its stones rushed down upon its swift journey to Edoras far below. To their right, dark and swathed in cloud, loomed the vast tumbled mass of great Dunharrow, but its peak and cap of snow they could not see, for they were crawling under the shadow of its knees. Across the valley upon the mountain-side lights were twinkling.

It was now Éomer, not Aragorn, who replied to Théoden's question 'But was it not the full moon last night?'; for Aragorn was no longer a member of the King's company.

'No, the night before,' said Éomer. 'Five days we have passed on the road: it has been slow since we took to the mountain-paths; five days remain until the day that you appointed for the muster at Edoras.'

'Then here at Dunharrow maybe we can rest a while,' said the King.

'If you would take my counsel, lord,' said Éomer, 'you would remain here until the war that threatens is over, lost or won. [*Struck out at once:* You have ridden far and taxed your strength in the war with Saruman. Victory will have little joy for me, or for your people, unless we can lay our swords at your feet.]'

'We will speak of that later,' said Théoden.

They rode on. Merry looked about him. He was tired, for he was riding himself now, on a sturdy hill-pony furnished for him at Helm's Deep; but he had enjoyed the journey among the passes and high dales, the tall pine-woods, and the bright waterfalls. He loved mountains, and the desire to see and know them had moved him strongly when he and his friends had plotted to go with Frodo, far away in the Shire.

He rode with the King's company, and often he had jogged along beside Théoden himself, telling him of the Shire, and the doings of hobbit-folk. They had got on well together, although much of Merry's language was hard for Théoden to understand. But all the same, and in spite of the honour, he was lonely, especially at the day's end. Aragorn had ridden on far ahead with the swifter riders, taking Legolas and Gimli; and he missed Pippin deeply. The fellowship seemed now altogether scattered.

They came now in the dusk to a stone bridge across the Snowbourn ...

It would be interesting to know why (at this stage in the development of the narrative, when they would all meet again at Dunharrow) Aragorn with Legolas and Gimli and others went on ahead (see note 9), but no explanation is given.

Text C now follows B very closely, and is largely identical with it. The mention of Legolas and Gimli riding with Merry is of course removed. Of the ancient men of Dunharrow it is said that 'their name was lost', and that here they 'had their refuge and hidden fane'; 'those were the days when Sauron first was lord, and Baraddur was founded; but they had not served him, making here a refuge that no foe could take.' The 'wide upland slope' is again named 'the Lap of Dunharrow', and it is again said to open on the west; 'There there was a sheer brink that fell some hundreds of feet down to the Snowbourn. Up this the winding path climbed. Inside the amphitheatre (?) was clasped by sheer walls of rock rising at the back to a great precipice; and the walls'

Here text C stops; there is thus no mention here of the falling stream referred to in A (where it is actually the Snowbourn) and B and shown on one of the accompanying sketches, nor of the relations of the men of Dunharrow with the men of Gondor.

A fourth text (**'D'**) followed, in which the actual words of the opening of 'The Muster of Rohan' in RK were quite closely approached for the most part, but this extends no further than a single page, ending with Merry's 'listening to the noise of water, the murmur of dark trees, the crack of stone, and the vast waiting silence that brooded behind all sound.' The most notable feature of this brief text is the following passage:

To their right, dark and swathed in cloud, loomed the vast tumbled mass of [*struck out immediately:* great Du] mighty Starkhorn, [*struck out:* the grim mountain,] but its gnarled and jagged peak they could not see, for they were crawling under the shadow of its knees. Across the valley upon the lap of the great mountain lights were twinkling.

At this point, it is clear, the great mountain 'Dunharrow' became the Starkhorn, and though the text does not extend far enough to make the matter certain the last sentence of this extract suggests strongly (especially from the use of the word 'lap') that the Hold of Dunharrow, in which lights were twinkling, was situated on the lower slopes of the Starkhorn.

The next stage seems to have been two pages of notes in very rapid pencil ('E'), some but not all of which my father overwrote clearly in ink, and against some names and words putting queries.

When the Eorlingas came first to Dun Harrow they had found only one old man living in a cave, speaking in a strange tongue. None could understand him. Often he spoke and seemed to desire to tell them something, but he died before any could read his words. Where were all the rest of his folk?

Aragorn and Éowyn meet the King. They say that Riders are mustering at Dun Harrow – Gandalf's command: he had passed by Edoras some days ago. Many have already come in – and many strange folk. I do not .... understand how, but a summons went forth long ago. Rangers have come and Dunlanders and messengers from the Woodmen of Mirkwood.

They say that but for the shadow of the new war they would make a feast of victory. Even so they will feast and rejoice because of the King's return.

Torchlit stone hall.

Merry sat beside Théoden as promised.

The following was overwritten in ink, apparently only to clarify the pencilled text (parts of which can be made out), not to alter or expand it. Several of the names have queries against them in the ink overwriting, and some of the pencilled words my father could not interpret.

Éowyn bears wine to him, bidding him drink and be glad.

Even as Théoden drinks the cup, the messenger of Minas Tirith arrives. ? Barahir ? Halbarad.

He asks for ten thousand spears at once! The Swertings have come. The forces of Sauron have crossed the Nargul ? Pass and raised the men of Harad and of ? Umbor. A fleet has put out from the Havens of Umbor – once Gondor's, but long lost – and sailed up the Anduin and reached Anárion, at the same time more enemies have crossed the river and taken the fords of Osgiliath again – won back hardly in the winter. [*In margin, ink over pencil:*] Swertings are only just moving, and a few preliminary ravages of Lebennin. Spies report a great fleet ? [*concluding pencilled words were illegible*]

Théoden replies that that is more than he could have mustered in a ? [*pencilled word was illegible*] at his height, and before the war with Saruman.

Éowyn says that women must ride now, as they did in a like evil time in the days of Brego son of [*mark showing name omitted*] Eorl's son, when the wild men of the East came from the Inland Sea into the Eastemnet.

[*Pencilled text struck through and not overwritten:*] Théoden decides to pass over the [*struck out:* Rath] Scada pass to the vale of Blackroot into Lebennin and fall on enemy in rear.

[*Ink over pencil:*] Aragorn [*in margin:* Éomer?] begs leave to take a force over the Scāda Pass and fall on the enemy's rear. 'I will go with you in my brother's stead' said Éowyn [*added:* to King Théoden].

[*Ink text original:*] As had been promised him at Isengard, Merry sat beside [*written above:* near] the King himself. On either side of the King were Éowyn and Éomer, and Aragorn beside Éowyn. Merry sat with Legolas and Gimli not far from the fire and spoke together – while all about rolled the speech of Rohan.

[*Ink over pencil:*] They had been bidden to the King's table but said that the lords would wish to talk high matters, and they wished to talk together. ? Legolas ? [*in margin:* No, King surely?] tells history of Dunharrow: how the men of Dunharrow lived in the valley; how Dunharrow was furnished; how the Kings of the Mark had once dwelt here – and still returned once a year in autumn. But Théoden had not kept this custom for several years. The Feast-hall had been long silent [*pencilled text:* But Théoden had not done so for many years].

Éowyn brings wine.

[*Ink text original:*] Remembering his promise at Isengard, Théoden summoned Merry and set him at his left hand at the high table upon the stone dais. On the King's right sat Éowyn[12] and Éomer, and at the table's end Aragorn. Legolas and Gimli sat beside Merry. The three companions spoke much together in soft voices, while all about them the speech of Rohan rolled loud and clear.

These notes – very much a record of 'thinking with the pen' – have several curious features. The conception of the Hold of Dunharrow as a great redoubt of the Kings of the Mark, with a hall of feasting in its caverns (whence came the lights twinkling on the mountain-side), reappears from text A, and the last survivor of the ancient people of Harrowdale emerges.

Aragorn (with Gimli and Legolas) has ridden on ahead to Dunharrow, as in text C (p. 241); and in these notes is the first mention of the coming south of a body of Rangers. Éowyn's reference to the assault on Rohan long before, when in the days of Brego 'the wild men of the East came from the Inland Sea into the Eastemnet', is a sign that the history of Rohan had been evolving unseen. In LR (Appendix A (II), 'The Kings of the Mark') Eorl the Young fell in battle with the Easterlings in the Wold of Rohan, and his son Brego, builder of the Golden Hall, drove them out. In the outline 'The Story Foreseen from Fangorn' (VII.435) and in drafting for 'The King of the Golden Hall' (VII.445) Brego, builder of the hall, was the son of Brytta. In the present notes Brego is the grandson of Eorl, and a blank is left for the name of his father.

Among other names that appear here, I cannot certainly explain the queries that my father set against the first occurrence of *Umbor* and against *Nargul (Pass)*.[13] For *Anárion* as the name of a region of Gondor see VII.309–10, 318–19; *Anárion* on both the First Map and my 1943 map is given not only to *Anórien* (north of Minas Tirith) but also to the region south of Minas Tirith. For the former, *Anórien* appears already in the draft A of the opening of 'Minas Tirith', p. 231. The *Scāda Pass* leading over the mountains into the Blackroot Vale is not named on any map.[14] It is here that the possibility first appears that Aragorn (or Éomer) will lead some part of the forces mustering at Dunharrow across the mountains, rather than ride to Minas Tirith along their northern skirts, in view of the news brought by the messenger from Gondor (see further pp. 252–3). The name proposed here for the messenger, *Halbarad* (beside *Barahir*), has appeared already in the original draft A of 'The Muster of Rohan': see p. 236 and note 10.

A new version of the narrative ('F') was now begun, clearly written at the outset but soon collapsing into a scrawl; in this the story extends rather further. In the opening passage of this text lights still twinkle across the valley 'on the lap of the great mountain'; Éomer still informs Théoden that the moon was full two nights before, that they have passed five days on the journey, and that five remain to the muster at Edoras; and the Riders still cross the Snowbourn by a stone bridge (not as in RK by a ford), here described as 'a bare arch, wide and low, without kerb or parapet'. The horns blown from far above answering the blast blown as the King's company passed over the bridge now become 'a great chorus of trumpets from high above' that 'sounded in some hollow place that gathered them into one great voice and sent it forth rolling and beating on the walls of stone.' When this was written, as will be seen shortly, the 'hollow place' was the interior of the Hold of Dunharrow – in the sense that my father originally intended by that name: the rock-ringed recess or 'amphitheatre' and the great caverns in the cliff; but the description survived into RK (with the addition of the words 'as it seemed' after 'some hollow place'), when the Hold of Dunharrow was used to refer to the Firienfeld, the wide upland reached by the twisting road, where the upper camps were set. There is no mention (at this point) of Gandalf's passage through Edoras, nor of the great encampment of Riders in Harrowdale (cf. RK pp. 66–7, and see note 16); after the words 'So the King of the Mark came out of the west to Dunharrow in the hills' the text continues at once with 'Leading up from the valley there was a road made by hands in years beyond the reach of song.'

The description of the climbing road here reached virtually its form in RK, and now appear the Púkel-men described word for word as in RK apparently without any previous sketching. But they were called by the Riders of Rohan *Hoker-men* (Old English *hocor* 'mockery, derision, scorn') – changed subsequently to *Pookel-men*.[15]

I give the remainder of this text in full.

After a time he [Merry] looked back and found that he had mounted some hundreds of feet above the valley, but still far below he could dimly see a winding line of riders crossing the bridge. Many men had followed Théoden from Westfold to the muster of Rohan.[16]

At last they came to a sharp brink and the road passed between walls of rock and led them out onto a wide upland: the Lap of Starkhorn men called it, [rising gently beyond the sheer wall of the valley towards a great northern buttress of the mountain >] a green mountain-field of grass and heath above the sheer wall of the valley that stretched back to the feet of a high northern buttress of the mountain. When it reached this at one place it entered in, forming a great recess, clasped by walls of rock that rose at the back to a lofty precipice. More than a half-circle this was in shape, [and its entrance looked west, a gap some fifty yards wide between sharp pinnacles of stone >]

its entrance a narrow gap between sharp pinnacles of rock that opened to the west. Two long lines of unshaped stones marched from the brink of the cliff [up to the slope to the Hold-gate >] towards it, and [in the middle of the Hold one tall pointed stone stood alone >] in the middle of its rock-ringed floor under the shadow of the mountain one tall menhir stood alone. [Beyond it in the eastern wall >] At the back under the eastern precipice a huge door opened, carved with signs and figures worn by time that none could read. Many other lesser doors there were at either side, and peeping holes far up in the surrounding walls.

This was the Hold of Dunharrow: the work of long-forgotten men.[17] No song or legend remembered them, and their name was lost. For what purpose they had made this place, a town, or secret temple, or a tomb of hidden kings, no one could say. Here they had dwelt under the shadow of the Dark Years, before ever ship came to the mouths of Anduin or Gondor of the Kings was built; and now they had vanished, and only the old Hocker-men [*later* > Pookel-men] were left, still sitting at the turnings of the road.

As the King climbed out upon [the Lap of Starkhorn >] the mountain's lap, and Snowmane paced forward up the long avenue of stones, riders came down to meet him, and again the trumpets sang. [*Struck out:* Now Merry saw that they were blown inside Dunharrow, and understood the great echo that they made.][18]

He looked about and marvelled, for there were many lights on either side of the road. Tents and booths clustered thick on the slopes and the smokes of little fires curled up in the dim air. Then again the trumpets rang, echoing in the hollow of the Hold, and riders came forth to meet him [Théoden] as Snowmane paced forward up the long avenue of stones.

As they drew near Merry saw to his delight that Aragorn rode at their head, and beside him was a woman with long braided hair, yet she was clad as a warrior of the Mark, and girt with a sword.

Very glad was the meeting of the lady Éowyn with Théoden the King and with Éomer her brother; but Merry did not wait for leave, while they spoke together he rode forward.

'Trotter, Trotter,' he cried. 'I am glad to see you again. Is Pippin here? or Legolas and Gimli?'

'Not Pippin,' said Aragorn. 'Gandalf has not been here [*later* > to Dunharrow], but Legolas and Gimli are here. You may find them in Dunharrow [*later* > the Hold] if you like to go and look, but don't wander in through the doors if they are not in the open. Without a guide you will get lost in that place, and we might spend days looking for you.' Merry rode on up the line of stones and Aragorn turned back to the King.

'Is there any news, Aragorn?' said Théoden. 'Only this,' said Aragorn. 'The men of Rohan are mustering here as you see. The Hold is full and the fields round about will soon be covered over. This is Gandalf's doing. It seems that he passed by Edoras going East many days ago and gave word that no great gathering of men should be held on the edge of the plain, but that all should come to meet you here. Many have already come, and with them many strange folk not of Rohan. For in some manner the rumour of war has long been abroad and men from far away say that they have had summons / a word that all who hate Mordor should come to Edoras, or to Minas Tirith. There are Dunlanders here, and some even of the Woodmen from the borders of Mirkwood, and wandering folk of the empty lands; and even some of the Rangers of the North, last remnant of Elendil's race: my own folk: they have come seeking me.'

'And you, Éowyn, how has it fared with you?'

'Well, Théoden King,' she answered. 'It was a long weary road for the people to take from their homes, and there were many hard words but no evil deeds. Then hardly had we come to Dunharrow and ordered ourselves when tidings came of your victory, and the fall of Isengard. There was great rejoicing, though I thought the tale had grown as it travelled along the road, until Aragorn came back as he promised.[19] But all have missed you, lord, especially in the hour of victory. It is overshadowed now by new fear, yet not dimmed altogether. Tonight all are preparing the feast. For you do not come unexpected. Aragorn named the very hour at which we might look for you. And behold you come.' She clasped his hand. 'Now I will admit, Théoden, brother of my mother, that it is beyond any hope I had when you rode away. This is a glad hour. Hail, Lord of the Mark, may I never again be taken from your side while you live still and rule the Eorlingas. Father you are to me since Éothain my father fell at Osgiliath far away.[20] Come now – all is prepared for you. And though Dunharrow is a dark place, full of sad shadow, tonight it shall be filled with lights.'

So they passed on, through the pinnacles of the gate, and

beside the Middle-stone, and dismounting before the dark portal they went in. Night gathered outside.

Far within Dunharrow there was a great cavern enlarged by many hands [*added later:* at different ages] until it ran back deep into the mountain, a great hall with pillars of living stone. At the far end it rose by [?steep short steps] to a platform of rock that rose far up above the light of torch. There was no hearth and no louvre for the smoke that could be seen; but fires of pinewood were lit all down the centre between the pillars, and the air was full of the scent of burning pinewood, but the smoke rose and escaped through fissures or channels that could not be seen. Torches blazed on wall and pillar. Three thousand men could stand there when the hall was cleared; but at the feast when all the benches and tables were arranged five hundred sat that night at the King's feast.

Here this text ends, and was followed, no doubt at once, by a second version ('G') of the latter part of F, beginning at the description of the Hold of Dunharrow (p. 245) and ending at the same point ('some five hundred sat that night at the King's feast').

While the description of the Hold was repeated virtually unchanged from F (as emended) – the 'Hoker-men' or 'Hocker-men' become 'Pookel-men' – the story that follows was rearranged and expanded. Merry does not now have any speech with Aragorn when he appears with Éowyn, and it is Éowyn that Théoden first addresses; in her reply she says:

There were hard words, for it is long since war has driven us from the quiet life of the green hills and the fields; but there have been no evil deeds. We had scarcely come to Dunharrow and all was still in turmoil, when tidings came of your victory at Helm's Deep. There was great rejoicing, and many at once went back to the lowlands, caring nothing for rumours of greater perils to come. I hindered as many as I could, for I thought that the tale had grown as it travelled – until Aragorn returned, yesterday morning, even as he said. Then we learned of the fall of Isengard and many other strange happenings. And we missed you, lord, desiring to make merry. ...

The remainder of her words are as in F, but she does not now mention her father. When she has finished speaking the text continues:

Now they rode on. Aragorn was beside the King, and Éowyn rode beside her brother exchanging many glad words. Merry jogged along behind, feeling forlorn: Aragorn had smiled at him, but he had no chance to get a word with him, or find out what had become of Legolas or Gimli, or Pippin.

'Have you gathered any tidings by the way, Aragorn?' asked the King. 'Which way did you ride?'

'Along the skirts of the hills,' said Aragorn. 'Being few we did not take to the mountain-paths, but came to Edoras and then up the Harrowdale. No enemy has been to Edoras or harmed your house. A few men have been left to hold the walls, and send word if any evil thing is seen in the plains. But the men of Rohan are mustering here, as you see. The Hold is full, and the uplands round about are covered with the camps of men. This is Gandalf's doing. We found that he had passed by Edoras before us, riding East, and had given orders in your name that no great gathering should be held on the edge of the plains, but that all men should come to meet you here. Most were willing enough. The dark shadow that we saw flying to Isengard was seen there also; and it, or another like it, has been seen twice again, darkening the stars. They say that men cower with fear as it passes, men who have never feared any enemy before.

'Not all your folk that can come have assembled yet, for the Last Quarter of the Moon was the day set; but most have already arrived. And with them have come also strange folk that are not of Rohan. For in some manner, the rumour of war seems to have gone far abroad long days ago, and men in distant countries have heard the word go forth that all who hate Mordor should come to Edoras or Minas Tirith. There are tall warriors of Dunland, some that fought against you, and some that never listened to Saruman, hating the Orcs far more than the Rohir! There are even Woodmen from the borders of Mirkwood, and wanderers of the empty lands. Last and fewest, but to me not least, there have come seven Rangers out of the North, my own folk, remnant of Elendil's race: they have sought me here.'

'How many spears and horses can we muster, if sudden need should come?' asked Théoden.

'Somewhat short of ten thousand,' answered Aragorn: 'but in that count I reckon only men well-horsed, fully armed, and with gear and provision to ride to battle far away, if needs be. As many again there are of men on foot or with ponies, with sword and shield, or bowmen and light-armed men of the dales: a good force to defend strong places, if war should come to the land of Rohan itself. If your Riders leave the land, then, lord, I should gather all your home-keeping men in one or at most two strong places.'

'It is my purpose to hold the Hornburg and Dunharrow,' said Théoden. 'I have left Erkenbrand and three hundred good men in Helm's Deep, together with many stout country folk, and yeomen of Westfold; and men skilled in the mountains are to keep watch on the tracks and passes that lead from there to here. The guard at Edoras I shall strengthen, commanding them to hold it as long as they may, and defend the mouth of Harrowdale. But here, where now the most part of my people who are willing to leave their homesteads and seek refuge is now gathered, I will leave the main host of my men that do not ride away. Not while any crumb of food remains will any foe overtake us here.'

'Not without wings,' said Aragorn.

So at length they passed the pinnacles of the gate, and the tall Middle Stone, and dismounted before the dark portals of Dunharrow. The king entered, and they followed him. Night drew down outside.

The description of the great hall in Dunharrow was scarcely changed from that in the text F (p. 248). The platform of stone at the far end was 'reached by seven shallow steps'; and 'two thousand men, maybe, could have stood in that place' when no tables and benches were set out.

It is interesting to observe that the picture in crayon of 'Dunharrow' in *Pictures by J.R.R. Tolkien* (1979), no. 29, reproduced as second frontispiece, represents this original conception: the dark cleft to which the double line of standing stones leads is (as I think) the 'gate of the Hold', the 'Hold' itself, the 'recess' or 'amphitheatre' with doors and windows in the cliff at the rear, being in this picture invisible.

Lastly, there is a typescript ('H') typed in the same 'midget type' as was used for the text 'C' of 'Minas Tirith' (see p. 233); this is only a little longer than the other, and the two texts are so closely similar in every respect that I think it certain that they come from the same time – i.e., this typescript of the present chapter belongs with all this original material for the opening of 'The Muster of Rohan', composed before my father again abandoned work on *The Lord of the Rings* towards the end of 1944.

It is therefore remarkable that in this typescript (which in other respects closely followed the previous version F, pp. 244–6) my father had already abandoned an essential element in the conception he had devised. No lights now twinkled on the far side of the valley as the King and his company came into Harrowdale; and after the description of the Pukelmen (so spelt) at the turns of the climbing road the text reads thus:

At last the king's company came to a sharp brink, and the road passed between walls of rock and led out onto a wide upland. The Firienfeld men called it, a green mountain-field of grass and heath high above the sheer wall of the valley. Beyond it was a dark wood that climbed steeply on the sides of a great round hill; its bare black head rose above the trees far above and on it stood a single pinnacle of ruined stone. Two long lines of unshaped stones marched from the brink of the cliff towards it and vanished in the gloom of the trees. Those who followed that road came in the sighing darkness of the Firienholt to a huge doorway in the side of the black hill of Firien;[21] signs and figures were above it, worn by time, that none could read. Within were vast caverns, so men said, though in living memory none had ever dared to enter. Such was the dark Dunharrow, the work of long-forgotten men.

Then follows the passage cited from text F on p. 246 ('No song or legend remembered them ...'), which was little further changed in RK (p. 68); and the typescript breaks off at the words 'As the king climbed out upon the upland field'.

What was the thought that lay behind this change, whereby 'dark Dunharrow' was now set within 'the black hill of Firien', a pinnacle of stone on its bare head, and became, so far from a place of feasting for the lords of Rohan, a place of fear that no man dared to enter? Perhaps my father felt that there was too much likeness between Dunharrow as first conceived and Helm's Deep: 'There are caves in Helm's Deep where hundreds may lie hid' (TT p. 134), 'Behind us in the caves of the Deep are three parts of the folk of Westfold ... great store of food, and many beasts and their fodder, have also been gathered there' (TT p. 136). Perhaps also the idea that Aragorn would pass over the moun tains by the Scāda Pass, as proposed in the notes E (p. 243), had already led to a new idea, that his road would lead *through* Dunharrow (cf. the outline V in the next section, p. 262). However this may be, I believe that it was here that my father laid aside *The Lord of the Rings*, at least in the actual written evolution of the narrative, until a further year and a half had passed.

There remains a further difference to notice in this last text from the preceding versions. To Théoden's question 'Was it not the full moon last night?' Éomer now replies: 'Nay, lord, the full moon will rise tonight four hours after dark. Tomorrow ere evening you shall come to Edoras and keep tryst with your Riders.'

(iii) Sketches for Book Five

I give here first (the most convenient place for it) a brief text of especial interest that stands quite apart from the outlines that follow, those being of much larger narrative purview and concerned to work out a coherent chronology for the extremely complex story to come. This text is found on a single page torn into halves and preserved separately among the manuscripts of 'The Siege of Gondor' at Marquette University – the reason for this being that my father later used the reverse of one half of the torn sheet to draft a revision of the opening of that chapter; but the original text belongs with the initial work on Book V studied here, and represents in fact a very early stage in that work. It is written in rapid pencil and is in places very difficult to make out, but the first part of it (as far as 'Muster in Minas Tirith') was overwritten clearly in ink, and so far as I can see my father scarcely altered the underlying text, his sole purpose being clarification. The whole page was struck through. At the head is written in pencil '250 miles', which probably refers to the distance from Edoras to Minas Tirith.

Evil counsels for evil days.

Éomer rides away and the king laments – for the snow is still deep and the wind over the Scāda has been the death of many a man.

Now it is to be told that King Théoden rested a day in Dunharrow and rode then to Eodoras and passed thence with five ? thousand riders, fully armed and horsed, and took the road to Minas Tirith. Others were to follow.

In ? five days they came within sight of Minas Tirith (Feb. 15 ?).

Merry's first sight of Minas Tirith from afar.

The plain below the hill covered with camps.

It would be better geographically if the main attack were made to come from the direction of Kirith Ungol – and the Swertings only a diversion, which nearly turns the scale.

Muster in Minas Tirith. [*Here the overwriting in ink ends.*]

People come from Belfalas and Dol Amroth and from the Five Streams of Lebennin in [?Anárion].[22] [?There came] Inram the tall from the vale of ....[23] and Nosdiligand[24] and the people of the Delta and Benrodir prince of [?Anárion], and the remnants of the folk of [?Ithilien] across the [??vale], and .....

from Rhovanion ..... men of the East,[25] and Rangers from the empty North, and even some of the folk of Dunland. [*Written against this passage in the margin*: King of Rohan Men of Rohan come *after* the assembly. Only Aragorn rode .. to it.]

And the counsel of Denethor was to retake the Fords [*of Osgiliath*] and drive back the Orcs. So they sounded their trumpets and flew the red banner from the tower and rode to meet the enemy. And the enemy could not withstand the swords of Gondor, and before the sword of Elendil they fled like ... But Gandalf stood on the hill and [?watched afar]. Then comes the fleet of the Swertings [> Harns] up from the Delta and the Swertings come up through Ithilien.

They watch for the men of Rohan who [?are late]. Men of Rohan camp nearby and charge in the morning. Then the Nazgûl come

Here the text stops abruptly. In its opening ('Éomer rides away ...') it is closely associated with a passage in the notes E in the preceding section, where is found the only other reference to the Scāda Pass, leading over the mountains to the Blackroot Vale on their southern side (see pp. 243–4): 'Aragorn [*in margin:* Éomer?] begs leave to take a force over the Scāda Pass and fall on the enemy's rear.' Thus the present text, where it is Éomer who takes this road, preceded – in this opening passage – the definitive emergence of the story that it was Aragorn who 'went with his rangers over the mountains' (see outline III on p. 260) or 'passed into the mountains with his Rangers' (see outline V on p. 262). On the other hand, in this earliest form of the 'catalogue'[26] of the peoples of Southern Gondor mustering in Minas Tirith mention is also made of men of Rhovanion, and Dunlanders, and 'Rangers from the empty North' coming into the city; whereas in the notes E (p. 242) it is to Dunharrow, not to Minas Tirith, that 'Rangers have come and Dunlanders and messengers from the Woodmen of Mirkwood' (and similarly in Aragorn's account to Théoden at Dunharrow in the text F, p. 247: 'There are Dunlanders here, and some even of the Woodmen from the borders of Mirkwood ...').

The present text seems then evidence of a fleeting stage in which certain important narrative ideas had emerged, but when their potential significance for the whole structure of Book V had not yet been realised. From the host mustering at Dunharrow, intending to ride to Minas Tirith by the Anórien road, a detachment is separated and passes over the mountains in order to come down swiftly into Southern Gondor (and this is above all on account of news of the great fleet approaching from the South, whose coming had long been foreseen, and which seems to have been originally the chief menace in the assault on Minas Tirith: see VII.435, 437). And Rangers come out of the North. These elements were of course essential to the story of 'the Grey Company' and all that flowed from it. But those who leave the main host of the Rohirrim are here led by Éomer, not Aragorn; and the Rangers come not to Dunharrow, but to Minas Tirith.

But if this is so, the stage was certainly fleeting. Apparently, even as he wrote this brief text my father began to move in a new direction. The Orcs before the city 'fled before the sword of Elendil' – and that can only mean that it was Aragorn who came over the mountains and so reached Minas Tirith before the main host out of Rohan. The marginal note ('Men of Rohan come *after* the assembly. Only Aragorn rode ... to it', where the illegible word might be 'in' but does not look like it) was obviously written concurrently with the passage that it adjoins, since in the sketch of the war that then follows the Men of Rohan are obviously *not* present at the 'assembly' at Minas Tirith.

In the conclusion of the text there seems to be no suggestion that the city was laid under siege. Of course it is very easy to misinterpret these allusive and elliptical outlines, in which my father would pick out salient 'moments' and pass over others equally essential to the narrative in silence; but although 'the siege of Minas Tirith by the Haradwaith' is mentioned in 'The Story Foreseen from Fangorn' (VII.437) I think that no siege is mentioned here because none existed, or at any rate not in a form significant for the narrative. The force of his remark 'It would be better geographically if the main attack were made to come from the direction of Kirith Ungol – and the Swertings only a diversion, which nearly turns the scale' must surely be that he had supposed hitherto that in the strategy of the Enemy the attack from the South was to be the major blow against the city. In the sketch of events given here the attack out of Mordor is repulsed with rapid victory by the forces riding out of Minas Tirith (which included Aragorn); but Gandalf 'stood on the hill' (of the city) and (if I read the words aright) 'watched afar': '*then* comes the fleet of the Harns up from the Delta and the Swertings come up through Ithilien' – and 'nearly turn the scale'. And so here, where (so far as record goes) the charge of the Rohirrim in the morning first appeared, it is against the attack from the South that the horsemen ride. If the city had been in anything like a state of siege, it was surely besieged no longer when they came.

Of the names that appear in this text, *Eodoras* can be no more than a casual reversion to the earlier form. On *Anárion* (?) see note 22. The reference to 'the Five Streams of Lebennin' is remarkable, since in the first full text of the chapter 'Minas Tirith', deriving from the period of renewed work on Book V in 1946, Lebennin is still 'the Land of Seven Rivers' (see p. 278). So far as I know, neither *Harns* (presumably = Haradwaith, Haradrim), nor the names of the rulers in Southern Gondor, Inram the tall of the Morthond Vale (? – see note 23),

Benrodir prince of Anárion (?), Nosdiligand of the people of the Delta, ever appear again.

There are half a dozen outlines sketching out the content of 'Book Five and Last' – at this stage my father was determined that *The Lord of the Rings* should extend to one further 'part' only: as he wrote to Stanley Unwin in March 1945 (*Letters* no. 98): 'It is divided into Five Parts, of 10–12 chapters each (!). Four are completed and the last begun.' It is not easy to determine the order in which these outlines were written down, and though the sequence in which I give them seems to me probable other arrangements are possible. There is however fairly clear evidence that all belong with the abandoned openings of 'Minas Tirith' and 'The Muster of Rohan' in October 1944.

The outline that I give first, numbering it 'I', obviously belongs to the earlier time, in view of the date of Gandalf's arrival at Minas Tirith: 'Feb 5 or 6' (see the Note on Chronology at the end of this chapter); and the date February 8 of Théoden's arrival at Dunharrow appears to agree with the third version C and the fifth version F of the opening of 'The Muster of Rohan' (*ibid.*). A part of this text, all of it originally written in pencil, was overwritten in ink, but the part that was not is here and there altogether illegible.

(I) Book V

Gandalf comes with Pippin to Minas Tirith. Feb 5 or 6 [*later* > 6].

Faramir. The allies come in. Urgent messages are sent to Théoden.

(Messages[27] must bid Rohirrim assemble at Edoras as soon as may be after the Full Moon of Feb. 6. Théoden reaches Dunharrow Feb. 8. Edoras Feb. 10 ...)[28]

Denethor only willing to hold his walls. Knowing war drawing near he has long sent out summons to allies. They are coming in. But the messengers to Théoden, his chief ally, have not returned yet. Gandalf tells of Théoden's war. Gandalf and Pippin on battlements. See shadow as Nazgûl sweep over river. Faramir comes on night of Feb. [7 >]8. At same time [> Next day] comes news of war at Osgiliath. Orcs led by Nazgûl have crossed river. Fleet from Umbar is approaching mouths of Anduin.

Faramir supports Gandalf's policy of attack by sortie *on the plain*. The first battle. The mountaineers drive the orcs back and burn ships. But orcs [?win through]. Nazgûl. Minas Tirith forces driven back. Still Gandalf .... [?on] the battlements.

Théoden leaves Edoras Feb. 11 with Éomer and Éowyn. Ents drive off the attack in north of Rohan. They drive back orcs out of west [?Anórien] and [*struck out:* Feb. 15 Last Quarter.] Reach battle Feb. 15.[29] Siege relieved by the Rohirrim and the allies of Lebennin. Gandalf comes forth and the enemy driven off. Théoden slain and Éowyn slays the King of the Nazgûl and is mortally wounded. They lie in state in the white tower.[30] Gandalf ..... [?Aragorn]. Cross the River at Osgiliath. Elves and Ents drive Orcs back. They reach Minas Morgul and press on to Dagorlad. Parley with Sauron.

Another outline, 'II', gives a brief, and increasingly brief, pencilled synopsis of each of the ten chapters that were to constitute Book V and complete *The Lord of the Rings*.

(II) Bk. V

1. Gandalf goes to Minas Tirith. Mustering of forces. War breaks out. Gondor driven back. No sign of Riders.

2. Théoden comes to Dunharrow. Beacons. Messengers arrive from Minas Tirith. Also from far afield reporting orcs across the river in Wold.

Théoden rides on the evening of Feb. 8.[31] Éowyn goes with him. Gamling is left in command in Westfold. The old seneschal of Edoras in Eastfold (Dunharrow).

Aragorn and Éomer ride to beat off orcs. They come back and rejoin main body reporting that Ents and Lórien Elves have driven back the north thrust. They ride to Minas Tirith.

3. Charge of the Riders of Rohan breaks siege. Death of Théoden and Éowyn in killing the Nazgûl King. Gondor destroys ships of Harad and crosses into Ithilien.

4. Sack of Minas Morgul. Victorious Gandalf [?pursues] on to Dagorlad. Elves of Lórien and Ents come from North. Parley with Mor..[32] Sauron's messenger.

5. Frodo from high tower sees the coming of the hosts of the West and the great assembly of secret army of Sauron.[33]

Rescue of Frodo by Sam.

[?This army] goes out, as he and Sam pass into Gorgor all is still and empty and the noise of the war is far away.

Gandalf is ambushed in Kirith Ungol and comes to edge of defeat.

6. Destruction of the Ring. Fall of Baraddur. Allies enter Mordor. Rescue of Frodo by Eagle.

7. Return to Gondor. Crowning of Aragorn. Funeral of Théoden and Éowyn.

The Hobbits depart north. [*Struck out:* Pass Lórien and]
Fall of Sauron.
Galadriel's land ruined.[34]

8. Rivendell.
9. Shire.
10. Epilogue. Sam's book.

There is no clear indication in this synopsis or in synopsis I that

Aragorn entered Gondor by a different route (indeed in II, § 2 the reverse seems to be implied).

This page carries also two notes deriving from the same time as the synopsis by chapters. One of these reads:

> Gandalf keeps back, not to reveal himself. As the siege grows and the armies of Gondor are pressed back he looks in the Palantír. He catches sight of Frodo in tower and then Sauron cuts in. Gandalf gives a great shout and hurls the Stone from the battlements. It slays ? a captain. Gandalf is now revealed. He rides forth. Nazgûl come. [?Host] comes out of Dagorlad.

Above the third sentence is written: 'Sauron holding the coat'. – With this note cf. the words 'Episode of the Palantír and Gandalf' in outline A for 'Minas Tirith', p. 231. This is the original germ of the story of Denethor and the Palantír of the White Tower, and also perhaps of that of the revelation of Aragorn to Sauron in the Hornburg.

The second of these notes is as follows:

> The Firien (Firgen) [*added:* or the Halifirien] is a hill surrounded by a dark pinewood (the Firienholt). In it is a great cave, the Dunharrow. No one has ever been in the cave. It is said to be a *haliern*,[35] and to contain some ancient relic of old days before the Dark. ?
>
> It is 22 miles up Harrowdale from Edoras.

This statement clearly agrees with the idea of Dunharrow that entered in the typescript H (p. 251), where the hill, clothed in a dark wood but with bare head, is named *Firien* and the wood *Firienholt*; and where it is told that 'in living memory none had ever dared to enter' Dunharrow. Perhaps this synopsis II and accompanying notes immediately preceded H.[36] The addition 'or the Halifirien' is not obviously later than the rest of this note on Dunharrow; it was presumably rejected at once, for in the companion typescript C of 'Minas Tirith' the names of all the beacons are in the final form, ending with 'the Halifirien on the borders of Rohan' (p. 233).

On the same piece of paper as synopsis II is a small sketch-map very hastily drawn in ink; this is reproduced on p. 258. At the top is Edoras at the entrance to the long valley of Harrowdale, through which flows the Snowbourn, rising in the Starkhorn at the head of the valley. The distance from the Starkhorn to Edoras is marked as 75 miles; on the First Map (IVE, VII.319), where the valley runs south-west, the distance between Edoras and the mountain against which is written 'Dunharrow' is also 75 miles.[37] About half-way up the valley the path taken by Théoden and the Riders, following the course of the mountain-stream, is seen descending into Harrowdale from the west; this path crosses the stream before it joins the Snowbourn (whereas in all early versions of the opening of 'The Muster of Rohan', including

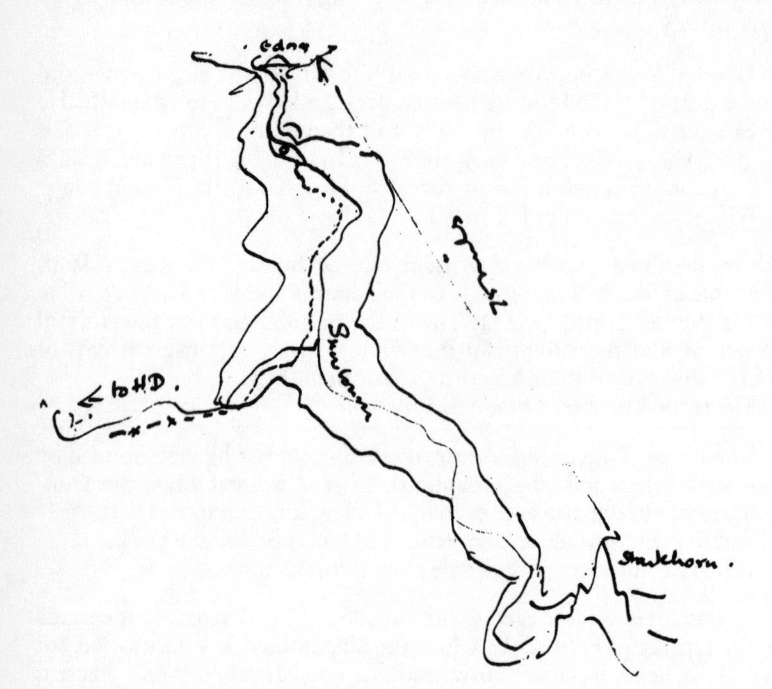

Gandalf keeps back – not to reveal himself. ~~[illegible]~~ As the siege grows and the armies of Gondor are pressed back he looks in the Palantir. He catches sight of Frodo in [illegible] and the Sauron [illegible] [Sauron trying to catch.] Gandalf gives a great shout and hurls the stone from the battlements. The [illegible] ? [illegible] Gandalf is now revealed. [illegible] come. [illegible] out of Dagorlad. [illegible]

Harrowdale

the typescript H, the stone bridge is over the Snowbourn itself), and turns north towards Edoras, ending at a place marked by a small circle but without a name. The circle is enclosed within two lines forming an oval shape. It can be seen in the original that the lower line is the course of the Snowbourn as first drawn, and that the upper line was put in with a subsequent stroke. However these markings, and the detached crescent line above them, are to be interpreted, there can be no doubt that this is the site of Dunharrow; both from the fact that the path leads to it, and from the statement in the time-scheme D (p. 141): 'Théoden comes out of west into Harrowdale *some miles above Dunharrow*, and comes to Dunharrow before nightfall.'

As regards the distances, if the Starkhorn is 75 miles from Edoras, then Dunharrow on this map is considerably less than 22 miles from Edoras (as stated in the note on the same page, cited above), indeed scarcely more than half as far; but perhaps the discrepancy can be accounted for by supposing that it was 22 miles on foot by a winding track, whereas the 75 miles is shown as a linear distance between two points.

An explanation of this curious stage in the evolution of the geography of Harrowdale can be found by combining the evidence of synopsis II, the time-scheme D, and the narrative opening of 'The Muster of Rohan' in the typescript H. Abandoning the idea that Dunharrow was a cavernous hold opening onto the green mountain-field that was called the Lap of Starkhorn (p. 245), and that within it there was a huge feasting-hall, to be used that very night to celebrate the King's return, my father at the same time moved its site far down the valley towards Edoras, and made it a cave or caves in a hill ('Firien') some 50 miles or so from the Starkhorn.

A third outline ('III') also sets out a scheme for Book V by chapters, but does not proceed very far.

(III) Book V

Ch. 1. Gandalf and Pippin reach Minas Tirith (Feb. 6 morning). They see Denethor. Reasons for the beacons: (a) news from scouts in Ithilien. (b) news reached Denethor on Feb. 5 that fleets of Southrons had set sail. Gondor musters its forces. Pippin sees full moon rising and wonders where Frodo is. No sign of Rohan.

2. Théoden comes to Dunharrow. Pukel men. (Feb. 6 [> 5]). Beacons and messengers [*added:* morning 6]. Tidings of orc-invasions of Wold. Théoden rides out on night of Feb. 8 [> 6]. Éomer and Éowyn ride with him. Gamling is left in command in Westfold. The old seneschal of Edoras in Eastfold. [Aragorn and Éomer ride north to beat off orcs. They come back >] Éomer rides north to beat off orcs. He comes back and rejoins main body,

reporting that Ents and Lórien Elves have destroyed the northern diversion. They all ride to Minas Tirith. Where is Aragorn? He went with his rangers over the mountains.

3. Great Darkness. Faramir returns (8). Host of Morghul crosses River (9). Southron fleets assail the south of Gondor (10 [> 9]). Gondor defeated and besieged (10 [> 9]). Gandalf in White Tower does not yet reveal his power or ...... [?name].

Final assault on Minas Tirith [*added:* [11 >] 10 night]. Nazgûl appear. Pelennor wall is taken. Sudden charge of Rohan breaks siege. Théoden and Éowyn destroy Nazgûl and Théoden falls [*struck out:* Feb. 12]. Aragorn arrives (having crossed the mountains with his rangers, he drove off the Southrons). Aragorn enters Minas Tirith and meets Denethor and Faramir.

4. [*Added:* 12] Gandalf and Aragorn and Éomer and Faramir defeat Mordor. Cross into Ithilien. Ents arrive and Elves out of North. Faramir invests Morghul and main force comes to Morannon. Parley.

A suggestion that Aragorn should cross the mountains into Gondor is found in the notes E on p. 243; in these notes is found also the first mention of the coming of Rangers from the North, referred to also in the narratives F and G (pp. 247, 249). The Púkel-men entered in F (p. 245), where they are called *Hoker-men*, *Hocker-men*; in G they are *Pookel-men* (p. 248), and in typescript H *Pukelmen* (p. 251).

The text that I give next, 'IV', is reproduced on p. 261. This is a very battered page[38] of great interest, since it carries what is undoubtedly the earliest drawing of Minas Tirith, around which is written an outline in faint pencil. The line that runs up to the right of the White Tower indicates the mountain behind the city, with the name *Mindolluin* written across the summit. Whether my father already conceived the 'Hill of Guard' to be joined to the mountain mass by a shoulder cannot be said.

The outline reads as follows (with contractions expanded and some punctuation added):

(IV) Gandalf and Pippin reach Minas Tirith dawn. Description of Minas Tirith and its huge 'cyclopean' concentric walls – it is in fact a fort and town the size of a small mountain. It has 7 circles with 7 – 6 – 5 – 4 – 3 – 2 – 1 gates before the White Tower is reached.

They are challenged on the borders of the Cityland, Pelennor,[39] about which ruins of an old wall ran. Gandalf [?carries messages] from Rohan and speaks some pass[?word] and they let him by in wonder. So he rides up to the 6th court and dismounts. There Pippin is re..... They pass into High City (Taurost) and so come before Denethor who at first does not recognize Gandalf.

1

G and P reach M T dawn.. Descr. of M.T and its huge 'cyclopean' concentric walls — it is in fact a fort and town the size of small mountain; it has 7 circles, with 7–6–5–4–3–2–1 gates before the White Tower is reached.

[illegible] [illegible] the borders of Cirion. [illegible] [illegible] [illegible] [illegible] [illegible] Gandalf [illegible] [illegible] for [illegible] Rohan and speaks [illegible] [illegible] [illegible] [illegible].

[illegible] [illegible] [illegible] [illegible] [illegible]. The P is [illegible]

[illegible] [illegible] [illegible] [illegible] ([illegible]) [illegible] [illegible]. Denethor [illegible] [illegible] [illegible] Gandalf. Denethor [illegible] [illegible]

News. Denethor [illegible] [illegible] [illegible]. [illegible] [illegible] [illegible] [illegible] [illegible] [illegible].

Throne empty. D. has seat in front. [illegible] comes in after G [illegible] [illegible] has a [illegible] letter from [illegible] ([illegible] of D. [illegible] [illegible] [illegible] for [illegible] but not [illegible] [illegible] Ring

The earliest sketch of Minas Tirith

Denethor comes out to his [?throne]. News. Denethor has lit the beacons because what his spies tell. Faramir. Boromir.

Throne empty. Denethor has seat in front. He comes in after Gandalf arrives. He has a secret letter from Faramir (telling of Boromir's death and meeting with Frodo, but not overtly mentioning Ring).

This seems to have been my father's first setting down on paper of his conception of Minas Tirith.

The next two outlines ('V' and 'VI') were developed from III, and are very closely related: they were certainly written at the same time. From the rejected sentence in VI 'He has a secret' it is seen that my father had IV in front of him, for in that text appears 'He has a secret letter from Faramir'. The rejected reference in V to 'Dunharrow under the Halifirien' relates this outline to the note on Dunharrow in II (see p. 257). There is thus good reason to think that V and VI derive from 1944 rather than 1946, and it is notable that in V appears the first glimpse of the story that would emerge as the passage of the Paths of the Dead.

(V) Book V

Gandalf and Pippin ride to Minas Tirith (3–4, 4–5 arriving at sunrise on 6). Interview with Denethor – reasons for the beacons: a great fleet from south is approaching mouths of Anduin. Also messages from secret scouts in Ithilien report that 'storm is about to burst'.

Muster of Gondor (Forlong the Fat etc.). Pippin on the battlements sees the full moon; and thinks of Frodo.

Théoden reaches Dunharrow [*struck out:* under the Halifirien] (Feb. 5 evening). Púkel-men. They find muster already begun and not at Edoras. Rangers have come! Gandalf had been at Edoras and issued orders: Nazgûl crossed the plain (3–4 and on 4). Beacons are reported that night. Messengers arrive in morning. Théoden prepares to ride. Gamling in charge at Helm's Deep. Galdor the old seneschal[40] of Edoras in Eastfold. Éowyn rides with Éomer and Théoden.

Théoden sets out at nightfall (6). At Edoras they hear tidings of invasion of Wold. ? Éomer rides off north but rejoins main host later with news that the Ents have come out of Fangorn and destroyed this N. diversion. They pass on at all speed into Anórien.

Aragorn is not there. He had fallen into converse with the messengers of Gondor and getting guides from the men of Harrowdale had passed into the mountains with his Rangers.

Great darkness over land (Feb. 8). Faramir comes. Host of Morghul crosses Great River at Osgiliath (night of 8) and assails

Gondor (9). At same time S[outhron] fleets come up the Great River and send a host into Lebennin, while another host from Morannon crosses River to north on a boat-bridge and links with the Morghul-host. Gondor is defeated in night battle 9–10. Gandalf in White Tower does not yet reveal himself. [*In margin:* Gandalf looks in Palantír?] Black hosts gather about the wall of Pelennor. Morning of 10 Nazgûl are seen: men fly. At sunrise on 10 there is a sound of horns. Charge of Rohan. Rout of the enemy. [*Scribbled in margin:* Éomer wounded.] Théoden is slain by Nazgûl; but he is unhorsed[41] and the enemy is routed. [*Added:* Gandalf leads charge in white.] Théoden is laid in state in tomb of kings. [*Struck out:* Great grief of Merry. Meeting of Merry and Pippin.]

[*Added:* News comes that fleet is coming up River. .....] News comes from South that a great king has descended out of the mountains where he had been entombed, and set such a flame into men that the mountaineers (where the purer blood of Gondor lingered?) and the folk of Lebennin have utterly routed the Southrons, and burned [> taken] their ships. The fleet sailing up the River is an ally! Aragorn reaches Osgiliath by ship like a great king of old. (Frodo's vision?)[42] Meeting of Gandalf and Aragorn and Faramir at Osgiliath evening of 10.

Closely related to outline V is the following text ('VI'), which I incline to think was written second.

(VI) Gandalf and Pippin ride to Minas Tirith (3–4, 4–5, 5–6) arriving at the Outer Wall of Pelennor at daybreak and seeing sunrise on the White Tower on morning of Feb. 6. On night of 5–6 they see the beacons flare up, and are passed by messengers riding to Rohan. Pippin sees moonrise about 9 p.m.

Description of Minas Tirith and its 7 concentric walls and gates. Gandalf and Pippin come into the presence of Denethor. Empty throne. Denethor has a seat in front. [*Struck out:* He has a secret] They exchange news. Reasons of Beacons: news of scouts in Ithilien that 'storm is coming'; Southrons are marching in; most of all – a great fleet from South is approaching the mouths of Anduin. Muster of Rohan [*read* Gondor] is going apace – catalogue.

(7) Great Darkness spreads from East. Faramir returns. Pippin on the battlements.

Théoden reaches Dunharrow (5 evening). Merry sees Púkelmen. They find Muster has already begun, owing to special instructions by Gandalf, who had stayed at Edoras on 4 and owing to passage of Nazgûl. Rangers have come! [*Struck out:* Aragorn and Éomer already there?] That night the beacon lights are reported. In morning messengers arrive from Gondor.

Théoden gets ready to ride. Éowyn and Éomer go with him. [*Struck out:* But Aragorn (after secret converse with Aragorn takes Merry]

Here outline VI ends, but the lower half of the page is taken up by a map, which is redrawn in part and discussed in a note at the end of this chapter.

NOTES

1 The illegible word might be *already*, in which case my father omitted the words *been riding*. The word I have given as *four* might be read as *five*.

2 The words *by nightfall tonight* are perfectly plain, but my father must have intended something else, since it was now several hours after nightfall. In the outlines V and VI (pp. 262–3) the messengers from Minas Tirith reach Edoras the following morning (6 February).

3 As in text B, the moon rises 'round and full out of the eastern shadows' ('now almost at the full,' RK). — At this stage the beacons were fired on the last night of Gandalf's ride; in the final form it was on the night preceding the last (the journey taking four nights), and so when Pippin woke in the dawn beside the wall of the Pelennor 'Another day of hiding and a night of journey had fleeted by' (RK p. 20). This sentence was added to the text of the chapter much later.

4 Possibly this means 'longer than the time that they had in fact taken'.

5 Here and subsequently, and again in text B, the river's name is written *Snowborn*, but at two of the occurrences in A the *u* was inserted.

6 At this point my father drew in the text a very simple little sketch of the 'upland field' set into the mountain's side, essentially the same as the lower of the two sketches on the page reproduced on p. 239, but without the falling stream.

7 My father first wrote 'ale of Háma', i.e. his 'funeral-ale', funeral feast (cf. *bridal* from *bride-ale*, marriage feast). He changed this to ... *ale of Háma*, intending some compound term of the same sense, but I cannot decipher it.

8 This is a reference to Théoden's words to Merry and Pippin at the end of 'The Road to Isengard': 'May we meet again in my house! There you shall sit beside me ...'

9 This contradicts the statement a few lines above that 'Éowyn comes forth and greets Théoden and Aragorn.' The story that Aragorn (with Legolas and Gimli) had gone on ahead and

reached Dunharrow before Théoden is not present in text B, which undoubtedly followed A; it appears however in the time-schemes C and D (pp. 140–1).

10 *Halbarad* first appeared in *The Lord of the Rings* as the name of Shadowfax: see VII.152, 390.

11 The Sea of Nurnen, the Nargil Pass, and the River Harnen all appear on the First Map (Map III, VII.309). — The text ends with a reference to Umbar that I cannot decipher.

12 *Éowyn* was struck out, and *wine!* written in the margin; which I take to mean that Éowyn was not seated, for she bore the wine.

13 The queries might mean that my father was uncertain of the correctness of his interpretation of the pencilled forms (in the one case it might be *Umbor* or *Umbar*; in the other the second vowel of *Nargil, Nargul* cannot now be read under the ink overlay). But this does not seem very likely. Both these names appear in text A (p. 237), where *Nargil* is clear, though *Umbar* could be read as *Umbor*. *Umbar* and *Haven of Umbar* appear on the First Map (VII.309) and on the map that I made in 1943; and on the latter the pass through the southern mountains of Mordor is named *Nargil* (on the First Map the name was pencilled in roughly and is hard to read, but was apparently *Narghil*, VII.310).

14 As originally drawn, a pass over the mountains in this region is clearly defined on the First Map: see Map IV[A], square P11 (VII.314), connecting to Map III, square Q11 (VII.309). Here the Blackroot rises in an oval lake. With the superimposed portion Map IV[D–E] (VII.319) the connections become unclear, especially since a different convention was used in the representation of the mountains, but at any rate there is no clear indication of a pass. The 1943 map retains the oval lake and the broad pass, but its relation to the First Map is here difficult to interpret (VII.320). Possibly it was to this feature that my father referred in his note on that map (VII.321 note 1): 'The White Mountains are not in accord with the story'. On late maps, as is to be expected, no pass breaks the line of the mountains.

15 In the *Guide to the Names in The Lord of the Rings* (*A Tolkien Compass*, ed. Lobdell, p. 200) my father noted of the name *Púkel-men*: 'It represents Old English *púcel* (still surviving as *puckle*), one of the forms of the *puk-* stem (widespread in England, Wales, Ireland, Norway and Iceland) referring to a devil, or to a minor sprite such as Puck, and often applied to ugly misshapen persons.'

16 In place of this, RK has: '. . . a winding line of Riders crossing the ford and filing along the road towards the camp prepared for them. Only the king and his guard were going up into the Hold.'

17 RK has here: 'Such was the dark Dunharrow, the work of long-forgotten men'; cf. text H, p. 251.

18 At this point my father's writing suddenly becomes very much more rapid and rough.

19 Cf. 'The King of the Golden Hall' in VII.447, where Aragorn says: 'If I live, I will come, Lady Éowyn, and then maybe we will ride together.'

20 I think that Éowyn's naming her father *Éothain* is most likely to be a mere slip, for *Éomund* father of Éomer and Éowyn was established (VII.393 etc.), and *Éothain* was the name of Éomer's squire (VII.400–2); but see further p. 350 and note 13. In LR Appendix A (II) it is said that Eomund, chief Marshal of the Mark, was slain in the year 3002 in pursuit of Orcs on the borders of the Emyn Muil.

21 Old English *fyrgen*, *firgen* 'mountain'; the word *fyrgen-holt* 'mountain-wood' occurs in *Beowulf*, line 1393. — Afterwards, when the Firien had become the Dwimorberg and the Firienholt the Dimholt, the Firienfeld remained (RK p. 67).

22 This name undoubtedly begins with *An*, and the word preceding it is almost certainly 'in'; equally certainly it is this same name that appears below, as the land of the prince Benrodir. The remaining letters of the name are uninterpretable as they stand, but their vague shapes do not exclude 'Anárion', and this name, found on the First Map (VII.309) of the region south of Minas Tirith, appears in the notes E on p. 243: 'A fleet has put out ... and sailed up the Anduin and reached Anárion' (see further p. 244).

23 This lacuna is where the page is torn across, cutting through a line of text. It might perhaps be read, but very uncertainly, as 'from the vale of Morthond and his ... sons, dark-haired, grey-eyed'.

24 *Nosdiligand*: the second and third letters of this name are not perfectly clear, but can hardly be other than *os*. Without striking through the first syllable my father wrote another form above, apparently *Northiligand*.

25 The illegible words might just possibly be 'fugitives' and 'representing'.

26 My father called it a 'catalogue': pp. 229, 263.

27 These messages, distinct of course from those just referred to, must have been sent from Isengard or Helm's Deep.

28 The illegible word might possibly be 'morn(ing)'.

29 It is not clear whether 'Reach battle Feb. 15' refers to the Ents or to the Rohirrim; but in any case the Ents were certainly present after the siege of Minas Tirith was relieved ('Elves and Ents drive Orcs back'; cf. also outline II §4 'Elves of Lórien and Ents come from North', and similarly outline III §4). Thus the original idea that 'tree-giants' (see VI.410), or Treebeard (see VII.211, 214), played a part in the breaking of the siege survived at least in the

idea that Ents were present in the last stage of the war in the South, though this would never receive narrative form. See further pp. 343, 345–6, 361.

30 Cf. the notes given in VII.448: 'Probably Éowyn should die to avenge or save Théoden.' These notes contain also the suggestion that the mutual love of Éowyn and Aragorn should be removed.

31 This is the date given in the time-scheme D (p. 182); see the Note on Chronology following.

32 The last two letters of this name might be read as *du*, sc. *Mordu.*

33 With this cf. the outline 'The Story Foreseen from Fangorn' (VII.438): 'Then return to Frodo. Make him look out into impenetrable night. Then use phial ... By its light he sees the forces of deliverance approach and the dark host go out to meet them'; also p. 230 in this book.

34 Cf. the outline given in VII.448: 'They pass by round Lórien' (on the homeward journey), with the later addition (VII.451 note 18): 'No. They learn (in Rivendell?) that Nazgûl razed Lórien ...'

35 Old English *haliern* (*hálig-ern* or *-ærn*) 'holy place, sanctuary'. Cf. my father's note on *Dunharrow* in the *Guide to the Names in The Lord of the Rings* (*A Tolkien Compass*, ed. Lobdell, p. 183): '*Dunharrow.* A modernisation of Rohan *Dūnhaerg* "the heathen fane on the hillside", so-called because this refuge of the Rohirrim at the head of Harrowdale was on the site of a sacred place of the old inhabitants (now the Dead Men). The element *haerg* can be modernised in English because it remains an element in place-names, notably *Harrow (on the Hill).*'

36 Outline II was written on the same thin yellowish paper as was used for text H of 'The Muster of Rohan' and text C of 'Minas Tirith' (the two pages in the 'midget type'). This paper was also used for the time-schemes C, D, and S. See note 38.

37 On my father's later large-scale map of Rohan, Gondor and Mordor (on which my map published in RK was based) the distance from Edoras to Dunharrow (at the head of Harrowdale) is 16 miles and from Edoras to the Starkhorn 19 miles.

38 Outline IV was written on the same paper as that referred to in note 36.

39 *Pelennor*: see p. 277.

40 *Galdor* was preceded by *Ealdor*.

41 In outlines I, II and III it is said that Théoden and Éowyn (who is not mentioned here) 'slew' or 'killed' or 'destroyed' the King of the Nazgûl.

42 Frodo's vision of a ship with black sails and a banner bearing the emblem of a white tree (FR p. 379) was added afterwards to the text of 'The Mirror of Galadriel'.

Note on the map accompanying outline VI

This map, drawn fairly rapidly in pencil (with the rivers in blue crayon), covers the White Mountains and the lands to the south of them; it is laid out like the First Map in squares of 2 cm. side. In my redrawing I have numbered the uppermost horizontal line of squares O 9–14 according to the First Map, although there is some discrepancy, and continued this numbering throughout, where the discrepancy becomes much greater. This is done deliberately in order to emphasize the curiously anomalous nature of this map among my father's later maps to *The Lord of the Rings*. Comparison with the First Map (VII.309, 319) and those published in LR will show substantial shifts in the geographical relations: thus Ethir Anduin is further to the east, directly south of Rauros, and the Havens of Umbar are shown as much less far to the south, and east of Tolfalas. On no other map is this so.

I strongly suspect that (for whatever reason) my father made this map from memory, and that it played no further part in the geographical evolution; and I think that its starting-point and primary purpose was to depict the region (pencilled more heavily than other parts of the map) between Harrowdale and the source of Morthond: with the emergence of the story that Aragorn passed *through* the Mountains into Gondor the map of *The Lord of the Rings* needed to be altered to show that there was no pass in this region (see note 14 above). It will be seen that the southern rivers have been substantially changed, though by no means reaching the final form: Morthond of the First Map is now named Ringlo, while the new Morthond flows east into the delta of Anduin. Erech is marked, south of the rising of Morthond, as is also Pelargir on Anduin (neither of which is mentioned in any of these outlines).* Harrowdale is shown running south-east, as on the little map reproduced on p. 258.

The map as squared out on the page extended through five vertical lines of squares east of Osgiliath (cf. VII.309), but these were apparently left blank. Subsequently my father attached a moveable portion covering O 13–14, P 13–15, and at the same time very roughly drew in the outlines of the mountains encircling Mordor, which here form more nearly a complete wall on the east than on any other map. The Dark Tower is shown as standing on a 'peninsula' thrust out southwards from the Ash Mountains, with Mount Doom to the north-west of it, very much as on the Second Map as originally drawn,

* Pelargir was first placed at the top of the delta of Anduin. On the First Map (VII.309) a pencilled dot within a circle was placed beside Anduin at the point where rivers flow in from east and west on R 13: this is obviously Pelargir, and was no doubt entered at this time. Another pencilled dot within a circle was put in to the east of the original Morthond on First Map Q 12 (just to the right of the *i* of *Enedwaith*), and this is evidently Erech.

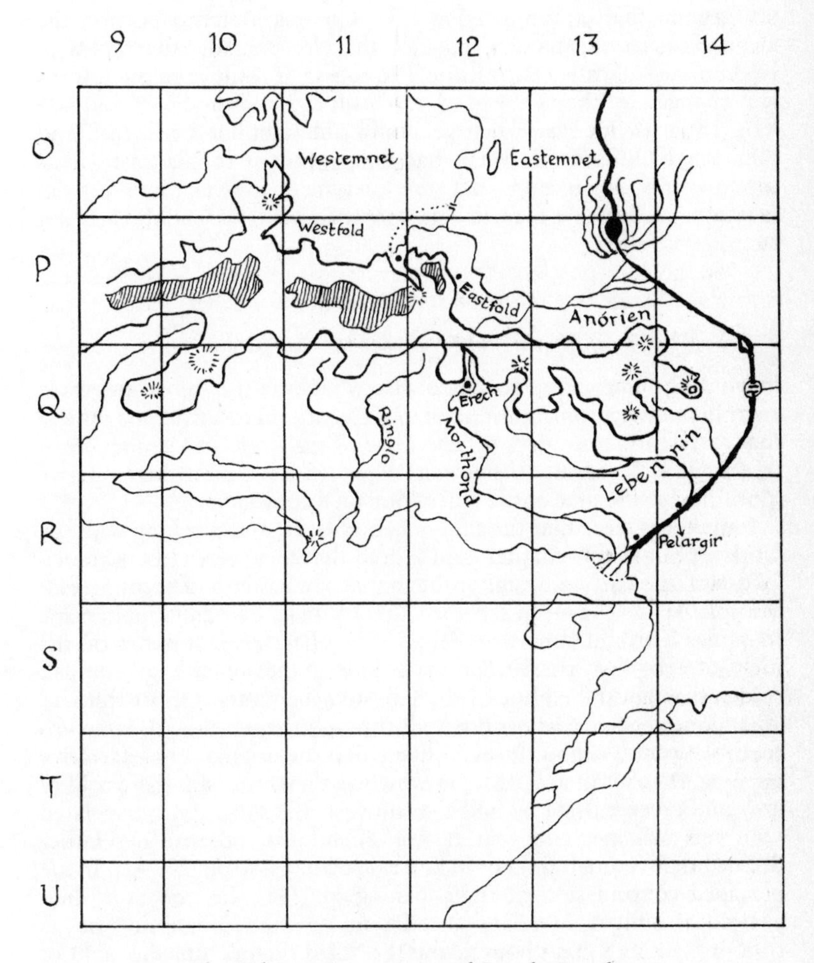

The White Mountains and South Gondor

pp. 435, 438. I have not attempted to redraw this added portion, for the pass into Mordor (here called Kirith Gorgor) was apparently moved eastwards from the position in which it was first drawn, resulting in a confusion of lines that I cannot interpret; and Osgiliath was now moved a good way to the north, so that it lies north-east of Minas Tirith (as is shown on the Second Map, p. 434, and on my large-scale map of Rohan, Gondor and Mordor published in RK, but not on my general map accompanying LR). On this attached portion the Dead Marshes are named, but not the Nomenlands; the rapids in Anduin are still called *Sarn Ruin*. The course of Anduin below Rauros was changed on the new P14 to flow as it does on the First Map (see VII.319) in a wide easterly curve, not in a straight line south-east (and thus the mouths of Entwash had to be shifted to the east). This supports my suggestion that the present map was drawn from memory: in this one area it was corrected by reference to the First Map.

Note on the Chronology

(i) Pippin and Frodo see the Full Moon

It would be interesting to know just what was the 'most awkward error in the synchronization ... of movements of Frodo and the others' that arrested the progress of *The Lord of the Rings* in October 1944 (see p. 234). It seems to me most likely to have been their relative 'positions' at the time of the Full Moon on 6 February.

I think it is clear that the time-schemes C, D, and S belong with the work set out in this chapter, and indeed that they were closely associated with the chronological problem that my father had encountered: see pp. 141–2, 234–5. In scheme C (p. 140) Gandalf and Pippin came to Minas Tirith at sunset on Feb. 5. They had left Dol Baran on the night of Feb. 3–4, passed Feb. 4 'in hiding' (presumably at Edoras), ridden through the night of Feb. 4–5, and then after a short rest had 'abandoned secrecy' and ridden all through the next day (Feb. 5) to reach the city at sunset. It seems likely that the original brief narrative opening (A) of 'Minas Tirith', in which as they rode 'still the world of grey and green rushed by and the sun rose and sank', was associated with this scheme, and that it was abandoned because my father decided that Gandalf did not in fact ride by day (see pp. 231–2). In the pencilled continuation of that opening (p. 231) the new story had entered: it is night, two days since Pippin 'saw the sun glinting on the roof of the king's great house', and the 'third riding', thus the night of Feb. 5–6. They see the beacons and the westbound messengers, but the moon is not mentioned; and it is obvious that in this story they will arrive at the wall of the Pelennor in the morning (Feb. 6). This is the story in scheme D (p. 141), except that there the beacons and the messengers are seen on the second night of the ride (Feb. 4–5). In that scheme the Full Moon 'rises about 9.20 p.m. and sets about 6.30 a.m. on Feb. 7. Gandalf rides all night of 5–6 and sights Minas Tirith at dawn on 6th.'

It was a datum of Frodo's journey that he came before the Black Gate at dawn of Feb. 5, leaving at nightfall; and he was in Ithilien (the episode of the stewed rabbit) and was taken by Faramir to Henneth Annûn on Feb. 6 (the night of Full Moon, which Frodo saw in the small hours of Feb. 7 setting over Mindolluin). In my father's letter of 16 October 1944 he said that among the alterations made to resolve 'the dislocated chronology' he had increased the journey from the Morannon by a day; this alteration was made to scheme D, and was present in scheme S as first written (see pp. 141–2). But the alteration was made by pushing Frodo's journey back by a day, so that he came before the Morannon on Feb. 4; he still comes to Henneth Annûn on the 6th. Therefore, when he looked out from the Window of the West and saw the moon setting, Gandalf and Pippin were already in Minas Tirith; the time-schemes are explicit (and it was presumably on this basis that in outline III, p. 259, Pippin in Minas Tirith on the evening of the 6th 'sees the full moon rising and wonders where Frodo is'; similarly in outline V, p. 262, and also in the outline given in the next chapter, p. 276).

In the second draft (B) of the opening of 'Minas Tirith' (p. 232) Pippin on the night of Feb. 5(–6) saw the full moon rising out of the eastern shadows as he rode with Gandalf; and in the third draft (C, in 'midget type', p. 233) Pippin wonders where Frodo might be, 'little thinking that Frodo on that same night saw from afar the white snows under the moon.' Surely my father's intention here was to relate Pippin's thought to Frodo's at Henneth Annûn (as in RK); but there was a day out. Was this the chronological problem?

On the face of it, apparently not; for the modifications made to the chronology did not correct it. On the other hand, that my father was concerned with precisely this question is seen from an isolated page of notes on diverse subjects, one of which casts some very cloudy light on the matter:

> Whole of Frodo's and Sam's adventures must be set back *one day*, so that Frodo sees moon-set on morning (early hours) of Feb. 6, and Faramir reaches Minas Tirith on night of the 7th, and Great Darkness begins on 7th. (This can be done by making Frodo and Sam only wander 4 days in the Emyn Muil.) The next night Frodo would see from far away the full moon set beyond Gondor and wonder where he was in the mists of the West, and the war-beacons would be hid from him in the darkness of the world.

This is very difficult to understand. Frodo's adventures are to be set back by a day, and he will see the setting of the moon (not yet quite at the full) from Henneth Annûn in the later night of Feb. 5–6, when

Pippin was on the last lap to Minas Tirith, and thought of him. But then why is it not till the next night (Feb. 6–7) that Frodo thinks of Pippin (if 'him' is Pippin), and why is it on this night that the beacons of Gondor are burning?

(ii) Théoden comes to Harrowdale

In the second version (B) of 'The Muster of Rohan' (p. 237) Aragorn agrees with Théoden, as they enter Harrowdale, that the moon was full the night before, and he says that they have been four (changed from five) days on the road, so that six remained before the day appointed for the muster at Edoras. In time-scheme C (p. 140) Théoden reaches Helm's Deep from Isengard soon after dawn on Feb. 4, and he leaves Helm's Deep on Feb. 5 (when also 'Aragorn rides on ahead with Gimli and Legolas': this appears in the third narrative C, p. 241). Nothing further is said about Théoden's movements in time-scheme C; but if the two texts are combined we get the following chronology:

Feb. 4 Théoden reaches Helm's Deep soon after dawn
Feb. 5 Théoden leaves Helm's Deep
Feb. 6 Full Moon
Feb. 7 Théoden reaches Harrowdale at dusk
Feb. 13 Date appointed for the muster

If this is correct, the 'four days on the road' include the day spent at Helm's Deep.

In the third version C (p. 240) Éomer says that the moon was full on the night before the last, that five days have passed on the journey, and that five remain until the muster; and all this is repeated in the next version (F) in which the passage appears (pp. 244–5). In these versions the journey has taken one day more, as it appears:

Feb. 5 Théoden leaves Helm's Deep
Feb. 6 Full Moon
Feb. 7
Feb. 8 Théoden reaches Harrowdale.

Time-scheme D (pp. 141, 182) gives the following chronology (with which the fully 'synoptic' scheme S agrees):

Feb. 4–5 Aragorn rides by night to Edoras, which he reaches in the morning, and passes up Harrowdale
Feb. 5 Théoden leaves Helm's Deep
Feb. 6 Full Moon rises about 9.20 p.m. Théoden comes to Dunharrow before nightfall
(Feb. 7 Théoden prepares to ride to Gondor. Messengers from Minas Tirith arrive
Feb. 8 Théoden rides from Edoras)

This is the chronology of the typescript text H (pp. 251–2), to the extent at least that the moon is full (rising four hours after dark) on the night of Théoden's arrival in Harrowdale: the journey through the mountains now took only two days. It is not the chronology of *The Tale of Years* in LR, in which Théoden set out from Helm's Deep on March 6 but did not reach Dunharrow until March 9.

The date appointed for the muster at Edoras as deduced above from the original narrative openings of the chapter, Feb. 13 (a week after the full moon of Feb. 6), is presumably to be associated with the change in the second manuscript of 'The Road to Isengard' from 'before the waning of the moon' to 'at the last quarter of the moon' (see pp. 27, 40). In the text H (p. 252) Éomer says to the King that 'Tomorrow ere evening you shall come to Edoras and keep tryst with your Riders'; with this perhaps cf. outline I (p. 255): 'Messages must bid Rohirrim assemble at Edoras as soon as may be after the Full Moon of Feb. 6.'

III
MINAS TIRITH

'I hope after this week actually to – write,' my father wrote to Stanley Unwin on 21 July 1946 (*Letters* no. 105); and it is clear that he did – at any rate on 7 December of that year he said that he was 'on the last chapters' (whatever that may have meant). Another synopsis of the proposed content of 'Book V' shows much further development in the narrative of the opening chapters, and I incline to think that it belongs to 1946 and was set down as a guide to the new work now beginning; I therefore give it here rather than with the outlines that I believe to date from 1944 (pp. 252 ff.). My father had now re-ordered earlier chapters, and so numbered the first of Book V in this synopsis '44' (not '41': see p. 226 note 49).[1] The text was written in pencil and then overwritten in ink: the underlying text was far briefer, but is barely legible except at the end, where the overwriting ceases.

Book V

Ch. 44 (1). Gandalf (and Pippin) rides to Minas Tirith and see[s] Denethor. Pippin on walls. Coming in of last allies. Great Darkness begins that night.

45. King and Aragorn (with Merry, Legolas, Gimli) ride to the Hornburg. Overtaken by the Sons of Elrond[2] and 30 Rangers seeking Aragorn (probably because of messages sent by Galadriel to Elrond). King rides to Dunharrow by mountain roads. Aragorn (Legolas and Gimli) and Rangers go by open road. Aragorn reveals he has looked in Palantír, and seeks the Paths of the Dead. King arrives at Dunharrow dusk 2 days later[3] and finds Aragorn has gone on Paths of the Dead. Errand riders of Gondor come. Muster of Rohan takes place in Harrowdale (by Gandalf's orders) not Edoras, and King sets out next morning for Edoras.

46. Pippin on walls. Several days later when Host of Morghul is victorious. News comes through of flanking attacks on Lórien and by Harad in South. A great army has crossed into Wold of Rohan. They fear Rohirrim will not come. Dark grows but even so the Nazgûl cause a greater darkness. Gandalf shines in the field. Pippin sees the light of him as he and Faramir rally men. But at last the enemy are at the gates, and the Nazgûl fly

over the city. Then just as gate is giving way they hear the horns of Rohan!

47. Go back to Merry. Charge of Rohan. Orcs and Black Riders driven from gate. Fall of Théoden wounded, but he is saved by a warrior of his household who falls on his body. Merry sits by them. Sortie saves King who is gravely wounded. Warrior found to be Éowyn. The Hosts of Morghul reform and drive them back to the gate. At that moment a wind rises, dark is rolled back. Black ships seen. Despair. Standard of Aragorn (and Elendil). Éomer's wrath. Morghul taken between 2 forces and defeated. Éomer and Aragorn meet.

48. Gandalf and Denethor learn of the defeat of the flank attacks by Shadow Host[4] and by Ents. They cross Anduin victorious and invest Minas Morghul. Gandalf and Aragorn come to Morannon and parley.

49. Return to Frodo and Sam.

At this point the overwriting in ink ceases – perhaps because my father saw that at this rate he was going to be very hard put to it to complete the story in 'Book Five and Last' (p. 219). In the pencilled underlying text he had had this programme for the last seven chapters:

48. Gandalf comes to the Black Gate.
49. Frodo and Sam come to Orodruin.
50. .... and return.
51. Feast at Minas Tirith.
52. Funeral at Edoras.
53. Return to Rivendell. Meeting with Bilbo.
54. Sam's Book and the passing of all Tales.

It was perhaps immediately before he turned to the chapter 'Minas Tirith' again that my father set down a further and very precise outline, which follows here (the figures refer of course to the dates in the month of February).

Gandalf and Pippin ride to Minas Tirith (3/4, 4/5, arriving at sunrise on 6). Pass Fords of Isen and reach mouth of Deeping Coomb about 2 a.m. (4). Come at daybreak to Edoras. Gandalf remains there during daylight. 2nd Nazgûl passes over Rohan (it left Mordor about midnight 3/4 but spies out plain and flies low over Edoras in early morn[ing]).[5] Gandalf rides again on night of 4/5 and passes into Anórien, where he lies hid in hills during daylight (5). Riding for third night (5/6) they see the beacons flare out, and are passed by messengers on swift horses speeding from Minas Tirith to Edoras. They reach the Pelennor Wall at first dawn, and after speech with guards pass through and sight Minas Tirith in the sunrise (6). They pass up through the 7 concentric walls and gates to the White Tower. Pippin sees white houses and domes on the slopes of the mountain above the city. Gandalf explains they are the 'houses of the kings' – i.e. dead tombs. (Before the gate of the White Tower they see the ruin of the Tree, and Fountain?) They are admitted to the audience chamber, and see the throne. Denethor comes in, and does not sit in the throne, but on a smaller chair lower down and in front. Interview with Denethor and his grief at news of Boromir. They learn reason of beacons: a great fleet has been sighted coming from Umbar to mouths of Anduin. Also messages from spies etc. in Ithilien report that 'storm is about to burst'. Denethor is vexed that no aid has come from Rohan. Gandalf explains the situation. Also warns Denethor that help may even now be delayed as almost certainly Rohan will be attacked on eastern flank north of Emyn Muil. He counsels Denethor to muster what he can at once. 'The muster has already begun,' said Denethor. (Forlong the Fat etc., but too few come from Lebennin owing to threat of sea-attack.)

Pippin on the battlements has talk with a sentinel. He sees the moonrise on night of 6 (about 8.45 p.m.) and thinks of Frodo.[6]

Aragorn takes Legolas and Gimli and Merry and proposes that what is left of the Company shall be reunited. He says his heart now urges him to speed, for the time of his own revealing approaches. They may have a hard and dangerous journey, for now the real business is beginning, beside which the battle of the Hornburg is but a skirmish by the way. They agree and Aragorn and his company leave Dolbaran ahead of the king at about midnight. Merry rides with Aragorn, and Gimli with Legolas. They go fast and reach Westfold at daybreak (4) and [*struck out at once:* do not turn aside but go straight] see the 2nd Nazgûl flying.

A great deal of the first part of this derives directly from earlier outlines, but by no means all (thus it is here that the great tombs of Minas Tirith are first mentioned, and it is here that Pippin's friend of the Citadel guard – Beregond in RK – first appears). The concluding portion of the outline, however, telling that Aragorn with Merry, Legolas and Gimli left together from Dol Baran ahead of the king about midnight, reaching Westfold at dawn of the following day and not so very many hours after Gandalf, is an odd and surprising development.[7] But it seems to have been abandoned at once, without further issue.

Taking up the opening chapter 'Minas Tirith' again, my father followed closely the abandoned opening (the text C in 'midget type') so far as it went, and the new text still differs from RK pp. 19–21 in the points mentioned on p. 233, except that the leader of the men at the Pelennor Wall is now Ingold, not Cranthir.[8] Written for most of its length rapidly but generally legibly in ink, the draft extends almost to the end of the chapter; and from the point in the story where C ended (in the conversation with the men repairing the wall), for which my father had only very sketchy notes, he advanced confidently through the account of Minas Tirith seen across the 'townlands', the structure of the city, the entry of Gandalf and Pippin, the 'audience' with Denethor, and Pippin's meeting with Beregond (not yet nor for a long time so named). This draft underwent countless changes afterwards, yet from its first writing the story was present in all essentials of narrative structure, of atmosphere, and of tone. In what follows it can be assumed that every significant feature of description and conversation in the chapter was present in the draft unless something is said to the contrary. On the other hand I do not record all the small touches that were added in later: for example, Denethor does not in the draft text lay down his rod in order to lift the horn from his lap; Pippin is not said to receive back his sword and put it in its sheath; chairs are brought for Gandalf and Pippin, not a chair and a stool; the room in which they were lodged had only one window, not three; and so on.

As noted earlier, the text C stops just before Gandalf tells Cranthir / Ingold that 'you are overlate in repairing the wall of the Pelennor' (p. 233; RK p. 21), so that this name does not appear. In the new draft Gandalf, in his words with Ingold, speaks of 'the wall of Pelennor' – but it appears immediately afterwards that this was the name of the wall itself:

Gandalf passed now into the wide space beyond the Pelennor. So the men of Gondor called the wall that was built long ago after Ithilien fell into the hands of the Enemy.

The name appears also in several of the outlines that I have attributed to 1944 and given in the last chapter: 'Pelennor wall' (p. 260), 'the wall of Pelennor' (p. 263), 'the Outer Wall of Pelennor' (p. 263), but in the light of the present draft these are ambiguous; on the other hand, in outline IV (p. 260) occurs 'the Cityland, Pelennor, about which ruins of an old wall ran', which is not at all ambiguous. On the face of it, my father twice changed his mind about the meaning of this name; for in RK (p. 22) the wall is named *Rammas Echor* and the Pelennor is again the name of the 'fair and fertile townlands' of Minas Tirith (see pp. 287–8).

The description in the draft continues:

It went in a wide circle from the mountains' feet and back to them, always distant some seven leagues from the First Gate of the City that looked eastward. Thus it enclosed the fair and fertile townlands on the long green slopes falling to the River, and at its easternmost point overlooked from a frowning bank the marshy levels. There it was loftiest and most guarded, for on a walled causeway the road from the fords of Osgiliath, a league away, came in through a great gate between two towers. But few men save herdsmen and tillers dwelt in the townlands, for the most part of the people of Gondor dwelt in the seven circles of the city of Minas Tirith, or in the deep vales of the mountains' borders; and away southward in Lebennin the land of Seven Rivers lived a hardy folk between the mountains and the mouths of Anduin and the Sea; and they were reckoned men of Gondor, yet their blood was mixed and if their stature and faces told the truth came more from those men who dwelt in the dark hills in the Dark Years ere the coming of the kings.

But now the light of day grew, and Pippin looked up ...

Thus the townlands were at first conceived altogether differently, as a great half-circle centred on the city and always with a radius of seven leagues, whereas in RK the enclosing wall was at its furthest point four leagues from the city and at its nearest little more than one.[9] In this draft text there is no mention of Emyn Arnen, of the Harlond, of Lossarnach, of Belfalas, or of Imrahil of Dol Amroth, and Lebennin is still 'the land of Seven Rivers' (see VII.310–12, and pp. 252, 254 in this book).

Pippin's first sight of Minas Tirith and Gandalf's encounter with the guards at the Great Gate is very much as in RK (p. 23), except that in the following passage from RK the bracketed part is absent:

> but to his right great mountains reared their heads, [ranging from the West to a steep and sudden end, as if in the making of the land the River had burst through a great barrier, carving out a mighty valley to be a land of battle and debate in times to come. And there where the White Mountains of Ered Nimrais came to their end] (and) he saw, as Gandalf had promised, the dark mass of Mount Mindolluin ...

Also, the Tower of Ecthelion is here called the Tower of Denethor (see p. 281).

In the draft text the description of Minas Tirith is as follows:

For the manner of Minas Tirith was such that it was builded upon seven levels each carved in the hill, and each had a wall, and in each wall was a gate. But the gates were not made in a line, for the outer and lowest gate was in the east, but the next faced half south and the third half north, and so on, so that the pave[d] way that led up without break or stair turned first this way and [then] that way across the face of the hill, until the seventh gate was reached that led to the great court and citadel on the levelled summit about the feet of the crowning tower. And that gate also looked due east, being there seven hundred feet above the plain before the walls, and the tower on the summit was three hundred feet from base to pinnacle. A strong citadel indeed it was and not to be taken by a host of men if there were any within that could hold weapons, unless some enemy could come behind and scale Mindolluin and so come behind upon the shoulder that joined the Hill of Guard to the mountain mass. But that shoulder which was at the height of the fifth wall was walled right up [to] the precipice that overhung it, and there stood the great domed tombs of bygone kings and lords, at once memorials and fortresses if need should come.

In the original hasty sketch of Minas Tirith reproduced on p. 261 the gates appear to be arranged in two lines meeting at the uppermost level, the one proceeding from the Great Gate (1 – 3 – 5 – 7), and the other proceeding from the second gate (2 – 4 – 6 – 7).[10] In the text just cited the configuration described in RK is present, with the Great Gate facing east, the second gate south-east, the third north-east, and so on up to the entrance to the Citadel, again facing east. On this page of the draft (reproduced on p. 280) my father drew a plan in which this arrangement is shown. The upper figure on the page is in fact two conjoined: the smaller area at the upper left (marked with 'M.T.' and 'summit of Mindolluin') was that first made, and this was struck out with three transverse lines. — It will be seen that the 'vast pier of rock whose huge out-thrust bulk divided in two all the circles of the City save the first' (RK p. 24), causing the mounting road to pass through a tunnel each time it crossed the line from the Great Gate to the Citadel, was not yet present.

Pippin's sense of the diminishment and decay of Minas Tirith, with its great silent houses, is told in the draft in words closely similar to those of the passage in RK (p. 24);[11] but the accoutrement of the guards of the Seventh Gate is thus described:

The guards of the gate were robed in white, and the[ir] helms were of strange shape, shining like silver, for they were indeed of *mithril*, heirlooms from the glory of old days, and above either cheekpiece were set the wings of sea-birds. Upon the breast of their surcoats were embroidered in white a tree blossoming like snow and above it a silver crown.

paved ways that lead up without break or stair and wound first this way and that way across the face of the hill, until the Seventh Gate was reached that lead to the great court and citadel on the levelled summit about the feet of the crowning tower. And that gate also looked due east, being ~~[illegible]~~ there seven hundred feet above the plain before the walls. and the tower ~~[illegible]~~ at the summit was three hundred feet from base to pinnacle. A strong citadel indeed it was and not to be taken by a host of men if there were any within that could hold weapons, unless some enemy could come behind and scale Mindolluin and so come behind upon the shoulder that that joined

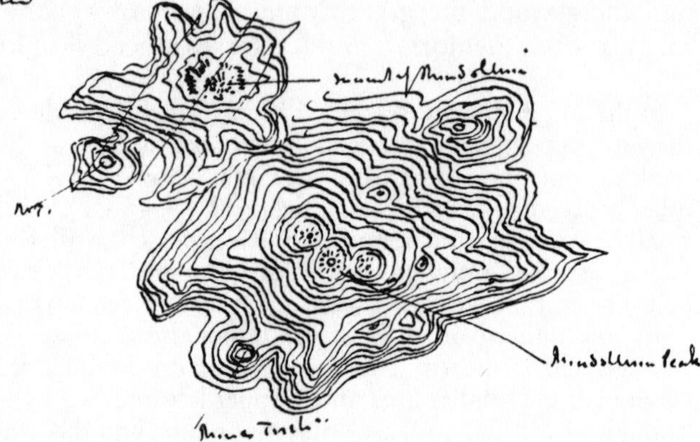

the hill of guard with the mountain mass. But that shoulder that was at the height of the fifth wall was walled up to the precipice that overhung it. And there stood the great domed tombs of bygone kings and lords, [illegible] [illegible] [illegible] [illegible] [illegible] come.

Pippin gazed in wonder at the great stone city. It was ~~[illegible]~~ greater and more splendid than anything he had dreamed of. Greater and stronger than Isengard, and far more beautiful. Yet it was in

Minas Tirith and Mindolluin

It is added here that beside the guards of the Citadel one other wore this livery of the heirs of Elendil: 'the warden of the door of the hall of the kings aforetime where now dwelt the Lord Denethor'; and at the door there is one 'tall guard' ('the tall silent door-wardens', RK). Perhaps the change in the colour of the livery from white to black was on account of the white tree embroidered on the coats.

The dead Tree in the court of the Fountain, with Pippin's recollection of Gandalf's words *Seven stars and seven stones and one white tree*, and Gandalf's warning to him to bear himself discreetly before Denethor, survived into the final text with very little change; but Gandalf says only of Denethor and Boromir: 'He loved him greatly, too much, perhaps', and does not add 'and the more so because they were unlike' (yet later, when they have left Denethor, he says, much as in RK: 'He is not quite as other men, Pippin, and whatever be his ancestry by some chance the blood of the men of Westernesse runs true in him, as it does in his other son Faramir, and yet not in Boromir whom he loved most. They have long sight.'). And of Aragorn he says that 'if he comes it may be in some way that no one expects. And Denethor at least does not expect him in any way, *for he does not know that he exists*.'

The great hall was conceived from the first almost exactly as the description of it stands in RK (p. 26): the great images between the pillars, reminding Pippin of 'the kings of Argonath',[12] the empty throne, the old man in the stone chair gazing at his lap. Only the carved capitals of the pillars are not mentioned; on the other hand the floor of the hall is described: 'But the floor was of shining stone, white-gleaming, figured with mosaics of many colours' (see p. 288). The name of Denethor's father, Ecthelion, entered here, with only momentary hesitation (earlier in the draft the White Tower is called the Tower of Denethor, not as in RK the Tower of Ecthelion; p. 278).[13]

When Pippin cried 'that is the horn that Boromir always wore!' this dialogue follows in the draft:

'Verily,' said Denethor. 'And in my turn I wore it, and so did each eldest son of our house far back into the mists of time, before the failing of the kings, since [Mardil >] Faragon father of Mardil hunted the wild oxen of Araw[14] in the far fields of Rhûn. But we heard it blowing dimly in the North twelve days ago,[15] and now it will blow no more.'

'Yes,' said Pippin. 'I stood beside him as he blew it, and it shook the woods; but no help came. Only more orcs.'

Pippin's account of Boromir's death, his offer of his service to Denethor, and the swearing of the oath were very largely achieved in the draft text,[16] save in one notable point: it is Gandalf, not Denethor, who speaks the words of the oath: '"Take the hilts," said Gandalf, "and speak after me." The old man laid the sword along his lap and Pippin laid his hand on the hilts and said slowly after Gandalf ...' The oath and its acceptance were scarcely changed from the original formulation in the draft, except only in the point that Denethor did not there name himself 'Steward of the High King'.

The words between Denethor and Gandalf that follow (RK p. 29), and Pippin's perception of the tension between them, and of Gandalf's greater power (though veiled), reached immediately the final text in almost every point; but Pippin's reflection on Gandalf's age and being took this form: 'Whence and what was Gandalf: when and in what far time and place [was he born >] did he come into the world and would he ever die?' His passing thought 'Treebeard had said something about wizards, but even then he had not thought of Gandalf as one of them' does not appear; it is not said that 'it was Denethor who first withdrew his gaze'; and Denethor says only 'for though the Stones are lost', without adding 'they say'.

In the margin of the page that bears this passage my father wrote: 'For his wisdom did not consider Gandalf, whereas the counsels of Denethor concerned himself, or Gondor which in his thought was part of himself'. There is no indication where this was to be placed, but I think that it would follow 'Pippin perceived that Gandalf had greater power, and deeper wisdom – and a majesty that was veiled.'

The interview with Denethor ended far more abruptly in the draft than in RK (pp. 30–1): at Denethor's words 'Let your wrath for an old man's seeming folly run off, and return to my comfort' there follows only: '"I will return as soon as may be," said Gandalf. "But I crave sometime words with you alone." And he strode from the hall with Pippin running at his side.'

After Gandalf had left the house in which they were lodged Pippin encountered a man clad in grey and white who named himself Beren son of Turgon (Beregond son of Baranor, clad in black and white, in RK). In their opening conversation and visits to Shadowfax and the buttery a number of small alterations and additions were made to the narrative later, but all are slight points: for example, Beren says to Pippin that 'It is said that you are to be treated as a guest for this day at the least', and that 'Those who have had heavy duty – and *guests* – take somewhat to refresh their strength in the mid-morning'; Pippin does not express his disappointment at seeing no inns in Minas Tirith; and the following curious dialogue was afterwards removed (cf. RK p. 34):

'... For now I may say that strange accents do not mar fair speech, and hobbits are well-spoken folk.'

'So Denethor, I mean the high Lord, said.'

'Did he indeed?' said Beren. 'Then you have received a mark of favour such as few guests have got from him.'

The keeper of the buttery was named *Duilas* (?), with a later pencilled alteration to *Garathon*.[17] Pippin tells Beren: 'I am only a boy in the reckoning of our people, for I am only twenty years old and we are not held to be grown-up as we say in the Shire for a dozen years more.'[18]

As Beren and Pippin looked out from the walls, 'Away down in the vale-bottom 7 leagues or so as the eye leaps, the Great River now flowed grey and glittering, coming out of the north-west and curving south-west till it was lost to view round the shoulders of the mountains in a haze and shimmer' (see pp. 288–9), whereas it is distant 'five leagues or so' in RK (p. 36): on this difference see p. 278. Immediately after this the original draft jumps, in relation to RK, from 'far beyond which lay the Sea fifty leagues away' to '"What do I see there?" asked Pippin, pointing due eastward down to the river'; thus the entire passage is lacking in which Pippin sees the traffic of waggons crossing the Pelennor and turning south, and Beregond explains to him that they are taking 'the road to the vales of Tumladen and Lossarnach, and the mountain-villages, and then on to Lebennin.' But from this point the conversation of Beren/Beregond and Pippin to its conclusion, as it stands in RK (pp. 36–40), was achieved, roughly indeed, but with scarcely any significant detail lacking, and often very close to the final text: the darkness in the East,[19] the passage of the Nazgûl far overhead, Beren's account of the battles for the crossings at Osgiliath,[20] of Denethor's far sight,[21] of the approach of the great fleet manned by the corsairs of Umbar,[22] of Faramir, and his invitation to Pippin to join his company for that day.

At this point the story told in the draft becomes altogether different from that of RK, and I give the remainder (very roughly written) of this earliest text in full:

Gandalf was not in the lodging, and Pippin went with Beren of the Guard, and he was shown to the others of the third company and welcomed by them, and made merry with them, taking his midday meal among them in a little hall near the north wall, and going here and there with others until the evening meal, and the closing hour, and the lowering of standards. Then he himself after the manner of Gondor soon went to his bed. Gandalf had not come or left any message. He rolled into bed and soon slept. In the night he was awakened by a light and saw Gandalf in the room outside the alcove. He was pacing to and fro. 'When will Faramir return?' he heard him mutter, as he peered out of the dark window. Then Pippin went to sleep again.

The next day still no commands came from Denethor. 'He is full of cares and busyness,' said Gandalf, 'and for the moment you are out of his mind. But not for good! He does not forget. Make use of your leisure while you can. Have a look round the City.'[23]

Beren was on duty and Pippin was left alone; but he had learned enough to find his way to the hatches at midmorning. For the rest of the time until noon he walked in the sixth circle, and visited Shadowfax, taking him some morsels that he had saved, which Shadowfax graciously accepted. In the afternoon Pippin walked down the ways of the City to the lowest circle and the great East Gate.

People stared much at him as he passed, and he would hear calls behind him, and those out of doors cried to others within to come see Mithrandir's halfling; but to his face most were courteous, saluting him gravely after the manner of Gondor with outstretched hand and a bowing of the head. For who he was and much concerning him was now noised through Minas Tirith.

He came at last by windy ways and many fair alleys and arches to the lower circles where there [were] many smaller houses. And here and there he saw children – and he was glad, for to his eyes it had seemed that too many of the folk of Minas Tirith were old. He passed a larger house with a pillared porch and steps and boys were playing there. As soon as he saw him one of the boys leapt down the steps into the street and stood in front of Pippin, looking him up and down.

'Well met,' said the lad. 'Are you not a stranger?'

'I was,' said Pippin. 'But they say I am now a man of Gondor.'

'Man!' said the boy. 'How old are you, and what is your name? I am ten already and soon shall be five feet high. Look, I am taller than you. But then my father is a soldier, one of the tallest.[24] I shall be a soldier too. What is your father?'

'Which question shall I answer first?' said Pippin. 'My father is like me a hobbit not a man, and he owns the land and fields round Whitwell near Tuckborough on the edge of the Westfarthing in the Shire. I am 21 years old[25] so I pass you there, though I am but four feet four, and that is reckoned a good height in my land, and I do not hope to better it much. For I shall not grow upward much before I come of age; though maybe I shall thicken and put on some weight, or should, if food were plentiful for travellers in the wild places.'

'Twenty-one,' said Gwinhir, and whistled. 'Why, you are quite old. Still, I wager I could stand you on your head, or lay you on your back.'

'Maybe you could if I let you,' said Pippin with a laugh. 'We know a trick or two of wrestling in my little country. But I do not much like standing on my head; what, if it came to a sticking point, and nothing else would serve, I have a sword, master Gwinhir.'

'A sword, have you?' said Gwinhir. 'Then you must be a soldier. Though you don't look like one.'

'I am and I do not indeed,' said Pippin. 'But when you have seen more than 10 years, if you live long enough, young friend, and survive the days that are coming, you will learn that folk are not always what they seem. Why, you might take me for a kind-hearted fool of a stranger lad. But I am not. I am a hobbit and the devil of a hobbit, companion of wizards, friend of Ents, member of the Company of Nine of whom your lord Boromir was one, of the ... of the Nine I should say, and I was at the battle of the Bridge of Moria and the sack of Isengard, and I wish for no wrestling or rough play. So let me be lest I bite.'

'Ai, Ai,' said Gwinhir. 'You do sound fierce, a ferret in the garb of a rabbit. But you have left your boots behind, master, maybe because you have outgrown them too quickly. Come on, good ferret, bite if you like,' and he ... up his fists. But at that moment a man came out from the door and sprang down into the street and grabbed the lad by the back of his tunic.

'What is this, Gwinhir, you ruffling young fool,' said the man. 'Will you waylay anything in the street that seems smaller than yourself? Will you not choose something larger? Shame on a son of mine, brawling before my doors like a young orc.'

'Nay, nay, not like an orc, Master Thalion, if that be your name,' said Pippin. 'I have seen enough orcs and all too close to be in any error. Here is nothing but a warlike lad spoiling for something to do. Will you not let him walk with me a while, and be my guide? For I am new come and there is much to see while the sun still shines. ....'

'I have already heard that the halflings are courteous of speech, if that one that came hither with Mithrandir is a sample,' said Thalion.[26] 'Yes indeed, the young ruffian shall go with you if you wish. Go now and keep a fair tongue in your head,' he said to Gwinhir, giving him a smart blow on his seat. 'But see that he returns ere the closing hour and the dusk.'

'I wanted a game,' said Gwinhir to Pippin as they set off. 'There are few lads of my age in this quarter, and such as there are are no match for me. But my father is stern, and I was near to a beating just now. When he says "orc" 'tis an ill omen for one's back. But you got me off very finely, and I thank you. What shall I show you?'

'I do not know,' said Pippin, 'but I am going to the East Gate, and we shall see.'

As they drew near the East Gate there was much sound of running and bustle, and Pippin thought he heard horns and trumpets blowing. For a moment his heart beat for he thought it might be a signal that war had begun. But Gwinhir cried out. 'They are come. Some of the folk from beyond the walls that have been rumoured. Hasten now, they'll be riding [?in by] the East Gate.

Here the draft ends, abandoned. Why my father rejected this story one can only surmise; a clue is perhaps to be found at the point in the text where Pippin, at the end of his first day (6 February) in Minas Tirith (spent in the company of Beren and other men of the Guard), 'after the manner of Gondor soon went to his bed' (p. 283). Here my father added a note on the manuscript in pencil, reminding himself to look up what had been said of the weather in the story of Frodo and Sam in Ithilien, and saying that 'if possible' the sunset of 6 February should be 'ominous': 'Darkness began next morning, a fiery haze.' When he wrote this he may have intended to rewrite the story only to the extent that Pippin should see the 'ominous' sunset as he went back to his lodging on the first night, and then when he woke next morning the great pall should have overspread the sky: in deepening darkness he would make his way down to the Great Gate, and encounter the aggressive Gwinhir. Or it may be that it was when writing this note that he decided to change the structure of the story, and abandoned the draft. At any rate, he evidently decided that it would be better to compress the whole story of this chapter into a single day, concluded by the first presage of the Darkness approaching and the smouldering sunset at the closing of the gates, when the last of the men of the Outlands had entered the City. Chronological considerations may have played a part in this.

He now turned back to the point where Beren invited Pippin to join his company for that day, and began anew. This new drafting was written in soft pencil at great speed, and would be hard indeed to interpret and often altogether illegible were the new text not so close to the final form: the story becomes that of RK in virtually every point[27] and largely in the same words. But it peters out shortly before the end of the chapter, at the words 'But the dying sun set it all afire and Mindolluin was black against a dull smoulder' (RK p. 44).

Beren now becomes *Barathil*, changed in the course of the writing of the text to *Barithil*; his father's name does not appear. His son was named Bergil from the first. The Street of the Lampwrights has the Elvish name *Rath a Chalardain* (*Rath Celerdain* in RK); and Pippin is called *Ernil a Pheriannath* (*i* for *a* in RK).

The 'Homeric catalogue', as my father called it (p. 229), of the reinforcements entering Minas Tirith[28] from the Outlands was written out twice, the first form being jumbled and unclear, and at the second writing (beginning after the arrival of Forlong, at the words 'And so the companies came and were hailed and cheered ...', RK p. 43) it becomes remarkably close to the form in RK. I have the strong impression that the new names that appear here were devised in the composition of this text. Forlong the Fat, however, had appeared several times previously, pp. 229, 262, 276. He was here first said to be, as in RK, 'lord of the vale of Lossarnach',[29] but *Lossarnach* was struck out and replaced by 'the Ringlo away in Lebennin' (see Map III in VII.309). Yet this is immediately contradicted in both forms of the text, where we find just as in RK 'the men of Ringlo Vale behind Dervorin, son of their lord, striding on foot: three hundreds.' In the first form the vale is called Imlad-Ringlo. Duinhir and his five hundred bowmen from the Blackroot Vale (Morthond Vale and Imlad Morthond in the first form) is named (but not his sons, Duilin and Derufin in RK). After them come the men of 'Dor-Anfalas [*changed from* Belfalas], the Langstrand far away': see again Map III in VII.309, where 'Belfalas (Langstrand)' is the region afterwards named Anfalas. Their lord is Asgil-Golamir (Golasgil in RK). Then the hillmen of Lamedon, a name that first appears here; the fisher-folk of the Ethir; and Hirluin the Fair from the green hills of Pinnath Gelin, also first occurring here (but he is at first said to be from Erech). The Prince of Dol Amroth, kinsman of the Lord of Minas Tirith, bears the token of a golden ship and a silver swan; but he is given no name.

There is no other initial drafting extant (except for a roughly pencilled slip giving the revised conclusion of the conversation with Denethor, RK pp. 30–1). The first complete text is a typescript: I think it all but certain that my father made this before he proceeded much, if any, further in the narrative.

The title of the chapter as typed was: *Book V Chapter XLIV: Peregrin enters the service of the Lord of Minas Tirith*. For the most part the differences between the original draft and RK noticed above (pp. 277–83 and notes) were retained in this text: some but by no means all of these were changed in pencil on the typescript. Thus Gandalf's ride still took three nights, not four. The description of the 'townlands' of Minas Tirith remains as it was (pp. 277–8), with the sole difference that the *Pelennor* now becomes the name of the townlands, and the wall is named *Ramas Coren* (changed in pencil to *Rammas Ephel*).[30] On the other hand, the passage cited on p. 278 concerning the River is now present as in RK, except for the sentence 'And there where the White Mountains of Eredfain came to their end' (changed on the typescript to Ered Nimrais). The White Tower remains the Tower of Denethor; and the description of Minas Tirith remains as it was in the draft, with no material difference save in the height of the Tower, here said to be two hundred, not three hundred feet. Thus the great out-thrust pier of rock was still absent, and it was not introduced into this text. On the reverse of the preceding typescript page is a plan of the city, reproduced on p. 290; here appears the name *Rath Dínen*, and also *Othram or City Wall*, of the wall of the outermost circle, pierced by the Great Gate.[31]

In the account of the great hall the description of the floor is retained from the draft, and that of the capitals introduced, thus:

> Monoliths of black marble, they rose to great capitals carved in many figures of strange beasts and leaves; and far above in shadow the wide vaulting gleamed with dull gold. The floor was of polished stone, white-gleaming, inset with flowing traceries of many colours.

This was repeated in the following typescript; but in the final typescript, from which the text in RK was printed, the sentence was compressed: '... gleamed with dull gold, inset with flowing traceries of many colours.' Since there is no indication on the second typescript that any change was intended, it seems certain that this was a casual 'line-jumping' error, causing the 'flowing traceries' to be ascribed to the vaulting.

Denethor now names the father of Mardil *Orondil* (*Faragon* in the draft, *Vorondil* in RK). It is still Gandalf, not Denethor, who speaks the words of the oath which Pippin repeats; but the conclusion of the conversation between Gandalf and Denethor (also found in preliminary drafting, p. 287) is now present, and differs from the form in RK only in that after Gandalf's words 'Unless the king should come again?' he continues: 'That would be a strange conclusion. Well, let us strive to keep some kingdom still against that event!'

Barathil, *Barithil* of the second draft (p. 287) is now *Barithil*, becoming in the course of the typing of this text *Berithil*; he is the son of Baranor, as is Beregond in RK. The man at the buttery hatch is now Targon, as in RK.

In the description of the view eastward from the walls of Minas Tirith the Anduin is still some seven leagues away, and as it bends 'in a mighty sweep south and west again' it is still 'lost to view *round the shoulders of the mountains* in a haze and shimmer' (p. 283). The italicized words were afterwards struck from the typescript; the reason for this can be seen from a comparison of Map III in VII.309 with the large map of Rohan, Gondor and Mordor in *The Return of the King*, where the view of the Great River from Minas Tirith is not impeded by the eastern end of the mountains. The passage in RK which was absent from the draft, describing the traffic across the Pelennor, is now present and reaches the final form in every point, save only that Berithil here says: 'That is the road to the vales of Tumladen and Glossarnach' (see note 29); but this was changed in pencil to *Lossarnach*, and later in the text Forlong the Fat is named 'lord of Lossarnach'.[32]

Of the part of the text covered by the second draft (pp. 286–7) there is little to note, since the final form was already very largely achieved. In the 'catalogue' of the peoples of the Outlands the lord of Anfalas (so named) is now Golasgil, as in RK, but the prince of Dol Amroth is still not further identified. The conclusion of the chapter, not found in the draft, is here almost exactly as in RK. After the words (RK p. 45) 'The lodging was dark, save for a little lantern set on the table' my father first typed: 'Beside it was a scribbled note from Gandalf', but he barred this out immediately and substituted 'Gandalf was not there'. The chapter ends: 'No, when the summons comes, not at sunrise. There will be no sunrise. The darkness has begun.'

NOTES

1 Book V, Chapter 1 'Minas Tirith' is the 44th chapter in *The Lord of the Rings*. 'The Departure of Boromir' had now been separated off from 'The Riders of Rohan', 'Flotsam and Jetsam' from 'The Voice of Saruman', and 'The Forbidden Pool' from 'Journey to the Cross-roads'.

2 This is the first appearance of the Sons of Elrond (see VII.163–4, and p. 297 in this book).

3 According to time-schemes D and S (p. 272) Aragorn reached Edoras and went up Harrowdale on the morning of February 5, while Théoden came to Dunharrow at nightfall of the 6th.

4 This is the first reference to the part played by the Dead Men of Dunharrow. For the earliest hint of the story see outline V on p. 263: 'News comes from South that a great king has descended out of the mountains where he had been entombed, and set such a flame into men that the mountaineers ... and the folk of Lebennin have utterly routed the Southrons and burned [> taken] their ships.'

5 This was the Nazgûl (as the chronology was at this time) sent out from Mordor after Pippin looked into the *palantír* of Orthanc, passing high overhead and unseen 'about an hour after midnight'

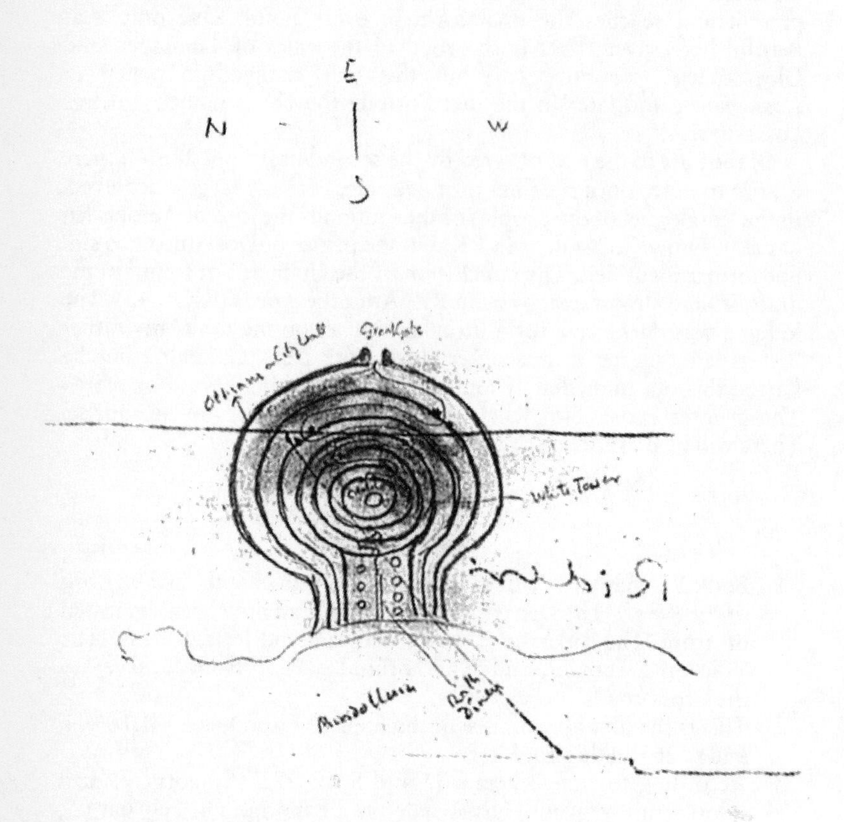

Plan of Minas Tirith

when Frodo, Sam and Gollum had not long left the pit among the slag-mounds: see pp. 119–20.

6 *Pippin on the battlements ... sees the moonrise on night of 6 ... and thinks of Frodo*: see p. 271.

7 I presume that the rejected words at the end of the outline 'do not turn aside but go straight (on)' mean that they passed the mouth of the Deeping Coomb and did not go up to the Hornburg. According to time-scheme D (p. 140) Gandalf reached Edoras at dawn on February 4, and he stayed there throughout the daylight hours. If Aragorn and his companions rode on at all speed making for Edoras, without any long halt, they would have caught him up!

8 Thus the passage in which Pippin thinks of Frodo remains the same as in text C, though with a difference in wording: 'little thinking that Frodo would see from far away the white snows under that same moon as it set beyond Gondor.' Gandalf's journey still takes three nights, not four as in RK.

9 On the First Map (Map III in VII.309) the distance from Minas Tirith to Osgiliath is about 70 miles (more than 23 leagues); and on the map made in October 1944 that I have redrawn on p. 269 it is still about 50 miles (which, since in the present draft the fords of Osgiliath were a league from the Pelennor wall, would give a radius of some 15 and a half leagues). In the note that my father wrote about my 1943 version of the First Map (see VII.322 note 1) he said that 'the distance across the vale of Anduin [should be] *much* reduced, so that Minas Tirith is close to Osgiliath and Osgiliath closer to Minas Morgul'; and the distance from the city to the Rammas Echor in the direction of Osgiliath is 10 miles on my map published in RK (on the original map on which mine was based 12 miles, agreeing with 'four leagues' in the text of RK, p. 22).

10 In the drawing the seventh gate faces in the same direction (north-east?) as the second gate, but the drawing may be defective: gates 1 – 3 – 5 – 7 are in a line.

11 In the draft, when Gandalf and Pippin came to the Seventh Gate, 'the sun that looked down on Ithilien and Sam busy with his steaming pan and herbs glowed on the smooth walls and the marbled arch and pillars.' It was the morning of February 6, the day on which Frodo and Sam encountered Faramir and went to Henneth Annûn. In RK the sentence is different: 'the warm sun that shone down beyond the river, as Frodo walked in the glades of Ithilien ...' — for on the day that Gandalf and Pippin arrived in Minas Tirith (March 9) Frodo and Sam reached the Morgul-road at dusk.

12 This is the first appearance of the name Argonath (see VII.359–60, 362).

13 In LR (*The Tale of Years*) it was the Steward Ecthelion I who rebuilt the White Tower in the year 2698, more than three centuries before this time; Denethor's father Ecthelion was the second Steward of that name (which derives from the legend of the Fall of Gondolin: see II.212, footnote). — 'The tower of Denethor' was named in the chapter 'The Palantír', p. 77.

14 *Vorondil father of Mardil* in RK, p. 27; and see LR Appendix A (I, ii). — A space was left for the name of the god, apparently filled in immediately, first with *Ramr* which was struck out before completion, then with *Araw*. On *Araw* beside *Oromë* see the *Etymologies*, V.379, stem ORÓM.

15 *twelve days ago* (*thirteen days ago* in RK): see p. 150 and note 10. In *The Tale of Years* the dates are February 26 (death of Boromir) and March 9 (Gandalf reaches Minas Tirith).

16 Denethor says of Pippin's sword: 'Surely it is a sax wrought by our own folk in the North in the deep past?', where RK has 'blade' and 'kindred'. The word *sax* (Old English *seax*, dagger, short sword) was the final choice in the draft after rejection of 'blade', 'knife' and 'dagger'.

17 Many other pencilled alterations were made to this part of the manuscript, mostly to clarify the writing, which is here rather rough. Among these the following may be noted: as Beren and Pippin sat on the seat beside the battlement Beren said: 'We thought it was the whim our lord to take him a page boy', and this was changed by the addition of 'after the manner of the old kings that had dwarves in their service, if old tales be true.'

18 *only twenty years old* was changed in pencil to *little more than twenty years old*. In RK Pippin told Beregond that 'it will be four years yet before I "come of age", as we say in the Shire.'

19 Of the shadow in the East it is said in the draft: 'Maybe it was mountains looming like clouds on the edge of sight ... 100 miles away'; cf. RK p. 37: 'Perhaps it was mountains looming on the verge of sight, their jagged edges softened by wellnigh twenty leagues of misty air.'

20 Where in RK (p. 37) Beregond tells that the Fell Riders won back the crossings 'less than a year ago', and that after Boromir had driven the enemy back 'we hold still the near half of Osgiliath', in the draft Beren says: 'And the Fell Riders but a little while ago [?two] years or more won back the crossings and came [?over] into this western land. But Boromir drove them back. And still we hold the crossings.'

21 Beren says as in RK that 'some say that as he sits alone in his high chamber in the Tower at night ... he can even read somewhat of the mind of the Enemy'; he does not speak of 'wrestling', nor add the words 'And so it is that he is old, worn before his time.'

22 The coming of the great fleet from the south is referred to in all but one of the outlines given in the last chapter. In the draft Beren says of the Corsairs of Umbar that they have 'long forsaken the suzerainty of Gondor' ('long ceased to fear the might of Gondor', RK). And he says of the fleet: 'Now that will draw off much help that we might look to from Lebennin south away between the mountains and the Sea, where folk are numerous.' Thus Belfalas is not named, as it is in RK ('from Lebennin and Belfalas', p. 38). The name *Belfalas* was originally applied to the coastal lands in the west subsequently named *Anfalas* (*Langstrand*): this change was made to the First Map and the 1943 map (VII.309–10). Precisely where my father placed Belfalas when Anfalas was substituted is not clear, but his note correcting the 1943 map (VII.322 note 1) says: 'Lebennin should be Belfalas'. That Belfalas was in the region of the Mouths of Anduin might seem to be suggested by the passage describing the journey of the funeral boat in drafting for 'The Departure of Boromir' (VII.382): 'and the voices of a thousand seabirds lamented him upon the beaches of Belfalas'; but Belfalas seems to have retained its original sense up to this time, since it was replaced by Dor-Anfalas in drafting for the present chapter (p. 287). On the Second Map (by a later addition) it is placed as on the map published in LR (see pp. 434, 437).

23 At this point my father scribbled down some very rough notes in pencil, but the following paragraph ('Beren was on duty ...') was then written over them, so that they are hard to read: 'rude boy of the City Gates password *Gir.. edlothiand na ngalad melon i ni [?sevo] ni [?edran].* Sees the hosts ride in from Lebennin.'

24 Written in the margin here: 'He is called Thalion, and my name is Ramloth.' Beneath *Ramloth* is written *Gwinhir*, and at the first occurrence of the boy's name in the actual narrative my father began *Ram*, changed it to *Arad*, and then wrote *Gwinhir*. — *Thalion* 'steadfast' was the 'surname' of Húrin.

25 *I am 21 years old:* see note 18.

26 Added here: 'But do not speak so darkly.' I do not know what this refers to. Perhaps Pippin's concluding sentence, consisting of three or four wholly illegible words, was equally obscure to Thalion.

27 The greeting of Gondor is still 'with outstretched hand', not 'with hands upon the breast'; and Pippin still says that he is 21 years old (see note 25).

28 For the earliest form of the 'catalogue', bearing little relation to this, see p. 252. The name Forlong the Fat is written on the manuscript of 'The Story Foreseen from Fangorn', p. 229, but this is obviously not contemporary with that outline.

29 *G* was written before *Lossarnach*, but struck out before *Lossarnach* was entered: see p. 289.

30 This passage was afterwards rejected and replaced by a carefully written rider, introducing the description as it stands in RK p. 22, with the name Rammas Echor, and mention of Emyn Arnen, the Harlond, Lossarnach, 'Lebennin with its five swift streams', and Imrahil of Dol Amroth 'in the great fief of Belfalas'. As this rider was first written, 'the quays and landings of the Harlond' were 'the quays and landings of Lonnath-Ernin'.

31 The two cross lines above and below the word 'Rider' reversed show through from the other side of the page: this is the rider referred to in note 30. — The reference to the sun looking down on 'Sam busy with his steaming pan and herbs' (see note 11) remained, but was altered in pencil to 'the warm sun that shone down beyond the River, as Frodo saying farewell to Faramir walked in the glades of Ithilien' (in RK the words 'saying farewell to Faramir' are absent). The altered text represents the synchronization discussed in the Note on Chronology below, whereby Frodo left Henneth Annûn on the same morning as Gandalf reached Minas Tirith.

32 The treatment in this text of other differences of detail between the original draft and RK may be mentioned here. The description of the livery and helms of the guards of the Citadel (p. 279) now becomes precisely as in RK; but Gandalf's words 'And Denethor at least does not expect him in any guise, for he does not know that he exists' remain. Denethor still declares that the horn was heard blowing upon the northern marches twelve days ago (note 15), and he still calls Pippin's sword a *sax* (note 16). Berithil is still clad in grey and white, and his reference to 'the old kings that had dwarves in their service' remains (note 17). Pippin tells him that he has 'not long passed twenty years' (note 18), and later tells Bergil that he is 'nearly twenty-one' (p. 284). Of the mountains in the East it is said that 'their jagged edges [were] softened by wellnigh a hundred miles of misty air' (note 19). Berithil says that 'the Fell Riders, but two years ago, won back the crossings' (note 20); his words about Denethor in the Tower are now precisely as in RK (note 21); and he says that the Corsairs of Umbar 'have long forsaken the friendship of Gondor', and again does not mention Belfalas as a source of aid to the city (note 22).

Note on the Chronology

In the chapter 'Journey to the Cross-roads' (pp. 175 ff.) Frodo and Sam left Henneth Annûn in the morning of February 7 and reached the Osgiliath road at dusk of that day. During the night of February 7–8 the air became heavy, and dark clouds moved out of the East during the morning of the 8th; they reached the Cross-roads at sunset, and saw the sun 'finding at last the hem of the great slow-rolling pall of cloud'.

In the present chapter Gandalf and Pippin arrived at Minas Tirith at sunrise on February 6, and in the note added to the original draft (see p. 286) my father said that the sunset of that day was to be ominous, with the Darkness beginning next morning, the 7th. There is thus a day out between 'Journey to the Cross-roads' and 'Minas Tirith'. (In the outlines for Book V given in the last chapter the Darkness begins on the 8th in outlines III and V, but on the 7th in outline VI.)

I cannot certainly explain this. Presumably my father had introduced a change in the chronology of the movements of Frodo and Sam in Ithilien, or at any rate intended to, and it may be that the rather obscure note given on p. 271 is connected with this: 'Whole of Frodo's and Sam's adventures must be set back *one day*, so that Frodo sees moon-set on morning (early hours) of Feb. 6, and Faramir reaches Minas Tirith on night of the 7th, and Great Darkness begins on 7th.' This gives the following relations (and see note 31 above):

Feb. 6 Frodo leaves Henneth Annûn; reaches Osgiliath road at dusk.
Gandalf reaches Minas Tirith. Ominous sunset.

Feb. 7 Great Darkness begins. Frodo reaches Cross-roads at sunset.

See further the note on chronology on pp. 321–2. — The final synchronization of the stories east and west of Anduin was differently achieved, with extension of Gandalf's ride to Minas Tirith from three nights to four (p. 264 note 3), and of Frodo's journey from Henneth Annûn from two days to three (p. 182). Thus in *The Tale of Years* in LR:

March 8 Frodo leaves Henneth Annûn.

March 9 Gandalf reaches Minas Tirith. At dusk Frodo reaches the Morgul-road [= Osgiliath road]. Darkness begins to flow out of Mordor.

March 10 The Dawnless Day. Frodo passes the Cross Roads.

IV

MANY ROADS LEAD EASTWARD (1)

The original draft ('A') for Chapter XLV (Book V Chapter 2, afterwards called 'The Passing of the Grey Company') was written in pencil in my father's roughest script, and extended only as far as Théoden's words about the Rangers: 'thirty such men will be a strength not to be counted by heads' (RK p. 48). At this stage, I think, he wrote a brief outline for the next part of the chapter which takes up from the point reached in A.

The night was old and the East grey when they came at last to the Hornburg and there rested.

Rangers say that messages reached them through Rivendell. They suppose Gandalf or Galadriel or both?

Merry sat at the king's side in Hornburg, regrets that Pippin was away.

They prepare to ride by secret ways to Dunharrow. Aragorn does not sleep but becomes restless. Takes the Orthanc stone to the tower of the Hornburg and looks in it.

He comes out of the chamber looking very weary, and will say naught but goes to sleep till evening.

'There is evil news,' he said. 'The black fleet is drawing near to Umbar [*sic*]. That will disturb counsels. I fear we must part, Éomer. To meet again later. But not yet. How long will it take to Dunharrow?' 'Two days. If we ride on the 5th we shall reach there by evening of the 6th.'[1]

Aragorn fell silent. 'That will do,' he said.

The reverse of this page is a contoured map of the White Mountains, ruled in squares of 2 cm. side, extending some 90 miles east and west of Edoras, with no features (other than mountain peaks) marked save the Morthond and the Stone of Erech in the south and Edoras and the Snowbourn in the north. Harrowdale here runs a little west of south, in contrast to the map redrawn on p. 258 where it runs south-east, and Erech is a very little east of south from Edoras (assuming that the map is oriented north-south). A pencilled note against the Stone of Erech gives a distance: '62 miles as crow flies from Dunharrow' (where the second figure seems to have been changed from 3); and in the margin is written: 'Scale 4 times main map'. Whichever map my father was referring to[2] this would mean that 1 mm. = 1.25 miles; and a dot pencilled in subsequently very near the head of Harrowdale and obviously representing the place of Dunharrow is at a distance of 51 mm. from the Stone of Erech (= 63.75 miles).[3]

He now returned to the opening of the chapter and overwrote the brief pencilled text in ink, so that it is obscured.[4]

The new draft ('**B**') in ink, as far as the point where the underlying pencilled text ends, reaches that of RK (pp. 46–8) in all but a few points. In the opening paragraph of the chapter it is said of Merry's possessions only that 'he had few things to pack', and this was bracketed; at the head of the page my father wrote: 'Hobbit packs lost at Calembel? replenished at Isengard' (for *Calembel* see the Index to Vol. VII, s.v. *Calenbel*). To Aragorn's words 'But why they come, and how many they are, Halbarad[5] shall tell us' Halbarad replies: 'Thirty we are, and the brethren Elboron and Elbereth are among them. More of us could scarcely be found in these dwindling days, as you well know; and we had to gather in haste. We came because you summoned us. Is that not so?' To which Aragorn replies: 'Nay, save in wish.'[6]

The coming of the sons of Elrond with the Rangers is referred to in the outline given on p. 274. It is interesting to see that the names first given to them, *Elboron* and *Elbereth*, were originally those of the young sons of Dior Thingol's Heir, the brothers of Elwing, who were murdered by 'the evil men of Maidros' host' in the attack on Doriath by the Fëanorians (*The Annals of Beleriand*, in IV.307, V.142); they were thus the great-uncles of the sons of Elrond. But the names *Elboron* and *Elbereth* of Dior's sons had been replaced by *Elrûn* and *Eldûn* (IV.325–6; V.147, 351–3; VI.68).

The new draft B continues on from the point reached in the pencilled opening, but the passage that immediately follows in RK (in which Elrohir son of Elrond delivers his father's message to Aragorn concerning the Paths of the Dead, and Aragorn asks Halbarad what it is that he bears) is entirely absent. The text continues (RK p. 48):

The night was old and the East grey when they rode at last up from the Deeping Coomb and came back to the Hornburg. There they were to lie and rest for a while and take counsel.

Merry slept, until he was roused by Legolas and Gimli. 'The sun is high,' said [Gimli >] Legolas. 'Everyone else is out and about. Come and look round. There was a great battle here only three nights ago. I would show you where the Huorn-forest stood.'

'Is there not time to visit the Caves?' said Gimli.

'I have given my word to go with you,' said Legolas. 'But let that be later and do not spoil the wonder with haste. It is near the hour of noon, and after we have eaten we are to set out swiftly, or so I hear.'

Merry sighed; he was lonely without Pippin and felt that he was only a burden, while everybody was making plans for a business he did not much understand.

'Aragorn has a company of his own now,' said Gimli. '[He seems changed somewhat, and some dark care is on him. But [he] looks more like a king than Théoden himself.][7] They are stout men and lordly. The Riders look almost like boys beside them; for they are grim and worn for the most part, such as Aragorn was. But he seems changed somewhat: a kingly man if ever there was one, though some dark care or doubt sits on him.'

'Where is he?' said Merry.

'In a high chamber in the tower,' said Gimli. 'He has not rested or slept, I think. He went there soon after we came here, saying he must take thought, and only his kinsman Halbarad went with him.'

Merry walked about with Legolas and Gimli for a while, while they spoke of this and that turn of the battle; and they passed the ruined gate and the mounds of the fallen, and they stood upon the dike looking down the Coomb. The Dead Down stood black and tall and stony amid the trampled grass. The Dunlanders and other men of the garrison were busy here and there, on the dyke and in the fields or on the battered walls. At length they returned and went to the meal in the hall of the burg. There Merry was called and was set beside the King.

The conversation of Merry with Théoden, leading to the offer of his service and its acceptance, is virtually the same as in RK (pp. 50–1) and need not be cited. Then follows:

They spoke together for a while. Then Éomer said: 'It is near the hour we set for our departing. Shall I bid men sound the horns? And where is Aragorn? His place is empty and he has not eaten.'

The horns were sounded and men got ready to ride, the Riders of Rohan now in a great company, for the King was leaving but a small garrison in the Burg, and all that could be spared were riding to the muster with him. A thousand spears had already ridden away at night to Edoras; and yet now there were still some three hundred or more that had gathered from the fields about.

In a group by themselves were the Rangers. They were clad in dark grey and their horses were rough-haired. Hoods were over the[ir] helms. They [?wore] spear and bow and sword. There was nothing fine or splendid in their array, no sign or badge, save this only, that each cloak was pinned on the left shoulder by a silver brooch shaped like a rayed star.[8] Dark and sombre and proud men they looked.

Presently Éomer came out of the gate of the Burg, and with him came Halbarad and Aragorn. They came down the ramp and walked to the waiting horses. Merry sitting on his pony by the King was startled by Aragorn. He looked grim, grey-faced, weary, old, and leant a little on Halbarad.

'I have evil tidings, lord,' he said standing before the King. 'A grave peril unlooked for threatens Gondor. A great fleet is drawing near from the south, and will cut off all but scanty help from that region. From Rohan alone can they expect much help now. But I must take new counsel. I fear, lord, and Éomer my friend, we must part – to meet again, maybe, or maybe not. But how long will you take to reach Dunharrow?'

'It is now an hour after noon,' said Éomer. 'On the evening of the second day from now we should come there. That night the moon will rise full, and the muster that the King commanded will begin the day after.'[9]

Aragorn fell silent as if considering. 'Two days,' he said. 'It cannot be much speeded. Well, by your leave, lord, I will forsake this secrecy. The time for it is passed for me. I will eat now and then I and my rangers will ride as swift as steed may go direct to Edoras. We shall meet at Dunharrow ere we part. Farewell. May I commit my friend and charge Meriadoc to your care?'

'No need,' said Théoden, 'he has sworn himself to my service. He is my esquire.'

'Good,' said Aragorn. 'All that you do is kingly. Farewell.'

'Goodbye, Meriadoc,' said Gimli, 'but we're going with Aragorn. It seems that he needs us. But we'll meet again, I think. And yours for the present is the better road, I think. Jogging on a nice pony, while I cling on behind Legolas and try to keep pace with these Rangers!'

'Farewell,' said Merry regretfully.

A horn was sounded and the Riders set forth, and rode down

the Coomb, and turning swiftly west [*read* east] took a path that skirted the foothills for a mile or so and then turned back in among the hills and slopes and disappeared.

Aragorn watched until the King's men were far down the Coomb. Then he turned to Halbarad. 'I must eat,' he said, 'and then we must speed on our way. Come Legolas and Gimli. I would speak to you as I eat.'

'Well,' said Aragorn as he sat at the table in the hall. 'I have looked in the Stone, my friends. For my heart [foreboded that] told me that there was much to learn.'

'You looked in the Stone!' said Gimli, amazed, awestruck, and rather alarmed. 'What did you tell – him?'

'What did I tell him?' said Aragorn sternly, and his eyes glinted. 'That I had a rascal of a rebel dwarf here that I would exchange for a couple of good orcs, thank you! I thought I had the strength, and the strength I had. I said naught to him and wrenched the Stone from him to my own purpose. But he saw me, yes and he saw me in other guise maybe than you see me. If I have done ill I have done ill. But I do not think so. To know that I lived and walked the earth was something of a blow to his heart, and certainly he will now hasten all his strokes – but they will be the less ripe. And then I learned much. For one thing, that there are yet other Stones. One is at Erech and that is where we are going. [*Struck out:* At the Stone of Erech Men shall ... be seen.][10] Halbarad bears this message:

Out of the mountain shall they come their tryst keeping;
at the Stone of Erech their horn shall blow,
when hope is dead and the kings are sleeping
and darkness lies on the world below:
Three lords shall come from the three kindreds
from the North at need by the paths of the dead
elflord, dwarflord, and lord forwandréd,
and one shall wear a crown on head.[11]

And that is an old rhyme of Gondor which none have understood; but I think I perceive somewhat of its sense now. To the Stone of Erech by the paths of the Dead!' he said rising. 'Who will come with me?'

The last two sentences were inked in over pencil, and the rest of the text consists of jottings in ink and pencil. These begin:

So now all roads were running together to the East and the coming of the War. And even as Pippin stood at the Gate and saw the Prince of Dol Amroth ride into the city with his banners the King of Rohan came down out of the hills.

This is the beginning of 'The Muster of Rohan' in RK.[12] It is followed by a sketch of the Starkhorn, and then by rough drafting developing the conversation of Théoden and Éomer as they came into Harrowdale nearer to its form in RK. On the significance of this see pp. 306–7.

This draft was followed (as I judge, immediately) by another ('C'), numbered 'XLV' but without title, more clearly written, but not much advancing on its predecessor. At the beginning of the chapter, Merry 'had few things to bring, for the hobbits had lost their packs at Calembel (Calledin), and though Merry and Pippin had found some new ones at Isengard and had picked up a few necessaries, they made only a light bundle' (see p. 297). In the conversation of Legolas, Gimli and Merry at the Hornburg (RK p. 49) Legolas now speaks of the sons of Elrond, still named Elboron and Elbereth (and it is only now actually made clear who these were, cf. p. 297): 'Sombre is their gear like the others', but they are fair and gallant as Elven-lords. And that is not to be wondered at, for they are the own sons of Elrond of Rivendell.' From Merry's question 'Why have they come? Have you heard?' the conversation then proceeds as in RK, with Gimli quoting the message that came to Rivendell and ascribing it to Gandalf, and Legolas suggesting that it came more likely from Galadriel.[13] Aragorn's horse Roheryn, brought by the Rangers (RK p. 51) has not yet entered (when he left for Edoras he still rode Hasufel), nor is Merry's pony (Stybba in RK) yet given a name; but the sons of Elrond are described in the same words as in RK, and their armour of bright mail cloaked in silver-grey (thus apparently contradicting Legolas' earlier remark 'Sombre is their gear like the others'', where in RK he says 'Less sombre is their gear than the others'').

When Aragorn came from the gate of the Burg the new text follows the earlier closely (pp. 299–300), but he does not name the 'grave peril unlooked for' that threatens Gondor, and he no longer says 'We shall meet at Dunharrow ere we part', but 'I shall be gone ere you come there, if my purpose holds'. His account of his looking into the *palantír* of Orthanc is somewhat developed, though his sarcasm to Gimli remains; from his words 'If I have done ill I have done ill, but I do not think so' this text continues:

'To know that I lived and walked the earth was a blow to his heart, I deem, for he knew it not till now. But he has not forgotten the sword of Isildur or his maimed hand and the pain that lives ever with him. That in this very hour of his great designs the heir of Isildur should be revealed and the sword of

Elendil – for I showed him that – will disturb his counsels. Certainly now he will hasten all his strokes, but the hasty stroke goes often wild.

'And I learned much. For one thing, that there are other Stones yet preserved in this ancient land. One is at Erech. And thither we are going. To the Stone of Erech, if we can find and dare the Paths of the Dead.'

'The Paths of the Dead?' said Gimli. 'That has a fell name! Where does it lie?'

'I do not know yet,' said Aragorn. 'But I know much old lore of these lands, and I have learned much myself in many journeys; and I have a guess. To prove it we shall ride fast ere the day is much older. But harken, here is an old rhyme of my kindred, almost forgotten. It was not said openly, but Halbarad tells me that the message that came to Rivendell ended so. "Bid Aragorn remember the dark words of old:

Out of the mountain shall they come their tryst keeping;
At the Stone of Erech their horns shall blow ..."'

The only differences in this form of the verse from that in the previous draft B (p. 300) are: *horns* for *horn* in line 2; *lost* for *dead* in line 3; *shadow* for *darkness* in line 4; and *man* for *lord* in line 7.

This text C was very substantially altered, by pencilled changes, and by the substitution of rewritten pages to replace existing ones. I doubt that much time if any elapsed between the initial writing of the manuscript and the making of these changes: my impression is that the text as first written ended at this point, with 'the dark words of old', at almost the same point as the preceding draft B ended (p. 300), and that my father at once began to develop it further.

The points in which B differed from RK, mentioned in note 6, were now all altered to the final form (save that the name *Dúnadan* had not yet arisen); and while *Elboron* remained, *Elbereth* was changed to *Elrohir*. The passage (RK p. 48) in which Elrohir delivers Elrond's message to Aragorn, and Halbarad speaks the message of Arwen accompanying her gift, is still altogether lacking; but after the description of the Rangers (RK p. 51) the following was inserted:

Halbarad their leader carried a tall staff, upon which it seemed was a great standard, but it was close-furled and covered with a black cloth bound about it with many thongs.

A major rewriting[14] was inserted into the C manuscript at the point where Aragorn came from the gate of the Burg; the text of RK is now much more nearly approached, yet not reached, for Aragorn seeks knowledge of the Paths of the Dead, whereas in RK (p. 52) he does not.

'I am troubled in mind, lord,' he said, standing by the king's stirrup. 'Strange words have I heard and I see new perils afar off. I have laboured long in thought, and now I fear that I must change my purpose. But tell me, Théoden, what do you know in this land of the Paths of the Dead?'

'The Paths of the Dead!' said Théoden. 'Why do you speak of them?' Éomer turned and gazed at Aragorn, and it seemed to Merry that the faces of the Riders that sat within hearing turned pale at the words, and he wondered what they could mean.

'Because I would learn where they are,' said Aragorn.

'I do not know if indeed there be such paths,' said Théoden; 'but their gate stands in Dunharrow, if old lore be true that is seldom spoken aloud.'

'In Dunharrow!' said Aragorn. 'And you are riding thither. How long will it be ere you come there?'

'It is now two hours past noon,' said Éomer. 'Before the night of the second day from now we should come to the Hold. That night the moon will rise at the full, and the muster that the king commanded will begin the day after. More speed we cannot make, if the strength of Rohan is to be gathered.'

Aragorn was silent for a moment. 'Two days,' he murmured, 'and then the muster of Rohan will only be begun. But I see that it cannot now be hastened.' He looked up, and it seemed that he had made some decision; his face was less troubled.

'Well, by your leave, lord, I must take new counsel. For myself and my kindred, we will now be secret no longer. For me the time of stealth has passed. I will make ready now, and then with my own folk I will ride the straight and open way with all speed to Edoras, and thence to Dunharrow, and thence – who shall say?'

'Do as you will,' said Théoden. 'Your foes are mine; but let each fight as his wisdom guides him. Yet now I must take the mountain-roads and delay no longer. Farewell!'

'Farewell, Aragorn!' said Éomer. 'It is a grief to me that we do not ride together.'

'Yet in battle we may meet again, though all the hosts of Mordor should lie between,' said Aragorn.

'If you seek the Paths of the Dead,' said Éomer, 'then it is little likely that we shall meet among living men. Yet maybe it is your doom to tread strange ways that others dare not.'

'Goodbye, Aragorn!' said Merry. 'I did not wish to be parted from the remnant of our Company, but I have entered the King's service.'

'I could not wish you better fortune,' said Aragorn.

'Goodbye, my lad,' said Gimli. 'I am sorry, but Legolas and I are sworn to go with Aragorn. He says that he needs us. Let us hope the Company will be gathered again some day. And for the next stage yours will be the better road, I think. As you jog on your pony, think of me clinging here, while Legolas vies at horse-racing with those fell Rangers yonder.'

'Till we meet again!' said Legolas. 'But whatever way we chose, I see a dark path and hard before each of us ere the end. Farewell!'

The text then continues with Merry's sad farewell, and the departure of the Riders down the Coomb (in this text spelt throughout *Combe*), but Aragorn's words with Halbarad about Merry and the Shire-folk are absent. Aragorn's account of the Orthanc-stone was now rewritten again, with various minor changes bringing the text still closer to that in RK (his words 'The eyes in Orthanc did not see through the armour of Théoden' are however not present: see p. 77 and note 17). But in answer to Gimli's objection 'But he wields great dominion, nevertheless, and now he will move more swiftly' he replies in this revised version:

'The hasty stroke goes often astray,' said Aragorn. 'And his counsels will be disturbed. See, my friends, when I had mastered the Stone I learned many things. A grave peril I saw coming unlooked-for upon Gondor from the South that will draw off great strength from the defence of Minas Tirith. And there are other movements in the North. But now he will hesitate, doubting whether the heir of Isildur hath that which Isildur took from him, and thinking that he must win or lose all before the gates of the City. If so, that is well, as well as an evil case may be.

'Another thing I learned. There are other Stones yet preserved in this ancient land. One is at Erech. Thither I will go. To the Stone of Erech, if we can find the Paths of the Dead.'

'The Paths of the Dead!' said Gimli. 'That is a fell name, and little to the liking of the men of Rohan, as I saw. Where do they lie, and why must we seek them?'

'I do not yet know where they lie,' said Aragorn. 'But in Dunharrow it seems that we may learn the answer. To Dunharrow at the swiftest, then, I will go.'

'And you would have us ride with you?' said Legolas.

'Of your free will I would,' said Aragorn. 'For not by chance, I deem, are we three now left together of the Company. We have some part to play together. Listen! Here is an old rhyme of my kindred, almost forgotten, never understood.

The days are numbered; the kings are sleeping.
It is darkling time, the shadows grow.
Out of the Mountain they come, their tryst keeping;
at the Stone of Erech horns they blow.
Three lords I see from the three kindreds:
halls forgotten in the hills they tread,
Elflord, Dwarflord, Man forwandréd,
from the North they come by the Paths of the Dead![15]

Why does this point to us, you may ask. I deem it fits the hour too well for chance. Yet if more is needed: the sons of Elrond bring this word from their father in Rivendell: "Bid Aragorn remember the Paths of the Dead."'

'Come then!' Aragorn rose and drew his sword and it flashed in the twilight of the dim hall of the Burg. 'To the Stone of Erech! I seek the Paths of the Dead! Come with me who will!'

Legolas and Gimli answered nothing, but they rose also and followed Aragorn from the hall. There on the green waited silently the hooded Rangers. Legolas and Gimli mounted. Aragorn sprang on Hasufel. Then Halbarad lifted a great horn and the blast of it echoed in Helm's Deep; and they leapt away, riding down the Combe like thunder, while all the men that were left on Dike or Burg stared in amaze.

The last page of the manuscript carries the words pencilled at the end of version B (p. 300): 'So now all roads were running together to the East ...', the paragraph that opens 'The Muster of Rohan' in *The Return of the King.*

At this point my father typed a fair copy, which I will call 'M',[16] very closely based on the manuscript C as revised. This text, numbered 'XLV', bore the title 'Many Roads Lead Eastward'. Only a few passages need be noted. I have mentioned (p. 304) that after the departure of Théoden from the Hornburg 'Aragorn's words with Halbarad about Merry and the Shire-folk are absent' in C revised; but the forerunner of the passage in RK (p. 53) now appears:

Aragorn rode to the Dike and watched till the king's men were far down the Combe. Then he turned to Halbarad. 'There go three that I love,' he said, 'and not least the hobbit, Merry, most dearly. For all our love and dooms, Halbarad, and our deeds of arms, still they have a great worth, that greatheart little people; and it is for them that we do battle, as much as for any glory of Gondor. And yet fate divides. Well, so it is. I must eat a little, and then we too must haste away ...'[17]

Secondly, after Aragorn's words, 'If so that is well, as well as an evil case can be' (p. 304) he now continues:

'... These deadly strokes upon our flanks will be weakened. And we have a little room in which to play.

'Another thing I learned. There is another Stone preserved in the land of Gondor *that he has not looked in*. It is at Erech. Thither I will go. ...'

And lastly, Aragorn now introduces the 'old rhyme' in these words: 'Listen! Here is an old rhyme-of-lore among my kindred, almost forgotten, never understood: it is but a shard of the rhymes of Malbeth, the last Seer of our folk in the north' (see note 15). The verse differs from the form in C revised (p. 305) in lines 2–4, which here read:

It is darkling time, the shadow grows.
Out of the Mountain he comes, his tryst keeping;
At the Stone of Erech his horn he blows.

From the point where 'Aragorn sprang on Hasufel' the typescript M continues thus:

... Then Halbarad lifted a great horn, and the blast of it echoed in Helm's Deep, and with that they leapt away, riding down the Combe like thunder, while all the men that were left on Dike or Burg stared in amaze.

So now all roads were running together to the East to meet the coming of war and the onset of the Shadow. And even as Pippin stood at the Gate of the City and saw the Prince of Dol Amroth ride in with his banners, the King of Rohan came down out of the hills.

Day was waning. In the last rays of the sun the Riders cast long pointed shadows that went on before them. ...

The paragraph 'So now all roads were running together to the East ...' had been written at the ends of texts B and C (pp. 300, 305), from which it was already clear that my father had in mind a chapter that should fall into two parts: first, the story of the return of Théoden and Aragorn to the Hornburg and Aragorn's looking into the *palantír* of Orthanc, followed by the separate departures of Théoden and the Riders and of Aragorn and the Rangers; and second, the story of Théoden's coming to Dunharrow. The paragraph 'So now all roads were running together to the East' was devised as the link between them (and provided the title of the chapter in the typescript, which I have adopted here). In terms of RK, this 45th chapter of *The Lord of the Rings* consisted of 'The Passing of the Grey Company' (pp. 46–56) and 'The Muster of Rohan' (pp. 64 ff.); but all account of Aragorn and the Rangers after they had left the Hornburg was to be postponed.

By the time typescript M was made, much further work had been done on what it is convenient to call by the later title 'The Muster of Rohan', extending it from the point reached in October 1944, as detailed in Chapter II ('Book Five Begun and Abandoned'). I shall therefore postpone the second part of 'Many Roads Lead Eastward' to my next chapter; but the subsequent history of the first or 'Hornburg' part may be briefly noticed here. The typescript M, retitled 'Dunharrow', became the vehicle of much of the later development (doubtless at different times) as far as the departure of Aragorn and the Rangers from the Hornburg, with such changes as *Parth Galen* for *Calembel* (and a proposed name *Calembrith*), *Elladan* for *Elboron*, the introduction of the passage (RK p. 48) in which Elrohir and Halbarad deliver the messages from Elrond and Arwen ('the Lady of Rivendell'), and of Aragorn's account (RK p. 55) of the oathbreaking of the Men of the Mountains and the words of Isildur to their king. Nonetheless, the verse of Malbeth did not at this stage reach the alliterative form in RK:

'... Listen! This is the word that the sons of Elrond bring to me from their father in Rivendell, wisest in lore:

'"Bid Aragorn remember the Paths of the Dead. For thus spoke Malbeth the Seer:

When the land is dark where the kings sleep
And long the Shadow in the East is grown,
The oathbreakers their tryst shall keep,
At the Stone of Erech shall a horn be blown:
The forgotten people shall their oath fulfill.
Who shall summon them, whose be the horn?
For none may come there against their will.
The heir of him to whom the oath was sworn;
Out of the North shall he come, dark ways shall he tread;
He shall come to Erech by the Paths of the Dead."'

At the stage represented by the further development of this typescript with its manuscript additions my father added (as the pagination shows), in a roughly written continuation that is however close to the form in RK, the story of the coming of the Grey Company (not yet so called) to Dunharrow, and the meeting that night, and again next day at dawn, of Aragorn and Éowyn (RK pp. 56–9).[18] It is clear from the pagination that at this stage the muster in Harrowdale was still to be included in this chapter ('Dunharrow'); and that the passage of the Paths of the Dead was not yet told in this part of the narrative.

NOTES

1 A note in the margin of this text says 'Night of 3, day of 4th', i.e. they came to the Hornburg at dawn of the 4th of February. The chronology envisaged here was presumably that Théoden would leave the Hornburg early on the 5th. See note 9.

2 On the First Map 'Dunharrow' was the name of the mountain afterwards called Starkhorn (VII.319 and p. 240 in this book); the distance from that 'Dunharrow' to the spot added later to mark the position of the Stone of Erech (p. 268, footnote) is 18.5 mm or 92.5 miles. Precisely the same, though I think that this is by chance rather than design, is found on the anomalous map redrawn on p. 269 for the distance from Erech to a little mark in Harrowdale that probably represents Dunharrow. The Second Map (p. 434) gives (probably) 45 miles; and this is also the distance on my father's large-scale map of Rohan, Gondor and Mordor (and on my reproduction of it published in *The Return of the King*).

3 A wooden ruler that may have been the one used by my father at this time gives 50 mm. = 62.5 miles.

4 Taum Santoski has been able however to read a good deal of it, especially in the latter part of the text where the arrival of the Rangers is described: here there is no difference of any significance between the original draft and the overwriting in ink. Of the opening passage of the chapter less can be made out; but it can be seen that Aragorn, in answer to Legolas' question 'Where?' ('And then whither?' in RK) replied: 'I cannot say yet. We shall go to the Hold of Dunharrow, to Edoras I guess for the muster that the King ordered in [three > ?four] nights' time from now. But that may prove too tardy.' He seems not to have said anything equivalent to 'An hour long prepared approaches'; and in answer to his question 'Who will go with me?' it is Merry alone who replies: 'I will. Though I promised to sit by the King when he gets back in his house and tell him about the Shire.' To this Aragorn replies: 'That must wait, I fear – [?indeed] I fear it shall

prove one of the fair things that will not come to flower in this bitter spring.'

5 For earlier applications of the name *Halbarad* see p. 236 and note 10.

6 A few other details in which the text differs from RK may be mentioned. Aragorn's reply to Merry's remark about his promise to Théoden remains as it was (note 4). In the encounter with the Rangers Merry's thoughts are not reported; Halbarad does not name himself *Dúnadan*; and neither Aragorn nor Halbarad dismount at first – not until the 'recognition' do they leap down from their horses.

7 The brackets are in the original.

8 In *The Tale of Years* (LR Appendix B) the entry for the year 1436 in the Shire Reckoning states that the King Elessar, coming to the Brandywine Bridge, gave the Star of the Dúnedain to Master Samwise. In my note 33 to *The Disaster of the Gladden Fields* in *Unfinished Tales* (pp. 284–5) I said that I was unable to say what this was. This is a convenient place to mention that after the publication of *Unfinished Tales* two correspondents, Major Stephen M. Lott and Mrs. Joy Mercer, independently suggested to me that the Star of the Dúnedain was very probably the same as the silver brooch shaped like a rayed star that was worn by the Rangers in the present passage (RK p. 51); Mrs. Mercer also referred to the star worn by Aragorn when he served in Gondor, as described in Appendix A (I.iv, *The Stewards*): 'Thorongil men called him in Gondor, the Eagle of the Star, for he was swift and keen-eyed, and wore a silver star upon his cloak.' These suggestions are clearly correct.

9 The chronology is now thus:

February 4 Théoden and Aragorn reach the Hornburg at dawn. In the afternoon Théoden and the Riders leave for Dunharrow, and soon after Aragorn and the Rangers leave for Edoras.

At the Hornburg Éomer says: 'On the evening of the second day from now we should come there [to Dunharrow]. That night the moon will rise full.'

February 6 Full moon. Théoden arrives at Dunharrow at dusk.

10 In a later text (see p. 397) the black Stone of Erech, brought from Númenor, was not a *palantír*, but a *palantír* was preserved in the Tower of Erech. In the present text (and in the subsequent revisions, pp. 302, 304–5), on the other hand, the most natural interpretation of the words seems to be that the Stone of Erech was itself the *palantír*. On the sites of the *palantíri* as originally conceived see pp. 76–7. — Against Aragorn's speech is pencilled in the margin: 'He has not forgotten the sword of Isildur. Doubtless

he will think that I have got the treasure.' Cf. the subsequent text (p. 304): 'But now he will hesitate, doubting whether the heir of Isildur hath that which Isildur took from him.'

11 I have punctuated this verse according to the subsequent version of it, which is almost identical. In the fourth line my father wrote *over earth*, changing *earth* to *the world*, and I have substituted *on* for *over*, as in the following version. — *forwandréd*: worn and weary from wandering.

12 The original texts of the abandoned opening of 'The Muster of Rohan' began 'Day was (fading) waning'; the paragraph cited ('So now all roads were running together to the East ...') precedes 'Day was waning' in RK.

13 In the message that came to Rivendell the wording in this text is: *The Lord Aragorn has need of his kindred. Let the last of the Kings of Men in the North ride to him in Rohan*, where RK has *Let the Dúnedain* ... In a rejected form of this passage preceding it in the manuscript the wording is: *Let all that remain of the* [struck out: *Tarkil*] *Kings of Men ride to him in Rohan.*

Legolas' support for his opinion that it was Galadriel who sent the message, 'Did she not speak through Gandalf of the ride of the Grey Company from the North?', is absent here. The reference is to 'The White Rider' (TT p. 106) and Galadriel's verse addressed to Aragorn spoken to him by Gandalf in Fangorn:

Near is the hour when the Lost should come forth,
And the Grey Company ride from the North.
But dark is the path appointed for thee:
The Dead watch the road that leads to the Sea.

It was at this stage in the evolution of the story that Galadriel's message in verse to Aragorn was changed from its earlier and altogether different form: see VII.431, 448.

When the three companions went down from the broken gates they 'passed the new mounds of the fallen raised on the Gore' ('on the greensward', RK p. 50); and 'the Riders were assembling upon the Gore' ('on the green', RK p. 51). Cf. the description of the Hornburg in the chapter 'Helm's Deep' (TT p. 134): 'About the feet of the Hornrock it [the Deeping Stream] wound, and flowed then in a gully through the midst of *a wide green gore*'; also the drawing of Helm's Deep and the Hornburg in *Pictures by J. R. R. Tolkien*, no. 26.

14 An odd detail may be mentioned here. In his conversation with Legolas and Merry Gimli says in the C version, as first written: 'I played a game which I won by no more than one orc' (cf. RK p. 49). This was now altered to: 'and here Legolas and I played a game which I *lost* only by a single orc', and this survived into the first typescript. But in the second completed manuscript of 'The Road to Isengard', written long before this time, the text is

precisely as in TT, p. 148: '"You have passed my score by one," answered Legolas.'

15 A rejected version of this form of the verse is also found in the manuscript: in this the first two lines read:

The Shadow falls; the kings are sleeping.
It is darkling time, all lights are low.

The remainder of the verse is the same as that given in the text. Although Aragorn describes it only as 'an old rhyme of my kindred', the words 'Three lords I see' perhaps suggest the utterance of a seer; and Aragorn attributes it in the following text (p. 306) to 'Malbeth, the last Seer of our folk in the North' (cf. RK p. 54, where he declares that the wholly different verse that he recites in this place was spoken by 'Malbeth the Seer, in the days of Arvedui, last king at Fornost'). — In none of these texts is there any indication of what the 'tryst' might be. In the outline given on pp. 274–5 there is mention of the defeat of the Haradwaith by 'the Shadow Host'.

16 The reason for calling the typescript 'M' is that as will be seen shortly it covers, in a single chapter (XLV), both the story of Aragorn at the Hornburg (preceded by texts A to C) and the story of the Muster of Rohan (preceded by texts A to L).

17 This was changed on the typescript to read: '"There go three that I love," he said, "and the halfling, Merry, most dearly. ... and for them also we do battle, not only for the glory of Gondor. And yet fate divides us. ..."'

18 It is said in this continuation that Aragorn came to Edoras 'at dusk on the next day' (February 5), and that they did not halt there but passed up Harrowdale and came to Dunharrow 'late at night'; and Aragorn says to Éowyn on the following morning (February 6) that Théoden and Éomer will not return 'until the day is old'. See note 9.

V
MANY ROADS LEAD EASTWARD (2)

When my father made the typescript (M) of the long chapter 'Many Roads Lead Eastward' he had not only written a good deal of what afterwards became 'The Passing of the Grey Company': he had also greatly extended the story that would later become 'The Muster of Rohan' from the opening abandoned in October 1944. A new text of the latter (following the last of the earlier ones, that in 'midget type' which I have called H, p. 250) takes up at the point where Éomer says 'Harrowdale at last!' (RK p. 65); this I will call 'J'. Tolerably clearly written in ink, it extends only as far as Merry's wonderment at the line of standing stones across the Firienfeld (RK p. 68), the last lines being roughly pencilled, and then peters out into a brief outline; but so far as it goes the first part of 'The Muster of Rohan' in RK was now achieved almost word for word, except just at the point where it breaks off.[1] The text ends thus:

At last they came to a sharp brink, and the climbing road passed into a low cutting between walls of rock and passed up a slope out onto a wide upland. The Firienfeld men called it, a green mountain field of grass and heath above the deep-delved valley, on the lap of the great mountains behind: the Starkhorn southward, and westward [*read* northward][2] the many-peaked mass of Iscamba[3] Irensaga [*written above:* Ironsaw], between which lower, but steep and grim, stood the black wall of the Dwimorberg, rising out of thick slopes of sombre firs / pines. Towards this marched from the very brink of the stairs to the dark edge of the wood a line a double line [*sic*] of standing stones. Worn and black, some leaning, some fallen, some cracked or broken, they were like old teeth. Where they vanished into the wood there was a dark opening into a cavern or recess in the [?western] side. Just within dimly seen was a tall standing pillar.

Merry looked at this strange line of stones and wondered what they could be. He

Éowyn says Aragorn has gone by the Paths of the Dead.

The huts and pavilions of the hold.

To the king's pavilion come the messengers of Gondor.

The king promises 7 thousand horse to ride as soon as may

be. At same [time] messengers come from Eastemnet saying that an orc-host has crossed the river, below the Limlight.

It is a gloomy evening repast.

The morning is dull and overcast, and gets darker.

On this page, which is reproduced on p. 314, are two rapid pencilled sketches which amply illustrate the final conception of Harrowdale and Dunharrow.

It is to be remembered that at this time the further story of Aragorn and the Grey Company, their coming to Dunharrow and their entering the Gate of the Dead, was not present in the narrative: the present passage was to be the first account of the Dwimorberg, the Firienfeld, the line of standing stones, the Dimholt, and the great monolith before the Dark Door. When afterwards the structure of the narrative was changed my father largely retained this description in the chapter 'The Muster of Rohan' (RK pp. 67–8): he treated the coming of the Grey Company to Dunharrow two nights before the arrival of Théoden in a single sentence ('they passed up the valley, and so came to Dunharrow as darkness fell', RK p. 56), and said almost nothing of the scene – they 'sat at supper' with Éowyn, 'as Aragorn came to the booth where he was to lodge with Legolas and Gimli, and his companions had gone in, there came the Lady Éowyn after him and called to him', and that is all. The approach of the Company to the Dark Door next morning is described with a mysterious brevity: the double line of standing stones across the Firienfeld is mentioned cursorily, as if their existence were already known to the reader: 'A dread fell on them, even as they passed between the lines of ancient stones and so came to the Dimholt' (RK p. 59).

The text J was followed by another, '**K**', beginning at the same point ('Harrowdale at last!'); this was clearly written in ink as far as the point where Éowyn says to Théoden: 'And your pavilion is prepared for you, lord, for I have had full tidings of you' (cf. RK p. 68). In this text the description of the Firienfeld runs as follows (the passage here set between asterisks was rejected, but is not marked in any way in the manuscript):

The Firienfeld men called it, a green mountain-field of grass and heath, high above the deep-delved valley [> course of the Snowbourn], on the lap of the great mountains behind: the Starkhorn southwards to the right, and [westward in front >] northward to the left the many-peaked mass of Irensaga Ironsaw, between which there faced them, darkly frowning, the grim black wall of Dwimorberg, rising out of thick slopes of sombre pines. *[Towards these woods >] Across the wide field there marched, from the brink of the stair to the dark edge of [illegible] valley loomed up mournfully into dusk. After a while he looked back and found that he had already climbed several hundreds of feet above the valley, but still far below he could dimly see a winding line of riders crossing the ford and filing along the road, towards the camping place [illegible] camps prepared for the king [illegible] Chief King's guard was going up with him.

At length they came to a sharp brink, and the climbing road passed into a [illegible] cutting between walls of rock and passed up a slope out on to a wide upland. The Firienfeld men called it, a green mountain field of grass and heath high above the deep delved valley, on the lap of the great mountains behind. The Starkhorn northward and southward the [illegible] mass. Irensaga between which was lower, but steep and [illegible] the blackness of the Dwimorberg [illegible] out of a thick slope of sombre firs pine. Towards this marched from the brink of stones to the dark edge of the wood a line a double line of standing stones. Worn and black some leaning, some fallen, some cracked or broken like old teeth. [illegible] there was a dark gap [illegible] a cave or recess [illegible] at the inner side [illegible] [illegible] seen was a little standing pillar.

He looked at the strange line of stones and wondered what they could be. He

[illegible] Stranger [illegible] Paths of the Dead.

[illegible] and [illegible] of the [illegible]

[illegible] King's [illegible] comes [illegible] of [illegible]

The King's [illegible] house [illegible]

[illegible] comes from [illegible] over the river [illegible]

[illegible]

[illegible] and [illegible]

Starkhorn, Dwimorberg and Irensaga

the woods, a double line of standing stones, worn and black. Some leaning, some fallen, some cracked or broken, they looked like rows of old and hungry teeth. Where they entered the wood there was a [dark opening >] way in the trees: just within dimly to be seen was a tall standing pillar and beyond it the dark opening of a cavern or great door.* Dividing the upland into two there marched a double line of standing stones that dwindled in the dusk and vanished into the trees. Those who followed that road came to a dark clearing amid the sighing gloom of the Firienholt,[4] and there like a shadow stood a single pillar of stone, and beyond a huge doorway in the side of the black cliff. Signs and figures were set about it that none could read, worn by the years and shrouded from the light.[5] In long memory none had dared to pass that door. Such was the dark Dunharrow, the work of long-forgotten men. ...

The text then continues very close indeed to RK (p. 68), ending with Éowyn's words to Théoden 'I have had full tidings of you', which do not stand at the foot of a page. The next words, '"So Aragorn has come," said Éomer' (RK p. 69), stand at the head of a new page, and there follows a manuscript pencilled in my father's most impossible handwriting, effectively indecipherable except insofar as later versions provide clues – as is however largely the case here. This further text can be regarded as a continuation of K. It carries the narrative of 'The Muster of Rohan' as far as the conclusion of Théoden's words with the errand-rider of Gondor, RK p. 73; and while it is naturally rough and hasty in expression, and would be greatly refined, the story was effectively present from the first. The following passage, however, I cite in full, following Éomer's words (cf. RK p. 70) 'For the road we have climbed is the approach to the Door. Yonder is the Firienholt. But what lies beyond no man knows.' For the earliest reference to the old man of Dunharrow see the notes ('E') given on p. 242.

'Only legend of old days has any report to make,' said Théoden. 'But if these ancient tales are to be believed, then the Door [?in] Dwimorberg leads to a secret way that goes under the mountains. But none have dared ever to explore it since Baldor son of Bregu dared to pass the Door, and came never back. Folk say that Dead Men out of ... Years guard the way and will suffer none to come to their secret halls. But at whiles they may be seen [?rush]ing out like shadows and down the Stony Road. Then the men of Harrowdale shut fast their doors and shroud their windows and are afraid. But seldom do the Dead come forth, and only at times of great peril.'

'Yet it is said in Harrowdale,' said Éowyn quietly, 'that they came forth in the moonless nights [?just past].'

'But why has Aragorn gone that way?' said Merry.

'Unless he has spoken to you his friend, then you have heard as much as we,' said Éowyn. 'But I thought that he had changed much since I saw him in Meduseld.[6] Fey he seemed to me, and as one that the Dead call.'

'Maybe,' said Théoden. 'Yet my heart tells me that he is a kingly man of high destiny. And take comfort in this, daughter, since comfort you seem to need in your grief for this passing guest. It is said that when the Eorlingas came first out of the North and passed up the Snowbourn seeking strong places of refuge in time of need, that Bregu and his son Baldor climbed the Stair of the Hold and [?passed] to the Door; and there there sat an old man aged beyond count of years, withered as old stone. Very like to the Púkel-men he was as he sat upon the threshold of the dark Door.

'Nothing he said until they sought to pass him and enter, and then a voice came out of him as if it were out of a stone, and to their amazement it spoke in their own tongue. *The way is shut.*

'Then they halted and looked at the old man whom [?the king] had at first taken for [??an image] such as stood at the turnings of the Stair. But he did not look at them. *The way is shut* the voice said again. *It was made by those who are Dead and [??for] the Dead [??to] keep until the time comes.*

'*And when will that be?* said Baldor.

'But no answer did he ever get. For the old man died in that hour and fell upon his face, and no other [??words] of the ancient dwellers in the mountains did [?our] folk ever learn. Yet maybe the time has come and Aragorn will pass.'

'And whether the time is [?come] or no,' said Éomer, 'none can discover save by daring the door. A [?true]-hearted man was Aragorn, and still against hope I hope to see his face once again. Yet our roads lie' And then he paused, for there was a noise without of men's voices and the challenges of the king's guard.

Then Dúnhere entered and announced the coming of the messenger (or messengers)[7] of Gondor. In his opening words Dirgon, as he is called here (Hirgon in RK), says: 'Often you have aided us, but now the Lord Denethor begs for all your strength, and all your speed, lest Gondor fall. Then would the tide sweep over the fields of Calenardon.'[8] From Théoden's words 'And yet he knows that we are a scattered people and take time to gather in our riders' the text runs far more briefly than in RK to the end of his speech with the messenger. Dirgon does not speak again, and Théoden refers only, and briefly, to the war with Saruman and the lesser number of Riders that he can send; concluding 'Yet all is more advanced than I hoped. We may ride on the [?third] day from now.'

A further pencilled text ('L'), as fearsomely scrawled as K or worse, takes up after a short gap for which there is no drafting with Merry's words: 'I will not be left behind to be called for on return' (RK p. 73). It is curious that this text is headed 'XLVI' (without title), whereas the typescript M, obviously developed from L, includes this story of the departure of the Riders from Harrowdale as the conclusion of 'XLV: Many Roads lead Eastward'. I can only suppose that my father briefly intended to begin a new chapter with Merry's words, but thought better of it.

The opening of the text L is very close to RK pp. 73–5. The darkness that has spread out of the East and reached far into the western sky is described in the same words; the first messenger from Gondor is now named Hirgon, and the second (never named) is present – but this latter says of the darkness only: 'It comes from Mordor, lord. It began last night at sunset, and now the great cloud lies on all the [?land] between here and the Mountains of Shadow, and it is deepening. By the fire-signals war has already begun.' To this Théoden replies: 'Then the die is cast. There is no longer need or profit in hiding. We will muster at once and wait not. Those who are not here must be left behind or follow. ...'

Merry's story at this point was somewhat different from its form in RK. After his expostulation to Théoden ('Then tie me on to one, or let me hang on a stirrup ...') the text, hurled onto the paper, continues:

Théoden smiled. 'You shall ride before me on Snowmane [?rather than wander in the plains] of Rohan. Go now and see what the armourers have prepared for you.'

'It was the only request that Aragorn made,' said Éowyn. 'And it has been granted.'

With that she led him from the pavilion to a booth at some distance among the lodgings of the king's guard, and there a man brought out to her a small helm and a coat of mail and a shield like to the one that had been given to Gimli.[9] 'No mail we had to fit you nor time to forge a hauberk for you,'[10] she said, 'but here is a short jerkin of leather and a shield and a [?short] spear. Take them and bear them to good fortune. But now I have .... to look to. Farewell. But we shall meet again, my heart foretells, thou and I, Meriadoc.'

So it was that amid the gathering gloom the King of the Mark set out. Not many hours had passed, and now in the half-light beside the grey rush of the Snowbourn he sat proudly on his white horse, and five [and] fifty hundreds of Riders, besides men ..... with spare horses bearing light burdens, [?were ranged]. They [?were to ride down] to Edoras and [?thence out and away] along the well-beaten road eastward, pass along the skirts of the hill[s] to [?Anórien] and the walls of Minas Tirith. Merry sat on his pony that was to bear him down the [?stony] valley, and after that he was to ride with the king or some other of his company.

A trumpet sang. The king raised his hand, and without any sound of voice, silently, without shout or song, the great ride began. The king passed along the lines followed by Merry and Éomer and the errand-riders of Gondor and Dúnhere, and then his guard of twelve picked spearmen. To Éowyn he had said farewell above in the Hold.

It is clear, from Théoden's 'You shall ride before me on Snowmane rather than wander in the plains of Rohan. Go now and see what the armourers have prepared for you', and from the words 'Merry sat on his pony that was to bear him down the stony valley, and after that he was to ride with the king or some other of his company', that at this stage Merry was to go with the Rohirrim to Minas Tirith openly, with the concurrence of Théoden, and without any assistance from Éowyn. This does not mean, of course, that Éowyn was not present among the Riders in disguise, although no covert reference is made to her in this original account of the departure from Harrowdale; and indeed her death before Minas Tirith had been long foreseen (see VII.448; also the outline given on p. 256 and especially that on p. 275). In any case, a further draft for the story of the departure follows in text L:

First there went twelve of the king's household-men [?and] guard, picked spearmen. Tall and stern they looked to Merry, and one among them, less tall and broad than the others, glanced at the hobbit as he passed, and Merry caught the glint of clear grey eyes. He shivered a little, for it seemed to him that the face was of one that goes knowingly to death. The king followed with Éomer on his right and Dúnhere on his left. He had said farewell to Éowyn above in the Hold. Merry followed with the errand-riders of Gondor and behind went twelve more of the guard. Then in [?ordered] lines the companies of the riders turned and rode after them as was appointed. They passed down the road beside the Snowbourn, and through the hamlets of Upbourn and Underharrow where many sad faces looked from dark doors. And so the great ride to the East began, with which the songs of Rohan were busy for many lives of men thereafter.

Here the text L ends, and here the typescript M ends also.

In this second part of the chapter 'Many Roads lead Eastward' the typescript text shows great refinement in detail over these exceedingly rough and obviously primary drafts, but no texts are found to bridge them; and it seems possible that the developed form in M was actually achieved on the typewriter (there are in fact several passages that could suggest this). To a great extent the text of RK in 'The Muster of Rohan' was now present; but there remained still some differences, and among these I notice the following.[11]

Éowyn now says of the coming forth of the Dead (see p. 316): 'Yet it is said in Harrowdale that they came forth again in the moonless nights but little while ago, a great host in strange array, and none saw them return, they say.' The old man beside the Dark Door is still said to resemble one of the Púkel-men.[12] On the front of Hirgon's helm 'was wrought as an emblem a small silver crown' ('star' in RK). The second, unnamed errand-rider from Gondor says here of the darkness spreading out of Mordor: 'From my station by the beacon of Minrimmon I saw it rise', where in RK he says: 'From the hills in the Eastfold of your realm I saw it rise'. Notably, the conversation between Merry and Théoden now takes this form:

Théoden smiled. 'Rather than that I will bear you with me on Snowmane,' he said. 'I guessed your words before you spoke them. But at the least you shall ride with me to Edoras and look on Meduseld, for that way I shall go. So far Stybba can bear you: the great race will not begin till we reach the plains.'

'And over the plains with you to the end of the road your squire will ride,' said Éowyn. 'That you know in your heart, and others also have foreseen it. Come now, Meriadoc, and I will show you the gear that is prepared for you. It was the only request that Aragorn son of Arathorn made of us ere he departed.'

With that she led the hobbit from the king's pavilion to a booth among the lodges of the king's guard near by; and there a man brought out to her a small helm and a spear and round shield, and other gear.

The account of the departure follows that in text L (p. 318); the Rider who looked at Merry as he passed is still among the twelve household-men that preceded the host, 'somewhat less in height and girth than the others'; and nothing is said of what arrangement had been made for Merry after the departure of the host from Edoras.

The chapter 'Many Roads Lead Eastward' ended, both in manuscript and typescript, at the ride of the Rohirrim down Harrowdale: 'And so the great ride to the East began, with which the songs of Rohan were busy for many lives of men thereafter' (p. 319; RK p. 76). The conclusion of 'The Muster of Rohan' as it stands in RK was added later, but not much later (at least in terms of the progress of the narrative: what halts and of what duration took place in the writing of Books V and VI there seems no way of telling); it first appeared, in fact, as the opening of Chapter XLVII, 'The Ride of the Rohirrim', and I postpone it to that place (p. 349).

NOTES

1 On a rejected page in this manuscript, however, Théoden expresses some amazement at the scene in Harrowdale: 'The king looked with surprise about him, for there was a great concourse of men ... "What is the meaning of this?" asked the king. "Was not the muster set to begin tomorrow at Edoras?"' Then a man, unnamed, explains how this is due to Gandalf, and a note follows: 'Gandalf must tell the king as he rides off that he will order the muster at Dunharrow and speed it up. That will necessitate altering remarks about the full moon' (see the Note on Chronology below). This rejected page then concludes with a brief passage that depends on the note: 'So they saw that Gandalf must have done as he promised. The muster was here, not at Edoras, and already the greater part of the men of Rohan were assembled.'

The words 'Gandalf must tell the king as he rides off' can only refer to his leaving Dol Baran on Shadowfax after the Nazgûl passed over; but no such change was in fact introduced in that place.

At the foot of this rejected page is written: 'Éowyn tells of Aragorn's coming and his departure. The Paths of the Dead. The road of Monoliths.'

2 *westward* was, I think, no more than a slip. It was repeated in the following text (p. 313) but corrected, probably at once.

3 *Iscamba:* cf. Old English *camb* (Modern English *comb*), comb, crest (as of a cock, a helmet, etc.).

4 For the name *Firienholt* of the later *Dimholt* see p. 251 and note 21.

5 For the origin of this sentence see p. 246. It reappears in changed form in 'The Passing of the Grey Company' in RK (p. 59), where the Company halted before the Dark Door: 'Signs and figures were carved above its wide arch too dim to read, and fear flowed from it like a grey vapour.'

6 The first part of the name of the Golden Hall is so scrawled that it could be read in almost any way, but it is clearly not *Wínseld*, the earlier name, and is almost certainly the first occurrence of *Meduseld*.

7 Apparently there were two messengers, for while the writing is so fast that no detail of letter is entirely certain, my father seems to have written 'Men are here, errand-riders out of Gondor.' Théoden's reply could be equally well read as 'Let him come' or 'Let them come'. But only one man enters. — The war-arrow that he bears is green-feathered (black in RK).

8 The name *Calenard(h)on* emerged in the course of writing the chapter 'Faramir': see pp. 155–6, with notes 18 and 22.

9 The reference is to 'The King of the Golden Hall', TT p. 127: '[Gimli] chose a cap of iron and leather that fitted well upon his round head; and a small shield he also took. It bore the running horse, white upon green, that was the emblem of the House of Eorl.' This passage, in which is recounted also the arming of Aragorn and Legolas 'in shining mail', was added on a rider to the fair copy manuscript of 'The King of the Golden Hall'.

10 Thus the provision of a coat of mail for Merry, referred to in the preceding sentence, was immediately denied.

11 The following names and name-forms in the typescript may be mentioned. The *Firienholt* remains, for later *Dimholt*. *Brego* is now again spelt thus, not *Bregu*, but his son's name is here *Bealdor* (changed to *Baldor* on the typescript): both of these are Old English variants. The path down from the Dark Door ('the road of Monoliths', note 1) is again called 'the Stony Road', capitalised, as in the text K (p. 315). Hirgon speaks of *the Harad*, where RK has *the Haradrim*.

12 In RK (p. 71) the old withered man is said to have been once 'tall and kingly'. Cf. *The Lord of the Rings* Appendix F (*Of Men*): 'The Dunlendings were a remnant of the peoples that had dwelt in the vales of the White Mountains in ages past. The Dead Men of Dunharrow were of their kin.'

Note on the Chronology

In the last of the texts (H) of the abandoned opening of 'The Muster of Rohan' Théoden asked if the moon had not been full on the night before, and Éomer replied that on the contrary the moon would be full that night (pp. 251–2, 272–3). In the first of the later texts (J) Théoden himself says 'Tonight the moon will be full, and in the morning I shall ride to Edoras to the gathering of Rohan', and this remained into the typescript M.

In 'The Road to Isengard' the date of the muster at Edoras was changed over and over again according to the shifting chronology. For the earliest texts see p. 27 and note 6; the second fair copy of that chapter had 'before the waning of the moon', changed to 'at the last quarter of the moon'. This was retained in the following typescript, but there changed subsequently to 'on the first day after the full moon' – which is the date in the present texts. (In 'The Road to Isengard' in TT, p. 150, the date of the muster is to be 'the second day after the full moon', and so at the beginning of 'The Muster of Rohan' in RK, p. 65, Théoden says: 'Last night the moon was full, and in the morning I shall ride to Edoras to the gathering of the Mark.')

In the note on text J (see note 1 above) it is said that 'Gandalf must tell the king as he rides off [from Dol Baran] that he will order the muster at Dunharrow and speed it up', and that this 'will necessitate altering remarks about the full moon.' I do not understand this. If my father was referring to the passage in 'The Road to Isengard' in which the date of the muster is set, this would seem to have no relevance: for Gandalf was proposing, in view of the coming of the Nazgûl, to *change* the arrangement that had been made and 'speed up' the muster.

All these later 'Muster of Rohan' texts agree that the moon was full on the night that Théoden came to Harrowdale (February 6); cf. p. 299 and note 9. This was the night following the day on which Gandalf and Pippin reached Minas Tirith at sunrise; the sunset of that day was 'ominous', and the Darkness began on February 7 (p. 295). With this the present texts agree: the second errand-rider from Gondor, arriving on the morning of the 7th, says that the Darkness 'began last night at sunset' (p. 317), and the departure of the Riders from Dunharrow takes place in deepening gloom. It is interesting to see that in text K, as Merry sat alone in his tent on the Firienfeld, 'Slowly night came on, and the half-seen heads of the mountains were crowned with small stars in the West, but the East was dark and shadowy, *and the moon did not appear until late at night*'; whereas in the typescript M (where it was still the night of full moon) the moon is not mentioned. The natural presumption is that the moon was hidden by the vast cloud spreading out of Mordor.

How my father was at this stage relating the full moon of February 6 to Frodo's movements is not clear to me. In *The Tale of Years* in LR the full moon was on March 7 (since Frodo left Henneth Annûn on March 8, and he saw the full moon setting before dawn on the morning of his departure: 'The Forbidden Pool', TT pp. 292–3), and Théoden came to Dunharrow on the evening of March 9; but with this the king's words in 'The Muster of Rohan', RK p. 65, 'Last night the moon was full', do not accord, and should have been 'Two nights ago'. This in turn would require alteration of the date set for the muster in 'The Road to Isengard' (see above).

VI
THE SIEGE OF GONDOR

My father's first start on this chapter was a brief, roughly pencilled text ('**A**') which he then wrote over in ink, so that a good deal is lost, especially of the latter part of it; but Taum Santoski has managed to recover quite enough to show that the ink overwriting ('**B**') followed it for the most part very closely. I shall here describe B rather than A, noting subsequently passages in which A is significantly different.

Text B (numberless and titleless) begins as does Chapter 4 in *The Return of the King* with 'Pippin was roused by Gandalf', and extends through the paragraph beginning 'It was dark and dim all day' (RK p. 80). After Pippin's question 'Why did you bring me here?' the text differs from that of RK:

'Because it was not safe to leave you behind,' answered the wizard. 'Safe for others, I mean. It is no safe place here for you or anyone else, as you'll probably soon discover. But you brought it on yourself.' Pippin said no more.

Before long he was walking with Gandalf back again down the long cold passage to the doors of the Tower Hall. Within Denethor sat in a grey gloom, like an old patient spider, Pippin thought, and looking as if he had not moved since he dismissed his new esquire the day before. He beckoned Gandalf to a seat, but Pippin was left standing for a while unheeded. Presently the old man turned to him with a cold smile, whether of mockery or welcome Pippin could not tell.

'And why have you come, Peregrin son of Paladin?' he said.

'I was told that you wanted me, sir,' said Pippin, 'to, well, to learn my new duties.'

'Ah yes,' said Denethor. 'It is to be hoped that you spent yesterday well and to your liking, if less in eating [*struck out:* and sleeping] than you might wish. Today you shall take your turn to wait on me. I have little more now to do, until my son Faramir returns with tidings. And if there comes no ill news and the great ones' (he looked at Gandalf) 'do not occupy all my leisure, you shall talk to me. Can you sing?'

Pippin's apologetic account of the songs he knew and his horror at the thought of singing a comic song of the Shire before the grim

Steward of Minas Tirith follows as in RK, as does Denethor's discussion with Gandalf, the arming and clothing of Pippin,[1] and the darkness over the city, up to 'as if all the Vale of Anduin waited for a ruinous storm.' Then follows:

His duties he found irksome and dull, so much so that he would even have welcomed a chance to sing one of his comic songs. But he was not asked to sing, and indeed few spoke to him at all.

Here the overwritten text B ends. In the underlying pencilled text A the discussion between Gandalf and Denethor did not concern Rohan, but was on the subject of the immediate strategy: though very little of it can be made out, the phrase 'Gandalf had already been urging on the Steward' and the name 'West Osgiliath' can be read. After Pippin had returned from the armoury it is said that he spent the day idly, 'for Denethor sat mostly behind closed doors'; and at some point during the day 'There was a clamour in the city. Faramir had returned. Pippin witnesses the greeting of Denethor and Faramir.'

The pencilled and the overwritten texts end at the same point on the page, although in substance they had diverged.

My father evidently doubted the rightness of beginning the chapter in this way, for at the head of the first page of this 'doubled' text he wrote in pencil: '? Begin with Pippin and Berethil[2] talking again on wall on eve[ning] of 9th. . . .' This was in fact overwritten by part of the B text in ink, and as a result some further words of the note cannot be read; presumably therefore my father had (but only temporarily) abandoned the idea that the chapter might open differently.

At the end of the 'doubled' text the following notes were written in pencil:

? Sunset – a gleam far off. Gandalf says there is hope still in the West.

Next day there is a council and soon Faramir departs. Pippin has more talk with Berethil and hears that Faramir has gone to Osgiliath. Time passes slowly. Ill news comes on 11th March (next day) that there is a Fell Captain on the enemy's side. He has won the Crossings and Faramir is driven to Ramas Coren.[3] Still the darkness grows. It is like a slow disease, thought Pippin.

Some time on 9th Pippin must look out from the walls and see Nazgûl (6 or 7) flying over Pelennor, and see them pursue a few riders. But Gandalf rides out – and saves them. It is Faramir! Just in time. Great joy in City. Faramir sees Pippin as he comes up to the Citadel, and is astonished.

In these notes is the first appearance of the final calendar, the month being now March instead of February. Whether it entered at this very time or somewhat earlier cannot be said: but the last actual date found in the texts is February 5–6 in the outline for a part of 'Many Roads Lead Eastward' given on p. 296, so that the change had at any rate been made not long since. The conception of the month 'lost' in Lórien had now been abandoned: see VII.367–9. The relative dates have however not been changed: in the note suggesting a different way of opening the chapter Pippin and Berethil are to be talking on the wall of the city 'on the evening of the 9th', which would be February 7 according to the former dating (see the Note on Chronology at the end of this chapter).

My father now returned to the idea of a different opening, and began a new draft ('C') in which the matter of the opening already written was omitted or compressed, and referred to only in retrospect. This draft was written in thick soft pencil, in ink over pencil, and in ink with pencilled corrections and clarifications, and is throughout a formidably difficult manuscript. I have no doubt that it all proceeded from the same time and impulse.

This new text is numbered 'XLVI', without title; it begins with the words 'It had been dark all day; from the sunless dawn until the evening the heavy gloom had deepened ...', and continues essentially as in RK pp. 80–1 as far as 'now he was one small soldier in a city preparing for a great assault, clad in the grim and sombre manner of the Tower of Guard'; but there is no reference to the errand of Berethil (Beregond) across the Pelennor, nor to the last gleam of the sun as it escaped from the pall of cloud (see below). Then follows:

For in the morning Denethor had summoned him, and bidden him to take up his duties as the lord's esquire; and he had been sent straight to the armouries where already clothes and gear were made ready for him by Denethor's command.

In some other time and place he might have taken pleasure in his new array, but he knew now too clearly that this was a deadly serious matter, and no masquerade in borrowed plumes. The small coat of black mail seemed heavy and burdensome, and the helmet with its wings weighed on his head. Black too was the tunic or surcoat that he now wore above his mail, except where upon the breast was broidered in white the device of the Tree. He had been permitted to retain the grey cloak of Lórien [*added:* when not on duty], but that was now cast aside on the seat beside him, for the air was close. He turned his gaze away from the darkling plain far below, and yawned, and then he sighed.

In Pippin's complaint to Berethil and their words about the Darkness, the failure of Faramir to return across the River and Gandalf's anxiety, and the sudden cry of the Nazgûl, the draft reaches the text of RK pp. 81–2 almost word for word (save only that Pippin does not name the Prince of Dol Amroth as present at the deliberations with Denethor, and he says that Gandalf left the council before the evening meal, where RK has 'noon-meal'); but when Pippin climbs on to the seat and looks out there enters the description of the last gleam of sun that shone also on the head of the ruined king at the Cross-roads, omitted at its place in RK (on the synchronisation see the note at the end of this chapter). Then again the draft reaches the final text in almost every turn of expression in the description of the Nazgûl swooping on the horsemen, the distant sound of Faramir's horn call, and the radiance of the White Rider racing towards them, as far as Pippin's wild shouting 'like an onlooker at a great race urging on a runner who is far beyond encouragement.' At this point my father stopped and set down a brief outline:

Gandalf saves Faramir. Faramir sees Pippin at gate of Citadel and wonders – Gandalf introduces them, and takes Pippin along to Denethor's council. So Pippin hears a lot and hears Faramir accept orders to go to Osgiliath. Denethor and Faramir marvel at Gandalf's power over Nazgûl. Gandalf says things are still not so bad – because the W[izard] King has not yet appeared. He reveals that he is a renegade of his own order ... [?from] Númenor. 'So far I have saved myself from him only by flight – for many an age he has lain in hiding or sleep while his master's power waned. But now he is grown more fell than ever. Yet it was foretold that he should be overthrown, in the end, by one young and gallant. But maybe that lies far in the future.'

He hears about Frodo and Sam. Also how Faramir crossed from Tol Varad (the Defended Isle) [> Men Falros] with three companions, and came on horse. The rest of the 'task force' he had despatched to the Pelennor Gate.

Last half of chapter must deal with situation after taking of Pelennor, the battle of Pelennor and the fall of the Gate.[4]

The draft continues with 'And now the swooping dark shadows were aware of the newcomer' (RK p. 83), and again the final form is closely approached, if with rougher and less full expression, through the coming of Faramir with Gandalf to the Citadel, his wonderment at seeing Pippin, and his story told in Denethor's private chamber. Only Pippin's emotion when he first saw Faramir was at this time different from the form in RK (pp. 83–4): the passage 'Here was one with an air of high nobility such as Aragorn at times revealed . . .' is lacking (and remains absent in the following fair copy manuscript).

From the point where Faramir reached the story of his meeting with Frodo and Sam I give the draft text in full, for though in many respects it closely approaches that of RK there are also many differences, and some are very noteworthy.

As the tale of his meeting with Frodo and Sam was unfolded, Pippin became aware that Gandalf's hands were trembling as they clutched the carven wood; white they seemed now and very old, and as he looked at them suddenly with a thrill of fear he knew that Gandalf – Gandalf himself was afraid, mastering a great dread, and not yet daring to speak. At last when Faramir told how he had parted with the travellers and that they were resolved to take the road to Kirith Ungol his voice fell, and he shook his head and sighed. But Gandalf sprang up. 'Kirith Ungol and Morghul Vale,' he cried. 'The time, Faramir. When was this, do you say? Tell me, tell me. When did you part with them? When would they reach the Morghul Vale? When did this darkness begin? Do you not see – that it may be a sign that all is indeed lost?'

'I spoke with them yestermorn,'[5] said Faramir. 'It is nigh on [20 >] 7 leagues from Henneth Annûn to the road that runs from M[inas Morghul] to Osgiliath, [and from the nearest point up that road west [*sic*] of our landing place it is 5 or 6 leagues to the Vale of Dread >] and if they went straight southward then they would find the road some 5 or 6 leagues west of the Vale of Dread. But the darkness came soon; I deem [?under cover] of that very night, long ere they could reach the vale. Indeed I see your fear; but it is clear to me that the Enemy had long planned this war, and the hour was already determined and nought to do with the errand of the travellers.'

Gandalf paced up and down. 'Yesterday morn?' he said. 'Then you have been swift. How far hence is the place where you parted?'

'Maybe 75 leagues[6] as bird flies,' said Faramir. 'But I *am* swift. Yestereve I lay at Men Falros, the isle in the river northward which we hold in defence, and on the hither bank we keep horses. As the darkness drew on I saw that haste was needed. So I rode hither with the four men that could be horsed, and sent the rest of my company to strengthen the guard at the fords of Osgiliath. Have I done ill?'

'Ill!' said Denethor, and suddenly his eyes blazed. 'Why do

you ask? Do you need my judgement? Your bearing is lowly as is fitting, but it is long since you turned from your own way at my counsel. You have spoken skilfully and discreetly, but have I not seen your eyes fixed on Mithrandir, seeking to learn how much you should say? He has your heart in keeping.

'My son, your father is old, but he is not yet a dotard. I can see and hear as was my wont, and not much of what you have left unsaid or half said is now hidden. I know the answer to the riddling words and to other riddles besides. Now I understand the ...[7] of Boromir and his [?death].'

'If you [are] angry, father,' said Faramir, 'tell me what other courses you would have had me take.'

'You have done as I should have expected, for I know you well,' said Denethor. 'Ever your desire is to be lordly and generous as a king of old – gracious and gentle. And that well befits men of high lineage who sit in power amid peace. But in these black hours gentleness may be bought with death.'

'So be it,' said Faramir.

'So be it,' said Denethor; 'but not by your death only. The death also of your father and of all your people whom it will be your part to rule ere long – now Boromir is no more.' He paused, clutching his [?wand].

'Do you wish then,' said Faramir, 'that our places had been exchanged?'

'Yes, I wish that indeed,' said Denethor. 'Or no,' and then he shook his head; and rising suddenly laid his hand on his son's shoulder. 'Do not judge me harshly, my son,' he said, 'or think that I am harsh. Love is not blind. I knew your brother also. I would wish only that he had been in your place, if I were sure of one thing.'

'And what is that, my father?'

'That he was as strong in heart as you, and as trustworthy. That taking this thing he had brought it to me, and not fallen under thraldom. For Faramir, and you Mithrandir, amid all your far flung policies, there is another way that is not yours nor Boromir's. It is one thing to take and wield this power for one's own victory – you, Mithrandir, may think what you will of me –'

'What I think of you is at least one part of my mind that you do not seem to have read,' said Gandalf.

'As you will, but I have in this as much wisdom as yourself,' said Denethor. 'I would not use it. On the other hand, at this hour to send the bearer, and such a one, helpless into Mordor itself, or as my son to let him go with that burden to Kirith Ungol, that also seems to me folly patent.'

'What then is wisdom?' said Gandalf.

'To do neither,' answered Denethor. 'Certainly not to risk the maker recovering it to our final ruin. To keep it – hidden, deep hidden, yet not used – hidden beyond his grasp until at last [?either] he wins all by war and we are dead.[8] Would that I had that thing now: in the deep chambers of this citadel, and then we should not shake with dread ...'

The remainder of the conversation between Gandalf and Denethor reaches effectively the form in RK, p. 87 (but Gandalf says: 'had you taken this thing by force or daunting you would not have escaped'; 'if you had received this thing, it would have overthrown you', RK). The episode ends thus in the draft:

He turned to Faramir. 'What news from the garrison at Osgiliath?'

'I have sent the company from Ithilien to strengthen it, as I said,' replied Faramir. 'It will be there, I think, that the first assault will fall.'

He rose, and suddenly he swayed and leant upon his father. 'You are weary, my son,' said Denethor. 'You have not spoken of your ride from Men Falros – and the dreadful wings.'

'I do not wish to,' said Faramir.

'Then do not so,' said Denethor. 'Go now to sleep, and think that such things shall not come here within shot of our bows – not this night at least. Tomorrow will need new counsels.'

Gandalf's talk with Pippin after they returned to their lodging as it stands in RK (pp. 88–9) was closely approached here,[9] and I cite only one brief passage:

'... But in truth I believe that the news that Faramir brings has more hope in it than seemed at first. For if Frodo was still so far away yestermorn, then that which I hoped might be has probably happened. The Enemy has made war in haste *without* the Ring and thinking that it is with us. And even if all goes as he plans, and it will not if I can prevent it, he will have his eyes in many places, far from his own land. There is a gleam of hope there. So I told Aragorn when we rode to Rohan.[10] But still, I did not expect it so soon. Something else has happened to stir him.'

The draft text now races towards its more and more illegible conclusion. Some passages were added in ink, and these I include, marking them as such, since they clearly belong to much the same time. The last section opens with 'The next day came like a brown dusk' (RK p. 89), and continues very much as in the final text as far as the departure of Faramir to Osgiliath and the mutterings against Denethor.

'The Lord drives his son too hard, and now he must do duty for the one that is dead as well.' [*Added in ink:* But in truth Faramir went at his own will, and he it was that most swayed the council of the captains.][11] The council of the Lord had decided that with the threat in the South their force was too weak to make any stroke of war on their own part. They must man the defences and wait. Yet ever Faramir had urged that their outer defences must not be abandoned, and the River was the one that the Enemy should buy most dearly. It could not be crossed by a great host north of Men Falros because of the marshes, and away south in Lebennin it became too broad without many boats. So now he was gone again, taking such few men as Denethor would spare to strengthen the force that held the western ruins of Osgiliath. [*Added in ink:* 'But hold not too long so far afield,' said Denethor as he went out. 'Though you slay ten times your number at the crossing, the Enemy has more to spare. And your retreat will be hazardous. And do not forget that ... danger in the North. Not one army only will be sent at this time from the Black Gate.']

Hardly had he gone when a rider came in reporting that a host was approaching and ... had reached East Osgiliath. [*Added in ink:* and a Black Captain of great terror [?came] there out of Minas Morghul.] With that ominous news ended Pippin's third day in the Tower.

The next day the darkness, though perhaps little more, weighed yet heavier on men's minds, and it seemed that slowly fear grew. Late in the day evil news was brought by riders. The passage of the Anduin had been won. Faramir was retreating to the Pelennor Wall and the fort[s] that guarded the entrance of the causeway into the townlands; but he could not hold them long. He was much outnumbered and had 4 leagues or more of open land to cross with few defences when he must give back again.

'Mithrandir's help fails now,' said some. For Gandalf had ridden down to Osgiliath at Faramir's side.[12] But others said

'Nay, he has never given any, not of such a kind. He is not a captain of war.'

But late that night he returned riding with the last wains filled with wounded men. 'They have paid dearly for the causeway,' he said, 'although they had prepared all things well. They have been building barges and boats secretly in East Osgiliath to the ruin of Ithilien's trees. But the river is now half choked with them. But he has come whom I feared.' 'Not the Dark Lord,' cried Pippin. 'No, he will not come except in triumph,' said Gandalf. 'He wields others as his weapons. I speak of one whom you have met. The Wizard King, captain of those you called the Black Riders. Most fell of all the servants of the Dark Tower. But he has not [*struck out (?):* yet] taken to winged steeds. [In him I am not overmatched, and yet still I am matched, for he was a member of our order before evil took him.][13] Now his fury and malice are grown to the full, and men fly before him. [*Written in ink at the head of the page:* But the Wizard King has not shown himself. He wields far behind a great fear that will drive his soldiers whither he will, even to cast themselves into the River that others [?can] walk on their bodies. But he will come forth yet.]'

So the storm broke at last.

The next day the causeway fort[s] fell and Faramir began his desperate retreat across the Pelennor, [*in ink, replacing a passage in pencil:* the enemy pouring through the wall behind and sweeping away the ... rearguard. Fires glowing red in the mist could be seen far off, and once and again [a] red flash and then slowly a dull rumble would come rolling across the darkened fields. The ... were destroying the wall and blasting great breaches in it so that they could enter at any point. Soon the tide of war [?would cross]. The companies of Gondor could be seen [?hastening] back. And with that out of the][14] And now the Nazgûl [?stooped again] and the retreat became a rout, and [?many] men threw away spear and shield and sword and ran shrieking, or flung themselves to the ground and were trampled.

Then there was a sortie from the city led by the Prince of Dol Amroth kinsman of Faramir and his folk, and Gandalf at his side. In the [?notch] of time they came up, and [?two] miles from the city drove back the enemy, making great slaughter, for the enemy cavalry were [?few] and [?little] ...; the Nazgûl [?would (not) stand] the onslaught of Gandalf, for their Captain was not with them.

So now the City prepared for a last siege. The Pelennor wall was abandoned, and all that could be [?withdrawn] behind the gates. Orcs and [?wild horsemen] roam[ed] the townlands lighting the black night with fires, and the more bold rode within earshot of watchers on the walls, crying with hideous voices, and many bore upon their spears the heads of men they had slain and hewn.

Here the draft C ends. It was followed by a fair copy manuscript ('D'), in which the text of RK was very largely achieved: but it took a great deal of further work to reach it. This manuscript can be seen as divided roughly between the part that was based on C, and the part that extended beyond the point where C ended. Like the draft, it is numbered 'XLVI', but has no title; and the chapter again begins with the words 'It had been dark all day.'

In the first part it is notable that while my father went to great pains with the detail of expression, and clearly intended it to stand, in all those passages in which Denethor showed himself less coldly obdurate and hostile to Faramir than he became in *The Return of the King* the original draft was followed closely. His sudden softening in response to Faramir's question 'Do you wish then that our places had been exchanged?' (p. 328) remains:

'Yes, I wish that indeed,' said Denethor. 'Or no.' And then he shook his head, and rising swiftly he laid his hand upon his son's bowed head. 'Do not judge me harshly, my son,' he said quietly, 'or believe me more harsh than I am. I knew your brother well also. Love is not blind. I could wish that Boromir had been at Henneth Annûn when this thing came there, only if I were sure of one thing.'

'Sure of what, my father?'

'That he was as strong in heart and selfless as you, my son. That taking this thing he would have brought it here and surrendered it, and not fallen swiftly under its thraldom. For, Faramir – and you too, Mithrandir, amid all your wide webs and policies – there is a third way, that is neither the folly of wizards nor the lust of warriors. ...'

It is certain that there was no element of embittered banter in these words, 'That he was as strong in heart and selfless as you, my son.' Denethor was coldly watchful as always of those he spoke to, but he expressed the true bearing of his mind. His gentler good-night to Faramir, with a suggestion of a comforting word (p. 329), remains; and in this brief passage it can be seen how Denethor's harshness towards Faramir was enforced in later revision by the slightest of touches: as in the movement from 'You are weary, my son' to 'You are weary, I see.'

Again, in the debate on the following day (p. 330), it is still Faramir who argues that an attempt must be made to hold the outer defences at the line of the Anduin (but so far does the new writing go towards the actual words of RK (pp. 89–90) that when my father came to revise the passage he had little more to do than to give the speeches to different speakers). In this version the speech made by Prince Imrahil (RK p. 90), warning of another host that may come from Mordor, is given to Gandalf, and it is Faramir who is adamant and concludes the debate with words that afterwards became his father's:

> 'Much must be risked in war,' said Faramir. 'But I will not yield the River and the fields of Pelennor unfought, unless my father commands me beyond denial.'
>
> 'I do not,' said Denethor. 'Farewell, and may your judgement prove just: at least so much that I may see you again. Farewell!'

When he rejected this account of what happened at that meeting of the council my father wrote in the margin of the page: 'This must be altered to make Faramir only go to please his father against his own counsel and to "take Boromir's place".' And on a slip of paper he wrote a brief statement of how, and why, the existing portrayal of Denethor's relations with Faramir must be changed:

> The early conversation of Faramir and his father and motives must be altered. Denethor must be *harsh*. He must say he did wish Boromir had been at Henneth Annûn – for he *would* have been loyal to his father and brought him the Ring. (Gandalf may correct this.) Faramir grieved but patient. Then Denethor must be all for holding Osgiliath 'like Boromir did', while Faramir (and Gandalf?) are against it, using the arguments previously given to Denethor. At length in submission, but proudly, to please his father and show him that not only Boromir was brave [he] accepts the command at Osgiliath. Men in the City do not like it.
>
> This will not only be truer to previous situation, but will explain Denethor's breaking up when Faramir is brought back *dying*, as it seems.

The first part of this passage was struck through, as far as 'Faramir grieved but patient', and the second part allowed to stand; but this was then rejected also. Finally the whole was marked with a tick, when my father at length decided that this was how it should in fact be.

Also on this slip is a note written independently: 'Something should be said between Gandalf and Pippin about the scene between Faramir and his father', but this suggestion was not taken up.

Not only in these passages, but in almost all the points where the draft C differed from RK, the manuscript D, as my father first wrote it, retained his first conceptions.[15] When (in relation to further progress in the narrative) the very substantial alterations to this part of the chapter in D were carried out I cannot say for certain. After this, the text as it stands in RK was present in all essentials; but at this stage my father was still uncertain whether or not to adopt the 'longer opening', as he called it, in which the chapter opens with Gandalf's waking Pippin in their lodging (see pp. 324–5).[16]

Drafting for the latter part of the chapter is not as coherent and continuous as it is for the former. My impression is that having written the fair copy manuscript D on the basis of the draft C so far as it went, or so far as it usefully went, my father then simply went on with it, writing sections of draft *pari passu* with progress on the fair copy, which was itself in places the primary composition. There is no way of knowing over how long a period all this work was spread.

The last part of C, from 'The next day the darkness, though perhaps little more, weighed yet heavier on men's minds' (p. 330), where the draft text became very cursory and rushed, was developed to the form in RK (pp. 91 ff.): Gandalf does not now ride down to Osgiliath with Faramir, and the account of the barge-building in East Osgiliath and the fear of the Black Captain is given by the messenger; it is only at this news that Gandalf leaves the City, returning at mid-morning on the next day with the wains bearing the wounded, and there follows his conversation with Denethor (RK pp. 91–3), here set 'in a high chamber near the summit of the White Tower'. In this all is almost as in the final form; but Denethor, revealing the mail in which he was clad beneath his long cloak, says nothing of it (he does not reveal that he wears it night and day), and Gandalf still as in the draft (p. 331) reminds Pippin who the Black Captain is: 'You have met him, Peregrin son of Paladin, though then he was far from home, veiled to your eyes, when he stalked the Ringbearer. Now he is come forth in power again, growing as his Master grows.' Gandalf now names him 'King of Angmar long ago', and this is the first appearance of the conception of the Kingdom of Angmar in the texts of *The Lord of the Rings*. To Denethor's 'Or can it be that you have withdrawn because you are overmastered?' (causing Pippin to fear that 'Gandalf would be stung to sudden wrath') the wizard answers 'lightly' ('softly' in RK); and after 'But our trial of strength is not come yet' he recalls a prophecy concerning the fate of the Lord of the Nazgûl different from that in the brief outline given on p. 326:

'... And if words spoken of old come true, he is not doomed to fall before warrior or wise [> men of war or wisdom]; but in the hour of his victory to be overthrown by one who has never slain a man [> by one who has slain no living thing]. ...'

In RK this becomes: 'not by the hand of man shall he fall, and hidden from the Wise is the doom that awaits him' (cf. RK p. 116). At the end of this conversation Denethor says: 'Some have unjustly accused you, Mithrandir, of delighting to bear ill news'; before 'unjustly' my father pencilled 'no doubt', but afterwards removed both qualifications.

For all the story of the sortie for the rescue of Faramir and the out-companies and the mounting of the siege there is preliminary drafting, in which almost all features of the final narrative were already present.[17] In the fair copy there is a remarkable addition pencilled in to the description of the Nazgûl circling over the City on the first day of the siege:

The Nazgûl came once more, slaves of the Nine Rings, and to each, since now they were utterly subject to his will, their Lord had given again that ring of power that he had used of old.

This survived into the first typescript, where it was afterwards replaced by the words in RK (p. 97): 'The Nazgûl came again, and as their Dark Lord now grew and put forth his strength, so their voices, which uttered only his will and his malice, were filled with evil and horror.'

In initial drafting for the last part of the chapter the central story of Denethor's madness can be seen emerging as my father wrote (torrentially, with scarcely-formed letters).

And Faramir lay in his chamber wandering in fever, dying as it was said, while his father sat beside him and heeded little the ending of the defence. It seemed to Pippin, who often watched by his side or at the door, that at last something had snapped in the proud will of Denethor: whether grief at the harsh words he spoke before Faramir rode out,[18] or the bitter thought that whatever now should happen in the war, his line too was ending, and even the House of the Stewards would fail, and a lesser house rule the last remnant of the kings of men.

So it was that without word spoken or any commission from the Lord, Gandalf took command of the defence. Wherever he came men's hearts were lifted and the winged shadows passed from memory. Tirelessly he went from Citadel to the Gate, from north to south about the wall, and yet – when he had gone the shadow seemed to close on men again, and vain it seemed to resist, to wait there for cold sword or cruel hunger [*sic*].

And so they passed out of a dim day of fear to the shadow of desperate night. Fire now raged in the lowest circle of the City. The garrison on the walls was well nigh cut off, those that indeed had not already fled. And then in the middle night the assault was loosed.

[Messengers came to the high tower and Denethor looked at them. 'The [?outer] circle is burning, lord,' they said, 'men are flying from the walls.' 'Why?' said Denethor. 'It is well to burn soon than late. I will go now to my own pyre. Farewell, Peregrin son of Paladin, your service has been short. I release you from it, unless you would still use your sword in defence of what is lost. Go now if you will to him that brought you here, to your death.'

He rose and bidding men take up Faramir's bed and follow him left the White Tower and paced slowly, pausing only for a moment at the ... tree, passed out of the Citadel, and going laid himself in the house of tombs under the shadow of Mindolluin with Pippin by his side.]

This passage that I have enclosed in square brackets was an addition to the manuscript, but it can be seen clearly from the manuscript that my father inserted it while he was actually writing the description of the black horseman and the destruction of the Gate. A later note scribbled against the passage reads: 'Pippin follows the cortège until it enters the tombs and then flies down in search of Gandalf. Meets Berithil and together they go through the city. Pippin arrives in time to see Gandalf and the Sorcerer King.'

The vanguard passed over narrow ways between the trenches and suffered loss where they bunched, but too few archers left on the walls. [?Front of war] not in the north or south, but a great weight came to the gate. The ground was choked with bodies but still they came on.

There Gandalf stood. And then over the hill in the flare of the fire a great Black Horseman came. For a moment he ... halted menacing, and lifted up a great ... sword red to the hilt. Fear fell on all .... Then great rams went on before, but the steel only shook and boomed. The Black Captain ..... lifted again his hand crying in a dreadful voice. In some forgotten tongue he spoke crying aloud words of power and terror. Thrice the rams boomed. Thrice he cried, and then suddenly the gate as if stricken by some blast burst [?asunder], and a great flash as of lightning, burst and fell, and in rode the Lord of the Nazgûl. But there waiting still before the gate sat Gandalf, and Shadowfax alone among the free horses of the earth did not [?quail] but stood rooted as an image of grey marble.

'You cannot pass,' said Gandalf. 'Go back to the black abyss prepared for you, and fall into nothingness that shall come upon your Master.'

The Black Rider [?lay *for* laid] back his hood and ..... crown that sat upon no visible head save only for the light of his pale eyes.[19] A deadly laughter [?rang] out.

'Old fool,' he said. 'Old fool. Do you not know death when you see it? Die now and curse in vain. This is my hour of victory.' And with that he lifted his great sword. [*Added:* And then suddenly his hand wavered and fell and it seemed that he shrank.] And [> For] in that very moment away behind in some courtyard of the city a cock crowed. Shrill and clear he crowed, recking nothing of wizardry or war, welcoming only the morning that far above the shadows of death was now coming once again.

And as if in answer there came from far away another note. Horns, horns, horns, great horns of the north wildly blowing. The riders of Rohan had come at last.

From short passages of further drafting, either separate or pencilled on the fair copy manuscript itself and then overwritten, the final form of the story was largely reached, and there is nothing to notice in this development. But as the fair copy was left to stand there remained a few differences from RK. The account of Pippin's watching beside Denethor and Faramir remained essentially as it was in the initial draft (see p. 335), where Denethor himself does not speak, and the cause of his devastation is expressed as a surmise of Pippin's: 'Grief maybe had wrought it: grief at the harsh words he spoke when Faramir returned [> remorse for the harsh words he spoke that sent Faramir out into needless peril],[20] and the bitter thought that, whatever might now betide in war, woe or victory beyond all hope, his line too was ending ...'

The description of the journey of the bearers of Faramir, with Denethor and Pippin, after they had passed through the gate of the Citadel, begins thus (cf. RK pp. 99–100):

Turning westward they came at last to a dark door, used only by the Lord of the City, for it opened on a winding way that descended by many curves down to the narrow land under the shadow of Mindolluin's precipice where stood the tombs of the Kings and their Stewards.

But from this point the text reaches effectively the form in RK in the description of the descent to Rath Dínen, the Silent Street.[21] The passage just cited reappears in the first typescript of the chapter, with the addition that the door was 'in the rearward wall of the sixth circle'; but the final text was entered on the typescript in a rider, and here the name of the door appears: '*Fenn Fornen*, for it was kept ever shut save at times of funeral'.[22]

Pippin's encounter with Berithil as he fled from the horrifying scene in Rath Dínen begins differently from its form in RK (p. 101):

'Whither do you run, Master Peregrin?' he said.

'To find Mithrandir,' answered Pippin.

'Then have you left the service of the Lord so soon? We hold that it is the duty of those who wear the black and silver to remain in the Citadel of Gondor whatever else may chance, until death release them.'[23]

'Or the Lord,' said Pippin.

'Then he sends you on some errand that I should not hinder. But tell me, if you may, what goes forward? ...'

The text then continues as in RK; but Pippin was still permitted at this fateful moment a more Shire-like turn of phrase: 'Something is wrong with him', he says of Denethor (where in RK he says 'He is fey and dangerous'), and he tells Berithil: 'Don't bother about "orders" and all that!'

Lastly, it is worth remarking that the importance of the Prince of Dol Amroth was enlarged as the chapter evolved. In the draft C Pippin did not name him among the 'great persons' present at the council held before Faramir's return from Henneth Annûn (p. 326), and this remains the case in the fair copy D. The Prince's intervention in the deliberations before Faramir went to Osgiliath is absent in the first version of D (p. 333): it enters with the revision (where he is called 'Dol Amroth'). His bringing of Faramir to the White Tower was never added to D (note 17). And in drafting for the latter part of D he is not mentioned as accompanying Gandalf in his tireless permabulation of the City (p. 335) – the passage in which he is introduced here (RK p. 98), with the reference to there being 'Elvish blood in the veins of that folk, for the people of Nimrodel dwelt once in that land long ago', was in fact written into the D manuscript as an afterthought soon after my father had passed this point. At this stage the name *Imrahil* had still not emerged (see pp. 287, 289).

NOTES

1 The account of Pippin's livery is in every point as described in RK, save only that the silver star on the circlet of his helm is not mentioned.

2 *Berethil* is clearly written so, *Berithil* in the first typescript of 'Minas Tirith', p. 288; after further occurrences of *Berethil*, however, *Berithil* reappears.
3 *Ramas Coren*: earlier name of the Wall about the Pelennor (p. 288).
4 I have inverted the order of the last two paragraphs of this outline.
5 On this and subsequent references to days and times see the Note on Chronology below.
6 75 leagues from Henneth Annûn to Minas Tirith: 25 leagues in RK. The distance on my father's large map of Rohan, Gondor and Mordor which I redrew in *The Return of the King* is about 23 leagues. The figure 75 in the present text is however perfectly clear, although the following text D, directly based here on the present draft, has 25. On the First Map the distance can be very roughly computed to something in the region of 75 miles, and I suppose that my father, working very fast, simply wrote 'leagues' for 'miles'.
7 The illegible word seems to begin with *d* and might be *duty*, but the writing is so unclear that it might be *dealings*, or some other word. In the following text, where Denethor still says that he knows 'the answer to the riddling words', the sentence is replaced by 'Poor Boromir!' > 'Alas for Boromir!'
8 The word I have given as '[?either]' is in fact hard to interpret in any other way. Possibly the sentence was left unfinished. The following text has the reading of RK (p. 87), 'save by a victory so final that what then befell would not trouble us, the dead [> being dead].'
9 Pippin says of Frodo: 'Just think, he was alive at least up to this time yesterday, and not so far away across the River!' I do not know why Pippin should say 'at least up to this time yesterday', since Faramir had said that he had parted with Frodo and Sam 'yestermorn'. The following text has: 'he was alive and talking to Faramir only yesterday'. — In Gandalf's reckoning of the time he says: 'Let me see, he would discover some four days ago that we had thrown down Saruman – and had the Stone,' where RK has 'five'. See the Note on Chronology below.
10 The following text has: 'So I told Aragorn, on the day when we met again in Fangorn and rode down to Rohan.' The reference is to 'The White Rider', TT p. 100: 'For imagining war he has let loose war, believing that he has no time to waste ... So the forces that he has long been preparing he is now setting in motion, sooner than he intended.'
11 Cf. the original outline on p. 326: 'Pippin ... hears Faramir accept orders to go to Osgiliath.'
12 In RK (p. 91) Gandalf does not leave the City until news comes of Faramir's retreat to the wall of the Pelennor.

13 The square brackets are in the original.

14 Here the passage in ink breaks off; the sentence would have continued with the sortie from the Gate.

15 I note here a few details. All the references to date remain as in the draft. The distance from Henneth Annûn to Minas Tirith becomes 25 leagues (see note 6). Peregrin's friend is Berithil (see note 2; Beregond only entered at a late stage). The island in Anduin receives momentarily the name *Cairros*, changed immediately to *Andros* (and later to *Cair Andros*).

16 This appears from a note written on a slip in which the existing opening of the chapter (see p. 325) was rewritten. In this revision was introduced the fact of Berithil's having just returned from an errand over the Pelennor 'to *Bered Ondrath*, the guard-towers upon the entrance of the causeway'. This name was subsequently lost.

17 I notice here two features in which the narrative differed from that in RK, and a few other details. The account of Prince Imrahil's bringing Faramir to Denethor in the White Tower, and the light seen flickering in the high chamber (RK pp. 94–5), is absent not only from the initial draft but also from the fair copy D; and the last men to come into the City before the Gate was shut (RK p. 95), reporting the 'endless companies of men of a new sort' who held the northward road or had gone on into Anórien, are not said to be led by Ingold in the draft.

In both draft and fair copy the 'wild Southron men' of RK (p. 95) are 'wild eastlanders'. The wall of the Pelennor is still called Ramas Coren in both texts where RK has 'the Rammas' (p. 95), with '(? Corramas)' added at the time of writing. In the sentence (RK p. 94) 'And in his arms before him on his horse he [the Prince] bore the body of his kinsman, Faramir son of Denethor' a word is written above 'kinsman' in the draft text which looks like 'cousin'; this seems to have been struck through. The genealogy of the house of Dol Amroth is found in LR, Appendix A (I, iv): Denethor married (late) Finduilas daughter of Adrahil of Dol Amroth. Elsewhere it is recorded (see *Unfinished Tales* p. 248) that Adrahil was the father of Imrahil, so that Imrahil (brother of Finduilas) was Faramir's uncle.

18 This is curious, because in the D manuscript as written (when it was Faramir who imposed his own will on the council in his demand to lead a force to Osgiliath) Denethor (as reported) spoke no harsh words to Faramir, and indeed bade him farewell with the words 'may your judgement prove just: at least so much that I may see you again' (p. 333). This may suggest that the later version of this episode was already in being, in which Denethor says: 'But I will not yield the River and the fields of the Pelennor unfought – not if there is a captain that will do my will, and quail

not' (cf. RK p. 90).

19 The handwriting here is such that many words could not be interpreted at all in isolation, without context or other clues, but 'save only for the light of his pale eyes' seems tolerably clear. Cf. p. 365.

20 See note 18.

21 The name *Rath Dínen* appears on the plan of the city reproduced on p. 290 from the first typescript of the chapter 'Minas Tirith', where however the conception of it was decisively different.

22 Other names are written beside this rider: *Fenn Forn the Closed Door*, *Fenn uiforn the Ever Closed*, also *Uidavnen* and the word *davnan*.

23 These words, slightly changed, were afterwards spoken by Gandalf to Pippin at the beginning of the chapter 'The Pyre of Denethor' (RK p. 126).

Note on the Chronology

The new 'calendar' (i.e. with dates in March instead of February, see p. 325) can be equated with the old from the date of the first day of the Darkness, Pippin's second day in Minas Tirith, which had been February 7 and is now March 9. I presume that my father calculated this on the basis that all months now had thirty days. Thus proceeding from 26 December = 26 January, the day of Frodo's flight (see VII.368), there are the following equations: December 31 = February 1; January 1 = February 2; January 29 = February 30; January 30 = March 1; January 31 = March 2; February 1 = March 3.

The chronology, however, is still not that of LR (see *The Tale of Years*). At this stage Faramir says (on 9 March) that he had parted with Frodo and Sam at Henneth Annûn on the morning of the previous day ('in the morning two days ago', RK p. 85), and he says that the Darkness began to come over that night ('yestereve', RK). The relation between the two chronologies can be set out thus:

	The present chronology	*The chronology in LR*
March 7	Frodo taken by Faramir to Henneth Annûn.	Frodo taken by Faramir to Henneth Annûn.
March 8	Frodo leaves Henneth Annûn. Gandalf reaches Minas Tirith.	Frodo leaves Henneth Annûn.

March 9	The Dawnless Day. Faramir rescued on the Pelennor. Frodo reaches the Cross-roads.	Gandalf reaches Minas Tirith.
March 10	Faramir goes to Osgiliath.	The Dawnless Day. Faramir rescued on the Pelennor. Frodo reaches the Cross-roads.
March 11	Faramir retreats to the Causeway Forts.	Faramir goes to Osgiliath.

Thus the horns of the Rohirrim are heard at cockcrow on March 14 in the chronology of the present texts, but on March 15 in LR. At this stage Frodo still takes two days, not three, from Henneth Annûn to the Cross-roads (see p. 182), and Gandalf takes three nights, not four, from Dol Baran to Minas Tirith (see p. 264 note 3).

Gandalf, speaking to Pippin on the night of 9 March, reckons that it was now four days since Sauron discovered 'that we had thrown down Saruman – and had the Stone' (note 9), whereas in RK (p. 88), on 10 March, he reckons the time as five days. He is referring to 5 March (= February 3), and the difference is again due to the longer time taken on his ride.

VII
THE RIDE OF THE ROHIRRIM

A single manuscript page (**'A'**) gives an outline for the narrative of this chapter. It was written in ink over a pencilled text – which at this stage had again and unhappily become my father's frequent method of composition. The figures introducing each paragraph are of course the dates in the month of March.

(9) Théoden leaves Dunharrow on 9th. He rides 25 miles to Edoras. After a halt there and reviewing the garrison he sets out East. At first they go slow to conserve strength. Merry is given leave to go to war, and is assigned to ride with one of the king's guard: the one who seems young and light and so less burden to his steed. He is silent and never speaks. They halt not far from where the Snowbourn runs into Entwash 25 miles from Edoras – they bivouac in dense willow-thickets.
(10) They ride steadily and halt now nearly 100 miles from Edoras.
(11) They ride again. When 125 miles out about midday fugitives and late joining riders bring news of attacks in North, and of forces crossing above Sarn Gebir[1] into the Wold of Rohan. Théoden decides that he has left sufficient garrison (or all possible) in his strong places, and must ride on: soon the marshes of Entwash mouth will cover his flank. They cross into Anórien (of Gondor) and camp under Halifirien (160 [miles]). Mysterious drums are heard in the woods and hills. Théoden resolves to ride warily, and sends out scouts.
(12) They halt some 230 miles on at dusk (64 miles or a day's ride from Pelennor). They camp in the skirts of the Forest of Eilenach out of which rises Eilenach Beacon. Scouts return with the errand-riders of Minas Tirith (who had ridden ahead but found entrance closed). There is a great camp of enemy under [Amon Dîn >] Min Rimmon about [25 >] 50 miles west of the Pelennor or about [40 >] 14 miles further on:[2] Orcs are roving along the road. Dark men of Eilenach come in. They decide to push on by night. Suddenly they see fires ahead and hear cries. A great *hoom hom* is heard. Ents! Treebeard cries Merry. The enemy camp is in confusion. Dark men of Eilenach

have attacked it, and suddenly coming out of North after a victory over Orcs in Wold ([250 >] 225 miles) Treebeard and a company of Ents. The Rohirrim come round to rear [and] sweep the remnants away N.W. into marshes. They halt under Min Rimmon and take counsel of war.

(13) Morning of 13th. Scouts report that siege is now [?strait] and great fires and engines are all about walls. They ride about 20 miles and [?hide] in the woods and hills of Amon Dîn ready to move at night and attack with dawn.

(14) At dawn they charge. Rammas has been destroyed at this point.

At the foot of the page, in pencil, is a list of distances: *Eilenach* 215 (written beneath: 219); *Min Rimmon* 245 (written beneath: 246); *Amon Dîn* 270; *Rammas* 294; *Minas Tirith* 306.[3] Beside this list is a note: 'Camp just west of Min Rimmon (243 miles) on night of 12th.'

The names of the beacons in their final forms and final order (which I count eastwards from Edoras) had appeared long before in the abandoned opening C of 'Minas Tirith' (p. 233; repeated in the first text of the chapter), but now the order has been changed:

Early texts of 'Minas Tirith' and LR	*The present text*
1 Halifirien	1 Halifirien
2 Calenhad	2 Calenhad
3 Min Rimmon	3 Erelas
4 Erelas	4 Nardol
5 Nardol	5 Eilenach
6 Eilenach	6 Min Rimmon
7 Amon Dîn	7 Amon Dîn

I can offer no explanation for this other than the obvious but not entirely convincing one that my father had misremembered the order as it stood in the 'Minas Tirith' text, and that afterwards, looking back through the papers, he returned to it.

So in the outline A the Rohirrim camped on the night of March 12 'in the skirts of the Forest of Eilenach out of which rises Eilenach Beacon', and here 'the dark men of Eilenach' enter the story, forerunners of the Woses or Wild Men of the Woods, though nothing is said of them other than that they attacked the enemy camp (the drumming in the hills is heard, however, from the camp under Halifirien on the previous night, March 11). Thus the Forest of Eilenach is the forerunner of the Druadan Forest, but Eilenach Beacon is the fifth, and beyond it are still Min Rimmon and Amon Dîn.

Treebeard and the Ents reappear, coming south 'after a victory over Orcs in the Wold', and clearly they play a part in the attack on the camp

(I take it that the meaning of the text at this point is 'Dark men of Eilenach have attacked it, and so also have Treebeard and a company of Ents suddenly coming out of the North'). In the early outlines for Book V there are several references to the southward march of the Ents after the destruction of the Orcs on the Wold (see p. 255 and note 29), but these all specifically refer to their arrival (together with Elves from Lórien) *after* the siege of Minas Tirith had been broken: there has been no suggestion that they appeared earlier, in Anórien.

Merry is here 'given leave to go to war, and is assigned to ride with one of the king's guard: the one who seems young and light and so less burden to his steed.' This is presumably the story that my father had in mind at the end of 'Many Roads Lead Eastward' (see p. 318), where one among the guard, noticeably slighter in build (and certainly Éowyn), looked at Merry as the ride began from Dunharrow: this Rider would be *assigned* to carry the hobbit.

Two pages of pencilled text are hard to place since they are very largely illegible on account of subsequent overwriting in ink; but they are very noteworthy, since from what little can be read it is seen that my father was here developing the story of the coming of the Ents into Anórien from the outline just given. The narrative envisaged clearly ran into difficulties, and was decisively abandoned, without any repercussions in the development of the chapter; for this reason it seems most probable that they should be placed here. The ink overwriting that so obscured them bears no relation to the pencilled text beneath.[4]

On one of these pages (which I take to be the first in order since the arrival of Treebeard appears, whereas on the other he is already present) Treebeard's call of *hoom hom* (or something similar) is heard; 'Merry sprang up. "Treebeard!" he cried. Treebeard comes with good news. The Ents and the Huorns had ..... the invaders on the Wold and driven them into the River.' Fragments of the following sentence refer to rumour of the ride of the Rohirrim having reached the Ents, and to their great march southwards to aid the king. 'Friendship and reward the king offered. But he asked only leave when war was over to return to Fangorn and there be troubled by ..... For reward he would take .....'

No more than broken fragments can be discerned in the remainder of this page, but these suggest uncertainty of direction. 'They plan to divide into three. The Ents would come on the camp from the north first while the main host ...'; 'and so come down to the plain [?somewhat] behind the camp between it and the leaguer of the city'; 'Or remove the host of orc-men'; and later: 'In that case the wild men slay orcs but also turn against king. But the riders brush them aside and reach Amon Dîn ...'

The other page begins thus: 'But the wild men were nowhere to be seen. At the first sight of the Ents they had cried out shrieks of fear and fled back to vanish into the hills ..... what dark and distant legends out of [?elder] days held their minds enthralled none could say. But Treebeard soon found for himself what he needed .... a [?pool] under the side of Amon Dîn fed by a spring [?above]. There he stood and [?laved] himself while the king and his captains held council under the trees.' After '"Both ... and warriors are needed, lord," said Éomer' follows: 'Some few at least must have escaped eastward to give warning of our approach.' Does this refer to the Wild Men?

From the rest of this page scarcely anything useful can be gleaned, but the sentence 'The wild men lead them again along hill-paths' is clear; which is puzzling, since there seems not to be enough text intervening to explain the reversal of the story just given.

Nothing more is found anywhere touching on the appearance of the Ents in Anórien, and the reason for their disappearance can only be guessed at. It seems to me possible that something on the following lines may lie behind it. The vast armies at the disposal of Mordor made it a certainty that a host would be dispatched beyond Minas Tirith into Anórien in order to block any attempt from Rohan to come to the aid of the city: this could be said to be a datum of the story. But an assault on the orc-camp would necessarily constitute a major episode, and my father wanted such an episode at this juncture no more than did the Rohirrim. The Wild Men, who (as 'the dark men of Eilenach') had entered in outline A as attackers of the orc-camp, found their rôle in leading the Rohirrim by forgotten roads through the hills known only to themselves, so that the orc-camp was entirely circumvented. The Ents therefore had no clear function left to them. This is of course pure speculation; there are no notes found pertaining to the question. But at any rate the explanation cannot be that my father had come to feel (independently of the immediate story as it was emerging here) that Treebeard should not appear again in person until the reunited Company met him once more on the homeward journey: see p. 361.

My father had great difficulty with the question of how Merry went to Minas Tirith, and indeed with finding a satisfactory opening to the chapter. The previous chapter in the narrative sequence ('Many Roads Lead Eastwards') had ended with the host of the Rohirrim passing down Harrowdale; now something must be told of the halt at Edoras – but at the same time he would prefer to pass over the uneventful first days of the ride and begin the chapter at a later point.

His first solution, in a very brief and very rough text ('**B**'), was to open with the Riders halted on the third night (March 11) below the Halifirien, where, as in the outline A, the mysterious drums are heard in the hills, and to introduce the halt at Edoras as a retrospect of Merry's as he reviewed his situation, lying under the trees in the darkness.

It was so dark that Merry could see nothing as he lay rolled in his blankets; but though it was an airless windless night all about was the soft whisper of endless dark trees. He lifted his head. There it was again, a sound like faint drums in the wooded hills and mountain-steps to the south, drums that stopped and seemed to be answered from other places. He wondered if the watchmen heard it. Though he could not see them he knew that all round him were companies upon companies of the Riders. He could smell the horses in the dark, and hear now and again their stamping and shifting on the soft needle-clad ground. They were bivouacked in the pinewoods that clustered about the dark Halifirien: a great hill, flat-topped, standing out from the [?main] range beside the road from Edoras on the borders of Anórien.

He was tired but could not sleep. He had ridden now for three days since the dark morning of the muster at Dunharrow, and at each halt the darkness seemed to deepen, and his heart and spirits to fall lower. There was now no song or speech on the way in all the great host of Rohan. At Edoras they had halted for a while and then at last he obtained the king's permission to go on to battle with him. He now wondered why. It was arranged that he was to ride before one of the king's guard, and it seemed that the young man whom he had noticed had claimed him, since he was lighter of build than the others, so that his steed was less burdened. At any rate as they rode forth at last from Edoras Merry had been helped up to this man's seat, and there he had [?sat] ... while men were riding, but never a word did his companion utter, at mounting or dismounting or on the way.

All the last part of this text (from 'At Edoras they had halted ...') was struck out, and the following substituted: 'and already he wondered why he had been so determined to come against [?even] the king's command. Not a word more since the first day had Grímhelm spoken [?whether] at mounting or dismounting or on the road.'

My father had come to the conclusion that Merry had *not* been given permission by Théoden to come with the host of Rohan to Minas Tirith; and he had decided also – perhaps for this reason – that the halt at Edoras had best be recounted in direct narrative. He therefore began a new opening for the chapter in another extremely rough manuscript ('C'), entitled 'The Ride of the Rohirrim':

The king came to Edoras in the gathering dark, though it was but noon. There he halted and said farewell to his golden hall and the people of his house. Merry begged not to be parted from him.

'This is no journey for Stybba,' said Théoden. 'We ride to war, and in such battle as we hope to make what would you do, Master Holbytla, sworn swordthain though you are and greater of heart than of ...?'

'As for that, who can tell?' answered Merry. 'And why did you take me as swordthain if I was to be left behind when my lord rides to war?'

'If the battle were here we would see how you bore yourself,' said Théoden, 'but it is 100 leagues or more to Mundbeorg[5] where Denethor is lord. And the first thing for my swordthain to do is to hear the commands of his lord.'

Merry went out unhappy and looked at the lines of horses. The companies were already being ordered for the start. Suddenly a Rider came up to him, and spoke softly in a whisper. 'Where will wants not, a way opens, say we,' he said. 'So have I found myself.' Merry [?looked] ... rider of the king's guard whom he noticed before. 'You wish to go where the lord of the Eorlingas goes?'

'I do,' said Merry. 'Then you shall ride before me,' said the Rider. 'Such good will shall not be wasted. Say nothing more, but come.'

'Thank you indeed, thank you sir – I do not know your name.'

'Do you not?' said the Rider softly. 'Then call me [Cyneferth >] Grímhelm.'[6]

(9) So it was that when the king set forth again before Grímhelm sat Meriadoc the hobbit, and his great grey steed made little of the burden, for Grímhelm was less in build than most of the guard though lithe and well-knit in shape. That [?evening] they camped in the willow thickets where Snowbourn ... into Entwash 12 leagues or more east of Edoras.

The text then tails off into scrawled and partly illegible notes about the next two days' journey: on the third day, with the date March 11 (cf. outline A, p. 343), 'men rode in joining the muster late, and they brought rumours of war in the North and of Orcs crossing into the Wold above Sarn Gebir'; to which news Éomer said: 'Too late to turn back or aside.'

It was now, as the name Grímhelm shows, that the conclusion of the text B, with the story that Merry rode with the king's permission, was rejected (p. 347).[7]

My father evidently decided now (probably, as I have suggested, because he did not wish to treat each day of the ride from Edoras in consecutive narrative) that this passage, recounting the king's denial of Merry's request and Grímhelm's stepping secretly into the breach, had best be placed at the end of 'Many Roads Lead Eastward' ('The Muster of Rohan'); and the next text ('D')[8] was marked 'Place this at the end of Chapter II of Book V'. The alliterative song *From dark Dunharrow in the dim morning* had not yet arisen. The 'young rider of the guard' still names himself Grímhelm, but with an alternative *Derning*, and a further suggestion *Dernhelm*. The conclusion of the passage in RK (p. 78, the end of 'The Muster of Rohan') is now present, with mention of the Folde and the Fenmarch, but whereas in RK four beacon-hills are named after Halifirien (Calenhad, Min-Rimmon, Erelas, Nardol) here there are only three: Calenhad, Erelas, Nardol, with omission of Min-Rimmon (see p. 344).

Rough workings for *From dark Dunharrow in the dim morning* are found, and the song was then incorporated into a further text ('E')[9] ('to be added to Chapter II of Book V'). The Rider who bears Merry is here still called Grímhelm (with 'Dernhelm?' written beside); and four beacon-hills are now named, but still with the omission of Min-Rimmon: Calenhad, Erelas, Nardol, Eilenach (because, when this was written, Eilenach had already been passed when the story told in 'The Ride of the Rohirrim' begins).

Finally, the alliterative song with the following text was copied in a fine manuscript and attached to the typescript M of 'Many Roads Lead Eastward': here the song is all but in final form.[10] There are now no differences from RK in the conclusion of the earlier chapter, except that Dernhelm remains 'a young rider of the guard'.[11]

The development of the new opening of 'The Ride of the Rohirrim' (i.e., when the story of the halt at Edoras had been removed) is particularly hard to analyse. There is here no continuous primary text followed by a continuous second version: my father wrote in a series of overlapping and partly discontinuous stages, some of which are in pencil overwritten in ink. I shall not attempt here to describe this complex in detail, especially since much of it is repetition, as my father sought to find a satisfactory articulation of existing elements in the story.

In the earliest brief text of this new start to the chapter (in pencil, but largely legible despite the overwriting) the host of the Rohirrim is 'bivouacked in the pinewoods that clustered about Minrimmon Beacon'. Merry hears a sound like faint drums in the wooded hills. They had been riding for four days, and were now less than a day's ride from the walls of the Pelennor. Scouts sent ahead had returned with the errand-riders of Gondor and reported that Minas Tirith was besieged, that another host was holding the approach to the City, and that a part of that force was marching west along the road. 'Suddenly Merry heard the soft whisper of Dernhelm again. Not a word more had he spoken since Edoras, either at mounting or dismounting or upon the way. "Come!" he said. "We ride again by night. Battle comes to meet us."' Here this text ends. It is clear that 'Minrimmon Beacon' has now replaced 'Eilenach Beacon' of the outline A (p. 343);[12] and in the ink text written over it (with the chapter number 'XLVII') Min Rimmon Beacon is 'a tall hill standing up from the long ridges of the forest of Taur-rimmon'.

In a second pencilled text, again overwritten but again largely legible, the scouts report that the enemy host was encamped on the road 'between Amon Dîn and the walls'. Dernhelm is now more communicative, for when the night riding has begun Merry ventures to put a question to him, and gets an answer. 'Drums, Dernhelm. Do you hear them, or am I dreaming? Is that the enemy?' Dernhelm replies very much as does Elfhelm the Marshal in RK (p. 105) after he stumbled over Merry in the dark, though more briefly: 'It is the wild men of the hills. In many wooded vales they live secretly, but most in this region, remnants of the Dark Years. They go not to war for Gondor or the Mark, and ask but to live wild. But now the darkness troubles them and the coming of orcs: they fear lest the Dark Years be come again. Let us be thankful. For they have offered service to Théoden. They are now our guides.' Here this text ends in its turn.

Ink overwriting advances the story: Éothain 'captain of the guard'[13] stumbles over Merry lying on the ground, and it is he who tells Merry about the meaning of the drums: 'Those are not orc-drums. You hear the wild men of the hills: so they talk together. In many wooded vales of these regions they live few and secretly.' Éothain makes no mention of the use of poisoned arrows by the Wild Men, and nothing is told here of any colloquy with one of them. The text concludes (from the end of Éothain's words to Merry):

'... Let us be thankful; for they have offered service to Théoden. They have spied on the enemy, and will guide us, they say, by cunning paths.'

'Where?' said Merry.

'That we shall learn ere long, I doubt not,' said Éothain. 'But I must hasten. The guard is to lead a flank march, and I must soon be ready.' He vanished in the dark, and at that moment 'Come,' said the soft voice of Dernhelm in Merry's ear. 'We ride again. I am ready.'

Soon Merry found himself riding again, slowly, warily. The guard led the way but beside each horse walked with long strides strange shapes of men, hardly to be seen in the gloom, and yet somehow Merry was reminded of the Púkel-men of

Dunharrow. Guided by these unlooked for friends they turned away southward towards the hills, filing among the trees, and then turning again moved further along hidden tracks through narrow dales and over the shoulders of dark hills.

No words were spoken. Hours seemed to pass, and yet still the night held on.

A new draft in ink (the one that was written over and so obscured the pencilled text concerning the Ents and the Wild Men, p. 345) takes up at the point where the captain of the guard (here left unnamed and referred to as 'X') stumbles over Merry. He tells him that the Wild Men of the Woods 'still haunt Rimmon Forest, it is said'; he does not mention their poisoned arrows, but he says that 'even now one of their headmen is being taken to the king.' From here the story moves confidently into the conversation of the king and Éomer with the headman Ghân-buri-Ghân (so named unhesitatingly from his first appearance), near the end of which this text ends. Already in this draft the final form is very nearly achieved, with Ghân-buri-Ghân's names for the orcs (*gorgûn*), and for Minas Tirith (*Stonehouses*).[14] Of the ancient road made by the men of Gondor through the hills he says this:

'... They went to Eilenach with great wains. Forgotten now, but not by wild men. Paths in hills and behind hills. Long road runs still under tree and grass behind Rimmon down to Dîn, and so back to horsemen road.'

It is to be remembered that at this stage the Rohirrim were bivouacked in the forest of Taur-rimmon, out of which rose the tall hill of Min Rimmon Beacon, and that the order of the last three beacons was Eilenach, Min Rimmon, Amon Dîn (see p. 344). It is natural therefore that Ghân-buri-Ghân should speak of the old wain-road to Eilenach running 'behind Rimmon down to Dîn' (see below).

Turning now to the first completed text, this manuscript begins as a fair copy of the draft work already described, but for the latter part of the chapter (from the end of the conversation with Ghân-buri-Ghân) it is based variously on overwritten pencilled text and independent passages of preliminary drafting in ink. In this manuscript the chapter as it stands in RK was largely reached, and there are only relatively minor matters to mention. It is numbered 'XLVII' and titled '(i) The Ride of the Rohirrim'; beside this my father wrote afterwards 'and the Battle of the Pelennor Field', then struck it out.

The Rohirrim are still camped in 'Taur-rimmon Forest' from which rises Min Rimmon beacon. Ghân-buri-Ghân tells of the wains that went to Eilenach passing 'through Rimmon', where he clearly means 'the forest of Rimmon'; and he speaks as in the draft of the lost road that lies 'there behind Rimmon and down to Dîn'. Changes made to the manuscript in these passages produced the text of RK (pp. 104, 106–7), but this development is rather puzzling. The host now lies in the Druadan Forest out of which rises Eilenach Beacon; and Ghân-buri-Ghân now says that the wains went 'through Druadan to Rimmon'; but his words about the old road remain unchanged from the draft, 'there behind Rimmon and down to Dîn'. If we suppose that after the order of the beacons had been changed the ancient wain-road went all the way to Min Rimmon (and the change of 'They went through Rimmon to Eilenach' to 'They went through Druadan to Rimmon' was not casually made: my father wrote *Rimmon* twice and twice crossed it out before finally settling on this name), it nonetheless seems strange that Ghân-buri-Ghân, in the Druadan Forest, should say 'there behind Rimmon', since Min Rimmon was now the third beacon, not the sixth, and some seventy-five miles to the west of Eilenach.

The Rider who stumbles over Merry is now again named Éothain (see p. 350), but he is now 'captain of Éomer's company (éored)'. By subsequent correction he becomes 'Déorwin, chief of the king's knights since Háma's death', and he speaks to Merry of 'the Druedain, Wild Men of the Woods', who 'still haunt Druadan Forest, it is said.' The name *Druedain* is not found in the published LR (in the present manuscript it was afterwards replaced by *Woses*), but reappears in *Unfinished Tales*. At a later stage, the Rider who fell over Merry and cursed him for a tree-root became Elfhelm, while Déorwin (Déorwine) survived in the story, still as chief of the king's knights, to be slain in the Battle of the Pelennor Fields, his name remembered in the song of the Mounds of Mundburg (RK pp. 120, 125). Elfhelm makes his first appearance by correction to the present manuscript, taking over from Éomer the speech beginning 'We need no further guides ...' (RK p. 109): here he is described as 'one of the captains'. In the typescripts of the chapter, where he has replaced Déorwine as the stumbling Rider, he is called 'captain of the company with which he [Merry] was riding'; the change to 'the Marshal, Elfhelm' was made when the book was in proof.

After Éomer's counsel that the Rohirrim should rest now and set out again at night, and the words 'To this the king assented, and the captains departed' (RK p. 109), my father set down a brief outline:

On the grass way they find Hirgon's body and dead horse – facing back west. They are drawing near the Rammas when they meet a runner in the dark and take him captive; but he proves to be a soldier of Gondor that escaping through a postern has slipped through the leaguer and run for 14 miles. He falls dying of wounds and exhaustion. 'Too late you come!'

he cried. 'The first circle is burning and abandoned. The Lord will not give heed to the defence. Great siege towers and engines. They are bringing up a huge Ram for the Gates.'

Then suddenly as he looked at the flame far off the heart swelled in Théoden, as of one who is fey, and without more counsel he seized a great horn and blew it, and all the horns in the host took up the challenge. Then without more debate the Rohirrim poured in upon the fields of Gondor like a great torrent.

This passage was struck through; and from this point the development becomes for a stretch entirely obscure, a mosaic of repetitions and overwritings leading to the final text; but this was not achieved until after the manuscript was completed – the pagination shows that a page was added in here subsequently. Before this, the story was still that Dernhelm rode as a member of the king's guard, in the leading *éored* (see note 17); with the addition on the added page of the statement (RK p. 110) that 'Elfhelm's company came next, and now Merry noticed that Dernhelm had left his place and in the darkness was moving steadily forward until at last he was riding just in rear of the king's guard' that story is seen to be abandoned: Dernhelm had been riding from Edoras in the second *éored*.

On the added page is a small map. This marks the Druadan Forest and Stonewain Valley, the Anórien road, Eilenach (in its final position as the sixth beacon) and Amon Dîn, the 'Grey Woods' south-east of Amon Dîn, Mindolluin, Minas Tirith, and Osgiliath. The island of Cair Andros is shown, though not named, and most notably the Anduin now bends strongly west below Osgiliath, so that the walls of the Pelennor run along its bank for a stretch, and then turns still more sharply southwards (but the hills of Emyn Arnen are not shown): on this see p. 438. In one respect only does this map differ from the large-scale map of Rohan, Gondor and Mordor, and that is in the relation of Minas Tirith to Osgiliath.[15] Here the road across the Pelennor runs due east to the Causeway Forts (marked with small circles), and Osgiliath is due east of the city, whereas on the large map it lies to the north-east, and the road runs likewise; see the Second Map, pp. 434, 438.

In the remainder of 'The Ride of the Rohirrim' the final form was achieved in this manuscript almost word for word:[16] the speech of Wídfara about the change in the wind, the disposition of the companies of the Rohirrim,[17] Merry's fear that the king would quail and turn back, his great cry (with echoes of the Old Norse *Völuspá*) 'Arise, arise, Riders of Théoden ...', and the likening of Théoden to 'Oromë the Great in the Battle of the Valar when the world was young.'

Lastly I must mention the interesting name *Forannest*. Isolated notes show my father working out this name, without giving any indication of its reference,[18] and on a page of the earliest drafting for the chapter, written above and perhaps associated with the sentence 'They were less than a day's ride from the Rammas', *Forannest* appears again, followed by the words 'North entrance [?in]'. That *Forannest* (whatever the name actually means) was the 'north-gate in the Rammas' (RK p. 111) is made certain by an isolated slip[19] giving the distances, east of Edoras, of the Mering Stream and the seven beacons; for here, following Amon Dîn, appears *Forannest (Rammas Echor)*.

NOTES

1 *Sarn Gebir:* the rapids in Anduin.

2 In the pencilled text the enemy camp is near Amon Dîn, and the distances are greater: 245 or 250 miles to the halt in the Forest of Eilenach, 285 to Amon Dîn.

3 The distance from the Rammas to Minas Tirith given here (12 miles or 4 leagues) obviously refers to the distance from the city to the point in the wall where the Rohirrim entered (where the North Road from Anórien ran into the townlands); and while in RK (p. 22) the city was four leagues from the wall at the widest extent of the Pelennor (in the direction of Osgiliath) and the north gate in the Rammas rather less ('maybe ten miles or more', RK p. 111), my father had now abandoned the original conception that the Pelennor had at all points a radius of seven leagues (see pp. 277–8, 287). Cf. also the draft for 'The Siege of Gondor' (p. 330), where it is said that when Faramir was forced to abandon the Causeway Forts he had '4 leagues or more of open land to cross', i.e. across the Pelennor.

On the Second Map a line of five dots (shown on the redrawing, p. 434) runs northwest from Minas Tirith. These might seem rather too far north of the mountains to represent the beacons; but that they do so is seen from the fact that the distance measured in a direct line from Edoras to that nearest Minas Tirith is 270 miles, to the next 245 miles, and to the next 218 miles. These are virtually the same as the distances given here for Edoras to Amon Dîn, Min Rimmon, and Eilenach. On the other hand the distance on the Second Map from Edoras to the Rammas is about 285 miles, and to Minas Tirith about 295.

4 My references to and citations from the overwritten pencilled texts, here and subsequently, are very largely based on the work done on them by Taum Santoski.

5 In the following text of this passage the distance from Edoras to Minas Tirith becomes 'a hundred and one leagues', changed at once to 'a hundred leagues and two', as in RK. On my father's large-scale map of Rohan, Gondor and Mordor the distance in a

direct line is 302 miles, but he noted against a pencilled line connecting them '304'. — On the form *Mundbeorg* 'hill of protection' for *Mundburg* in LR see VII.449 note 7.

6 *Cyneferth* has the very common Old English name-element *cyne-* 'royal'; *Grímhelm* means 'visored helm', cf. *gríma* 'mask', the name of Wormtongue.

7 On a torn half-sheet, subsequently used for other writing on the reverse, are the remains of a time-scheme which is very difficult both to read and to place in sequence, especially since some dates are lost and can only be deduced from those that are left. It seems that Théoden here remains a whole day at Dunharrow before setting out on the 10th of March, and on the 11th, after news has come in of an Orc-host entering Rohan from north of the Emyn Muil, Éomer leaves the host, rejoining it on the 12th. Against March 10 (?) is written: 'Merry insists on going to war and is taken up by [Grim >] Dúnhere who rides with the King, *Éowyn*, and Éomer.' It is hard to know what to make of this. A possibility is that my father had briefly decided to abandon the story of the 'young rider of the guard' (Éowyn), for Éowyn will now come openly to Minas Tirith, while Merry, equally openly, is taken by Dúnhere, chief of the men of Harrowdale. In support of this is the abandoned name *Grim-* (for *Grímhelm*?), and perhaps the underlining of *Éowyn*. But this seems to me very unlikely. It seems more probable that this text represents *earlier* ideas for this element in the story: not only is Merry permitted to go with the host, but Éowyn rides also as a matter of course (in which case the name *Grim-* is without significance, for *Grímhelm* had not yet arisen). In support of this is the diversion of Éomer northwards, mentioned in several of the early outlines for Book V, but not subsequently.

8 This text was in fact 'doubled', pencil overwritten in ink; but much of the pencilled form was left clear, and it shows no significant difference from the version in ink.

9 In this first finished version of *From dark Dunharrow in the dim morning* line 2 reads (as also in the first workings) *fate defying rode Fengel's son*, alliterating on *f*, with *Thengel?* in pencil in the margin (*with thane and captain rode Thengel's son*, RK). Both *fengel* and *þengel* were Old English poetic words for 'king, prince', and since *Thengel* as the name of Théoden's father appears in early texts of 'The Riders of Rohan' and 'The King of the Golden Hall' (VII.399, 402, 441) the appearance of *Fengel* here may have been inadvertent.

Line 8 reads *where deep once he drank ere darkness fell*, changed to *where long he had lived ere the light faded*. In line 10 *faith compelled him* preceded *Fealty kept he*. Line 12, where the original workings had *five days and nights*, changed to *four nights and days*, retains the latter (*five* in RK). Line 14 reads *through Folde and Fenmarch past Firienlode*: *Firienlode* is clearly a river, and so perhaps the original name of the Mering Stream, which flowed through the Firien Wood. In line 16 *Minas Tirith* is *Mundberg*(see note 5; *berg* and *beorg*, 'hill, mountain', were Old English variants).

10 This text still has *Four nights and days* for *Five*, and *Mundberg* for *Mundburg* (see note 9).

11 This was subsequently altered on the manuscript. I presume that my father's thought was that for Éowyn to be disguised as a member of the king's own guard, and distinct among them by slightness of build, would obviously make her presence more readily detected; but see p. 369.

12 Cf. the note at the end of outline A (p. 344): 'Camp just west of Min Rimmon on night of 12th'. — The phrase 'bivouacked in the pinewoods that clustered about (Minrimmon Beacon)' was first used of the Halifirien (p. 347). In the final form it would be used of Eilenach, when that became again the sixth beacon (RK p. 104).

13 The name *Éothain* now appears in a third application (see p. 247 and note 20), for this Éothain, captain of the guard, can hardly be the same Rider as Éomer's squire in 'The Riders of Rohan' (see p. 266 note 20).

14 The appearance and clothing of Ghân-buri-Ghân are not described: 'There sat Théoden and Éomer and before [them] on the ground was a strange squat shape of a man. Merry felt that he had seen him before, and suddenly he remembered: the Púkelmen of Dunharrow. Almost it seemed that here was one come to life. Looking about he saw that in a ring just outside the light squatted other similar figures, while Riders on guard stood in a circle behind.' Ghân-buri-Ghân 'spoke after a fashion the Common Speech as it was in Gondor.' At the point where this draft ends he replies to the king's offer of reward and friendship thus: 'No need. Ghân-buri-Ghân himself go with you [?lord]. If he leads into trap you will kill him. If he lead well then we say farewell and ask only to be left in the woods.'

15 Whereas on the large map the Anduin bends southward after Cair Andros and is running north-south at Osgiliath, on this map it continues south-east after Cair Andros and then swings back south-west to Osgiliath. No features are shown here other than the course of the River itself.

16 The fair copy was here written over a pencilled text. Most of this Taum Santoski has been able to read, and it is seen that the final text was already closely approached.

17 After 'The first *éored* drew up behind him [Théoden] and about him on either side' (RK p. 111) this text continues: 'Elfhelm was

away on the right ...': thus the words 'Dernhelm kept close to the king, *though* (Elfhelm's company was away on the right)' are lacking. This implies that the story was still present that Dernhelm rode as a member of the leading *éored* with the king's household-men (RK p. 110), not as one of Elfhelm's company; see p. 353.

18 Rejected forms in these notes are *fornest*, *Anfornest*, together with words *nesta*, *nethra*, *nest*, the last with meanings (apparently: the writing is very obscure) 'heart, core'.

19 The reverse of this slip (which is the lower half of a torn page) carries the following text:

> ... war would be useless, disastrous .... something much simpler, smaller and more desperate.
>
> 'I see you have something in mind,' said Thorin. 'What is it?'
>
> 'Well, this first,' I answered: 'you will have to go on your quest *secretly*, and that means you must go yourself, without messengers or embassies, and go with only a few faithful kinsmen or followers of your house. But you will need something more. There is a piece missing from the plan.
>
> For I needed thought. Thorin's tale had roused memories in my mind. Many years before I had been to Dol Guldur, as you know. You will know what I mean since you know Bilbo's story. I remembered the unhappy dying dwarf in the pits of Dol Guldur and the torn map and old key. Except that he was of Durin's folk of Erebor (as the map showed) I had no idea who he was. Of some importance perhaps since he was bearing a Ring, though he might have come by it in many ways. None but the Dwarves, and only a few of them, know who were the possessors of their great rings. But I had other far more perilous business on hand, and after I escaped from Dol Guldur many urgent cares. I stowed the things away till perhaps time would show their meaning. Now it had done so. I saw that I [had] heard the last wandering words of Thráin II Thrór's son, though he could not speak his own name or his son's. By what toughness of resistance he had kept these small things hidden in his torments, I do not know. But I think that

Comparison with *The Quest of Erebor* in *Unfinished Tales* will show that these passages are the forerunners of two in that (see p. 332 for the first, p. 324 for the second). My father said (*Unfinished Tales* p. 11) that this account of Gandalf's 'was to have come in during a looking-back conversation in Minas Tirith'; the present text may perhaps be assigned therefore to a time when *The Lord of the Rings* was approaching completion, if not actually finished; and this is supported by the reference to Thráin II (see VII.160). Since the notes on distances are obviously a secondary use of the page, it would follow that the name *Forannest* was not abandoned, but was merely not used in the published work.

It is strange that Gandalf says here of the unknown Dwarf in Dol Guldur that he was 'of some importance perhaps since *he was bearing a Ring*, though he might have come by it in many ways' – and the following sentence 'None but the Dwarves, and only a few of them, know who were the possessors of their great rings' must imply that it was one of the Seven Rings of the Dwarves. But the story that Thráin's ring was taken from him in the dungeons of Sauron goes back to the earliest sketch for 'The Council of Elrond': 'But Thráin of old had one that descended from his sires. We do not now know where it is. We think it was taken from him, ere you found him in the dungeons long ago' (VI.398). It is surely incredible that at this stage my father should have entertained the idea that Thráin had managed to retain his ring in Dol Guldur. I can only suppose therefore, though it is not a natural interpretation of the words 'he was bearing a Ring', that he meant that Thráin told Gandalf that he *had been* the bearer of one of the Seven Rings of the Dwarves – even though he was so far gone that 'he could not speak his own name or his son's.' In the later form of this passage in *The Quest of Erebor* Gandalf did not discover in Dol Guldur who the Dwarf was, yet he did learn that he had been the possessor of a great Ring: 'Nearly all his ravings were of that. *The last of the Seven* he said over and over again.'

VIII
THE STORY FORESEEN FROM FORANNEST

I have called this outline 'The Story Foreseen from Forannest' (the north gate of the Pelennor Wall) because it takes up at the point in the narrative where the Rohirrim poured through the outwalls of Minas Tirith in that place. But it will be seen that a part was foreseen for Denethor in no way consonant with the story of his madness and suicide, and this outline must come therefore from before the writing of at any rate the latter part of 'The Siege of Gondor', in which that story entered as the original draft was in progress (pp. 335–6).

A briefer, rougher form of this outline is found, extending only as far as the coming of the Host of the West before the Morannon. This my father rejected immediately and began on the fuller outline given here. A few differences in the first form are given in the notes.

The second form of the outline was given a heading 'Gandalf, Rohan, and Aragorn'; this was added to the text subsequently.

15 [March]. Horns of Rohan heard in the morning. Great charge of the Rohirrim through breach in north of Ramas-Coren. Rohirrim reach field before Great Gate, and men of Minas Tirith throw out enemy. But Wizard King takes to air and becomes Nazgûl,[1] rallies host of Morghul, and assails king. Théoden falls from horse sorely wounded; he is saved by Merry and Éowyn, but sortie from Gate does not reach them in time, before Éowyn is slain.[2] Grief and wrath of Éomer.

Éomer leads Rohirrim in a second reckless charge; but at that moment there is a cry from the city. A black fleet is seen coming to Haramon.[3] Men are landing. Then as final despair comes on, and Rohirrim give back, [west >] south wind rolls back cloud, and noon-sun gleams through. Aragorn unfurls his great standard from ship-top. The crown and stars of Sun and Moon shine out.[4] Men cry that Elendil has come back to life or Nume....[5]

Éomer charges again and the enemy is routed and so Éomer and Aragorn meet again on the field 'though all the hosts of Mordor lay between'.[6]

By evening of 15th [*in pencil* > 14] in a bloodred sun victory is complete. All enemy is driven into or back over Anduin. Aragorn sets up his pavilion and standard outside gate, but will not enter city, yet. Denethor comes down to greet the victors. Théoden dies. He bids farewell to Gandalf, Aragorn, Éomer and Merry. Théoden and Éowyn laid for a time in the royal tombs.

Words of Aragorn and Denethor. Denethor will not yield Stewardship, yet: not until war is won or lost and all is made clear. He is cold and suspicious and ? mock-courteous. Aragorn grave and silent. But Denethor says that belike the Stewardship will run out anyway, since he seems like to lose both his sons. Faramir is sick of his wounds. If he dies then Gondor can take what new lord it likes. Aragorn says he will not be 'taken', he will take, but asks to see Faramir. Faramir is brought out and Aragorn tends him all that night, and love springs between them.[7]

Aragorn and Gandalf counsel immediate action. Gandalf does not hope to conquer Mordor or overthrow Sauron and his tower. 'Not in these latter days, nor ever again by force of arms.' Yet arms have their place; and sloth now might be ruinous. Gandalf advises at least the taking and destruction of Minas Morghul.[8]

[N.B. Sauron already troubled by news of the victory of the Ents on March 11th – Ents another detail left out of his plans – first hears of Frodo on 15 of March, and at the same time, by Nazgûl, of the defeat in Pelennor and the coming of Aragorn. He is wrathful and afraid, but puzzled, especially by news of Frodo. He sends the Nazgûl to Kirith Ungol to get Frodo, but thinks chiefly of his war, and suspecting that Gondor will follow up victory he plans a counter-attack and withdraws all his forces to Morannon and Kirith Gorgor.]

The hosts, as many as are unhurt, of Rohan and Gondor, with Rangers, set out on 16th [*in pencil* > 17] and cross Anduin, and find Osgiliath empty. On 17th they march on Minas Morghul and the van (Riders of Rohan and Rangers and Gandalf) reach it on 18th [*in pencil* > 19] noon and find it dark and deserted. They burn the fields and Gandalf destroys its magic.[9] They now plan to march on the Morannon. A guard is set on Road, lest an army come up from South, or Sauron lets any sortie out through Kirith Ungol (no very great force could come that way in a hurry). They have now, however, to go more slow, and keep all their host together, moving only at the speed of infantry. The footmen come up on 19th. On 20th they set out for Morannon (120 [*in pencil* > 100] miles by road). They march through empty lands unassailed 20, 21, 22, 23, 24 and reach Morannon – just as Frodo [is beginning the ascent of Orodruin > is crossing Kirith Gorgor >] draws near Orodruin. There they to joy and surprise are joined by Ents, with new forces (out of North, including Elves of Lórien).

[Ents had victory on 11 March. It appears that Treebeard was told by Eagles sent by Galadriel of the assault on Lórien and the crossing of host to the Wold of Rohan on 7th. Treebeard and many Ents set out at once at great speed and cover over 200 miles, coming down on the enemy camp at south end of Downs in Eastemnet on 11 March; they destroyed many and drove rest in rout back over Anduin, where they had made bridges of boats above Sarn Gebir (about where Legolas shot down Nazgûl) – but in too great disarray to destroy the pontoons. So Ents cross. Treebeard is here joined by Elves of Lórien. They pursue the enemy round north and east of Emyn Muil and come down on the Hard of Dagor-lad (300 miles and more from Down-end to Morannon by this route): they move swiftly but mostly at night, for away here the Darkness is not over sky, only a great blackness is seen in the South, extending in breadth from Rauros to Linhir.[10] They arrive at same time as Gandalf.]

Now follows the Parley [*added:* on 25th]. Aragorn and Éomer wind horns before the Morannon, and summon Sauron to come forth. There is no answer at first, but Sauron had already laid his plans and an embassy was already coming to the Black Gate. The Wizard King? He bears the Mithril coat and says that Sauron has already captured the messenger[11] – a *hobbit*. How does Sauron know? He would of course guess from Gollum's previous visits that a small messenger might be a *hobbit*. But it is probable that either Frodo *talked in his drugged sleep* – not of the Ring, but of his name and country; and that Gorbag had sent tidings. The messenger jeers at Gandalf for sending a weak spy into the land where he dare not go himself, since his wizardry is no match for the Master. Now Sauron has the messenger, and what happens to him depends on Gandalf and Aragorn. He sees their faces blench. And jeers again. 'So!' he says – 'he was dear to you, or his errand was vital? So much the worse for you. For he shall endure slow torment of years, and then be released when broken, unless you accept Sauron's terms.'

'Name the terms,' said Gandalf, and tears were in his eyes, and all thought he was defeated and would yield – and of course be cheated.

The terms are that the Hosts of Gondor and Rohan shall withdraw at once beyond Anduin. All land east of Anduin to be Sauron's for ever, solely; and west of Anduin as far as Misty Mountains shall be tributary to Mordor and swear vassalage: Gondor and Rohan: as far as the river Isen. The Ents shall help rebuild Isengard and be subject to its lord – not Saruman, but one more trustworthy!

Gandalf replies, 'Yea, and what surety have we that Sauron will keep his part? Let him yield first the prisoner.' (That is awkward for the ambassador as in fact Sauron has not got him! But he laughs.) 'Take it or leave it so,' he said.

'We will take it,' said Gandalf, '— this the mithril-coat in memory. But as for your terms we reject them utterly.' Horror of Pippin and Merry if they are present? 'For in any case you would not keep them. Do as you will. And let fear eat your heart – for if you so much as set a thorn in the flesh of Frodo you shall rue it.' The ambassador laughs, and gives a dreadful cry. Flinging off his garments he vanishes; but at that cry the host prepared in ambush sally from the mountains on either side, and from the Teeth, and pour out of the Gate. The host of Gondor taken at unawares wavers, and the leaders are surrounded. [*Added in pencil:* All the Nine Nazgûl remounted[12] swoop down; but the Eagles come to give battle.]

At that moment (25th) the Ring goes into Crack of Doom and the mountain vomits, and Baraddur crashes, and all things done by Sauron are cast down, the Black Gates fall. The Host of Mordor is dismayed, and flees back for refuge into Kirith Gorgor. The victorious host of Gondor and Rohan pours in in pursuit.

[*Remainder of the text is in pencil:*] Gandalf knows that Ring must have reached fire. Suddenly Sauron is aware of the Ring and its peril. He sees Frodo afar off. In a last desperate attempt he turns his thought from the Battle (so that his men waver again and are pressed back) and tries to stop Frodo. At same time he sends the Wizard King as Nazgûl[13] to the Mountain. The whole plot is clear to him. ? He blasts the Stone so that at that moment the Orthanc-stone explodes: it would have killed Aragorn had he had it in hand?

Gandalf bids Gwaihir fly swiftly to Orodruin.

This account of the Parley before the Black Gate may be compared with that in the outline 'The Story Foreseen from Fangorn', written years before (pp. 229–30).

As I have said, this text certainly preceded at any rate the latter part of 'The Siege of Gondor', in view of what is told here of Denethor. On the other hand, it equally clearly followed the initial drafting of 'The Ride of the Rohirrim', since the Ents here crossed the Anduin north of the Emyn Muil after their victory in the Wold of Rohan and came south to the Morannon through the lands east of the River: their appearance in Anórien had already been rejected.[14] While I have necessarily treated these chapters as separate narrative entities, whose development from initial draft to virtually final form proceeded without interruption, I think it is in fact very probable that my father moved back and forth between them.

NOTES

1 *But Wizard King takes to air and becomes Nazgûl.* These words can only mean that *Nazgûl* refers specifically to the Ring-wraiths *as borne upon 'winged steeds'*. But my father cannot have intended this. I presume that since in this part of *The Lord of the Rings* the Ringwraiths were 'winged', and their power and significance for the story lies in their being 'winged', he had nonetheless made this equation, and so slipped into saying that when the Black Captain (Lord of the Nazgûl) himself mounted on one of the monstrous birds he 'became a Nazgûl'. This occurs again at the end of the outline.

2 On the death of Éowyn see p. 318.

3 At the equivalent point in the first form of the outline there is a note in the margin: 'Pelennor wall here only 10 miles away and the wall right above stream which bends round the Hills of Haramon.' *Haramon*, the original name of Emyn Arnen, appears on the Second Map: see pp. 353; 434, 438.

4 The first form of the outline has: 'Sungleam shines on the [Tree >] Crown and stars of Sun and Moon.'

5 The first four letters of this name are certain, but it can scarcely be *Númenor*; the likeliest interpretation is *Numerion*.

6 The first form of the outline has here: 'Enemy is caught between Aragorn and the Dúnedain and Éomer and so Éomer and Aragorn meet.' This is the first time that the name Dúnedain is met with *ab initio* in the texts.

7 Of this passage, from 'Aragorn sets up his pavilion and standard outside gate', there is very little in the first form of the outline: 'Denethor comes down to welcome Aragorn; but will not yield the Stewardship, until all is proven and war is lost or won.

Aragorn agrees.' Then follows: 'Aragorn and Gandalf counsel immediate action.'

8 This passage is the first germ of 'The Last Debate'.

9 The first form of the outline has 'They burn the poisoned fields'; and distances are given: 'Minas Tirith to Osgiliath 26 miles. West edge of Osgiliath to Minas Morghul [50 >] 60 miles?' (with 55 written above 60).

10 This is the first reference to Linhir (see pp. 436–7).

11 It is curious and confusing that Sauron's messenger should refer to Frodo as a 'messenger'.

12 Earlier in this outline my father had questioned whether the ambassador was not in fact the Wizard King himself, and he appears again at the end, dispatched by Sauron to Orodruin (his fate on the fields of the Pelennor was therefore not yet finally decided). Since at the end of the parley the ambassador casts off his garments and vanishes, he was certainly a Ringwraith; is this the meaning of 'All the Nine Nazgûl remounted'?

13 On the implication of *he sends the Wizard King as Nazgûl* – that *Nazgûl* means specifically the winged Wraiths – see note 1. On the other hand, *All the Nine Nazgûl remounted* (note 12) carries the opposite implication.

14 It cannot be actually demonstrated that the story of the coming of Treebeard and the Ents to Anórien did not follow, and supersede, their appearance at the Black Gate; but this seems extremely improbable.

IX

THE BATTLE OF THE PELENNOR FIELDS

I give first a remarkable writing entitled *Fall of Théoden in the Battle of Osgiliath*. It is clearly written in ink, with only a few changes made at the time of writing; there are also a small number of pencilled corrections, which I show as such.

Then Théoden gave a great shout 'Forth Eorlingas!' and spurred Snowmane rearing into the deeps of the great shadow. But few followed him; for his men quailed and grew sick in that ghastly shade, and many fell upon the ground. The light of his golden shield grew dim. Still he rode on, and darts flew thick about him. Many fell before his spear, and almost he had reached to the standard of the Haradoth [> Haradhoth], when suddenly he gave a great cry, and fell. A black arrow had pierced his heart. And at the same moment Snowmane stumbled forward and lay still. The great shadow descended. Slowly the huge vulture-form [> Slowly as a settling cloud it] came down, lifted its wings, and with a hoarse croaking cry settled upon the body of the fallen king, digging in its talons and stooping its long [*added:* naked] neck. Upon its back there sat a shape. Black robed it was, and above the robe there was a steel crown, borne by no visible head save where between crown and cloak there was a pale and deadly gleam as it were of eyes.[1] But Théoden was not alone. One had followed him: Éowyn daughter of Éomund, and all had feared the light of her face, shunning her as night fowl turn from the day. Now she leapt from her horse and stood before the shadow; her sword was in her hand.

'Come not between the Nazgûl and his prey,' said a cold voice, 'or he will bear thee away to the houses of lamentation, beyond all darkness where thy flesh shall be devoured and thy shrivelled mind be left naked.'

She stood still and did not blench. 'I do not fear thee, Shadow,' she said. 'Nor him that devoured thee. Go back to him and report that his shadows and dwimor-lakes[2] are powerless even to frighten women.' The great bird flapped its wings and leapt into the air, leaving the king's body, and falling upon her with beak and claw. Like a shaft of searing light a pale sword cold as ice was raised above her head.

She raised her shield, and with a swift and sudden stroke smote off the bird's head. It fell, its vast wings outspread crumpled and helpless on the earth. About Éowyn the light of day fell bright and clear. With a clamour of dismay the hosts of Harad turned and fled, and over the ground a headless thing crawled away, snarling and snivelling, tearing at the cloak. Soon the black cloak too lay formless and still, and a long thin wail rent the air and vanished in the distance.

Éowyn stepped to the king. 'Alas, Théoden son of Thengel,'[3] she said. 'But you have turned the tide. See, they fly. The enemy is broken by fear. Never did an old Lord of Men die better. You shall sleep well, and no Shadow nor foul thing assail your bed.'

Then there was a sound of a great ...[4] and the men of Minas Tirith and of the Mark released from the Shadow swept up, the light reborn was strong on their swords and spears. They drove the enemy into the River. Some stayed by their king.

I think that my father wrote this well before the period of composition we have now reached, and I would be inclined to associate it (very tentatively) with the outline sketches for Book V, where the event described here is several times referred to, and especially with Outlines III and V. In these, in contrast to what is said in I and II (p. 256), there is no mention of Éowyn's wounding or death: 'Théoden and Éowyn destroy Nazgûl and Théoden falls' (III, p. 260); 'Théoden is slain by Nazgûl; but he is unhorsed and the enemy is routed' (V, p. 263). Although in my father's narrative sketches silence is a bad guide, it is possible that these brief statements are nonetheless to be associated with what is certainly a notable feature of the present text, that there is no suggestion that Éowyn was in any way hurt in the encounter with the Lord of the Nazgûl or after (while Théoden is felled and dies without speaking). A difficulty with this view is that in Outline V the Nazgûl King is 'unhorsed', whereas in 'The Fall of Théoden in the Battle of Osgiliath' his descent on a 'huge vulture-form' is at the centre of the story. Since the 'vultures' are referred to as 'winged steeds', it is possible that the word 'unhorsed' was used in this sense, though that does not seem very likely.

It is obvious that no part was foreseen for Merry in the great event; and it seems that (in strong contrast to the final story, RK p. 117) it was the beheading of the great bird that in itself caused the defeat and flight of the Lord of the Nazgûl, deprived of his steed.

Whatever its relative dating, the piece certainly gives an impression of having been composed in isolation, a draft for a scene that my father saw vividly before he reached this point in the actual writing of the story. When he did so, he evidently had it before him, as is suggested by the words of the Lord of the Nazgûl (cf. RK p. 116).

When my father came to write the story of the Battle of the Pelennor Fields he all but achieved the form in which it stands in *The Return of the King* in a single manuscript ('**A**'). He adopted here the method of building up the completed narrative through massive correction and interpolation of his initial text; and the greater part if not all of this work clearly belongs to the same time. Beneath the writing in ink on the first page of this manuscript there is however a pencilled text, and this bears further on the subject of Théoden and the Lord of the Nazgûl.

This underlying text is largely illegible on account of the ink overwriting, which is closely-packed, but from what can be seen it seems not to have differed greatly (the opening paragraph of the chapter, mostly legible, is very close to the ink version on top of it) – as far as the passage where the golden shield of Théoden is dimmed, horses reared and screamed, and men falling from their horses lay upon the ground. But then follows: 'And through the ranks of the enemy a wide lane opened.' The rest of the pencilled text is almost entirely lost, but isolated words and phrases can be made out: 'There came riding ..... a great ..... [*struck out:* The Black Captain] ..... stood ..... the Black Captain robed ..... and above the robes was a crown ..... ' This can scarcely mean anything other than that the Lord of the Nazgûl did *not* descend upon the battle borne upon the back of a great vulture.

Various statements have been made on this subject, beginning with that in Outline V, cited above, that the Nazgûl was 'unhorsed'. In the rough draft of 'The Siege of Gondor' (p. 331) Gandalf, speaking to Pippin of the Wizard King, says that 'he has not [*struck out(?):* yet] taken to winged steeds'; in the outline 'The Story Foreseen from Forannest' (p. 359) 'the Wizard King takes to the air and becomes Nazgûl'; and of course there is the evidence of 'The Fall of Théoden in the Battle of Osgiliath'. That my father should at this stage have abandoned, however briefly, the story of the Winged Nazgûl descending upon Théoden is certainly surprising; but it seems plain that he did so.

The first manuscript A has no title, and was paginated continuously with 'The Ride of the Rohirrim'; a subsequent fair copy manuscript ('**B**') was afterwards given the number and title 'XLVIII The Battle of the Pelennor Fields'. The opening passage in A is distinct from the form in RK:

But it was no orc-chief or brigand that led the assault on Gondor. Who knows whether his Master himself had set a date to the darkness, designing the fall of the City for that very hour and needing light for the hunting of those that fled, or fortune had betrayed him and the world turned against him? None can tell. Dismayed he may have been, cheated of victory even as he grasped it. Cheated, not yet robbed. He was still in command, wielding great power, Lord of the Nazgûl. He had many weapons. He left the Gates and vanished.

There is no mention of Dernhelm in the passage 'He [Théoden] slackened his speed a little, seeking new foes, and his knights came behind him. Elfhelm's men were among the siege-engines ...', where RK has 'and his knights came about him, and Dernhelm was with them.' This shows, I think, that Dernhelm was still conceived to have been riding with the king's knights throughout the journey from Edoras.[5]

When the Lord of the Nazgûl says to Éowyn[6] 'No living man may hinder me!' she replies, as the text was first written: 'I am no living man. You look upon a woman. Éowyn I am, Éomund's daughter. You stand between me and my kin. Begone! For though I have slain no living thing, yet I will slay the dead [> yet I will slay the Undead].' This rests on the earlier form of the prophecy concerning the Lord of the Nazgûl: 'he is not doomed to fall before men of war or wisdom; but in the hour of his victory to be overthrown by one who has slain no living thing' (pp. 334–5). This was changed on the manuscript to: 'Begone, if thou be not deathless! For living or dark undead, I will hew thee, if thou touch me.'

In the passage that follows, Éowyn's hair is described as 'shorn upon her neck', and this survived through the fair copy B into the first typescript, where it was changed to the reading of RK (p. 116): 'her bright hair, released from its bonds'. And Merry's thought is directly reported: 'I must do something. If only I can get away from those eyes!'

After the great cry of the Lord of the Nazgûl as he departed there follows: 'And far up above [?the] Nazgûl hearing that cry were filled with great terror, and fled away to Baraddur bearing ill tidings.' This was not taken up into the fair copy (B).[7]

At Théoden's death the text here is briefer, and no reference is made to the taking up of the banner from its dead bearer and the sign made by the king that it be given to Éomer: 'Grief and dismay fell upon Éomer as he leaped from the saddle and stood by the king. Slowly the old man opened his eyes again. "Hail, King of the Mark!" he said. ...' In the fair copy B the banner-bearer is named Guthwin (Guthláf in RK).

Of Merry's sword it was first said in this text: 'So passed the sword of the Barrow-downs, work of Westernesse. Glad would he have been to know its fate who wrought it slowly long ago, for the sorcerer-king he knew and the dread realm of Angmar in the ancient North, hating all his deeds.' The text of RK (pp. 119–20), 'who wrought it slowly long ago in the North-kingdom when the Dúnedain were young ...', was substituted, probably at once.[8]

The passage (RK p. 120) recording the burying of the carcase of the great beast and of Snowmane, with the horse's epitaph, is absent; and the great rain that came from the sea ('it seemed that all things wept for Théoden and Éowyn', recalling the grief for Baldr) likewise, being added in only on the first typescript. A page of the manuscript (A) in which the encounter of the Prince of Dol Amroth with the bearers of Théoden and Éowyn is described, and his discovery that Éowyn was still alive, was rejected and at once rewritten; in the rejected form occurs this passage in the words of the Prince (still given no other name) with the bearers:

'Bring him to the City,' he said. 'The gate is wide open, and by his own deed the way thither is made free.' And then he rose and looked on Éowyn and was amazed. 'Here is a woman!' he said. 'Do even the women of Rohan come to war in our aid?' he asked.

'It is the Lady Éowyn sister of King Éomer,' they said. 'And we do not know how she came here, but it seems that she took the place of one of his knights. [*Rejected at once:* Dernhelm ... a young kinsman of the king.] It is a grief beyond words to us.'

This is the only trace of the idea that Éowyn escaped detection by substituting herself for a young Rider among the king's knights actually named Dernhelm. No doubt it arose here and was abandoned here; probably because of the meaning of the name (*derne* 'hidden, secret'; cf. the earlier name by which Éowyn was to ride, *Grímhelm*, p. 355 note 6).

In the rewritten version of this passage the text of RK is reached, and here at last appears the name *Imrahil* of the Prince of Dol Amroth, entering apparently without any hesitation as to its form.

Among the horsemen of Gondor (RK p. 121) appears Húrin the Tall, 'Warden of the City', changed at once to 'Warden of the Keys'. In an immediately rejected version of the passage in which the new hosts streaming in from Osgiliath are described it was said of the Black Captain: 'He was gone, and the Nazgûl in fear had fled back to Mordor bearing ill tidings' (see note 7); but this was lost in the rewriting of the passage, where appear Gothmog lieutenant of Morghul,[9] the Variags of Khand (both names written without any precedent forms), and the black 'half-trolls' of Far Harad.[10]

The course of Anduin, as seen by the watchmen on the walls when the black fleet approached (RK p. 122), was first described thus:

For south away the river went in a knee about the out-thrust of the hills of Emyn Arnen in lower Ithilien,[11] and Anduin bent then in upon the Pelennor so that its outwall was there built upon the brink, and that at the nearest was no more than [five >] four miles from the Gates; [*added:* and quays and landings were made there for boats coming upstream from the Outlands;] but thence the river flowed southeast for three leagues and all that reach could be seen in line by farsighted men on high. And they looking forth cried in dismay, for lo! up the reach of Arnen a black fleet could be seen ...

Striking out this passage my father noted against the first part of it: 'This is now told before in XLIV' (i.e. the chapter 'Minas Tirith'). He was referring to a rider introduced into the first typescript of that chapter (see p. 294 note 30) entirely recasting the original description of the Pelennor and the Outlands (pp. 278, 287) to its form in RK (p. 22), where the bend in Anduin about Emyn Arnen appears. This rider was already in existence, though obviously belonging to this phase of writing, as is seen from the name *Lonnath-ernin* of the landings, subsequently changed (presumably at this very juncture) to *Harlond.* In the present text the passage just cited was removed immediately, and the much briefer passage as found in this place in RK (p. 122) follows in the manuscript, with the name *Harlond.*[12]

The great banner of Aragorn is described in the same words as in RK (p. 123), except that in the sentence 'for they were wrought of gems *by Arwen daughter of Elrond*' the italicised words are absent. In the fair copy manuscript (B) 'by Finduilas Elrond's daughter'[13] was added in the margin, changed later to 'Arwen daughter of Elrond'. Aragorn is named 'Elessar, Isildur's heir'; and when men leapt from the ships to the quays 'There came Legolas and Gimli wielding his axe, and Halbarad with the standard, and Elboron and Elrohir with stars on their brow, and the dourhanded Dúnedain, Rangers of the North; and in the hand of Aragorn Branding was like a new fire kindled, Narsil reforged[14] as deadly as of old, and about his helm there was a kingly crown.' Thus *Elboron* still survived, for *Elladan* (see pp. 297, 302), the change being made on the fair copy. *Branding*, for *Andúril, Flame of the West*, remained until changed on the first typescript; while 'about his helm there was a kingly crown' was not replaced by 'upon his brow was the Star of Elendil' until the book was in proof.

At the end of the chapter as first written Duinhir of Morthond is named among the fallen, whereas in RK it is his sons, 'Duilin and his brother' (Derufin), who were trampled by the *mûmakil.*[15] Grimbold of Grimslade is not named (though he has appeared in 'The Ride of the Rohirrim'), and instead the sentence in which he is named in RK reads: 'Neither Hirluin the Fair would return to his green hills, nor Elfhelm to Eastfold [*written above:* Westfold],[16] nor Halbarad to the Northlands, dourhanded Ranger.'

In the alliterative song 'The Mounds of Mundburg' (not yet so named) there was much variation in the recording of those who died in the Battle of the Pelennor Fields. The earliest complete, though still very rough, form of the song reads:

As long after a maker[17] in Rohan said in his song:

We heard in the hills the horns ringing,[18]
of swords shining in the South kingdom:
steeds went striding to the Stoningland
a wind in the morning, war at sunrise.
There Théoden fell, Thengling mighty,
life and lordship long had he wielded
hoar king and high, Harding and Grimbold,
Dúnhere and [Elfhelm >] Marculf, Déorwin the marshal.
Hirluin the fair to the hills by the sea,
nor Forlong the great to the flowering vales
ever of Arnach in his own country
returned in triumph, nor the tall bowman
doughty Duinhir to the dark waters,
meres of Morthond under mountain-shadows.
Death in the morning and at day's ending
lords took and lowly. Long now they sleep
under grass in Gondor by the Great River.
Red it ran then. Red was the sunset,
the hills under heaven high snowmantled
bloodred burning. Blood dyed the earth
in the Field of Mundberg in the far country.

Another rough text, moving nearer to the final form in some lines but petering out before the conclusion, has in the line corresponding to the 8th in the version just given *Dúnhere and [Elfhelm >] Guthwin, Déorwin the marshal.* Guthwin was the banner-bearer of the king (see p. 368). The first good text reaches the final form (with the name Rammas Echor in the last line) in all but the names of the dead Riders:

Harding and Guthwin,
Dúnhere and Marculf, Déorwin and Grimbold,
Herufare and Herubrand, Horn and Fastred,
fought and fell there in a far country;
in the mounds of Mundberg under mould they lie
with their league-fellows, lords of Gondor.[19]

NOTES

1 Cf. the initial drafting for the end of 'The Siege of Gondor' (p. 337): '. . . crown that sat upon no visible head save only for the light of his pale eyes.'

2 *dwimorlakes*: 'illusions, phantoms'. Old English *(ge)dwimor*, *-er*; cf. Wormtongue's name *Dwimordene* of Lórien in 'The King of the Golden Hall' (TT p. 118), and *Dwimorberg*. In the present chapter in RK (p. 116) Éowyn calls the Lord of the Nazgûl 'foul dwimmer-laik', *-laik* being the Old Norse ending *-leikr* corresponding to Old English *-lāc*, here 'modernised' as *-lake*.

3 *Théoden son of Thengel*: see p. 355 note 9.

4 The word is most naturally read as 'sound', in which case my father inadvertently repeated it instead of the word he had in mind, e.g. 'riding'.

5 The statement in 'The Ride of the Rohirrim' that 'Dernhelm had left his place and in the darkness was moving steadily forward until at last he was riding just in rear of the king's guard' (p. 353) was added after the writing of the present passage; see also p. 356 note 17.

6 Éowyn calls the Lord of the Nazgûl 'foul dwimmerlake', where *-lake* was changed subsequently to *-lord*. See note 2.

7 Cf. 'The Story Foreseen from Forannest', p. 360, in which it is said that Sauron heard from the Nazgûl of the defeat on the Pelennor and the coming of Aragorn.

8 For the first appearance of *Angmar* see p. 334, and of *Dúnedain* p. 363 note 6.

9 The name *Gothmog* is one of the original names of the tradition, going back to *The Book of Lost Tales*; Lord of Balrogs, slayer of Fëanor and Fingon.

10 *Khand*, *Near Harad*, and *Far Harad* were roughly entered on the Second Map.

11 *Emyn Arnen* has replaced *Haramon* (see p. 359 and note 3). On the origin of the great bend in the Anduin around the hills of Emyn Arnen see p. 438.

12 As first written, those who saw the black sails cried out: 'The Corsairs of Umbar! See! The Corsairs are coming. They have overrun Amroth and Belfalas and Lebennin are destroyed!'

13 In the First Age *Finduilas* was the daughter of Orodreth King of Nargothrond; she plays a major part in the *Túrinssaga*.

14 *Narsil reforged*: although it has been said that Aragorn gave the name *Branding* to the Sword of Elendil after its reforging (see VII.274 and note 19), its ancient name has never been told until now.

15 In the account of the men of the Outlands entering Minas Tirith given on p. 287 Duinhir is mentioned, but not his sons.

16 In LR Elfhelm was not slain in the Battle of the Pelennor Fields, but survived to command the three thousand Riders of Rohan who were sent to 'waylay the West Road against the enemy that was in Anórien' (RK p. 158; the leader of this force was not named in the First Edition, but Elfhelm is named in both editions as among those who stood before the gates of Minas Tirith when the Captains of the West returned, RK p. 244).

17 *maker*: used in the long since lost sense 'poet'.

18 *We heard of the horns in the hills ringing* is a variant entered at the time of writing both in this text and in that following.

19 *Guthwin* was later changed to *Guthlaf* on this manuscript (see p. 368). *Herufare* is written so (for expected *-fara*) both here and (apparently) in a scrap of rough drafting for the passage; *Herefara* in RK.

X
THE PYRE OF DENETHOR

The original brief draft of this chapter ('**A**'), mercifully written fairly legibly in ink and not in pencil subsequently overwritten, extended from 'When the dark shadow at the Gate withdrew' as far as 'There was no guard at the gate of the Citadel. "Berithil has gone then," said Pippin' (RK p. 127). The final text was naturally not reached in every turn of expression or every detail, but apart from the absence of the meeting with Prince Imrahil as Gandalf and Pippin rode up from the Gate on Shadowfax there is no narrative difference of any significance.[1] At this point my father stopped and set down a brief outline ('**B**').

? Porter dead at Closed Door. ? They see fire and smoke below as they hurry down the winding road. Berithil has rebelled, and taking some of the guard has fought with the household men. Before they could gain entrance to the tomb, one of these dashed back and set a torch in the wood. But Berithil was just in time to save Faramir. But Denethor leaped back into the flames and was now dead. Gandalf closed the door. 'That ends a chapter!' he said. 'Let the Stewards burn – their days are over.' Light is growing fast. Faramir is borne away to the house where women were who remained in city to tend sick.

A large question mark was placed against the first part of this, and it was evidently rejected as soon as written and replaced by the following:

? Berithil and guard had gone and stopped the burning. Gandalf reasons with Denethor. 'I have seen' says Denethor 'ships coming up Anduin: I will no more yield to an upstart – and even if his claim be true of the younger line: I am Steward for the sons of Anárion not of Isildur – than [to] my dark foe.'

The development from this point is hard to be sure of, but I am almost certain that the next step was the following outline ('C'), written in ink around and through (but not over) a much rougher outline also in ink (briefer but essentially the same, with mention of the *palantír*):

Gandalf and Pippin hear clash of arms as they hasten down

the winding road to Rath Dínen. When they reach the Tombs they find Berithil holding the door alone against the household-men, who wish to obey Denethor's orders and come and set fire to the pyre. From within comes Denethor's voice commanding Berithil by his oaths to let them enter.

Gandalf sweeps aside the men and goes in. He upbraids Denethor, but Denethor laughs at him. Denethor has a *palantír*! He has seen the coming of Aragorn. But he has also seen the vast forces still gathered in Mordor, and says that victory in arms is no longer possible. He will *not* yield up the Stewardship 'to an upstart of the younger line: I am Steward of the sons of Anárion.' He wants things to be as they were – or not at all.

Gandalf demands the release of Faramir, and when Denethor attempts to slay him ('he shall not live to bow down!') Gandalf strikes the sword from his hand, and lets suddenly be seen his power so that even Denethor quails. Gandalf bids the men lift up Faramir and bear him from the chamber.

Denethor says 'At least so far my rule still holds that I may determine my own death.' He sets fire to the wood which is oil-drenched. Then he leaps onto the stone bed. He breaks the wand of his Stewardship and lays the pieces on his lap, and lies down taking the Stone between his hands. Then Gandalf leaves him. He closes the door and the flames roar within. They hear Denethor give a great cry, and then no more. 'So passes the Stewardship of Gondor!' said Gandalf. It is said that ever after, if anyone looked in that Stone, unless he had great strength of will, he saw only two old hands withering in flames. [*Added:* Gandalf bids Berithil and household men not to mourn – or be too downcast. Each side has tried to do their duty.]

They now bear Faramir to the house of the sick. As Gandalf and Pippin climb back up the road they hear the last shriek in the air of the Nazgûl. Gandalf stands still a moment. 'Some evil has befallen!' he says, 'which but for the madness of Denethor I could have averted. So far is the reach of the Enemy. But we know how his will had entry to the White Tower. *By the Stone.* Though he could not daunt Denethor or enslave him, he could fill him with despair, mistrust and unwisdom.' When Faramir is placed under care with Berithil as guard they meet the funeral cortège. Where is Merry? Pippin volunteers to try and find Merry.

Most of the essential ideas of the chapter were present here – and one that was rejected: Denethor knew who was aboard the black fleet and what his coming meant (see pp. 378–9). This knowledge he derived from the *palantír*; and since it is present also in the brief preceding outline B the existence of the *palantír* in the White Tower must be presumed there also.[2]

At this stage, I think, my father began on a new text of the chapter ('D'), continuing as far as Gandalf's words concerning 'the heathen kings' (RK p. 129). The final text is here very closely approached[3] until near the end (which is very rough and has various alternative readings):

Then Gandalf showing now a marvellous strength leapt up on the faggots and raising the sick man bore him out of the deadly house; and as he was moved Faramir moaned and spoke his father's name.

Then Denethor stepped forward and the flame died in his eyes and he wept, and he said: 'Do not take my son from me. He calls for me.'

'He calls for you,' said Gandalf. 'But you cannot come to him save in one way. You must go out to the battle of your City putting away despair and risking death in the field; and he must struggle for life against hope in the dark ways of his fever. Then perchance you may meet again. / For unless you go out to the battle of your City putting away despair and risking death in the field you will never speak again with him in the waking world.'

'He will not wake again,' said Denethor. 'His house is crumbling. Let us die together.' / 'At least we can go to death side by side,' said Denethor. 'That lies not in the will of the Lord of this City or of any other,' said Gandalf. 'For you are not yet dead. And so do the heathen kings under the dominion of the Dark Lord, to slay themselves in pride and despair or to slay their kin for the easing of their own death.'

In RK this is followed by 'Then passing through the door he took Faramir from the deadly house and laid him on the bier on which he had been brought, and which had now been set in the porch. Denethor followed him ...'; for it is clear that Gandalf, bearing Faramir, had halted at Denethor's words 'Do not take my son from me!', and only now moved through the door. But in the text just given it is said that Gandalf bore Faramir 'out of the deadly house' as soon as he had lifted him from the pyre.

It was perhaps at this stage that my father wrote a single discontinuous page ('E') beginning with the words 'Gandalf now takes Faramir'. Here as in RK Denethor follows him; but no further words are spoken until, after a long hesitation while he looks on Faramir, he declares that he will rule his own end, and his death follows immediately. It is curious that Denethor is here said to die clasping the *palantír*, yet there is no drafting of the scene in which he reveals his possession of it.

Gandalf now takes Faramir.

Denethor now followed him to the door. And he trembled, looking in longing at his son and hesitating. Yet in the end his pride and wilfulness overmastered him and he was fey again. 'At least in this you shall not defy and snatch my power away,' he said. And stepping suddenly forth he seized a torch from the hand of one of his servants, and moving back thrust it among the wood, which being drenched in oil roared at once into flame and a black smoke filled the house. Then Denethor leaped again onto the table amid the fire and fume, and breaking the staff of his stewardship on his knee he cast it into the flames and laid himself back on his pillow clasping the *palantír* with both hands to his breast.

Gandalf in sorrow and horror turned his face away and came forth, closing the door. For a while he stood in thought silently upon the topmost step. And they heard the roar and crackle of the flames within; and then Denethor gave a great cry, and afterward spoke no more, nor was seen again by mortal man.

'So passes the Stewardship of Gondor!' said Gandalf. And he turned to Berithil and the lord's servants. 'Do not mourn overmuch,' he said. 'For the old days have passed for good or evil. And be not grieved with your own deeds. For all here, as I see it, have striven to do as they judged right, whether in obedience and the keeping of vows or in the breaking. For you servants of the Lord owed obedience only to your Lord, but Berithil owed also allegiance first to the Lord Faramir the captain of the guard. So let now all hate or anger that lies between you fall away and be forgotten. Bear away those who have fallen in this unhappy place. And we will bear Faramir to a place where he can die in peace if that is his doom, or find healing.'

So now Gandalf and Berithil taking up the bier that stood still in the porch before the doors set Faramir upon it and slowly bore him away to the houses of the sick, and the servants came behind bearing their fellows. And when they came at length through the closed door Gandalf bade Berithil who had the key to lock it. And as they passed into the upper circles of the City there was heard in the air the cry of the Lord of the Nazgûl as it rose and passed away for ever. And they stood for a moment stricken with wonder.

This was followed (again with some doubt as to the sequence) by another discontinuous page ('F') that takes up in the course of Gandalf's reply to Denethor's words 'Do not take my son from me! He calls for me':

'... But he now must strive for life in the dark ways of his fever seeking healing; and you must go out to the battle of your city, risking death, if it must be, in the field. This you know well in your heart.'

But Denethor laughed. And going back to the table he lifted from it the pillow that he had lain on. And lo! in his hand he bore a *palantír*. 'Pride and despair!' he said. 'Did you think that [the] eyes of the White Tower were blind?' he said. [*Added in pencil, without direction for insertion:* This the Stone of Minas Tirith has remained ever in the secret keeping of the Stewards in the topmost chamber.] Nay, nay, I see more than thou knowest, Grey Fool ...'[4]

The page then continues very close to the final text (RK pp. 129–30), except in the view taken of Denethor's knowledge of Aragorn and the black fleet. In RK, as final proof that the power arrayed against Minas Tirith is too great for any withstanding, Denethor declares to Gandalf that 'even now the wind of thy hope cheats thee and wafts up Anduin a fleet with black sails.' He therefore does not know who is aboard. But (after Gandalf's reply 'Such counsels will make the Enemy's victory certain indeed') he goes on to accuse him of commanding Pippin 'to keep silence', and of installing him as a spy in his chamber; 'and yet in our speech together I have learned the names and purpose of all thy companions. So! With the left hand thou wouldst use me for a little while as a shield against Mordor, and with the right bring up this Ranger of the North to supplant me.' As the text stands in RK it is not clear what Denethor means by 'with the right hand'; for he does not know that it is the 'upstart' Aragorn who is coming up the Great River.

From the present text F, however, it is clear what Denethor did originally mean by 'with his right hand'. Here, he does not mention the black fleet in the first of these speeches; and in the second he makes no reference at all to Pippin – so that it is not from Pippin that he has learned of Aragorn's coming. But then he goes on: 'But I know your mind and its plots. Do I not see the fleets even now coming up Anduin! So with the left hand you would use me as a shield against Mordor, and with the right hand bring up this Ranger of the North to take my place.' Here it is obvious that he does know who is aboard (with his left hand, one might suppose, he gestures towards Osgiliath and with his right towards Pelargir); and he knew it from use of the *palantír*, as is expressly stated in the outline C (p. 375): 'Denethor has a *palantír*! He has seen the coming of Aragorn.'

This text (F) ends thus:

'But who saith that the Steward who faithfully surrenders shall have diminishment of love and honour! And at the last you shall not rob your son of his choice, slaying him in your proud wickedness while yet healing is in doubt. This you shall not do. Yield me now Faramir!'

It is hard to know what these last words imply, since at this point Gandalf must have already raised Faramir from the stone table and moved towards the door. It seems possible that some drafting has been lost, which would have made clearer the evolution of the final structure in this chapter.

At any rate, my father now began another text ('G'), for which he used the initial pages of D (p. 376), but soon diverged into new manuscript, roughly written but now completing the chapter; and here the substance and structure of RK was reached with few differences. The manuscript had originally no title, but at some point he wrote on it 'XLVIII The Pyre of Denethor': at that stage, presumably, he was treating 'The Ride of the Rohirrim' and 'The Battle of the Pelennor Fields' as one chapter (see pp. 351, 367). 'XLVIII' was subsequently changed to 'XLIX' and 'V.6'.[5]

As first written, the different view of Denethor's knowledge of Aragorn and the black fleet was preserved, though changed later on the manuscript to the final form (on this question see pp. 390–1). Gandalf still said 'So passes the Stewardship of Gondor' for 'So passes Denethor, son of Ecthelion'; and in his address to Berithil and the servants of Denethor who stood by he said: 'But Berithil of the guard owed allegiance first to his captain, Faramir, to succour him while he lived' (cf. p. 377). This was changed on the manuscript to read:

'... For you servants of the Lord owed obedience to him only. And he who says: "my master is not in his mind, and knows not what he bids; I will not do it", is in peril, unless he has knowledge and wisdom. But to Berithil of the guard such discernment was a duty, whereas[6] also he owed allegiance first to his captain, Faramir, to succour him while he lived.'

This was preserved in the fair copy ('H') that followed, and was not rewritten to the form in RK (p. 131) until the typescript stage was reached. At the end of this passage my father wrote, as in D, that Gandalf and Berithil bore Faramir to 'the houses of the sick', but he changed this to 'the Houses of Healing', with the Elvish name *Berin a*

Nestad, changed at once to *Bair Nestedriu*, both of which were struck out; but a little later in the chapter ('So now at last they passed into the high circles of the City, and in the light of morning they went towards the houses that were set apart for the tending of men hurt or dying', cf. RK p. 131) the name *Bair Nestedriu* reappears. In the fair copy H there is no Elvish name for the Houses of Healing in the first of these passages, but at the second the form *Bair Nestad* is found. In the first typescript, in this same passage, the name is *Edeb na Nestad*, which was struck through.

At this time the story was that Gandalf and Pippin rode through the Closed Door on their way to Rath Dínen (see note 3). Now, as Berithil and Gandalf bore the bier, 'behind them walked Pippin and beside him Shadowfax with downcast head'; and when they came back to the Door (here called 'the Steward's Door' as in RK; 'the Stewards' Door' in the fair copy) Gandalf sent Shadowfax back to his stable, dismissing him in the same words that in RK (p. 127) he used when they first came to the Door.

At the point in the narrative where the dome of the House of the Stewards in Rath Dínen cracked and fell, and 'then in terror the servants fled, and followed Gandalf', my father set down an outline, which was struck through.

Gandalf must say something about the Stone. How it was kept in Tower but only *kings* supposed to look in it.[7] Denethor in his grief when Faramir returned must have looked in it – hence his madness and despair. For though not yielding to Enemy (like Saruman) he got an impression of the Dark Lord's overwhelming might. The will of the Lord thus entered the Tower, confused all counsels, and kept Gandalf from the field. All this takes about 1½ hours to nearly 8 o'clock? So as they come out into the upper circles they hear the dreadful shriek of the Nazgûl's end. Gandalf forbodes evil. Does Gandalf look out from a high place? When [he] has put Faramir in the sick quarters with Berithil as his servant and guard, Gandalf and Pippin go back down towards the Gates and meet the cortège with bodies of Éowyn and Théoden.[8] Gandalf takes charge; but Pippin goes in search of Merry; and meets him wandering half blind. Eventually Gandalf and Pippin stand on battlement and watch progress of battle. Gandalf says he is not needed there so much as with the sick. Pippin (and Gandalf?) see the coming of Aragorn and the fleet. Eventually the captains return after victory at the Red Sunset.

Council must follow next day. Is any account of Aragorn's march put in at council?

The text in this manuscript (G) was then continued to the end; and when my father came to record Gandalf's words about the *palantír* of Minas Tirith they took this form:

'... Alas! but now I perceive how it was that his will was able to enter among us into the very heart of this City.

'Long have I guessed that here in the White Tower, as at Orthanc, one of the great Stones of Sight was preserved. Denethor did not in the days of his wisdom ever presume to use it, nor to challenge Sauron, knowing the limits of his own powers. But in his grief for Faramir, distraught by the hopeless peril of his City, he must have dared to do this: to look in the Stone. He hoped maybe to see if help was drawing nigh; but the ways of the Rohirrim in the North were hidden; and he saw at first only what was preparing in the South. And then slowly his eye was drawn east, to see what it was willed that he should see. And this vision [*struck out:* true or false] of the great might of Mordor, fed the despair that was already in his heart until it rose and engulfed his mind.'

['That fits well with what I saw,' said Pippin. 'The Lord went away from the room where Faramir lay; and it was when he came back that I first thought he was changed, old and broken.'

'It was in the very hour that Faramir was brought back that many saw a strange light in the topmost chamber of the Tower,' said Berithil.

'Alas! then I guess truly,' said Gandalf.] 'Thus the will of Sauron entered into the Tower; and thus I have been delayed here. ...'

The passage that I have enclosed in square brackets was an addition, but pretty clearly one made at the time of writing. In the fair copy manuscript of 'The Siege of Gondor' the passage describing how Prince Imrahil brought Faramir to the White Tower after his rescue, how Denethor then went up to the secret room under the summit of the Tower, and how a light was seen flickering there (RK pp. 94–5), was absent: see p. 340 note 17. It was no doubt at this time that it was added. The fair copy H retains the form of the passage just given; it was not until later that it was revised to introduce Gandalf's guess that Denethor had looked many times into the *palantír*, and Berithil's corroboration 'But we have seen that light before, and it has been rumoured in the City that the Lord would at times wrestle in thought with his Enemy.' In the original manuscript of 'Minas Tirith' he had said to Pippin as they sat on the battlements that Denethor was reputed to be able to 'read somewhat of the mind of the Enemy' as he sat in his high chamber at night, but he did not then add the words 'wrestling with him', nor 'And so it is that he is old, worn before his time' (RK p. 37; p. 292 note 21). Thus Pippin's words, preserved in RK, 'it was only when he returned that I first thought he was changed, old and broken' were written when my father believed that it was only now and for the first time that Denethor had dared to look into the Seeing Stone of Minas Tirith.

NOTES

1 Gandalf says here: 'Is it not a law in the City that those who wear the black and silver must stay in the Citadel unless their lord leaves it?' And Pippin replies: 'He has left it.' For a previous use of this passage in a different context see p. 338 and note 23.

2 Cf. the original manuscript of the chapter 'Minas Tirith', p. 281: 'And Denethor at least does not expect him in any way, *for he does not know that he exists.*' This in fact survived through all the typescripts and was only changed on the proof to the reading of RK: 'Though if he comes, it is likely to be in some way that no one expects, *not even Denethor.*'

3 A minor narrative difference is that when Gandalf and Pippin came to the Closed Door on Shadowfax they rode through it, though on the steep winding road beyond 'they could go only at a walk.' In RK Gandalf 'dismounted and bade Shadowfax return to his stable' (see p. 380).

4 When writing a very rapid draft my father would move from 'thou' to 'you' in the same speech, but his intention from the first was certainly that in this scene Denethor should 'thou' Gandalf, while Gandalf should use 'you'. In one passage confusion between 'thou' and 'you' remains in RK (Denethor's speech beginning 'Hope on then!', p. 129). Here in the fair copy manuscript my father wrote: 'Do I not know that you commanded this halfling here to keep silence?'; subsequently he changed 'you commanded' to 'thou commandedst', but presumably because he disliked this form he changed the sentence to 'Do I not know that this halfling was commanded by thee ...' At the same time he added the sentence 'That you brought him hither to be a spy within in my very chamber?', changing it immediately and for the same reason to 'That he was brought hither ...' For some reason the 'you' constructions reappeared in the first typescript, and so remained.

5 'V.6', not 'V.7' as in RK, because 'The Passing of the Grey Company' and 'The Muster of Rohan' were still one chapter, 'Many Roads Lead Eastward'. The fair copy manuscript (H) was also numbered 'XLIX' and 'V.6', with the title '(a) The Pyre of Denethor'.

6 The meaning of *whereas* here is 'inasmuch as', 'seeing that'.
7 I take this to mean, in a colloquial sense of 'supposed', 'it was only the kings who were held to be permitted to look in it', rather than 'it was only the kings who looked in it, as it was thought.'
8 The story now was that Éowyn was still alive: p. 369.

XI
THE HOUSES OF HEALING

On the same page that my father used for the original opening draft (A) of 'The Pyre of Denethor' (p. 374) he also wrote a brief passage for another place in the narrative, beginning: '"Well, Meriadoc, where are you going?" He looked up, and there was Gandalf.' This was, I feel certain, the opening of a new chapter; and since it stands first on the page, with the opening of 'The Pyre of Denethor' below it, it seems to me likely that my father for a moment thought to continue the narrative after 'The Battle of the Pelennor Fields' in this way. But however this may be, he subsequently on another page (numbered 'a') wrote a new opening ('A mist was in Merry's eyes of tears and of weariness when they drew near to the ruined Gates of Minas Tirith'), and joined this on to the first opening (now numbered 'b') already in existence. This first part ('a') of the brief composite text is already very close indeed to the opening of the chapter in RK; the second (earlier) part 'b' differs from the text of RK in that it is Gandalf, not Pippin, who finds Merry wandering in the streets of the City:

'Well, Meriadoc, where are you going?'

He looked up, and the mist before his eyes cleared a little,[1] and there was Gandalf. He was in a narrow empty street, and no one else was there. He passed his hand over his eyes. 'Where is the king?' he said, 'and Éowyn, and —' he stumbled and sat down on a doorstep and began to weep again.

'They have gone into the Citadel,' said Gandalf. 'You must have fallen asleep on your feet and taken a wrong turning. You are worn out, and I will ask no questions yet, save one: are you hurt, or wounded?'

'No,' said Merry, 'well, no, I don't think so. But I cannot use my right arm, not since I stabbed him. The sword has burned away like wood.'

Gandalf looked grave. 'Well, you must come with me. I will carry you. You are not fit to walk. They should not have let you. But then they did not know about you or they would have shown you more honour. But when you know more you will pardon them: many dreadful things have happened in this City.'

'Pardon them? What for?' said Merry. 'All I want is a bed if there's one to have.'

'You'll have that,' said Gandalf, 'but you may need more.' He looked grave and careworn. 'Here is yet another on my hands,' he sighed. 'After war comes the woe and hopeless oft seems the task of the healer.'

At this point the part 'b' ends and is followed by 'When the dark shadow at the Gate withdrew Gandalf still sat motionless', the opening of 'The Pyre of Denethor', as described above.

My father now wrote an outline, obviously before the story had proceeded further.

Pippin meets Merry wandering half blind and witless – (as in scene previously written: but *not* humorous). Merry also is taken to sickhouse (Faramir, Éowyn, Merry).

[King Théoden is laid on bier in Hall of the Tower covered with gold. His body is embalmed after the manner of Gondor. Long after when the Rohirrim carried it back to Rohan and laid it in the mounds, it was said that he slept there in peace unchanged, clad in the cloth of gold of Gondor, save that his hair and beard still grew but were golden, and a river of gold would at times flow from Théoden's Howe. Also a voice would be heard crying

Arise, arise, Riders of Théoden
Fell deeds awake. Forth Eorlingas!

when peril threatened.][2]

Now the Captains return. But Aragorn sets his pavilion in the field before the gate and will not enter without permission and sends in word begging leave to enter and speak with the Steward. They tell him that the Steward is dead by his own hand and the Lord Faramir sick, to death. Then he lays aside all the badges of Elendil, and enters as a plain man. Aragorn meets Pippin and Gandalf and asks after Merry. He is given news of Éowyn. Great joy of Éomer.

All that night Aragorn tends the sick, for the Kings of Gondor had both a craft and a power of healing, and by this [?latter] it was made clear that the true king was returned. Faramir opens his eyes and looks on Aragorn and love springs between them. Merry too recovers.

Counsel [*read* Council] of the Lords. Gandalf warns them that what Denethor had said is true: there was no final victory in arms against the Enemy. We fought here as best we could, because we had to; and it is so appointed in this world that resistance must be made to evil without final hope. But when we take arms *to attack* we are using that power which is pre-eminently found in the Ring, and it would be logical to do as Denethor desired in that case: to use the Ring. So indeed we should probably [?now] have victory and overthrow Sauron. But only to set up another. So that in the end the result would be as evil, if different, or possibly worse, as if Sauron recovered the Ring. Therefore have I .....[3] recovery in order that for a great age victory should be otherwise.

But we must still use such power as we have. And not delay. Sauron must still be kept busy and deem we have the Ring.

Another page of outline-notes, very roughly pencilled, probably followed this.

Long sojourn of rest in Minas Tirith and coming of Finduilas?[4] [*written above:* and Galadriel].

Hobbits all go home via Rohan: funeral of Théoden, and then through Gap and up west of Misty Mountains to Rivendell and then home.

Yes, said Sam, as he closed the Book. That all happened a long time ago.

Aragorn will only enter as lord of the Forod, not as king.[5]

Lords ride in, and see Théoden lying in state. Where is Gandalf? He comes in late [*or* later] and tells of Théoden's fall,[6] and Yoreth's words.

They go to Houses of Healing, and Aragorn asks for *athelas*. He heals the sick. Yoreth says he must be king. After supper he heals many sick.

Council next day. Gandalf's advice. Merry wakes up feeling nearly well. While Council is [?on] Gimli, Legolas and Pippin talk. They ..... and hear of the love of Éowyn for Aragorn at Dunharrow. And of the great ride to Pelargir.

The lords ride east: 1000 Rohirrim, Dol Amroth and [?so on]. And a first force to hold Morgul. They ride into shadow of ambush. Peril.

A complete draft (**'A'**) for the chapter now followed, written rapidly but legibly in ink. In the first part of the chapter there are passages of marked divergence from the story that followed. The manuscript A was followed by a fair copy **'B'**, for which some pages were taken out of A, including the opening page bearing the chapter number and title: 'Ch.L The Houses of Healing', the number changed subsequently to 'XLIX (b)'.[7]

The first divergence in A from RK comes with Gandalf's words when he came on Pippin and Merry on the pavement of the main street up to the Citadel (RK p. 135):

'He should have been borne in honour into this City,' he said. 'Greater was the wisdom of Elrond than mine. For if I had had my way neither you nor he, Pippin, would have set out; and then far more grievous would the evils of this day have been. Faramir and Éowyn would be dead, and the Black Captain would be abroad to work ruin on all hope.'

This was repeated in the fair copy B, and (with loss of the final sentence 'Faramir and Éowyn would be dead ...') in the following typescripts: the change to 'He has well repaid my trust: for if Elrond had not yielded to me, neither of you would have set out' was not made until the book was in proof. This is decidedly strange: for the form of the Choosing of the Company in *The Fellowship of the Ring* (p. 289), in which it was through Gandalf's advocacy *against* Elrond that Merry and Pippin were included, had been reached long before in the second version of 'The Ring Goes South' (VII.164). Earlier than this, it is true, Gandalf had also been opposed to their inclusion ('Elrond's decision is wise', he had said, VII.115), but only here, and again in 'The Last Debate' (p. 415), is there any suggestion that it was Elrond who advocated their inclusion in opposition to Gandalf.

In the passage that follows, after the account of the 'leechcraft of Gondor' and the unknown malady named 'the Black Shadow' that came from the Nazgûl, the text of A is much briefer than that of RK (p. 136):

And those that were so stricken fell slowly ever into a deeper dream, and from fever passed to a deadly cold and so died. But Faramir burned with a fever that would not abate.

And an old wife, Yoreth ...

Thus there is no reference here to the morning wearing away and the day passing to sunset, while 'still Gandalf waited and watched and did not go forth'; and after Yoreth had uttered the old saying that 'The hands of the king are the hands of a healer' A diverges altogether from the later story.

'Mithrandir is wise and skilful,' said another. 'In this at least he is not a king,' said the old wife. 'He has done much for us, but rather his skill lies in the teaching of men, to do what they can or should.'

But Gandalf seeing that all was done that could be done for the present arose and went out, and calling for Shadowfax rode away.

But Pippin and Berithil found themselves together little needed while the sick were yet in peril, and while such errands as were needful were done by the boys, Bergil and his friends, who had been saved from the wreck of the Rath a Chelerdain and sent up hither. So they went to the roof of the house that stood above the battlement of the wall, and they looked out. The battle now raged upon the fields; but it was far from the walls, and all the enemy had now been drawn away from the City; and they could not mark how fortune went: nought but a dust and a smoke in the distance away southward, and a far crying of horn and of trumpet. Yet so it was that Pippin with the farsighted eyes of his people was the first to descry the coming of the fleet.

'Look, look, Berithil!' he cried. 'The Lord was not all demented. He saw something in truth. There are ships on the River.'

'Yes,' said Berithil. 'But not such as he spoke of. I know the ...[8] of those ships and their sails. They come from Umbar and the havens of the Corsairs. Hark!'

And all about them men were crying in dismay: 'The Corsairs of Umbar!'

'You may say what you like and so may they,' said Pippin, 'but this I will say for my lord who is dead: I will believe him. Here comes Aragorn. Though how, and why in this way I cannot guess. Here comes the heir of Elendil!' he shouted; but no one, not even Berithil, took any heed of his small voice.

Yet true he proved. And at last it was known in the City. And all men were full of wonder. And so hope grew as the day rose to noon and waned, and at last it came to the red sunset. And watchers looking out saw all the fields before them dyed as with blood, and the sky above them was bloodred, and at last ere the red burned out to evening ash-grey over the fields of the Pelennor rode the captains in victory to the City.

Aragorn and Éomer and Imrahil now drew near the City with their captains and knights; and when they came before the Gates Aragorn said: 'Behold the setting of the sun in fire ...'

Aragorn's words are then as in RK p. 137, and his speech with Éomer that follows; but with Imrahil's intervention the original text diverges again:

And the Prince Imrahil said: 'Wise are your words, lord, if one who is kinsman of the house of the Stewards may venture to give counsel. Yet I would not have you remain at the door like a beggar.'

'Then I will not,' laughed Aragorn. '[*added:* I will enter as one.] The banner shall be furled and the tokens no more displayed.' And he bade Halbarad [> Elladan][9] to furl the standard, and he removed the crown and stars[10] and gave them to the keeping of the sons of Elrond. And he entered the City on foot clad only in a grey mantle above his mail and bearing no other token save the green stone of Galadriel, and he said: 'I come only as Aragorn Lord of the Rangers of Forod.'[11]

And so the great captains of victory passed through the city and the tumult of the people, and mounted to the Citadel, and came to the Hall of the Tower seeking the Steward.

The description of Théoden lying in state follows as in RK (pp. 137–8), but then the story of his afterlife in the mound at Edoras is introduced and expanded from the outline given on p. 385; I cite it here from the fair copy B, where the text is all but identical to A except in the words heard from the mound.[12]

And thus, it was said in song, he remained ever after while the realm of Rohan endured. For when later the Rohirrim bore his body away to the Mark and laid it in the mounds of his fathers, there, clad in the cloth of gold of Gondor, he slept in peace unchanged, save only that his hair still grew and was turned to silver, and at times a river of silver would flow from Théoden's Howe. And that was a token of prosperity; but if peril threatened then at whiles men would hear a voice in the mound crying in the ancient tongue of the Mark:

> Arísath nú Rídend míne!
> Théodnes thegnas thindath on orde!
> Féond oferswithath! Forth Eorlingas!

Then follow the questions of Imrahil and Éomer in the Hall of the Tower, whereby they learn that 'the Steward is in the Houses of Healing' (thinking that this means Denethor), and Éomer learns that Éowyn is still living, just as in RK, except that when Éomer leaves the hall 'the others followed him' ('and the Prince followed him' RK), because Aragorn is present.

And when they came forth evening had come, with many stars. And even as the light waned Gandalf returned alone out of the East up the road from Osgiliath, glimmering in the twilight. And he went also to the Houses of Healing, and he met the Lords before its doors. And they greeted him; and they said: 'We seek the Steward and it is said that he is in this house. ...'

In the passage that follows there are differences from RK, in that Aragorn does not only now appear as 'the cloaked man' come with Gandalf, unrecognised until he steps into the lantern-light. Thus Imrahil says: 'Shall it not be the lord Aragorn?', and Aragorn replies: 'No, it shall be the Lord of Dol Amroth until Faramir awakes. But it is my counsel that Mithrandir should rule us all in the days that follow and our dealings with the Enemy.' Then Gandalf speaks as in RK of his sole hope for the sick resting in Aragorn, and quotes the words of Yoreth.

When Aragorn encounters Berithil and Pippin at the door Pippin says: 'Trotter! How splendid. There, Berithil, you see Denethor was right after all.' The last sentence was struck out, and replaced by Pippin's words in RK (p. 139): 'Do you know, I guessed it was you in the black ships. But they were all shouting *Corsairs* and would not listen to me. How did you do it?' And when Imrahil says to Éomer 'Yet perchance in some other name he will wear his crown', Aragorn overhearing replies: 'Verily, for in the high tongue of eld I am Elessar, Elfstone, the renewer.'[13] Then lifting the green stone of Galadriel he says: 'But Trotter shall be the name of my house, if ever that be established; yet perhaps in the same high tongue it shall not sound so ill, and *tarakil*[14] I will be and all the heirs of my body.'

In the following passage the first section that I have enclosed in square brackets is so enclosed in the manuscript, with a query against it, though it was used in RK; the second section in square brackets has a line drawn round it in the manuscript with a mark of deletion and a query against it. In the fair copy the first is again put within square brackets, and the second does not appear.

And so they went in. [And as they passed towards the rooms where the sick were tended Gandalf told of the deeds of Éowyn and Meriadoc. 'For,' he said, 'long have I stood by them, and at first they spoke much in their sleep dreaming, before they sank into a yet deeper darkness. Also it is given to me to see many things afar off.] [And when there came a ...[15] cry from the fields I was near to the walls and looked out. And even as I did, the doom long foretold came to pass, though in a manner that had been hidden from me. Not by the hand of man was the Lord of the Nazgûl doomed to fall, and in that doom placed his trust. But he was felled by a woman and with the aid of a halfling;[16] and I heard the fading of his last cry borne away by the wind.']

It will be seen that there were major differences in the structure of the story as told in A from its form in RK. In the first place, the distant view of the battlefield seen by Pippin and Berithil from the roof of the Houses of Healing is told in direct narrative, and thus the coming of the black fleet up Anduin is repeated from 'The Battle of the Pelennor Fields'. Since Pippin and Berithil were present at the House of the Stewards in Rath Dínen they had heard Denethor accuse Gandalf of intriguing to displace him: 'But I know your mind and its plots. Do I not see the fleets even now coming up Anduin! So with the left hand you would use me as a shield against Mordor, and with the right hand bring up this Ranger of the North to take my place' (p. 378). This knowledge Denethor had acquired from the *palantír*. The idea that Denethor knew that Aragorn was in command of the ships of the Corsairs was changed on the draft manuscript (G) of 'The Pyre of Denethor' (p. 379), and in the fair copy of that chapter, already as first written, his knowledge of Aragorn is derived as in RK from his conversations with Pippin: his sight of the black fleet becomes for him an overpowering proof of the futility of resistance to Mordor. The present text must therefore have preceded the fair copy of 'The Pyre of Denethor'.

In the form of the story in A Pippin has a reason for declaring that Aragorn is coming with the fleet ('There, Berithil, you see Denethor was right after all', p. 390) and for shouting 'Here comes the heir of Elendil!' when everyone was crying 'The Corsairs of Umbar!' (p. 388); in RK he can have no reason at all for his words to Aragorn ('Do you know, I guessed it was you in the black ships'), nothing but a strange presentiment.

In the second place, Gandalf leaves the Houses of Healing long before sunset and disappears on Shadowfax. Aragorn does not refuse to enter Minas Tirith with Éomer and Imrahil; and thus he is present at the door of the Houses of Healing when Gandalf comes back, returning alone 'up the road from Osgiliath' in the dusk (p. 389). Nothing is told of his errand (but I think it can be seen what it was from the B version of this part of the story, to be given shortly). In the changed story he did not leave the Houses of Healing until sunset, and his errand was to bring Aragorn in from outside the walls: this being a sudden decision inspired by the words of Yoreth. In the A version he does not appear to take any particular account of her words, and he leaves when he sees that 'all was done that could be done for the present'; yet when he returns he says as in RK that 'only in [Aragorn's] coming have I any hope for those that lie within', quoting the words of Yoreth.

A remarkable short text evidently belongs to this phase in the development of the story, as is seen from the fact that Aragorn has entered the city without Gandalf, who is looking for him. This text is found on an isolated slip in my father's worst handwriting, which he partly elucidated in pencil (with some queries), and slightly changed, in not quite his worst handwriting.

'Did you ride with the Rohirrim?' said Gandalf.

'Nay indeed,' said Legolas. 'A strange journey we have had with Aragorn by the Paths of the Dead, and we came here at the last in ships taken from our foes. Not often has one the chance to bring news to you, Gandalf!'

'Not often,' said Gandalf heavily. 'But my cares are many in these days, and my heart is sad. I am growing weary at last, Glóin's son, as this great matter draws to the final edge of its doom. Alas! alas! How our Enemy contrives evil out of our good. For the Lord of the City slew himself in despair seeing the black fleet approach. For the coming of the fleet and the sword of Elendil secured the victory but gave the last stroke of despair to the Lord of the City. But [?come], I must still labour. Tell me, where is Aragorn? Is he in these tents?'

'Nay, he has gone up into the City,' said Legolas, 'cloaked in grey and secretly.'

'Then I must go,' said Gandalf.

'But tell us in return one thing first,' said Gimli. 'Where are those young friends of ours who cost us such great pains? It is to be hoped that they were not [?worsted] and they are still alive.'

'One is lying grievously sick in the City after a great deed,' said Gandalf, 'and the other stays beside him.'

'Then may we come with you?' said Gimli.

'You may indeed!' said Gandalf.

This encounter on the fields of the Pelennor was lost, and nowhere else is Gandalf's meeting with Legolas and Gimli after they parted at Dol Baran recorded.

As the fair copy B was first written, Gandalf's earlier departure from the Houses of Healing and the scene in which Berithil and Pippin see the black fleet from the roof were retained;[17] but there are two significant differences. After Yoreth's words it is now said: 'But Gandalf *hearing this saying*, and seeing that all was done that could be done *by the leechcraft of Gondor*, arose and went out'; and the conversation of Berithil and Pippin is now changed:

'Look, look, Berithil!' he cried. 'The Lord did not see only visions of madness. Here come the ships up the River that he spoke of. What are they?'

'Alas!' answered Berithil. 'Now I can almost forgive his despair. I know the fashion of these ships and their sails, for that is the duty of all watchmen. They come from Umbar and the Haven of the Corsairs! Hark!'

And all about them men were now crying in dismay: 'The Corsairs of Umbar!'

Pippin's heart sank. It seemed bitter to him that after the joy of the horns at dawn hope should be destroyed again. 'I wonder where Gandalf has gone,' he thought. And then another question arose in his mind: 'Aragorn: where is he? He should have come with the Rohirrim, but he doesn't seem to have done so.'

'Berithil,' he said, 'I wonder: could there be any mistake? What if this was really Aragorn with the Broken Sword coming in the nick of time?'

'If so, he is coming in the ships of our enemies,' said Berithil.

It seems that Pippin's thought here, 'I wonder where Gandalf has gone' giving rise to the question 'Aragorn: where is he?', taken with the more explicit statement concerning Gandalf's departure, makes it certain that he had gone, as in the later story, to find Aragorn and (because 'the hands of the king are the hands of a healer') to bring him urgently to the Houses of Healing.[18] But why Gandalf did not return till dusk, after Aragorn had entered the city, is not explained.

At this point my father struck from the B manuscript all that followed 'and then passed to silence and a deadly cold, and so died' (RK p. 136; see p. 387) and replaced it with the text that stands in RK, with Gandalf leaving the Houses of Healing at sunset, his thought and purpose now perfectly plain: 'Men may long remember your words, Yoreth; for there is hope in them. Maybe a king has indeed returned to Gondor; or have you not heard the strange tidings that have come to the City?' To the point we have reached in A ('Also it is given to me to see many things afar off', p. 390) the fair copy B (apart from the passage concerning Théoden's Howe at Edoras already cited, and a few points that are mentioned in the notes) then has the text of RK.

The latter part of the chapter in A was written with remarkable fluency – or, at any rate, the text as it stands in this original draft[19] was scarcely changed afterwards. The only notable divergence from RK is found in the passage where Aragorn, Éomer, and Gandalf speak beside Éowyn's bed; for while the actual words of RK (p. 143) are present, what became Gandalf's speech is given to Aragorn. He begins: 'My friend, you had horses and deeds of arms ...', and continues to '... a hutch to trammel some wild thing in?' (where Gandalf ceases in RK), and then (without the sentence 'Then Éomer was silent, and looked on his sister, as if pondering anew all the days of their past life together') goes on, from the point where he begins in RK: 'I saw also what you saw. And few other griefs amid the ill chances of this world ...' Above 'said Aragorn' at the beginning of the speech my father wrote, almost certainly while still writing this manuscript, 'Gandalf?'; and subsequently he made in pencil the changes that give the passage the form that it has in RK.

Beyond this there are only details to mention. The herb-master, in his discourse concerning the plant *kingsfoil*, declares it to be named *athelas* 'in the noble tongue, or to those who know somewhat of the Númenórean — ', 'Númenórean' being changed later both on A and on B to 'Valinorian' (and afterwards to 'Valinorean'); and Aragorn replies: 'I do so, and care not whether you say now *asea aranaite* or *kingsfoil*, so long as you have some.' The form *aranaite* became *aranion* on the final typescript.

When Aragorn leaves Merry (RK p. 146) he says: 'May the Shire for ever live unwithered and unchanged. For this, maybe, more than all else, I hope and labour';[20] the last part of this, from 'and unchanged', being struck from the fair copy.[21]

The chapter in A ended with Gandalf's words with the Warden of the Houses of Healing: '"They are a remarkable race," said the Warden, nodding his head. "Very tough in the fibre, I deem." "It goes deeper than the fibre," said Gandalf.' The conclusion of the chapter in RK is roughed out in a pencilled text that was subsequently overwritten by material belonging to 'The Last Debate' (cf. note 19), but some of it can be read. Where the fair copy B has (as in RK) 'and so the name which it was foretold at his birth that he should bear was chosen by his own people', this first draft has 'and so his own choice was fulfilled [?in] the title chosen long before.' The final passage is largely illegible, but the following can be seen: 'And [?in the morning] when he had slept a little he arose and ..... called a council and the captains met in a chamber of the Tower ...' The fair copy ends as does the chapter in RK, with Aragorn leaving the city just before dawn and going to his tent; and pencilled beneath the last words of the text is this note: 'Aragorn will not go in the City again. So Imrahil, Gandalf and Éomer hold council [in the] tents with the sons of Elrond.'

NOTES

1 *and the mist before his eyes cleared a little*: this was added after the 'a' part of the text was written and joined on to 'b'.

2 This passage is enclosed within square brackets in the manuscript.

3 A first illegible word here almost certainly begins *res* and ends *ed*, but cannot as it stands be read as *resisted*. A second word could be 'the' or 'his'.

4 For a previous mention of Finduilas Elrond's daughter see p. 370.

5 Cf. the first narrative text (A) of the chapter, p. 389: 'I come only as Aragorn Lord of the Rangers of Forod.'

6 *and tells of Théoden's fall:* i.e. (I take it) the manner of Théoden's fall, of which Gandalf knew (cf. the second passage in square brackets on p. 390).

7 The first text A was paginated continuously on from 'The Pyre of Denethor', as also was the fair copy B. At some point my father wrote on the opening page of 'The Houses of Healing' (this page being common to both texts) the chapter number 'L', i.e. separating it from 'The Pyre of Denethor'; but the number 'XLIX (b)', following 'XLIX (a)' for 'The Pyre of Denethor' (see p. 382 note 5), again makes them subdivisions of a single chapter, without an overall title.

8 The word might, just possibly, be 'crewmen'. B has 'fashion' (p. 392).

9 Halbarad was named among the slain in the original drafting of 'The Battle of the Pelennor Fields' (p. 371).

10 *he removed the crown and stars:* the word 'and' was struck out; the replacement is illegible, but may be 'of' with another word struck out, i.e. 'crown of stars'. In B this becomes simply 'the crown'; altered on the first typescript to 'the crown of the North Kingdom', this survived into the proof, on which it was altered to 'the Star of the North Kingdom'. Cf. 'The Battle of the Pelennor Fields', p. 370, where 'about his helm there was a kingly crown' was replaced on the proof by 'upon his brow was the Star of Elendil'.

11 Cf. RK p. 138 (at a different point in the narrative): 'I am but the Captain of the Dúnedain of Arnor'. In the fair copy manuscript, at the same point in the narrative as in RK, Aragorn says: 'I am but the Captain of the Rangers of Forod'.

12 In the first text A the verse is in modern English in the same words as in the outline on p. 385. In both A and B the passage is enclosed in square brackets.

13 In B the text remained almost the same: 'Verily, for in the high tongue of old I am Elessar, the Elfstone, and the Renewer', and this is the reading of the First Edition of LR. In the Second Edition *Envinyatar* was added before 'the Renewer'.

14 *tarakil:* the fourth letter *(a)* is not certain, but is very probable, especially in view of the form in B, where the text remained the same as in A but with *Tarakon* here. This was altered to *Tarantar*, which survived into the first typescript, where it was altered to *Telkontar* (> *Telcontar* on the proof).

15 The word begins with *gr(e)*, but is certainly not *great*. Possibly the word intended was *great*, but the last letters, which look like *ry*, were due to the following word *cry*.

16 On the doom of the Lord of the Nazgûl see pp. 334–5, 368.

17 It is said of Bergil and his friends in this version (see p. 388): 'When the fire-bolts had fallen in the City they had been sent [to]

the upper circle; but the fair house in the Street of the Lamp-wrights had been destroyed.'

18 Cf. also the brief outline given on p. 386: 'Where is Gandalf? He comes in late and tells of Théoden's fall, *and Yoreth's words*.'

19 A part of the conclusion of the chapter, from '"He [Merry] lies nearby in this house, and I must go to him," said Gandalf' to 'For I have not slept in such a bed since I rode from Dunharrow, nor eaten since the dark before dawn' (RK pp. 145–6), is in fact extant in a preliminary pencilled text, subsequently over-written by a text in ink that belongs to the story of 'The Last Debate'. This draft, most of which has been read by Taum Santoski, shows no significant differences from the more finished version in A.

20 Cf. Aragorn's words to Halbarad at Helm's Deep, p. 306.

21 I collect here a few other details. For 'whether Aragorn had indeed some forgotten *power of Westernesse*' (RK p. 144) A, and at first B, had 'art or wizardry'. The name *Imloth Melui* in Yoreth's recollection of her youth (RK p. 142) appears thus from the first; and as in RK (p. 146) Aragorn says to Merry that the herb-master will tell him that tobacco is called '*westmansweed* by the vulgar, and *galenas* by the noble', where the pencilled draft that is extant for this portion of the chapter (note 19) has 'pipeweed' and 'sweet *galenas*'. For the name *galenas* see p. 38.

XII
THE LAST DEBATE

At some time before he began work on this chapter my father set down an outline entitled 'The march of Aragorn and defeat of [the] Haradrim.' This must have preceded 'The Battle of the Pelennor Fields', since the name *Haramon* appears, not *Emyn Arnen* (see p. 370 and note 11);[1] it was almost certainly a companion to the outline 'The Story Foreseen from Forannest' (pp. 359 ff.), but is obviously best given here. At the head of the page my father afterwards pencilled a note asking whether it might not be a good idea 'to have part of this told by a man of Morthond Vale', but nothing ever came of this. Pencilled changes made to the text are shown.

Aragorn takes 'Paths of the Dead' morning of 8 March, passes tunnels of mountains. (This tale will have to be told in brief later, probably at feast of victory in Minas Tirith – by Gimli and/or Legolas.) They see skeleton in armour of Bealdor son of Brego.[2] But except for dark and a feeling of dread meet no evil. The tunnels become the issuing caverns of Morthond. It is dusk [> afternoon] of 8 March when Aragorn and his company come out into the uplands of the head of the Vale of Morthond; and ride to Stone of Erech.[3] This was a black stone, according to legend brought from Númenor, set up to mark the meeting place of Isildur and Anárion with the last king of the dark men of the Mountains, who swore allegiance to the sons of Elendil, vowing to aid them and their kin for ever, 'even though Death should take us.' The stone was enclosed in a now ruined ring-wall and beside it the Gondorians had anciently erected a tower, and there had been kept one of the *palantíri*. No men went near the tower. Rumour of terror flies through the vales, for the 'King of the Dead' has come back – and behold behind the *living men* a great host of shadow-men, some riding some striding but all moving like the wind, are seen.

Aragorn goes to Erech at midnight, blows horns (and dim shadow horns echo him) and unfurls banner. The star on it shines in the dark. He finds the *palantír* (unsullied) buried in a vault. From Erech he sets out [*added:* dark] morn of March 9 [*added:* at 5 a.m.]. For [*read* From ?] Erech to Fords of Lameduin (say Linhir?) is 175 miles direct, about 200 by road.[4]

Great terror and wonder precedes his march. At Linhir on Lameduin men of Lebennin and Lamedon are defending passage of river against Haradwaith. Aragorn reaches Linhir at evening on March 10 after two days and night[s] forced riding with host of shadow behind in the deepening dark of Mordor. All fly before him. Aragorn crosses Lameduin into Lebennin at morning of March 11 and hastens to Pelargir [*added:* 100 miles].[5]

From this point the outline, becoming very rough, was struck out and replaced, immediately, by a new text on the reverse of the sheet of paper. At the head of this page is the following brief passage concerning Frodo and Sam, which (while certainly written at the same time as the outline of Aragorn's journey) probably already stood there:

Rescue of Frodo. Frodo is lying naked in the Tower; but Sam finds by some chance that the elven-cloak of Lórien is lying in a corner. When they disguise themselves they put on the grey cloaks over all and become practically invisible – in Mordor the cloaks of the Elves become like a dark mantle of shadow.

Then follows, returning to the outline:

Aragorn crosses into Lebennin on March 11th (morning) and rides with all speed to Pelargir – the Shadow Host follows. The Haradrim fly before him in dismay. Some hearing news of his coming in time get their ships off and escape down Anduin, but most are not manned. Early on 12th Aragorn comes on the fleet driving all before him. Many of the ships are stuffed with captives, and they are partly manned (especially the oars) by captives taken in raids on Gondor, or slave-descendants of captives taken long before. These revolt. So Aragorn captures many ships and mans them, though several are burned. He works feverishly because he knows that doom of Minas Tirith is near, if he does not come in time. That night the Shadow Host vanishes and goes back into the mountain valleys, and finally disappears into the Paths of the Dead and is never seen again to come forth.[6]

He sets out at 6 a.m. on 13 March, rowing. On the south plain of Lebennin the Anduin is very broad (5–7 miles) and slow. So with many oars they make about 4 miles an hour and by 6 a.m. on 14th are 100 miles on way. It is 125 miles by river from Pelargir to that place where Anduin takes a west-loop round the feet of Haramon, a great hill in South Ithilien, and bends into the Pelennor, so that here the Ramas-Coren is but 15 [> 5] miles from the City,[7] and stands right on the water brink. Just before that point the river course runs nearly North-South (slightly N.W.) and points straight towards Minas Tirith so that watchers can see that reach – about 10 miles long.[8]

On morning of the 15th [*written above:* 14] a wind rises [*added:* at dawn] and freshens from S.W. The cloud and gloom begins to roll back. They hoist sails and now go with [*struck out:* more] speed. About 9 a.m. they can be seen by watchers from Minas Tirith who are dismayed. As soon as Aragorn catches sight of the city, and of the enemy, he hoists his standard (the White Crown with the stars of Sun and Moon on either hand: Elendil's badge).[9] A sun-gleam from the S.E. lights it up and it shines afar like white fire. Aragorn lands and drives off enemy.

Especially notable here is the recurrence of the idea that appeared in 'Many Roads Lead Eastward' (pp. 300, etc.): there was a *palantír* at Erech (in the earlier chapter Aragorn seemed to say that the Stone of Erech was itself the *palantír*, p. 309 note 10). This Stone replaced that of Aglarond (pp. 76–8), so that there were still five *palantíri* in the South.

When my father came to write the chapter his intention – and achievement – was that in it should be recounted not only the debate of the commanders following the Battle of the Pelennor Fields but also the story of the journey of the Grey Company as recounted by Gimli and Legolas to Merry and Pippin – and that it should then carry the story on to the arrival of the Host of the West before the Morannon. The manuscript, or manuscript corpus, was originally entitled 'The Parley at the Black Gate'.[10] It was a huge labour to achieve the final arrangement, entailing draft upon draft upon draft, with the most complicated re-use of existing pages, or parts of them, as he experimented with different solutions to the structural problem. It is more than likely that when this great mass of manuscript and typescript left his hands it was already in dire confusion, and its subsequent ordering into wholly factitious textual entities made it seem that in 'The Last Debate' my attempt to discern the true sequence of the writing of *The Lord of the Rings* would finally founder. But it has proved otherwise, and since no significant element seems to have been lost out of the whole complex the sequence of development in fact emerges here at least as clearly as in some far less difficult parts of the narrative. But of course to describe in detail each textual pathway would demand far more space than can be allowed to it.

It seems that before my father began the coherent drafting of the chapter – while he was in fact still writing 'The Houses of Healing' – he set down a form of the speeches at the opening of the debate that had arisen in his mind and would not be postponed.[11] Since a great deal of this does not appear in RK I give it in full.

'My lords,' said Gandalf. '"Go forth and fight! Vanity! You may triumph on the fields of Pelennor for a day. But against the Power that now arises there is no victory." So said the Steward of this City before he died. And though I do not bring you counsels of despair, yet ponder the truth in this. The people of the West are diminished; far and wide the lands lie empty. And it is long since your rule retreated and left the wild peoples to themselves, and they do not know you; and [they] will come seeking new lands to dwell in. Now were it but a matter of war between Men, such as has been for many ages, I would say: You are now too few to march East either in wrath or friendship, to subdue or to teach. Yet you might take thought together, and make such boundaries, and such forts and strongholds, as could long be maintained and restrain the gathering tide [> ?wild]. But your war is not only against numbers, and swords and spears, and untamed peoples. You have an Enemy of great power and malice, and he grows, and he it is that fills all the hearts of the wild peoples with hate, and directs and governs that hatred, and so they are become no longer like waves that may roll at whiles against your battlements, to be withstood with valour and defeated with forethought. They are rising in a great tide to engulf you. What then shall you do? Seek to overthrow your Enemy.'

'Overlate should we begin that task!' said Prince Imrahil. '[Had Minas Morgul been destroyed in ages past, and the watch upon the Black Gate maintained   We slept, and no sooner had he re-entered the Nameless Land]   We slept, and awoke to find him already grown beyond our measure. And to destroy him we must overthrow first all the allies that he has gathered.'

'That is true,' said Gandalf. 'And their numbers are too great, as Denethor indeed saw. Therefore this war is without final hope, whether you sit here to endure siege upon siege, or march out to be overwhelmed beyond the River. Prudence would counsel you to await onset in strong places, for so at least shall the time before the end be made a little longer.

'But now into the midst of all these counsels of war comes the Ring. Here is a thing which could command victory even in our present plight.'

'I have heard only rumour of this,' said Imrahil. 'Is it not said the One Ring of Sauron of old has come back to light, and that if he regain it then he will be as mighty as he was in the Dark Years?'

'It is said so and said truly,' answered Gandalf. 'Only he will be more mighty than of old and more secure. For there is no longer any land beyond the Sea from which help may come; [and those who dwell beyond even the West will not move, for they have committed the Great Lands to the keeping of Men.]'[12]

'But if we should find the Ring and wield it, how would it give us victory?' asked Imrahil.

'It would not do so all in a day,' answered Gandalf. 'But were it to come to the hand of some one of power [?or] royalty, as say the Lord Aragorn, or the Steward of this City, or Elrond of Imladrist,[13] or even to me, then he being the Ringlord would wax ever in power and the desire of power; and all minds he would cow or dominate so that they would blindly do his will. And he could not be slain. More: the deepest secrets of the mind and heart of Sauron would become plain to him, so that the Dark Lord could do nothing unforeseen. The Ringlord would suck the very power and thought from him, so that all would forsake his allegiance and follow the Ringlord, and they would serve him and worship him as a God. And so Sauron would be overthrown utterly and fade into oblivion; but behold, there would be Sauron still ..... but upon the other side, [a tyrant brooking no freedom, shrinking from no deed of evil to hold his sway and to widen it].'

'And worse,' said Aragorn. 'For all that is left of the ancient power and wisdom of the West he would also have broken and corrupted.'

'Then what is the use of this Ring?' said Imrahil.

'Victory,' said [Gandalf >] Húrin Warden of the Keys.[14] 'At least we should have won the war, and not this foul lord of Mordor.'

'So might many a brave knight of the Mark or the Realm speak,' said Imrahil. 'But surely more wisdom is required of lords in council. Victory is in itself worthless. Unless Gondor stand for some good, then let it not stand at all; and if Mordor doth not stand for some evil that we will not brook in Mordor or out of it, then let it triumph.'

'Triumph it will, say or do what we will, or so it seems,' said Húrin. 'But after many words still I do not hear what is our present purpose. Surely, it is but a plain choice between staying here and marching forth. And if those who are wiser or more farsighted than I tell me there is no long[er] hope in waiting here, then I for one am for marching forth, and taking doom by the outstretched hand. So we may give it a wrench at the least before it grips us.'

'And in this at any rate I approve Húrin's words,' said Gandalf. 'For all my speech was leading to just such counsel. This is not a war for victory that cannot be won by arms.[15] I have rejected the use of the Ring, for that would make victory the same as defeat. I have (like a fool, said Denethor) set the Ring at a great risk that our Enemy will regain it, and so utterly overwhelm us; for to retain it would be to risk the certainty that ere the last throes came upon us one among us would take it, and so bring about at least as great an evil. But still we have set our hands to war. For resist we must while we have strength – and hope. But now our salvation, if any can be achieved, does not rest upon our deeds of arms, yet it may be aided by them. Not by prudence, as I say, of the lesser wars of Men. But by a boldness, even a rashness, that in other case would be folly. For our hope is still, though daily it grows fainter, that Sauron has not recovered the Ring, and while that is so he will be in doubt and fear lest we have it. The greater our rashness the greater his fear, and the more will his eye and thought be turned to us and not elsewhere where his true peril is. Therefore I say we should follow up this victory as soon as we may and move East with all such force as we have.'

'Yet still there must be prudence,' said Imrahil. 'There is scarce a man or horse alive among us that is not weary, even those that are not sick or hurt. And we learn that there is an army left unfought upon our north flank. We cannot wholly denude the city, or it will burn behind us.'

'True enough, I would not counsel it,' said Gandalf. 'Indeed for my design the force we lead East need not be great enough for any assault in earnest upon Mordor, so long as it is great enough to challenge a battle.'

Turning now to the primary manuscript of the chapter, this is itself a massive complex of rejected and retained material, but it cannot be satisfactorily separated into distinct 'layers', and I shall treat it as a single entity, referring to it as 'the manuscript'.

The opening achieves almost word for word the form in RK pp. 148–9, beginning 'The morning came after the day of battle' and continuing as far as Gimli's remark to Legolas: 'It is ever so with all the things that Men begin: there is a frost in spring, or a blight in summer, and they fail of their promise.' A servant of Imrahil then guided them to the Houses of Healing, where they found Merry and Pippin in the garden, 'and the meeting of those friends was a merry one.' The narrative then moves directly into the debate: as in RK (p. 154) Imrahil and Éomer went down from the city to the tents of Aragorn, and there conferred with Gandalf, Aragorn, Elrohir and Elladan. 'They made Gandalf their chief and prayed him to speak first his mind'; and as in RK he began by citing the words of Denethor before his death, bidding his listeners ponder the truth of them. But now he went on, following and condensing a passage in the draft just given:

'The peoples of the West are diminished; and it is long since your rule retreated and left the wild peoples to themselves; and they do not know you, and neither love nor fear will long restrain them. And you have an Enemy of great power and malice, who fills all their hearts with hatred, and governs and directs that hatred, so that they are no longer like waves that roll at whiles against your walls to be thrown back one by one: they are united, and they are rising as a great tide to engulf you.

'The Stones of Seeing do not lie, and not even the Lord of Barad-dûr can make them do so ...'

The remainder of Gandalf's speech, with the interventions of Imrahil,[16] Aragorn, and Éomer, was achieved through a series of drafts that need scarcely be considered more closely, except for one version of Gandalf's reply to Éomer (RK pp. 155–6). In this, after saying that the Dark Lord, not knowing whether they themselves possessed the Ring, would look for those signs of strife that would inevitably arise among them if they did, Gandalf goes on:

'Now it is known to you that I have set the Ring in peril. From Faramir we learn that it passed to the very borders of Mordor before this assault began, maybe on the first day of the darkness. And, my lords, it went by the way of Morgul. Slender indeed is the hope that the bearer can have escaped the perils of that way, of the horrors that wait there; still less is the hope that even if he comes through them to the Black Land he can pass there unmarked. Six days have gone, and hourly I watch the signs with great dread in my heart.'

'What are these signs that you look for, an enemy ... you on our ...' asked Imrahil.

'Darkness,' said Gandalf. 'That is my dread. And darkness began, and therefore for a while I felt a despair deeper than Denethor. But the darkness that is to be feared is not such as we have endured: it would need no clouds in the air; it would begin in our hearts feeling afar the power of the Ringlord, and grow till by sunlight or moonlight or under heaven or under roof all would seem dark to us. This darkness was but a device to make us despair and it has, as such deceits will, ... our enemy. The next sign is strife among the lords.'

A following draft reaches Gandalf's argument as it appears in RK, but here he adds to those signs that Sauron will have observed: 'He may also have seen in the Stone the death of Denethor, and since he judges all by himself he may well deem that a first sign of strife among his chief foes.' In the same text, after saying that 'we must at all costs keep his eye from his true peril', he adds: 'A single regiment of orcs set about Orodruin could seal our ruin' (in a subsequent version: 'A mere handful of orcs at watch on Orodruin would seal our doom').

At the end of the debate, following Aragorn's words (RK p. 158) 'no gates will endure against our Enemy if men desert them', an initial draft has a development that was not pursued:

Then even as they debated a rider came in search of Éomer. 'Lord,' he said, 'word has come from Anórien from the north-roads. Théoden King, when we rode hither, left men behind to watch the movements of enemy at Amon Dîn. They send word that there has been war far away in the Wold, and thence come strange tidings. For some say [the very woods have] that wild things of the woods have fallen on the orcs and driven them into the River and the rapids of Sarn Gebir. But the army that was on the road has heard this news, and also of our victory here, and is afraid, and is even now hastening back.'

'Ha!' said Éomer. 'If they dare to assail us they will rue it. If they seek to fly past they shall be smitten. We must cut off this finger of the Black Hand ere it is withdrawn.'

The numbers of those who should set out from Minas Tirith were differently conceived, for 'the great part of these should be horsed for swifter movement' (in contrast to RK: 'the great part of this force should be on foot, because of the evil lands into which they would go'): Éomer leading three thouand of the Rohirrim, Aragorn five hundred horse and fifteen hundred foot, and Imrahil a thousand horse and fifteen hundred foot; and there was no suggestion that any force of the Rohirrim were sent to 'waylay the West Road against the enemy that was in Anórien' (RK p. 158). The manuscript was however subsequently corrected and the muster as enumerated in RK introduced, with three thousand of the Rohirrim left behind.

After the words 'And he drew forth Branding and held it up glittering in the sun' (which is where in RK 'The Last Debate' ends), the original chapter then continues with a transition back to Legolas and Gimli: 'While the great captains thus debated and laid their designs, Legolas and Gimli made merry in the fair morning high up in the windy circles of Minas Tirith.' Legolas' sight of the gulls flying up Anduin follows, and the emotion that they stirred in him, are described in much the same words as in RK; but the conversation that follows is altogether different. At this stage no account had been given of the Paths of the Dead; in the outline at the beginning of this chapter (p. 397) my father had suggested that the story would be told 'at feast of victory in Minas Tirith', and had mentioned that in tunnels under the mountains the company saw the 'skeleton in armour of Bealdor son of Brego', but that except for the dark and a feeling of dread they met no evil.

There is at first both a draft and a more finished version; I give the latter, since it follows the former very closely.

'... No peace shall I have again in Middle-earth!'

'Say not so!' said Gimli. 'There are countless things still to see there, and great work to be done. But if all the Fair Folk, that are also wise, take to the Havens, it will become a duller world for those that are doomed to stay.'

'It is already rather dull,' said Merry, sitting and swinging his legs as he sat on the brink of the wall. 'At least it is for hobbits, cooped up in a stone city, and troubled with wars, while their visitors talk and nod together about their strange journey, and tell no one else about it. I last saw you at the Hornburg, and then I thought you were going to Dunharrow,[17] but up you come on ships out of the South. How did you do it?'

'Yes, do tell us,' said Pippin. 'I tried Aragorn, but he was too full of troubles, and just smiled.'

'It would be a long story fully told,' said Legolas, 'and there are memories of that road that I do not wish to recall. Never again will I venture on the Paths of the Dead, not for any friendship; and but for my promise to Gimli I would vow never to go into the White Mountains again.'

'Well, for my part,' said Gimli, '[wonder was stronger than fear >] the fear is past, and only wonder remains; yet it cannot be denied that it is a dreadful road.'[18]

'What are the Paths of the Dead?' said Pippin. 'I have never heard them named before.'

'It is a path through the Mountains,' began Gimli.

'Yes, I saw the door from a distance,' Merry broke in. 'It is up in Dunharrow, in the mountains behind Théoden's town and hall at Edoras. There is a long row of old stones leading across a high mountain field to a forbidding black mass, the Dwimorberg they call it, and there is a cave and a great opening at the foot of it, which nobody dares to enter. I think the Rohirrim believe that inside there dwell Dead Men, or their shadows, out of a past long before they came to that land.'

'So they told us,' said Legolas, 'and they forbade us to go in; but Aragorn could not be turned from it. He was in a grim mood. And that fair lady that lies now in the Houses below, Éowyn, wept at his going. Indeed at the last in the sight of all she set her arms about him imploring him not to take that road, and when he stood there unmoved, stern as stone, she humbled herself to kneel in the dust. It was a grievous sight.'

'But do not think that he was not moved,' said Gimli. 'Indeed, I think Aragorn himself was so deeply grieved that he went through all perils after like a man that can feel little more. He raised her up and kissed her hand, and then without a word we set out,[19] before the sun came over the black ridges of the mountain. I do not know how to put it into words, but even as we passed the last great standing stone a dread fell on me, of what I could not say, and my blood seemed running cold. I lifted my feet like lead across the threshold of that darkling door; and hardly had we passed within when a blindness of very night came upon us.

'Madness it would seem to try and take horses on such a road, but Aragorn said that we must attempt it, for every hour lost was perilous. We had to dismount and lead them, but I do not think they would have gone far, if it had not been for Legolas. He sang a song that went softly in the darkness, and though they sweated and trembled they did not refuse the road. I am speaking of our horses that the Rohirrim gave us;[20] the horses of the Rangers, it seemed, were so faithful to them that nothing would stay them if their masters were beside them.

'We had brought a few torches, and Elladan [> Aragorn] went ahead bearing one, and Elrohir [> Elladan] with another went at the rear. Bats flew over us, and [> We saw nothing, but] if we halted there seemed an endless whisper of voices all about, that sometimes rose into words, though not of any tongue that I have ever heard. Nothing assailed us, and yet steadily fear grew on us, as we went on. Most of all because we knew, how I know not but we knew, that we could not turn back: that all the black road behind us was packed with things that followed us but could not be seen.

'So it went on for some hours, and then we came to a sight that I cannot forget. The road, for so it was: no mere cavern-track, had been wide, so far as we could judge, and though it was utterly dark the air was clean. But now we came suddenly into a great empty space through which the way ran on. The dread was so great on me that I could hardly walk. Away to the left something glittered in the gloom as Aragorn's torch went by. ...

It will be seen that when my father transformed this story told by Gimli of the Paths of the Dead and placed it much earlier in the book (while in 'The Last Debate' merely referring to it as having been told to Merry and Pippin by Legolas: 'Swiftly then he told of the haunted road under the mountains,' RK p. 150), he retained Gimli as the one through whose experience the passage of the tunnels is described.

Gimli described the mailclad skeleton clutching at the door in almost the same words as are found in 'The Passing of the Grey Company' (RK pp. 60–1), with the addition that on the helm and the hilts of the sword there were 'north-runes'. But Aragorn here named the dead warrior:

'"Here lies Baldor son of Brego," he said, "first heir of that Golden Hall to which he never returned. He should be lying now under the flowers of Evermind[21] in the Third Mound of the Mark; but now there are nine mounds and seven green with grass, and through all the long years he has lain here at the door he could not open. But whither that door led, and why he wished to pass, none now shall ever know."

At this stage in the evolution of the book Théoden had told at Dunharrow how Baldor son of Brego passed the Dark Door and never returned (p. 315; cf. 'The Muster of Rohan' in RK, p. 70). But with the removal of the story of the Paths of the Dead from the present chapter to 'The Passing of the Grey Company', the discovery of the skeleton of Baldor came to stand *before* Théoden's words about him at Dunharrow; and this I suppose was why my father changed the passage. It was certainly not because he concluded that Aragorn did not know who he was. In the passage in RK it is clear that he did know, though he did not name him; for he knew that he had lain there in the dark 'through all the long years' as the burial mounds of the Kings of the Mark were raised one by one.

There are now nine mounds and seven at Edoras.[22] In the original draft of this passage the text is interrupted at Aragorn's words 'Here lies Bealdor son of Brego' by a very roughly written list of the Kings of the Mark, set down in two columns, thus:

1 Eorl
2 Brego (Bealdor)
3 Aldor
4 Fréa
5 Fréawine
6 Goldwine
7 Déor
8 Gram
9 Helm
10 [Bealdor > Folca >] Fréalaf Éowyn's son (sister-son of king)
11 [Brego >] Háma
12 Walda
13 Folca
14 Folcwine
15 Fengel
16 Thengel
17 Théoden

The names Folca and Folcwine replaced rejected forms that I cannot make out. It will be seen that these are the names found in Appendix A (II, *The House of Eorl*) to *The Lord of the Rings*, with the sole exception of the eleventh king Háma (in LR the eleventh king was Brytta: this name has already appeared in early texts as the father of Brego, VII. 435, 445, but is here absent). Beneath is written a long series of Old English names, many of them those that appear in the list of kings above, together with others, such as *Beorn*, *Brytta*, *Hæleth*, *Léod*, *Oretta*, *Sigeric*, *Sincwine*, &c. I suppose that it is possible that this series of names was written first, though it stands second, and that the names of the kings in the numbered list were selected from it. At any rate, it looks very much as if it were at this very point that the First Line and the Second Line of the Kings of the Mark, and their names, came into being.[23]

Beside the names of the kings are written dates. My impression (not having studied the actual original page) is that only the dates of Fengel, Thengel, and Théoden belong with the writing of the manuscript page and the list of kings, but that these certainly do so. The dates are:

Fengel	born 1268, died 1353
Thengel	born 1298, died 1373
Théoden	born 1328, died 141[?8]

The last figure in the date of Theoden's death is unfortunately obscure, but is certainly not 9. The dates of these kings in LR are 2870–2953, 2905–2980, and 2948–3019, which in the Shire Reckoning become 1270–1353, 1305–1380, and 1348–1419. It is clear then that at this stage in the writing of *The Lord of the Rings* my father was working with a chronology that is esentially similar to that of LR in respect of Rohan – but the actual numerical years are given according to the Shire Reckoning.[24]

Gimli does not record any words of Aragorn's to the Dead that followed:

'And so we turned away and left the dead untouched, and passed out of the hall that was his tomb, and hurried on, for behind us now fear seemed treading ever closer. And just when we felt that we could endure no more, and must either find an ending and escape, or else turn and run back in madness to meet the following fear, our last torch sputtered out.

'Of the next hour or hours I remember little, save a blind groping dread that pressed behind us, and a rumour that came behind like the shadow of the noise of endless feet, as horrible as the ghosts of men themselves. And we stumbled on till some of us were crawling on the ground like beasts.

'Then suddenly I heard the trickle of water ...

Allowing of course for the difference in mode of narration (e.g. 'Then Legolas turning to speak to me looked back, and I can remember still the glitter in his bright eyes before my face', cf. RK p. 61), the story of the emergence of the Company from the caverns and descent down the Vale of Morthond was little changed afterwards. Legolas takes up the narration at:

'The Dead were following,' said Legolas. 'A great grey host I saw come flowing behind us like a shadowy tide: shapes of men there were, and horses, and grey banners like shreds of cloud, and spears like winter thickets on a misty night. "The Dead are following," I said. "Yes, the Dead ride behind," said Elladan. "Ride on!"'

It seems that Gimli then takes up the tale again with 'And so we came at last out of the ravine as suddenly as if we had issued from a crack in a wall', for he refers to himself as 'Gimli of the Mountain' in his description of the ride to Erech. Elladan's answer to Gimli's question in RK 'Where in Middle-earth are we?' does not appear; it is here Gimli who describes the course of Morthond (with the explanation 'so I was after told'). He says that the river 'flows at last to sea past Barad Amroth[25] where dwells Prince Imrahil'; and he does not refer, as does Elladan in RK, to the significance of the name *Blackroot*. The ride to Erech is described thus:

'Bells I heard ringing in fear far below, and all the people fled before our faces; but we being in haste rode swiftly as though in pursuit, until our horses were stumbling weary, and [*struck out:* I at least,] even Gimli of the Mountain, was spent. And thus just ere the midnight hour – and black it was wellnigh as in the caverns, for though we did not know it yet the darkness of Mordor was creeping over us – just ere midnight we came to the Hill of Erech.'

On the Darkness out of Mordor coming over the sky as the Company rode to Erech see the Note on Chronology at the end of this chapter. – The text at this point becomes the primary draft, and continues:

'And what is that?' asked Merry.

'You should ask Aragorn,' said Gimli, 'or the brethren: they know, as is fitting, all the lore of Gondor of old. It is a black stone, they say, that old tales tell was brought[26] in ages past from Númenor before its fall, when its ships would come to the west shores of the world. And it was set upon a hill. And thereon the King of the [*struck out:* Dark] Men of the Mountains had sworn [> once swore] allegiance to the West; but afterwards the [?Shadow] Men fell again under the dominion of Sauron. Isildur came to the Stone of Erech, when he gathered strength to resist the power of Mordor, and he summoned the Men of the Mountains to come to his aid, and they would not.

'Then Isildur said to their king of that day: "Thou shalt be the last. Yet if the West prove mightier than thy black Master, this curse I set on thee and thy folk: to rest never till your oath is fulfilled. For this war shall last down many ages, and you shall be summoned once again ere the end." And they fled before the wrath of Isildur, and did not dare to go forth to war on Sauron's part. And they hid themselves in secret places in the mountains and seldom came forth again, but slowly died and dwindled in the barren hills.

This account of Gimli's to Merry and Pippin at Minas Tirith is the forerunner of Aragorn's to Legolas and Gimli at the Hornburg (RK p. 55). I think that it may very well have been at this point that the story of the breaking of their oath to Isildur by the Men of the Mountains first emerged, and that it was now that Aragorn's words at the Hornburg were enlarged to include it.

Gimli continues:

'But afterwards, in the days of Gondor's later power, men set a ring-wall about the Stone of Erech, and built beside it on the hilltop a tall dark tower, and there was guarded the seventh *Palantír*, which now is lost.[27] The tower is ruinous and the ring-wall is broken, and all about the land is empty, for none will dwell near the Hill of Erech, because it is said that at times the Shadow-men will gather there, thronging about the ruined wall, and whispering. And though their tongue is now long forgotten, it is said that they cry "We are come!" and they wish to fulfill the broken oath and be at rest. But the terror of the Dead lies on that hill and all the land about.

'Thither in the blackness before the storm we came. And at last we halted. And Elladan blew his silver horn, and Elrohir unfurled the banner that at the Hornburg he bore still wrapped in grey [*later* > black];[28] and dark as it was the stars glinted on it, as it was spread on a wind like a breath of ghosts coming down from the mountains. Nothing could we see but the seven stars of Elendil, and yet we were aware of a great host gathered all about us upon the hill, and of the sound of answering horns, as if their echo came up out of deep caverns far away.

'But Aragorn stood by the banner and cried aloud. "The hour is come at last, and the oath shall be fulfilled. I go to Pelargir, and ye shall come behind me. And when all this land is clean, return, and be at peace! For I am Elessar, Isildur's heir of Gondor."

'Then there was a silence, and no whisper or rustle did we hear as the night wore away. We lay within the ruined ring-wall, and some slept; though we felt the terror of the Dead that hedged us round.

At this point a revised version begins, and I follow this, since it adheres very closely to the initial draft (see however notes 33, 34, and 35).

'Then followed the weariest journey that I have ever known, wearier than our hunting of orcs over wide Rohan on our feet; three days and nights and on into another day with little pause or rest.[29] No other mortal men could have endured it and fought at the end of it, save only the Dúnedain, these Rangers of the North. They are as tough as dwarves, I swear it, though none of my kin should believe me. Almost I wished I was an elf and had no need of sleep, or could both sleep and wake at once, as it seems that Legolas can.

'I was never in that land before, and I could not tell you much of our road, even if you wished to hear. But it is, I reckoned, some 60 leagues as birds fly from Erech, over Tarlang's Neck[30] into Lamedon, and so, crossing Kiril and Ringlo, to Linhir beside the waters of Gilrain, where there are fords that lead into

Lebennin. And from Linhir it is a hundred miles, if it is a step, to Pelargir on Anduin.[31]

'The next morning day did not dawn, as you will remember well, but it must have been before the sun rose above the vapours of Mordor that we set out again,[32] and east we rode to meet the gathering gloom; and ever close behind us came the Shadow Host, some riding, some striding, but all moving silently and with the same great speed, and when they overtook our horses, though we pressed them to their utmost, the Shadow Host swept about us wide on either flank, and some went on ahead.

'Terror and wonder ran on wings before us, and all that was left of the folk of Lamedon hid, or fled to the woods and hills.[33] Thus we came at nightfall of the second day from Erech to Linhir. There the men of Lamedon had been contesting the passage of Gilrain with a great strength of the Haradrim, and of their allies the Shipmen of Umbar, who had sailed up Gilrain-mouth and far up the waters of Anduin with a host of ships and were now ravaging Lebennin and the coast of Belfalas. But defenders and invaders alike fled at our approach. And thus we crossed into Lebennin unopposed, and there we rested, and sorely we needed it.

'Next day we made our greatest endeavour, for Aragorn was pressed with a great fear lest all that he did would prove too late. "I counted on two days more at the least," he said; "but those who challenge Sauron will ever fall short of their reckoning. Now already Minas Tirith is beset, and I fear it will fall ere we can come to its aid."

'So we rose ere night had passed, and went as swift as our stouthearted horses could endure over the flat plains of Lebennin; and behind us and about us the host of the Dead flowed like a grey tide.

'Great rumour of dismay went on before us. I do not know who set the tales on the wing, but as we learned after among both friends and foes the tidings ran wild: "Isildur has come back from the dead. The dead are come to war, but they wield living swords. [The Lord of the Ring has arisen!]"[34] And all the enemy who heard these things fled as best they could back to Anduin, for they had many ships there and great strength; and we hunted them out of the land: all that day and through the next night, with few brief halts, we rode. And so we came at the bitter last to the Great River again, and we knew ere we came that it was near, for there was salt in the air. The mouths of Anduin were indeed still far away south and west of us, but Anduin is even at Pelargir so great and wide that almost it seems a slow-flowing sea, and countless birds are on its shores.

'It was day, I guessed, by the veiled/hidden sun – the fourth since we left Dunharrow – when we reached those shores, and saw the fleets of Umbar. And then we had to fight, at last. But fear was our mightiest weapon. Many of those who learned of our coming had already gone aboard and thrust off and escaped down Anduin to the the Sea. But the enemy, whose main task it was to ravage South Gondor and prevent help going north to the City, had been too wide-scattered for all to escape so. And while they marched abroad their ships were left with small guard. But there were among them captains sent by Mordor, and orc-chieftains, and they were not so easily dismayed, and they endeavoured to hold their men to a defence. And indeed the Haradrim are a grim folk, and not easily daunted by shade or blade. But their resistance did not last long. For now seeing that we were indeed come to aid them, many of the more stouthearted men of the land gathered to Aragorn. And on the ships the slaves rebelled. For the Corsairs of Umbar had in their ships many new-captured prisoners, and the oarsmen were all slaves, many taken in Gondor in petty raids, or unhappy descendants of slaves made in years gone by. Before the fifth day was over we had taken well nigh all the fleet, save some ships that their masters set ablaze; and all the enemy that were not slain or drowned were gone flying over the [?borders] into the desert that lies north of Harad.[35]

Here the revised version stops, at the foot of a page, and my father struck out the whole page (which begins at 'So we rose ere night had passed', p. 412) and wrote a pencilled note:

> No fight, but Shadows [?flow into] the ships and all men leap overboard except the chained captives. But Rangers went to each ship and comforted the captives.

He then rewrote the page – and this was obviously done immediately – beginning at the same words.

'So we rose ere night had passed, and went as swift as our stouthearted horses could endure over the green plains of Lebennin darkling under the shade of Mordor; and all about us the Host of the Dead flowed on like a grey tide. Still the rumour of our coming went before us and all men were dismayed, and none neither foe nor friend would wait for our approach. For the darkness weighed on the allies of Mordor, not being orcs or folk bred in the Black Land, and those that could fled back to Anduin, where they had gathered many ships. Thus we hunted them from Gondor all that day and on through the next night, halting seldom and sleeping not at all, until we came at the bitter end to the Great River.'

'I knew it,' said Legolas, 'long ere we reached it, for there was salt in the air. And my heart was troubled for I thought that I drew near the Sea, but indeed the Mouths of Anduin were far away to the south. ... '

This is only the second time that Legolas has spoken since Gimli's story of the journey began. He speaks now of the great breadth of Anduin as Gimli had done (p. 413);[36] and (following the note at the end of the previous version of this section of the story) he goes on:

'... But fear was the only weapon that we needed, for the grey host passed on to every ship whether drawn up or anchored in the tide, and all the men that were in them fled, or leaped overboard, save the slaves of the oars that were chained, or captives under hold.'

Legolas describes how to each of the greater ships one of the Rangers went to comfort the captives, bidding them put aside fear and be free (RK p. 152).

'And when all the fleet was in our hands Aragorn went up on that ship which he took for his own and let sound many trumpets, and the Shadow Host withdrew to the shores, and stood in great array there silently, and there was a red light in the gloom, for some of the enemy had fired their ships ere they abandoned them.'

Aragorn's words to the Dead ('Now I will hold your oath all fulfilled') are close to those in RK (p. 153).[37] It is 'a tall figure of shadow', not as in RK said to be the King of the Dead, that steps forth and breaks his spear. The remainder of the story is very much as in RK, though here told by Legolas: the rest of the Company that night 'while others laboured', the release of the captives from the ships, the coming of the men of Lebennin (but Angbor of Lamedon is not named), the slow passage by oar up Anduin (but it was 'the fifth morning, that is the day before yesterday' that the fleet set out from Pelargir: see the Note on Chronology at the end of this chapter), Aragorn's fear that they would be too late ('for it is forty leagues and two by river from Pelargir to the landings under the Pelennor wall'), and the red glow to the north from the burning of Minas Tirith. Legolas' discourse ends, as does Gimli's in RK, with 'It was a great hour, and a great day, whatever may come after', to which Gimli replies: 'Yes, whatever come after. Yet for all our victory the faces of Gandalf and Aragorn look grave. I wonder what counsel they are taking in the tents below. For my part I wish it were all well over. Yet, whatever is still to do, I hope I may have part in it, for the honour of the folk of the Lonely Mountain.' To this was added later: '"And I for the folk of the Wood," said Legolas.' Then follows:

His [> Their] wish was granted. Two days later the army of the West that was to march forth was all assembled on the Pelennor. The host of orcs and easterlings had turned back out of Anórien and harried and scattered by the Rohirrim had fled with little fight towards Cair Andros ...

This is the beginning of 'The Black Gate Opens' in RK, but with a major difference from the subsequent story: for here Pippin as well as Merry was left behind.

... To their bitter grief the hobbits were not in that riding.

'Merry is not fit for such a journey yet,' said Aragorn, 'even if he could ride a swift steed. And you Peregrin will lighten his grief if you stay with him. So far you have kept even with one another as well as your fortunes allowed – and indeed if you did no more to the end of your days you have earned honour, and justified the wisdom of Elrond.[38] And indeed we are all in like peril. For though it may be our part to find a bitter end before the gate of Mordor, if we do so, then you will have your chance or necessity also of a last stand either here or wherever the black tide overtakes you. Farewell!'

And so despondently Merry and Pippin stood before the ruined gates of Minas Tirith with young Bergil and saw the great army mustered. Bergil was downcast and grieved at heart, for his father was commanded to march and lead a company of the men of Imrahil. For he having broken his oaths could no longer remain in the guard of the Citadel, until his case was judged.[39]

The trumpets rang and the host began to move. [First rode Aragorn and Gandalf and the sons of Elrond with the banner and the knights of Dol Amroth. Then came Éomer with the [?chosen] Riders, and afterwards came those of his men that were on foot, and men of Lebennin, and last the great companies of Minas Tirith led by Imrahil.][40] And long after it had passed away out of sight down the great road to the Causeway the three stood there, until the last glint of the morning sun on spear and helm twinkled and was lost.

At this point my father decided that Pippin did in fact go with the host to the Black Gate, and he began anew at the words 'His [> Their] wish was granted' following the end of 'The Tale of Gimli and Legolas', continuing as before with 'Two days later the army of the West that was to march forth was all assembled on the Pelennor.' The text then continued both in initial draft and in a fair copy to the end of the story afterwards called 'The Black Gate Opens', with continuous pagination all the way through from the meeting of Gimli and Legolas with Imrahil before they went to the Houses of Healing. It is thus clear that the whole of the last part of Book V was in a completed (though not final) and coherent form before any structural reorganisation of the narrative took place. The structure was:

Gimli and Legolas meet Imrahil and go to the Houses of Healing.
The Last Debate.
The Tale of Gimli and Legolas in the garden of the Houses of Healing.
The journey to the Morannon and the Parley.

The next stage was the decision to reorganise the narrative so that 'Gimli's Tale' should stand independently – and therefore precede the Debate. To this end my father wrote a tentative conclusion for 'The Tale of Gimli and Legolas':

And so ended the tale of Legolas and Gimli concerning the ride of Aragorn by the Paths of the Dead, which long was recalled and sung in Gondor in after days, and it was said that never again were the Shadow-men seen by mortal men on mountain or in vale, [and the road from Dunharrow was free to all who were willing to take that way. Yet few did so, for the memory of fear abode there still; and none ever dared to open Baldor's door. *Struck out immediately:* A tomb they made for him in that dark place and so built it that none could come at that door.]

The passage that I have bracketed was replaced, probably at once, by the following:

but the stone of Erech stood ever alone, and on that hill no bird would alight nor beast feed; and the memory of fear still abode in the dark ways from Dunharrow, and few were willing to take that road; and none ever dared to open Baldor's door.

Concomitantly with this the words 'Their wish was granted' (following the end of 'The Tale of Gimli and Legolas' and beginning the story of the march from Minas Tirith) were circled, with a direction to omit them if this 'end-piece' to the 'Tale' were added to it; and a note was scribbled on the manuscript beside the opening of the debate (p. 403): 'It might be better to take out the debate (shorten it) and put it at the beginning of the Parley chapter.' Thus the decision was taken to divide the chapter as it stood (entitled 'The Parley at the Black Gate', p. 399) into two: the first to be called 'The Paths of the Dead' and consisting solely of the tale told to Merry and Pippin in the garden of the Houses of Healing, the second to be called 'Parley at the Gate' and beginning with the debate in Aragorn's tent.

Relatively little adjustment of the existing material was needed to achieve this. From the point in the narrative where Gimli and Legolas found Merry and Pippin ('and the meeting of those friends was a merry one') my father simply dropped the transition to the debate (see p. 403) and continued with the conversation in the garden of the Houses of Healing (see p. 405 and RK p. 149): 'For a while they walked and talked, rejoicing for a brief space in peace and rest under the fair morning high up in the windy circles of the City.' The conversation leading into the 'Tale' was somewhat changed. In contrast to the earlier version Merry is no longer represented as being ignorant (as he could not have been) of Aragorn's passage under the mountains (see p. 405 and note 17). After Pippin's words 'Come, Legolas! You and Gimli have mentioned your strange journey with Trotter about a dozen times already this morning. But you haven't mentioned anything about it' this dialogue follows:

'I know some of the story and I guess some more,' said Merry. 'For I hear that you came in ships from the South. So I know that somehow you must have got through, though in Dunharrow all the people were afraid, and Éowyn I thought had been weeping. Come now! The sun is shining and we can bear it. Tell us about the Paths of the Dead!'

'The sun may shine,' said Gimli, 'still there are memories of that road that I do not wish to recall. Had I known what was before me I think that not for any friendship would I have taken those paths.'

'For my part,' said Legolas, 'I do not fear the Dead; but I hate the darkness under earth far from hope of the sky. It was a dreadful journey!'

'The Dead?' said Pippin. 'The Paths of the Dead? I have never heard of them before. Won't you tell us some more?'

'It is the name of a road that goes through the mountains,'

said Merry. 'I saw the Gate, as they call it, from a distance when I was in Dunharrow ...'

Merry then continues as he does in the earlier version, and is followed by Legolas and Gimli describing the departure and Éowyn's distress (cf. p. 406 and note 19):

'... I think the men of the Mark believe that inside there dwell the shadows of Dead Men, out of a past long before they came to that land.'

'So they told us,' said Legolas. 'And that lady who lies now below in the Houses, Éowyn, she begged Aragorn not to go in; but he could not be turned from it. He was in haste, and in a stern mood.'

'And at the last when she saw that he would go,' said Gimli, 'then she begged to come with us! Indeed she knelt before him. Yet she is a proud lady. I wondered much what it all might mean, and I was grieved; for she was young and much troubled. But he raised her up and kissed her hand and without more words we departed. Yet I saw that he, too, was greatly grieved.'

The earlier version was for the rest of its length very largely repeated: that is to say, the original pages were retained with their pagination altered and some passages rewritten. Legolas now plays a larger part in the narration, describing the ride to Erech (see pp. 409–10), at which point Gimli re-enters: '"Yes, indeed, and never shall I forget!" said Gimli, taking up the tale again. "For the terror of the Dead lay on the hill and all the land about it"'; he continues much as in RK pp. 62–3, but he does not say that Isildur set up the Stone of Erech at his landing ('It looked as if it had fallen from the sky, but it was brought out of the West, we were told'), and he still repeats the story (p. 411) that when the Shadow-men gathered about the Stone 'sometimes a cry would be heard in our speech:[41] "We have come!"' The tower and ring-wall on the Hill of Erech, and the *palantír*, have now disappeared.

For the second of the new chapters my father wrote a new opening, beginning (cf. p. 403) 'In the meanwhile Imrahil sent for Éomer and went down with him, and they came to the tents of Aragorn...' To this he added the existing pages of the manuscript recounting the course of the debate, which ended at 'And he drew forth Branding and held it up glittering in the sun' (p. 405), and then the manuscript of the story of the journey to the Morannon and the Parley. On the new opening he pencilled the title 'Parley at the Gate' and the chapter number 'LI', so that 'The Paths of the Dead' was 'L' (see note 10). The structure was now (see p. 416):

The Paths of the Dead Gimli and Legolas go to the Houses of Healing, and Merry and Pippin hear the tale of the journey of the Grey Company from Dunharrow to the Battle of the Pelennor Fields.

Parley at the Gate 'The Last Debate', ending with Aragorn's drawing the sword of Elendil; the journey to the Morannon, and the parley with the Lieutenant of Barad-dûr.

It was probably now that my father made a typescript of the two chapters, the text diverging very little from the manuscript material as now reorganised;[42] but he treated them as subdivisions of a single chapter, without an overall title, and with the puzzling number 'XLIX' (see note 10): (i) 'The Paths of the Dead' and (ii) 'Parley at the Black Gate'.

The subsequent history of the chapter is textually exceedingly complicated, but I shall treat it briefly. The first typescript was very heavily revised, and two large sections of it were written out anew in a separate manuscript. The effect of all this was to bring the narrative closer in very many points to the texts in RK, and indeed much of the earlier part now required little more than grammatical alteration to bring Gimli's story to the direct author's narrative in 'The Passing of the Grey Company.'[43]

In the ride from Erech over Tarlang's Neck into Lamedon the deserted town of Calembel upon Ciril (so spelt, with C) appears,[44] and the blood-red sunset behind Pinnath Gelin (RK p. 63): the final chronology had now entered (see the Note at the end of this chapter). Angbor of Lamedon is now named, but the new text differs here from that of RK (p. 151):

'Then Aragorn said to Angbor their captain who alone stayed to meet him: "Behold! I am not the King of the Dead, but the Heir of Isildur, and I live yet for a while. Follow me, if you wish to see the end of this darkness and the downfall of Mordor."

'And Angbor answered: "I will gather all men that I may, and follow after you swiftly." His was a stout heart indeed, and I grieve that he fell beside me, as we clove our way from the Harlond.

In RK (p. 153) Angbor of Lamedon came to Pelargir but did not go up Anduin in the black fleet; he is last referred to by Aragorn in the debate in his tent (p. 157) as marching at the head of four thousand men from Pelargir through Lossarnach and expected soon to arrive at Minas Tirith.

To Legolas' words about the Sea (p. 414) he now adds his second reference to the gulls (RK p. 151): 'Alas! for the wailing of the gulls. Did not the Lady tell me to beware of them? For they cannot be forgotten.' He is thinking of Galadriel's message to him, spoken by Gandalf in Fangorn (TT p. 106):

Legolas Greenleaf long under tree
In joy thou hast lived. Beware of the Sea!
If thou hearest the cry of the gull on the shore,
Thy heart shall then rest in the forest no more.

For Galadriel's original message to Legolas, and its application, see p. 22.

There is an interesting passage immediately following in this revised version. In the version given on p. 413 there was fighting on the shores, for 'there were captains sent by Mordor, and orc-chieftains, and they were not so easily dismayed, and they endeavoured to hold their men to a defence. And indeed the Haradrim are a grim folk, and not easily daunted by shade or blade.' This was rejected, following a note that there was in fact no fighting at Pelargir: '*But fear was the only weapon that we needed*, for the grey host passed on to every ship ... and all the men that were in them fled, or leaped overboard' (p. 414). My father now went back on this decision.

'I soon forgot them [the gulls] for my part,' said Gimli. 'For at last we came to a battle. The Haradrim were driven now to despair, and could fly no longer. There at Pelargir lay the fleets of Umbar, fifty great ships and many smaller vessels beyond count. Some few of our enemies reached their ships and put off, seeking either to escape down the River or to reach the far shores; and some they set fire to. But we came too swiftly upon them for many to slip from us so. We were joined by some of the hardier folk of Lebennin and the Ethir, but we were not many when the corsairs turned to bay; and seeing our weakness their hearts revived and they assailed us in their turn. There was stern work there in the twilight by the grey waters, for the Shadow Host halted and wavered, unwilling at the last, as it seemed, to make war on Sauron. Then Aragorn let blow a horn and cried aloud, saying that if they broke their oath a second time

Here my father stopped and rewrote the passage to a form not essentially different from that in RK, where the Shadow Host is still said to have 'hung back at the last', but with no explicit suggestion that they were reluctant to fulfil the oath, and where for the living there was no need for 'stern work in the twilight by the grey waters'.

At this time my father also wrote an experimental version 'with entrance to the Door told at end of Chapter II of Book V' – that is, at the end of 'Many Roads Lead Eastward'. This begins: 'But Aragorn and his company rode across the high mountain-field upon which was set the refuge of the Rohirrim; and the paths were laid between rows of standing stones hoar with age uncounted. The light was still grey, for the sun had not yet climbed over the black ridges of the Haunted Mountain ...' It must be presumed that the story of the coming of the Grey Company to Dunharrow, and Aragorn's parting from Eowyn, had now been added to 'Many Roads Lead Eastward' (see note 19). The text ends thus: '... a groping blindness overcame him, even Gimli Glóin's son the Dwarf, who had walked in many deep places under earth. So the Grey Company dared the forbidden door, and vanished from the land of living men.'

Although this shows that my father was pondering the possibility of removing some part of the story told in the Houses of Healing and rewriting it as direct narrative in its chronological place, the following typescript is a text of the whole 'Tale of Gimli and Legolas' incorporating all revision to that time, and ending with the words 'and none ever dared to move Baldor's bones' (cf. p. 416).

There followed a rough manuscript in which the first part of the 'Tale' was written out as direct narrative, to stand in its chronological place in the earlier chapter, thus greatly shortening the material of the end of Book V. A further typescript has the structure of 'The Last Debate' in RK, with the story of the passage of the Paths of the Dead removed and only mentioned as having been told, though here it was still Gimli who told it:

> 'Alas! I had heart only for myself,' said Gimli, 'and I do not wish to recall that journey.' He fell silent; but Pippin and Merry were so eager for news that at last he yielded and told them in halting words of the dreadful passage of the mountains that led to the black Stone of Erech. But when he came to the Day without Dawn he ceased. 'I am weary recalling that weariness, and the horror of the Dark,' he said.
>
> 'Then I will say on,' said Legolas.[45]

The structure of the narrative in RK had been at last achieved, with the debate in the tent of Aragorn following in the same chapter the end of the story told to Merry and Pippin in the Houses of Healing.[46] I see no way to determine at what stage all this later work was done.

NOTES

1 On Haramon see p. 359 and note 3. The reading 'the Hills of Haramon' (plural) in the outline 'The Story Foreseen from Forannest' is certain, in contrast to the 'great hill' referred to in the present text.

2 For Bealdor (Baldor) son of Brego see pp. 315–16, and on the spelling of the name p. 321 note 11.

3 A pencilled note in the margin reads: '25 miles. Dunharrow > Erech 55.' Presumably '25 miles' refers to the distance from the issue of the Paths of the Dead to the Stone of Erech. On the distance from Dunharrow to Erech see pp. 296–7 note 2.

4 By '(say Linhir?)' I suppose that my father meant that since the road to Pelargir crossed the Lameduin (later Gilrain) at Linhir, 'Linhir' would do as well as 'Fords of Lameduin'. Linhir appears also in 'The Story Foreseen from Forannest' (p. 361); it is marked on the Second Map (see p. 437) at some distance above the head of the estuary of Lameduin, the direct distance from here to Erech on this map being 36 mm. or 180 miles.

5 From Linhir to Pelargir direct is 2 cm. or 100 miles on the Second Map.

6 The rejected portion of the outline has here: 'The Haradwaith try to fly. Some take ship back again down Anduin. But Aragorn overtakes them and captures most of the ships. Some are set fire to, but several manned by slaves and captives are captured.' (Then follows the passage about the Gondorian captives.) 'Aragorn embarks with men of South Gondor; the Shadow Host disperses, pursuing the Haradwaith about the vales.'

7 Cf. 'The Battle of the Pelennor Fields', p. 370: 'south away the river went in a knee about the out-thrust of the hills of Emyn Arnen in lower Ithilien, and Anduin bent then in upon the Pelennor so that its outwall was there built upon the brink, and that at the nearest was no more than [five >] four miles from the Gates.' In 'The Story Foreseen from Forannest' (p. 363 note 3) the Pelennor Wall is at this point ten miles away from the City.

8 On the Second Map it is 125 miles (the figure given in the text) up river from Pelargir to the angle of the 'knee' in Anduin (see note 7), and thus the straight stretch of ten miles 'just before that point', visible from Minas Tirith, is the 'leg' below the 'knee'. In the further continuation of the passage from 'The Battle of the Pelennor Fields' cited in note 7 (see p. 370) the length of 'the reach of Arnen' is given as 'three leagues'; but on the Second Map, on which both these passages were based, it is substantially longer. In RK (p. 122) 'Anduin, from the bend at the Harlond, so flowed that from the City men could look down it lengthwise for some leagues.'

9 Cf. 'The Story Foreseen from Forannest' (p. 359): 'Then as final despair comes on, and Rohirrim give back, [west >] south wind rolls back cloud, and noon-sun gleams through. Aragorn unfurls his great standard from ship-top. The crown and stars of Sun and Moon shine out.'

10 The opening page of the manuscript bears the chapter-numbers 'XLI', 'L', 'L(b)', and 'XLIX', all of which were struck out except the last. 'XLI' is an obvious slip (for 'LI'?), since the chapter could

not possibly bear this number; but it is hard to see how it could be 'XLIX' either (see p. 386 and note 7).

11 This draft for the debate follows immediately on an abandoned sentence of 'The Houses of Healing', thus:

Gandalf and Pippin then came to Merry's room and there saw Aragorn stand

'My lords,' said Gandalf. ...

The text that follows is written in ink over pencilled drafting for 'The Houses of Healing'.

12 This sentence is bracketed in the original, as also is that a little further on ('a tyrant brooking no freedom ...').

13 *Imladrist:* cf. p. 139 note 14 and p. 165 note 5.

14 My father struck out 'Gandalf' immediately. He then wrote 'Warden of the Keys' but put dots for the name, writing in 'Húrin' before he had gone much further. It would seem therefore that this was where the name arose, but since 'Húrin' appears in the first manuscript of 'The Battle of the Pelennor Fields' (p. 369) it seems clear that my father had merely forgotten momentarily here what name he had chosen for him.

15 Gandalf cannot have said this. Either *not* must be removed or *cannot* > *can*.

16 In a draft for this passage Imrahil called Dol Amroth *Castle Amroth*; this was repeated in a following draft, where it was changed to *Barad Amroth* (and finally *Barad* > *Dol*).

17 Merry of course knew that Aragorn did go to Dunharrow (cf. RK pp. 69–70; the final text of 'The Muster of Rohan' was now largely in being, p. 319). See p. 417.

18 This passage contrasts greatly with RK, where it is Gimli who will not speak of the Paths of the Dead, and Legolas who says 'I felt not the horror, and I feared not the shadows of Men, powerless and frail as I deemed them.' See p. 417.

19 I think that the parting of Aragorn and Éowyn would not have been recounted so fully by Legolas and Gimli here if the story of the coming of the Grey Company to Dunharrow already existed in the earlier chapter (RK pp. 56–9); see p. 308.

20 *our horses that the Rohirrim gave us:* 'horses', because Aragorn's horse was still Hasufel (pp. 301, 305–6); when Roheryn, his own horse brought from the North by the Rangers, was introduced, it was only Arod, the horse bearing Legolas and Gimli, that was of Rohan, and he alone is mentioned in the equivalent passage in RK ('The Passing of the Grey Company', p. 60).

21 In the early drafts for 'The King of the Golden Hall' the mounds of the kings at Edoras were first described as 'white with nodding flowers like tiny snowdrops', the flowers being subsequently *nifredil* (VII.442–3). In RK ('The Passing of the Grey Company', p. 61) Aragorn calls the flowers *simbelmynë*, but cf. 'The King of

the Golden Hall' (TT p. 111), where Gandalf says: 'Evermind they are called, *simbelmynë* in this land of Men, for they blossom in all the seasons of the year, and grow where dead men rest.'

22 In the first manuscript of 'The King of the Golden Hall' Legolas said of the barrows at Edoras: 'Seven mounds I see, and seven long lives of men it is, since the golden hall was built' (see VII.442 and 449 note 4). This was changed on that manuscript to the reading of TT (p.111): '"Seven mounds upon the left, and nine upon the right," said Aragorn. "Many long lives of men it is since the golden hall was built."'

23 If this is so, it was of course at this time that the first manuscript of 'The King of the Golden Hall' was emended to say that there were 'seven mounds upon the left, and nine upon the right' (see note 22).

24 The dates of the kings before the last three were so much changed and confused by overwriting that I can form no clear idea of what my father intended: it is at least plain, however, that they correspond in their pattern to those in LR – as adjusted for the Shire Reckoning.

25 *Barad Amroth*: see note 16. Later *Barad* was changed to *Dol.*

26 As first written, but immediately rejected, the text continued from this point: '... was brought from Númenor, and marks still the place where Isildur met the last king of the Dark Men of the Mountains, when he established the bounds of Gondor. And there he swore an oath, for Isildur and Elendil and his sons [*sic*] had the gift of tongues as many of the Númenóreans, and the tongues of men ..... [?of the wild] were known to him, for'

27 The ring-wall and tower on the Hill of Erech, in which was kept the *palantír*, are referred to in the outline given on p. 397; it is told there that Aragorn actually found the *palantír* of Erech, in a vault of the tower.

28 It is strange that it should be Elrohir who unfurled the banner (and bore it at the Hornburg), for from the first mention of the banner (p. 302) it was as in RK Halbarad the Ranger who bore it (and it was covered in a black cloth). — In RK (p. 63) no device could be seen on it in the darkness.

29 On this and subsequent references to the days of the journey see the Note on Chronology at the end of these Notes.

30 Tarlang's Neck is seen on the Second Map, though it is not named. For the geography of these regions see pp. 433 ff.

31 Sixty leagues in direct line from Erech to Linhir, and a hundred miles from Linhir to Pelargir, agrees with RK (p. 150): 'ninety leagues and three' from Erech to Pelargir.

32 *we set out again:* i.e. from Erech. — It is approximately here that the part of Gimli's story that was transferred to 'The Passing of the Grey Company' ends, and the part that remained actually

reported in 'The Last Debate' begins; there is some overlap in RK (pp. 63, 151).

33 At this point there follows in the initial draft:

'... But when we came over Tarlang's Neck Elladan and two Rangers rode ahead and spoke to any that they could find willing to stay and listen to them, and told them that a great help was coming to them against the Shipfoes and the Southrons, and that it was not the King of the Dead but the heir of the Kings of Gondor that had returned. A few listened and believed, and at the crossings of Kiril we found food and fodder set for our need though no man had dared to stay beside it, nor any fresh horses for which we hoped.

34 The square brackets are in the original. The initial draft text has here:

'"... but they wield living swords." And some cried [*struck out:* though they knew not what it meant]: "The Lord of the Rings has arisen".'

In the margin of this page in the draft text my father subsequently wrote the following remarkable passage:

'Indeed all the folk of Lebennin call Aragorn that.'

'I wonder why?' said Merry. 'I suppose it is some device to draw the eyes of Mordor that way, to Aragorn, and keep them from Frodo'; and he looked east and shuddered. 'Do you think all his great labour and deeds will be in vain and too late in the end?' he said.

'I know not,' said Gimli. 'But one thing I know, and that is, not for any device of policy would Aragorn set abroad a false tale. Then either it is true and he has a ring, or it is a false tale invented by someone else. But Elrohir and Elladan have called him by that name. So it must be true. But what it means we do not know.'

There is nothing on this page of the draft, or indeed anywhere in the manuscript, that this can refer to but the cry 'The Lord of the Rings has arisen'. I have found only one scrap of writing that seems to bear on this. Under the text in ink of a piece of rough drafting (that referred to in note 39) for the beginning of the story of the march from Minas Tirith are a few furiously pencilled lines, parts of which can be read:

Galadriel must give her ring to Aragorn (..... to wed Finduilas?). Hence his sudden access of power .... [?that won't work. It will leave] Lórien defenceless also Lord of the Ring will be too ...

This raises many more questions than it answers; but it cannot be unconnected with the strange suggestion that in Lebennin Aragorn was called 'The Lord of the Ring(s)'. I do not know whether it is significant that in the first draft the *s* of *Rings* was not written consecutively with *Ring*, but was added to the word – maybe immediately. This however only raises the question why, if Aragorn was called 'The Lord of the Ring' because it was thought that he possessed a Ring, did my father change it to 'The Lord of the Rings'? The only and rather desperate suggestion I can make is that he wished to mark the confusion of mind on the part of the people who uttered this cry (cf. 'though they knew not what it meant' in the draft text).

35 The initial draft has here: 'and all of the enemies that were not slain or drowned were flying away over the Poros into Lothland desert.' This name is not perfectly clear, but I take it as certain in view of the occurrence of Lothlann on the First Map (VII.309, 313); the form *Lothland* is found in the *Quenta Silmarillion* (V.264, 283). On the Second Map (p. 435) the region south of Mordor is named, but in pencil now so faint that it is hard to be sure of the name: the likeliest interpretation is 'Desert of Lostladen' (cf. the *Etymologies*, V.370, stem LUS).

36 Legolas says in this second version that the day they came to Pelargir was 'the fifth of our journey', whereas in the previous version (p. 413) 'it was the fourth since we left Dunharrow'; but I think that both expressions mean the same (see the Note on Chronology below).

37 The original primary draft reaches this point:

> 'And when all was won Aragorn let sound a host of trumpets from the ship that he took for himself, and behold the Shadow host drew near to the shore, and all others fled away. But Aragorn set a line of torches along the shore and these they would not pass, and he spoke to the Dead Men: "Now I will count the oath fulfilled," he said, "when every stranger of Harad or of Umbar is hunted out of this land west of Anduin. When that is done go back and trouble never the valleys again – but go and be at rest."

With this cf. the rejected portion of the outline given at the beginning of this chapter (note 6 above): 'The Shadow Host disperses, *pursuing the Haradwaith about the vales*.'

38 *and justified the wisdom of Elrond:* see p. 387.

39 In a rough draft for this passage Aragorn speaks to Berithil: 'It is not yet my part to judge you, Master Berithil. If I return I will do so with justice. But for this present you shall leave the guard in the Citadel and go out to war.'

40 The square brackets are in the original.

41 *in our speech* was corrected to *in the old speech of Númenor*, then changed back to *in our speech*.

42 Legolas now plays no part in the narration until Pelargir is reached.

43 The story in this version is expressly to be Gimli's: at the

beginning, in response to Pippin's 'Won't you tell us some more?' he says: 'Well, if you must hear the tale, I will tell it briefly.' As in the unrevised typescript (note 42) Legolas says nothing until he breaks in on Gimli at his mention of the Great River ('I knew it long ere we reached it', p. 414); but by an alteration to this revised version he breaks silence at Gimli's words '[we] went as swiftly as our stouthearted horses could endure over the plains of Lebennin':

> 'Lebennin!' cried Legolas. All the while he had kept silence, gazing away southward, while Gimli spoke; but now he began to sing: *Silver flow the streams from Celos to Erui* ...

The text of his song is at once in the final form. In RK it is Legolas who tells the whole story up to this point, and Gimli who here takes it up.

44 The place where Kiril was crossed was named on the Second Map *Caerost on Kiril* (p. 437).

45 On the back of the last page of this typescript is the following remarkable passage, on which I can cast no light. It is written in a fine ornate script, together with other odds and ends of phrases in the same script, characteristic of my father's habit of 'doodling' in this way (cf. VII.379):

> Then spoke Elessar: Many Guthrond would hold that your insolence merited rather punishment than answer from your king; but since you have in open malice uttered lies in the hearing of many, I will first lay bare their falsehood, so that all here may know you for what you are, and have ever been. Afterwards maybe a chance shall be given you to repent and turn from your old evil.

46 The title that my father first chose for the chapter when the final structure had been reached was 'Tidings and Counsel': the 'tidings' of Gimli and Legolas, and the 'counsel' of Gandalf at the debate of the lords.

Note on the Chronology

In the outline 'The march of Aragorn and the defeat of the Haradrim' (pp. 397–9) the dates of Aragorn's journey are as follows:

March

8	(morning)	Enters the Paths of the Dead
	(midnight)	Comes to Erech
9	(early morning)	Leaves Erech under the Darkness from Mordor
10	(evening)	Reaches Linhir
11	(morning)	Crosses River Lameduin into Lebennin
12	(early morning)	Reaches Pelargir

13	(early morning)	Sets out up river from Pelargir
14	(early morning)	100 miles up river
15	(early morning)	Wind rises and sails hoisted on the ships; c. 9 a.m. fleet is seen from Minas Tirith

The latter part of this chronology seems obviously unsatisfactory, in that the fleet is 100 miles up Anduin in the early morning of March 14, and yet nothing is said of any further journeying on the 14th: the last stretch is accomplished under sail on the morning of the 15th. Against this date (p. 399) my father wrote '14'; and in the companion outline 'The Story Foreseen from Forannest' (p. 360) the charge of the Rohirrim on the 15th was likewise changed to the 14th – which was the date in 'The Siege of Gondor', p. 342.

With the date of Aragorn's entering the Paths of the Dead cf. pp. 309 and 311, notes 9 and 18 (February 6 = March 8). The Dawnless Day is still March 9 (cf. p. 342).

In the manuscript of 'The Tale of Gimli and Legolas' this chronology is preserved – with March 14 as the date of the Battle of the Pelennor Fields. Thus Gimli tells that the Company came to Erech 'just ere the midnight hour – and black it was wellnigh as in the caverns, for though we did not know it yet the darkness of Mordor was creeping over us' (p. 410), and again (p. 412): 'The next morning day did not dawn' (in the margin of the manuscript the figure 9 is written here). 'At nightfall of the second day from Erech' they came to Linhir (and here 10 is written in the margin). They 'rose ere night had passed' (i.e. before dawn on March 11) and rode across Lebennin, 'all that day and through the next night'; and Gimli says that 'it was day, I guessed, by the hidden sun – the fourth since we left Dunharrow' (p. 413) when they reached the shores of Anduin at Pelargir, i.e. the morning of March 12. 'Before the fifth day was over we had taken well nigh all the fleet', which as will be seen in a moment means 'the fifth day of the journey', i.e. March 12.

The first version of the events at Pelargir ends here; in the second version Legolas says (note 36) that the day they reached Pelargir was 'the fifth of our journey' (March 12), that they rested that night 'while others laboured' – but also that the fleet set out up Anduin 'on the fifth morning, that is the day before yesterday' (March 13). This shows clearly that Legolas was distinguishing between 'the fifth day of our journey' (March 12) and 'the fifth morning since we left Dunharrow' (March 13) – so also in RK (p. 153) 'the sixth [morning] since we rode from Dunharrow' is the seventh day of the whole journey. Since it was now the day after the Battle of the Pelennor Fields, and the fleet left Pelargir on 'the day before yesterday', the battle took place on March 14.

The difference of this chronology from that of LR is therefore thus:

The journey of Aragorn

Day	March	*The present chronology*	*Chronology of LR*
1	8	Reaches Erech at midnight	The same
2	9	The Dawnless Day	
3	10	Reaches Linhir	The Dawnless Day
4	11		Reaches Linhir
5	12	Reaches Pelargir	
6	13	Sets out from Pelargir	Reaches Pelargir
7	14	Battle of the Pelennor Fields	Sets out from Pelargir
8	15		Battle of the Pelennor Fields

In the chronology of the manuscript text Aragorn's journey from Dunharrow to Pelargir took four days and nights, reaching the Anduin on the fifth day, and setting out up river on the morning of the sixth day. In LR Aragorn took three days, not two, from Erech to Linhir, and so five days and nights to Pelargir. Thus in the manuscript (p. 411) Gimli says that from Erech 'then followed the weariest journey that I have ever known ... three days and nights and on into another day', whereas when in RK (p. 150) Legolas speaks of the great ride from Erech to Pelargir he says: 'Four days and nights, and on into a fifth, we rode from the Black Stone'.

Lastly, whereas in the manuscript text the Darkness out of Mordor came over the sky during the night of March 8, and 'the next morning day did not dawn', in RK (p. 151) 'one day of light we rode, and then came the day without dawn' (and in the earlier passage at the end of 'The Passing of the Grey Company', RK p. 63, in the evening of the day on which they left Erech at dawn 'the sun went down like blood behind Pinnath Gelin away in the West behind them', and 'the next day there came no dawn').

XIII
THE BLACK GATE OPENS

As I have explained in the last chapter (p. 416), the story of the journey to the Morannon, the parley with the Lieutenant of Barad-dûr, and the attack on the Host of the West in the slag-hills before the Gate, was written before my father made any move to break up and reorganize the presentation of the narrative in the single very long chapter, which would ultimately be distributed between 'The Passing of the Grey Company', 'The Last Debate', and 'The Black Gate Opens'.

For the conclusion of Book V he had in fact already written some time before a very full outline ('The Story Foreseen from Forannest', pp. 360–2), and this, when he came to write the narrative, he followed remarkably closely. Already present in the outline were the coming of the vanguard to Minas Morghul and the burning of the lands about, the silence that followed the summons to Sauron to come forth, the embassy from the Dark Tower already prepared, the display of Frodo's mithril coat, the blackmailing terms for the surrender of Frodo, Gandalf's refusal to treat and taking of the mithril coat, and the hosts lying ready in ambush. The chief differences from the final story were the coming of the Ents (with Elves of Lórien) to the Morannon (with an express declaration by the ambassador of Sauron that the Ents shall help to rebuild Isengard), uncertainty whether Merry and Pippin were present, and the person of the ambassador: doubtfully identified as the Wizard King (implying a different view of the outcome of his encounter with Éowyn and Merry in the Battle of the Pelennor Fields), but certainly a Nazgûl ('flinging off his garments he vanishes').

For the narrative there is both initial draft and fair copy, which doubtless belong to the same time, since the first two pages are common to both: from the point where the first text became quicker and rougher my father replaced it; but in the first draft the story as it stands in RK was already present in almost every point. Aragorn's dismissal of the faint-hearted (as it is described in *The Tale of Years*) was however (in both texts) Gandalf's, and the cause of their faint-heartedness more immediate (cf. RK p. 162):

... and they could descry the marshes and the desert that stretched north and west to the Emyn Muil. And now the Nazgûl swept down over them unceasingly, and often daring within bowshot of the earth they would plunge shrieking down, and their fell voices made even the boldest blench. Some there were who were so unmanned that they could neither walk nor ride further north.

This survived into the fair copy, where it was replaced by the text of RK (p. 162), in which the Nazgûl did not closely approach the Host of the West until the final attack on the Slag-hills. In the draft text it is said that 'some 500 left the host' and went off south-west towards Cair Andros.

No more is said in the draft of the history of the Lieutenant of Baraddûr,[1] the nameless Mouth of Sauron, than that 'It is told that he was a living man, who being captured as a youth became a servant of the Dark Tower, and because of his cunning grew high in the Lord's favour ...' In the fair copy this was repeated, but was changed subsequently to: 'But it is said that he was a renegade, son of a house of wise and noble men in Gondor, who becoming enamoured of evil knowledge entered the service of the Dark Tower, and because of his cunning [and the fertile cruelty of his mind] [and servility] he grew ever higher in the Lord's favour ...' (these phrases being thus bracketed in the original). In RK (p. 164) the Mouth of Sauron 'came of the race of those that are named the Black Númenóreans'.[2]

NOTES

1 First written 'the Lieutenant of Morgul', but this may very probably have been no more than a slip.

2 A few other minor points may be mentioned together. The Morgul Pass (RK p. 161) is called 'the Pass of Kirith Ungol' in the fair copy, and the Pass of Cirith Gorgor (RK p. 162) is 'the Pass of Gorgoroth' in both texts, changed to 'the Pass of Kirith-Gorgor' in the fair copy. In the draft text Damrod of Henneth Annûn reappears again, with Mablung, as a leader of the scouts in Ithilien (RK p. 162); the host can see from their camp on the last night the red lights in the Towers of the Teeth; and in Gandalf's concluding words to the Mouth of Sauron (RK p. 167) he retains the words he used in the original outline (p. 362): 'Begone! But let fear eat your heart: for if you so much as set a thorn in the flesh of your prisoner you shall rue it through all ages.'

Note on the Chronology

In *The Tale of Years* in LR the following dates are given:

March 18 The Host of the West marches from Minas Tirith.
19 The Host comes to Morgul-vale.
23 The Host passes out of Ithilien. Aragorn dismisses the faint-hearted.

24 The Host camps in the Desolation of the Morannon.
25 The Host is surrounded on the Slag-hills.

In both manuscript texts the same indications of date are given, and in the same words, as in RK, except in one point. The Host here left Minas Tirith on 17 March (this date being written in the margin), and since this was two days after 'the Last Debate', which itself took place on the day after the battle, the date of the Battle of the Pelennor Fields was here the 14th of March, not the 15th (see p. 428). In the present versions, however, the difference of one day in the date of the departure from Minas Tirith is soon lost, for this reason: where in RK (p. 160) the first day's march ended five miles beyond Osgiliath, but 'the horsemen pressed on and ere evening they came to the Cross Roads' (i.e. 18 March), it is said here that '*Next day* the horsemen pressed on and ere evening they came to the Cross Roads' (i.e. 18 March); and it was again 'on the next day' that 'the main host came up' (with the date '19' in the margin). Thus where it is said in RK (p. 161) 'The day after, being the third day since they set out from Minas Tirith, the army began its northward march along the road', it is here 'the fourth day', with the date '20' written in the margin.

	The present version	*The Return of the King*
March 17	March begins, and ends at Osgiliath	
18	Horsemen reach the Cross Roads before evening	March begins, and ends near Osgiliath, but the horsemen go on and reach the Cross Roads before evening.
19	Main host comes to the Cross Roads	
20	The host begins northward march	

It may be noted lastly that where in RK (p. 163) on the night of 24 March 'the waxing moon was four nights old', here it was 'but three days from the full moon' on the night before the day on which the Ring was destroyed.

XIV
THE SECOND MAP

Whenever this map was first made, it was certainly my father's working map during the writing of Book V of *The Lord of the Rings*.[1] The first stage in its making was carried out in black ink, but black ink was also used later, and since it was not drawn and lettered at its first making with the meticulousness of the earlier stages of the First Map it is scarcely possible to isolate the layers of accretion by this means. Red ink was also used for a few alterations, and in the final stage of its useful life corrections and additions were very roughly made in blue ink (also in blue crayon and pencil).

The single sheet of paper on which it was made is now, after so much use many years ago, limp, torn, wrinkled, stained, and rubbed, and some of the later pencillings can scarcely be seen. It is ruled in squares of 2 cm. side (= 100 miles), the squares being lettered and numbered according to the First Map. In my redrawing I have divided it into a western and an eastern portion, with the central vertical line of squares (14) repeated.

The attempt to redraw it posed difficulties. In places there is such a cobweb of fine crisscrossing and competing lines (the 'contours' are very impressionistic) as to bewilder the eye, and the redrawing had to be done while holding a lens; even so, I have certainly not followed every last wiggle with fidelity. Here and there it is hard to make out what the markings actually are or to interpret what they represent. In the region south of the White Mountains the map is so extremely crowded, and there are so many alterations and additions of names made at different times, that (since a primary aim of the redrawing is clarification) I have found it best to omit a number of names and explain the changes in the account of the map that follows; and for the same reason I have shown the new course of Anduin at Minas Tirith but not the new sites of Barad-dûr and Mount Doom. The redrawing is therefore avowedly inconsistent in what is shown and what is not, but I think inevitably so; and the following notes are an essential part of its presentation.

I refer to the map of Rohan, Gondor and Mordor published in *The Return of the King* as 'the large LR map'.

The account of the Rivers of Gondor written on this map has been given in Vol. VII (p. 312) in a discussion of peculiarities in the original conception of the southern rivers, but since in reducing my redrawing

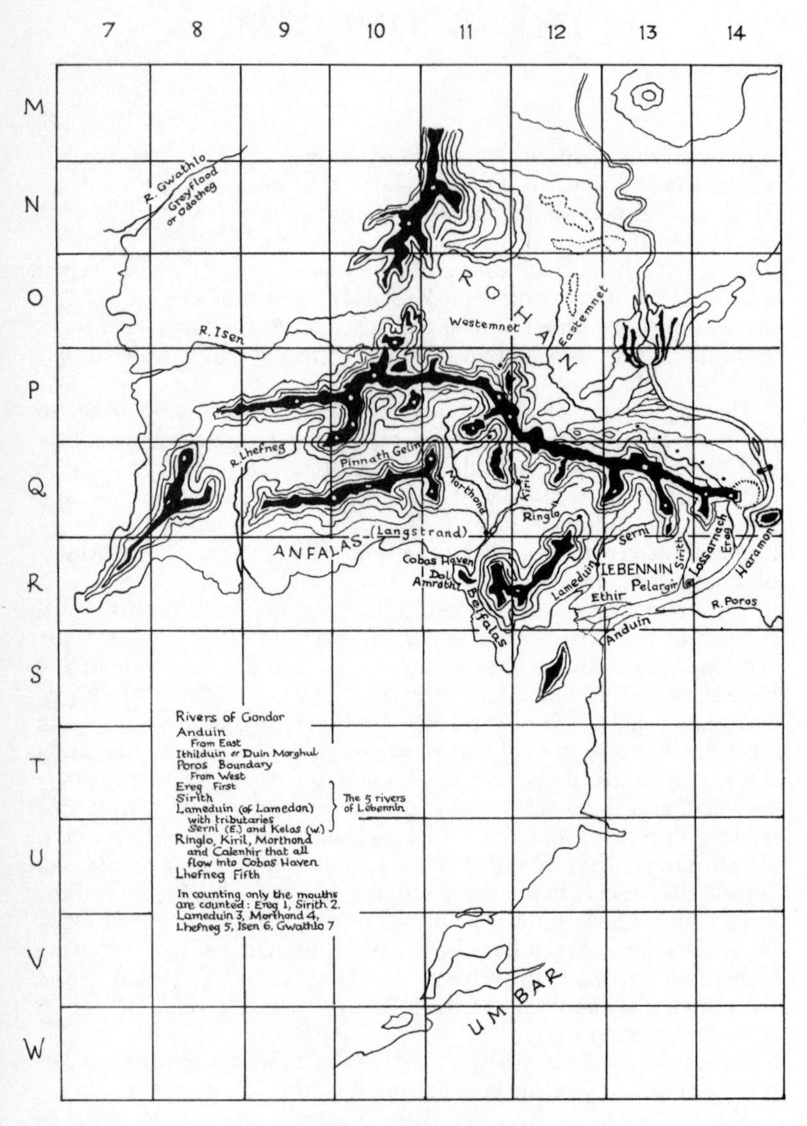
7
8
9
10
11
12
13
14
M
N
O
P
Q
R
S
T
U
V
W
R. Gwathlo
Greyflood
or Odotheg
ROHAN
Westemnet
Eastemnet
R. Isen
R. Lhefneg
Pinnath Gelin
Morthond
Kiril
Ringlo
ANFALAS-(Langstrand)
Cobas Haven
Dol Amroth
Belfalas
Lameduin
LEBENNIN
Serni
Sirith
Lossarnach
Ereg
Haramon
Pelargir
Ethir
Anduin
R. Poros
UMBAR
Rivers of Gondor
Anduin
From East
Ithilduin or Duin Morghul
Poros Boundary
From West
Ereg First
Sirith
Lameduin (of Lamedon)
with tributaries
Serni (E.) and Kelas (W.)
The 5 rivers of Lebennin
Ringlo, Kiril, Morthond
and Calenhir that all
flow into Cobas Haven
Lhefneg Fifth
In counting only the mouths
are counted: Ereg 1, Sirith 2,
Lameduin 3, Morthond 4,
Lhefneg 5, Isen 6, Gwathlo 7

The Second Map (West)

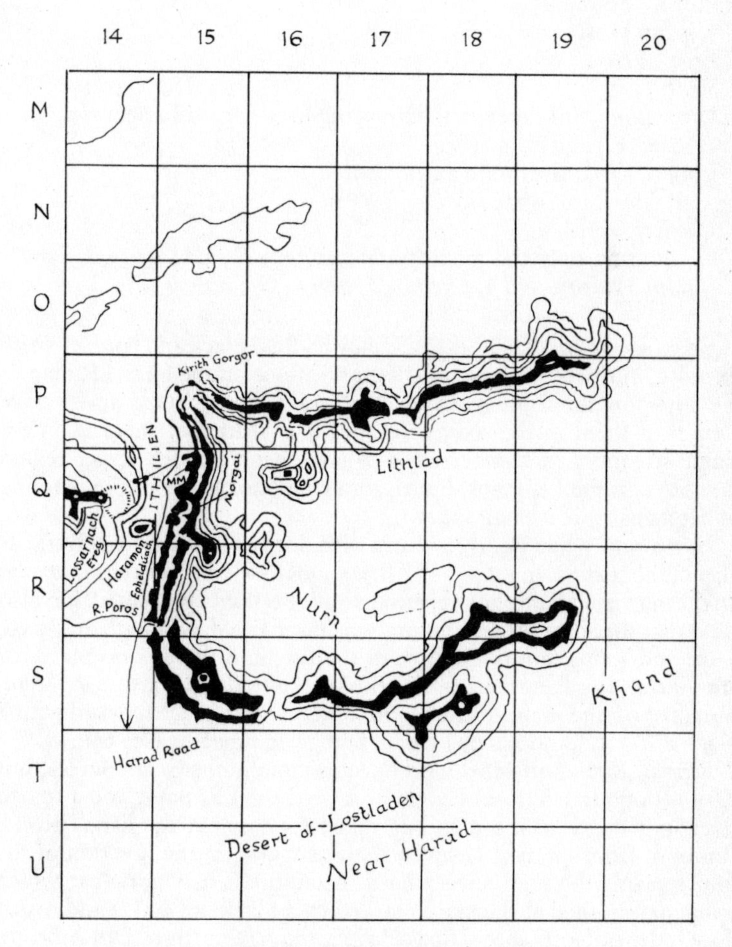

The Second Map (East)

to the size of the printed page the writing becomes extremely small I repeat it here:

Rivers of Gondor
Anduin
  From East
Ithilduin or *Duin Morghul*
Poros Boundary
  From West
Ereg First
Sirith
Lameduin (of Lamedon) with tributaries
  Serni (E.) and *Kelos* (W.)
  [The 5 rivers of Lebennin]
Ringlo, *Kiril*, *Morthond* and *Calenhir* that
  all flow into Cobas Haven
Lhefneg Fifth
In counting only the mouths are counted: *Ereg* 1, *Sirith* 2, *Lameduin* 3, *Morthond* 4, *Lhefneg* 5, *Isen* 6, *Gwathlo* 7

Ereg (later *Erui*) has now essentially its final place and course; *Sirith* likewise, but with no western tributary (*Kelos* on the large LR map) – the lines on the map in this valley are a dense maze and I have simplified them in the redrawing, but it is clear that there is only a single stream. *Lossarnach* seems to have been a much larger region than it is on the LR maps, but this may be due merely to the lettering of a long name in a small space.

Lameduin, while clearly written with final *-n* in the list of rivers (as also in the text given on pp. 397 ff.) is equally clearly written *Lamedui* on the map itself, and should perhaps have been so represented. It is also clear that there are three tributary streams marked, although only two, *Serni* and *Kelos*, are referred to in the list (and there is no place for another in 'the five rivers of Lebennin'); only the easternmost, *Serni*, is named on the map. All three join together at a place marked with a black dot (R 12), though this was at first given no name (see below).

Ringlo, *Kiril*, and *Morthond* have essentially the final courses; but Kiril is not a tributary of Ringlo as it is on the LR maps, and a fourth river, unnamed on the map but called *Calenhir* in the list of rivers, comes in from Pinnath Gelin to the westward. At the junction of the four streams the map is very hard to interpret: it is not clear which rivers have joined at the place marked by a black dot (Q 11) and which flow independently into Cobas Haven, the bay north of Dol Amroth. Beside the dot (in small lettering as if referring to the dot) was originally written *Lamedon*, which was struck through, and which I think was probably a simple error (in view of *Lameduin* many miles to the east). Above *Lamedon* was written *Linhir*, also struck through. The earliest reference to Linhir in the texts is found in the outline 'The

Story Foreseen from Forannest' (p. 361), where the Darkness out of Mordor is seen by the Ents as 'a great blackness ... extending in breadth from Rauros to Linhir': this could imply the earlier position, above Cobas Haven, but perhaps more probably the later, on Lameduin (Gilrain). The crossing of Ringlo was a later addition in red ink.

The name *Lamedon* was written a second time across R 13 (beneath *Serni* and above *Lebennin*), and this placing obviously consorts with the river-name *Lameduin*. In this position it was again struck out, *Lameduin* changed to *Gilrain*, and *Linhir* written against the dot on R 12 where the three streams join. *Lamedon* was later written in a third and final location (but see note 2) at the top of Q 12, across the upper waters of Kiril and Ringlo.

The emergence of the new geography can be traced in the texts. In the outline 'The march of Aragorn and defeat of the Haradrim' (see pp. 397–8 and note 4) occurs the following:

> Erech to Fords of Lameduin (say Linhir?) is 175 miles direct, about 200 by road. ... At Linhir on Lameduin men of Lebennin and Lamedon are defending passage of river against Haradwaith.

When this was written Lamedon still lay north of Ethir Anduin, a northward region of Lebennin, and 'the men of Lebennin and Lamedon' had withdrawn westwards to the line of the river, which they were attempting to hold. But already in the original drafts for the story of the ride of the Grey Company in 'The Last Debate' (see pp. 411–12) they passed 'over Tarlang's Neck into Lamedon', Lameduin has become Gilrain, and (as in RK, p. 151) it was the men of Lamedon who contested the passage of Gilrain against the Haradrim.[2]

The dot near the bottom right-hand corner of P 11 marks *Erech* (named on the original); this was an addition, as was the river flowing down from Erech to join the course of Morthond as originally marked on P–Q 11. To the dot on the river Kiril (Q 12), a later addition, is attached the pencilled name *Caerost on Kiril*; this was the forerunner of *Calembel*, where Kiril was crossed (RK p. 63). Neither *Caerost* nor *Calembel* is found in the original manuscript of 'The Last Debate' (see p. 419). The other dot on Q 12, east of the crossing of Ringlo, is marked with the pencilled name *Tarnost*, which so far as I know does not appear elsewhere.

The name Belfalas was a late addition (see p. 293 note 22); and a note added early to the map directs that *Pinnath Gelin* should be made into 'lower Green Hills'.

The name *Odotheg* 'Seventh' of Gwathlo or Greyflood was changed in pencil to *Odothui*; on this name see VII.311–12. The last letter of *Lhefneg* was also changed: most probably it was first written *Lhefned* and then immediately altered to *Lhefneg*, the form of the name in the list of rivers written on the map.

North of the White Mountains a line of dots on squares P 13, Q 13–14 represents the beacon hills; on this see p. 354 note 3.

Moving eastwards to Q 14, the original course of Anduin can be discerned on the original, running in a straight line from below the confluence of Ereg to where the river bends north-west below Osgiliath. The great elbow in Anduin here and the hills of Haramon that caused it were superimposed later in blue ink, *Haramon* being afterwards struck out and *Emyn Arnen* substituted (with some totally illegible name preceding it). In the original text of the chapter 'Minas Tirith' (p. 278) there was no mention of this feature. It is shown (but without the hills around which the river bends) on the little map drawn on a page added to the manuscript of 'The Ride of the Rohirrim' (p. 353); and it first appears in the texts in the outline 'The Story Foreseen from Forannest' (see p. 359 and note 3): 'the [Pelennor] wall right above the stream which bends round the Hills of Haramon'. The name *Emyn Arnen* appears in the drafting of 'The Battle of the Pelennor Fields' (p. 370). I have very little doubt that it was indeed the development of the story of the battle that brought the great bend in Anduin around the hills of Haramon / Emyn Arnen into being; for so the black fleet could be brought right under the wall of the Pelennor, and victory assured in the face of disaster by the exceedingly dramatic and utterly unlooked for arrival, on the very field, of Aragorn with the Rangers and the sons of Elrond, and all the men newly gathered from the southern fiefs.

Osgiliath is now north-east of Minas Tirith (see pp. 269–70, 353). A note on the map says that 'Minas Morgul must be rather more north' (cf. the plan reproduced on p. 181 and the large LR map).

Within the confines of Mordor a major change was made in the last stage of the use of this map. The great peninsula of high land (Q 16) thrust out southwards from the Ash Mountains, on which stood Barad-dûr, was struck through, and Barad-dûr was moved north-west (to P 16). This was where Orodruin had stood as the map was first drawn.[3] Orodruin was moved to stand near the bottom right-hand corner of P 15. I have in this case preserved the original site of Barad-dûr in my redrawing, for the alterations were carried out very roughly. Other additions of this time were the rough outline of the Sea of Nurnen, the names *Lithlad*, *Morgai*, and *Nurn*, and also *Gorgoroth* of the vale running back from the Morannon. *Gorgoroth* was struck out, and in its place was pencilled here the name *Narch Udûn*.

NOTES

1 The fact that the track of Frodo's journey from the Emil Muil to the Morannon (not shown on my redrawing) is very carefully marked and probably belongs to the first 'layer' does not demonstrate that in its making this map goes back to the writing of Book

IV. For one thing, it seems unlikely that my father would have made the map redrawn on p. 269 if the Second Map had been already in existence.

2 A name in scarcely visible pencilling that is almost certainly *Lamedon* can be seen written right across Q 11–12 (from below the *r* of *Morthond* to east of the crossing of Ringlo), which suggests that Lamedon was at first a larger region.

3 When Barad-dûr was moved to the site of Orodruin the original markings were obliterated.

4 The names *Harad Road*, *Near Harad* (and an arrow directing to *Far Harad*), *Desert of Lostladen* (see p. 426 note 35), *Khand* (see p. 369), and *Umbar* were scribbled in pencil or blue crayon.

INDEX

In this book the variables are so many that the arrangement of the index, if it is to be more than a simple list of forms, becomes to some degree a matter of choice; for on the one hand there was a great deal of alteration and substitution among the names themselves, while on the other their application changed as the narrative, and the geography, changed. Thus for example the *Stone of Erech* was originally a *palantír*, but when it became a stone brought from Númenor the *palantír* (or *Stone*) of Erech was for a time still present; *Kirith Ungol* and *Minas Morghul (Morgul)* were several times shifted in relation to each other; and the Lord of Westfold was in succession *Trumbold*, *Heorulf (Herulf)*, *Nothelm*, *Heorulf*, *Erkenwald*, *Erkenbrand*, while *Westfold* was originally *Westmarch* and the original *Westfold* was a region in the west of the Misty Mountains. I hope at any rate that my attempt will be found accurate and serviceable for all the inconsistencies of presentation.

With constantly recurring names I have used the device employed in *The Return of the Shadow* and *The Treason of Isengard* whereby the word *passim* means that in a long run of references no more than one page here and there happens not to carry that name. Names occurring on the maps and on the pages reproduced from the original manuscripts are not indexed, and only exceptionally those in chapter-titles. Under the entry *Old English* are collected only special instances, and not of course the very large number of names in Rohan that are in fact Old English.